THE

# BOY SOLDIER;

OR,

## GARIBALDI'S YOUNG CAPTAIN.

A Novel.

ILLUSTRATED WITH NUMEROUS ENGRAVINGS.

LONDON:
GEORGE HOWE, RED LION COURT, FLEET STREET, E.C.

MDCCCLXXI.

# THE BOY SOLDIER;

## *Or, Garibaldi's Young Captain.*

DEPARTURE OF THE BOY SOLDIER.

## CHAPTER I.

"HURRAH FOR GARIBALDI !"—THE RIOT AT BROMLEY HALL ACADEMY—REV. JONATHAN GRAVESTONES AND HIS BODY OF TEACHERS ASSAIL THE INSURGENT SCHOLARS — THE SCHOOL-ROOM BARRICADED — THE STUDENTS' WATCH-WORD, "LIBERTY OR DEATH !"—DESKS, STOOLS, AND BENCHES USED FOR BREASTWORKS—THE "GREAT BATTLE AT BROMLEY HALL"—CUT HEADS AND SORE BONES—CAPTAIN FRANK, LEADER OF THE STUDENTS' BAND — THE GARIBALDIANS VICTORIOUS — YOUNG FLINT, THE SPY AND INFORMER !

"HURRAH for Garibaldi !"

"Nine times nine, and one cheer more for the brave Garibaldians !"

"Up with the Red, White, and Green !"

Such were the shouts of the students at Bromley Hall Academy, when the news arrived there of the then approaching war for Italian Independence.

"Silence in the classes !" roared old Gravestones, the reverend president, rising from his desk. "Silence there, or I'll punish the first boy that raises his voice again !"

"Hurrah for Garibaldi !"

"Garibaldi for ever !" shouted twenty voices on the instant.

"Silence ! I say, Frank Ford, and all the rest, or I'll lock you up and punish you !"

"Three cheers for the brave Italian !" said Frank Ford.

The cheers were given with such a triumphant shout that it alarmed the whole Academy.

"Down with school tyrants !" said Frank Ford, brandishing a long ruler, and waving his handkerchief.

"Seize that youth, Mr. Shanks !" said the president to his chief tutor. "Joel Flint, assist him. Knock the young scoundrel down if he resists !"

Joel Flint, the sly, cunning lawyer's son, the chief spy and informer on the whole school, rushed at his old enemy, Frank Ford.

On the instant, young Frank jumped upon his desk, and knocked Joel down with the ruler !

"H-o-o-ray ! h-o-o-ray !" said the boys, with a wild shout of joy. "Down with the Spy ! down with the Sneak !"

"Seize him, Mr. Shanks ! seize him ! Knock the young villain down !" cried the angry and tyrannical old master, seizing a small, stout riding-whip from the desk, and advancing to thrash the noisy youths.

"Stand back, Mr. Shanks, stand back ! We do not wish to hurt you," said Dick Fellows, jumping to Frank Ford's side. "Stand back, sir, we do not wish to hurt you. It is old Gravestones we have a grudge against. He and his wife half starves the scholars, and we won't stand it any longer."

"What is that I hear ?" roared the master, getting red in the face. "What ! to be insulted in my own place in Bromley Hall Academy by a dozen unruly boys ! What next ! Seize every one of them, I say, and birch them till they bleed again ! Rush on to them, Mr. Shanks !"

"Do you hear that, boys? We are to be half starved, robbed of our pocket money, refused holidays, and then be birched till we bleed again. Will you submit to *that* ?"

"No ! Never !" was the shout of about twenty sturdy youths, out of some one hundred or more, who were at that moment assembled together.

"Lock the doors, my boys, lock the doors," said old Gravestones, whip in hand ; "they shan't escape my vengeance *this* time. I know them every one. Seize your sticks and rulers, boys, and help your master and the tutors to subdue these vile young rebels. Every one who does so shall receive a shilling, and two days' holiday."

This promise was received with loud shouts by many who recognised Joel Flint as their chief and leader.

Joel himself, though bleeding from the nose, and with a black eye, quickly locked the doors, and seized a poker.

"Come on lads," said he, "we'll give them Garibaldi !"

In a moment the whole Academy was in the greatest uproar.

Chairs, tables, benches, stools, writing desks, and all were thrown down, and the fight commenced in earnest !

The red-faced, pot-bellied master, whip in hand, led the way, and laid about him right and left, with more vigour than judgment.

Many of his blows fell upon his own favourite scholars, who were all well-known "sneaks."

Some shouted, others yelled ; ink-stands, copy-books, dictionaries, slates, spelling-books, Latin grammars, Greek lexicons, all were used as weapons or missiles.

Blows were freely exchanged on both sides.

Screams, yells, and cheers were heard on every side.

Some were limping about with sore shins.

Others had received nasty knocks with rulers from Frank Ford's band of young Garibaldians.

All was a perfect Babel of confusion and noise.

Some tried to escape through the windows, but they were too high from the ground.

Others rushed to the doors, but they were locked, and the keys were in the gaunt and angry master's pockets.

Shouts of triumph and defiance rang out from Frank Allen's brave band of twenty.

"Seize them, lads ; seize them," cried Joel Flint, "give them no quarter, they have always been 'the cocks of the school' in everything."

"Do you hear that ?" shouted Frank Ford and Dick Fellows. "No quarter, mind ; let 'em have it ! Have no mercy on the half-starved, craven crew."

Joel mounted on a desk and aimed a terrible blow at Dick Fellows with a long poker, which, had it hit him, must have killed him on the spot.

At that moment, however, Frank Ford reared himself up, and, with all his strength, gave the sneak, Joel, such a "nose-ender" with his right fist as knocked him headlong off the desk head over heels among his noisy followers.

"Hurrah ! boys, the Sneak shuns the combat," said Dick Fellows, with a loud shout. "Give it to 'em."

"Let 'em have it."

"Fire away ! Don't spare 'em."

"Down with mouldy bread and sour milk !"

"Fight for your rights."

"They have stolen our pocket money and half starved us," said first one and then another of the twenty young Garibaldians.

The master and his tutors now knew not what to do.

Frank Ford and his comrades defied all attempts to secure them.

Some of the scholars were crying and bawling in various corners.

Others had black eyes and bloody noses, presenting altogether not a very enviable or inviting appearance.

This partial defeat only exasperated the master, his assistants, and monitors all the more.

They would not give in, nor own that they had been beaten by a score of rebellious youths.

"Surround 'em! surround 'em!" bawled Joel at the other end of the large, long room, who had now got possession of the coal skuttle and was throwing coals about with great violence.

One large lump, which he had aimed at Frank Ford's head, just missed it, and smashed a large globe that stood near by.

A cheer rose from the young Garibaldians as they perceived this trick of the Sneak.

"Two can play at that game," said Tom, Frank's brother.

The young Garibaldians now fought their way to the coal cupboard, which was at their end of the room.

"Don't let 'em get at it," shouted old Gravestones, who with his friends was unable to storm the strong barricade of desks and benches the young Garibaldians had raised against them.

"Fight 'em, lads; fight 'em," said he, "but don't let 'em secure the coal cupboard, or they'll smash everything in the school."

Dick Fellows with Frank Ford led on a dozen of their followers, and the fight for the much-coveted coals was hot, desperate and short.

At length they gained possession of it, and beat back their opponents.

A shout of triumph was raised.

"Three cheers for Garibaldi!"

"Liberty or death!"

"Down with oppression and tyranny!"

The coal cupboard was a very large one, and filled with coals.

This proved a mine of wealth to the young Garibaldians.

They showered dozens of lumps upon the heads of their assailants, and the fight now became hotter than ever.

Coal dust was thrown into the eyes of those nearest to them, while lump after lump, and cobble after cobble, was fired in all directions, greatly to the master's anger and dismay.

Perceiving the destruction on all sides from the lumps of coal, he shouted out,

"Surrender! Give up quietly, and I'll let you off.

"Never!"

"No surrender!"

"Hurrah for Garibaldi and liberty!"

"If you will *not* submit, you young imps of the devil, I will *make* you," said the master, with an angry oath.

With a determined rush he dashed at the young Garibaldians' barricade.

But a shower of coal dust was thrown fairly into his eyes, and, for the moment, almost blinded him.

With a yell of pain he retreated to the door, stamping and swearing.

He opened the door in order to escape.

His wife and two daughters stood outside in terror and alarm.

As soon as they saw the black and grimy appearance of the master, with several large bumps about his head and face, they screamed with dismay and fainted on the landing.

The master not heeding them was about to pass by and go downstairs when his foot caught in his wife's dress.

He fell headlong over the bannisters on to the landing below.

Perceiving the retreat of the master the tutors and scholars were about to follow his example in order to get out of harm's way.

This the young Garibaldians perceived.

With a loud shout they issued from behind their barricade, and charged their opponents with such ferocity that they drove them all helter skelter before them down stairs, freely dealing blows to the right and left until the school-room was cleared, and they remained masters of the well-fought ground!

"Ho-o-ray!" they shouted again and again.

"Three cheers for Garibaldi!"

The demand was responded to, and they made the Academy ring again with their loud and deafening shouts!

* * * * *

But while all this riot was in progress among the young Garibaldians, what must be said of Tony Waddleduck, or "Paunchey," the "Fat Boy" of the school, as Hugh Tracy and others called him?

Tony, fat, dreamy and sleepy as he always was, had just laid his head down on his desk for an afternoon nap when the row began.

He had eaten too much at dinner; his pockets were crammed with cakes, apples, and whatever he could buy, beg or steal, and at the moment when he should have been helping Frank, Dick Fellows and the rest, he was curled up all of a heap in his own particular corner, and snoring as loudly and soundly as a young prize hog.

"Wake up, Tony. Look out, Paunchey," said first one and then another of the young Garibaldians, when they found themselves furiously attacked by Joel Flint, and other fierce antagonists.

"Wake up, Tony! Now then, young Paunchey," shouted Tom Ford, "don't you see that war has commenced? Wake up; this won't do you know if you think of joining Garibaldi in Italy; come, Paunchey, roll up your sleeves, and let's see what you can do."

"Eh? What?" said Tony, gaping and yawning, still half asleep, and not feeling at all inclined to be roused up. "Eh? what? Oh, let me alone, I want to sleep."

This was said in such a plaintive voice by the fat boy that young Tom Ford roared with laughter.

"Sleepy, eh? Why, you're always eating and sleeping," said Tom Ford; "I never saw such a chap; no wonder you're all fat, and bursting out your clothes, Tony. Come, take this stick, and fight like a man; we are nearly overpowered."

"Fight! Why, I might get a slap on the head."

He was about to close his eyes again and drop off to sleep, when a heavy dictionary was shied at his head.

Tony did not see it coming, but he felt it when it *did* come, for it left a bump of respectable looking size on his forehead, and made "Paunchey's" eyes dance again with surprise.

With a yell of anger he roused himself up, while, with a large apple in one hand, which he munched from time to time, and a long ruler in the other, he jumped over the barricade of desks, and his fat, puffy, pudding-bag looking person was soon lost among the friends and followers of the master and Joel Flint.

Tony, the fat boy, was a big youth for his age, and, though sleepy and lazy, would fight light a trooper—when he couldn't get out of it!

When old Gravestones rushed out of the school-room in despair, and fell over his wife and tumbled down stairs, the first person to raise a shout of triumph was Job Parsons the page, or "Buttons," as he was generally called by the students, from three rows of large brass buttons with which his tight-fitting jacket was ornamented.

Buttons' hair was generally unruly, and all he

could do with soap, comb, and brush would never keep his front locks from always standing on end.

"Now's my time for a jolly good feed!" thought Buttons. "The boys will be blamed for all that disappears. Now's your time, Job; the preserves await you!"

He did not like the master much, or any of the family, for they half-starved him, and were perpetually knocking him about and abusing him.

Poor Job, the unfortunate "Buttons," had no friends save the young Garibaldians, and when he heard of the riot, and of the master's disgrace, he raised a faint shout of joy, and forthwith rushed to the larder to help himself to all the luxuries he could lay hands upon while the noise and confusion lasted.

He remained in the larder quite long enough to demolish a bottle of jam, and his face was smeared all over with it.

He was just finishing his stealthy repast when he heard the heavy fall of some one down stairs.

He dropped the jam-pot with a loud smash upon the floor, and rushed out in alarm.

He had awful fears of the master catching him in the act of petty peculation, and he shivered in his shoes!

"Oh, crikey!" said Buttons, when he saw his master sprawling and groaning upon the floor. "Oh, here's a go! he's half killed! what a jolly lark! I wish it had been Missus though, or that ugly tutor, Shanks! Here's a spree! the young Garibaldians have raised the standard of revolt! I hear 'em! Oh! that's their cry! "Liberty or Death!" just so. I could tell Frank Ford's voice among a thousand. Hooray! I'm one on 'em, too. Here goes to strike against short commons and tyrants!"

So saying, Job, or the enthusiastic "Buttons," rushed into the kitchen, tumbled over the cat, upset the cook, and seized the rolling-pin!

So armed, he dashed upstairs, bent on giving Joel Flint "one for himself" on the sly.

But though the young Garibaldians had defeated the grim old master and his half-starved assistants they had not come out of the battle without losses of one kind or another.

Dick Fellows had his left arm in a sling.

Another one had a huge bump on his head.

A third had a very suspicious black mark under his eye, and so with others, who, more or less, had received as hard knocks as they had given.

"Hurrah for Frank!" some shouted, in boisterous mirth.

"Yes, three times three for 'Gallant' Frank, captain of the Garibaldians!"

"Three times three for 'Gallant' Frank!" roared a number of merry voices.

"What shall we do next?" shouted some.

"They have gone down to fetch the village constables!" cried others.

"Who cares for the Bobbies?" laughed Frank Ford. "There are only three in the village, and we are able to beat off any dozen of them."

"So we can, so we can."

"Let 'em come, that's all; we'll show e'm what stuff English boys are made of, won't we, lads?"

"Bravo, Frank; we'll follow you anywhere."

"Then let's go and liberate our companions the master and assistants have locked in the library," said Frank; "we must not let them suffer for us, shall we, boys?"

"No, no!" roared many voices.

"To the library! to the library, lads! Follow me!" said Gallant Frank, long ruler in hand.

"Bravo, boys! Lead the way, Frank! we'll show old Gravestones whether he can half starve us, and do what he likes," said Dick Fellows.

"Lead on, 'Roaring' Dick!" sang out a dozen merry voices, "To the library, lads! to the library!"

With a loud, wild shout that echoed throughout the whole Academy, Frank Ford and his brother Tom, followed by Dick Fellows—"Roaring" Dick, as he had been christened—and a number of other determined youths, rushed out of the large schoolroom, and mounted the stairs.

On their way they were vigorously opposed by Joel Flint, old Gravestones, the master, and a body of assistant tutors.

These worthies had been so roughly handled in the recent *melée* that they did not at all relish the idea of any fresh encounter.

But Joel Flint, who had a deadly hatred of Frank Ford and his friends, as will be afterwards seen, hit right and left as the young band of Garibaldians attempted to mount the steep, broad staircase towards the library.

"That's it, Joel! that's it Joel!" cried the master, "have no mercy on the young blackguards!"

"Go and fetch the village constables, quick!" roared out Mr. Shanks, the long-legged, herring-bodied, half-starved, cadaverous-looking head tutor. "Go and fetch the constables, boys; quick!" he shouted, "or we shall all be murdered!"

A blow from Frank's ruler soon laid this long, lean gentleman flat and sprawling on the floor.

"Come on, lads," cried Frank, "mount the stairs, and fight your way up, our companions of the band *must* and *shall* be liberated."

"Bravo! bravo!" shouted his campanions.

"Three cheers for Garibaldi!"

"One cheer more for Garibaldi's young captain, brave Frank Ford!"

After much hard fighting the young Garibaldians fought their way upstairs towards the library, the prison-house of their young companions.

When they arrived almost at the top of the landing another and a stranger episode took place.

Mrs. Gravestones and her scraggy daughters, with the aid of several servants, procured several buckets of water and slops.

From their elevated position on an upper landing they could see the whole battle raging below.

With shouts and shrill cries of passion, these infuriated females stood ready to shower the water and slops down on the young Garibaldians.

"Throw it down, wife! throw it down!" said Gravestones, with upturned face.

"Now's your time, madam!" screamed out Joel Flint; "now's your time! Drown 'em! drown em!"

At the word of command Mrs. Gravestones and the other females poured down the water and slops!

But they missed their aim.

So excited were they that it all fell upon the master, assistants, and Joel Flint, buckets and all!

Old Gravestones and his friends now retreated slowly, and shut themselves in the library, followed by Joel and the rest.

The Garibaldians were disappointed at this trick, but not discouraged.

They rushed at the door, and hammered at it with all their might, but without making any impression upon it.

Joel, the cowardly cur, with the master and his chief assistant, Shanks, no sooner got into the library than they began to vent their vengeance upon several of the young Garibaldians who were prisoners there.

These Joel hit and cuffed with all his might.

None of them were half his own size, or near his own age, for he was a tall, gaunt, ugly youth of eighteen, while neither Frank Ford nor any of the Garibaldians were more than fifteen or sixteen.

The cries of the young prisoners reached the ears of their comrades outside on the landing.

"To the rescue, lads! to the rescue!" shouted "Gallant Frank" and "Roaring Dick."

This appeal was answered by a deafening, determined cheer from their followers, which so terrified the mistress, her daughters, and servants, that they locked themselves in their bed-rooms, and barred the doors.

"Do you think they'll dare to break into the library?" gasped old Gravestones, looking deadly pale.

"Dare? Aye, they'll dare anything, the young imps of the devil! Don't you hear them cheering?" said Shanks.

"I do. The school will be nought else than ruins if they go on in this way, Mr. Shanks," sighed Gravestones. "Do you hear that other cheer down stairs?"

"I do."

"What can it mean?"

Shanks, the long-legged tutor, did not know, but the truth was this:—

Frank Ford, finding that his followers increased more and more every moment, sent his brother Tom below, to lead the insurgents there.

Tom Ford was in his glory.

He addressed the boys in a few stirring words.

Standing on the steps of the Hall-door he said,

"We have revolted against the master, boys, because he half starves us."

"Bravo!"

"That's true!"

"He keeps our pocket-money, and illtreats us!"

"He does! he does!"

"The band of Garibaldians have risen in insurrection against his miserly, stingy ways!"

"Quite right!"

"Don't we pay well for our board and schooling?"

"We do, of course!"

"Then, shall we be treated like niggers or Hindoos!"

"No, never!"

"Then strike for Liberty and Justice! Join the Garibaldians under Gallant Frank and Roaring Dick!"

"We will! we will!"

"Follow me, then! Three cheers for Garibaldi!"

The cheers were given lustily, and with a right good hearty will.

"Down with tyrant masters!"

"Ho-o-ray!"

"Follow me, lads," cried Tom Ford.

"To the larder! to the larder!"

"To the wine cellar! that's the place, there's plenty of wine there; but *we* don't get any of it."

"That's true; our relations send it to us: but we don't get any of it."

"Old Gravestones drinks it all."

"Liberty and justice!"

"Hurrah for Garibaldi!"

Locks and bars in the cellar doors were wrenched off, and the doors themselves broken open.

Wine, fruits, pastry, beer, ale, and quantities of edibles were seized and consumed on the spot!

Chief and foremost among them all were the Fat Boy and Buttons. These two youths were now in their glory!

The entire school was now almost in the hands of the young Garibaldians, who carried everything before them.

"Lock and bolt the school gates, lads," said Tom Ford. "Don't let any of the villagers in."

This was quickly done, and to prevent any one climbing over the wall, several of the band stood sentry upon it ready to give the alarm should any one attempt to climb over to the rescue.

But while a large number of the students were thus engaged below in the cellars, and lower parts of the house, Frank Ford and his companions were having a dreadful fight.

They got into the library by bursting open the door, and the contest there became fierce, hot, and determined.

The prisoners no sooner saw their friends than they turned upon the master and his assistants with great fury.

With a well-timed aim gallant Frank hurled a heavy book at the master's head which struck him fairly between the eyes, and his nose swelled up on the instant to treble its ordinary size, and that was by no means very small.

With eyes blackened and swollen, and face and shirt front smeared with blood, the master jumped into the midst of his assailants, and fought his way towards a small private door, and vanished none knew whither.

Mr. Shanks, Joel Flint and a score of overgrown boys beat a retreat, and hastened from the spot, shouting, "Fire! fire!" "Murder!" "Thieves!" "Robbers!" "Police! police!" in wild, discordant voices.

Mr. Caspar, a favorite tutor among the boys, finding that he could not restore order or harmony, gave up his cane to Frank Ford, and left the spot laughing, and loudly cheered by the young Garibaldians.

Shanks, however, managed to escape the same way as the master had done, through the small private door of the library.

"Hang the luck!" said Roaring Dick, in disgust. "He has escaped us!"

"I'd give a sovereign to have him here, the brute!" said Frank Ford, in anger. "Oh, I *would* pound him!"

"Can't we break that door in and seize them both?" Frank suggested.

"Of course we can; here goes. Come on, lads," Dick replied, and they all assailed the small private door with redoubled energy and fury.

"It could not be forced!"

*It was lined with iron, doubly bolted and barred!*

"*There is some mystery here!*" said Frank, in a whisper to Dick.

"*I am sure of it,*" was the almost inaudible reply of young Fellows.

There *was* a mystery!

A dark, deep, cruel secret it was.

Well might the master, and Shanks, his slavish, cruel, hireling assistant, tremble with fear when they heard the fiery students banging against that iron door!

## CHAPTER II.

THE MIDNIGHT MURDER—CONSPIRACY TO DISINHERIT OLD FORD'S NEPHEWS—THE HAUNTED HOUSE—POLICEMEN ON THE WATCH—THE UNKNOWN ASSASSIN—THE HIDDEN TREASURE—VILLAINS FOILED.

THE night was intensely dark, and black, heavy clouds rolled lazily in the heavens.

Sudden faint flashes of lightning darted through the sky, and low, rumbling, distant thunder gave token of an approaching tempest.

All was quiet in the streets at the west end of London; scarcely a single person was abroad, and a solitary policeman could be seen here and there in his heavy overcoat and shining cape slowly and drearily walking his lonely beat.

The appearance of all things in the heavens and in the streets betokened the fast approach of a terrific storm of thunder, lightning, wind and rain.

It was late.

The bells of neighbouring churches had tolled the hour of ten, and their solemn sounds fell upon the ear with a melancholy cadence.

The winds sighed mournfully at times, and then again at intervals increased in violence till they screamed aloud as if the cold bleak winds were peopled with a thousand mysterious voices high in rage and anger.

Suddenly, and when least expected, the lightning flashed with almost blinding brilliancy.

Its fiery forks struck a solitary tree in the large garden of a two-story house, which stood alone and far apart from others in the street.

The tree was instantly shivered into a thousand splinters, and deafening thunder peals burst right over the house with tremendous power and unearthly grandeur, shaking tiles off the roof, breaking window panes, and causing more than one chimney pot to topple over and fall into the yard and garden with a teriffic crash.

The policeman, to escape the deluging rain that now poured forth from the heavens, stood in a neighbouring doorway.

He was in full view of the lonely, tumble-down-looking house, which, as we have said, stood far from the street, surrounded by a large garden, and he perceived that the solitary tree which had stood near the entrance gate had been felled to the earth.

Ere many minutes had elapsed he was joined by his sergeant, a red-faced policeman, with enormous sandy whiskers, and he, too, crept into the doorway out of the pouring rain.

"Terrible storm, Tomkins?" said the sergeant to "61 Z."

"Yes, sir; just such a night as 'ud suit some on 'em to crack a crib."

"Just so, just so, Tomkins; but I don't think any of that craft will trouble *your* beat. What are you looking at across the way?"

"Well, sir, I've been for some time a looking at that there house opposite, that old, two-story red brick building standing there all alone in that big wilderness of a garden. I don't like the looks o' that place much; what a dark, dingy, miserly, cut-throat-looking place it is!"

"Just so; that's what they call the 'Haunted House;' it's gone under that name ever since I entered the 'force,' and that's a good many years ago."

"But it ain't haunted, is it?" said Tomkins, who had come from the country, and had not long been in the "force."

"Haunted, no; but there's been some very queer stories told about it, *I* can tell you."

"Well, I don't know whether it be haunted or not," said Tomkins; "but I *have* heard of haunted houses afore now, and it strikes me that that is, if there ever was one. You should have seen how the lightning struck that tree down in the yard; it shivered it all to pieces in a minute; the light was so brilliant for a short time that I thought it would blind me."

"So the old tree has fallen at last, eh?" said the sergeant. "Well, I thought it would one o' these stormy nights. It has been shaky and withered this many a year."

"See how that single light moves about in the second floor window," said Tomkins. "I never much liked the looks o' that place."

"So it does. Somebody sick, I suppose."

"Who lives there?"

"Oh, a miserly old devil named Ford. The house belongs to him; he's only got two servants, a red-headed slavey for cook, housekeeper, and general servant, and a man—a sort of half-butler, half-gardener, half-anything. Both of 'em look as thin as starved rats, for the old man is so stingy."

"Is he rich?"

"Rich? No; he can't be very well to do, or he wouldn't live as he does. He had a horse once; but he soon sold him, 'cause he couldn't abear to buy him beans or oats."

"He must be an old miserly hound, then."

"I believe you. He gives his servants five pounds a year, and allows 'em seven bob a week to keep themselves, so I hear, and thinks it quite enough to get fat on."

"61 Z" whistled very low at this, as if it were too hard to believe.

"Fact, though," said the sergeant. "Did you ever see him?"

"No, never. He's a curiosity whoever he is."

"No; nor anybody else, as I've heard of. Nor the servants either much. The old cook goes out every night to buy sixpennorth o' "pieces" at the market-stalls for the governor's grub, I've heard; but the half-starved, hang-dog-looking butler isn't seen at all. He tends on the old devil night and day, so I hear."

While they thus spoke together, "61 Z" nudged the sergeant, and said in a whisper,

"Did yer see that?"

"What, the shadow o' the man passing the blind?"

"Yes."

"Is that the butler, I wonder?"

"I dare say it is; but come, the rain has given over. We must make a move."

So saying, the two policemen left the doorway, and resumed their duties.

They walked leisurely down the street, and their heavy footfalls soon died away.

The church clocks struck eleven.

While the two officers had stood out of the rain looking at the Haunted House, as it was called, the proper name of which was "Red Lodge," their conversation had been overheard by a man, who, like themselves, had crouched in the dark recesses of a spacious, overhanging, beetle-browed doorway near by.

This person was a tall, stout, middle-aged man, and wore a large cloak that enveloped him completely from head to foot.

He had walked up the street unseen by the officers, and his boots were encased in gutta percha goloshes, so that his footsteps could not be heard.

He was on his way to "Red Lodge;" but he wished to enter it unseen.

The voices of the policemen had prompted him to hide near them, and listen to all they said.

So well did he crouch in the deep dark doorway, that their sharp eyes had not perceived him.

Had they by accident turned their lamps upon him, he would have opened the street door, and entered, for he had lodgings in that house; but for reasons of his own, did not wish to enter that night.

In truth he had lodgings at *several places.*

This house was No. 56, Barlow Place, and from his third floor front room he had a full view, both night and day, of "Red Lodge," and of all who entered or left the so-called Haunted House.

From some strange cause, he had hired lodgings also in a house in the next street, the back garden of which communicated with the garden of No. 56, Barlow Place.

He also had an office in the city, and at each of these three places he *was known by a different name.*

In the city he wore a moustache.

At Barlow Place he only wore whiskers.

At his other lodgings opposite, No. 56, he was always clean-shaved, and with not the least sign of a hair upon him!

*He* had very *great* reasons for this strange conduct, and so suspicious was he of everything and everybody that he feared least his own shadow even might, by some strange chance, reveal to the world who and what he was, or what his intentions were.

When the policemen had gone far out of all hearing, he glided from his place of concealment like a guilty shadowy thing, and crept across the road towards Red Lodge.

He crouched low as he passed under the wall which surrounded this Haunted House, and made his way towards the back entrance of the lodge.

For a moment he listened, and seemed fearful of being seen or heard.

A low whistle—a very faint note—was borne upon the wind

He stopped.

Presently a man appeared at the back gate, and opened it.

"All right," said the man, a strange, villanous-looking fellow, with a hairy cap.

"Is the dog dead?"

"Yes."

"I thought so."

"I did for him with a piece of poisoned meat. The cook is out."

"And the butler, too?"

"I've seen nothing of him all night."

"How long have you been here?"

"Two hours or more."

"Is the coast clear?"

"It is."

"Have you listened at the old man's door?"

"I have."

"Is there any one with him?"

"Old Davy the butler has been with him all the time, I think."

"What have they been talking about?"

"He says he has been much worse since he called in Dr. Warner."

"Oh! indeed! who *is* this Dr. Warner?"

"Don't know; never saw him. He has altered his will once more."

"The devil! he is always altering it."

"That's no matter; it won't hurt us much, I think."

"Not a particle."

"But are you sure he ordered all his securities and leases to be turned into ready money?"

"Yes; I heard him tell the lawyer so last evening."

"And he is to call with the money to-night?" you said.

"Yes; in bank-notes."

"All right. The prize is ours, my boy. When are the two lads expected home?"

"In an hour or two. He has been raving about Frank and Tom all night, and has left them everything."

"There won't be much left for any one, after *we* have had our hands upon it. He's worth half a million altogether."

"Half a million, and all in one pile!" said the villain, in astonishment.

"Yes, perhaps so; if the lawyer does what the old man has told him, he will bring it with him to-night."

"Then, I had better stay about here, and be ready to help you?"

"No occasion. Do you go and watch in front of the house. Mind no one sees you."

"All right."

"Have you laid hands on anything yet?"

"Well, not o' much value," said the ugly rascal; "but, as I was looking about, I prigged this out of his nephew's room."

"What?"

"Why, this, you see," said the ruffian, exhibiting a gold-handled dagger. "It's a pretty little thing, and I thought as how it might prove useful in case any one should tap me on the shoulder, and say, 'Look here, Bill, you're wanted.'"

"Let me see it. Why, this is young Frank's?"

"I know it is. I took it out of his room, as he's not at home. I thought a boy like him wouldn't want such a thing as a dagger."

"You need not take that away; we musn't play our game for such trifles as this. I will return it."

"Just as you like, but you'd better keep it; it might come in useful if you were disturbed, you know."

"Nonsense," said the elegant stranger, in a soft voice; "there is no work of *that* kind needed."

He made a motion to his rough companion, who left the spot noiselessly.

He looked after him to see that the ruffian had disappeared, when he rapidly passed one hand across his face, and in a second his false whiskers and moustache disappeared!

He next pulled off his wig, and placed all these articles in his hat.

With noiseless step he ascended to the sick man's chamber, and listened at the door.

He peeped through the key-hole, and saw old Davy nodding, half asleep, in an easy chair, beside the sick man's bed, who was groaning and moaning, and faintly calling for his nephews, Tom and Frank.

Slipping off his cloak, he placed it with his slouched hat in a small cupboard on the landing.

He next produced a new opera hat, flat as a pancake, from under his waistcoat, and put it on.

So changed did he now appear that it would have puzzled any one to have recognized him.

He touched Davy, who woke up out of his doze with a sudden start, and for a moment looked as if he beheld an apparition.

"Hullo, doctor, is it you?" he said.

"Yes, Davy, I have taken so great an interest in Mr. Ford's desperate case that I could not sleep till I had called again."

"Werry kind o' you, sir, but I don't think as how all the medicine in the world 'll do him any sort o' good now, sir. He's werry low, sir, werry low; he's fast asleep."

"Does he speak much, Davy?"

"Oh, yes, sir, he raves enormous about his nephews, Tom and Frank."

"Why, Davy?"

"Why, you see, sir, both o' them young gents are his brother's orphan children, and wild, harum-scarum young devils they are too; and for all Mr.

Ford can do, he can't keep the young beggars at school."

"Why, not?"

"Why, they is always talking of Garibaldi, and swears they'll go and help him to fight in the cause of them organ-grinding, hurdy-gurdy Italians, as comes about the streets with performing monkeys."

"Oh, indeed," said Dr. Warner, with a ghastly smile, showing his large white teeth. "I suppose, then, that they have often quarrelled with their uncle?"

"Oh, yes, werry often."

"Indeed! you are *sure* of that?" said the doctor, with a fiendish smile; "it is very important to be remembered."

"Indeed, doctor."

"Oh, yes, I have heard that they threatened Mr. Ford's life once if he dared to disinherit them."

"It's the fust time as *I* ever did then, doctor. He's got plenty o' money, and I know he is going to leave it all to Tom and Frank."

"And nothing to you?"

"Not a farthing."

"That's very hard, considering how long you have been a good and faithful servant to him."

"Werry bad, sir—werry bad it is. I suppose I shall go to the work'us when he's "snuffed out," as they say—have a brown coat, metal buttons, a hoil-skin hat, and a broom. Ah, your's *is* a Christian heart, doctor, and no mistake; you are a *real* gentleman."

"Are you sure Mr. Flint, the lawyer, will call to-night?" asked Warner, doubtingly, and with a very anxious look.

"Sartin, doctor."

"The old man sleeps well, you say?"

"Uncommon well, sir, and it's a pity to wake him up till the lawyer comes, for he'd better have a good long sleep afore he dies."

"Just so, Davy; quite right. Do you remain here, then, till Mr. Flint comes. I will return home, and call after all the law business is over."

"Quite right, sir; just as you please."

"If he is restless, and wakes, give him some of that medicine I left and plenty of wine—it will compose the old man. If he should call out when you are not in the room you needn't be alarmed."

"Oh, no, sir, I've got used to that. He does shout out in his sleep awful sometimes, though."

The doctor left the room, and as he did so, cast a sidelong glance at Davy, who, as soon as Dr. Warner had gone, helped himself very freely to the sick man's wine.

The doctor imagined he would be sure to do this, and had dropped into the tumbler a small drug while talking to him.

Dr. Warner stood peeping through the keyhole, and observed Davy help himself to wine, and smiled, for in less than two minutes Davy began to yawn and twist about uneasily in his chair."

"So far all works well," said the doctor, "and now, if Flint only does *his* part, our fortunes are made. What a time he is in coming."

While thus musing on the landing in the dark, the doctor felt some one touch him on the shoulder.

A cold tremor ran through his body.

He clutched the dagger his ruffian companion had given him, and would have dealt a deadly blow, so excited had he now become.

"It's me," said a faint voice.

"You, Flint?"

"Yes. How is he?—have you given him the fatal dose you spoke of?"

"Ye-e-s," said the doctor, with chattering teeth.

"Then all is well," said Flint.

"Where are the deeds and cash you were to have brought with you? Have you turned everything into ready money?"

"Yes."

"Where is it?"

"In his room. I left the bundle of notes safe under his pillow this afternoon."

"Why, Davy said you were to call to-night with the money, and finish making his will, altering it in favour of his nephews, Frank and Tom."

"I know he thought so, and so did the old man himself. But do you think I was going to do it? No, not me, because I knew *you* would do for him before midnight, according to promise, and then it would be too late for any alteration to be made."

"Just so, a good thought. But why leave such a vast sum under his pillow, Flint?"

"Ain't the nephews coming to his death-bed? I have written for them."

"Well?"

"Both of us will then be sent out of the way, and, as it is well known that the old man has often had violent quarrels with them, they will be suspected, and——"

"I understand," said Warner; "but the money had better be secured first."

"Oh, there is no need to fear, no one would suppose that any vast sum would be concealed in such an unlikely place as beneath his mattress under the pillow."

"Well, what do you propose to do?"

"Why, let us both watch until the nephews arrive, and, directly they are in the house, let's accuse them of having poisoned their uncle, and have them arrested."

"It is not a bad plan," said the doctor, "I accede to it."

"Where will *you* watch?" asked Flint.

"At the back of the house."

"Well, so be it; and I at the front; we cannot help but catch them."

So arranging, the lawyer and doctor descended the stairs.

"I have nicely played the game with Warner," said Flint. "Frank and Tom will *not* return. I went down to the school and saw old Gravestones, and arranged everything. I knew that both of them were harum-scarum boys, and wished to go to Italy; to get them out of the way I gave them £500 each, in the master's care, to leave England, telling him that their uncle, the old miser, had changed his mind, and had made them sole heirs to his vast property, and that he was well in health. They are on their way now to the south coast, I should think, and will soon reach Italy; but they won't live long there, I fancy, among the knife-using Italians; my son Joel has plans of his own; *he* knows what he's up to, and will soon rid the world of the two brats, while I, in the meantime, will change my residence, and, with old Ford's money, which I have safe in my office, will live for the rest of my days in ease."

Thus musing, Flint, the crafty lawyer, hurried away from the spot, saying,

"As Warner has poisoned him so much the better, but he'll find nothing beneath the old man's pillow save a bundle of worthless papers. What matters, this sham doctor will never see *me* again."

The lawyer hurried through the streets at a rapid rate towards his dingy offices in the city, and was soon out of sight.

"What an ass Flint was to put the money in such a place," thought Warner. "But his idea of the boys returning and being found in the dead

"'I AM PURSUED BY FURIES,' HE CRIED."

man's room, and in possession of the treasure which the will says was left to *us* in equal shares, will damn them before any jury and screen us. But Flint supposes he is dying. He is *not* though; he will live if something is not done. Suppose I were to use his nephew's dagger? That would be still greater proof against them. And then to seize the treasure unknown to Flint, eh? Ah! a capital plan; but how to do it? Let me see, let me see," thought Warner; "they are expected home at twelve to-night! It does not want many minutes to that time now. Still the old cook has not yet returned. A good thought; I will wait until she rings; the back doors are fastened; she can't get in. Old Davy will go down and open the door; while doing that I can slip in, and—and——"

Warner did not speak aloud his thought, but after a moment's reflection, he said,

"I will do it; the treasure shall be mine, and mine alone! Why should I share it with Flint? No, I will not; as I will do the deed let the booty be mine. The lawyer is timid, I am not; he shall not share with me; in twelve hours I will be far from the spot. No one knows me. Flint all through this affair has been crafty, but he shall find me to be more cunning than himself."

At that moment there was heard a loud ringing at the bell.

"'Tis the cook," said Warner. "Let me see if the noise will wake Davy."

He peeped at the key-hole, and saw Davy stirring.

"Now's my time," said he, putting on his former disguise, namely the false wig, whiskers, moustache, slouched hat and cloak.

"It must be done," he said, as he peeped through the keyhole, dagger in hand.

At that awful moment the solemn sounds of Big Ben were heard.

Slowly boomed forth the mystic hour of twelve!

Warner felt the blood creeping through his excited heart like icicles.

A deathly damp oozed from his brow.

He could scarcely breathe.

He had not gazed at the sleeping man more than a second when he was horrified at what he then saw in the sick man's room.

A youth in a mask, dressed much like himself, entered old Ford's bed-chamber, knife in hand!

The young stranger seemed to have glided in through the wainscotting in some mysterious way, and with noiseless step.

He hurried to the bedside of the old man, who now suddenly awoke.

With a loud shout and scream of alarm and horror, old Ford rose bolt upright in his bed.

The young assassin was for a moment surprised, and he hesitated what to do.

"Spare me! spare me!" the old man cried.

The youth rushed upon him with an angry oath, knife in hand.

Old Ford seized his upraised arm with a grip of frenzied energy.

A fearful struggle for life or death ensued.

"Spare me! spare me!" the old man gasped.

"You know me not," the villain hissed.

"I do! I do! You are my nephew—my nephew—I will bequeath all to you, but spare my life."

"Down, miser, down!" said the desperate assassin, with an oath. "Die—die like a dog!" he said.

The next moment, he plunged a long thin steel weapon into the old man's side, who fell back with a loud groan, dying.

With a low, fiendish laugh the assassin rushed towards the chamber door to escape.

There stood Davy, concealed and gazing on the frightful scene, almost distilled to a jelly with fear and trembling.

"Oh, heavens! it is—it is—I know him!" he said, and fell on the landing, fainting, as the assassin rushed past him and dashed down the stairs.

---

## HAPTER III.

THE OLD GARDENER'S SECRET — THE ANCIENT ROOM — CONSTERNATION OF JONATHAN AND SHANKS — THE REVOLVING CUPBOARD — THE SURPRISE—THE DISCOVERY.

"OH, heavens, Shanks! surely those wild devils will not dare to break into *this* room?" said old Gravestones, with looks of terror upon his pale and haggard face.

"I don't know, sir," said the red-haired Shanks, with a bitter smile upon his bloodless lips; "but it appears to me, now that they have got the upper hand of us, that they'll attempt anything."

"But if they find out——"

"No fear of *that*, sir," Shanks replied. "They will have to go through many rooms before they get to *theirs*."

"But they might, you know; and, if our secret is found out, they would kill us."

"Then we must *fight*," said Shanks. "They are but youths, you know, and one determined man is worth more than any dozen of the young brats."

The Rev. Jonathan did not quite understand this, for he had fought against the young Garibaldians for a full hour, he knew, and had got much the worst of it.

"I'd give a hundred pounds to see Frank Ford or Dick Fellows lying dead at my feet!" said the master, bitterly.

"Have you any arms—a pistol or sword?"

"No, nothing."

"Then I fear if they do break in upon us, we may get roughly handled, for nearly all the boys have joined them now."

"So it seems, from their wild shouting. Look out of window, Shanks, and see what they are doing."

Shanks did so.

The instant he did so his red head was recognised by the boys below, and a shower of apples, potatoes, stones, and such like, were thrown up at him.

"They have ransacked all the cellars, sir," said he.

"The young imps of the devil!" said the master; "I'll have all the young villains transported."

During all this time Frank's followers had been hammering at the iron door, but without success.

They might have remained outside a long time, but just as Frank and Dick were about to give up the task in despair, old Giles, the bandy-legged gardener, appeared on the stairs, radiant with smiles.

"Don't speak my name, Frank," said he, "but I'm right glad you've served old Jonathan out at last; I knew it would come to this before long. Where is he?"

"In the small room with the iron door. Is that the place he keeps his money?" said Frank, in a whisper.

"No, lad; but that room leads to another where he keeps a great secret."

"A great secret? What do you mean?" asked Dick.

"What I mean is this, lads; but mark me, don't let any more than two on ye know it at once. He's got a great secret in one of the rooms in this house."

"Has he?"

"Yes; and a *live* one," said Giles, with a knowing wink, "at least, they were alive when *I* last saw 'em, poor devils."

"What do you mean, Giles?"

"I mean nothing, my lads; but he thinks there is only *one* way into that room of secrets, but he's much mistaken, *I* know another," said Giles, "and if you wants to know all about it, why, I'll show you the way; but, mark ye, lads, come this way, and when you have found it all out there's only one thing I'll ask of ye."

"What is it, Giles?"

"Why, this, *don't you kill Mr. Jonathan!*"

So saying, Giles led Frank and Dick away to the end of the corridor, and pulling out a rusty key opened a door.

It was a small, empty room, damp, mouldy, and full of rat holes.

"Well, what have we to do here?" Frank asked. "There is nothing here, Giles."

"Perhaps not, Master Frank; but there *is* in the next room."

So saying, old Giles went to an old worm-eaten cupboard, and opened it.

When he had done so he turned round and said,

"If you make any noise old Jonathan will hear it; the small room with the iron door is next to the one we are now going into. I'll peep in first, and see if he is inside."

With an ease which surprised Frank and Dick, Giles crawled into the cupboard, and removed a small piece of wood from the back of it, which gave him an insight into the next room.

"No one there," said Giles. "Come into the cupboard."

"We can't; it isn't large enough."

"But you *must* squeeze yourselves in."

"What for?"

"You'll see what for in a minute."

Frank and Dick crept into the cupboard with much labour.

In an instant it turned on a pivot!

They found themselves in the next room!

The sight which they then saw filled them with surprise and indignation.

## CHAPTER IV.

THE CAPTIVES RESCUED FROM A LIVING TOMB—AN IMPORTANT CONVERSATION OVERHEARD—THE DARK CONSPIRACY—THE HAPPY RELEASE—FINDING OF THE MONEY SAFE—THE DISTRIBUTION OF COIN.

HUSH-S-S-H!" said old Giles, with a finger on his lip in token of dead silence.

Frank and Dick looked on the scene before them with beating hearts, and cheeks flushed with anger.

In a corner of that small, dark, damp, and comfortless room lay a boy and girl asleep!

They were reposing on a dirty straw mattress upon the floor, and covered with a ragged counterpane.

A single chair, on which stood a small basin of water, with soap and a dirty towel, was the only article of furniture in the place.

A pitcher of water, and an old stale mouse-eaten loaf was near the bed.

The girl appeared to be about fourteen years of age, a pale, pallid, pretty girl she was, with long, black, wavy hair, beautiful eye-lashes, and pouting lips, which disclosed in sleep her matchless teeth.

She was thin and haggard from want, neglect, and cruelty, yet, for all this, as we have said, she was pretty, nay, captivating, and as she smiled in sleep she affectionately threw a slim, white, delicately-formed hand and arm around her brother's neck, and caressed him unconsciously.

The boy seemed to be a little younger than his sister.

He had a manly face, but marks of sorrow had left deep lines upon it.

Frank and Dick looked on in wonder.

"What mystery is this?" asked Frank, in an almost inaudible whisper.

"I will tell ye all by-and-bye," said old Giles, with a deep sigh.

"But we must rescue and save these poor creatures," said Frank.

"Silence, I say," old Giles answered, "silence, or all is lost. Jonathan may overhear us, and then all our good intentions would be foiled. They *shall* be rescued, but not now. See how they sleep, poor dears! Old Jonathan puts drugs in their food so as to make 'em sleep as much as possible. Hush-sh! don't you hear him talking in the next room?"

Frank listened, and heard his own name mentioned.

This excited his curiosity intensely, and he put his ear to the key-hole.

"If that young imp of the devil gets possession of my private desk I am lost," said Jonathan to Shanks.

"Why so, sir?"

"I received a letter from Flint this morning, together with 1,000 pounds in bank notes."

"Indeed?"

"Yes."

"Might I ask what for, sir—for what purpose?"

"That secret remains with me, Mr. Shanks. When you have married my daughter Sophia you will be a blood relation, and I can then explain all, but suffice it to say I have made up my mind that neither of them shall receive a penny of it. I will keep it for my myself, and transport the young rascals for theft or on some other false pretence; it is easily done. I know that such a turn of affairs would greatly please Flint, their uncle's lawyer."

"It is well Mr. Caspar never knew anything of those two brats, sir."

"Just so, just so; nobody knows a word about it, Shanks, but you, myself and my wife. Did you give them that sleeping draught as usual this morning?"

"Yes."

"That's right, let 'em sleep away their life; they won't get very fat on what *I* give 'em, eh, Shanks?" said Jonathan, with a fiendish grin.

"I think not," Shanks replied; "but it is a very great responsibility, sir."

"I know it, but I am well paid for it, you know. Those two half-starved brats are worth £1,000 a year to me."

"Indeed!"

"Yes; I have had 'em here this last eight years or more. They haven't been out of that room once since. I don't know how it is, but they *won't* die, Shanks."

"No, they seem to linger on, sir. I don't know what keeps life in 'em; I'm sure their allowance of bread and water, and their daily sleeping-draughts can't make e'm very fat."

"I wish they *would* die, you know, Shanks, because if they did it would be a thousand or two in my pocket, but *why*, you know, is a dead secret to any one but me at present."

* * * * *

Frank heard all this conversation with a beating heart.

The first impulse of his noble nature was to liberate the boy and girl, and then have Jonathan arrested.

But he thought that after all he had done in causing the riot, and breaking up the school, his word would not be trusted by any one of a jury.

He knew not what to do, and turned his head to consult Dick Fellows.

At that moment the boy and girl awoke.

They smiled gladly when they beheld their old and long-tried friend Giles, but were astonished at seeing Frank and Dick.

The young girl blushed, and hid her face beneath the bed-clothes, as her gaze met that of Frank.

"Silence!" old Giles whispered to them. "Make not the slightest noise, as you value your lives. I have brought these two young gentlemen to assist me in carrying you both away."

At these words the girl and boy stared wildly for a moment, and then streams of silent tears flowed from their eyes.

"Thank Heaven!" they sighed.

While Giles was meditating what to do Frank's heart leaped into his mouth with excitement.

The sight of the pale, pretty girl filled him with joy and enthusiasm.

He knelt down, and clothing the girl in an old ragged blanket, took her up in his arms like a child, and kissed her affectionately often and often, as he said in a whisper,

"I will save her, if I die for it!"

Dick Fellows instantly did likewise with the boy.

Old Giles was thunderstruck at the strength Frank and Dick thus unexpectedly displayed.

He could not have believed it possible.

But all they did was done so quietly that old Jonathan, in the next room, could not hear them, not even a footstep.

In a few seconds they had passed through the cupboard before described, and were free from the dingy, dreary prison.

"This way, this way, lads," cried old Giles. "Take them out by the back door. My cottage is not far off; no one will suspect them there."

Frank and Dick descended the back staircase, each with his precious burden, and, unobserved even by the riotous students, who were merrily and noisily carousing below, staggered away through the orchard, and reached the old gardener's cottage in safety.

Old Giles's wife was amazed.

She held up her aged hands in wonder and astonishment.

"There is no time for words or explanations now, good wife," said Frank. "Clothe this girl and boy as best you can; they must fly from this place at once."

"Night would be safest," said Giles.

"At nightfall, then, let it be," said Dick.

Not stopping to speak more at that moment, Frank and Dick returned to their friends, but said not a word of their strange discovery of the imprisoned and half-starved boy and girl.

"Now's the time for our pocket-money, lads," said Frank. "I've found out all about it. Follow me; *I* know where the master's safe is. He has been robbing all of us this many a day. Whoever wants his money, let him follow me."

The word "money" acted like a charm upon the young insurgents, and with a loud shout they followed Frank and Dick to the private room of old Jonathan.

Foremost among them all was the red, excited Fat Boy, who was puffing and blowing like a grampus.

As soon as they reached the door of the master's private room they burst it open.

Inside were discovered Mrs. Gravestones and her daughters.

Madam and her two scraggy daughters rushed from the room screaming with alarm.

The desks were soon broken, and in one of them was found a memorandum-book which contained every item of money received for the students, but none of which had ever been given to them.

"Here it is, lads, here it is!" said Frank. "Here's the little book which proves what a scoundrel old Jonathan is! Listen!"

And in great excitement Frank Ford read as follows:—

"'Received for Dick Fellows, £200; ditto for Hugh Tracy, £300; ditto for the young scamps, Frank and Tom Ford, £500 each, a penny of which they shall never receive!'

"Do you hear *that*, lads? You *now* see how great a villain the old wretch is. But listen:—

"'Received for the "two brats," £400.'"

"Who are the two brats?" asked many.

"Ah, that is a great mystery as yet," said Frank, with a knowing wink. "It will all come out in a short time; won't it Dick?"

"I believe you, my boy," answered Dick.

"Here's some more items," said Hal; "the old devil seems to have his knife in all the young Garibaldians. Listen:—

"'Received from Steve Gray's parents, £300 in all, a penny of which he shall never have.'

"There are twenty other items here, lads, shall I read 'em?"

"No, no!"

"Where's the money?"

"Let's find it, and divide as the book says."

"Agreed! agreed! Hurrah, for gallant Frank! It's no theft to take our own!" said many.

"Three cheers for Garibaldi's young captain!"

"Here's the safe, lads," said Frank, opening a cupboard. "Pull it out, and burst it open."

"No need of that," said Hugh Tracy, "here's the key; I took it out of the old woman's pocket."

In less than a minute the safe was lugged out of the lower compartment of a cupboard and opened.

The money was found!

With the book in hand Frank Ford called off the amounts due to each youth, and which Hugh Tracy and Dick Fellows handed over to the rightful owner.

"Now what shall we do?" asked a dozen voices.

"Pack up your trunks, lads, as quick as possible, and let's away," said Frank Ford. "I shan't stop within these walls two hours longer."

"Nor I! nor I!" shouted a score of voices.

"I'm off to join Garibaldi!" shouted Frank.

"Bravo! bravo! So will I! And I! And I!" roared more than a score, right lustily.

"A steamer starts for Italy to-morrow, lads," said Hugh Tracy; "it leaves Southampton with several bands of volunteers. Who will go?"

"All of us! Every one!" resounded on all sides.

"Then, let us pack up, and get off as soon as possible."

"Agreed! Who shall lead us?"

"Frank Ford!"

"Garibaldi's young captain!"

"Bravo! bravo! so he shall!"

"Then, let each one go his own way, and meet to-morrow evening at Southampton," said Frank. "I will lead you!"

"Agreed! agreed!"

Within a short time nearly all the students were prepared to depart.

It was arranged among the young Garibaldians that all were to meet at Southampton on the following evening, so that by going different ways and by different conveyances their flight from Bromley Hall Academy might not be so much noticed.

Ere long, then, a goodly number of students had departed, some by railroad and others by the river steamers which were not far away from the academy.

Frank and Tom Ford made up their minds to visit London that night, but what their object there might be they told to no one.

Frank and Tom, together with Dick Fellows and Hugh Tracy, stayed behind for some time until they could procure a conveyance in which to bear away Annie Morton and her brother Joe, the two youthful prisoners they had rescued that day.

Frank jumped upon the box, and, whip in hand, drove off at a rapid pace.

Tom was inside with the poor, friendless orphans, while Dick Fellows and Hugh Tracey sat upon the roof, and waved their handkerchiefs in triumph, as they dashed along on their way to London.

It was well that Frank and his friends departed when they did, for a dozen stout and determined constables arrived at Bromley Hall Academy, armed to the teeth, and well primed with old ale.

But the birds had flown.

The sight of his private desks and money-safe broken open and rifled, caused Gravestones to curse.

"Follow me, Shanks, follow me; my worst fears are aroused. If our secret has been discovered we are ruined!"

Up stairs they went, both together, and darted into the room. It was empty!

With a shout of long pent-up rage, he foamed at the mouth, and stamped and swore until almost black in the face.

"Idiot!" he said, addressing Shanks, "I *knew* that this would come to pass. Why did you thwart me?"

"*I* did not interfere with your plan, sir," Shanks answered, meekly.

"Liar!" stammered old Jonathan.

"Sir?"

"Don't stand there sirring me."

"I do not understand——"

"Not understand, eh, when I call you fool! liar! idiot! ass! eh?"

"Rev. sir——"

"Rev. devils!" said Jonathan, stamping with rage. "I am undone; I must fly! The two birds have flown; I tell you this, sir, is *your* doings!"

"Mine, sir?"

"Yes, yours. Take *that*, sir, for your pains," said he, and at the same moment hit Shanks a violent blow in the face, which knocked him down.

With a loud laugh of mingled rage, disappointment, and venom, he flung open the door, and darted out of the room, saying between his teeth, and in a hissing tone—

"I must away to London at once, or all is lost! and reach it I will before midnight chimes from the tower of St. Paul's."

In a low, hissing tone he added,

"*I will have ample revenge!*"

## CHAPTER V.

THE ALARM—DESPERATE SITUATION OF WARNER—THE DEAD MAN'S DYING GRIP—THE STRUGGLE FOR LIFE OR DEATH—THE DAGGER USED—THE TREASURE GONE—THE PARCHMENTS—THE ASSAULT OF THE POLICE—THE SECRET PANEL—THE ESCAPE, AND FEARFUL FALL—WHO AND WHERE IS THE MURDERER?

FOR a second or two Warner was struck dumb with astonishment!

"Who could the assassin be?" he thought. "Was it one of the nephews? They were both expected home that night, and at twelve o'clock. It *must* be one of them. Yet he knows nothing of the concealment of the treasure. What a fool he is; how lucky it is for me! It will save me doing the nasty job, and yet I can secure the treasure, for he is dead!"

Thinking thus, he opened the door and entered old Ford's room.

With hasty steps he rushed towards the old man.

To get at the treasure he had to raise the body.

In hurry and excitement he did so!

He threw his arms around the old man, and lifted up the body!

In doing so, a quantity of blood spurted from the wound!

Old Ford was *not* dead!

With a dying, convulsive grasp he seized Warner by the throat with a grip of steel!

Warner was almost paralysed with fear.

"Help! help!" faintly sighed the old man. "Murder! he is here! Help! help! I am dying!"

Warner struggled violently to get free from Ford's suffocating grasp, but could not.

He became black in the face, and was nearly choked.

To add to his horror and fright, there were now heard loud noises outside in the street!

They approached nearer and nearer.

Hurried heavy footsteps were heard upon the stairs

"This way! this way!" said the voices.

"Murder! help! murder! villains! police! murder!" shouted Davy, at the top of his voice.

"Death and damnation!" gasped Warner, struggling desperately to release himself from the dead man's hold. "I must be quick or the blood-hounds will be upon me!"

With all the energy of death and despair staring him in the face, he made one last and desperate effort.

With young Ford's dagger he cut, and slashed, and jagged at the dead man's hand.

He was free!

He hurled the body upon the floor.

It fell with a heavy sound.

"I have time yet," he gasped, in great haste. "The treasure shall not escape me."

He threw the pillows about, and searched for the miser's fortune.

It was not there—neither in cash or notes.

With a terrible oath of disappointment he seized a small bundle of papers he found there.

"Haste! haste!" cried Davy. "He is here! he is here!"

The noise of feet clattering up the front stairs aroused him into energy.

"It was Davy who has caused all this alarm," he said. "He shall die for it!"

He rushed towards the helpless old butler, and would have stabbed him on the spot.

The glimmer of a policeman's lantern upon the stairs quickly approaching the landing made his heart sink within him.

He had not time to slay old Davy, so slammed the chamber door and locked it.

"I am surrounded and hemmed in on all sides," he said, "but I will fight dearly for my life. Which way did that young assassin enter?"

On the instant he sounded the walls in every direction and on all sides.

"Break the door!" "Burst it open!" "Rush in upon him, my men!" "Take care; he is armed!" "Dash in upon him!" "Kill him like a dog, if he dares resist!"

Such were the confused sounds of angry voices outside.

Truncheons battered at the door with dull, heavy sounds.

But the door was old, heavy, doubly-barred, and made of stout English oak.

It seemed to resist all the efforts of those pushing against or battering at it.

"Here's an axe! here's a strong axe!" said one.

"Give it to me," said the sergeant.

"Hand it this way," said 61 Z, who had now arrived upon the scene.

Crash! crash! bang! bang! went the axe at the door.

Warner now felt like a man who had not many minutes to live.

He sounded the walls in every direction, and yet he could not find the secret entrance through which the assassin had got in.

The door was fast giving way to the terrible blows delivered on it by the powerful arms of two or three determined officers.

There was no light in the room, and Warner could see by the fitful rays of their lanterns through a broken panel how fierce and determinedly the constables were working to get in.

"One moment more, and the hounds are upon me," said the desperate villain.

Least when he expected it, the door fell in upon the floor with a loud crash.

The officers and others rushed into the room.

Several of them stumbled over the dead man's body, and were smeared with blood.

Warner, unseen, retreated behind the bed-curtains, and fell against a panel of the wainscoting.

It gave way!

A single panel turned on its hinges!

He fell through it, whither he knew not.

It was a tremendous fall!

The secret panel closed on its hinges again.

The officers were foiled!

The villain escaped!

## CHAPTER VI.

THE ALARM—THE PURSUIT—BILL BARNEY, THE HALF-BRED PUG—CABBY AND HIS SUSPICIOUS FARE—OLD FLINT IS FLEECED—CABBY DRIVES OLD FLINT HOME, AND THINKS HE SMELLS A MOUSE.

OLD FLINT, the cunning, foxy lawyer, had not gone far on his way home when he overtook two policemen. They were Sergeant Ruff and policeman Tomkins, No. 61 Z.

"I don't care what anybody says, sergeant," Tomkins observed, "I always did and always shall think that that there house is no good, and so that's flat. It looks like a murderer's den to me, and always did. It's so gloomy, and stands out o' the way of all other houses, as if it had a guilty conscience, and didn't want to be stared at much."

Sergeant Ruff laughed, as he remarked quietly,

"Ah, my boy, you haven't seen as much o' this here world as I have. When you've been six-and-twenty years in the force you'll not be so taken up with the look o' houses as the physogs o' cracksmen and the like."

"That may be, Sergeant Ruff," Tomkins answered, "but no good 'll come out o' that 'ere queer-looking place, if I'm any judge, for it looks to me more like a genteel 'smasher's crib,' or some respectable 'fence,' than anything else. And talking of queer-looking faces, I must say I see two or three o' sich like about and around my beat to-night as I never seed afore."

"Ah! indeed! you never mentioned it before, Tomkins. Was to-night the first time you observed them?"

"No. Me and Smithers, 47 Y, whose beat joins mine at top o' the street, have noticed it all this week; but, barring the looks o' the chaps, I didn't see anything worth talking of. Nothing was done, you know. All my beat and his was quiet and snug; but I didn't fail to make a note or two in my book, for the inspector's use, if required."

"Quite right, Tomkins, quite right."

The two policemen walked on slowly, and Flint heard no more, for he hastily turned down a bye-street without being seen by either of the officers.

He had not gone many yards—in truth, he had but just turned the corner out of view—when his heart beat wildly, and his limbs trembled so violently that he could scarcely walk.

"Mur-d-e-r! mur-d-e-r!" faintly cried some distant voice that was borne on the passing breeze.

He stopped near the entrance to a mews, and under its dark shade he listened with distended eyes.

"Mur-d-e-r! mur-d-e-r!" were the ominous sounds which greeted his astonished ears.

In an instant he heard the rapid footsteps of the two officers running up the silent street.

In a few moments, several rattles were sprung.

The echo grated upon his ears, and seemed to cut his very heart strings asunder.

A flash of lightning—a vivid unearthly, blinding flash—crossed the street.

A terrific peal of thunder crashed over his head.

"The vengeance of heaven follows me!" he moaned, and sank down in his hiding-place more dead than alive.

"Murd-e-r! murd-e-r!" still rang out through the streets with heart-chilling echoes.

The policeman's rattle was sprung again and again.

A cold sweat oozed from his body, and his teeth chattered like one attacked with deadly ague.

From all directions he heard heavy-booted policemen running towards the scene of blood!

He perceived two of them rapidly approaching the spot where he then stood.

His heart almost leaped into his mouth, and he could have shouted out aloud with mental torture.

"The deed is done! Ford is dead! I know it—I feel it!" he gasped. "Warner has been true to his word, and I have been false to mine! No matter. Oh! that I were safe in my office—a thousand pounds to be anywhere but here."

The two officers he had heard approaching him slackened their pace, out of breath, as they came nearer to the mews.

"I am betrayed!" he moaned. "Warner is caught, and has confessed all. I am a dead man! they have tracked me!"

He fell in the corner in which he stood; but the two officers passed him by.

Oh! what a relief it was to Flint.

He felt as if a ton weight had been lifted off his shoulders.

"I must be quick," he muttered. "The whole neighbourhood will be aroused in a few moments."

As he spoke he heard windows raised in all directions, and could plainly catch the distant sound of voices murmuring in the direction of old Ford's house.

By a lucky chance a four-wheel cab came into the street at a slow pace.

The horse and driver seemed drenched with rain.

"Drive on cabby, be quick!" said the voice of some one inside; "drive sharply, I tell you, and I'll pay you well."

"All right, sir," said cabby, an old man, clay pipe in mouth, muffled up to the nose in endless handkerchiefs and wrappers; "all right, sir, I'll go as fast as I can," and whipped up his poor jaded beast accordingly.

All the whips in the world, however, would not have forced that poor, weak and broken-winded animal to hold up his head and go faster.

It was not in him, and cabby knew it, for he was a "long night man," and any sort of horse is considered good enough for a stormy night, whether it be lame, broken-winded, or even half-dead.

"Drive on, cabby, drive on," said the impatient gentleman inside.

"All right, sir, don't be in a hurry; as fast as I can, sir. 'Orses ain't steam engines, you know, sir, and I don't wish mine to bust his biler."

"Oh, that I had a cab," said Flint, half-aloud, just at the moment when a rough costermonger-looking fellow was passing him.

"Hullo!" said the rough-looking stranger, "what's all this, eh? Why, blow me, if there ain't an old gent knocked all of a heap in the corner here. Hi, cabby!"

The rough-looking fellow approached old Flint and raised him up.

"Rather queer, sir; nasty night, ain't it? A little too much wine, I take it. I thought so. Hi, cabby!"

Thus hailed in a very noisy style the cabman stopped.

His fare, however, was so disgusted that he opened the door and slipped out without the driver perceiving it.

"What d' yer want a 'ailing me? Don't yer see as how I've got a fare."

"Well, if you has, it licks me," said the rough-looking fellow, looking into the cab, and laughing; "you must a been havin' a snooze, old 'un; there's nary party inside as I sees on, but there *is* a hold party jest here as vants a lift up; he vishes to go to the city."

The old cabman cursed and swore at the trick played on him by the stranger, and, in a very loud manner observed,

"Jest to think as how that there party should a come puffin' and a blowin' up to the rank, and 'drive like the devil!' says he, and then, cause a 'orse isn't a hexpress engine, he hooks it. I vish I honly 'ad 'is 'ead 'ere," said cabby, making pretence of having a man's head under his left arm, "I vish I honly 'ad 'is 'ead 'ere, *that's* all, he's a werry suspicious-looking article, whoever he vas."

After a few seconds old Flint recovered himself and explained that the dreadful thunder and lightning had discomposed him for a moment and that he had fallen and cut his cheek."

"Jest so, sir," said cabby, winking at the rough-looking stranger; "jest so, sir, it *is* werry quver weather; unkimmon I might say."

"The old gent vishes to be took to St. Paul's," said the rough-looking fellow, with a knowing wink at cabby.

"All right, master, jump in."

Flint walked slowly to the cab and got in, but not before giving several quick, inquisitive glances at the stranger and cabby, who were whispering together.

"I thinks as how I've seen *your* mug afore," said cabby to the stranger, in a very dry and quiet way.

"Has yer," said the stranger, "an vhot of it?"

"Just so."

"Vhere?"

"At the Bailey," said cabby, in a faint whisper, and winking. "Any swag?"

"Not a ha'porth?"

"Gammon! Bill Barney, the pug, ain't soft. Vhere shall I see yer to-morrow, Bill," said cabby, with much earnestness, "at the station, eh?"

"The 'Cat and Bagpipes,'" said Barney, with a look of anger.

"Vhat time?"

"Arternoon."

"On the square, Barney; honour?"

"Oh, in course."

"All right; I'll be there."

So speaking together cabby drove off with his fare, muttering,

"Who'd a thought a seein' *him* up here in this genteel part o' the town; summat's up, or it ain't Barney's fault. I suppose I shall see all about it in to-morrow's '*Tiser*."

Barney looked after the cab for a moment, and then glanced at a handsome gold watch and chain he pulled out of his capacious pocket.

"The old cock looked werry queer though; but vot's the use o' the time o' day to *him?* Lor, how easy it slipped out of his pocket, to be sure, this 'ere pocket-book an' all."

Barney looked at the treasures with a fond eye, and then, after a moment of deep thought, ran after the cab.

He soon overtook it, and, with great agility climbed up behind without being heard or seen while rumbling over the noisy stones.

"I must not be seen around that *there* quarter in a hurry," he said to himself; "the sooner I gets out o' the way the better. Nobody knows *my* lodgin's, and if they does, vhy, I can get a dozen to swear I didn't leave my crib all night; aye, I could have a dozen halibis for a pint o' gin, and square it with 'em all in less nor no time."

So thinking—cabby of Bill Barney, and the latter of cabby—the vehicle drove on through Lincoln's Inn Fields, where Barney, unobserved, slipped off into a quiet street, and walked rapidly towards his "crib" as he called it, down one of the numerous dirty streets and alley ways of Drury Lane.

## CHAPTER VII.

MYSTERY FOLLOWS MYSTERY — THE DOUBLE MURDER — THE HEADLESS BODY — FIRE IN THE COURT—THE BODY RESCUED BY LONG TOM THE COSTER AND "BRUDDER BONES" —VISIT OF THE UNKNOWN.

THE old cabman drove his unknown "fare" through the streets, perfectly unconscious that Barney the "fighting cove" had been riding behind.

"This 'ere's a jolly rum go, an' no mistake," he mused, as he "touched up" his jaded animal occasionally, with a low "ge-et alorng, will yer?"

"I begins for ter think as how there's some nice little game on hand. Howsomedever, I'll give 'im a call to-morrer or next day, and see vhat's in the vind."

While thinking thus, old Flint inside pulled the "check string," and the "four wheeler" stopped.

"Vhat now, sir?" asked cabby.

"Are there any public-houses open, cabby?" Flint asked, in a weak voice.

"Vell, it's rayther early, guv'nor, but I dare say as how there's one or two in the Garden."

"Then, drive there; I feel faint. You needn't go right into Covent Garden, you know, but stop at the corner of the street."

"All right, sir."

Once again cabby cracked his whip, and turned his horse's head in the direction of the market.

Ere long they reached Long Acre, when the cabman stopped.

"We are quite near enough to a public-house now," said Flint, nervously. "Do you go, and bring me a half pint of brandy; you can keep the change for yourself," he observed, handing cabby a crown-piece.

For a moment the cabman imagined that "the old gent was arter doin' ov 'im out on his fare," but when he had "collared the dollar" he felt easy, and went to the nearest public-house for the brandy.

When he returned Flint had disappeared.

The lawyer, it would seem, watched cabby into the public-house, and saw him stop for a second or two and speak to a policeman.

Flint's heart leaped into his mouth!

"What if he suspects me!" thought the old lawyer.

His resolution was taken immediately.

He slipped out of the cab, and darted down one of the many, dirty dark and narrow streets that lead to the Seven Dials.

Having gained this neighbourhood, he knew not for a moment which of the streets to turn down towards his abode, in Green Court, Strand.

Ultimately the rattling of cab wheels startled him like a hare.

With a quick step he trudged through the blinding rain, which now began to fall, and soon found himself in Drury Lane.

With more courage than was his wont, he chose one of the numerous dirty, narrow side streets.

Through the slush and half-putrid garbage he trudged, picking his way through the carts, barrows, baskets, and what not, belonging to a numerous family of "costers" abiding there, and soon found himself in Lincoln's Inn Fields.

With a fast beating pulse, he stood for a moment out of the rain under a doorway, and reflected on what he had better do next.

"Shall I go to my lodgings or to the office?" he thought.

The rain abated a little, but it was still pitch dark.

He crossed over towards the railings, and crept close to them on his way towards Carey Street.

As he did so he distinctly perceived the figure of a man hurriedly gliding through the drizzling rain on the opposite side of the way, in the same direction as himself.

For a moment Flint stopped, and allowed the man to go ahead of him.

This the unknown did, and was soon lost to view.

In a few moments Flint resumed his quick walk towards his lodgings, situated in Green Court not far off; but when about to turn down the court, he heard and saw some one violently pulling the bell at the very house in which he lived.

He knew not who it was, but thought it wise to stop and listen.

A neighbouring door was open in the court.

This afforded him shelter.

He peeped out, and soon perceived that the landlady of his house opened the door, candle in hand.

"Who do you want?" asked the landlady, in a sharp, cracked voice, and by no means gratified at being thus disturbed in her slumbers. "Who do you want at this unnat'ral time o' night?"

"Does a Mr. Flint live here, ma'am?" asked the stranger, politely.

"Do you mean *Old* Flint?" asked the angry landlady; "if so I understands yer; but we doesn't know any *Mister* Flints here. What do yer want of him?"

"Oh, nothing in particular," the stranger replied, "only——"

"Well, then, if it's nothing in partic'lar, why do yer come at this time o' the mornin' for?"

"Is he in?"

"No, he isn't, and——"

"Where *is* he, then? Has he lost anything?"

"How should *I* know; who do you take me for, eh? I'm not his wife, nor mother neither; the old miser can't have lost much, I wouldn't give twopence for all he's worth."

"Hasn't he an office somewhere, ma'am?"

"Perhaps he has, and perhaps he hasn't; but if he has it can't be worth much, or he wouldn't live in Green Court. I takes it his office ain't much better than a dust-hole, if he *has* any."

"He may have an *object* in living here," said the stranger, in an emphatic manner. "Well, it doesn't matter for the present. Good night, I'm sorry for troubling you; I shall call again."

The landlady slammed the door in the stranger's face, who slowly left the court.

Flint, from his dark place of concealment, eyed the stranger as he passed.

"It isn't Warner," he thought; "who can it be?"

In a few moments he let himself into his lodgings with a latch-key.

To his no small amazement he found his own room door ajar.

For a moment he hesitated what to do; but, at last, thinking he had forgotten to shut it when he went out, he screwed up his resolution, and entered.

Yet, as he did so, he kept muttering to himself, in the dark,

"It wasn't Warner, yet who *can* it be?"

As thus he whispered, an echo seemed to say to him,

"Who *can* it be?"

As he sat in his dark room he felt cold shivers creeping all over him.

"*Lost* anything? What could he mean? *Me* lose anything? Not very likely, indeed; no one knows what I have got hidden away in my office; the old iron safe is crammed with one thing and another of value. What shall I do now? pack up my papers and leave, or stop till morning? Morning," he thought, "perhaps Warner will be here before then."

All this time Flint felt the cold shivers thrill through his very heart.

He felt as if he was surrounded by ten thousand devils.

Whichever way he cast his eyes in the darkness, he thought he saw Warner standing over the helpless body of the murdered Ford.

He opened an old cupboard, and, from a bottle, took a hearty drink of gin.

This, for a moment, seemed to cheer him; but still he felt his heart quaking with fear.

The darkness of his little room seemed intolerable to him.

The very air seemed peopled with unclean spirits shouting "Murder! Mystery!" in his ears.

His very soul seemed appalled, and he could have shouted out aloud with mental fright and anguish.

He lit his lamp.

He next turned towards his bed to seek for something hidden beneath the clothes.

Upon a sudden he started back with horror at what he saw.

He gasped for breath.

His eyes seemed to start from their sockets.

His teeth chattered with fear.

The whole of the veins in his face, hands and neck were swollen with horror.

The lamp dropped from his hand upon the floor with a smash.

In an instant the oil ignited in all directions around him.

This he knew not at the moment, for his heart, soul and mind were deadened with fright and horror.

He sank upon his knees with hands clasped before him.

"Oh, horrible!" he gasped, with a foaming mouth, and fell prostrate on the floor.

The sight he had seen, indeed, was terrible—horrifying!

*A headless body lay gory and ghastly in his bed!"*

*No. 2 will be ready next Friday. Orders should be given early.*

# THE BOY SOLDIER;

## OR, GARIBALDI'S YOUNG CAPTAIN.

His clothes were all soaked with blood!

For a moment or two he lay prostrate and helpless upon the floor.

The flames, which now began to encircle him, aroused him from his almost deadly stupor.

He jumped to his feet like a lunatic.

"I am a dead man!" he gasped. "I am pursued by avenging furies! I am doomed!"

Trembling in heart and limbs, with every thought concentrated in his own safety, he closed his door and locked it, and took the key with him.

He noiselessly descended the stairs and escaped into the street.

In a second he had disappeared with the fleetness of a hare.

Within a few moments the flames burst forth from his room in one broad sheet, and the whole court was in an uproar.

"Fire! fire!" were the sounds which Flint heard in all directions.

Still he ran on.

He was almost blind with excitement, and ran full butt against a policeman.

"Hillo! what's up? You look frightened!" said the policeman. "What have you been up to, eh, old 'un?"

"N-n-nothing," gasped Flint. "There is a fire broken out! Don't stop me; I'm going to fetch the engines."

"Fire! where?"

"In Green Court," gasped Flint. "Don't stop me!"

"All right," said the policeman. "Look sharp; you're sure to earn a crown."

Flint ran one way and the policeman another.

Soon a bright flame burst forth from the court.

But there was still another cry which startled both Flint and the policeman more that that of "fire!"

It was the wild shout of—

*Murder!*

Which now broke forth from the court as a headless body was dragged, half charred, out of Flint's room by the brave exertions of Long Tom, a coster, and "Bones," otherwise Joe Banks, who travelled about the town and country, sometimes as a "tumbler," and at others as one of a band of "niggers," both of whom lived near by.

"Murder!" thought the policeman, as he hastened towards the fire. "Then that old man did it!"

## CHAPTER VIII.

MARK, THE FOSTER-BROTHER, TURNS SOLDIER—PLOTS AGAINST NELLY LANCASTER—THE SWORN AND DEADLY FOE—SPIES ENGAGED BY JOEL—THE FAT BOY AND BUTTONS IN ECSTACIES—THE JOURNEY—OLD FLINT'S PLOT DISCOVERED—THE BANKER'S DAUGHTER.

ACCORDING to a previous arrangement made with the young Garibaldians, Frank and his brother Tom proceeded straight to London the same night they left Bromley Hall, but for what purpose they told no one.

Dick Fellows hinted that they had gone to see their old uncle before leaving England.

Hugh Tracy, however, thought differently, for neither Frank nor Tom had ever been on very good terms with "the old miser," as they called him.

In fact, the truth was they had had violent quarrels with him.

It was also rumoured among the young Garibaldians that they had had frequent "rows" with the old man, and it was said their uncle did not much care what they did or where they went to.

Be that as it may, and let the opinions of his young comrades be what they might, both Frank and Tom appeared upon the scene again at the appointed time and place, greatly to the delight of the "Fat Boy," and young "Buttons," both of whom entered heart and soul into the proposed trip to Italy to join Garibaldi.

The "Fat Boy" didn't much care about the prospect of fighting the Austrians, it is true, although he was no coward when "cornered" and compelled to use his fists, or any weapon that was handy.

In truth, he saw nothing else in the proposed expedition than pilfering, and plundering, and sacking villages and towns for the sake of booty, devilment, and good living.

Fat as he was, he was always ripe for a lark and fun of any kind, but his chief delight was in "feeding" well upon the fat of the land, and of sleeping any number of hours he could get.

"Buttons," on the other hand, was quite the reverse of the Fat Boy.

While "Fatty" was round, unwieldy, slow, and possessed of an unlimited appetite, young Buttons was quick, slim, always wide awake, tricky, and slimy as an eel—here, there, and everywhere at once.

He delighted in adventure of any sort, was active as a cat, and cunning as a young ape.

"Buttons" was much beloved by all the young Garibaldians, would go anywhere, or do anything for them, was up to all sorts of larks and madcap freaks with policemen and servant-girls, was always getting in and out of scrapes of all kinds, and fond of singing songs.

When Frank and Tom joined their comrades it was observed that the former looked pale, nervous, and full of anxiety, but this soon disappeared, and although he shunned all mention of London and of his uncle, he soon regained his usual flow of good-humour and "dash."

Some proposed that they should start by the steamer from Southampton to Italy.

This proposition was opposed by Frank, who whispered mysteriously about policemen being on the look-out for them there to arrest them.

Buttons immediately proposed that they should knock down the first "bobby" that dared oppose them.

Fatty, for his part, didn't care which route was selected so that it was easy and pleasant, and didn't involve much jolting about.

After a lengthy conference between Frank and other young leaders it was decided to pass over to France, and take a steamer that was to sail from Marseilles with a crowd of disguised volunteers who were bound for Garibaldi—young men who had for the most part at one time or another been in the French army.

This was agreed to by all unanimously, and particularly by "Fatty," who had loving, longing dreams of French fruits and famous French wines and brandies, commodities which young Paunch greatly delighted in whenever his limited allowance of pocket-money would "run to it."

Away then they started by rail for Dover, and a merry, noisy party they were, singing and shouting, smoking and drinking all the way, greatly to the annoyance and alarm of sundry old ladies and gentlemen who were fellow-passengers.

Buttons had never been on the railway before.

The luxury and ease of a "first-class" carriage were delightful to him, and his mirth and noisiness knew no bounds.

Dick Fellows, Hugh Tracy, Tom Ford, and the other young leaders sang patriotic songs until almost hoarse with shouting.

But Frank was dark, silent, and moody.

He had the pale, restless look of one who was fearful.

His face was sorrowful, and almost haggard.

*He seemed at times like one who had dread remorse for some fearful crime.*

He was thoughtful of what Joel Flint had said before they parted during the riot and heat of conflict at school—

"Frank, I am your mortal enemy, and until death! I will follow you like an evil genius throughout the bounds of the whole earth!—you cannot, you *shall* not escape me! I will ruin you—nay, blast your name and character wherever you go! When you shall be branded as a traitor I will laugh with scorn; when you stand in the felon's dock, a convicted thief and assassin, my revenge will be complete, *but not till then.* Fly where you will, you shall be followed night and die! We are sworn enemies! *I will drive you to madness and despair!*"

This fearful curse Frank well remembered, but why Joel entertained such an inveterate hatred he could not tell.

Their natures were opposite.

Joel was much older, but still they heartily detested each other, and were deadly enemies from the first moment they had ever met.

A strange fatality hung over them.

One was clever, the other a dunce.

Frank was loved by more than one fair damsel, where Joel was despised.

Young Flint could never attain distinction or honour of any sort while Frank was in the field, and this he knew.

Frank was beloved by all, and Joel the reverse.

The best and the bravest at Bromley Hall chose Frank for their leader.

While Joel was deep in cunning, and a coward at heart, Frank was open, brave, and generous to a fault.

Joel hated his school-fellow with the bitterness of a devil.

Frank despised Joel, and treated him with supreme contempt.

But while Frank had friends who would fight for him to the death, Joel also had a band of followers who, in secret, obeyed all his orders.

Joel had *money*.

How or by what means he got it need not now be said.

With this money he bought up spies—dark daring fellows it were well to avoid; but of this Frank and his band of young Garibaldians knew nothing.

*They little dreamed that there were active spies and informers in their ranks!*

But this was true.

Joel Flint had two of his friends among Frank's followers.

Well, then, might Frank, as he sat in a first-class carriage on his way to Dover, smoking a cigar, remember Joel's ominous, poisoned-tainted threat,

"When you are branded as a traitor, I will laugh with scorn! When you stand in the felon's dock, a convicted thief and assassin, my vengeance will be complete! *but not till then!*"

* * * * *

Dover was soon reached, but directly the train arrived, and after his companions were comfortably provided for in a cosy inn not far from the steamboat pier, Frank hired a horse and dashed off into the country towards a neighbouring village.

What his object was none knew, not even his brother Tom.

His presence for some time was not missed, and when it was very little comment was made thereupon, for, during the last day or two, Frank's behaviour had been so mysterious and unaccountable that no one could imagine what troubled him.

As to the Fat Boy and Buttons, they vigorously laid siege to an immense veal pie, nor did either "give in" until the savory dish was demolished and abundantly washed down with ale, after which, Fatty and Buttons indulged in a cigar, and soon were "gloriously tight," singing and brawling loudly, but not very musically.

At a furious rate Frank galloped and soon arrived at the village.

He dismounted at the "Red Lion," tied up his horse to a post, and bent his steps hurriedly towards a humble cottage.

Before he reached it, however, his approach was perceived by a strong, rosy-faced youth, about his own age and size, who rushed forth from the cottage to meet him.

"What, Frank!"

"Brother Mark!"

Such were the greetings of the two foster-brothers.

For it must be explained that Frank and Tom Ford were twins.

Their mother had disappeared suddenly, unaccountably, and mysteriously, when they were but a month old, and they had been reared from the breast by "good old Mother Tilton," and at the same time as Mark, her only son.

While Frank and Tom's father lived, "Mother Tilton," as she was affectionately called by the twin brothers, was well provided for by their father, but he, a captain, had been, as it was supposed, drowned at sea, and therefore the two boys were left to the care of their old miserly uncle, who had been murdered in the "Red House." "Mother Tilton" had almost been forgotten and uncared-for by any one save Frank, who, at times, sent her small sums of money to help her along.

This was discovered by their uncle, old Mr. Ford, who forbade his nephew's generosity.

But Frank took no notice of his uncle's order, and gave the poor woman all he could spare or scrape together from his pocket-money.

For it must be confessed that though Mark Tilton was far below his foster-brother's sphere in life, being but a plough-boy working on neighbouring farms, Frank loved him intensely, if not even more than his own twin-brother Tom.

A long time had elapsed since they met each other before, but Frank had written to him often, and poor Mark so loved him that he had frequently begged to be taken in his service as "a servant," so as to be near him.

The idea of Mark being a servant to him, Frank would never think of, if even his means had been ample enough to support one, but he sighed to think that such a generous-hearted lad as Mark was, should be doomed to the toil and drudgery of such labour as "a poor plough boy."

When they met, therefore, and shook hands, Frank turned very red, while tears gushed from poor Mark's eyes, who was much tempted even to act like a girl and kiss his foster-brother.

"Did you take the letter to the seminary?" Frank asked, hurriedly.

"I *did*, brother," Mark answered, with a trembling voice, and lowering his eyes

"Well, speak out, Mark," said Frank, with a heaving bosom, and biting his nether lip; "speak out; don't be afraid, no one hears us. Did she refuse to see me?"

"No."

"Then shall we meet at the old spot?"

"No, no," answered Mark, clasping both Frank's hands.

"No? And why not?"

"She is not there."

"Not there?" said Frank, turning pale; "not there? What mean you?"

"She has been removed."

"Removed! Oh, Heavens! where? Speak!"

"Nay, do not blame me, Frank. I have often taken your notes to Nelly, as you know, and always sent you her loving answers."

"I know it. But speak, explain; where *is* she? How is this?"

"I do not know, brother Frank; all I could find out was that she had been removed."

"Why?"

"Because her father, the banker, discovered that you loved each other. Mr. Flint was down here t'other week, and, I fear me, he has not mended matters much between you and her rich old daddy."

"*Him* again," said Frank to himself; "it seems to me I am always to be thwarted by one or the other of them, father or son; curse 'em. Who told you this?"

"Polly, the young housemaid."

"Then you brought my letter back."

"No; I did not learn all this until I had delivered it."

"Ha!" said Frank, with a rising colour, "am I, then, betrayed?"

"*I* did not betray you, Frank, I'd suffer death first."

"Then where is my letter?"

"They sent it off to her father."

"Who will, of course, tell all to Flint, and he to his triumphant son."

"But she cares nothing for him."

"That remains to be proved," said Frank, with a sigh; "he may do me much mischief, but if he dares step in between me and Nelly Lancaster I'll kill him like a dog."

"And right, too," said Mark; "and so would I if any one dared interfere with me and little Polly, the young housemaid at the seminary; so help me, bob, I would."

"So Polly told you all this?"

"She did, and said as how she'd found out that Nelly, for a time, had been removed out of your way to a seminary, at a place in France called Marseilles."

"Marseilles! 'tis the very place I'm going to, Mark," said Frank, with a flushed face. "I'll find her if I search for my whole life; she never shall give her hand and heart to that dastard, Joel Flint. I know what his father is aiming at, and striving for. I cannot be mistaken."

"*You* going to France?" asked Mark, in surprise.

"France, yes; and from there to join Garibaldi. If I do not find Nelly I care not if I'm shot dead in the first battle we're engaged in."

"Fight for Garibaldi," said Mark, looking thoughtful, "going to help him for the cause of liberty?"

"Yes, Mark."

"Then I am one in the same cause, Frank; come, take me," Mark said, with a flushed face, and full of enthusiasm.

"*You*, Mark?"

"Yes, *me*. Come, say the word, Frank; we are foster-brothers, you know, and have been nourished at the same mother's breast; we have laughed together, played together, slept together, quarrelled and fought together. Why not let me go with you, and, if need be, let us *die* together!"

In a moment the two foster-brothers clasped each other in their arms, and tears flowed down the cheeks of both.

"So be it, then, Mark," said Frank; "yours is in truth a true, bold heart; come, then, let us live together, and, as you say, 'if need be, let us *die* together.'"

## CHAPTER IX.

ELLEN LANCASTER'S HIDING-PLACE DISCOVERED—MEETING OF THE LOVERS—PERILOUS POSITION OF FRANK FORD—MUTUAL VOWS—THE FAT BOY AT SEA—HE HAS A GLORIOUS SALT-WATER BATH—BUTTONS TURNS NURSE.

THE prospect of a short sea voyage across the English Channel, from Dover to Calais, greatly delighted Buttons and the Fat Boy, who never in their lives before had seen salt water.

The first thing that the Fat Boy did, therefore, to prepare himself for such a trip was to stuff himself at the inn with edibles and drinkables to such an extraordinary extent that he seemed swollen out to double his ordinary size.

In truth his clothes were much too small for him at any time, but on the present occasion his buttons went popping off in all directions, and he looked like some enormous pudding when helped on board by Buttons and some other good-natured Garibaldians.

Young Buttons went so far in his mirth as to hint the necessity of "ducking" the Fat Boy in the sea-water, but this proposition roused the corpulent youth from his half-sleepy state, and he threatened a thousand things against the mischievous but frolicsome page.

When they got on board, and the steamer had started, all went well for a time, and the young Garibaldians sang songs in right merry style assisted in no small degree by the stentorian lungs of Mark, and the small voice of Joe Morton, the rescued boy, who seemed to be the gayest of the gay among them.

Poor Joe felt delighted that his sister had been placed in a comfortable home in London by Frank and Hugh Tracy, and seemed to care little for himself, since he was now on his way to Italy, where, as he said, his only brother had gone to long before.

A few hours of fast travelling by steamboat and an express train found the young Garibaldians safe at Marseilles, full of fun, and ripe for mischief.

Buttons soon recovered from his salt water bath when they arrived at Calais.

Not so the Fat Boy, however.

He would *not* recover, but had to be carried about by his comrades, who heartily swore at him.

It was not until he had been put into a warm and comfortable bed in Marseilles, and several draughts of good old brandy had been imbibed that he showed any signs of vigorous life again.

Buttons was ordered to sit by his bedside and attend him.

This he did faithfully enough, nor did he forget to help himself to many of the good things which were especially prepared for the fat volunteer.

Even in sleep Fatty thought of the sea, and all of a sudden, while dreaming, he imagined himself to be desperately swimming for his life.

In one of these moods he struck out his hands so violently and vigorously that he knocked Buttons and the astonished French landlord sprawling on the floor.

But while the young Garibaldians were strolling about the town in their red shirts and plumed hats, seeing all the sights, and smoking cigars, Frank went forth in all haste to seek Nelly Lancaster at the English Seminary.

After much exertion he discovered her hiding-place.

His heart beat wildly with excitement.

She was found!

He espied her at a first floor window of the English Seminary, looking out upon the glorious sunset.

"Nelly!" he cried.

In an instant she recognised him!

With a faint scream and tearful eyes she gazed down upon him.

How was he to reach her?

She was far beyond his reach, he knew, and his heart throbbed with anguish.

"Are you alone?" he asked.

"Yes," was the faint reply of the sobbing girl. "I cannot get out, Frank!"

"No matter," said Frank; "if you cannot get out *I* can get in, my lassie."

On the instant his resolution was formed.

He clambered up the water-pipe with the agility of a young monkey as he was.

In a few moments, and before Nelly could raise any cry of alarm, he stood with one foot on her balcony, yet still holding on to the water-pipe for support.

In an instant the pipe fell to the ground with a loud smash!

Frank's position was perilous in the extreme.

Both his feet slipped from under him.

Next moment he would have been dashed to the ground!

He clung to the balcony, and for a second swung between earth and air!

With a terrible struggle he exerted all his strength, and Nelly helped him to climb.

He secured a firmer hold, and soon placed one knee outside the railing.

This saved him.

He clutched the balcony rail afresh with a grip of iron, and nearly wrenched it out of its place in the stone-work.

He was safe!

In an instant he and Nelly were clasped in each other's arms, and there, in the silence of that room, and beyond all hearing or prying eyes, Frank told again his tale of love in her not unwilling ear.

Nelly leaned her head upon his breast, and with many kisses sealed the vow "to love him, and him only until death!"

## CHAPTER X.

FRANK'S PARTING WITH NELLY LANCASTER—THE RESOLVE—A GIRL'S LOVE AND DEVOTION—THE SHIP'S DEPARTURE.

It must not be supposed that Frank and Nelly Lancaster were allowed to remain long undisturbed, during their loving interview in that snug quiet room of the English Seminary, for it must be confessed that they were several times disturbed.

During their conversation Nelly confessed to him her fears that he was beset and surrounded by many enemies, the chief of whom was Joel Flint.

She knew not why, but she felt alarmed for Frank's fate, and shed many many tears when he told her that he and his young band had resolved to join Garibaldi, and help to fight his battles for liberty and freedom!

How Frank and his young affianced bride contrived to escape from the Seminary that evening, and the exciting adventure which ensued must remain for another chapter to tell.

Suffice it for the present, however, to say that they *did* manage to elude the vigilance of the master and mistress as well as the many teachers of the Seminary, and that Nelly went forth to the steam-boat pier to see her lover and his friends depart.

A sorrowful and painful moment for Nelly was her parting with Frank Ford. Yet he kissed her oft, and wiped her tears away, promising at the same time to write to her constantly, and inform her of all that happened.

"I know that I shall achieve honour and distinction, Nelly," said he, "and that ere long will return safe and sound to claim you for my own, and at the same time to shame my old uncle, who has ever predicted the very worst career for me."

"But what if you are hurt, Frank?" sighed Nelly. "Perhaps in some far distant battle-field you may lay wounded and dying, and with no one to assist or tend you."

"Never fear, dear one," said Frank, placing his arm tenderly round her slim and tapered waist, "never fear, my own one, when dangers are greatest, I will think of you, who art my angel and guiding star. As long as you love and pray for me, no great harm can befall me."

"Why not let *me* come, Frank?" Nelly asked, with a flushed cheek.

"*You*, darling?"

"Yes, *me*."

"You are but a girl, and would quail before the many scenes of strife and bloodshed which I shall have to go through."

"You mistake me, Frank. I should *not* quail or tremble. I am an English girl, remember, and though but a girl, I could face and encounter any danger while with *you*."

"It must *not* be, Nelly," said Frank, with a choked utterance. "No; it must not be. I know that you love me, and dearly too; but if a single hair on your sweet head were harmed through me, I should die with shame and remorse. Come, Nelly dear, think no more of this your mad intention. Remain true to me, continue your studies at the Seminary, and wait patiently till I return."

"But why go at all?"

"Why, Nelly?"

"Yes, why?"

"Am I not dependent on my uncle for education? Am I not looked upon by him as a burden? I am called a poor beggarly orphan by all who know me, and shall I longer remain a recipient of his charity, or the charity of any one, while my heart prompts me to seek my own fortune, and achieve both a name and fame?"

"Do not go," still Nelly sighed. "Do not, Frank, run into these dangers for *my* sake; do not."

"I must, Nelly. I shall return one of these days, honoured and loved by all. Would you not love me all the more for that? ("If I do *not*," Frank thought to himself, as he deeply sighed, "I shall die upon the battle-field.") "Besides," Nelly, he continued, "you are rich. Your father is an immensely wealthy banker. He hates the very sound of my name."

"I know he does, Frank; but *I* do not," said Nelly, in a sweet voice.

"I know that, my own one," said Frank, "and it is only to prove to all that I love you for yourself, and not for money, that I now go. It is to show to all that I *am* worthy of your love that I thus jeopardise my life to gain honour and renown."

"Have you heard the news?" Nelly asked.

"What news?"

"Before my father sent me here I heard it said that Joel Flint was going to be admitted into my father's bank, and that ere long he would become one of the partners."

"I guessed as much," said Frank, biting his lip. "Oh, that I were rich, so that I might be always near to you, Nelly!" he sighed; "but the fates forbid. But come, there is no time to lose; the signal is up and flying at the mast-head; the vessel will depart ere many minutes, Nelly, dear. Painful as it is, we must part; all my friends you see yonder are gathering around the companion-ladder; one more kiss—one long and loving embrace, Nelly and then——!"

Even as he spoke, Nelly fell into his arms and nearly fainted.

* * * * *

Within five minutes Frank and his friends ascended the vessel's side, and ere long the steamer gracefully glided from her berth and put to sea.

Loud were the cheerings of the young Garibaldians, but Frank stood upon the paddle-box waving his handkerchief, and long after they had left the wharf he could see Nelly standing there weeping and sobbing.

"He will not let me go," sighed Nelly, sobbing, as she stood looking after the steamer with streaming eyes, "he will not let me go because I am a girl. But," she said, after a long pause, "I *will* go! Yes, I too will share his danger, but he shall never know it."

The parting indeed was painful to both; but

destiny divided them, and ere they met again strange and startling adventures fell to the lot of both.

What those exciting adventures were we shall quickly see.

## CHAPTER XI.

THE FIRST EXPLOIT—SEIZURE OF THE SCHOONER YACHT "KAISER"—THE SPIES AT WORK—THE CONFLICT—THE VICTORY—INCREASING DANGERS—THE ITALIAN COLOURS HOISTED—FATTY HAS ANOTHER BATH.

THE steamer sped on her way merrily towards the shores of Italy, and all the Garibaldians on board enjoyed themselves vastly in all manner of ways.

The captain, who was an Italian in the French mail service, advised all the young Garibaldians to disguise themselves, for the vessel had to call at the Austrian port of Trieste before reaching the harbour of Ancona, where the Italian fleet lay.

When they were but two days' journey from Trieste, and while pleasantly journeying up the Adriatic Sea, Frank called his friends together and addressed them privately.

"We are all bound on a dangerous expedition," said he, "and before we join Garibaldi it is necessary that you should formally elect some one to lead you."

"We have chosen you for our captain," cried all *but two.*

"Yes, that is very well," Frank replied, "but you had better vote upon the subject. Let each of you write upon a slip of paper the name of the one you have most confidence in as your intended captain, and afterwards there cannot be any dispute; as far as I am concerned, I care not who is captain—whether it be Dick Fellows, Hugh Tracy, or any other, so that the selection is properly settled by vote."

"Agreed! agreed!" shouted all; "we will vote for it at once."

In a moment each one wrote the name of his choice on a slip of paper, but without signing his name thereto.

These were all cast into a hat and afterwards examined.

Except *two (!)* all had voted for Frank as their chosen captain, and the choice was hailed with loud applause.

Who these two were who had voted against him no one could discover!

Murmurs were heard against them, whoever they were, but it could never be discovered, for each and every one swore that they had voted for Frank and no one else.

So well did the two spies conceal their guilt that no one could ever have suspected them of the base designs they had in view.

"Well, comrades," said Frank, when the election was over and ratified, "you have elected me to a very honourable, responsible, and dangerous post; but you may rely upon it I will never disgrace you. Remember, we are English boys, and must show to all that we are not only brave, as all Englishmen are, but prove to them that we are a little more than brave. Wherever the most danger is, there let us be; and, with our banner unfurled, prove to all that Garabaldi has not misplaced confidence in us."

"We will! we will! Three cheers for General Garabaldi!"

"And now," said Frank, "since you have elected me of your own accord, I will read to you a letter, which I received from Garibaldi while in Marseilles."

Amid loud applause, Frank read as follows:—

WHEREAS the King of Italy having been graciously pleased to appoint me, Guiseppe Garibaldi, Generalissimo of all the Volunteer Forces raised for the Liberation of Venetia, I have, under the powers conferred on me, accepted the services of a Gallant Band of English Boys, raised and commanded by Frank Ford, otherwise known as the "Boy Soldier," who will in future be known as "Garibaldi's young Captain," and whose deeds, with those of the Band under his command, will add fresh lustre to the English boys' name, and prove worthy of ranking beside the laurels gained at Cressy, Agincourt, Waterloo, and a thousand others.

(Signed) G. GARIBALDI.

Lonato, July, 1866.

Disguised as they now were, the young Garibaldians could not be taken for any other than ordinary passengers.

As they approached the Austrian port of Trieste it was arranged that they should land, and in the night seize some Austrian vessel, and make sail towards Ancona.

"For it won't do for us to arrive among the Italians like empty-handed beggars," said Hal. "There are many schooners lying in the bay, and nearly all of them carry a couple of guns. Suppose we seize one in the night, and, under cover of the darkness, escape into some Italian port, and make a present of our prize to Garibaldi?"

This proposition was received with loud applause and great enthusiasm.

The French steamer arrived at Trieste during the afternoon, and as they were entering the port Frank's quick eyes espied a beautiful, fast-sailing schooner lying a few yards from shore.

She had two brass guns on board, her colours were flying, and altogether she looked a very tempting prize.

When the steamer arrived at the wharf all the young Garibaldians landed, and strolled about the town enjoying themselves.

No one would for a moment have suspected that these good-looking, generous, and well-dressed English youths were Garibaldians in disguise.

Wherever they went they were well received.

Their passports were minutely examined by the hawk-eyed police on guard at the Custom-House; but these important papers were pronounced quite correct, and the youths were looked upon as so many young English travellers.

All their luggage had been directed to Ancona, so that when the steamer sailed again that evening they felt perfectly satisfied that their trunks, boxes and the like would be safely landed at the Italian port.

According to Frank's directions, all his followers gradually directed their footsteps towards that part of the port where the beautiful two-gun schooner lay.

"At midnight, when all is quiet, let us assemble by twos and threes under the long shed on the wharf near where the schooner lies," said Frank.

In the meantime, he, Hugh Tracy, and Dick Fellows strolled about until they came within a few yards of where the "Kaiser" was.

They found out that the beautiful schooner was the property of the Austrian admiral, who was on board a frigate out at sea.

All the schooner's crew, it was supposed, were ashore enjoying themselves.

There were but four men left on board during the evening.

Frank laid his plans, and hired two or three boats, which some of his band rowed down towards the appointed spot.

These were hidden under the deep shadows of the wharf until midnight should arrive.

But before midnight Frank changed his mind.

He knew not why nor wherefore, but he had a misgiving in his own mind that treachery was at work somewhere.

When the cathedral clock struck eleven, he selected twenty of his followers, and placed ten in each boat.

He, Hugh Tracy, Fellows, and Tom got into the third, and were about to leave the wharf, when Mark, Frank's foster-brother, jumped in also, and *would* share in the danger.

At a signal from Frank the three boats glided from their hiding-places like shadows and crept towards the schooner unobserved.

They floated with the tide until they were securely fastened under the lea.

All was breathless suspense and excitement.

The cathedral clock chimed the half-hour.

This was the signal for the boarding party.

In an instant Frank, followed by his brave companions, climbed up the vessel's sides, and in a moment swarmed on to the deck!

The men on deck were surprised—thunderstruck!

They at first supposed themselves to be in some dream.

They were not long undeceived.

Frank rushed at one, and knocked him down.

A hand-to-hand fight now began on all sides, for, contrary to all expectations,

*There were twenty stout Austrian sailors on board!*

Mark, the foster-brother, with more prudence than the rest, dashed down the hatches on the heads of the sailors who had not rushed on deck.

It was instantly fastened down, and securely.

By this move those below could not rush to the assistance of their friends on deck.

With no noise of any kind save the desperate clinking of swords, Frank and his followers continued the conflict until at last they had struck down the last man, and the "Kaiser" was theirs!

The young Garibaldians would have cheered oudly, but this Frank forbid.

The anchor was slipped in an instant—the beautiful little vessel began to move slowly and gracefully.

It was drifted towards the long shed.

In a moment all the young Garibaldians leaped on board.

A sail was raised, Mark, the foster-brother, took the helm, and soon they were on their way out to sea, with the Italian colors flying in the night winds!

This had scarcely been done, amid loud cheers—for Frank could no longer restrain them—when they perceived a great commotion on shore.

A large body of soldiers had just then marched down to the long shed, but were a few minutes too late!

"We have been betrayed!" said Frank, bitterly.

"Some one has informed upon us!" said Hugh, with an oath.

The soldiers fired, but their shots fell short.

Again and again they fired, but with no better result.

A cannon shot now came plunging over the schooner, and Fatty on the instant crouched very low out of the way behind a huge water-cask.

Another cannon shot came whistling along, and smashed the immense water cask, almost drowning the unfortunate fat youth hidden behind it.

Fatty groaned aloud.

Beyond this no damage was done.

The sails were quickly set, and off darted the schooner like a swallow on the wing, amid great cheering.

But all danger was not yet over.

They were pursued by another schooner which continually fired at the "Kaiser" but without effect.

Another and a greater danger was yet in store for them.

*They had to pass the Fort.*

Frank knew this, and prepared for the worst.

Instead of going away from the fort he crept close up to it.

This made several of the Garibaldians turn deadly pale for they knew the schooner would be treated to a whole broadside from the fort, and expected to be sunk on the instant.

Fatty and Buttons squeezed themselves into the smallest possible space under the bulwarks, so as to be out of the way.

But Frank's plans were right.

The schooner as she passed by the fort was so close to it, under the walls, that when the broadside was fired at them the shots whistled over head, for the gunners could not depress their guns so as to hit the gallant little craft!

Shot after shot, grape and canister shot, were showered down upon them, but not a single bullet touched any of them.

The sea rose around them on all sides, like immense water-spouts, shooting up in columns, but beyond a good ducking no harm was done and amid loud cheers the gallant little craft shot by the fort, and was soon far out at sea, pursued by two Austrian sailing vessels, whose shots were plunging all around them in the moonlit waters.

## CHAPTER XII.

THE LUMINOUS SKELETON AT BROMLEY HALL—THE GIPSY'S PROPHECY—STRANGE DISCOVERY BY OLD GILES, THE GARDENER—THE HAND OF THE HEADLESS MAN—THE APPARITION—THE RESOLVE FOR VENGEANCE.

THE distance from Bromley Hall Academy to London was inconsiderable.

The anxiety of old Gravestones for the safety and recapture of the brother and sister he had so brutally treated, and for so long a time, filled him with alarm.

There was a deep, dark mystery which hung around those two children, one, indeed, which old Gravestones would not have had the world know aught of for thousands of pounds.

He was sick at heart, therefore, as he journeyed towards London, and resolved upon having vengeance upon some one.

Who that one was will be hereafter seen.

While he was away, therefore—in truth, but an hour or two after his departure from Bromley—Mistress Gravestones called in the aid of all her servants to re-arrange the wild disorder of the academy.

Among those she first consulted was Giles, the old gardener.

Giles was glad of this, for it proved that no one knew of his having taken any part with the young Garibaldians.

Least of all did she imagine that Giles was the chief conspirator against her husband, and had discovered the two living secrets.

"I must not let her suppose that I knew anything about the two missing children, or else all my plans will prove fruitless for the future. How well the old hypocrites conceal their guilt, though! *I* must not be behindhand in cunning, and will wear as pleasant a face as they. I know what *they* are, but they don't know who *I* am."

Thus old Giles, the gardener, mused, and as he moved to and fro, he muttered,

"Bromley Hall is a very ancient place, and there are more secrets in it yet than many dream of, but if I live I will unearth them all."

If any one could have seen old Giles's face at that moment they would have been surprised, nay, startled at the terrible changes which came over it.

At one time he smiled, and looked as placid and innocent an old man as could ever be seen.

At other moments, however, his lips trembled, a deep, dark flush spread over his face rapidly, his eyes glared wildly around him, and he clenched his thick, bony fist with savage earnestness.

"*I have sworn it!*" he said, in an earnest savage whisper, when he found himself alone and far from all observation. "*I have sworn it! They know not who I am, ha, ha! I am old Giles the gardener, eh? Well, well, so let them think for the present. When my time comes they will find out their mistake! Frank and Tom Ford are to be their next victims, I see; but it shall never be!* Oh! that I had completed all my plans, and could cast my net around the villains all at once! Some are in my power now; but, patience, I have sworn to be revenged, and will be!"

Instead of helping the servants to repair the damage done by the riot to the house, furniture, &c., Giles stole away unobserved to the room where the girl and boy had been confined.

Here he rummaged about for some time, but found nothing worth the search.

Determined not to be foiled he entered the master's private library, which was still open.

But this he did not dare do until long after dark.

For a moment he listened as if uncertain how to act, for he heard footsteps moving quickly to and fro.

With great resolution, however, he entered, provided with a small dark lantern.

He did not go to the master's desk.

He touched not the open safe.

Parchments, deeds, mortgages, letters, and the like, lay strewn around in wild confusion.

Such things, however, had no charm for old Giles.

With the scent of a bloodhound he stood upon one particular plank in the floor!

He lightly stamped his foot, but for what purpose did not at that moment appear.

Shortly, however, the plank *rose* at the other end, slowly at first and by almost imperceptible degrees.

After a second or two it was suddenly raised four or five feet from its proper place by some mysterious means that Giles knew not.

He did not stop to inquire how or by what means the planking was thus raised, for he left the spot whereon he stood and looked into the hole thus disclosed.

He started back as if struck by a bullet.

*A perfect skeleton lay within!*

*It was robed in white satin, and decked in long faded wreaths of flowers!*

Dust and cobwebs hung over all—the body had been mouldering there for many, many years.

*There were blood marks on the white garments!*

They were rent and torn as if some violent struggle had taken place before death.

For some time old Giles, dark lantern in hand, stood gazing at the strange sight as if stupefied with wonder.

He knelt down after a time in order to take a fuller view of it.

The head had been severed from the body; it was not there.

A headless skeleton it lay, robed in blood-stained silk!

A deep, dark mystery it was, one that old Giles could not then solve, but as he gazed on the bleached bones tears rolled down his face as he sighed,

"'Twas twelve years ago this very night since first we missed her—would that the hour of vengeance had arrived."

Giles little dreamed, however, as he stood gazing on that silk-clad skeleton, artfully concealed beneath the floor, that on that self same night twelve years before the gipsies prophesied—

"Giles, there are dread secrets at Bromley Hall, and one shall be discovered by you years hence, many years; but remember, at that same moment that one secret is discovered at the Hall, another murder, another headless mystery, will lay exposed to view in a lonely court in London, both deeds of blood accomplished by the same hand."

Still gazing on the headless body, Giles turned deadly pale.

His lamp suddenly went out!

He trembled, and felt a sense of holy awe creep over him.

Minutes seemed like hours to him, and a cold sweat oozed from his brow.

He seemed scarce able to move or breathe.

Why had his lamp gone out?

Had any one observed him?

Thus thought he as he heard the winds sigh mournfully past the window and the rain patter against its many diamond-shaped panes.

A sudden flash of lightning dashed vividly through the dark and spacious room, which for a moment lit up everything in an unnatural manner.

A deafening peal of thunder instantly succeeded, and seemed to crash right over Bromley Hall, and shook it to its very foundation.

Then all was black again.

*Dark it was, indeed, except where the skeleton lay!*

*That* spot, however, from some awful cause, was *not* dark!

*Every bone emitted a pale, phosphorescent glow!*

The outline of each was clearly defined!

*The bones were a skeleton of bluish-white, glowing in the darkness of its prison chamber!*

This it was that made Giles stare with surprise, and caused him to tremble.

There was so much that was unnatural in this appearance that it made him quake again.

Suddenly he heard the door behind him violently thrown open!

It was a fearful moment to Giles.

He could not turn to look—he dared not!

He seemed rooted to the spot.

The footfalls of a man approached him!

A heavy hand was laid upon his shoulder!

He slowly turned his head.

He saw no one near!

Yet he felt that strong and heavy hand upon his shoulder!

The suspense was horrible—appalling.

A flash of lightning of dazzling brilliance filled the room again.

He looked around him wildly.

*It was the hand of a headless man!*

THE INTERVIEW WITH GARIBALDI.

## CHAPTER XIII.

THE CHASE—THE RUSE—THE SUCCESSFUL FLIGHT—ITALIAN COLORS RAISED—THE STRAY SHOT—HUGH TRACY AND FRANK AT WORK.

THE first exploit of the gallant band of young Garibaldians caused Captain Frank to be lustily cheered by his followers, who rent the air with their joyful shouts.

They rushed towards him and seized his hand with a firm and hearty grip of friendship.

Fatty, who still lay concealed in some out of the way place, far from harm's way, could not understand the meaning of so much shouting and bawling.

He imagined that they had yet to run the gauntlet of other Forts, and, as an occasional shot from the ships in chase whizzed overhead with a screaming sound, and plunged into the sea around the "Kaiser," he hid himself still more closely under the protection of the bulwarks, and almost squeezed the breath out of the body of young Buttons, who was by no means so fearful as his corpulent companion.

"U-u-gh!" groaned Fatty, aloud. "Oh, lors! here comes another shell, Buttons, don't yer hear it?" and with that he kicked and plunged as if he expected each moment to be annihilated. "Oh, lors! that dare-devil, Frank, will be the death of us all, I know he will. U-g-h! here it comes whistling along! I don't mind fighting, you know, Buttons," he said very confidentially, but in a sorrowful voice, "in fact I rather *like* a little of it, but them beastly cannon balls and screaming shells, Buttons, make my hair stand on end——"

"With fear?" asked the page.

"Fear? no, with astonishment," said Fatty, "that's all. Who told yer I was afraid, I should like to know?" he said, very valiantly.

"We shall get used to them things after a time," said Buttons, "when we reach Garibaldi; there's plenty of 'em there. They say the general don't care no more about 'em than so many pills!"

"Pills, eh?" sighed Fatty, "rather hard 'uns, I should fancy! I should never be able to digest one; I'd rather swallow a good sized apple-dumpling."

"Hillo, there!" said Frank, perceiving Fatty ensconced safely under the bulwarks, and with a smile upon his handsome face! "Hillo, there, what's up?"

"Oh, we're only having a quiet snooze, Captain Frank," said Fatty, with an air of great innocence and simplicity.

"Having a snooze, eh?" said he, laughing. "Can you sleep while all the shots and shell are flying about?"

"Sleep! lor' bless yer, yes. *We* don't mind it, do we, Buttons, eh!"

"Don't you?"

"No."

"Then you must be a brace of very brave boys," said Frank.

"So we are," said Fatty; "we don't care about the shots and shells, do we, Buttons?"

Buttons did not answer, for he felt very much ashamed at being thus discovered hiding.

"Well, then, if you don't fear the shot and shell so much the better," said Frank, "for I expect the next one that comes will knock both you into a——"

Fatty didn't wait to hear a single word more.

"Eh? Oh, lor!" said he, with staring eyes, "you don't mean that, Frank?"

"I do, though."

In an instant Fatty jumped from his hiding-place with the agility of a cat, and disappeared out of view.

He rushed down into the cabin, and locked himself in the pantry, among the plates, dishes, and jam pots!

* * * * *

Frank's position on board the yacht was a very dangerous one.

They were now sailing out to sea at a "clipping" pace, and the little vessel seemed almost to fly across the dark blue waters.

The two vessels pursuing them were losing ground each moment, but from the number of signals exchanged between them it seemed certain that they were determined to recapture the "Kaiser" if possible.

Mark, his foster-brother, had been born at Dover, and passed all his life near the sea.

He well knew how to manage a vessel, and it was under his direction that all the sailing arrangements were carried out.

He stood at the helm and steered her bravely, nor did he flinch when more than one shot rushed over head near him, and rent great holes in the mainsail.

Under his orders the yacht carried every yard of canvas she possibly dare do in safety, and as the gallant pretty little vessel dashed along it seemed like some snow-white bird upon the wing.

"I wish I could understand their signals," said Frank, to his foster-brother, "then we might know what was best to be done."

"It is easy enough, Frank."

"How?"

"I dare say if you search the cabin you will find an Austrian signal-book, which will explain all.

"A good thought; but what are we going to do with the number of prisoners we have safely secured under the hatches?"

"Leave that to me, Frank. Let a dozen or two of your boys stand guard over the hatches; if any of 'em dare show a head, or attempt to rush up, blow their brains out, that's all; if they are civil and peaceable, promise to land 'em at some spot on the coast of Dalmatia, looming up yonder leeward of us."

"But can it be done with safety?"

"If we make out their signals we shall soon know. Search for the signal-book; this is the admiral's yacht, remember, so there *must* be one somewhere on board."

Frank always had great respect for his foster-brother's advice and sound sense, and his behaviour ever since he had joined the young Garibaldians showed to all that he was a great acquisition to the whole party, for the greater the danger the cooler was Mark.

Giving orders to his men to guard well the hatches and keep a sharp look-out for any stray shot that came from the two pursuing vessels, Frank and Hugh Tracy descended into the cabin.

They went to work cautiously in their search, for they knew not as yet the ins and outs of the admiral's cabin, and thought perhaps that some of the crew from hidden places might rush out and murder them.

As they walked into the cabin both were struck with amazement at the beauty of all around them.

Pictures of great price, mirrors, chandeliers, carpets, gold and silver ornaments, massive clocks, chronometers, telescopes, books, and splendid glass were in profusion.

For a moment Frank and Hugh held their breath in wonder!

At that moment a tremendous crash of crockery-ware was heard in the pantry.

At the same moment a cannon shot whizzed right through the cabin.

It came in at one side and passed out the other, leaving huge holes and a mass of splinters on every hand.

In an instant afterwards Fatty rushed forth from his hiding-place, looking as pale as death, and with hair on end.

His face and hands were all smeared over with raspberry jam with which he had been quietly regailing himself.

With a loud groan he ran on deck, shouting he was shot, his companions mistaking the jam on his face for blood.

"A close shave that, Hugh," Frank said.

"Yes, and no mistake; if we intend to remain here long, we must grope about on our hands and knees."

Nothing daunted they began their search, and discovered a copy of the latest edition of the Austrian navy's signal-book.

This was a great prize.

"Do you continue your search," Hugh said; "Frank and I will go and endeavour to make out what those two vessels are saying to each other."

This he easily managed to do.

With a pair of splendid double-eyed sea-glasses, found in the cabin, Frank distinctly saw the number and colour of the various flags which the two vessels were hoisting and lowering.

These he called off as he perceived them, while Dick Fellows, with the signal-book, read out aloud their meaning.

"What are they talking about, Dick?"

"They say we can't escape, for we are running right into the jaws of the Austrian fleet, which is cruizing thirty miles eastward off the harbour of Ancona."

"The devil!" said Frank. "We must change our course, then."

"No, no, don't do anything of the sort, Frank," said the foster-brother; "if you sail towards the coast of Dalmatia yonder, you run greater risk. Stop till the moon sinks; in the darkness we shall be able to give them the slip or double on 'em."

"What are they saying now?" asked one.

"I make out that they fear we may land and rescue the Italian spy, who is confined in the coast-guard house, a few miles up the coast. They say the spy is a handsome girl in the pay of Garibaldi."

"Are you sure?"

"Yes, certain of it."

"What else?" asked Frank, eagerly.

"They can't make out why we don't fire back on them."

"A good thought!" said Mark, the foster-brother.

"What is!"

"Why, not firing on them."

"Why so?"

"Let your boys, Frank, pretend to be fighting among themselves."

"What's the use of that?"

"Never mind; you'll soon see. Watch their flags closely in the meantime, and, Dick Fellows, don't make any mistake in reading the meaning of the signals Frank calls off to you."

At a word from Frank the young Garibaldians began.to dance around the deck in a wild manner, as if they were fighting among themselves.

In an instant the two pursuing vessels began to signal each other again,

"I told you so," said Mark, laughing in high glee, "I told you so; up gotheir signals. Now, Frank, let's hear the news; what are they saying?"

Frank called out the name and number of each flag.

"By Jingo!" said Dick Fellows, in great glee; "they think we are fighting among ourselves."

"Are you sure?"

"No; now I come to look at the signals again, I find they say that the Austrian prisoners here on board have risen up in revolt against us!"

"Bravo! I thought they would," said Mark, the foster-brother.

"What shall we do next, Mark?" asked Frank.

"Haul down the Italian colours and hoist the Austrian flag over it; let them both fly together."

"What does that mean?"

"That the yacht is Austrian again."

"Oh, no, don't do that," cried several; "it would be cowardice!"

"But you *must*," said the foster-brother, "without you wish to run amuck among the Austrian fleet not far off."

This was accordingly done.

As soon as this was perceived by the two pursuing vessels, they hoisted other signals which read,

"Have you retaken her?"

"Say yes," cried the foster-brother. "Hoist Nos. 1 and 20."

This was done.

In a moment faint cheers were heard from the Austrian vessels.

"What shall we say now, brother?" Frank asked.

"Hoist signals to say 'we have retaken the "Kaiser," and will join the Austrian fleet; don't fire at us any more.'"

For a few moments Frank and Dick Fellows rummaged among the signal-flags in the box, and hoisted the proper ones.

They were quickly perceived.

Faint cheers were again heard from the Austrians.

A parting volley of blank cartridge was fired in token of joy, and in a few moments the two pursuing vessels changed their course, and sailed again for the harbour of Trieste, perfectly satisfied that all was right.

"I told you we should deceive them," said Mark, the foster-brother, in high glee, "if you followed my advice."

It was well, indeed, that Frank and the rest *did* follow his advice, for at that instant a steam-vessel was observed to have joined the chase which must, sooner or later, have overhauled them.

As it was, this vessel was informed by the others of the favourable turn things had taken on board the "Kaiser," and she, like the others, turned her head towards Trieste again, flying the signal,

"Well done, 'Kaiser.' Glad to see our own flag flying again. Have no mercy on the young Garibaldians!"

## CHAPTER XIV.

TERESA, THE CAPTIVE ITALIAN SPY—RELEASE OF THE PRISONERS—THE BAPTISM OF FIRE—THE RAVINE—THE SPY—THE AUSTRIANS ALARMED—THE FIRST VOLLEY—THE FAT BOY IN TROUBLE—THE SURPRISE—BRAVERY OF YOUNG BUTTONS—HE SCALES THE WALLS OF THE FORT.

WHILE Frank and his foster-brother, with Dick Fellows, were successfully deceiving the Austrian vessel, Hugh Tracy diligently carried out his search in the admiral's cabin.

The moon had now gone down upon the troubled sea, and all was darkness.

With lantern in hand, Hugh opened numberless boxes, and discovered many things that proved of great service to the young Garibaldians.

In one chest of immense size he discovered more than two hundred red shirts, and in another as many felt hats adorned with dark green plumes.

What this meant, Hugh could not understand, for they were Garibaldian uniforms.

In another chest he discovered several hundred American revolvers, quite new, and with plenty of ammunition.

In another, he found several cases of swords, and a few rifles which could discharge twenty shots in a minute.

Ammunition for these arms he found in abundance.

After turning over many desks and chests, he found a large quantity of gold coin, and much correspondence which came from Austrian spies in the Italian camps.

The rifles, revolvers, red shirts and hats he immediately distributed, according to Frank's orders, among the young Garibaldians, who hailed these treasures with loud shouts and cheers.

Such were the very things they most needed, and proved invaluable to all.

Frank himself now joined in the search.

He divided all the money he found among his followers.

Each one was well supplied with meat, bread and wine from the well-stored pantrys, and ere an hour had passed all the young soldiers were as merry as crickets, chief of whom was the Fat Boy, who, at the first mention of wine and good food, crawled from his hiding place among the empty water-casks.

After a time a loud knocking was heard at the main-hatchway.

This was raised a few inches.

A rough-looking seaman who spoke Italian, which Frank well understood, begged to be allowed to come on deck.

As the young Garibaldians were all well-armed, and did not fear any mutiny, this was allowed.

"What do you want?" asked Frank.

For a moment the Italian seaman looked astonished at the number of red-shirted youths around him.

Tears stood in his eyes, as he said,

"Now I understand all, my young friends. Every one of you belong to Garibaldi."

"We do," Frank answered, proudly.

"I see that from your dress, and, moreover, you are brave English boys?"

"Every one is English."

"And you forfeit all to fight for Italian liberty?"

"Yes, we do; and will sacrifice our lives if need be."

For a moment the Italian seaman hung his head.

At last he said,

"Let *me* join you?"

"You?"

"Yes, me. There are twenty more beside me in the hold, who hate the Austrian yoke. Some are Poles, some are Italians, some Hungarians, and some from other parts. We all love Garibaldi, and will fight for him if you will let us free."

"But why are you serving on board an Austrian vessel, then?"

"Because we have been forced to do so, my young captain."

"I have been sent by my comrades to ask this favour of you; will you grant it? Will you let us help to fight your battles for Italian independence? If you distrust us, sail away to the first Italian port you like, and then you will soon see how quickly we will keep our words, and join the volunteers."

For a moment Frank knew not what to do.

He was fearful of some plot.

"What proof can you give us of your sincerity?" Frank asked.

"Anything you demand."

"Do you know anything of the Austrian's intentions?"

"I do."

"Tell me them?"

"The Austrians seized one of Garibaldi's female spies—her name is Teresa Fazzi."

"Well?"

"She is now confined in the strong coast-guard house, near the light-house?"

"What light-house?"

"The one you see some fifteen miles away, there yonder, where the small light twinkles above the waves like a star."

"Is that the light-house?"

"It is. The coast-guard house is but a mile higher up the beach."

"How know you she is there."

"I saw her arrested this morning in Trieste. They removed her out of town for fear of any rescue being attempted. To-morrow she will be taken to Venice. She is a most important prisoner for the Austrians, and I fear me they will torture her to death but what they will extract every secret from her."

Here the Italian sighed, and hung his head.

"Why do you sigh?" Frank asked, with compassion in his voice.

"I saw her pass, and in my heart I vowed to attempt her rescue."

"You?"

"Yes, captain; we both belong to a Secret Society, having in view the deliverance of Italy from the Austrian yoke."

"How know you this?"

"She made certain signs which I could not mistake. We both belong to the same secret order, as I have told you, and could recognise each other anywhere."

"What order is that?"

"Nay, signor, I could not, I dare not, reveal that; it is too great a secret. Perhaps ere many days you yourself, nay, every one of your gallant young band, may belong to it, and then you will not only be surprised, but commend and admire my silence."

"Perhaps so; and what is your name?"

"Antonio Ricci. It is all important that Teresa be released, and to-night."

"Ah, indeed!"

"Yes, she ought to be at Ancona ere this, for she bears important information to Garibaldi."

"Well, if this be so, why not let us change our course, and assail the coast-guard house?" said Frank.

"Agreed! agreed!" shouted all.

"Then so be it. We might as well fight our first battle with the Austrains to-night as at any other time."

This proposition was received with applause by all the young Garibaldians.

The Italian seaman, Antonio, shed tears of joy when informed of their intention.

After a long consultation together, it was agreed to release the Italian prisoners, and arm them.

When this determination was made known to them by Antonio and Frank, the prisoners leaped for joy.

On their bended knees they swore to be faithful and true.

Some wept, others laughed with joy, while many kissed Frank's hands in token of humble submission, admiration, and loyalty.

They soon changed their hated Austrian uniform for a red shirt, and ere long the yacht "Kaiser," with her two brass cannon charged with grape shot, turned her course towards the light-house.

The plan, as agreed upon, was this:—

The yacht was to sail in towards the land, and, in a small inlet about two miles south of the light-house, land a part of the crew.

It would then sail an equal distance above the coast-guard fort and land the rest, leaving some one behind to guard the "Kaiser."

At a given signal, which was to be a red rocket fired from the yacht, both parties were to march towards the fort, and assail it on both sides at once.

A part of the Italian sailors and young Garibaldians, led on by Hugh Tracy and Dick Fellows, were the first party landed, while Frank Ford and the rest were also landed above the small fort.

There were *two* of the young Garibaldians left

behind to guard the yacht, and these two, unknown to Frank, were spies!

When the red rocket was fired by Frank he marched his men towards the fort through a small dry ravine which ran at the back of it.

He gave particular orders that every one should arm themselves with two six-barrelled revolvers and a cutlass; which they did, for every one of the youths, sailors included, knew very well that some hard fighting would be required ere they overcame the Austrian guard.

Tony, the Fat Boy, was among Frank's party, but, instead of arming himself with two revolvers, he had at least a dozen in his belt, all double-shotted, besides an immense sabre he had picked up in the cabin.

In truth, as he trudged along, puffing and blowing, and munching a piece of bread, he looked like a walking magazine of fire-arms, and, to add to his load, he filled a large havresack with bread and meat, and had over a pint of wine in his canteen!

He tried a cigar on the march, but it was too much for him, and made him groggy.

He drank of the wine freely to quench his thirst after eating an enormous quantity of salt beef, and, long ere a shot was fired on either side, the Fat Boy was pretty well "tight," and, as he said, "dying for a fight."

Young Buttons was made head of the commissariat department for the occasion, and was accompanied by several of the youngest of the Garibaldians whom Frank did not think it prudent to expose to the chances of the battle. They were well laden with refreshments, which, with young Button's assistance, they lightened at almost every step.

However, all things seemed to prosper this the first land exploit of the young Garibaldians, and they crept close up to the fort through the ravine without being observed.

They lay close to the ground waiting for Hugh Tracy's band to arrive and "open the ball" on the other side, and could plainly hear the Austrian sentinels challenging each other in their rounds.

Frank, in a whisper, explained everything to his followers, and all was in readiness for the surprise and attack, when Tony whispered to Frank, in a hurried manner,

"Do you see him?"

"Who?"

"Why, don't you see yonder one of our band talking to that Austrian soldier just above us on the hillock?"

Frank turned his eyes, and perceived a person dressed like one of the young Garibaldians, but who it was he knew not, conversing with an Austrian sentinel.

"Who can it be?" thought Frank. "Surely none of my party have been taken prisoners?"

He counted his men, and found them all right.

But while he turned deadly pale, and whispered "treason" to himself, he knew not what to do.

To fire, and shoot down the villain, whoever he was, would have been easy enough, but it might ruin his plans.

He sat considering what to do for some moments, when the sentinel and the stranger suddenly disappeared from view.

In less than two minutes drums were heard beating wildly in the coast guard fort!

A discordant jar of voices was heard—a loud, angry murmuring sound it was—which betokened that the enemy had been secretly informed of the expedition, and were hurriedly assembling to thwart it!

A few moments passed—awful moments of suspense they were to Frank—still not a shot was fired to indicate to him that Hugh Tracy and his band had commenced the fight.

"Hide yourselves in the darkness of the ravine," said Frank, in a whisper; "we mustn't begin till our comrades have arrived on the other side. Hide, I tell you, Fatty! Creep low behind the rocks and clefts; let no one breathe aloud!"

He had just said these words when a company of Austrian marines appeared at the head of the ravine.

The form of each man of them was clearly visible against the bright blue sky.

The officer at the head was sword in hand.

"If the young Garibaldians are down here," he said, with a loud laugh, "we can't very well miss them, comrades. The spy said they were here, but I don't see anything of them. Do you, my lads?"

"No, captain," said the soldiers.

"Well, no matter; in case there be any one lurking and prying about, we might as well give them a good volley."

"Oh, the villain!" Fatty sighed. "He's going to give us a 'good volley!' It's all up with us now, Buttons. Give us a swig at the wine afore we dies!"

"Hus-s-s-h!" said Frank. "Hold your tongue, you big donkey. Keep quiet and crouch low; they can't hit you."

"Oh, can't they, though? I know better than that. In a moment or two they'll make cat's meat of us all! Oh, lor! I feel the bullets drilling holes into me even now! Ugh! this is soldiering, is it?—to be made a target of, and mustn't fire a pouch in return! Well, I suppose it's all right; give us another drink of wine, Buttons; it's all up with us, and no mistake! Good-bye; take care of yourself. Remember Tony to all his old friends."

"Who goes there?" asked the Austrian officer of marines, interrupting Tony's whispered words. "Who goes there?" he repeated. "Friends or foes?"

"Friends or foes, eh? It's coming now, Buttons, look-out!" gasped Tony, coiling himself up behind a huge stone like an eel."

"Ready!" said the officer to his men.

On the command forty bright barrels were levelled at the ravine.

Fatty, in trying to creep closer under the rock, lost his balance, and fell into a hole hard by some fifteen feet deep.

"Fire!" was the next command.

On the instant a sharp report broke upon the night air, and forty bullets went whistling and pattering through the ravine.

Directly they had fired Frank listened, for he thought some of his men were hit.

But not a sound was heard, save a deep sigh from Fatty in the mud-hole.

"Bravo!" said Frank, half aloud. "Not one hurt. They stand it like fire-eaters."

"They can't be there," said the Austrian officer.

"I think not," said another, "or we must have hit them."

"So much the better, then. Let us return, and rejoin our companions."

They moved off with measured tread, but had not gone far when a loud noise of fire-arms was heard in the opposite direction.

"That's Hugh and Dick, for a thousand pounds!" said Frank. "Now's our time, my lads. Let's rush forth and help them; no cheering or shouting yet, mind. We must first get some one into the fort."

The firing between Hugh Tracey's party and the Austrians was now very rapid, and wild shouts from the Italian seamen rent the air.

"Follow me!" said Frank.

Sword in hand, he rushed forth from the ravine, followed by his men, silent and determined.

"The gate is open! rush into the fort and secure it!" shouted one.

They did rush towards it, but it was slammed in their face!

All, or nearly all, the garrison were out fighting; not a man was on the walls, and therefore Frank knew there was no time to be lost, or Hugh Tracy's party might be overpowered by numbers.

"Here, Buttons," said Frank, "do you want to distinguish yourself?"

"Of course. What's up, Master Frank?"

"Why, this; there is a female imprisoned in there, and we must find her out."

"Well?"

"Will you do it?"

"Of course; if you give me a couple of revolvers to defend myself. But how am I to get in, the gates are closed?"

"Oh, we'll soon manage that."

In a moment eight of the Italian seamen formed a platform with their bodies against the wall; upon their backs jumped four boys, who did likewise, on the top of those clambered two others, thus forming a perfect scaffolding of human bodies, up which young Buttons had to climb.

As they were on the dark side and at the back of the fort, this stratagem was not perceived by the Austrian guards.

Provided with a long rope Buttons mounted on the back of first one and then another of his companions, and was soon safe on the top of the wall, concealed by some projecting masonry, and out of sight.

In a moment the scaffold of bodies was destroyed, and as they marched off towards the spot where Hugh Tracy and his men were fighting, Frank, full of glee, pointed out a dark speck on the wall of the fort, which was creeping along like a huge cat.

It was Buttons crawling towards the roof of the prison!

## CHAPTER XV.

FLINT'S MOVEMENTS AFTER THE FIRE—UNEXPECTED MEETING WITH WARNER AND THE PUG—OVERHEARD CONVERSATION IN THE COFFEE SHOP—ARRIVAL OF TWO OFFICERS WHO SEARCH IT—THE THREE VILLAINS ESCAPE.

"WHERE can the murderer run, or hide from the sight of man his red-dyed hand?"

Such were old Flint's thoughts as he hastened away he knew not whither from Green Court.

Still, as he ran, blinded with agony and despair, cold perspiration oozed from his brow and his limbs shook under him.

Where could he go? He knew not.

Whichever way he went, he cast his eyes towards the sky and could see there the red glare of the flames of his own burning dwelling.

And as often as he thought of his small, dingy chamber, with its worthless furniture, and as often as his fiery brain reverted to the horrible spectacle of the headless body in his own bed, he groaned aloud with mental agony.

"Who was that stranger?" he thought, that called at his lodgings in so mysterious a way.

What could he want?

What did he mean by inquiring for him so familiarly by name?

What was his purpose in asking "if he had lost anything?"

What had he lost at all?

He knew not.

Was it Warner in disguise?

No, this could not be; the voice, the manner, the height, and walk of the person was not Warner.

Who else could it be?

"Was it a detective?" he thought, and, as he did so, his teeth chattered again.

But suppose it *were* a detective; how could he have found him out so quickly?

He had ridden home from old Ford's place and had not tarried on the way.

"Surely," he thought, "the police cannot have found out a clue already? But suppose they have arrested Warner," he sighed; "if such be the fact, then it explains all."

He stood under a doorway to let many persons pass who were hurrying towards the fire.

Engine after engine came tearing along towards Green Court, and policemen in squads were hurrying thither also.

He heard some of them say that the whole court would be burnt to the ground.

"I wish it may," sighed Flint.

A fireman coming from the conflagration was heard to report that a life was lost.

"Who could it be?" thought the lawyer.

"Is the party known?" asked a policeman of the fireman, as they walked on together.

"Yes," the latter replied, "the landlady says the missing man is an old chap named Flint; the headless body she swears looks very much like that of his son; but she's not quite certain."

"You don't mean that?" said the policeman.

"I do though. The old lady is frantic about the loss of her house; and swears she distinctly heard the old man go upstairs into his room but never come out again."

"But wasn't the old chap discovered when they pulled the body out into the court?"

"No; you see, the 'Coster' and the 'Darkey' were almost suffocated in pulling the body out. They had bundled out all the other lodgers into the court, when the landlady screams out, 'Old Flint is there still!'"

The Coster and Darkey volunteered to go into the house again to look after him.

This was before any fireman had come on the spot; but directly they reached the front door, the whole place fell in with a loud crash, leaving nothing but the four walls standing.

"It's a horrible affair."

"I believe you," said the fireman.

"And a mysterious one to boot," said the policeman. "There must have been murder, then?"

"Without a doubt."

"And so the father was buried alive in the ruins?"

"It seems so."

"This makes two murders as have occurred to-night," said the policeman, as he and the fireman passed out of hearing.

"My son! my only son, Joel," gasped the lawyer, "murdered!—his head cut off! It cannot be! And yet the old landlady has seen him before—the last time he came from Bromley Hall. Oh, heavens, it cannot be! and all this tragedy—this double tragedy—is the work of cursed gold! Oh, that I had never been born! Until I robbed the widow and fatherless, years and years ago, I never felt that hellish thirst for money which now consumes me. It is a curse upon me! My hands are blighted—my heart has turned to stone, and I am a blood-dyed villain for the sake of pelf!"

These words were uttered by old Flint with so much earnestness that his brain seemed all on fire.

Acts in his life, long years past, now flitted through his mind like so many revengeful demons.

He thought he could even hear voices of the dead shouting in his ears—

"You have robbed the orphan and widow; you have foresworn their right and title; you have conspired for their death. You have done all this for gold! gold! gold! Where is now the peace of mind and happiness you promised yourself would come when you had accomplished your last purpose on old Ford? Gold you wanted—gold you have—gold shall be your curse! Your ill-gotten wealth, like a mill-stone round your neck, shall pull you down to the lowest loathsome pit of hell!"

These thoughts, as they flitted through his fever-heated brain—these imaginary voices which shouted in his ears with the strength of the town crier—seemed to chill his very marrow, and his eyes emitted a fiery glow as if his aching brain was nought but a burning furnace inhabited by shrieking devils.

"Oh, the curse of money!" he groaned. "What would I not *now* give for a moment's peace and innocence! But my heart is seared with crime—my hands are red with blood—aye, as gory as Warner's! What shall I do?—confess all and then destroy myself?"

For a moment he reflected, and then laughed in a wild defiant manner.

"Kill myself!" he chuckled, "what an idiot I am to think of such a thing! No, no; courage, Flint, courage. What is man without money? I am not the *only* one who has gotten it dishonestly, and by blood, too. *They* live and prosper—why not *I?* Yes, so I will. I will live like a prince on the fat of the land, and drown all remorse in the best of wine."

Walking to a pump, he washed the blood off his hands and face—the blood which had flown from his cut face, and the dark gory stains on his hands, which had smeared them when fumbling the bed-clothes in his room.

This seemed to refresh him much.

He next went into a public house, and had a quartern of hot brandy and water. This was quickly and ravenously gulped down, when, to cheer himself still further, he went into a second and a third public house, and had a like quantity.

The effects of the brandy was soon apparent, so much so, that on his way through the streets he laughed and chuckled to himself, and began laying out his plans for the future.

In imagination he pictured to himself a palace-like residence, splendid parks and orchards, magnificent carriages and horses, and his son Joel a Member of Parliament.

"I must keep out of Warner's way, though," he thought, "or there will be murder between us. For this purpose, in case I might meet him on some dark night, I will always go armed—yes, I'll carry two revolvers, double-loaded, and a dagger. But, Lor, what should I fear him for? He'll never trouble me; the police are close to his heels by this time. I hope they'll hunt him down! Calcraft would then have a job. I wouldn't mind giving a strong pull at his legs myself. Ha, ha! He's the only one that knows anything about it; if I get *him* out of the way I can hold up my head with the best in the land. Flint, Mr. Flint, eh? Well, well, how I have deceived them all! Ha, ha! They may hunt for Mr. Flint as long as they like. Old Ford used to call me by that name, and I adopted it. Even Joel doesn't know anything to the contrary; he little thinks that his and my right name is Smidt. A fine old Dutch name, truly, and I'm not ashamed of it. The Dutch are the cutest and coolest villains out. Ha, ha! I will go over to Germany, and buy a grand title. Let me see, for a few hundred pounds I could be made a count, a baron, or even a duke. What would sound the best?—Count Smidt, Baron von Smidt, or—— Yes, that's it: Baron von Smidt, of—— Where shall it be? Oh, I know, old Ford has the title to an estate he bought there among his papers in my safe. I'll go by the title of that domain. All is mine now. Ha, ha! Money's the thing. Joel will marry a lord's daughter, or something grand, and we will live in princely style."

While thus thinking as he walked along, he stepped into a coffee shop that had just opened, and soon fell asleep over a cup of tea.

It was in a very low neighbourhood, dirty and ill-lighted.

He was aroused by the whispered conversation of two men, several boxes away.

"Don't speak so loud," said one; "that old chap might hear us."

"No fear," said the other. "He's sleeping as sound as a top."

Greatly to old Flint's surprise he heard these two men whispering about Ford's murder.

One was Warner, entirely changed in dress; the other, Bill Barney!

He was horrified to discover this, but still held his head low, and snored on as if fast asleep.

He heard Warner say that after he had "finished the old man" he looked for the treasure, but found none. He managed to escape, and rushed off to old Flint's lodgings just in time to find it all in flames. Here he met with Bill Barney, who had been roused out of bed by the clamorous noise of "fire!"

Warner appeared sadly disappointed that he could not discover what had become of the lawyer, whose throat he threatened to cut on the instant he met him unless he divided the booty.

A threat which the half-bred pug coincided in fully, as he murmured,

"Jest so; cut his wizzon fust, and chuck him in the Thames arter, is *my* adwice; no marcy on sich slimy coves as he is. Jest you on'y point him out to *me*, that's all, *I'll* soon 'do' for him."

At that instant two policemen came in and called for the landlord.

Warner and Bill Barney moved away from each other and began to read newspapers, hiding their faces as much as possible.

The two policemen wished to know if the landlord had let any of his beds the night before to any persons of suspicious appearance, "as there was a party which was wanted."

The landlord protested that though his shop was a dirty, dingy one, and situated in a very disreputable neighbourhood, he was sure that none of his beds had been let out to improper persons, men or women; an oath, by the way, which most coffee-shop keepers will willingly swear to, although they know, on the contrary, that after certain hours their rooms are frequented both by prostitutes and thieves more than any other class.

The two officers went upstairs to examine the apartments, for suspicious parties *had* been traced there.

Warner and Bill instantly left the shop, and, as the latter said, "hooked it."

Old Flint had been perspiring with fear, but also decamped very hastily, greatly to the surprise of the officers when they returned a few minutes afterwards.

They had not found the person they particularly "wanted," but they did not go away empty-handed, for they had discovered four thieves in the house—two professional pickpockets and their "gals," notorious prostitutes of the Haymarket, who drugged gentlemen and robbed them, as a genteel and lucrative mode of living.

These were lugged off to the station-house, kind reader, whither let us go, and see what was doing there regarding Old Ford's murder at the Haunted House.

## CHAPTER XVI.

SANGUINARY COMBAT IN THE DARK RAVINE—FIGHT FOR THE STANDARD—FATTY "THE FIRE-DEVIL"—EXPLOITS OF THE YOUNG LEADERS—MARK, THE FOSTER BROTHER'S DEED OF BRAVERY—THE VICTORY—THE CAPTURED FLAG—THE SURRENDER—THE AWFUL EXPLOSION.

FRANK had not gone far with his men when he perceived the dangerous position in which Hugh Tracy and his party were.

They, like himself, had journeyed up the ravine, and hid themselves for a time until the proper moment.

Shortly a company of Austrians appeared at the head of the ravine, which stopped Hugh's progress.

When he heard the firing, however, he made sure that Frank had been attacked, and therefore ordered his men to begin firing.

Nothing could have been better for the Austrians, who were very numerous.

They returned the fire, and for some time the young Garibaldians maintained their ground.

But they had to give way before superior numbers, and were slowly retiring down the ravine again, knocking over Austrians at every step.

The enemy, with loud shouts, and notwithstanding their number of killed and wounded, bravely followed, and were then fighting there at the moment when Frank's party arrived, and screened themselves from view in the edge of the ravine, right behind the Austrians.

He saw at a glance how matters stood, and in order to encourage his friends fighting below he and his party raised loud shouts and cheers for Garibaldi!

These shouts were recognised by Hugh Tracy's party, who answered them, and made the ravine echo again with their lusty cheers.

The Austrians were much surprised, but did not prove cowards.

They were now taken in front and behind by the young Garibaldians, who, on all sides, showered vollies of shot upon them without mercy.

The fight was now becoming hotter and more desperate each moment.

The Italian seaman who had joined Frank performed prodigies of valour.

Amid cheers, shouts, groans, and oaths, the combat continued.

The Austrians could not escape, they were assailed with such fury on either side that they knew not what to do.

"Surrender!" shouted Frank on one side.

"Never!" was the response.

"Then let them have it, lads," said Frank, and his followers fired faster than ever.

The poor Austrians did not know what to make of it. They were far more numerous than the young Garibaldians; but the latter seemed to fire six shots to their one; and no wonder, for most of them had breech-loaders, and rifles which could fire twenty times per minute, so that they literally poured balls into them like showers of hail stones.

Frank, though brave, was also wise. He did not madly rush into the thick of the fight, and thus leave his comrades without a commander.

He did much better than this.

The Austrian officer in command rode a horse which Frank made up his mind to have at all costs.

But how to get it he did not know.

Chance soon gave him an opportunity.

The Austrian ordered a part of his men to wheel about and charge Frank's party with the bayonet.

This they attempted to do.

But Jack was as good as his master, for Frank, nothing loth, cheered on his men, and with sword in hand dashed at the Austrian officer on horseback in front.

For an instant the mounted Austrian was astonished to see such a youth assail him.

But next moment their swords clashed, and it was a hand-to-hand encounter, short and desperate.

The officer tried to ride over Frank; but the youth was too nimble. He jumped aside, and the sword which was aimed at his head, clove the air!

With a loud laugh of triumph, Frank struck the officer on the sword-arm, and not only disabled but unhorsed him!

In a second Frank jumped upon the animal, and with a loud shout he galloped towards Hugh Tracy to give directions.

The Austrian flag was waving in the breeze amid fire and smoke.

On his way to Hugh, Frank made a dash at it.

He cut the bearer down, and the force of his blow severed the flag-staff in twain.

He was now surrounded on all sides.

The colours were snatched up by some brave Austrian, and Frank, though not disgraced, was obliged to fight his way out of the throng, whose bayonets were all pointed at his breast.

Frank at that moment was unhorsed.

The young Garibaldians seeing his danger rushed closer and closer on the foe with wild shouts.

The meeting was a deadly one.

With pistols, knives, bayonets, cutlasses, and rifles the combatants met breast to breast!

It was a fearful moment.

The fight was still terrible, intense and unequal, for the Austrians were far more numerous.

But this the young Garibaldians did not seem to care much about, for their foes were falling fast on every hand.

For a short time longer the sanguinary combat lasted, but the enemy were beaten at all points.

Some clambered up the rocks out of the ravine, and thus escaped certain slaughter.

Others hid themselves behind rocks, and in clefts, but the greater part still fought on bravely.

How long the fight might have lasted there was no telling, for the young Garibaldians discovered they had met men who were not cowards.

"Fatty," who, to his credit, it must be confessed, fought like a lion during the whole affair; many had fallen before his strong arm.

His arms, and sleeves, and face were all dyed with gore, and his hair stood on end as if with fright.

"The flag! The flag!" he cried, and rushed into the thickest of the fight. "We'll teach 'em what

# THE BOY SOLDIER;

## OR, GARIBALDI'S YOUNG CAPTAIN.

John Bull is made of, my boys! Hooray for the flag! On to it, boys!"

It is more than likely that the Austrians would have very soon found out what Fatty was made of, as he rushed in among them, were it not for Frank, Tom, Hugh, and Dick, who came to his aid.

Even they could not make much impression on the close ranks before them.

At that moment, more than a dozen took a deliberate and deadly aim at Frank, who was again on horseback.

They fired, and his horse fell.

It was not shot—it had been baulked in its stride by Frank's foster-brother, Mark, who saw the danger

This stumbling of the horse saved Frank's life.

On the instant several rushed at him to despatch him.

Mark, however, was near.

With a six-barrel revolver in one hand, and a cutlass in the other, he discharged the one right into their faces, while with the other he cut and cleaved a way for Frank out of the infuriated crowd.

The young captain remounted his horse on the instant, and dashed towards the standard, round which Hugh, Dick, Tom and Fatty were fighting like braves.

They could not secure it.

One after another did Fatty fire his many pistols,

and then threw them at his opponents' heads, until the Austrians began to imagine the fat boy was no less than the devil himself.

Vaulting on to the horse behind his foster brother Frank, Mark Tilton rose up, and, like an acrobat, jumped right into the middle of the combatants, and seized the flag.

A dozen swords were levelled at his head in a moment.

He slipped down to avoid them, and the next moment the flag was *his!*

The fight that now ensued was horrible.

"Surrender!" shouted Frank. "Surrender, and quarter will be given."

"Throw down your arms!" roared Fatty, puffing and blowing; "throw 'em down this instant, you thick-headed fools. Do you think you can fight against English boys, eh? Not you, you tallow-faced hounds; you must eat more roast beef and plum pudding first, eh, lads? Put down your arms, I tell you, or, by the Lord Harry, we'll spifflicate you all, and turn you into German sausages."

This speech from the "fire devil," as the Austrians called Fatty, as he stood blood-stained and furious before them, had the proper effect.

"Surrender!" shouted Frank.

"We do! We do!" was the sullen answer, as the prisoners threw down their arms.

In a few moments the firing had ceased on both sides.

Groans and and cries were heard on all sides, but these were drowned by the shouts and cheers of the triumphant young Garibaldians.

At that moment a bright flash swept upwards towards the sky.

A terrific explosion followed like the concentrated energy of a dozen earthquakes.

It shook the ground so violently that every one fell in amazement and horror.

The truth was quickly known.

Hissing shells went screaming through the air, and legs and arms flying in all directions!

*The Fort had blown up!*

---

## CHAPTER XVII.

AFTER THE BATTLE—FATE OF YOUNG BUTTONS—THE SPOIL AND PRISONERS—THE RUINED FORT—THE UNKNOWN SPY—THE ALARM—JOYFUL MEETING—RESCUE OF TERESA.

FOR a moment the young Garibaldians stood aghast and looked appalled at the frightful explosion which had shaken the earth.

They knew not what to think or how to act.

They had valiantly vanquished the Austrians, it is true, in this severe night encounter, but their hearts were sad at the extraordinary fate of poor Buttons.

The Italian seamen, who, a moment before, were loud in shouts, cutting and slashing at the Austrians, looked grim and sorrowful.

"Poor Teresa!" they sighed. "Alas! she deserved a better fate; she was one of Garibaldi's chief spies, and was worth more than her own weight in diamonds to the Italian cause of liberty."

Bloodstained and wounded as many of them were, they shed bitter tears for poor Teresa's luckless end.

The Fat Boy was in a frightful rage at the event, and he swore to be revenged on somebody for the page's death.

It was as much as Frank, Hugh, and Mark could do to keep him from shedding the blood of a black-looking Austrian officer, who sat near by, grinning at the awful occurrence.

"Poor Buttons!" said Fatty, sobbing and crying, "I'd 'a give anything rather than he should have been hurt—and so brave, too! The little beggar, he was a good sort, and no mistake; he'd always divide his grub with a fellar as wanted it. But he's gone now. What shall I do? what shall I do? Poor Job!"

Up to the moment of the explosion, no one of the young Garibaldians had given a thought to the worth, the bravery, or the laughter-making, frolicsome Buttons, but now that he was blown up in the fort while engaged in a dangerous enterprise, every one was loud in their praises of the poor friendless boy.

No one seemed more cut up than Mark, Frank's hardy foster-brother.

He did not speak, but as he sat down in the shade, out of the bright moonlight, tears flowed down his cheeks,

"Ah! Frank, I would rather have sacrificed an arm or a leg than have lost Job Parsons. He was the life and soul of the expedition, and a braver boy never stepped in shoe-leather than that same care-killing, laughter-loving page.

Frank and others had their own feelings about the matter.

They knew well that Job Parsons was a good-hearted, harum-scarum fellow, and they felt great sorrow for his loss.

But how could it be prevented?

It was not *their* fault that he had shoved himself forward, and volunteered on that hazardous enterprise.

They had endeavoured time and again to curb his wild, reckless doings, but it could not be done.

He *would* do this and that, despite all that might be said to the contrary, and if nothing else was to be done on board, he would clamber about the rigging of the yacht, like a nimble young monkey as he was, playing all sorts of tricks.

Now that he was gone his good qualities were discovered; but no one seemed more down-hearted about his unhappy fate than the Fat Boy and the foster-brother Mark.

"He could sing, dance, and fight," said one.

"Yes, and he could cook, wash, and tell a good story," said another, and as they lamented the fate of "poor little Buttons," as they now termed him, they felt deep and sincere sorrow for his sudden death.

But what must the young Garibaldians now do?

They had fought well, and were victorious.

They had a number of officers and privates prisoners; but the fort was blown up, and the true object of their mission—namely, the rescue of Teresa, the Italian spy—had failed.

"We must not remain here long," whispered an Italian seaman in Frank's ear; "we must not long remain here," he repeated, in a very solemn, and rather ominous tone. "You don't know these Austrians as well as I do."

"What do yo mean, Pedro?" Frank asked.

"I mean this, my young captain. The Austrians have a splendid code of signals."

"Well. what of that?"

"I have no doubt they know all about it by this time in Trieste."

"I do not understand you."

"Well, captain, I mean this. The fort did not blow up of its own accord."

"Well?"

"Before it blew up there must have been some good cause for it, and the telegraph was used to warn the garrison in Trieste of what was going on."

"Just so."

"Well, then, after they had telegraphed for more men, and for ships to be sent out to catch us, the magazine was fired, no doubt by the orders of superior officers, and I feel certain they have already got up steam, and are on their way hither with one or two vessels. We must leave this at once, or we may be all lost."

"Right, Pedro, right," said Frank. "Did you hear that distant gun just now?"

"Yes, captain, I did; it was that which made me speak thus boldly to you."

"What did it mean?"

"It is a system of signalling the Austrians have. They are on the alert all along the coast."

"But I don't like to give up all our prisoners, Pedro."

"You need not give liberty to all, my young captain," said the Italian.

"What, then?"

"Make all of them march through the rain towards the yacht, carrying their arms."

"Carrying their arms? They are more numerous than we are now, and might turn on us again."

"No, no, captain," said the Italian, smiling; "there is no fear of that if you do what I tell you."

"What is it?"

"Disarm two-thirds of them, make the other third carry all the guns and ammunition."

"I see, I see."

"Let the unarmed march in front with little escort, as those carrying the arms and ammunition will be too heavily loaded to offer any resistance. Let them march behind, surrounded by our men."

"Just so, Pedro; it shall be done."

"And quickly, captain, pray, for I hear the Austrian signal guns firing all along the coast; we shall not have much time to spare."

After a few moments' conference with the young leaders, it was resolved to follow Pedro's plan.

Two thirds of the prisoners were disarmed and marched in front, the remaining third carried the guns and ammunition of the remainder.

This was done so quietly and quickly that in a few moments all the Austrian prisoners were on their way to the yacht through the dark ravine, the wounded Garibaldians being carried by their comrades.

When the "Kaiser" was reached all the rifles, swords, ammunition, bayonets, and the like were piled on board, and, except the officers, all the Austrians were liberated.

The "Kaiser" was soon ready for sea, and all things were right for a pleasant start and a quick run over the Adriatic to Ancona.

"Where is Tom and Mark?" asked Frank, as he missed them when calling off the names of his followers.

"They have gone to look at the fort; they won't be long."

Ere many minutes Tom and Mark appeared in the distance, dragging between them a rough, drunken Austrian soldier, who was cursing and swearing and struggling to get away.

"Any sign of young Buttons?"

"Have you seen him anywhere?"

"How did it blow up?" asked first one and then another, in great haste and eagerness.

All that Mark and Tom could answer was that they had not seen the slightest sign of either one or the other of them.

"All I could learn," said Tom, "was that this wretch here had something to do with it, and have brought him here as a prisoner."

"Then let us set sail," said Frank.

In five minutes the yacht, with flowing sheets and a gentle breeze, rolled gracefully in the wind, and had left the shore more than a mile behind.

The fate of Buttons was still the chief topic of conversation.

"Who was that fellow we saw talking to the Austrian officer at the head of the ravine just before they fired on us?" asked one.

"Don't know."

"Wasn't it Buttons, think you?" said one of the two who had been left in charge of the boat. "It might have been, you know."

"What, Buttons turn traitor?" said the Fat Boy, indignantly. "Look here, Jenkins, don't you dare whisper anything o' that sort again in *my* hearing, or I'll knock you down."

Jenkins didn't utter another word, but moved off, biting his lip.

"Jenkins," said Frank, "did you and Smalls stay on board all the time we were away?"

"Yes, nearly all the time, captain," Jenkins answered; "but we just went on shore to have a little look at the fighting, and returned in a few moments again.

"Did you see anyone skulking around?"

"No."

"Nor any one go on board."

"No."

"How far did you go?"

"About a hundred yards off, that's all. Why?"

"Oh! nothing," said Frank, moodily, and walked towards the wheel, where Mark was steering.

The two or three wounded Garibaldians were all comfortably lying on deck, and all was peace and quiet again.

Most of them dropped off to sleep after the hard-fought battle they had gone through; but the Fat Boy was consoling himself with a cold fowl, and a bottle of wine, both of which he had "hooked" from one of the Austrian prisoners, who were grouped together in the head of the boat, and well guarded.

He was munching away, and paying very great attention to his bottle of wine, when some one crept slowly towards him and said in a whisper,

"You might give a fellow a bit I think, Tony."

"Wh-h-h-a-a-t!" gasped the Fat Boy in surprise, with his mouth half-filled. "Wh-h-a-a-t! is that you?"

"Yes, me."

"What! Buttons?"

"Yes, Buttons."

In a moment the Fat Boy seized Job round the neck, and began to blubber like a child.

The noise he made awoke all his comrades, who, when they discovered the cause, clustered round the page, shook him by the hand, and cheered loudly for his safety, while Fatty, like a rough bear, nearly hugged him to death.

"But how is this, Buttons? There is some mystery here. How did you escape?"

"What of Teresa? Did you discover her?"

"Not only discovered her; but rescued her," said Buttons. "She is now sleeping in the cabin."

"And neither of you got hurt?"

"Not the scratch of a pin."

Loud shouts rent the air on hearing this good news.

"But how did it all happen? how could you escape the explosion?"

"That remains to be told, Captain Frank," said Buttons, laughing. "When we are well rested, if you don't mind, I'll spin that yarn to all assembled."

"Agreed! agreed!" shouted the young Garibaldians, in high glee.

At that moment Mark pointed towards the south.

A steamer was approaching at full speed; but was yet some distance off.

They began to fire at the yacht; but their shot and shells fell wide of the mark and spurted up the water in heavy columns full half a mile wide from the "Kaiser."

"We are discovered," said Mark, "and chased. Tell the lads to hoist every stitch of canvas. We must fight our way out of this."

Bang! bang! went the enemy's guns; but the shots fell short.

"Hugh, load the two brass rifled guns," said Frank. "We'll just give the Austrian a taste of our quality when he comes near enough."

The guns were loaded, and Frank pointed them.

"Don't fire yet," he said. "Wait for the word from me."

"Aye, aye, sir," said the Italian gunners and young Garibaldians, full of enthusiasm.

Frank stood beside the guns, telescope in hand, ready to give the word of command.

## CHAPTER XVIII.

THE OLD IRON SAFE AND ITS TREASURES—PREPARATIONS FOR LEAVING ENGLAND—THE TELEGRAPH AND DETECTIVES WORK TOGETHER—"IS THAT THE MAN?"—THE MYSTERY NOT CLEARED UP—SUSPICION ON FRANK.

INSIDE the office sat a spruce, well-shaven inspector, pen in hand, while inside and outside of the little square room sat several policemen, most of them in plain clothes, wet, muddy, and tired with their work.

Drunkards, thieves, and riotous persons of both sexes came in, conducted by various officers; the charges against them were taken in a short, business-like manner, and the luckless individuals quickly confined in various cells of very small and uncomfortable dimensions.

This was nothing.

The telegraph from Scotland Yard was working rapidly, and the inspector knew very well that something more than common had taken place.

He read the message and seemed shocked.

It was about old Ford's murder at the Haunted House.

The "case" seemed a difficult one, but the inspector, after a moment's thought, called in Sergeant Gale, and police-constable Stiff.

Both these officers were in plain clothes.

Quiet, fatherly, innocent-looking fellows they were, with no flurry about them, and always took things very coolly.

Innocent as they looked, however, they were as sharp as needles, and it might be truthfully said, as it often had been said, that a thief or desperado might as well have the devil after him as either Gale or Stiff.

They received their instructions, and quietly left the inspector's little office, as if they were going to bed, instead, perhaps, of never seeing one for a week to come.

"It was a very difficult job," the inspector said; but then he knew that both Gale and Stiff were used to "difficult jobs" all their lives, and rather liked them than otherwise, as all good officers do.

They went their way, plunged into the dark streets around the police station, and vanished none knew whither.

* * * * *

Of all this Old Flint knew nothing.

He hurried homewards to his "office" so called, a two-roomed den, situated not far from Lincoln's Inn, which boasted of little more than an iron safe, piles of parchment, books, and cart-loads of legal rubbish; while in the front apartment stood a bed and wash-stand.

When he entered this office he sank back perfectly exhausted into an old arm-chair.

The shutters were up, but the grey light of morning stole through the cracks, and shed a dim uncertain light on all around.

All was quiet; nought but a mouse gnawing in the deserted cupboard, or rustling among books and papers on the floor and tables, broke the stillness of the scene.

With candle in hand he walked towards his iron safe, and opened it.

He drew a small stool towards him, and sat down to pore over his deeds and treasures.

His old eyes sparkled with delight as he conned the will and a number of valuable title deeds of his murdered client—Mr. Ford.

Bags there were also, filled with gold almost to bursting.

A small drawer was packed with diamonds of great price.

"All these are mine," he said, as he surveyed his treasures.

He took up a large bundle of bank notes, a very large bundle it was indeed.

"This is the result of the many sales of old Ford's property," he mused. "What a silly old fool he was to trust any lawyer with so much wealth. Well, I am no worse than the majority of my calling; they are very much like pawnbrokers; it's two to one if the client ever gets back what he entrusts to them, and then not till they've been well bled first—ha, ha! lawyers for ever. They call us spiders waiting for a fly; so we are, but the fly doesn't get off easier than a lawyer's patron."

These thoughts made the old man chuckle again.

He paid a visit to his mouldy cupboard, drank

heartily out of a bottle of gin he always kept there, and then locked up the safe again.

He slept for two or three hours, or at all events tried to sleep, and rose again as tired as ever.

He had great affairs to settle, however, which required all his cunning and firmness.

He dressed himself more carefully than was his wont, and went to a box-maker, and had there and then a strong deal box made according to his orders, such an one as would just contain the iron safe.

This was brought home and paid for.

He next put a large quantity of gold and notes into his pockets, packed the safe, and then went to a railway carrier's.

A van and two strong men soon arrived.

The safe was placed in the strong deal case, nailed firmly down, and directed to—

"Samuel Sneider, Esq., Dover. To be called for."

It was conveyed away to the railway station, and was to reach Dover that same evening.

"So far, so good," said Flint. "All my valuables are safe, at all events. In case anything should happen," he thought, "and I *don't* reach Dover, I'll drop Joel a line, in care of the master at Bromley Hall, and tell him all—that is if he is alive; for," thought he, "I can't believe that the body found is that of my own son."

The letter was written and sent off by post.

"Now," said old Flint, "my hardest task is to be done. I'd rather face the devil himself than do it; but if I don't wish to be ferreted out by the hawk-eyed detectives, and looked upon as an accomplice in old Ford's murder, I must go to the house at once and play the hypocrite."

The lawyer fortified himself with a hearty breakfast and several draughts of liquor, after which he called a cab and drove off to the Red House.

He got out of the vehicle some distance from the house, and walked up boldly towards it.

There were two policemen in the garden, who shoved him back and would not let him pass.

A wink from Sergeant Gale, who sat at the parlour window, told them how to act, and they allowed him to pass in.

"What—what in the name of goodness, is the matter?" gasped the lawyer, with well-feigned surprise, as he confronted Gale in the entrance hall. "What has happened? What are policemen doing *here*, I wonder?"

"Doing their duty, sir," answered Gale, scanning the lawyer from head to foot with a keen, quick glance that made old Flint wince again. "What do *you* want here? Who are you and what are you?" asked Gale.

Flint explained in a few words.

"Old Ford's lawyer, eh? Well, he won't want any *more* lawyers," said Gale, in a careless way.

"What do you mean? I've been his legal adviser for years."

"He's dead."

"What?"

"Murdered."

"Mercy on us, you don't mean that?"

"I do; murdered last night."

"Who did it?"

"That remains to be found out; but I don't think, between you and me," said Gale, laying his hand on the lawyer's shoulder, "I don't think it will be long before we lay hands on *one* of 'em."

The lawyer faintly smiled, and, do all he could, was unable to keep from shaking.

"Then there *is* more than one?" the lawyer asked.

"It looks like it, from the butler's statement."

"But his property, *his* property," said Flint, "What has become of that?"

"Stolen, I suppose; we found none."

"What, all his title-deeds and money stolen?"

"Was there any?"

"Any? why a vast amount in notes and parchments. He always concealed his most valuable papers under his pillow. All gone! Lord a mercy on us, what a strange world we live in! Who'd a thought it? Why, I came expressly according to his order this very morning to make out a new will in favour of his two nephews, Frank and Tom."

"Indeed!" said Gale, with twinkling eyes. "And where are these two youths?"

"At Bromley Hall."

"And were they, up to the present time, not mentioned in his will?"

"Yes; they have behaved very badly to the kind old man, and, so I hear, have often threatened him if he disinherited them."

"Just so," said Gale, making a note in his pocket-book. "Just so. Frank—Tom—Bromley Hall. Just so."

"I prevailed on the old man but yesterday to alter his will in favour of them, but he put the parchment under his pillow, and said he'd see about it by this morning. Poor man! good old soul! murdered, eh? Lord have mercy on us all!" said Flint, shedding tears. "In the midst of life we are in death! Heigho! that it should have come to this!"

Flint was allowed to proceed upstairs.

As he passed, Sergeant Gale whispered to the butler,

"No, sir, that's not him. He waren't near here since yesterday. That's nothing like the party I saw dash by me down stairs. It's not him."

"*That* the party you saw, Tomkins?" whispered Gale, to 61 Z.

Tomkins was "dead certain" he wasn't either of the men he had seen prowling around the neighbourhood for the past week, and equally sure was Sergeant Ruff.

Old Flint went upstairs with Davy, the butler, and viewed the body of the murdered man.

With many sighs and groans, he moaned and bewailed the old man's death, and with crocodile tears in his eyes, placed a crown piece in the butler's hands as he walked down stairs again.

"Mysterious affair, Sergeant Gale," said Ruff, afterwards.

"Just so—quite. We've found out, though, how the murderer escaped; through that panel at the back of the bed. Davy says he must have got in that way; but it seems there were two engaged on the job. One escaped at the front door, and the other, who evidently knew but little about the panel, missed the ladder, and fell into a cellar below, whence he escaped through a trap-door that opens into the back garden. We have traced the footsteps of the last one through the garden and mud as far as the cab-rank, but there we must stop for the present."

"Anything else?"

"We have found the nephew's dagger in the bed, and have missed several things out of Frank's room

—his gold watch among other trifles I have already had it stopped at all the pawnbrokers and goldsmiths; a keen eye is already on all the smashers and cribs of the Israelites."

"We may trace them, after all?"

"Perhaps so; I found a pair of gold studs on the floor, and a pocket-handkerchief also, which may give us a clue by-and-bye."

While speaking thus to his brother officer, Flint disappeared so suddenly as to excite the suspicions of Sergeant Gale, who directed a plain-clothes man to watch him, if possible.

This could not be done, however, for Flint disappeared like a shadow from the premises.

As he left the house, and faced Barlow Place, he looked up, without any object.

In the first floor he espied a man looking down upon him with fiery eyes.

***It was Warner!***

## CHAPTER. XIX.

KNAVE MEETS KNAVE—SUDDEN APPEARANCE OF OLD JONATHAN—THE QUARREL—THE COMPACT—THE WRITTEN CONFESSION—THE RESOLVE.

In great haste old Flint returned home, for the savage look of Warner, as he gazed out of window, sent a thrill of horror through the old lawyer's craven heart.

"He looks every inch a murderer," thought Flint, "and he would not be over scrupulous in finishing *me* off, if he got a chance. If he *got* a chance," mused the scoundrel, "but I'll take very great care he *doesn't* get a chance; if he does, it's all up with my prospects of wealth and happiness. I'd just as soon meet the devil himself as Warner at this present moment."

With the instinct of a doubly-dyed rogue as he was, he slunk into the first public-house he came to.

It was well that he had done so, for, as he peeped through the door, he perceived Warner, in a fresh disguise, dash past wildly, looking up and down the street in search of him.

"Luck attends me yet," said Flint. "And now for a cab."

He swallowed his brandy hastily, and perceiving that Warner had over-shot his mark a long way, and had hurried down the street, he jumped into a cab and drove off rapidly towards his office near Lincoln's Inn.

He paid the cabman and slunk through the bye streets until he was near his own office, and then darted upstairs with a quick step and unlocked his door.

"A few hours will settle all," he said to himself, as he sat in the arm-chair playing with his fingers, "a few hours will settle all. I shall be far away by this time to-morrow, and I defy any of them to discover me then."

While thus musing, the door behind him opened, and in stepped Jonathan Gravestones with noiseless foot.

When Flint by instinct turned round and perceived him, he was so shocked for a moment at the unexpected encounter that he staggered again and turned pale.

"Th-h-hat you, Jonathan? L-l-l-or' b-l-l-e-ss my soul, how you *did* frighten me!"

"Did I?"

"Yes, upon my word."

"Why?" asked the Rev. Mr. Gravestones, in a calm sepulchral tone.

"I don't know; but you *did*, though."

"It looks like it; why, you tremble even now."

"Do I? Lor' you don't say so."

"Yes, you gasped for a moment as if you saw a blood-stained murderer before you."

"A what?" said Flint, shuddering at Jonathan's cold manner.

"Why, a murderer; but I'm not one, am I, old Flint, eh? Ha, ha!"

"You, n-n-o-o. What makes you look so pale, Jonathan?"

"A great deal. We have been partners for years, haven't we, Flint?"

"Partners, Jonathan, in what? I don't understand you."

"You are very dull of comprehension, then, all at once. Do you forget the two brats?"

"Hus-s-s-h!" said Flint. "Let me close the door; we might be overheard. How did you find out my office, my dear Jonathan?" asked the lawyer, with a bitter smile.

"Why, as I had very important business with you, you know, I——"

"Yes, my dear friend, but it ain't necessary to mention any names, you know. *We* understand each other—walls have ears."

"Very well, then, as I wanted to see you regarding the two——"

"Yes, yes; go on."

"And as I could never get you to give me your right direction, I watched for several hours, and at last walked upstairs after you."

"Ha! ha!" laughed the lawyer, with an hyena-like grin, as if he would very much like to snap Jonathan's head off. "Really! And what do you want now you *have* come?"

"Money."

"Nonsense; did you not agree long ago to keep them for a certain sum per year, and so much extra when they—— You know."

"I did."

"*And are* they dead?"

"Yes."

"You don't mean that, my dear friend Jonathan," said Flint, squeezing him by the hand; "you don't mean that? Lor', you *don't* know what a relief it is to me to hear that!"

"I'm glad to hear it is a relief to you."

"When did it happen?"

"Yesterday."

"And you came up to London immediately to tell me of it?"

"I did."

"Oh, Jonathan! you *are* a friend," said the lawyer; "a friend indeed! Are they buried?"

"Yes."

"Where?"

"In the stream."

"Jonathan, your hand, my dear, dear boy. You could not have acted more wisely. If you had bought coffins and all such rubbish, why——"

"There would have been a very unpleasant investigation and such like; and we should have been presented with a rope by Calcraft, that is all."

"How funny you are, Jonathan. You always were a droll dog, you know, ha! ha! Ah," said Flint, pouring out a glass of spirits for himself and friend, "ah, I very seldom touch spirits of any kind, but I *must* drink a toothful to our joyous meeting, for a friend in need is a friend indeed."

"Just so, and that's the reason I came up to see you, Flint."

"About the money, I suppose?"

"Yes."

"Well, it isn't convenient for me to pay you such a large sum to day, Jonathan, but I can do the next best thing. I will pay you part in cash, and give you a check for the rest."

"That will do; draw it out."

Flint did so, but could scarce keep from laughing as he wrote it, for he knew his account at the bank had been closed weeks before.

But of this Jonathan knew nothing.

He looked at the check, and placed the cash in his pocket.

"And now that the two brats are disposed of what does it benefit you, Flint?"

"Not one farthing, my dear sir, not a groat."

"Then why have you taken so much care of them for years past."

"Merely a whim to oblige a distant friend."

"You must be a kind fellow, considering how much you have already paid *me* in their behalf."

Flint only smiled.

He thought to himself "I shall soon be out of his way."

While old Jonathan, on the other hand, chuckled to himself,

"This makes the second big pull I've had out of old Flint on account of that boy and girl; he little dreams they are *not* dead, though. I wish they were, for in that case I might have a little peace of mind; as it is they may turn up again at any moment, and I, having had most to do with them, shall run the risk of transportation for life. No matter, while Flint lives I am sure of money."

He did not mention anything about the school riot, but simply said that Frank and Tom had left.

"And Joel?"

"Oh, he's all right; he went to dine at the banker's yesterday, and intends to come to town shortly."

"I'm glad of that; Joel will do well wherever he goes. I have sent off a very important letter to him."

"At the school?"

"Yes."

"Oh, indeed, he's sure to get it; he's a fine lad, and brave as steel. He gave Frank and Tom such a trouncing yesterday, a real good thrashing it was. I didn't interfere, you know, for I hate those two Fords."

"I, too, hate them. I should not have much cared if he killed them both."

For a moment there was a dead silence.

Jonathan eyed Flint very closely, and the crafty lawyer did likewise.

"And so you arrived in town this morning, eh, Jonathan?"

"Of course I did. What makes you think I came last night?"

"Oh, nothing."

Another pause.

"Have you heard any news?" Jonathan asked in a very careless manner.

"What news?"

"About a very shocking murder which took place last night."

"Murder?"

"Yes; not only one, but *two*."

"Two?" gasped Flint, fairly taken off his guard.

"Yes. What makes you tremble?"

"Me tremble? I don't, on my honour."

"Your honour isn't worth much, Flint," said Jonathan, grinning.

"What do you mean? Why do you stare at me so?"

"There are two large placards posted on the walls already about the murders."

"Well, suppose there are, what's all that to do with me? What are you so hideously grinning at, Jonathan, surely you don't think that I——"

"There is £100 reward offered for each of them."

"Indeed! Well, and if so, what then?"

"*I* can find out *one* of the murderers."

"Can you, though, really?" said Flint, attempting an air of great indifference. "You must be very clever, then, or know something of the murders."

"No, not so *very* clever, Flint. But, as I was about to say, *I* can earn £100 by informing on one, and *you* can earn the other £100."

"*Me?*" said Flint, jumping out of his chair as if shot; "*me?* What the devil do you mean? Is the man mad, or what?"

"Perfectly sane. Sit down, Flint, and don't speak so loud, or I might——"

"You might. Go on, might what?"

"Why, choke you, and take the contents of yon heavy money box."

"Choke me?"

"Yes, and I *will*, if you are not civil. Sit down."

Jonathan spoke so calmly, and with such earnestness, that Flint turned deadly pale as he gasped,

"Come, come, Jonathan. No larks, you know. A joke's a joke; but——"

"This is a very *grim* joke, Flint; it's a hanging matter, you know. Who killed old Ford?"

"Old Ford killed! you don't say so?"

"None of your hypocritical surprise, Flint. You *know* he was murdered."

"Me? How should *I* know it? Poor old man! Murdered, eh?"

"Where is all his fortune, parchments, title deeds, and the like?"

"How should I know? I didn't do the bloody deed."

"I know you didn't; but you *procured* it."

"*Procured* it?"

"Yes; where are all the deeds and parchments."

"I gave them to old Ford, yesterday. I haven't got a penny's-worth belonging to him. If they are lost the murderer must have stolen them."

"Liar!" hissed Jonathan between his teeth. "You know you lie in your throat. You never gave him anything yesterday."

"Upon my——"

"There, don't damn yourself any more, Flint. I know you of old. We have been mixed up in crime too long together to boast much of honor or truth. Who was your cut-throat in the affair?"

"I know nothing about it."

"But you see I do. You haven't heard anything about the murder and conflagration in Green Court either, I suppose?"

"How should I? I never lived there. Where is it?"

"What about the headless body found in your bed, Flint?"

Flint's head sunk upon his bosom.

He felt almost choked with passion.

"Who and what are you?" he gasped, rising in anger. "Are you a fiend incarnate come to taunt me? Away, man! Annoy me no more. I know nothing of what you speak. Quit my place, I loathe you."

"How soon you have changed your tune. Sit down, Flint; let us talk over matters.

"Proceed. I hear, d——n you."

"There have been two murders. *You* are concerned in one, and I could explain the other, if necessary."

"Well."

"You have gained Ford's property and title deeds by one."

"No."

"Yes."

"Well, suppose it."

"No, I won't suppose it, for I *know* it."

"What, then?"

"I want half."

"What?" gasped Flint.

"Half."

"You must be dreaming, Jonathan."

"I was never more wide awake in my life."

"But suppose I do not?"

"I will denounce you to the police."

"And if I cannot at the present moment?"

"There remains then but one of two things, Flint," said Jonathan, suddenly rising, long dagger in hand.

"What! a dagger?—violence?"

"Yes, a dagger, Flint, that shall pierce your deceitful heart if you dare attempt to stir or raise any alarm."

"What would you have me do, then?" said Flint, trembling in every limb, as Jonathan stood over him, weapon in hand.

"Have you do?"

"Yes."

"You have not his wealth here, you say?"

"No."

"Then take up pen and paper."

"For what purpose?"

"To write a full and true confession of old Ford's murder on stamped paper. I will attest it as witness."

"Confession! what criminate myself?"

"Yes, or die. The confession will be held by me for four days. If in that time you do not produce a fair half of old Ford's treasures, I will deliver this in person at Bow Street. Choose—the confession or instant death!"

Flint was conquered.

He trembled like a leaf, and turned ghastly pale as he wrote the confession.

"There," said he, handing it to Jonathan, "will that do?"

"Yes."

"I have four days clear?"

"You have."

"In that time you shall see me."

"'Tis well; don't forget the hour—nine in the morning, on the fifth day, exclusive of this."

"I will not, you may rely upon it. I value my life more than wealth."

"Do so; or tremble!"

Jonathan cast a withering glance at Flint as he left the room, and shook the confession in his face.

"For the present, farewell, said he."

"Must there be, then, still *another* bloody deed?" mused Flint, when left alone. "Four days hence! What a world of time! I shall be hundreds of miles away; yet I'd give £10,000 to see that villain powerless at my feet. We shall see; four days will work wonders!"

## CHAPTER XX.

ANOTHER SEA-FIGHT—FATTY TURNS GUNNER, AND "TOUCHES OFF" A CANNON—HIS NOTIONS OF KICKING—THE AUSTRIAN SUNK.

For some time Frank and Hugh Tracy stood each at his gun, ready to fire.

The Austrian steamer came nearer and nearer, and endeavoured to get the yacht between them and the shore.

This was good seamanship, for there were many rocks against which the steamer must have struck.

But Frank did not want them to get such advantages.

Under Mark's directions, the yacht tacked and went before the breeze at a spanking pace, the steamer full tilt after her.

"We can't avoid it, lads," said Frank, "they are getting closer and closer; we must fight her while we have a plank standing."

"So we will! so we will!" shouted all in triumph.

"Then prepare, my lads!" said Frank; "buckle on your swords and pistol-belts!"

They did so in a moment, and all was ready for action.

"Look out, Frank; here it comes!" said Dick Fellows.

At that same instant a terrible shell whizzed right over them.

"Two can play at that game, my hearties," laughed Frank. "Let 'em have it, Hugh. Now then, ready?"

"Aye, aye!"

"Fire!"

At the same instant the two brass cannon were discharged.

Their shells screamed through the air in a beautiful luminous flight, and then came down smash upon the steamer's decks and exploded with a terrific report.

"That's it, my lads, load again," said Frank, "we've got the range. Let 'em have it! Never say die!"

In a twinkling the guns were reloaded with shells and again discharged with accurate aim.

This time the missiles struck the vessel just between wind and water, and stove in the side.

In an instant they bursted and blew up all the machinery, tearing the vessel fore and aft, leaving her a mere wreck upon the water.

Still the Austrians fought; they disdained to lower their flag to a mere yacht, and worked like brave men, firing gun for gun.

"Let me have a touch at 'em," said Fatty; "let me point the gun this time, Frank," said he; "you'll see, I'll send 'em all to Jericho."

Frank allowed Fatty to point the gun, which he did long and carefully.

"It's ready; touch it off!"

Some one "touched it off" accordingly, but the recoil of the gun knocked Fatty head over heels sprawling on the deck.

"Crikey! don't it 'kick?'" laughed Buttons.

"I believe you," said Fatty, growling, "harder than any horse as ever I ever come anear."

The shell, however, was well aimed, for it struck the Austrian fair amidships.

It was a true point-blank shot, and in a few seconds a terrible explosion took place.

Fatty's shot had hit the powder magazine!

In a second a column of fire and smoke rushed into the heavens. The young English boys rushed eagerly forward with anxious faces as they saw

THE NIGHT VULTURES AFTER THE BATTLE.

showers of shells fly through the air like so many fire-works.

Burning timbers lay flickering on the waters, and a dense mass of sparks fell all around.

The Austrian vessel had disappeared.

It had sunk!

Not a vestige of that proud, well-manned ship remained!

Every soul on board had perished!

"What do you think of that, boys, eh?" shouted Buttons. "Who'll say that Fatty can't hit a hay-stack, again? Hooray, for Garibaldi! Hooray for us English boys! Lor, I wish we could only meet a yacht full of Austrian boys as old as we are, eh, Fatty, my boy? We'd give 'em a rare doing in the shake of a sheep's tail."

"Yes, it's all very fine o' you shouting, Master Buttons," said Fatty, rubbing his seat of honour, and with a rueful face, "but I've a good mind to wallop you for laughing at me. The gun only kicked me, eh? If I was to kick you half so hard as it did me there would be nothing left of you. Don't you laugh at me any more, you little powder-monkey!"

"Want a cake, Fatty?" said Buttons, on the sly.

"I don't mind," said the Fat Boy.

And in a moment the two "pals" were as thick as two thieves again, and munching biscuits and

Italian sausages, of which Fatty was immensely fond, and could devour any possible quantity put before him.

"Fine, ain't it, Buttons?"

"I believe yer."

"Who wouldn't be a soldier?"

"Ah! just so; all but the knocks. When one of them there round cannon shots hits a feller aside of his nob it tickles him rayther."

"I should just say so; make him scratch his head a trifle, eh, Buttons? Any more sausage left?"

"Yes, here's another dose for you," said Buttons, handing him a "chunk" of about two pounds weight. "It wouldn't do for you to be a commissary."

"What's a commissary?"

"Why a chap as has the care of all the grub."

"That's just what I would like. I wouldn't look after myself first, eh, Buttons? Oh, no, not the slightest."

"If you were you'd eat up all the grub," said Captain Frank, who, some distance off, had been listening to the comical snarling of Master Buttons and Fatty, could not but smile as he whispered to Hugh Tracy,

"Hugh, just listen to Fatty and Buttons; they are very loving now, but in a minute or two they will be quarrelling like a couple of angry dogs."

"Yes," said Hugh; "but still they like each other."

"Like each other? I believe you, and would shed their blood for each other."

"Fatty seems to take to Buttons amazingly."

"Yes, and Buttons to him; they are a strange pair, always up to some devilment or other. Do you remember the trick Buttons played on him coming across the channel?"

"No; what was it?"

"Fatty was getting very sea-sick, and Buttons tried to coax him into some exercise in order to shake it off. 'You can't do this,' said Buttons, standing on one leg, and holding out the other with the right hand.

"'Can't I though?' said Fatty, who considers himself one of the nimblest fellows in the world. Can't I though? You just see.' I was standing by, and, after several tumbles, Fatty did it.

"'But you can't do this, though?' said young Buttons, standing on his head.

"'Yes, I can,' said Fatty, 'but the deck is too slippery.'

"'Well, do it on this tub,' said Buttons.

"Fatty did do it, but——"

"What makes you laugh?" said Frank.

"It would make the devil laugh to see what occurred."

"What was it?"

"Fatty's head knocked in the top of the tub, and he went up to the shoulders."

"In what?"

"In soap fat."

"You don't mean that?" said Frank, grinning.

"I do, though."

"But did young Buttons know it?"

"Of course he knew all about it, and it was done on purpose; but he never let out, for while Fatty was puffing and blowing and cleaning himself, the little imp of a page was laughing till the tears ran out of his eyes. Had Fatty ever suspected it was done on purpose, I fear he would have given Master Buttons a sound hiding, as much as he loves him. He is the very devil for practical jokes, and is the life and soul of all the Band."

After an hour or two of repose, Frank roused up Buttons, who, with Fatty, was lying snoring on the deck.

"Come, Buttons, you must go with me into the cabin. I want to see and speak to Teresa the spy," said he.

"Don't wake her up yet," said Buttons, "for she told me as we came on board that she hadn't had any sleep for several nights."

"Well, then, let the young maiden sleep on. Have you made her comfortable?"

"Oh, yes; she's in the admiral's bunk, and your brother Tom is at the cabin-door, guarding her from all intrusion."

"Right; and now that we are sailing merrily towards the port of Ancona, and no enemy in sight, suppose you tell us how you got on in the Fort."

"Yes, Buttons, let's have it," said the young Garabaldians, who now clustered around him and sat on the deck.

The Italian seamen seemed much interested to hear all about it, so they also formed part of the audience, Frank and Dick Fellows translating to them Button's story as fast as he told it.

In order to "whet his whistle," as Mark the foster-brother called it, Captain Frank gave Buttons a bottle of wine, which he stood beside him, but kept a close watch on Fatty, who once or twice very cunningly stole it, and helped himself.

"Well, here goes, gentlemen," said Buttons. "I'll tell you all about it, provided Fatty doesn't call me a liar half a dozen times in every minute, as he always does."

"I'll take care of that," said Hugh. "If Fatty dares touch your bottle or interrupt you, he shall be put on short commons for a week, the worst punishment we could inflict upon him, for we all know how he loves his bellyful."

"Well, then," said Buttons, "you left me on the wall of the Fort."

"Just so," said Fatty; "we know all about that."

"Silence, Paunchey," said Hugh, flourishing a ropesend. "Proceed, Buttons; we are all attention."

"Well, as I lay on the top of the wall, I began to feel very shaky and very nervous. I stayed there for some few minutes, and then began to crawl like a cat. I had a full view of the courtyard below, and could see the soldiers marching up and down. There were not more than half a dozen left in it, for all the rest had marched out through the gate to give battle to you in the ravine. The guards when left alone began talking to each other, and, thanks to the few lessons of German I learned from you, Captain Frank, at school, I found out that the female spy was confined in the colonel's house, which formed part of the Fort. How to get there I didn't know, but after a time I mustered up courage enough to crawl towards it on my hands and knees. I found a skylight open, and got into it. The place was all deserted; for every man was marched off to fight; everything seemed in confusion as if they had hurriedly got out of bed; watches and other valuables were lying about loose in the room, but I was so excited I did not touch anything."

"Oh, there's a crammer," said Fatty. "Wouldn't *I*, though?"

"Silence, Paunchey!"

"As I descended the stairs I got into a room where several officers had been playing cards and drinking wine. There were several purses lying there filled with gold coin. I took a good drink of the wine, and thinking that a little money might come in servicable, took the purses."

"Halves, then, say I," said Fatty. "Let's have everything on the square."

"Silence, thick-head!"

"Well, I went in and out of every room, but couldn't find the prisoner. I felt awful mad, and didn't know what to do. I got on to the wall again, and crawled further on, until I got to a dark, gloomy prison house, with strong iron bars over the windows.

"While doing this, I heard one of the soldiers say that they had removed Teresa out of the colonel's house to the prison for greater safety when the fight began. But which cell she was confined in I had no notion.

"From the distant shouts I began to imagine that our Band was getting the worst of it, for one of the soldiers said to another that they had better open the magazine, and get out more boxes of ammunition for their use.

"This they did, and very carefully. So sure did they feel about the safety of the Fort, that all of them, save one, who stood guard at the gates, pulled off their coats, and began to lug out cartridge boxes.

"'Now's my time,' said I, 'there is no one looking,' and with all the activity I was master of, I ran along the walls towards the prison house.

"I must have been seen by the sentry at the gate, for he shouted out,

"'Halt! Who goes there?'

"I lay flat behind a large stone, but didn't answer, and he fired.

"The bullet just grazed my clothes, and to deceive him, I screamed out as if shot dead.

"This seemed to satisfy the guard, and he loaded again, saying,

"'That was a good shot. I hit him, whoever he was.'

"In an instant the men came out of the magazine, and rushed towards the gate, and I could hear the guard tell his comrades that some deserter, perhaps, had tried to escape, and that he had knocked him off the wall as dead as a herring.

"This explanation seemed to satisfy the others, who returned to the magazine again.

"In the meantime I lay behind the stone, and not far from me could hear a soft, plaintive voice humming a tune.

"It was the voice of a female, and I swore to find out who and what she was.

"As I crawled towards the prison I saw a white handkerchief wave through the bars.

"'It must be Teresa,' I thought, and this gave me fresh courage.

"I crawled on until I was right on to the roof of the prison. There were no chimneys to get down, and what to do I did not know. As the moon was obscured, I dropped the end of my rope down.

"She seized it, and tugged it three times.

"'It must be her,' I thought.

"In a moment, I heard her singing again. She dared not speak out aloud, for fear of being overheard by the guard below, so she let me know what to do by putting her words into a song, which I made out was—

"'Happy night! the end has come; deliverance is nigh!'

"This was repeated three times rather quickly, and in a moment afterwards she sang the same words twice, very slowly, but in each case with great stress on the word 'end.'

"For a moment I could not imagine what she meant by repeating, 'Happy night! the *end* has come; deliverance is nigh!' in such different voices.

"'What if I am discovered and betrayed?' I thought. 'I don't understand her meaning.'

"In a few moments all appeared explained.

"It appeared to me that by singing the line three times she meant there were *three bars* to her window and that by repeating it *twice* slowly afterwards, she meant to let me understand she was in the second story of the three story building.

"This was correct.

"I tugged at the rope to let her know I understood her meaning, and found that the end was firmly fastened. I tied the other end to a lot of large spikes on the wall and slipped down, slowly and carefully."

"Crikey," said Fatty, "if you'd a fell, Buttons?"

"If so I should have been smashed to atoms on the stone court-yard, that's all."

"It would have been all up with your cocoa-nut then," said the Fat Boy.

"Silence, beef-eater!"

"Well, as I slipped down the rope the spikes above began to get shaky, and one of them fell on the head of a soldier below.

"He looked up; but the night was then so dark and windy that he didn't see me; he, perhaps, thought that the gale of wind which had just sprung up had loosened one of the tiles."

"It spoilt *his* 'tile,' I should think, and no gammon."

"Silence, Fatty!"

"I trembled for my very life, for I feared that the other end of the rope would give way.

"Just as I was descending and near the prison bars the rope slipped from the spikes.

"I fell!"

"To the ground?"

"No; I seemed to have had the strength of a lion; I felt the rope was loose, and I held out my hand to Teresa, whose arms were stretched through the iron bars.

"She clung to me with a grip of steel.

"It was for a few moments a terrible struggle for life or death.

"My eyes began to swin with fear, my brain reeled again. Had she not upheld me as I then was I should have been dashed to pieces!

"In a few moments I partly recovered myself.

"Teresa was almost fainting.

"She had supported all my weight with her outstretched arms, and I could see her eyes flashing like some wild woman.

"'Oh, holy mother!' she said, 'save the boy.'

"I felt filled with fresh courage, made a last vigorous effort, and clutched a single bar.

"Oh! the struggle to get up was awful; it was like a dozen deaths.

"I remember little of what took place, for I was so excited. All I know is that when I pulled myself into the window Teresa shrieked out,

"'Good God! I thank you,' and fell back into her cell.

"Her screams seemed to have excited the attention of some one below, who felt certain that something was up."

"Of course there was. Wasn't *you* up at the window?"

"Fatty, we'll put you on half rations if you don't keep quiet."

"Well, go on Buttons; take a drink of wine," said Hugh, "it will refresh you."

"I knew that no time was to be lost, so began tugging at the centre bar, and after a time Teresa recovered and assisted me.

The perspiration poured off me, and I puffed and blowed—well, like Fatty, when he pulled his head out of the tub of soap fat."

"None o' your chaff, Master Buttons," said Fatty, not at all pleased with the allusion.

"After about ten minutes the centre bar got shaky, and all at once it gave way, and both Teresa and I fell right on the prison floor, both of us still having old of the bar.

"I jumped to my feet in a moment, for I heard the footsteps of some one approaching up the stone stairs.

"'Oh, Mother of Heaven!' sighed Teresa, 'we are discovered! we are lost! It is the goaler!'"

"'Hush!' said I, 'do not weep!'

"'But you are but a boy,' she said. 'What can *you* do with a big soldier like he is?'

"'Well, you shall see.' If I am a boy, I'm an English boy,' said I, 'and a match any day in the week for any two Austrians.'"

"There's cheek! he ain't got no small opinion of his little self," said Fatty, "has he?"

"Order!"

"Silence!"

"Turn him out!" said several.

"Well, when I heard him coming to the door, I saw the light of his lantern through the keyhole, and had a peep at him, and a big, ferocious-looking devil he was.

"'He is suspicious,' said Teresa; 'he has visited me twice to-night. We are lost; you will be killed!'

"'Shall I?' said I. 'You'll see whether I am or not.'

"I laid hold of the iron bar, and held it over my shoulder ready to give him 'what for,' when he came in.

"I stood behind the door, and, as he opened it, I hid behind.

"He came in, and, just as he did so, I gave him such an awful bang across his long legs, and over he went sprawling on the floor.

"I stood over him with the iron bar, and threatened to kill him.

"He drew his sword like lightning, and was about to give me a dig, but I gave him a gentle tap on the head and knocked him senseless.

"I took the keys from him, locked the door, and descended the stairs, but not before I had coiled up the rope, for I knew that we dursn't go into the court-yard.

"As we went below, I espied an empty room, and went into it.

"The window was without bars of any kind, and looked into a garden outside the walls of the Fort.

"Tying one end of the rope to a fire grate, I showed Teresa how to escape.

"She was all game, and slipped down the rope like as if she had been Blondin.

"I saw her run off towards the ravine, and felt happy I had rescued her.

"But all was not done yet.

"'I must have satisfaction out of these Austrians,' I thought, and not knowing how the fight was going on, made up my mind to blow up the whole place before I went!"

"Game as a pebble he is," said Fatty, in a soft voice. "Here's his health;" at the same time seizing Buttons' bottle of wine, and taking a long drink ere it could be taken from him again.

"I boldly went down stairs to the kitchen and got some lucifer matches and a piece of rag burning in the ashes.

"'This will do the trick,' I says, so creeps out into the court-yard towards the magazine.

"The place was very large, and soldiers inside were working in the dark.

"They were lugging out boxes of cartridges and placing them on the parade ground.

"When the fourth man had gone out with a box I slipped in and hid myself.

"I placed the smouldering rag under a case of loose cartridges, put the matches near it, and near them put a handful of cartridges.

"I knew that the rag would take a full quarter of an hour in burning before it reached the matches, and the lucifers, once touched by the heat, would fire the cartridges, and then all was up.

"All this didn't take me a minute to do; and, like a lamplighter, I retraced my steps to the kitchen, siezed a roast fowl and a string of Bologna sausages, and slipped down the rope into the garden.

"You may be sure I ran as fast as my heels would let me until I reached the ravine, where I met Teresa, who was there waiting for me.

"I sat down for a moment or two out of breath, and began to think the soldiers had discovered the burning rag and put it out.

"But in case they hadn't, and fearful any of the stone-work might be blown near us, I looked out for a place of safety.

"I soon found a large, low, projecting rock, and there I placed Teresa and myself.

"I was just on the point of having a drink of wine out of my canteen when a sudden flash of light rushed up into the sky like a pillar of fire, and next moment was followed by a terrific explosion which shook the whole ravine.

"The Fort was blown up into the air, and cannon balls, shells, wheels, boxes, swords, muskets, and a thousand other things came down in a shower near where we sat.

"I never saw such a fine sight in all my life; and here I am safe."

This story of Buttons' adventures was listened to with great delight by all who heard it, and at its conclusion three hearty cheers were given for "Garibaldi's Young Soldiers—long life to them!"

Fatty, though, when he had helped to finish the page's bottle of wine, lolled back and was soundly snoring, while two of the boys, with tar and brush, were very quietly painting a pair of moustaches and whiskers on his round pudding face.

## CHAPTER XXI.

REJOICINGS OVER FRANK'S VICTORIES—ANCONA MAKES HOLIDAY TO MEET THE ENGLISH VOLUNTEERS—GARIBALDI VISITS THEM—THE PLACE OF HONOUR IN THE ARMY BESTOWED ON THE ENGLISH BOYS—JOEL FLINT'S EMISSARIES BEGIN TO WORK—THE PLOT AND PLAN.

THE sight of a yacht approaching the harbour of Ancona—a vessel which was well known to have belonged, if, as the Italians thought, it did not *then* belong, to an Austrian admiral—excited the suspicions of various men-of-war that were cruising off that port.

They steamed out to meet it; but, before they could fire a shot, Frank hoisted his ensign, and soon signalled to the Italian guard-ships how matters stood on board.

Deafening cheers was the answer to their signal flags, and the Italian men-of-war saluted the gallant little "Kaiser" and her crew with guns of welcome.

The telegraph on shore was soon at work, and long ere Frank cast anchor in the bay, the whole town poured forth to the landing-place to welcome the brave young Garibaldians.

According to orders, all the British boys dressed themselves out in their gayest and best uniforms; rifles on shoulders and with colours flying, they and the Italian sailors marched four abreast through the town.

Bells rang, people cheered, the streets were crowded, a regiment of Garibaldian volunteers marched out to escort them with bands and banners.

The whole city was joyful, and as Frank Ford, sword in hand, marched at the head of the English boy-band of soldiers, fair women waved handkerchiefs and kissed their hands in token of admiration to the brave boys.

The newspapers were filled that day with long accounts of "the capture of the 'Kaiser,'" and the heroism of such mere boys, as they were called.

The commandant of the town, however, had ample proof of the statements rumoured abroad, and seemed astounded at all he heard.

Wherever the boys went they were treated like conquerors; they were not allowed to pay for anything.

This just suited Fatty, who, as may be supposed, was in his glory, and almost danced his legs off that same night with lots of pretty girls at the Casino.

Frank and his gallant little band marched out to their camps, situated in a beautiful grove near the edge of the town.

Fatty was very sorry to leave Ancona and all its goodlings behind him.

Had it not been for Frank's positive orders he would willingly have remained in the city for a whole month, stuffing himself and capering about with young ladies.

But Frank was a soldier.

Merriment was all very well in its way; but the young Garibaldians had come to Italy to fight, not for pleasure, as he knew very well.

There were thousands of soldiers camped near them, and many Garibalbian volunteers also; but none of them could equal Frank's company in cleanliness, beauty of drill, and soldierly conduct.

After three days of hard work in drilling, Frank began to think of doing something.

He hated idleness.

He was a bold youth, and wanted excitement.

While his company were on parade one day, a loud flourish of trumpets and rolling of drums was heard in the distance.

Cheers and shouts from distant camps echoed on every side.

Frank could not make out what it all meant.

In a few moments, however, a cloud of dust was perceived in the distance.

One minute after a body of horsemen appeared.

Thinking it might be some general, Frank waited until the escort approached, and then the whole company, like one man, presented arms in fine style.

*It was General Garibaldi!*

He and his escort halted.

For a moment all was dead silence.

Garibaldi looked at the Boy Band with admiration.

They stood there as solid as a stone wall.

Not a boy stirred.

Garibaldi's lips trembled.

He wanted to say something, but could not.

He was pleased, surprised, astounded at the soldierly appearance of the youthful English Band.

A solemn pause ensued.

The boys were too good soldiers to cheer or break their ranks without a command from their captain, and he did not like to give the order without Garibaldi's permission.

The old Italian chief waved his hand.

"Shoulder arms! right face! arms aporte! break ranks!" said Frank, quickly.

In a moment the English boys rent the air with their shouts, and flocked around Garibaldi like children.

His officers never seemed tired of shaking hands with the Boy Band, while Garibaldi himself extended his right hand to Frank, and said in a tremulous voice,

"The war has scarcely begun, and yet you have immortalised yourselves! I have heard of all your bold achievements, and give you the place of honour among my volunteers. English boys, I thank you for your heroism and devotion to the cause of Italian liberty! For the present, farewell. In a few days we shall meet again. You are all ordered off to Lombardy, where it will not be long ere you meet the Austrians again face to face. Captain Frank Ford and the Company of English Boy Soldiers, I thank you in the name of Italy. May all honour and glory await you!"

Loud and prolonged cheers followed General Garibaldi as he rode off the ground, noisiest of all being Fatty and Buttons.

"He might have asked us to have something to eat and drink, eh, Buttons?"

"Garibaldi don't eat," said Buttons, grinning.

"What?" said Tony, with an astonished look.

"Fact, so I've heard."

"Gammon, Buttons."

"Well, if he does, he lives on gunpowder; and as to sleeping, they say he never does—least, so I've heard—and if he does sleep, he lies on a bed stuffed with bayonets instead of feathers."

Tony made a "drive" at Buttons, who was grinning like a young monkey; but that lively youth nimbly got out of the way.

"I hope Captain Frank will bring a fellow something home from the supper he's going to to-night," said Fatty. "I wouldn't mind a tuck-out of duck and green peas."

"So he's going to the officers' supper to-night, is he?" said one Italian to another, who had heard Tony's last remark. "Couldn't *we* manage to go there also?"

"Why not? We have uniforms—who will know us?"

"But are you sure that Captain Frank Ford *is* the person mentioned in your English letter?"

"I am positive."

"What do you propose?"

"Let us go to the supper, and trust to chance for the rest. The deed must be done."

"True, and quickly."

"Then, until to-night, farewell."

"Farewell."

Such was the brief conversation between two swarthy individuals who had strolled into the volunteers' camp.

Who they were no one knew, although dressed like officers of the Italian army.

*What* they were we shall very quickly see.

## CHAPTER XXII.

THE BANQUET--PROFESSIONAL DUELLISTS HIRED BY JOEL FLINT — THE INSULT — TONY IN RAPTURES.

THE night was beautiful and calm; the stars shone forth from pure Italian skies, while the horned moon peeped over the tree tops of the grove where the Boy Band were encamped.

Sounds of martial music fell upon the ear from a large and distant tent, in which a party of officers were assembled round the festive board doing honour to the arrival among them of Frank Ford and his gallant English boys.

Songs and toasts and cheers were heard, and loudest among them all could be heard some half dozen English boys who were at the table.

Here and there a sentinel could be espied in the margin of the wood, and as he silently walked his post, his bayonet glittered in the starlight.

Two men were seen to approach the banquet tent.

They stopped, and for a moment conversed in whispers.

"Any fear?" said one.

"Not the slightest."

"What soldier is on guard?"

"Pedro. He it is we shall have to encounter."

"But will he let us pass?"

"I have no doubt; leave that to me. Come."

They advanced towards the banquet tent, boldly.

"Halt! who goes there?" the guard shouted.

"Friend, with the countersign."

"Advance, friend, and give the countersign," said the sentry.

The two strangers approached.

"The countersign!" said the soldier, levelling his musket at them.

"The brave English Boys!"

"Right!" said the soldier. "Pass on."

"I told you that was the countersign to-night for all the volunteer camps."

"Who told you?"

"One of the young Garibaldians—one that Frank Ford little dreams of."

"How well he is watched."

"Young Flint is no fool."

"He pays us well though."

"Yes; and regularly."

"But shall we not be detected?"

"No; trust to me. You see I have two tickets to the banquet?"

"How did you get them?"

"From the same one who gave me the countersign."

"Excellent."

"They will take us for strange officers, that's all."

So saying, the two strangers walked into the tent, and took seats in a very cool style.

They were not noticed; song and laughter were the order of the night.

Frank was there, surrounded by Hugh Tracy, Dick Fellows, Mark, and a very large, red-faced youth, who it was easy to distinguish was Mr. Tony Waddleduck, who, with a face like a full moon, was bowing right and left, and drinking lots of the best wine.

For some time he had been mistaken by the Italian officers for Captain Frank, who treated him to a great display of bowing and hand-shaking, which Tony amply repaid, and made several visits to the wine tables long before his young captain arrived.

How he had managed to get a ticket of admission to the banquet was a mystery to Frank.

The truth was Tony had been strolling out for a walk, and the sweet, savory smell of costly eatables in a neighbouring tent assaulted his nose with so much order that he could not repress a sigh of regret.

"Oh! Buttons, if *we* were only the lucky ones, eh?" he thought, and scratched his big head for an idea.

He soon got one.

He boldly marched up to the cook, and bribed that functionary with a sovereign!

The sight of the precious coin delighted the chief cook, who soon managed to abstract a dinner ticket from the colonel's tent, and this he gave to the delighted Fat Boy.

This was how he got there; and, in order not to create any disturbance, Frank whispered to him to behave himself, and he might remain.

To say that Master Waddleduck enjoyed the eating part of the banquet would ill-express what he did and what he felt.

He whispered to Mark "that this was the happiest moment of his life," and, as he did so, sighed, and unbuttoned his jacket.

Knife and fork in hand he made sad havoc with all before and around him, never having time even to pass the time of day with his next neighbour.

After two courses had been gone through his vest was unbuttoned.

After the third course his shirt collar was unbuttoned, and his face was as red as a beet-root with eating.

In truth he astonished the waiters so much that they stood and looked at him in wonder. Two whole ducks, to start with, had mysteriously disappeared from the dish before him; one bottle of wine had washed them down.

Puddings whole were demolished, a perfect pyramid of tarts vanished like snow down his capacious throat.

In truth it might be said on this occasion that Master Tony had stuffed himself up to his shirt collars, for his eyes were staring out of his head, and he could scarcely breathe.

But still his jaws worked first on nuts and then on fruit until at last he was conquered, and fell asleep in his chair with a cigar in his mouth.

The chief toast of the evening was,

"Capt. Frank Ford and his Boy Band of Gallant Garibaldian Volunteers."

The whole company rose, glass in hand, and honoured the toast with three times three.

All we have said.

*Not* all.

There were two individuals who did *not* rise and drink.

They sat with an air of defiance, and with a smile of disdain upon their lips.

"Gentlemen," said the chairman, "I beg you all to rise to honour this toast."

Still the two strangers kept their seats. For a moment there was a pause.

"Why don't you rise, eh?" said he, looking daggers at the two strangers.

"We do not rise to drink the health of such persons as he is," was their cold, ironical answer.

"Sir," said Hugh to one.

"Sir," said Dick Fellows to another, indignantly.

"I repeat that we do not rise to drink the health of such a person as he is."

"What mean you?"

"Turn them out."

"Explain!"

"Who are they?"

"Pitch 'em out, waiters," shouted Fatty, waking up.

"Gentlemen, what means all this?" asked the president. "Explain!"

"Impudent dogs!" said Hugh, striking one of them in the face.

"Take that, fool!" said Dick to the other, tossing a glass of wine in his face.

In an instant all was a scene of noise, confusion, and uproar.

"What means this?" shouted the president.

"Satisfaction first and explanation afterwards," said the strangers, drawing their swords.

"I hope Capt. Ford will not allow any one else to fight for him," said one, with a sneer.

"No fear of that," said Fatty. "If he won't *I* will, so have at you when and where you will."

It is impossible to describe the tumult which now took place.

Swords were drawn, and blood would have flown upon the spot. But this was not permitted.

"Follow us," said the two strangers, "follow us, if you are not cowards."

Hugh, Dick, Frank, Mark, and Fatty were on their legs in a moment.

"When and were?" said Frank.

"By moonlight at midnight near the river. A little grove is there, we can settle our difficulty without interruption."

"So be it."

"Remember, midnight!"

"I shall not forget," said Frank.

"Who and what are they?" asked a dozen voices.

"I know not," said Frank. "They are officers; they have insulted myself and friends. Nothing remains but to wash it out in *blood!*"

## CHAPTER XXIII.

TREACHERY—THE AMBUSCADE—THE DUEL—BOY SOLDIERS TO THE RESCUE—SUDDEN SUCCOUR—TERESA—THE PISTOL SHOT—FRANK WOUNDED AND SAVED.

As may be imagined, the interruption to the banquet which the Garabaldian officers gave to Frank Ford and others of the English Boy Band, caused the greatest excitement in the camp.

Some attempted to dissuade Frank or Hugh from fighting. But this they would not listen to.

"We came among you as friends," said Frank, "and as friends you received us. If I am unworthy to command the Boy Band, then let me retire and be the least among them; but never shall it be said that their leader ever showed the white feather, or was any other than an English Boy Soldier."

"But who are they?"

"What are they?" asked first one and then another.

"Will you go out to fight men in mortal combat that you know nothing about?"

"They may be your enemies."

"They certainly are not my friends," said Frank.

"But I mean they may be jealous of you, they may have evil designs."

"That may or may not be, gentlemen, but all I know is, that they have come here among you dressed in the Italian uniform; they had the password and passed the guard; their tickets admitted them to the banquet, and that's all I know about it. I will meet them if I lose my life."

"But you must not," said Dick. "They insulted Hugh and I; we are the ones to settle this matter."

"True, true," said Fatty. "Rather than any harm should befal Captain Frank, *I* will have a 'go in' with them. The captain must *not* fight."

"But the captain *will*," said Frank, smiling. "Meet me in the grove beside the river at midnight; and, mark me, friends, let none of the Boy Band know a word of this, or they will be up in arms. If I fall I shall die like a true British Volunteer, and will show my back to no cravens, let them come in dozens even."

"If he does go, I shall go too," said Fatty, "and see fair play; if any on 'em tries to act foul, I'll pepper 'em without mercy."

So saying, he examined his revolvers, and double-loaded them.

He put the sharpest edge possible on his large sword, and made up his mind to "give some of the beggars particular fits."

Hugh and Dick tried to persuade Mark the foster-brother that there would be no fight after all; but he was loth to believe it, and in a few minutes slipped out of sight.

Frank sat in his tent, alone.

He was not afraid of the coming combat, for that was last in his thoughts.

But he could not help confessing that do what he might, or go where he would, he was thwarted always in his best intentions, and visibly surrounded by enemies.

"They are strangers to me," he thought, "and men, while I am but a boy. What harm have I done either of them that they should thus publicly insult me, and fasten this quarrel upon me? I have never done harm to any one in my life, yet why am I always harassed and annoyed?"

He knew not.

Yet, as he sat in the silent tent and thinking of his only love, little Nelly Lancaster, and planning out a pleasant and happy future for them both, a voice seemed to sigh near him—a voice he had heard once before—which seemed to say,

"I will follow you through the world like an evil genius! You cannot escape me! Never will I be content until I see you standing in the dock a branded felon, and swung to a tree as a murderer!"

His flesh creeped as he thought of Joel's fearful curse; but then his mind became calm again when he thought of Nelly Lancaster, "his guiding star," whose sweet look of innocence seemed to throw a mantle of heavenly protection around him.

One hour followed another quickly, and, as he knew, it was now near the hour of twelve.

He rose, and buckled on his sword and pistols.

Hugh and Dick were at hand, and all three left the tent together.

"If I—if I fall, Hugh," said Frank, "let no one say I died a cur, for you are witness I did not seek this meeting with these strange men."

"Your honour is safe *in* my keeping," said Hugh. "Trust me for that."

"And if—if I *should* fall, Hugh," said Frank, with a choked utterance, "undo my waistcoat, you will find a small miniature photograph; you may not know how I prize it. Give it—send it to Miss Lancaster at the English seminary at Marseilles; she gave it to me long ago."

While thus the two young friends spoke to each other in confidence, they approached the shady grove beside the river.

The far distant cathedral clock solemnly and faintly tolled the hour of midnight.

The echo fell sweetly on Frank's ear, whose thoughts were now all of Nelly Lancaster.

He, Hugh, and Dick wore long black cloaks, and as they advanced through the moonlight to the grove they espied three men there awaiting them.

"You are punctual, gentlemen," said one of the Italians.

"Yes," said Dick; "English youths generally are when there's a fight on hand."

"Oh, indeed," was the sardonic reply; "and what do you propose doing? Have three pairs of duellists, or one pair at a time?"

"Just as you please about that," said Hugh, carelessly throwing his cloak on the grass. "It's just as our captain likes."

"And I do *not* like it," said Frank, stepping forward. "The insult was intended for *me* not for Hugh or Dick."

"Captain Ford is quite right," said one of the Italians; "the insult *was* intended for him and no one else. As *you* had two friends we brought two."

"It little matters," said Frank, "if you had brought a dozen."

"But we have not brought a dozen. I hope, as an Englishman, you will believe us. There are only three."'

"Well, and now that we are altogether and bent on mischief, in what way have I ever offended you?"

"We will fight first, if you please, and make explanations afterwards."

"I am not an advocate for duelling, gentlemen; it is a thing very rare among Englishmen; I would rather shed my blood in some nobler cause than a common brawl."

"Captain Ford has the reputation for bravery."

"I have, and would prove it in any honourable cause; but to my English notions duelling is unmanly, brutal, and even cowardly; it does not show the bravery so much as the rashness of those who engage in it."

"Then you refuse to fight?"

"I do until you show cause."

"Then must I brand you as a coward," said the Italian, lifting his sword to strike Frank across the shoulder.

"Enough!" said Frank, whipping out his sword in a trice, and keeping his dark antagonist at bay. "Enough! you are mad, you thirst for blood! Then take your chance—have at you!"

So saying, Frank dashed at his unknown foe, and their weapons flashed in the moonlight like lightning.

With the fury of a tiger the Italian rushed on to Frank, and his eyes flashed fire.

Young Ford was so active, however, that he danced about with great nimbleness and a smile of confidence on his handsome face.

"You have made a mistake, signor," said he, laughing; "I am not a boy when I take sword in hand."

The Italian grinned ghastly in reply; but all he knew he could not even scratch Frank, who several times had punctured his enemy.

Meanwhile, while Frank was thus bravely fighting, Hugh and Dick drew their swords, and stood ready to protect their captain from any unjust interference.

The fight now became fast and furious.

The Italian thought that his superior strength would have soon beat Frank to the ground.

But failing in this, he ground his teeth in rage to find he had "caught a Tartar" in the modest English youth.

Not a word was spoken by the four seconds all this time, but it was evident that they were all very greatly excited, and little would have been required to draw them into the fight.

Frank, finding that his enemy's strokes were getting weaker and weaker, pushed him harder and harder.

With a loud laugh of mocking triumph he dashed at his tall antagonist, and after feinting once or twice, stabbed the Italian for the third time; the blood now gushed in purple streams.

This brought him on his knee in a second.

"Apologise, or die!" said Frank, standing over him, with upraised sword.

At that moment a pistol shot was fired by one of the Italian's seconds.

Frank was struck, and staggered back with a sharp cry of pain.

"Treachery!" he cried, and leaned against a tree.

In a second the truth was now revealed. Frank's death had been resolved on by fair means or foul.

With a savage oath Hugh and Dick rushed upon the two cowardly seconds, and the fight which then took place was fierce and desperate.

The Italians were excellent swordsmen, and for a long time kept Hugh and Dick at bay, although not without being probed more than once, and "pinked" in the arm.

Finding that Frank was faint, and almost helpless, the wounded Italian gave a shrill whistle.

A half-dozen ruffians answered his summons, who rushed out of their place of concealment in the grove.

But just as they did so they were met with great fury by Mark, Buttons, and the Fat Boy, who, unknown to any one, had climbed up a tree near by to witness the duel, and see "fair play."

Pop! pop! pop! went Fatty's revolver among the dusky villains, who were hit about the legs, and yelled with pain.

This only excited the brown-looking scoundrels all the more, who fought with the fury of fiends.

The grove was now all alive with combatants.

The clink of swords was incessant, but not a word or oath scarce passed the lips of any one of them, so deadly was the combat.

Frank, however, was faint with loss of blood, and lay under a tree.

Not far from him crawled his antagonist through the shade, with a long knife between his teeth.

Like a tiger-cat he crawled, bent on murdering the brave youth, who, unconscious, looked deadly pale, and fondly murmured from time to time the sweet name of his own beloved Nelly Lancaster.

Onward crept the assassin slowly, and his eyes flashed in the moonlight like two burning coals.

He foamed at the mouth.

His hair was wild and disordered.

He gasped with mad passion as now he had approached unseen within three feet of young Ford.

He leaned on one hand, and slowly raised the knife for the last fatal stroke!

His eyes danced with made delight.

His teeth shone like the fangs of a deadly viper.

"Now," said he, "is the moment of my triumph. "Thus shall the English dog die!"

The knife was about to descend with unerring aim into the heart of the unconscious boy, when—

The figure of a young girl emerged from behind the tree, pistol in hand!

The Italian saw her.

He trembled like a wounded snake.

The pistol was presented at his head!

It dazzled his eyes.

He gasped.

He foamed at the mouth.

"Teresa!" he gasped.

Crack! went the weapon.

He fell, with a loud groan, bleeding on the grass!

# THE BOY SOLDIER;

## OR, GARIBALDI'S YOUNG CAPTAIN.

THE DETECTIVES AT WORK.

### CHAPTER XXIV.

THE BATTLE BY MOONLIGHT—STRANGE SCENES—ACTS OF DARING—VICTORY—THE UNKNOWN FUGITIVE—TERESA GIVES LIGHT TO MANY THINGS.

The fight between the Boy Soldiers and the cowardly rascals who had planned Frank's assassination was fierce and desperate.

Like a young lion just uncaged Mark, the foster-brother, rushed into the thickest of the fray.

With one desperate stroke he cleaved the skull of the villain who had fired at Frank, and he tumbled to the ground all but headless.

Fatty could not fence well, but his strokes fell on all sides like as if he were felling a bull.

In his shirt-sleeves, the manner in which he always liked to fight, he rushed hither and thither, dealing terrible blows all around him.

"Give it to 'em, Fatty!" shouted Buttons, in great glee. "Let the sooty-faced devils have plenty of it! Don't spare the elbow-grease, my round-bellied friend!"

Hugh and Dick fought like true soldiers; and great cause had the cowardly villains to repent their treachery.

On all sides lay some one or other bleeding and groaning, but still the battle went on.

Finding themselves mastered and with no hope of making any impression on the brave Boy Soldiers, those who were able took to their heels and fled like deer from the spot.

They did not go, though, without a parting salute from Hugh, Dick, Mark, Fatty, and Buttons, and such a "popping" and "cracking" of fire-arms was never heard there before.

That their shots did some execution was plain, for several of the villains were seen to fall, but these were rescued by a fresh body of villains who had concealed themselves in the wood and were afraid to take part in the combat.

At this moment a fresh party of young Garibaldians came running on the scene.

In a moment everything was explained to them, and they dashed out of the grove after the scoundrels, bent on destroying every one of them.

Even little Joe Morton was there among the company, and although he could not yet shoulder a rifle, for he was not strong enough, he carried a revolver in each hand, and acted as bravely as any one.

"Who told *you* to come out of your shell?" said Buttons, to him. "You are a big youth to come out with a revolver in each hand!"

"Well, you ain't much bigger," said poor Joe, mildly. "Musn't I try to help Captain Frank when he rescued me and my sister from certain death?"

"That's all square enough," said Buttons, stretching himself up to his full height—not much above four feet; "but then, you see, you haven't smelt as much powder as *I* have."

"Well, if I haven't, I soon will," said Joe. "So here goes!"

With that, little Joe dashed out of the grove, pistol in hand.

They soon overtook their cowardly enemies, who were trying to get across the river.

The young Garibaldians, however, prevented this.

They arrived on the spot just in time to seize their boats.

"Who is that in that small boat pulling away for his life?" asked Hugh.

"I don't know," said Dick; "I didn't have a good look at him."

"It looks like Joel," said Buttons, "as much like him as two peas in a pod."

This idea was scorned by all, for each one thought Joel was too much of a coward to leave England for Italy.

"Whether it's Joel or not," said Fatty, "I'll give him a rare warming, see if I don't!"

Saying this, he took the two revolvers from Joe Morton, and let fly six shots at the suspicious-looking person in the boat.

A loud cry of pain was heard.

"That's hit him!" said little Joe, in great glee.

"Give him another dose of Morison's blue-pills!" shouted Buttons. "Hang the expense, Fatty, brimstone is cheap, and lead is dull as ever in the market—fire away!"

"Drill as many holes into him as there are in a sieve."

"Let daylight through his ugly carcase, Fatty!"

True to these repeated injunctions on all sides, Master Tony Waddleduck "fired away, Flannagan," as he called it, until the boat had drifted beyond his range.

But while Buttons, the Fat Boy and Joe were thus amusing themselves by dosing the unknown with "blue pills," as the bullets were called, and knocking splinters out of the unlucky boat, Hugh Tracy, Dick Fellows, and Mark, led on the young Garibaldians against the remainder of the ruffians, who were fighting hard to get away.

"Surrender, rascals! surrender!" shouted Hugh, sword in hand.

"Down with the villanous sweeps!" said Dick.

"Throw down your arms, or we'll give no quarter," shouted Mark, in stentorian tones.

"Never," said several.

"Fire away, then, boys! kill every mother's son of 'em!" said Hugh.

"Make short work of the treacherous devils!" said Mark.

"Aim low, lads," shouted Dick, "aim low. Make cat's meat of them all."

Many tried to jump into the river and swim away.

"Hillo, there, hillo!" shouted Fatty, running up breathless. "Come on, Buttons, here's a go, Tracy is driving all the poor devils into the river. Won't this be a fine place for eels, eh?"

"Come back, you black-headed villains, come back, or I'll scratch your heads with a charge of duck shot, my jokers," said Buttons.

True to his word he loaded his rifle with a handful of small shot and let fly at the swimmers.

"They won't want any combs after that, I think," said Fatty; "see how that big chap yonder is scratching his cocoa-nut!"

"Help! help!" shouted one unfortunate in the water; "help! help! I'm sinking!"

"Poor devil," said Buttons.

In a moment his heart melted.

He jumped into a boat in an instant and rowed off to rescue "the poor devil," as he called him.

The drowning man grasped the boat, in order to save himself, and clutched the gunwale with the energy of despair.

"Take care, Buttons, take care!" shouted Fatty.

He had scarcely got the words out of his mouth when the boat capsized!

"Thunder and lightning," growled Tony, "why, Buttons is overboard! The young devil! why didn't he let the Italian get in alone?"

In a moment his clothes were off.

He dashed into the water, and dived like a duck.

In a moment or two he appeared on the surface.

Buttons was nowhere to be seen.

Fatty cast an anxious look around him for the page.

He dived again.

So long was he under water that many thought he was drowned also.

Hugh and Dick jumped into a boat and rowed off.

Mark jumped into the water, clothes and all.

The moment was intensely exciting!

Like a huge Newfoundland dog Mark plunged with rapid strokes through the water.

At that moment the stranger who had escaped in the boat had reached the opposite bank.

He was seen to level a rifle at Mark.

Bang went his weapon, and his shot struck the water.

In a second Mark turned a complete somersault and disappeared.

In a moment, however, he was seen again, holding up the half-dead form of the page with one hand while he swam towards the shore with the other.

A rousing cheer hailed this gallant exploit.

In a few seconds Fatty's red face re-appeared on the surface of the water.

He saw how things stood with Buttons, and plunged after Mark, who was exhausted, and almost sinking from weakness.

"Give him to me, Mark; save yourself, my boy," said Fatty, puffing and blowing like a young whale.

Mark would not.

Fatty, however, seized Buttons by the heels, while Mark held up his head, and in this way they gallantly brought the brave boy to shore.

Fatigued as the brave young Garibaldians were, they easily captured nearly all the Italians who opposed them, and marched them off as prisoners of war.

Mark was wounded slightly by the rifle shot in the shoulder, but did not heed it much, but helped Fatty to revive young Buttons, which he soon did.

They carried him in a blanket, while Hugh Tracy and Dick Fellows cared for Frank, who was quickly put under the skilful care of a surgeon.

Then the procession marched back to their camp. Not one of their own party was killed, and as they passed the camps of other troops, they found them drawn up, and at that moment about to march out to the rescue of the brave band of English Boy Soldiers who had fought so well.

## CHAPTER XXV.

THE HEADLESS SPECTRE—SHANKS IN TROUBLE—OLD JONATHAN'S YOUNG WIFE—A WOMAN IN LOVE AND HATRED—CASPAR IS CAST FRIENDLESS ON THE WORLD—THE CONFESSION.

THE terrible aspect of the headless ghost standing so close beside him with his hand laid on the old gardener's shoulder was something so unexpected and horrible that Giles trembled in every limb, and felt almost distilled into a jelly.

"Heavens!" he gasped, as he looked at the headless apparition.

He would have sunk to the ground, but the grasp of the headless being held him up without the least apparent effort.

"In the name of all that's holy tell me who and what ye are?" said Giles, with a great effort.

The headless being stirred not.

Yet a voice, calm, sepulchral, and of thrilling tone, which came as if from the depths below, answered, slowly,

"I am the Mystery of Bromley Hall!"

"What would you have me do? Oh, speak! let me not die of fear," said Giles.

"Get thee hence to thy cottage, then; let not the master of Bromley Hall ever suspect that you know aught of his bloody secrets, else death will follow."

"I will."

"Be mute, know nothing, pretend silliness; vengeance will come, and thy aged hands shall help it on."

"I will obey."

"Mark me; whatever you are told to do, do ye without question, and, ere midnight chimes from the village clock, I will visit thee again——but stay not here one moment longer than necessary, or you are lost. Fasten down that panel in the floor; time will shortly reveal all to you. For the present, farewell!"

As he spoke, he raised his hand from Giles's shoulder, who covered his face with his hands as the figure appeared to *sink through the floor!*

For a few moments old Giles stood trembling with wonder and surprise.

"Was he dreaming?" he thought, "or had all this strangely horrible apparition been real?"

While he stood mute, and with trembling limbs, the panel of the floor was closed of its own accord!

The boards flapped to again as if fastened with springs, and made the old gardener start again, and return to consciousness.

His lamp had gone out; he was in total darkness.

For a moment he knew not what to do.

He groped about and found his extinguished lamp, but that was of no earthly use to him.

He was now startled afresh by the sounds of light footsteps approaching along the corridor.

It was by this corridor that he had to escape!

What was he to do?

He listened.

The footfalls were light and cat-like.

Were they those of man or woman?

He knew not.

Suppose he had been watched or tracked thither?

And suppose, also, that they had come to murder him?

All these things flitted through the old man's mind.

And he trembled, for he was weak and feeble, and unable to make any stout resistance in case of need.

Where should he hide?

While he thought of all these things he heard the suppressed breathing of some one near him.

"Is that you?" sighed a faint voice.

For a moment there was no answer.

"Is that you?" was repeated.

"Yes," sighed another voice not far off, as of some one approaching in the contrary direction.

Old Giles was in a fix; he was caught both ways, and knew not what to do.

At last he laid himself flat on the floor of the corridor, with his face downwards.

In a few seconds, through the intense darkness, he espied the shadowy form of a woman approaching on one side, and in the opposite direction the figure of a man.

They were both creeping along like guilty things, and as if afraid of the sound of their own footsteps, and were feeling the sides of the wall as they advanced.

"Who could they be? and what were their motives?" thought the old gardener.

What other horror was he about to witness?

He knew not, but held his breath.

At that instant some one stumbled over him, and fell with a loud noise.

In an instant Giles vanished from the spot.

It was the tutor Shanks and the mistress of Bromley Hall!

What could they want there at that lone hour, and in total darknes?

"Oh!" groaned Shanks, in pain, as he lay sprawling on the floor, "oh! that must have been a ghost or the devil himself."

"Silence, fool!" said the faint voice of Jonathan's guilty wife. "Hus-s-sh! Do you want to alarm the whole house?"

"Did you not see it?" said Shanks, trembling in every limb. "It flitted down the corridor like a spirit. The house is haunted; I know it is."

"Hus-s-sh, booby," was the female's answer. "Come this way; you are timid; be not a coward. Follow me."

Shanks crawled along in great pain, and followed his mistress into the very library old Giles had just left.

She locked the door upon them.

They were now alone.

"What want ye with me, mistress?" Shanks asked, in a doleful tone.

"Are you certain that Jonathan *did* go to London, and that he does not suspect our meetings?"

"I am."

"Then all is well; the children have escaped."

"Yes; and he knocked me down for it."

"That is of no consequence."

"Isn't it, though? I had a good mind to knock him down as dead as a herring with the poker."

"And if you had all our plans would have been useless."

"What do you propose? Let us fly from this place at once. The Hall is haunted."

The mistress of Bromley Hall curled her lip disdainfully as she thought,

"What a craven-hearted cur I have enlisted in my cause. I begin to hate and loathe him! Would that Caspar had listened to my whispered proposals instead of this red-headed ass; but he would not—he spurned me. What woman can forgive a man for *that*?" she thought. "He shall live to repent his high-born pride. I'll teach him that he cannot thwart me, and let him see how much he has lost in spurning the desires of his master's wife, the idiot! Yet how different is Caspar to this white-livered fool! He is my tool nevertheless; I will use him as such, and then when my own purposes are secured, I'll cast him from me. Oh, Caspar, Caspar," sighed the wicked wife to herself, "why did you ever darken the doors of Bromley Hall? Why did I ever see you, that my heart and soul and mind should thus be racked and torn both day and night? How handsome, noble and brave he is compared to this coward at my feet; but he spurned me, he loathes me. I will be revenged!"

As thus she thought the heart of the mistress of Bromley Hall heaved with mingled feelings of guilty passion and hopes of revenge.

"What do you wish, mistress?" asked Shanks, trembling, as he stood beside her in the darkness. "Why do we meet here again and run the risk of exposure?"

"Trembling fool!" thought madam. "He has the heart of a dog." And then, half-aloud, she said, "Your master has determined to dismiss you, Shanks."

"Me? Why?" he said. "It was to be Mr. Caspar."

"It remains with me which of the two shall go."

"Then, of course, seeing how much I have done for you, and how intimate we are, *I* will be the one to stay."

"Would you have Caspar expose us?"

"He knows nothing."

"That is doubtful. Have you not noticed his proud curling lip of late? I have, and could have knocked him down times and times again, only—only you were not *man* enough, Shanks. I could love any one who did me that service," said the mistress, who, as she looked back at the many secret advances she had made to the young and good-looking Caspar, and remembered his proud scorn, her heart and soul were heated to a burning pitch of revenge.

"Would you have Caspar leave, then, to triumph over us, Shanks?"

"No, how can he? Master will not give him a character; he cannot get another situation without one, and must go begging from door to door, or starve."

"But he would still have a tongue in his head, and might speak aloud his suspicions. What is to prevent him?"

"What, then, do you propose?"

"Could you not slip something into his trunks before he takes them away?"

"Money?"

"Anything would do; we could miss it, have him arrested, and his trunks searched; you could swear anything against him."

"Me?"

"Yes, you; are you afraid to tell a lie?" jeered the mistress of Bromley Hall, scornfully.

"No; but I shouldn't like to meet his gaze when in the dock."

"Why not?"

"Well, I don't know, but there is something about his proud looks I could not withstand under such circumstances."

"Then leave it to me, idiot; what a *man* fears to do a woman will; aye, and with a smile, too." She added, "He does not sleep in the hall to-night?"

"No."

"Then go your way; leave the matter to me. See me early in the morning."

Shanks skulked away from the library, and a cold sweat was on his brow.

He was a mean-spirited coward.

Every one in the Hall knew that he bitterly hated young Caspar the tutor—yes, hated him with the bitterness of gall.

He was a bright scholar, and the only son of a very poor gentleman, long dead, and it was whispered that young Caspar was the sole hope and support of his widowed mother.

Shanks dared not pick any quarrel with Caspar, for fear of instant punishment on the spot, and this only increased his hatred all the more.

It was because of Shanks's intense hatred that the mistress of Bromley Hall had picked him out as the instrument of her revenge.

"What will she want me to do next?" he thought, as he stealthily crept to his own chamber. "I tremble before that woman; she has murder in her eyes at times. How the devil we have managed to hoodwink her husband so long is a puzzle to me. She must be a witch or a she-devil; her passions are never satisfied. If old Jonathan knew all he would murder us both, I know."

Like a ghost or some evil spirit, the mistress went to her own room, and there, in the silence of the night, looked over her drawers.

She took from thence a jewel case, and wrapped several valuable diamonds in small pieces of paper.

With a bunch of small keys in her hand and a lamp, she stole away to Mr. Caspar's room.

No one was there.

She looked about with a pale face and quivering lips.

"Fanny loves him, and has long done so," she thought. "Sophia had a sneaking liking for him also. But what do *I* care for all that? *I* love him also!" said Madame, with a fiery eye. "They are not *my* daughters—they are the children of Jonathan's first wife. I am not within twenty years as old as he is. Why did I marry him? Aye, why I cannot tell. I was a poor French teacher, and he a rich, doting old fool. He was of high position in the world; I was not. I was determined to rise somehow or other, and so became mistress of Bromley Hall; but what a curse it is upon me! I loathe my husband's very name, and would laugh with delight to see him lying dead at my feet! Oh! the curse of pride! Oh! the intolerable weight of riches where there is no love! Why did I not marry some one young, handsome, and brave? I had the chance once; aye, a noble young soldier that adored me! But he lies buried in the Crimea. No one that I have ever seen, though, ever inflamed my heart as Caspar does. But he rejects me! he hates me! What care I for honour, for riches, for fair fame? Why, nothing! I would give the world to be free again; but the law binds me down to live with a man I hate! Oh, Caspar! Caspar! why force me to weep? why force me to transport you? I would fly to the ends of the earth with you, if you would but smile on me and hearken to my proposals! But no! he shuns me! I have dressed, and sang, and danced to please him. I have done everything that a Frenchwoman could do to win him; but no! he is like the rock—unchanging! Nought, then, remains but *revenge!*"

Lamp in hand she opened Caspar's trunks, and examined their contents.

She took out all his things and laid them on the floor, in order to replace them in proper order and to dull the young tutor's suspicions.

Among his bundle of letters she found several beautifully written in a female hand, and signed,

"Your loving, and ever true,
"Grenhock Hall." "MARION.

"Then this explains!" she gasped. "He is engaged! Grenhock Hall! It must be Marion Newman, the squire's daughter! It is a secret correspondence! What a discovery! She has incited me several times; yet I never suspected anything between them. How sly; and even to dupe *me!* Marion, you shall pay dearly for all this deceit! Perhaps she even suspects *me* of loving him. How lucky that I have found them out. I'll tell the squire. They shan't escape me!"

With that she placed the most tender and loving of Marion's notes in her own wicked and passion-tossed bosom with eyes glistening with rage.

Among other things she discovered Marion's photograph, which she tore up with a bitter smile and burnt the fragments over her lamp.

Next she found Caspar's own likeness among some loose papers, but this she kept.

Placing the diamond rings and other valuables in different parts of his trunks, artfully concealed, she replaced all his things as she found them, locked the boxes, and returned to her own room.

That night she passed like one harrassed by evil spirits, bent on perpetrating some fearful crime.

Next morning she rose late, and as she looked in the glass was astonished to find how haggard she appeared.

Dressing with great care, and making herself look as captivating as possible, she sailed into the breakfast room pale, calm, and looking more disdainfully than ever at Sophia and Fanny, her scraggy step-daughters.

"Has Mr. Caspar returned to the Hall?" she asked a servant. "If so, tell him I wish to see him in the parlour, and alone."

Mr. Caspar was waiting in the parlour when Madame entered it.

"My husband, Mr. Caspar," she said, "has gone to London on important business. He attributes the riot among the students to your influence."

She dared not confront the young tutor's steady look and handsome face, but actually trembled before him.

"He has told me to discharge you, sir, and refuses to give you a character."

A pang shot through his soul, for he thought of his poor, helpless mother.

For a moment there was a dead pause.

"And am I, then, to be turned helpless on the world?" Casper sighed. "Good heaven! what is to become of me? I have led a dog's life here for many months—aye, a living death—but have borne it all for *her* sake!"

"My husband's orders must be obeyed, Mr. Caspar. It is your *own* fault that you have not made friends, instead of enemies, at the Hall."

"How, Madame? I do not understand you!" said Caspar, in doubt.

"Had you hearkened to *me*," she began.

But her utterance became choked, tears gushed from her eyes, her bosom heaved; but still, as she sank into an easy chair, her face was rigid and pale; no sigh escaped her—it was smothered in its birth.

She looked the picture of death!

Fearful that some sudden sickness had overcome her, the young, pure-minded tutor hastened to her side, and proffered his assistance.

"Do not touch the bell!" she gasped. "Hand me some water; I shall be better presently; it is only a passing faintness."

He did so.

Her hands trembled; the glass fell, and was smashed on the floor.

To the young tutor's astonishment, she sank upon her knees before him, clasped both his hands in hers, and wept!

"What means this, Madame?" said Caspar. "You are unwell—seriously ill. I had better ring for Miss Sophia, or Fanny."

"No, do not touch the bell, on your peril!" she gasped. "I *am* unwell—my heart bleeds!"

"Madame, rise, I beg of you. Let me call some one. Suppose we were discovered thus?"

"I care not. Oh, Caspar, Caspar! pity me! pardon me! do not go and leave me thus lonely in this hated place!"

"Your husband, Madame——"

"Would he were dead! Listen to me, Caspar," she said, holding up her face, and with a convulsive effort. "Listen! Remain with me, or let me fly with you—*I love you!*"

## CHAPTER XXVI.

NIGHT VULTURES OF THE BATTLE-FIELD—TERESA CAUSES THE ARREST OF PEDRO, THE SENTINEL—REVELATIONS OF THE AUSTRIAN SPIES.

THE sudden and strange commotion that ensued after the battle of the English Boy Volunteers with the unknown band, after the three duels, did not subside in the Italian camp of Garibaldians until the safe return of Frank Ford and the other young leaders from the scene of action.

When the truth was fully made known that he had not only successfully fought his duel, but also vanquished a numerous band who had set upon him and his friends in such a cowardly manner, the Italian volunteers shouted with admiration.

Teresa, Garibaldi's chief female spy, knew more about the whole affair than any one else.

She did not disclose anything, however, to the noisy multitude of soldiers, but went straight to General Garibaldi's head-quarters, and informed the old hero of all that had happened.

"And do you mean, Teresa," the old general said, "that these mere boys, this band of young English volunteers, had the rash bravery to engage in conflict with twice their own number?"

"Yes, general, I do, and they vanquished them completely."

"Then this band of scoundrels must have been lying in ambush."

"They were. They crossed the river in many boats, for the most part dressed like Italian troops; but in a fortunate moment I discovered that they were a gang of hired assassins in the service of some Englishman, who has a deadly grudge against young Captain Ford; but his name I have not yet ascertained."

"I hope he has not escaped," said the old general, with a bitter smile.

"I am sorry to say that he has, general. When he found that the young Englishmen were beating all opposed to them, he, like a cowardly knave, left his hired villains in the lurch, and decamped; he even fired at some of the brave boys who were rescuing one of his own followers from a watery grave."

"Dastard that he was; would that the brave young English boys had captured him, then we might have known the secret plot which is afoot against young Captain Ford."

"I fear, general," Teresa replied, "that there is more than we can see on the face of it; but leave it to me, and I swear to unravel this plot and mystery ere long. There is one thing we can say, and no one dare dispute it, that this courageous band of English boy volunteers are the bravest of the brave."

"I know that," said the old general, with a smile, "I know what English boys are too well to dispute your words, Teresa. I have had English boys under my command in every—yea, in all my engagements on land and sea, both in Europe and South America, and more heroic youths never were than they are. English boys are equal to men of other nations. There is nothing that they will not attempt, and, I believe, nothing but what they can do. If we do not find some hazardous enterprise for them to undertake they will be sure to find out one for themselves," said Garibaldi, laughing. "Let us hope, however, that they will curb their fiery tempers, and be cooler than they generally are."

Teresa was delighted to find that General Garibaldi had formed such a high opinion of her young and gallant friends.

She did not tell him, however, what she had heard in the English camp, namely, that the Boy Band were getting tired of doing nothing, and that they had made up their mind on a series of daring adventures on Austrian territory, and that all arrangements were perfected for carrying them out.

This was true, however, as we shall shortly see.

When Teresa returned to the camp of the young English boys, she found that the general commanding had summoned a court martial to enquire into the late duel and subsequent encounter.

Frank was very weak from loss of blood, but yet able to walk.

Had it not been for Teresa's timely aid, he must have been slain.

All the young Garibaldians were safe; none of them were dangerously hurt.

Despite the labours of the court marshal, it was unable to fathom the cause of the late strange proceedings.

Pedro the guard was arrested; but he, like the rest, was sullen, and refused to reveal ought he knew of the unexpected and bloody encounter.

The two men disguised as Italian officers, though suffering from wounds received in the duel, were heavily ironed, as was also Pedro the soldier, who, without doubt, knew more about the plot than he cared, or perhaps dared, to reveal.

Next day, and greatly to the surprise and pleasure of the young English boys, Garibaldi sent an order for them to march to the Austrian frontier, where they would have ample opportunities for action.

They were ordered to the extreme front of the Italian line of frontier in Lombardy.

This news was hailed with joy.

Frank received his orders under seal from General Garibaldi himself.

A special train was got ready for them, and off they started with wild "hoorays."

At thirty miles per hour they rattled along towards Lombardy.

The people of towns and villages had heard of them, and met them at various stations with fruits, wine, cigars, and all things that money could buy.

This sort of thing greatly delighted Master Fatty and the comical Buttons, who danced and sang all the way in great glee.

Sometimes Fatty indulged in very wild capers.

He and Buttons and several other harum-scarem young devils climbed on to the roof of the carriages and amused themselves with singing and shouting, and dancing to the tune of a fiddle which one of the party could very well play.

The engineer and guard protested against such mad freaks, and appealed to Frank, but he only laughed and said,

"Never fear, they won't hurt themselves; let 'em have their way. They are brave as steel, and have more lives than a cat."

The spot which General Garibaldi had selected for them to watch and guard was a most dangerous one.

They were placed far in the front, and many miles from the general army, right in the teeth of the Austrians, who were strongly posted with a large army on the opposite bank of a small river.

To keep their movements as secret as possible, Frank would not let any of his men put up their tents or make any fires, lest the white canvas and smoke should be observed across the river.

Twelve youths were picked from the company, and posted under cover of night close by the river.

Fatty and Buttons were among them.

Fatty, for his bravery in the late fight, was made a sergeant by the unanimous wish of his comrades, and Buttons was likewise henceforth to be styled "corporal."

Frank, Hugh, Dick and Mark, as the chief officers, held a council of war the first night of their arrival.

Fatty and Buttons were bent on mischief.

As they lay beside the river wrapped up in their blankets side by side these two young devils made plans of their own.

They could hear boats passing and repassing on the river, heavily armed by Austrian guards, and, from a good knowledge of Italian and German, which both had more or less achieved at Bromley Hall, or during their recent travels, they were able to make out and understand the conversation they overheard.

"By Jingo, though, wouldn't it be a lark if we were to cross the river, and surprise some on 'em?' said Fatty. "What say you?"

"Captain Frank, perhaps, wouldn't like it."

"But how is he to know? I'm game."

"So am I."

"What say you, then, suppose we do have a jolly spree when the other guard relieves us, Buttons?"

"How many will form the party?"

"Oh, about a dozen."

"But we shall want horses."

"That's easily managed. Let us all swim across the river and 'nail' a dozen from yonder cavalry camp in the valley just before us."

"I don't mind. When will the next guard relieve us?"

"In about an hour."

"Then I will go and visit all our fellows on guard, and put them up to our move, shall I?"

"Yes; and tell 'em not to show themselves to the Austrians, for they are very vigilant on the river to-night. If they were to know we were so near 'em, Buttons, they would land a regiment in no time, and then it would be all U-P with us."

"All right, trust to me; I'll tell 'em."

So saying, Buttons crept away through the trees, and left Fatty at his post.

In a few moments the Fat Boy, while passing across the river—all the Austrian guards on the opposite bank—faintly heard the splash of approaching oars.

He cocked his big ears, and opened his eyes in wonder.

"Jerusalem!" he gasped. "Why, here's a boat and two men coming across. What are they up to, I wonder? What's their little game? Surely they can't have found us out already?"

Now, some boys in Fatty's position would have felt alarmed, and roused all the soldiers.

But *he* didn't.

"I'll see what they are up to first," he thought, "and if one lands I'll brain him, that's all."

He hid behind a huge tree.

The boat came nearer and nearer without noise, and managed to reach the Italian side through dense shadows without being perceived by any of the young Garibaldians on the look out, who might have fired. They reached the shore, and one man stepped out of the boat.

"You ain't afraid to go, are you?" asked he in the boat.

"Me? No. What makes you think so?"

"Why, you looked pale coming across, and seemed uneasy.

"Did I? Well, the truth was, as we came across I thought I saw the glitter of bayonets in these woods here."

"Bayonets? Ha! ha! what nonsense! Why, none of the Italians are within twenty miles of here; there are none outside of Milan, Crema or Brescia. Ha! ha! what would the Archduke Albrecht think if any one told him that his chief secret agent, Major Andre, was afraid to cross the river? Ha! ha!"

"Well, laugh as you will," the officer replied, "I dare say I don't look much like a major now, do I, with this peasant's dress on?"

"No; it's a capital disguise. Where are you bound for *this* time?"

"Milan; we have several Austrian agents there unknown to Victor Emanuel, who regularly supply the Court of Vienna with news of all military movements going on. The archducke has received much information of late, and he wants me to go and see with my own eyes whether the Italians are on the move or not, for a great battle is expected."

"Well, good luck to you, major," said the boatman, who was also an officer; "good luck attend you. When do you intend to return?"

"In ten days. If you do not see or hear of me in that time you may rest assured I have been discovered and cast into prison. Good night."

"Good night."

The Austrian watched the boat disappear, and then he clambered up the river bank with a quick and nimble step.

As he came nearer to Fatty it was clearly seen that he was a person of superior rank and condition. He was tall, powerful and active.

Fatty, behind his tree, eyed the major like a cat does a mouse.

The Fat Boy trembled with excitement, for the Austrian was near him.

"Halt!" said Fatty, suddenly darting out, sword and pistol in hand. "Halt! surrender or die! No gammon, mind yer!"

The Austrian was staggered.

In an instant he jumped on one side out of Fatty's way, and tumbled head over heels down the bank again and disappeared!

Fatty was astonished!

As well he might have been, for the Austrian tumbled with the ease of an acrobat!

"Who'd ever a thought it?" gasped Mr. Waddleduck, in amazement. "Why, he made a double sommersault backwards, and has broken his neck for certain. But where the deuce has he gone to? I should much like to capture him; he's the best tumbler I ever see, beats all the travelling circuses hollow!"

But while Tony stood looking down the steep bank after the missing Austrian, and knowing not what to do, he heard a scuffle going on in the bushes just below him, near the river.

"Hillo! what's that? Has a rattlesnake got hold of him? What a scuffle it is!"

"Help! help!" said a voice in English.

In a moment, as if aroused from his stupor of surprise, Tony slipped down the bank, and rushed to the rescue.

He was confounded to find that the Austrian was struggling with two of the Boy Band, who had perceived him.

One of them had been struck on the head with a stone. The Austrian was bleeding from a severe cut in the face, and lay on his back endeavouring to rid himself of a second boy, who was straddled across his chest, and had handcuffed him!

This boy was little Corporal Buttons!

"Thunder and lightning!" said Tony, "that ain't *you*, is it, Buttons?"

"Yes, it's me. Why didn't you crack him on the head when you had him? He's safe now. I perceived the whole affair. His fall stunned him. Jake Somers and I slipped down after him, and bound him hand and foot while but half-conscious He fought well, though, and almost kicked the life out of Jake. He tried it on with me; but I was too quick for him."

"Do-you-mean-for-to-tell-me that this is the chap as took a back sommerset," said Tony, looking at the prostrate Austrian in wonder, "and not dead yet? Well, all I've got to say is, that his bones must be made of cast-iron, and his body of indian rubber, that's all."

The Austrian still struggled to get away; but Fatty reasoned with him in a very peculiar manner.

"It's no use o' you plunging about in this ere style when you're tied legs and wings, my circus-jumping gentleman. Not a bit o' use in the world. I knows yer, and a very smart, active gentleman you are, without a doubt. They must have been good hands at gymnastics where you came from."

At the same time he pounded the Austrian in the ribs occasionally, to keep him quiet, and to find out whether he really was made of india-rubber.

With the assistance of others, Fatty and Buttons, and Jake Somers carried their prisoner up the bank, and marched him off to Frank's head-quarters.

From papers discovered on the prisoner, and which he had not time to destroy before pinioned by Jake and Buttons, much very valuable information was gleaned regarding the Austrian movements; but what it was Frank did not then reveal.

After a short consultation with Hugh, Dick, and Mark, Frank made up his mind to go on a secret expedition that same night.

## CHAPTER XXVII.

THE SECRET EXPEDITION BY NIGHT—THE FARM-HOUSE SURPRISED—MAJOR ANDRE'S SECRET—THE AUSTRIAN PAYMASTER HAS TO PAY DEARLY FOR HIS RIDE—SERGEANT FATTY AND CORPORAL BUTTONS TAKE A NIGHT GALLOP IN SEARCH OF PREY.

SERGEANT FATTY didn't like to be left out of it, whatever it was, nor did Buttons, hence, after much coaxing on the part of Tony, he and Job were allowed to form two of the party.

"But what are you going to do?"

"That will shortly be seen," said Frank. "Come, buckle on your pistols and swords, and follow me."

"Are we going on foot?" said Tony, dolefully. "I can't a-bear walking; it hurt's a fellow's corns so."

"No; we are not going to walk this time, we shall ride, Tony."

Fatty and the rest were delighted.

Frank picked out ten persons altogether, and went out of the camp towards the river.

"The capture of that spy is worth more than £10,000 to us, Tony," said Frank.

"How?"

"You will soon see. From his papers I have found out many things which will be quickly explained. Follow me in silence, and don't dare walk out of the wood."

After half an hour's walking, one after the other, in silence through the wood, Frank stopped.

"Here's the ford," he said. "Tuck up your trousers, and follow me! we shan't be seen."

In the greatest silence they did as commanded, and followed Frank, who was already in the river up to his knees.

In ten minutes they had forded the river.

But now the adventure began.

Keeping close under the high bank of the river, they crept up the stream for a considerable distance, and even passed several sentries without being seen.

In twenty minutes they came to an old farm-house.

No sounds were heard; not a soul was stirring, not even a watch dog could be seen.

"This is the house," said Frank. "Open the garden gate quietly. Enter the back way."

Hugh was the first to enter, followed by the rest, without the slightest noise.

At that instant a ferocious bull-dog rushed out of his kennel with a fearful growl, and was about to jump at Hugh's throat.

In a second Frank's sword flashed in the moon-light.

The dog's head was severed from the body at one stroke, and rolled on the ground!

Fatty and Buttons were inclined to laugh at the quick work their captain had made of the ugly beast, but Frank cautioned silence.

"Keep close to the wall," he said, "in the deep shadows, and be ready, pistol in hand, while I go to the front door."

With his sword-hilt Frank rapped at the door loudly.

"Hillo! house here! In the name of the emperor, open!"

In a few moments the bushy head of the farmer appeared at the window.

"Who calls house at this lonely hour?"

"I do; open instantly. I come from Major Andre."

"Major Andre?"

"Aye; come, come, old man, be quick, without you want the Italian light cavalry surrounding your house."

"Major Andre, eh?" muttered the farmer, as he descended the stairs. "Surely he can't have returned so quickly? There is some mystery here. I must be cautious with this stranger."

The door was half opened by the old farmer, who said,

"You come from Major Andre, do you?"

"Yes; you have a dozen horses here, fully equipped, and ready for the use of his friends?"

"So I have, youngster," said the old man, drily, "but not for you."

"Not for me? What mean ye?"

"I mean this, my boys, you have come to the wrong house; you are one of Garibaldi's English boys. Now, if you'll take my advice, you'll be off with yourself as soon as possible. I don't want to hurt you, seeing how young and foolish you are, but if you *must* know the truth, I'll tell you that I have not only the twelve horses, but the twelve men here."

"Twelve men?" said Frank, surprised, certain that he had fallen into a trap. "And where are they?"

"I'll soon let you see. You have played your part very well, but you ain't quite so old in the tooth as I am. If you don't believe me, and want to see 'em, I'll wake 'em up for you."

"Hold!" said Frank, who perceived that the old man was about to raise an alarm. "Hold, on your life!" said he, presenting a pistol at the old man's head.

"Two can play at that game, rash youth," said the old man, snapping a revolver full in Frank's face.

The weapon missed fire, and next moment Frank seized him by the throat, and flung him on the floor.

"Make the slightest noise, and you are a dead man!" he whispered in the farmer's ear. "Tell me on the instant where the men and horses are."

"Release your hands from my throat, and I will," the old man gasped.

"Then, do so, quickly."

"The men are Austrian hussars. They came to-night, and are sleeping in the hay-loft, over the barn. The horses are in the stable."

"What brought them here?"

"The Austrian commandant received information from an English gentleman that a desperate band of young Garibaldians would perhaps be sent into this part of the country; and, to guard his mail-bags and despatches, he sent twelve hussars here to escort it on its way from Vienna."

"Ah! an Englishman informed him, eh? Didn't you hear who he was?"

"A young man of property. His name I did not learn. He hates this young band of Garibaldians intensely. I myself heard him say he would give a thousand pounds for the head of Frank Ford, their captain."

"Very merciful and polite, I'm sure," said Frank, with a broad grin. "And when is this mail coach expected here? Does it carry money?"

"It does, and will call to-night. I expect it in about two hours."

"Enough, old man. Now, as you value your life, show the way to your stables," said Frank, putting a pistol at the old man's ear.

"Who is that? Who is below?" said the voice of a soldier, poking his head out of the hay-loft door not many yards away, "who is below, there? speak, or I fire!"

A sharp click of a pistol was at that moment heard!

"Answer him," said Frank, in a whisper; "but be careful. I am not alone, mark you!"

"Who is there?" said the soldier, again, harshly.

"It's—it's only *me*, lieutenant," the farmer feebly replied.

"Then, why didn't you say so before? I thought I heard scuffling going on in the doorway."

"Oh, no, nothing of the sort," Schwabe replied; "I was only a little restless and couldn't sleep."

"Retire to bed again and try," said the soldier. "But now you *are* up go into the stables and give an eye to my men's horses. Are they ready for an instant start? All saddled I hope?"

"Y-e-e-s, sir!" the farmer answered, with a trembling voice.

All this time Frank stood over him, pistol in hand, and the young Garibaldians were crouched in the shade ready for their captain's command.

"It was well you answered him as you did, farmer," Frank whispered, placing the cold barrel of the revolver to his temple. "Now, show the way to the stables."

Old Schwabe did so.

Frank followed him closely for fear of any treachery.

By a lucky chance heavy, black clouds now obscured the moonlight, and like shadows the young Garibaldians crept towards the stables.

It did not take a moment for them to adjust the stirrups and mount an animal each.

The stable-doors were cautiously opened.

"At the word of command, follow me!" said Frank. "Are all ready?"

"Yes."

"Then, away!"

In a trice Captain Frank put spurs into his horse's flanks and dashed into the farm-yard.

He was quickly followed by the rest, who, as they plunged after their daring leader, raised a loud shout of,

"Hurrah for Garibaldi! Hurrah for Captain Frank!"

They leaped the farm-yard gate in gallant style, in a free and easy, devil-may-care, break-neck manner, peculiar to young Englishmen, and were soon on the main road leading to Vienna.

The twelve hussars, who were aroused from sleep by the ringing cheers of the boys, rushed from the hayloft, half dressed as they were, and seized their arms, but before they could fire the bold boys were several hundred yards away.

"Ain't this fine?" said Fatty, who dearly liked horse-riding. "Spur up, Buttons; don't lag behind! This is rare fun; much better than tramping it, eh, corporal?"

"I believe you, sergeant," said Buttons, much elated, and galloping madly along. "We shall have capital sport with these nags."

They had not ridden more than a dozen miles when Captain Frank halted at the foot of a hill.

He placed three of his men in a wood on one side of the road, and three on the other; the remaining four he placed here and there on the roadside with instructions what to do in case of need.

He himself went up to the hill-top, spy-glass in hand.

He had not been long there ere he heard the rattle of wheels.

In the distance he saw a four-horse coach approaching very rapidly.

He expected that it would come up the hill, but it did not.

There were two roads, and the driver of the coach selected the one that ran round the hill.

Frank was annoyed; but he galloped back to his comrades, and they retraced their steps so as to meet the coach on the other road.

Half an hour's hard riding brought them to it.

All the young horsemen went out of sight into the woods, and waited patiently.

In about ten minutes the coach appeared.

But in its round-about journey it had been met by half a score of dragoons who had been waiting for it!

This was a discovery that greatly surprised Frank and his boys; but they had made up their minds to have the coach, at any price, and so, therefore, prepared for a fight.

Part of the dragoons rode some distance in front, as Frank could very well see with his glass, and he made up his mind to conceal his men, and dash in between the coach and its advanced guard.

"Do you see that canal yonder?" said Frank, pointing in the distance. "Well, that is used for canal boats now. The mail coach will have to cross the draw-bridge. Let four of you dismount, and lie near the bridge, and when the six dragoons in front have gone over, rush out and swing it backwards. Do it quickly and cleverly, that will stop the coach, and while all are surprised at the bold measure, the rest of us will secure the mails."

Four of the strongest boys were selected and galloped to the canal bridge, which was always lowered after boats had passed for the use of ordinary road traffic.

The rest concealed themselves.

In ten minutes the advanced guard of six dragoons galloped past, and went clattering over the bridge.

In an instant four stout youths rushed out from their places of concealment, and with all their strength quickly pulled up the drawbridge.

The coach was stopped on the instant, and in a second was surrounded by the boy volunteers.

The driver was knocked off his box by Hugh Tracy, who dismounted his own horse, and took the reins.

Frank Ford, with revolvers cocked, turned out the inside passengers, but not before he was obliged to fire once or twice, and bang several obstinate passengers on the head with his sword.

Dick Fellows and the rest dashed at the remaining dragoons with such force and vigour that two or three of them were unhorsed, and tumbled into the ditch.

Fighting now became general on both sides.

The dragoons who had crossed the bridge were unable to return, but they fired across the canal, and more than once hit several of their own friends.

The four youths who had drawn up the bridge now remounted, and galloped to Frank's assistance—foremost being Fatty, revolver in hand.

Frank was engaged in a desperate sword encounter with two ferocious Austrian officers, who fought like demons.

Had not Buttons knocked one of them on the head Frank would have been overpowered and slain.

On all sides the fight continued for some time; but gradually the boy volunteers got the upper hand, when, with a wild shout, they made a general charge and drove the Austrians helter skelter down the road right into the canal!

"Hoo-ray!" shouted Fatty in triumph. "That last charge licked 'em, eh, Buttons? like the last charge of the guards at Waterloo, and Alma, and Inkerman! Ho-o-ray for us! Three cheers for Captain Frank! Three cheers for old Garibaldi! Three cheers and a good hooray for everybody!"

It was a gallant fight while it lasted.

"It was what I call quick and devilish," said Buttons, wiping his perspiring face, and laughing. "Didn't the devils fight, though? Never mind, we've whopped 'em, and nobody's much hurt on our side."

But though Frank's foresight was the real cau e of victory in cutting off the advanced guard of dragoons, he took all the honors bestowed upon him in a very quiet and modest manner, and gave instant orders for a retreat into Italian territory.

The coach was reached, and, by moonlight, Frank discovered many important letters, and much gold and silver in the mail bags, together with sundry Austrian despatches of great value. He had not much time to read, but found that one of the despatches related entirely to important recent doings of his brother Tom and the Italian crew in the gallant yacht "Kaiser," which had sailed out of Ancona, and been "playing the very devil," among Austrian ships in the Adriatic.

## CHAPTER XXVIII.

THE TREASURES OF THE MAIL COACH—WHAT THE AUSTRIAN DESPATCHES SAID—THE GALLANT DEEDS OF THE YACHT "KAISER."—TOM FORD AND HIS BRAVE CREW—THE PURSUIT—FATTY TURNS CRACKSMAN—THE VOLLEY—THE ESCAPE—THE DESPERATE FIGHT—THE DESPATCHES ARE READ ALOUD.

FATTY, who was much tired with his long ride on horseback, coaxed Hugh Tracy to let him drive the four horses.

Hugh did not object, and Tony, full of glee, mounted the box, and whipped up his horses in true coachman-like style.

One or two of the young band, slightly hurt, were

placed inside, and all the spare horses were led by the bridle rein.

"Now," said Frank, "since we have accomplished the object of our expedition, let us make the best of our way to camp again, for there can't be a doubt but that the Austrians will soon be out in strong force, and will scour the whole country in search of us. Whip hard, Tony. Come, lads, don't spare your spurs, we must get to the other side of the river before sunrise, or its all up with us."

Fatty *did* whip hard, and shouted till he frightened his four horses into a mad gallop.

But at the same time it must be confessed that a great deal of his wild cuts and great earnestness arose from a very particular cause, which was this:

Young Buttons and he had discovered a small hamper of wine and edibles under the box seat, and, as might be expected, neither he nor his young chum the "corporal" breathed a word of it to any one until they had stuffed themselves almost to suffocation.

How much of the cold fowl and wine the sergeant and corporal made to disappear will never be known.

But little, nay, *very* little remained for the rest of the hungry volunteers, although Master Tony, with a knowing wink at the corporal, and his mouth full of ham, swore roundly that he was as innocent as a baby, and had never touched it.

The river was reached at last.

But how were they to cross it?

This was a puzzle to all.

"Here, Fatty," said Frank, laughing, "come down off that box; *you* will never sink, you are all blubber and wind; fat people float the longest, and you can swim like a duck; jump in and swim across, there's no danger, we aint pursued; try the depth, and find a ford if there is one."

Tony didn't much like the job, but he soon stripped and jumped in.

He swam about for some time, and going up the stream a little distance, found shallow water.

He carefully tried the depth across, and reported only three feet in the deepest part of the ford.

All the party turned to the spot, and following Tony, their leader and guide, were soon half-way across up to their middle in water, the coach in front.

While they were thus crossing, and congratulating themselves on their successful adventures, a loud clattering of horses' hoofs was heard approaching.

Turning towards the bank they had just left, they saw in the distance a full squadron of Austrian hussars approaching at a gallop.

"Crikey! we're in for it at last," said Tony, getting out of the water, and behind a tree as quickly as possible; "look out for your heads, lads, they will be sure to fire."

With the strength and energy of desperation the young volunteers spurred and whipped their horses vigorously, and were just on the point of gaining the bank, when a volley was fired at them.

This only roused the little band to greater exertions.

No one was hit, but the shots flew all around them, whistling very unpleasant tunes in Tony's big ears, as he hurriedly put on his clothes.

## CHAPTER XXIX.

### THE HAND TO HAND COMBAT—THE PURSUIT—THE OLD MAN OF THE MOUNTAIN—THE SURPRISE.

"LOOK out, lads!" said Frank, laughing, when all the party had safely landed on the other side; "look out, lads, these hussars will give us a rare peppering if we don't mind; lay low, and return their fire."

Crack! whiz! bang! went the rifles, and showers of shot whistled all around the boy band in a very unpleasant manner.

Crack! crack! c-r-r-ack! still went the Austrian guns, but they did no harm to the young volunteers, who were concealed behind trees or in the deep grass.

When they had been firing thus for some time their commandant was seen to leap his horse into the river.

"Follow me!" he shouted.

The trumpets brayed out hoarsely.

"Keep cool, lads," said Frank, "and do as I tell you. All of them will not dare to follow their brave leader. Don't fire at him, let us catch him alive; he's a gallant fellow whoever he is."

While Frank thus spoke a part of the Austrian hussars leaped into the river and followed their leader.

The rest remained behind.

"Ready?" said Frank, in a hoarse whisper.

"Aim!" he repeated, after a moment of intense excitement.

"Fire!"

On the instant the boy band "let loose" upon the Austrians with rifles and revolvers in rapid succession.

Dozens of the Austrian hussars were knocked over in the course of a few minutes, and all was confusion among them.

"Half a dozen of you follow me," said Frank. "Fatty, you make the best of your way down the river road with the mail coach; we will soon overtake you."

In a few seconds Frank and a half-dozen brave boys mounted their horses and leaped into the river!

The act was full of daring.

The Austrians were amazed.

In a moment, Frank, followed by M rk, Dick, Hugh, and some others, swam their horses right into the middle of the Austrians, and fought them hand to hand!

The Austrians on the bank feared to fire lest they might hit some of their own men.

Thinking that no half-dozen boy soldiers could do much with double that number of war-like hussars, they quietly sat on their horses awaiting the issue of the combat going on before their own eyes.

Never were men more mistaken than these same Austrians!

Frank and his brave boys defeated all opposed to them, and captured the commandant likewise!

This bold, brave deed was accomplished by the gallant Frank in a moment, for the Austrian officer made but one thrust at him, and in a second was disarmed and unhorsed.

Seeing their officer captured, the hussars hastened out of the water in dismay, and began to fire rapidly at the bold youths who had defeated them.

Frank and his followers were content with doing what they had done, and soon reached their own side of the river in triumph.

But now another episode occurred in this hazardous night's work.

The Austrians all along the river front were thoroughly alarmed, and the report of heavy firing brought artillery to the spot.

They could not cross it in time, but they opened fire so vigorously with shot and shell that more than once the mail coach was in great danger of being smashed upon the spot.

One shell went whizzing and screeching very close to Fatty's head, closer than he desired; and he whipped up his horses with the energy of desperation.

But which road had he to go?

This puzzled him.

There were several roads, but he knew not which to take.

They had accomplished wonders that night, but now all depended on finding the right road to their camps.

"Do you think the Austrian beggars will dare to follow us, Captain Frank?" asked Fatty, red, out of wind, and perspiring.

"Think, Tony?" Frank answered, laughing. "I am *sure* they will!"

"Oh, Je-rusalem!" groaned Tony. "What bloodthirsty scoundrels the white-coats are! Get along!" said he, whipping up his horses into a gallop.

They had not gone far, and knew not which way they were travelling, when some one shouted out loudly in front,

"Halt! halt! for your lives!"

Frank dashed forward to see who it was, determined to sell his life as dearly as possible, when he was again challenged,

"Halt! halt! for your lives!"

The band were now approaching a dense thicket, and all was dark.

"Who shouts halt?" demanded Frank, in a resolute tone.

"*I* do!" was the stern reply.

In an instant a grey-headed old friar stepped into view before him.

"Why detain us, old man? Who and what art ye?"

"A friar, as ye see by my garb; my object is to save your lives."

"Ah! Know you, then, who we are?"

"I do, brave youth. But, listen to me; you and your band are strangers in this part of the world, and know not the roads."

"'Tis true; and we are pursued!"

"No you are not."

"Not, say you?"

"No; but the Austrians have cut off your retreat, nevertheless. They have crossed the river lower down, and now occupy all the roads."

"How know you this?"

"From yonder hill I saw what took place between you and your enemies, and right bravely you fought; but they know more about the ins and outs of this country than you do. They crossed lower down; if you had not returned to the river and fought them, you would have had time to escape. But they full well knew the stubborn courage of you English boys; and that half hour gave them time to perfect their plans to cross the river at three points and cut off your retreat."

"And have they done so?"

"They have. From yonder hill-top I saw all their manœuvres. To save your life and those of all your band I have come here."

"There is hope for us, then?"

"There is, if you follow my advice; if you do not, not one of you will escape. Have you any prisoners with you?"

"One, an officer of hussars, in the carriage behind."

"Then bind him, bandage his eyes, firmly stuff cotton in his ears that he may not hear anything; do this quickly, mark ye, and follow me!"

"I will, old friar," said Frank, who immediately returned to his comrades and told them all.

Fatty, for one, grumbled, and gave it as his opinion that the old friar was perhaps an Austrian spy, who wished to lead them into an ambuscade.

But one voice among the many did not prevail.

The Austrian officer was bandaged, and his ears even were stuffed with cotton as directed, and in less time than it takes to tell it, the whole party, led by the old, grey friar, were quietly and stealthily creeping along an obscure path in the forest.

Frank, revolver in hand, walked beside his guide, determined to slay him if treachery was meant.

Every one of the party were prepared for the worst in like manner.

Slowly and cat-like the little band made their way through the woods, and for more than an hour they travelled thus without speaking above their breath.

They had gone a considerable distance in the darkness, like shadows, when one of the horses neighed!

"Who goes there?" said a gruff voice in the distance.

The ominous "click" of a rifle was heard.

"Who goes there?" was repeated in sterner tones.

"Basil," was the friar's answer.

"Who else?"

"Basil's friends."

"Approach, Basil, with friends, and give the countersign."

Frank and the friar advanced.

But, to the surprise of the young Garibaldians, they now discovered that they were surrounded by more than one hundred shadowy forms, who rose to their feet in the forest, each clothed from head to foot in black garments, and with rifles levelled at them!

## CHAPTER XXX.

MYSTERY ON MYSTERY—DETECTIVES ON THE TRACK—CASPAR IS ARRESTED—JONATHAN ASSISTS SERGEANT GALE.

POOR Caspar, the young, intelligent, handsome, and pure-minded tutor, hastened from Bromley Hall with all possible haste.

The behaviour of his mistress had been so criminal in all its meaning, that it shocked him, and he determined to leave the mansion instantly.

Not thinking that Mr. Shanks could be the vilehearted fellow he really was, Caspar shook him by the hand in a friendly way before parting, and hastened to the railway station in order to reach London as soon as possible, that he might inform his poor aged mother of all that had happened, and get employment of some kind to support her in her old age.

He made several resolves in his own mind what to do to get an honest living; but he was low, and in very depressed spirits.

When about twenty miles from London, a very respectable-looking old gentleman got into the same train, and soon entered into conversation with him.

When they arrived at the London terminus, however, this same old gentleman tapped him on the shoulder.

"Your name is Caspar, I believe?" said he.

"It is."

"You are, or rather were, a tutor at Bromley Hall Academy?"

"I was."

"You did not leave with a written character, I think?"

"No, I did not, sir; for some strange and unexplained reason, the reverend principal refused to give me one."

"Oh! indeed!"

"My back wages is also due; but that I do not expect to receive, for it has been said I favoured a revolt among the students, which caused much damage and disgrace to the Hall, and I do not think that the Rev. Mr. Jonathan Gravestones will ever give it to me, although I confess that a poor old lady—my mother—looks to it for her sole support."

"I don't doubt, young man, that all you say is true; but no one can ever expect to do well in the world and act towards his kind master and mistress in the manner you have done to yours."

"*I* have done? What mean you?" said young Caspar, with looks of surprise. "Who are *you* that you thus dare speak to me in such a threatening tone?"

"Oh! if you *must* know," said the stranger, smiling, "I will tell you. *I am a detective!*" he added, in a whisper.

"A detective?" Caspar asked in surprise, turning pale. "Good heavens! what can you have to do with *me*, then?"

"A great deal, young man. I take you on the charge of *robbery!*"

"Robbery!" gasped the young man, trembling from head to foot.

"Yes, that is the charge at present; but I daresay we may find out more about you in a few days. Come, don't stand there shaking like a leaf; we had better call a cab, and do the thing quietly; I shall not examine you here on the platform before all these people."

If a thunderbolt had fallen at his feet, Caspar could not have been more surprised.

A cab was called; Caspar's trunks were placed on top, and he was just about to step into it, when he espied Marion Newman, the squire's daughter, approaching him, with outstretched hands.

"Why, Caspar," she said, in surprise, "how is this? Left Bromley Hall? Come with me. Papa is on the platform. I know he would be glad to see you. Why, what makes you turn so pale and tremble? What has happened?"

Caspar could not speak from emotion.

"Well, miss," said the detective, in a subdued tone, "the case is this—this here young man is accused of robbery, and is my prisoner; that's how it is. I'm very sorry; but if you wish to see him, you can call any time at Bow Street, you know."

"Bow Street! Robbery! Caspar!" she gasped.

"Oh, do not believe it!" said Caspar. "I am innocent; it is false; some villain has laid this plan to ruin me. I am *not* guilty of this foul charge!"

By this time a crowd had collected round the cab, but the detective hurried his prisoner away, while Squire Newman and others now stood over his fainting daughter, unable to learn from her anything positive of all that had just occurred.

Pale, quiet, and like one in an oppressive dream, Caspar sat in the cab, and spoke not a word.

He and the detective soon reached Bow Street.

The prisoner was ushered into the presence of an inspector immediately, who, with pen in hand, sat at his desk.

"Who is this, Gamble?" said he.

"A telegraphic message came this morning from Bromley Hall Academy, sir, respecting this young gentleman, and I proceeded a few miles down the railroad to the sou'-west junction, in case he might get out there. The description given was most perfect. I did not tell him my business till I arrived in London."

"What is the charge?"

"For robbery, sir."

"Have you searched the prisoner?"

"Not yet, sir."

"Do so at once, and his trunks likewise."

In a moment Caspar's trunks were opened, and to his horror he found several valuable articles of jewellery were concealed among his clothes, consisting of diamond finger rings, and other articles of great price.

"Is that the property, Gamble?" the inspector asked.

"It is, sir."

"And who is my accuser?" Caspar gasped, with a trembling voice.

"The mistress of Bromley Hall for one, young man."

"For *one?* Are there any more?"

"Yes; from several articles found here, I fancy Mr. Shanks and Mr. Gravestones will be others."

"Merciful Heaven! how could all this come to pass?" sighed poor Caspar, his heart sinking within him.

He sank upon a bench, perfectly heart-broken.

"Madame Gravestones accuse me!" he whispered, half aloud; "and Shanks, too! Alas! what harm have I ever done to either that they should thus seek my ruin?"

While the inspector wrote down the charge, detective Gale entered the lobby, followed at some distance by the Rev. Master of Bromley Hall.

"Is *that* the man?" asked Gale, in a suspicious whisper, of the prim, sanctimonious Jonathan, as they both peeped in at the door.

"Yes," said Jonathan; "the cloak and slouched hat found in old Ford's (the murdered man's) house belong to *him*. I can swear to them. Question him.

"I will," said Gale; "but you stand where you are in the lobby. Don't let him see you."

This little conversation was unheard by Caspar, who was in too great distress of mind to notice that Sergeant Gale and his late master had unexpectedly arrived, and then stood at the doorway of the charge-room.

"Hello! what's all this?" said Gale, as he entered the room, in an off-handed manner, to his brother officers, who had charge of Caspar.

"Oh, nothing much—a runaway with his employer's property, that's all."

"He's got a pretty good stock of things, I see," said Gale, in a whisper. "Turn 'em over, Gamble, and see if you can find a slouched felt hat and a black cloak among them."

Gamble did so.

"Have you got *all* your things here, young man?" Gamble asked.

"I believe so, but I left Bromley in such haste I did not stop to examine them."

"I see you haven't a black cloak among them?"

"Then I must have left it behind," said Caspar, carelessly.

"Nor a slouched felt hat," said Gamble.

"Nor a black mask," Gale remarked, very carelessly.

"Oh, as to them, I don't value them much now," said Caspar, with a faint smile. "I only bought them to go to a masquerade ball with once, at the Town-hall, in Bromley."

"What character did you take?" Gale asked, with a pentrating look.

"A robber," said Caspar, faintly smiling.

"You did not take the part of an *assassin*, then, I suppose?" asked Gale, with a dry laugh, in which some of his brother officers joined.

"No."

"You are pretty clever, I dare say," replied Gale, "but not clever enough, perhaps."

"Is *this* your slouched hat?" said the hardened detective, opening a bundle he carried under his arm.

"Yes," said Caspar. "How and where did you get it?"

"And is this your mask?"

"It is. How came you by it?"

"And this is your cloak?" said Gale, showing it.

"It is. But why all this mystery and ominous words? If it is my cloak it has my initials on the back of the collar. Yes, that's it; 'Caspar,' you see, is marked on the lining; but—oh, God!" said he, looking at it again, and with trembling hands unfolding it, "it is my cloak; but—oh, God!" he gasped, "*it has blood on it!*"

Some strange and horrible suspicion now crossed his mind.

He fell fainting on the floor!

## CHAPTER XXXI.

THE DETECTIVES AT WORK—GALE AT BROMLEY HALL—SHANKS FLIES TO LONDON—ALARM AND TERROR OF JONATHAN—WATCHED NIGHT AND DAY.

THE appearances, or "circumstantial evidence," as it is called, were so much against Mr. Caspar, the young tutor, that, although he was locked up on the charge of robbery, only Sergeant Gale considered it well to look into the matter of old Ford's murder, and ferret out his connection with it.

"Where did you say this youngster came from, Gamble?" asked Gale.

"From Bromley Academy; he was a tutor there."

"You have found the missing property in his trunk, you say?"

"Yes."

"Let's have a look at some of it."

Gamble showed him some, the diamond ring in particular, as being the most valuable article of the lot.

Gale looked at the ring, wrapped up as it was found in tissue paper, and he smiled.

"Were all the articles so wrapped up?"

"Yes. Why do you smile?"

"The youth never stole 'em, that's all," said Gale.

"Why, we found 'em all in his trunk. What greater evidence would you have?"

"*He* never wrapped them up so carefully as this," said Gale. "They are done up too nicely and tidily for a man to do. This is a *woman's* work, Gamble."

"Think so?"

"Yes; a man's fingers didn't do it, you may rest assured."

"But he will have to prove that. Perhaps the lady's-maid might have done it, and gone shares with him."

"Not very likely, for I hear the mistress doesn't keep one. However, I shall be going down to Bromley Hall in a day or two, and will drop you a line as to what I think. Meanwhile, don't be in any hurry with the case, you can have him remanded for a week or two."

"But do you think he has had anything to do with this murder?"

"Ah! there you ask me too much. I have no doubt in the world that the cloak, and hat, and mask we found in the house belong to him; that he doesn't deny; but the question is, was he at Bromley Hall on the night of the murder?"

"If not, it looks ugly against him."

"Just so; but we mustn't be in any hurry to form conclusions. His things may have been stolen by some other party, but at present all is mystery. It's a perplexing case, I must say."

Take him altogether Gale wasn't a bad sort of man; his heart could be soft enough at times, but he was continually mixed up with thieves, housebreakers, forgers, murderers, and the like, and had been for many, many years, until at last he began to look upon all human nature with a distrustful and suspicious eye, and could scarcely be brought to believe in the honesty of his own brother.

When Caspar had been locked up Gale sauntered towards the cells, while the old turnkey, as if by accident, began to speak to the prisoner on several subjects in order "to pump" out of him all he knew regarding the late Mr. Ford.

Gale, who was out of sight, listened, but he could gain no information whatever.

Caspar was too low-spirited to speak much on any subject, and Gale, as he moved away, and when alone with the gaoler, said,

"It's no use asking any questions, the youngster has had no hand in the murder."

"Whether he has had or not I fear a jury would hang him on circumstantial evidence, if he couldn't prove that he slept at Bromley Hall."

"That remains to be seen," said Gale; "I'll discover that when I go down."

"When do you start?"

"To-morrow morning."

That same evening Sergeant Gale saw old Jonathan, but did not say anything about his intended journey.

Jonathan, however, was full of the murder, and the more brandy and water he drank the more his tongue rattled on with wonderful rapidity.

"So you think that either one of the nephews or Mr. Caspar did this?" asked Gale.

"Well, you know, I couldn't *say* for certain, but every one must confess things look very ugly against them."

"Just so, just so; but let me ask, Mr. Jonathan, when did *you* come up to London?"

"Me? why the very morning *after* the murder."

"On what business, pray?" Gale asked, smiling.

"Why to inform old Ford of the conduct of his two rascally nephews."

"Just so, just so."

"But I hope and trust that you have no suspicions about *me*, Mr. Sergeant?"

"You? Lor' bless you, no; not the least, Mr. Gravestones," said Gale, laughing.

Jonathan began to feel very uneasy and looked very pale.

He now wished that he had never come to London at all.

"Do you often come to town?"

"Not often."

"And where do you stay?"

"Why, generally at the 'Three Cripples,' Cripplegate. Why do you ask?"

"Oh, nothing; it's a good house. Do you remember where old Ford's lawyer lived?"

"His lawyer? No; I never thought he had one, he was too much of a miser for that."

"He *had* a lawyer, though, so Roger the old butler says. His name was Flint."

"Was it, though? How singular! why I had a pupil of that name at Bromley Hall."

"Did you?"

"Yes, he came up to London the same day the riot took place."

"Indeed!" said Gale, with a bright smile, "and where is he now?"

"I can't say; perhaps in London now, for all I know."

Gale's questions were put so keenly, that old Jonathan began to think it would be wise to have as little to say to him as possible.

Gale thanked Jonathan for the interest and trouble he had taken in relation to the murder, and bade him good night.

The first thing that Gale did, when he left, was to put plain-clothes policemen on Jonathan's track, to watch him night and day, while he went into the country.

Besides this, he leisurely strolled towards Green Court, and found that the coroner had held an inquest on the headless body dragged out of old Flint's room by "Brudder bones," and the costermonger, and had returned a verdict of "wilful murder against some person or persons unknown."

Outside the "Ship Inn," where the inquest was held, which this night was very extensively patronized by hundreds of idlers, he saw a band of negro minstrels playing, and "Brudder bones" among them, all in his glory. Gale spoke to him, privately, and told him to keep a bright look out for old Flint, who had suddenly and mysteriously absconded, the same time "tipping" him with a £5 note.

On the following afternoon Gale arrived in the village of Bromley. He was dressed like a respectable farmer, with false whiskers, riding-whip in hand, top boots, and big stomach.

He put up at an obscure inn, at the edge of the village, and strolled towards Bromley Hall.

He saw the mistress, and told her he came to visit the establishment, for he had a boy or two he intended to send there.

Madame was all smiles, and Shanks showed him over the building, not failing, of course, to describe the late riot among the scholars, and to use a great many words in speaking of the great bravery *he* (Shanks) had displayed throughout all that very trying occasion.

With an eye like a hawk, Gale looked at every thing, and everywhere; and discovered, not only that the late Mr. Caspar's room adjoined Shanks's, which was on the floor above the mistress's apartments, but also was sorry to learn, that

Caspar had *not* slept at the Hall on the night Gale named!

Poor Caspar! things looked very black against him on every side.

"I may as well enter my sons' names on your school list," said the farmer, with a rich, north-country twang.

He did so, and paid the fee, which was a sovereign each.

He gave Mr. Shanks a £5 note, which that long-legged gentleman took to his mistress, who gave a receipt therefore in her husband's name.

The change, three sovereigns, was wrapped up in a piece of tissue paper, just like the articles discovered in Caspar's trunks!

When Gale perceived the particular twist, so delicate and feminine like, which the tissue paper had, he smiled, and put the money in his pocket without examining it.

Mr. Shanks wished the gentleman to open the paper, to see that his change was right.

This he did not, but simply felt the three coins in there, and departed to his inn.

"Young Caspar never wrappod up those jewels we found in his trunks," thought Gale. "The mistress did it! But why?"

Aye, that was a question which puzzled the detective; but for the present he contented himself with writing up to London, and informing the inspector all about it.

During his survey of the building, he had caught a glimpse of old Giles working in the garden.

The old man had eyed him so closely and suspiciously that Gale made up his mind to have a chat with him.

This was not a very difficult matter to do.

He lounged about the Hall gate when dark, and, as luck would have it, met old Giles, who was going to the "Hare and Hounds" to have a mug of beer, a luxury which he could seldom afford to indulge in.

But old Giles, from causes we know, was very low spirited.

The apparition of the headless man at midnight had shaken his nerves to such a degree that, although he opened his mind to no one, he felt, by some unknown cause, *forced* to walk over to the "Hare and Hounds" to revive his drooping and shaken spirits.

A very few words and a pleasant greeting from the farmer-looking detective induced old Giles to go to the "Jolly Farmer," where the stranger was staying.

Giles was on his guard, however, and thought the stranger was too civil to be honest-minded, and not knowing but what he might be one of Jonathan's spies, he held his tongue very firmly.

But there was *another* person who did not much admire the stranger.

This was Mr. Shanks.

When evening came on, he also went into the village, and, just as he did so, perceived Giles and the stranger deeply engaged in private, and what seemed to him to be, a whispered confidential chat.

This aroused Shanks's suspicions.

He followed to the "Jolly Farmer," and stood outside the parlour and listened.

He did not catch much, but what little he heard made him resolve to inform Jonathan, his master, by by letter of all he imagined.

This was quickly done, and the letter posted to the "Three Cripples," Cripplegate, London, in all haste.

After he had posted it he repented having done so, for although Jonathan could understand what he meant, no one else could, perhaps, save some lynx-eyed officers, and this was what he feared.

Without saying a word, therefore, he called at the post office late at night, and asked for the letter again.

But it had gone, so the postmaster said.

It had gone, truly; but not before Gale had read the direction, and shown his authority for so doing to the surprised village post-master.

Shanks bit his lips with vexation, for he had never known the post to go out so early by several hours.

Gale was in the post office when Shanks called, and now *his* suspicions were more and more aroused.

Shanks, however, was as cunning as he was ugly.

He went to the railway late at night—not to the station, be it remembered—and sat down by a telegraph post in total darkness.

Within an hour a luggage train came up for a few moments, and stopped to water at Bromley, and when it started again at a slow, snail-like pace, as luggage trains usually do, particularly the last train for the night, Shanks got into one of the empty waggons unperceived, hid himself under the tarpaulin, and had a cheap ride to London, which he reached in a few hours.

It was not yet morning when he arrived, but, early as it was, he roused up Jonathan and told him all his suspicions.

"That job of the two young Mortons will be the ruin of us both," said Shanks, weary and tired.

Jonathan did not say much.

But he turned deadly pale, and a cold perspiration was on his brow.

His eyes glared like those of a wild beast as he bit his lips with anger.

"Surely that can't be Gale, the detective," he said, half aloud, when Shanks had left him. "If it is, he and Giles will search the Hall from top to bottom. Would that I had old Flint's throat in my hands! I'd strangle the old villain! But stay, this is the fourth morning; I have to see him today, and if he doesn't settle with me at once, I'll murder him!"

He rose, and dressed himself instantly.

With his shoes in hand he quietly descended the stairs, and opened the door of the private entrance.

He did this so suddenly that it startled a man who sat on the doorstep.

He closed it again instantly, and listened.

The man rose, and whistled quietly.

It was answered by some one over the way that Jonathan had not perceived.

A strange thought flashed across his mind, and made him quake.

"I am watched both day and night," he groaned. "I know it, I *feel* it! But how to escape? I must stay here no longer."

As fortune would have it, the "Three Cripples" was an old-fashioned inn, with a large stable-yard, much used by country carriers and the like.

He entered this place by the back door, and concealed himself in a waggon, which was already loaded and ready to depart in the morning.

He had not been there more than an hour when it *did* depart, and as the waggon rumbled through the old gateway, Mr. Jonathan peeped from his hiding-place, and perceived a man still sitting on the doorstep, and another opposite, hid in an overhanging doorway.

"There cannot be a doubt of what they mean," thought Jonathan; but when he slipped from the waggon he felt infinite relief.

"They shall never take me alive," he said, as he darted down a narrow bye street, and disappeared.

## CHAPTER XXXII.

### FLINT TURNS INFORMER, AND VANISHES—WARNER, PUGGY, AND JONATHAN DISCOVER IMPORTANT LETTERS—THEIR PERILOUS POSITION.

But there were other persons besides Jonathan who much desired to have a conference with old Flint, the cunning, foxy lawyer.

Flint knew this very well, but only laughed in his sleeve.

He felt certain that his "dear friend" Warner would not leave a stone unturned to find him, and he trembled at the idea of meeting him.

Warner had hitherto been foiled.

His heart, vile and wicked, was filled with dark designs against Flint, and the lawyer felt certain that murder would be committed on one side or the other if they ever met.

But Flint never intended that they *should* meet.

Warner, however, was restless, and resolved to find out the lawyer, if he searched for a twelvemonth after him.

Calling the Pug to his assistance, they made the strictest inquiries, and, at last, at the end of three days' search, found out old Flint's den.

They called at the house, but the old woman who lived in the kitchen could not give Warner "the stranger," as she called him, any positive information regarding Flint, but from what she said, he came to the conclusion that the iron safe and many other valuables had been removed from the so-called office.

He also learned that a gentleman (Jonathan) had promised to call on a certain day, and that Flint had as faithfully promised to meet him on important business. This was enough for Warner.

He and the Pug put their heads together, and the latter volunteered to get into the room, and stay there both night and day until Flint *did* come.

This he really did.

The morning on which Jonathan was to call arrived. Warner was early on the spot, and slipped up-stairs.

The Pug admitted him, and they remained many long hours together, but still no one came.

"Whenever the old villain enters we will seize him, and half strangle him," said Warner, with a bitter oath.

Like two determined villains bent on mischief, they watched and waited, priming themselves well with spirits for the task that was before them.

At the hour agreed upon with old Flint, Jonathan arrived.

He opened the office door without any fear or hesitation.

In an instant the Pug, who was hidden behind it, and knew not who Jonathan was, struck him a violent—nay, a terrific, blow on the jaw, which felled him to the floor like an ox!

# THE BOY SOLDIER;

## OR, GARIBALDI'S YOUNG CAPTAIN.

THE BOY SOLDIERS ATTACK THE AUSTRIANS.

Warner, who was in the front room, rushed to the spot to assist the Pug, who was pounding at Jonathan with all his might and main.

Warner was surprised at the mistake, and greatly amused at Jonathan's horror-stricken countenance, and said, calmly, but firmly,

"Don't hit him any more; but mark me, old man," said he, sternly, "do not speak above your breath, or I will not be answerable for your life."

Jonathan, bleeding from the nose and mouth, gazed about him with a wild, enquiring look.

"What means this brutal treatment?" he gasped.

"Who are you?" asked Warner; "quickly speak, or I'll strangle you."

"Why, this ere's the werry cove as I seed walking about with and talking to the 'slops,' the werry same. Oh, he's been unkimmon busy with the detectives this last two days; *I* twigged him. I dare say he's 'blown' all about old Ford's job, the white-livered old hound, and now we've got him!"

"Speak quickly?" said Warner. "What brings you here?"

"I had an appointment with Mr. Flint this morning."

"Is he coming here, then?"

"He said so."

"And where does he live?"

"I don't know."

"You lie, old man."

"On my honour I don't."

"Honour be d——d, that won't do. What did you come for?"

"To receive some money."

"How much?"

"Two or three thousand pounds."

"Then, in course, as you're goin' to get so much, you can do without these articles," said the Pug, easing Jonathan of his watch, chain, rings, and money.

"For mercy's sake don't take my money. It's all I've got in the world; on my honour, it is."

"Gammon, my old bloke," said the prig. "You keep still, and don't patter so much, or I might knock your eye out in a twinkling."

Jonathan groaned, for he felt he had got into the hands of two very desperate men.

"So you called to receive money, eh?" said Warner. "Well, that is just what *we* called for."

"'Zactly; and we is goin' to have it, too," said the Pug, putting Jonathan's watch into his own pocket. "We is going to have it, too, old 'un. No kid, mind yer."

While the villains were thus engaged with the unfortunate master of Bromley Hall, who lay on the floor helpless between them, they were startled to hear the approach of footsteps.

In a trice Warner locked the door, and took the key out.

They then dragged old Jonathan on the floor into the front room.

The footsteps approached nearer and nearer.

They sounded like those of two men and a woman.

"Hu-s-s-sh!" said a voice, as if in warning, outside.

Warner felt for his revolver.

The Pug clutched his keen knife.

"The beaks!" said he, in a whisper.

Warner put a finger on his mouth in token of silence.

He presented the revolver at Jonathan's head.

"Speak a word," said he, "and I'll blow your brains out."

In a moment the footsteps stopped at old Flint's door.

The handle was turned slowly, and the lock tried.

Again the lock was tried; but to no purpose.

"Any one at home?" said the old woman, in a cracked voice.

No answer.

"Come, open this door. Quick, or we'll burst it open," said a gruff voice without, for the first time speaking.

"'Slops,' as safe as houses," whispered Puggy. "Shall we hook it?"

Warner put a finger on his lips, and turned deadly pale.

"Come, open this door; no nonsense with us," said a second man's voice. "Open, or we'll break it open!"

Still no response.

Those within now stopped their breathing by placing their hands to their mouths.

"I think as how you are mistaken, gentlemen," said the old woman. "I'm sure you are, in fact; there's no one been, although I am *certain* the old gentleman will call this morning."

"At what time?"

"Well, *this* is about his regular time."

"Has he moved any of his things out lately?"

"Well, no, not as *I* knows on. I *did* hear him say, however, a day or two ago, that he should pack off, and sell a lot of his old books, and the like."

"And did he?"

"All I knows on is, that a very heavy box went off in a waggon a day or two since."

"Was it a safe, think you?"

"It was made of wood; and couldn't be a safe, for them things are made of iron; not that he wants an iron safe though, gentlemen, for between you and me, although I doesn't know your name nor your business neither, he is *such* a poor old miserly mortal, I don't think he's worth twopence."

"H-em!" said one of the two men.

"Well, we'll call again."

"Has any letters come for him since he's been away this last day or two?"

"Yes, several."

"Where are they?"

"I put 'em into his letter box through the slit of this door, as usual."

"You don't know where they came from, I suppose?"

"Lor' bless yer, no; I never looks at the postmarks on letters, nor into any gentleman's cupboard neither, as some prying folks do, for I'm above it."

"I dare say. Well, no matter, we'll call in two hours' time, and then if he has not arrived we'll break in the door."

"What! Are you policemen, then?" the old woman said.

"Whether we are policemen or not, it doesn't much matter to you, old lady. Keep your tongue quiet, it will be much better for all parties."

* * * * *

"Letters in the box, eh?" said Warner, when the sounds of footsteps had died away.

"Perhaps they has 'chink' in 'em," the Pug whispered. "Have a squint."

Without any noise Warner crept towards the letter-box; but it was locked.

He carried several skeleton keys with him, and soon opened it.

He found four letters, two of which were not directed.

His hands trembled as he looked at the direction on two of them, and he almost gasped for breath.

The first one was directed to the landlord of the house—"Care of Mr. Flint, Solicitor, &c.", and read:—

Dear Sir,—Before I left town I paid you a quarter's rent in advance, as I may not return *shortly*, for special reasons I need not name *now*, and as you may, perhaps, open my room to dust it, &c., I ask, as a particular favour, that you will send all letters found in my box to the several addresses on each.

Your friend,

Flint.

P. S.—You will find two letters in my box undirected. Open them, and deliver to the parties they are intended for, and much oblige your old tenant.

"The old villain has given us the slip," said Warner, with a bitter oath, as he threw down the first letter in great anger.

"What! hooked it?" said Pug, in a whisper.

Warner made no reply, but opened a second letter, which was directed to—

Rev. Jonathan Gravestones,
Bromley Hall Academy,
———shire.

Care of Mr. Flint, Solictor,
——— street, ——— square.

It read as follows:—

My dear friend Jonathan,—When last I saw you I made an appointment to meet you, but circumstances, over which I have no controul, prevents me keeping it.

I do not know when I shall have the honour and very great pleasure of seeing you again, but you may rely upon it, it will be a long, a *very* long time first. I may inform you, however, that I have finally settled all my affairs, and have got the *money*, which I intend to keep, and so, therefore, now wash my hands from all further dealings and business with you and for ever. I have retired from business at last, and if I have outwitted you it is simply because I am the cleverer of the two. I leave you all the burden of the two darling children now in your "more than paternal care," as your school advertisements say in the newspapers, and for *my* share take the money. Don't grin, my good friend Jonathan: but next time you try your knavery and extortion try it on with some one less sharp than your very old friend,

FLINT, THE LAWYER.

"The old scoundrel!" Warner groaned. "Oh! that I had him here for five minutes!"

"Who can this werry reverend old bloke be?" asked Puggy.

"That's *me*," sighed Jonathan, who was handed the letter, and read it with a suppressed groan.

"Who can these two undirected letters be for?" said Warner, as he opened them, and read very nervously—

To the Chief Inspector of Police, Bow Street.

DEAR SIR,—A frightened conscience, and a due regard for justice, compel me to inform you that information has come to my knowledge regarding old Ford's murder, which I think it my duty to reveal to you in order that the real culprits may suffer the just penalty of the law.

Important affairs call me away immediately to a far distant land, or I would have visited you personally and explained all I have heard regarding that cold-blooded and merciless murder; but I hope to return in a few months, and, if it is necessary, assist you all I can in the matter. I have already written a note asking you to call on Thursday morning, and get the information which I allude to, and, no doubt, you will find waiting for me there a tall, clerical-looking party you would do well to look after.

Yours,
FLINT, Solicitor, &c.,
A Friend of Justice.

"Oh! what a bitter old scoundrel," said Warner. "A friend of justice, too, eh!"

The fourth letter—the second one undirected—was opened by Warner with trembling hands.

Two photographs fell upon the floor.

One was a likeness of *himself*—Warner!

The other was a portrait of Jonathan!

The letter was a short one, and said—

These pictures are the portraits of two villains who deserve to hang at Newgate. I heard them conversing in a coffee shop one morning. They thought I was asleep, but their words convinced me that if they did *not* do the deed they know all about those who *did* do it.

A third party is concerned in it, a brutal, low, costermonger-looking fellow, half a fighting man, half a thief, who goes by the name of "Barney," "Puggy," the "Pug," or some such names. With these portraits you cannot fail to find them out, and run them to the gallows. The clerical-looking party is the master of Bromley Hall. Search his place, and you will be astonished at what you may discover.

In haste yours,
A FRIEND OF JUSTICE.

"Great heavens!" gasped Jonathan, as he heard the letter read, "why, he brings *me* into it!"

"I wish I could only get hold of his ugly mug for five minutes, I'd show him if I was only a half-bred pug," said Barney.

But while the three rogues, who had now become in some sort friends, were astounded at what they had discovered, three loud raps were heard at the door.

It was the "slops" again!

* * * * *

But while this scene was transpiring in old Flint's office, let us for a moment turn to Green Court, where the headless body was discovered, and dragged out of the burning dwelling by Long Tom, "the Coster," and Joe Banks, or "de Brudder Bones."

As will have been seen in a preceding chapter, the chief detective in the case, Serjeant Gale, had very great suspicion that, after all, the tragedy in the court, and the horrid murder of old Ford, might be traced to one and the same source.

This conviction startled the head officer.

The description of Flint, who had fled, was pretty accurately given by the old landlady, and by other lodgers; but no one gave such positive and conclusive information as Joe Banks, "Brudder Bones," the comic gentleman of a travelling nigger band.

Sergeant Gale knew the value of this, and, as we have before shown, he estimated "Brudder Bones's" ideas at their proper worth.

Joe Banks did not much like the job of "keeping his eye open" for the missing man; but still he felt a very great interest in ferreting out the missing individual, in order that justice might be done and the guilty one brought to light.

But how was this to be accomplished?

He had travelled about the streets of London, by night and day, for more than a week; but he could not perceive, in all his travels, any one like the missing lawyer.

He had seen old Flint often, but, although he danced and sang, as usual, and directed his footsteps into very unfrequented and unusual places, where he imagined the cunning lawyer to be hiding, he could not discover any features like those he was in search of.

Serjeant Gale frequently had interviews with "Ole Joe" or "Brudder Bones," but could not glean any information worthy of notice; but he did not forget to "tip Ole Joe" occasionally with a sovereign, if not more.

One morning, however, Joe Banks, with his face all nicely corked and blackened, and his attire very fanciful and gay, in a very broad "loud" check of red, white, and blue, repaired to his usual rendezvous to meet his sable brethren at a well-known but now demolished public-house under the pillars near St. Clement Danes, in the Strand.

He had nearly forgotten all about the mysterious affair in Green Court, and was indulging himself with a pint of humble porter to add sweetness and volume to his voice ere starting out on his usual afternoon rounds, when he was surprised to perceive near him Sergeant Gale, dressed up exactly like a nigger, with a tall white hat and long-tailed coat, and armed with a capital banjo.

Joe Banks at the moment was about to introduce his nose into a fresh pint of foaming porter and take a long "pull" at the malt and hops when Gale tripped up to him in a lively fantastic manner, struck up a capital chord on his instrument, and capered about to the tones of a lively nigger jig.

"Brudder Bones" stared for a moment and rolled his eyes in a most extraordinary manner.

"Dat you?" he gasped, with a red, open mouth, and in intense surprise.

"Yes, dat's me. How is you, Bones?"

"De Lord hab mercy on dis chile! You doesn't mean to come it on us in dat way, does yer?"

"I does, dough," was the reply of the strange nigger, with a broad grin.

"W-h-h-a-t, turn nigger? *You*, Ser——"

"Hu-s-s-s-h!" said the officer, with a knowing wink. "I am going out with you to-day."

"Gammon!"

"Positive."

"You don't mean dat?" said Bones, rolling his eyes. "What's yer little game *dis* time? You London detectives am de berry devil."

"Just so," said Gale, strumming his instrument, but whispering, "We are obliged to resort to a good many shifts and starts to get hold of our customers, you know. But don't you say a word."

"Why, by Golly, I thought it were Jack Jenkins, our banjo man; I did, on my soul. So you can play and sing, eh? Well, by golly, dat beats all—yah, yah!"

"Hus-s-s-h!" said Gale. "I've dressed myself just like Jack Jenkins; but he's locked up."

"Locked up?"

"Just so. He got drunk last night, and got seven days for thrashing two policemen. I have come to take his place. Don't you let out; none of the other chaps will know me."

"Dat's sure," said Bones, "you deceive de devil."

"That's what I thought; but don't you whisper a word of this to the other lads."

"De Lor' bress yer soul, dey wouldn't find you out in a week. But what's up now?"

"Why, the old chap, Flint, that absconded from Green Court."

"What, have yer copped him?"

"No; but I think we are on his track. Which round are you going to take to-day?"

"Well, de chaps think o' goin' round Regent Street, and them places."

"Why not go round Hatton Garden?"

"Lor' bress you, we can't yearn a penny in dat quarter."

"But there are a good many quiet old lawyers there."

"Dat's just it. Why, dey wouldn't give us a solitary mag if we was to sing for a month. Dey orders us off, and one ole gent come to the window with a gun and threatened to shoot us."

"Indeed! And how was *he* dressed? Anything like old Flint?"

"Lor' bress yer, no. Old Flint had whiskers; this ole cock hasn't got any at all. I'm sure it's not Flint."

"Perhaps," was the dry reply; "but do as I tell you, Joe; I'll pay you well enough. Here come your companions. Silence, mind!"

"Just so, massa; mum's de word!"

So well had Gale, the detective, studied the ways and habits of street "niggers" that he deceived the sable band, who did not for a moment suspect that the banjo was in any other hands than those of their old companion, Jack Jenkins.

After drinking down to the bottom of several pots of porter, and favouring the landlord of the public-house with a few artistic flourishes with toe and heel, the nigger band started on their rounds.

They called and performed at several places, but the more the detective sang and thrummed his banjo, the more was Joe Banks astonished at his talent.

"By golly, you beats de devil!" he whispered, more than once, in a quiet way, and burst out into frequent roars of laughter, which the by-standers seemed much to enjoy, for they showered coppers into Bones's hat more plentifully than was ever known before.

The tambourine player was in ecstacies at the unexpected display of Jack Jenkins's talent, and so successful were they in their rounds that Joe Banks vigorously attacked more than one foaming pot of porter at different public-houses, in order to drown his exuberant feelings.

After a time the black band of minstrels, in their walks, came to Hatton Garden, and opposite the very house where lived the pugnacious lawyer that Bones spoke of.

"Dat's de crib," said Joe, in a whisper, "but you must look out, for dat gun o' hisn is loaded, and he's more dan once threatened to shoot de whole lot of us."

"Never mind," said Gale, "give him another chorus."

So saying, the band struck up a chorus, and sang long and lustily.

The figure of an old man was seen peeping through the blind, and walking to and fro in his apartment in a state of great restlessness and annoyance.

"By golly! he'll let us have it after a bit," said Bones, grinning. "Look out, chaps!"

But still they sang on, and more discordantly than ever.

The occupant of the room was seen to frequently shake his fist at the minstrels, but they took no notice of him, and continued their noisy songs.

At last the window was thrown up, and the old man came in sight.

Directly Gale caught a clear view of the man's face his eyes glistened with delight.

"Now's the time," said Gale; "*I'll* give him a chant which shall shake his nerves, if he's got any."

"Go away, go away, you noisy vagabonds; be off this instant. How dare you interrupt and annoy people in this manner from day to day? Depart, I say. I'll call a policeman," the old man stammered out very fiercely.

Bones and the rest took no notice whatever of the old gentleman's anger, but continued singing all the songs they could think of, particularly the most doleful and sentimental ones, greatly to the parlour occupant's horror and disgust.

"Begone, you noisy rascals, begone," he said.

"Is that like his voice, Bones?" whispered Gale.

"Werry like; werry like, indeed, massa."

"Then here goes for *my* song, let's see how he likes it—join in the chorus."

But before he commenced the old man rushed to the window, gun in hand.* "Vanish," he said, cocking the weapon, looking angry and determined. "Go this instant, or I'll murder some of you."

"Dat won't do, massa," said Bones, laughing; "if you mean to do dat, you know, to dis ere darkie, you might give ole Massa Ketch a nasty job. Yah, yah! Now den, brudder Banjo, for dat ere new ditty o' yourn."

On this challenge, and despite the old man's angry curses, Gale commenced in a loud voice to sing a song, the chorus of which was—

Sing, sing, ye darkies, sing,
A mystery strange—a horrid thing,
A headless nigger was brought to light,
The murderer fled in the dead of night,
And never more was seen.

Had a thunderbolt fallen at the feet of the old man he could not have been more surprised.

He changed all manner of colours, trembled in every limb, tried to speak, but could not gasp out a single word, and at last dropped the gun, tottered from the window, looking pale as death.

"Ha, ha! It *is* Flint," said Gale, "I am on his track!"

## CHAPTER XXXIII.

BASIL, THE BANDIT CHIEF—KING OF THE MOUNTAINS—THE ITALIAN'S DECEIT—FRANK FOILS HIM—THE ROBBERS' CAVE—THE BANQUET—THE POISONED DRAUGHT—A GIRL'S DEVOTION—AGNESE THE BANDIT'S DAUGHTER.

DIRECTLY the Boy Soldiers found themselves so suddenly surrounded by the black-looking band, who, with levelled guns, stood on all sides of them, the truth flashed to Frank's mind that they had been artfully deceived by the supposed Friar Basil, and that he had conducted himself and followers

* See last week's illustration.

into the mountains among a lot of desperate and bloodthirsty brigands!

None of them, he guessed, understood English, so he spoke a few words to the boys, telling them of what he thought and what he intended to do.

"Leave the matter to me," he said, "and all will yet go well with us."

Then, addressing his guide, he said in Italian,

"Basil, we knew from the beginning that you were no friar, but a brigand chief, and that we relied on your honesty and honour is plain, otherwise we might have killed you, and continued our journey unmolested and uninterruptedly."

"Well! Now that you *do* know who I am, you cannot get out of the scrape without paying heavy ransom for yourself and followers," said Basil. "If you knew I was a brigand chief why were you so silly as to follow me hither, boy?"

"Boy!" said Frank, proudly, "'tis true I *am* a boy, and so are all here present among my followers, but we are men in action."

"Pshaw, mad youth, what are you mouthing at? You are entrapped, and there's an end of it. Ha, ha! hear how bravely this baby prattles, ha, ha!"

"You will find I prattle, as you call it, to some purpose when you hear me out."

"Hear you out! what means the bold boy?"

"I mean this. It is *you* who are entrapped, not us."

"Me! Basil, chief of the Black Banditti, King of the Mountain!" said the chief, surprised, "what mean ye? Speak, quickly; if I do but move my finger, every one of your followers shall lie helpless at my feet in their blood."

Frank mustered up his courage as he said,

"Yes, you, and all your band, are entrapped if you do not follow my advice."

"*Your* advice! Oh, oh! Why I and my men have been well paid to capture you by a rich young Englishman. I did think that some of the band I sent to your camps had done the job for me long ago, but I see they haven't."

"Then those with whom we fought and duelled were part of this band," thought Frank.

"Listen to me, Basil," he said, aloud; "we, boys as we are, are freebooters, like yourself and the black banditti you command."

"Ha! rivals, eh?"

"Rivals, but only in friendship, let me tell you, and to night we have learned that a large Austrian force would cross the river and attack you here in your mountain home."

"The lad is dreaming," said Basil.

"No, Basil, I am not; but knowing you were true Italians at heart, and *not* the bloodthirsty scoundrels report speaks of you, I beat back part of the Austrians, who mistook our party for some of yours."

This was false, of course, but the plain, truth-like manner of Frank perfectly disarmed the brigand chief, who looked astonished.

"This cannot be."

"But it is true. To prove it I can describe to a nicety the very man who paid you to look out for us and entrap us."

"Ha!"

"Yes, and his name, too, if necessary. Think you, if we did not mean honour and friendship to you and the Black Banditti, that we should have been foolish enough to have selected the very road that led to your mountain home?" said Frank, warming up. "And let me tell you more, Basil; the very young Englishman who hired you to murder us this very night had a long conference with the Austrian general in command across the river. He telegraphed the statement to the Archduke Albrecht at Verona. Your whereabouts and number were minutely described, and the latest order which the Archduke signed was for the purpose of ordering a large force to cross over to-night and surround you."

"Impossible!" said Basil, "the young Englishman could not have been such a cowardly traitor!"

"But he is, and I can prove it."

"The proof, then," said Basil, "and at once."

Among the papers Frank captured was an order very similar in purport to what he had now stated.

He found it, and in triumph handed it to Basil the bandit chief, who, as he supposed, could not read.

"My eyesight is not good, young man; read it for me," said the sullen and angry chief.

Frank did so aloud, and added much more to the order than the archduke said, or ever thought of saying.

When Basil heard the contents of the order he raved like a madman to think that one who had employed him should thus turn informer.

"Enough! you are right, young man. Your hand. I find you are true friends, and will treat you as such."

At a sign from Basil his dusky followers lowered their weapons, and retired.

"Follow me!" said the bandit chief.

Frank did so.

In a short time the Boy Soldiers found themselves in an immense cave, which contained many passages of great width, and intricate windings.

It looked more like an immense magazine of goods and fire-arms than anything else, but was excellently furnished.

Basil, with the pride of a bold bandit, took Frank here and there, in all manner of out-of-the-way places in this mountain cave, and showed him his various treasures.

The interior of the mountain seemed as if it had been hollowed out by nature for the home of some bold robber, for, except the small gateway through which they had entered, no other means of ingress or egress was discernible.

As Basil walked in front with a torch in hand, taking pride in displaying all his illgotten treasures, Frank perceived a dim ray of moonlight streaming into the cave at an immense distance from where they then were.

But he did not pretend to notice it.

"You see we can defy all the armies in the world here," said Basil. "No one can harm a single hair of mine while the front entrance in blocked up, and as to finding us, ha! ha!" laughed the grim chief, "that is impossible, for the forest road is so full of pitfalls and intricacies that it would puzzle the very devil to discover again the winding forest path by which I just brought you. Ha! ha! no fear of taking Basil either dead or alive. What think you, my bold lad?"

"You are perfectly correct, Signor Basil. I pity the Austrians who dare attack you in this stronghold."

"*I* don't pity 'em; let 'em come. I could show you our skull chamber where we have dozens of skulls arranged on the walls that were on Austrain or Italian shoulders once, and we mean to keep adding to the number, too, as long as they won't let us alone. What care I for Austrians or Italians? Not a bit. I treat 'em all alike; it's all fish that comes to *my* net, and if you and your boy followers hadn't proved yourselves friends you would have been all shot before morning, I can tell you; but what of that; it's nothing to me. What care *I* for killing and shooting? Not a bit. I've got several prisoners confined here now, and if their friends do not ransom them shortly, why, I shall chop their heads off, and get rid of them *that* way. I am king of these mountains, and defy the devil to take or dethrone me!"

After showing Frank into many places, Basil returned to a large chamber which was fitted up like a supper-room.

It was decorated on all sides with damask and velvet.

Chandeliers of sparkling beauty hung suspended from the walls.

All wore an air of comfort and elegance.

"This doesn't look much like a bandit's cave," said Frank, with a smile.

But as he smiled a faintness came over his heart he could not explain.

There was an air of mystery about the place that filled him with apprehension.

Basil's very politeness and kind attentions alarmed him.

For there was a hidden devil in the chief's eye which spoke of dark designs and infernal mischief.

"What means all this parade?" asked Frank. "Surely this table is not laid for me and my companions, bold Basil."

"That is just what it *is* prepared for," said the Italian, with a wicked smile.

"What, entertain strangers in such a mysterious way as this?"

"Oh, yes, we often give sulphur to our dear friends," said Basil, coolly; "sometimes we call it the death supper."

At the same moment he touched a bell twice.

From behind a screen that hid some other apartment he had not seen, a girl appeared, looking pale, timid, and beautiful.

"My handmaiden, young Englishman," said Basil, with a demonical grin; "the daughter of a captain I once had. Oh! you need not look surprised and sad, my young friend," said the bandit chief, curling his moustache as he observed Frank's sorrowful glance at the pretty girl. "You need not feel sorry for her, she is perfectly happy, ain't you, Annette?"

"Quite happy, padrone," said the girl, trembling the while.

"I told you so. Tell this young Englishman whether you are happy or not, Annette?"

"Quite happy, signor," said she, casting a furtive glance at Frank, and looking paler still. "Quite happy, signor."

"I told you so. Quite happy; how could she be otherwise with such good company as mine? I, Basil, Bandit Chief and King of the Mountains, ha, ha! I am going to make her my wife one of these days, when my old devil dies. She won't live long—I told her so long ago. She must die soon, or I'll make her. Ha, ha!"

"Your commands, good padrone?" said Annette, bowing before the black-looking rascal, but trembling in every limb.

"Tell my wife to serve up supper immediately."

"For whom, good padrone?"

"For whom? Why, for myself and this young man's friends. Begone, and do it quickly. When next you come in, let me see some colour in your cheeks, and no trembling lips, mind."

So speaking, Basil, on some pretence or other, went out of the apartment, and left Frank alone.

He had not been so for more than a minute when the curtains rustled and a second girl appeared—a beautiful creature about sixteen years of age, dressed in picturesque mountain costume.

She peeped through the tapestry curtains for a moment, and then whispered to Frank as she hurriedly approached him,

"My father means you no good. He must not see me thus warning you; I do so at the risk of my life. Annette, the captive, told me all."

"What mean you, fair one?"

"You are going to sup."

"Well?"

"Eat and drink to your heart's content; but, mark me, touch nothing that comes out of a bottle with a green seal; it contains poison, and will be served last."

"How can I avoid it, sweet maid?"

"Leave that to me, bold youth. If there is any wisdom left in me I will save you. I must away."

With these few words, Agnese, the bandit's daughter, flitted from the room like a shadow.

On that instant her father re-entered.

"Who was that that rustled the curtains just now?" he said.

"*I* did not observe it, worthy Basil," said Frank.

"But *I* did. Has any one spoken to you?"

"How should they?"

"'Twas well they have not."

With a surly look he rang the bell, and supper was soon served.

Frank and all his boy companions seated themselves round the table, and the meal began.

Basil was the gayest of the gay.

"If the Austrians come upon us to-night, they will not have to fight men with empty stomachs."

He touched the bell, during the repast, and Annette appeared.

"Tell Agnese to bring me my favorite bottle," said he; which expression seemed so very funny to many of his followers, who were also at supper there, that they laughed out loudly.

Agnese, looking pale as death, appeared with a single bottle, having a green seal, which she placed at her father's elbow.

With a look full of meaning at Frank, she said, "Father, the rest of the band are also at supper, in their own cavern, and are noisy for more wine."

"Then why ask me, slut? Let them have their fill. Show one of them to a cask, and let them draw as much as they like; if we want men to fight well, we must feed them well, and prime them well with good old wine. Eh! my young Englishmen?"

"Worthy Basil, quite right. John Bull is a great one for feeding well first, and fighting well afterwards."

This remark seemed greatly to tickle Basil, who played with the bottle having a green seal very fondly, but poured none out as yet.

Frank, in secret, warned all his followers to beware of drinking anything the bandit chief gave them; and they did so.

The supper was over, and the cloth soon removed; but it struck Frank as a very singular thing that every one except himself and his followers seemed to be fast getting tipsy.

Why this was he knew not.

He watched Annette and Agnese very closely as they brought in bottle after bottle of wine, and uncorked them, and still the thing remained a mystery to him.

During some noisy toast, in which Basil and his

chief men were indulging, Agnese poured out for Frank a fresh glass of wine, and as she did so, whispered—

"Be careful; they will be helpless by-and-bye, but when you are free again remember me."

Frank pressed her hand without speaking a word, and slipped off his own finger a diamond ring he wore.

"Let that be our pledge, dear Agnese," said he, in a faint whisper. "I shall never forget you, and will soon return."

From sips of wine, the bandit gentlemen got to bumpers, and it appeared very certain that if left to themselves for half an hour they would all be hopelessly and helplessly stupefied.

Frank and his companions, perceiving how things were going, kept up the laugh and joke, until the whole company became merrier and noisier, and well-nigh drunk.

"We-ll," said Basil, hiccupping, "before we part let us take a drop of cordial in our wine all round; it's a splendid sleeping draught." (With an ominous wink to his companions, who laughed boisterously at the great wit of their chief.)

"No, not yet, Basil, not yet; we haven't drunk half enough," said Frank. "Fill again before we have the cordial. Don't let it be said that English boys can beat an Italian brigand at wine-drinking."

"As you like. Well, fill glasses all round, and let's have a song; after that you young English boys shall have a drop of cordial to kill the wine, then we'll all have a sleep, and wake up fresh for the Austrians when they come upon us."

This was just what Frank desired.

"A song! a song!" he cried.

"Yes; that's it!"

"Let's have a song, Basil."

"Now for it, captain, your old favorite," said several swarthy brigands, half drunk, clapping their hands, "the one you composed on yourself."

With many hems and haws Captain Basil commenced his song, which was of such a tremendous length that all save himself and the Boy Soldiers were fast asleep, snoring in their chairs or stretched on the floor, before it was finished.

Basil had sung ten verses, and his voice got weaker and weaker, until at last he stopped dead still after just finishing the chorus, which was,

"They may call us bold villains, but 'tis my firm belief,
There's none half so gay as a brave mountain chief.
Then fill up your bumpers, and our toast it shall be,
'To all gallant craftsmen on land and on sea!'"

For a moment Frank and the rest sat uneasily in their chairs knowing not what to do.

At that moment Agnese whispered,

"I have drugged them, or they would have poisoned you all. Fear nothing, they are all insensible. Follow me."

"But there are many more outside."

"They are all stupefied with drink but Antony, and him I fear. Quick! quick! brave English youth, or all is lost!"

## CHAPTER XXIV.

THE FLIGHT—DESPERATE HAND TO HAND COMBAT—A VILLAIN'S SHOT—A SCOUNDREL'S PUNISHMENT—SAFETY OF THE BOY SOLDIERS.

"ANTONY, who is he?" asked Frank, passionately, as he followed his fair guide. "Think you I fear any *one* man?"

"Hu-s-s-h!" sighed Agnese, "you know him not. I hate him. I refused his hand, and he hates me. If he had any idea of the trick I have played upon my father and the whole band he would drive a poignard to my heart."

"Then let him only try," said Fatty, greatly pleased at the prospect of escaping from the "devil's den," as he called it; "let him try it on, that's all."

"Silence," said Frank, fiercely, "silence, Fatty, you know not with whom we have to deal. Discretion is the better part of valour."

Agnese, with soft steps, conducted Frank out of the cavern used as a banquetting hall, and had to pass through another and a much larger one.

She peeped in first, and found, as she had said, that all the band, without exception, were intoxicated and fast asleep.

She beckoned Frank and his followers on with a faint, timid smile.

"They had to step over the prostrate, helpless forms of several dozen of the band as they lay about fast asleep.

"This way," she said; "Annette and I have prepared your horses; everything is ready for your instant departure, but we have done this at the peril of our lives, for our hearts were sad to think so many brave youths should be sacrificed to my father's deadly passion and hate."

They had reached the outer door or gate of the bandit's cave when a rifle was fired at Frank's head by some one unseen.

It missed him, but hit Agnese slightly in the shoulder.

"Look to yourselves," she said, "I am not badly hurt, only grazed; look to yourselves, or all is lost; it is Antony!"

With the fury of a young lion, Frank rushed to the spot whence the shot was fired.

He then saw Antony, the solitary guard, sword in hand, and with flashing eyes.

The brigand would have raised a shout of alarm, but ere he did so Frank rushed upon him and seized him by the throat with a fiery, deadly grip.

This was the only person now visible.

"Get you to your horses," said Frank; "harness the horses to the carriage; leave this scoundrel to me."

His followers did so.

But little did they dream what a terrific struggle it was between Antony and Frank, their brave young captain."

But Frank's grip on the villain's throat was like that of a vice.

Antony struggled valiantly, but could not relax the hold young Ford had of him.

They wrestled and fell over and over again, and yet neither had the mastery.

At last, with a tremendous effort, Frank rolled his enemy over.

Antony, with the desperation of despair, managed to loose one hand.

He seized his pistol, and snapped it right in Frank's face.

The ball passed close to his temple.

With the vengeance and anger of a strong man young Frank drew his knife, and it glittered before the villain's eyes.

"Spare me! spare my life!" the ruffian groaned.

"Die, dog, die!" was the bitter response.

The long shining knife descended with unerring aim.

The brigand sank back dead.

Frank ran after his companions who were putting the horses to the carriage. Annette was assisting them, and as soon as she saw Frank she said—

"Your dangers are but beginning, you must every-one of you be prepared for instant action, for we know not whom we may meet. It may cost me my life, but yet I will risk it to save this gallant and youthful band of brave Garibaldi volunteers."

None of the Boy Soldiers could imagine which way the road led along which she was piloting them, but they had faithful confidence in their young guide.

They travelled down a long broad path round the side of the mountain.

No one spoke.

Nought was heard but the jingling of horses' harness and the creaking of the carriage springs.

For a full half hour they journeyed where they knew not, through the dense forest of the mountain, and at last came in sight of a fine level road.

"This is the road I wished you to take," said Annette. "Go straight on; you cannot miss your way; you are all well mounted and armed. As for me," she sighed, "I must return."

"But why, dear Annette," said Frank, gallantly, "why not flee from that den of thieves?"

"I dare not; at least, not without Agnese, who is more to me than a sister. We both sigh to escape the contamination of that wretched den, but dare not yet. Our plans are not completed."

"Your plans?"

"Yes. We are but two simple girls; Agnese is a little older than myself. But we have plans—brave, good plans; but she is hurt. I will not, I could not, desert her now. Her father would kill her did I escape. We will some day both flee together. But go! I cannot, I dare not, say more at present, but I shall return to my slavery with a firm hope, that, as we have saved the Boy Band, they may also save and rescue us."

So saying, the brave little Annette waved her hand and disappeared like a fairy up the mountain side.

It was no time for Frank or any of his band to moralize or feel regret.

Time was precious; morning was about to dawn, and yet they were far from their own camps.

With whip and spur the young Garibaldians sped along.

They had not gone far, however, when they heard the distant sounds of a fiery fusilade going on in the direction of their own camps.

This quickened the curiosity of all.

Onward they dashed along the road.

Their own camps were visible in the distance.

The nearer they approached the more certain they felt their companions had been set upon.

This was put beyond doubt when they approached still nearer and nearer.

They could hear the Austrians shouting.

The report of fire-arms, and the bright flash, was visible on every hand.

## CHAPTER XXV.

If ever the blood of English boys was aroused, it was on the present occasion.

"Now, comrades, to the charge!" cried Frank, his eyes flashing with the stern joy of battle. "Upon them! First powder, and then steel! Blench not, for the honour of old England! Viva Garibaldi! Morte ai Tedesche! Death to the Austrian tyrants! Huzza!"

"Huzza!" shouted the Boy Band, rushing along in a cloud of dust, amid which their bright swords gleamed like lightning flashes in the sulphury thunder cloud.

A roar of artillery, and a long, sharp crackle of musketry.

Suddenly the youthful cavalcade reined in their galloping horses.

"He is struck! he falls!" was gasped from every lip.

A clot of crimson appears on Frank's noble brow.

His horse caracoles; then the noble youth reels back in the saddle, and the next instant he is rolled in the dust.

ANNETTE SAVES THE LIFE OF FRANK FORD.

Mark leapt off his horse and in a moment had his young captain in his arms. "How goes it, Frank," said he, tenderly. "Are you badly hurt?"

"I think not," replied Frank, faintly, as they placed him beneath a tree; then, rising up he shouted, "Onward, lads, to the rescue of our brave boys, or all may be lost."

But for a moment let us explain what took place during Frank's absence from the camp.

* * * * *

As we have seen, a party of the Boy Soldiers had started out on a night adventure, or "a glorious raid;" but before they got home to camp again, as we know, they had gone through very perilous and daring scenes.

They did not expect, or even imagine that the Austrians knew where the Boy's camp was pitched; but this was discovered in a manner to be afterwards explained.

Long before Frank and his companions galloped to the rescue, their young companions had sustained a terrible onslaught by thrice their own number of the enemy.

The Austrians, perhaps, thought to achieve a very easy victory over the few boy soldiers in camp when they attacked them; but were miserably mistaken.

Frank, before he started on his night adventure, had collected six waggons, and with them formed a square sort of barricade.

"I don't think that any of you will be disturbed

until our return," said he; "but it is better to be prepared for all chances."

When the alarm *was* raised the wisdom of young Captain Frank's foresight was apparent.

All the young volunteers hastened to this rallying point.

They had plenty of spare arms with them, such as revolvers and rifles, and following the orders of Dick Fellows, all these spare weapons were doubly loaded, and placed close at hand ready for instant use.

The Austrians did not come on boldly with trumpets sounding, but stole into the camps as quietly as possible.

They looked around everywhere; but nowhere could they see any of the Boy Soldiers.

The Austrian commandant was puzzled.

"Where had the young Garibaldians retreated to?" he thought, as he brought up a full squadron right into the middle of the camp, and looked around annoyed at being foiled.

He had not long to wait for an answer.

All at once, and when least expected, Dick Fellows whispered to the boys,

"Now, lads, take good aim. Keep your heads low, and at the word, fire."

"Are you all ready?" he said.

"Yes," was the answer.

"Fire!"

No sooner said than done.

On the instant a terrific volley was poured into the Austrians.

All sides of the waggon barricade seemed suddenly lit up, and was vomiting fire and shot into the Austrians.

The enemy, although taken by surprise, were no cowards, and fired away with hearty goodwill and loud shouts.

Their shots, however, never hit the boys.

All the harm done was to knock splinters out of the waggons, behind which the young soldiers were concealed.

On horseback as they were, the Austrians hoped in some way to break down the barricade; but they could not.

"Surrender! surrender!" the Austrian officer shouted, in stentorian tones, "or we will exterminate every one of you."

A loud shout of derision was the only answer, as Dick Fellows, flag in hand, stood upright in the midst of the boys, and said aloud,

"English boys, never surrender! Hurrah! for Garibaldi and liberty!"

The combat had now lasted about twenty minutes, when the Austrians, finding they had lost many men, resolved to bring into action a light cannon which carried a six-pound shot.

"We'll soon smash down their barricade," said they, in boast.

One of their men galloped off, and soon returned, followed by the cannon.

"Surrender, lads, surrender!" the Austrian officer shouted again. "We don't want to kill you; throw down your arms!"

"Never!" was the answer.

"Then," said he to the artillery-men, "load, and fire rapidly; we'll soon demolish their rotten waggons; the pistol and sabre will do the rest."

It was at this exact moment, when loading their cannon, that Frank and his party arrived on the scene to the rescue at a furious gallop.

* * * * *

With swords flashing in the twilight of morning, the boys, now led on by Mark, dashed in upon the Austrians, shouting,

"Garibaldi for ever!"

The Austrians, taken in the rear by the gallant young soldiers, were amazed and panic-stricken.

They knew not for a moment what to do.

With firm resolves to conquer or die they met the onslaught with coolness and bravery.

The combat was now terrific.

With shouts and yells the Austrians tried to escape, after losing more than half their number, but they knew not which way to go.

They madly dashed in one direction; but when about to reach the road, near where the mail coach now stood, the Fat Boy blew a terrific blast upon a cavalry trumpet he had found in the carriage.

"Right about," shouted the Austrians; "these imps of the devil are calling up reinforcements; we shall be all cut to pieces if we attempt to retreat by that road!"

Panic-stricken, they wheeled right about, just in time to meet Mark and his band, who were now at their heels galloping in mad pursuit.

Another clash of swords, and another terrific running fight ensued.

Whichever way the Austrians tried to flee they met with obstacles.

Left to themselves and without any support the artillery-men were unable to protect their gun, and so abandoned it and fled.

One brave fellow did not run, however, and he was a sergeant.

With a valour worthy of a better cause he remained by the cannon, and was about to spike it so as to render it useless to its captors.

He had the spike in the touch-hole, and, with hammer in hand, was on the point of driving it home, when a well-directed shot from young Buttons hit him, and knocked the hammer from his hand!

"Now's our time, boys!" said Buttons, who was on foot, his horse having been shot from under him. "Now's our time, boys; some of you come out of the barricade, and help me to load it. We'll give the Austrians a rare warming in a minute!"

With a cheer several of the boys ran to his assistance.

With nimbleness the boys loaded the cannon with grape shot.

"Don't fire till we see those flying Austrians well clear of our boys; let me touch it off."

So saying, Buttons seized the strap which pulled the hammer down on the percussion cap, and waited a moment to watch a good opportunity.

It was not long in coming.

Mark and his brave boys had cut off the enemy's retreat by every road save by crossing the river!

This the Austrians perceived, and they madly galloped towards the stream.

At that instant Master Buttons levelled his cannon and took good aim.

"Now for it. Stand aside, boys; here's at 'em!"

On the instant he vigorously pulled the hammer down on the cap.

Next moment a terrific roar ensued, and grape shot flew into the enemy's ranks, cutting horsemen down like so many dry twigs!

"That's our parting to 'em," said Buttons. "They won't trouble us again in a hurry; at all events, not to-night We'll now have a bit of grub in peace, eh, Fatty?"

"I believe, you my boy," said Fatty, in a weary manner.

"Tired to death," the boy band were too much of soldiers to neglect any precaution.

"They have found us out," said Mark, "and we

must get out of this place as soon as possible; the whole Austrian army confronts us across the river. Stuff your havresacks full of food," he said, "empty the barrel of wine into your canteens, pack the waggons with all haste; we must retreat. We are too weak to stay here; the Austrians will be over here in thousands to-morrow, you'll find."

Although some did not much like this order to retire they followed out the orders to the letter.

Fatty was annoyed, but crammed *two* havresacks full of "grub," as he called it, and stuffed his stomach almost to suffocation as well, not forgetting "to pay his very particular respects," as he said, to the barrel of wine.

In less than half an hour the young volunteers struck their tents, packed their waggons, and were soon far from the river, in high glee at their late gallant exploits.

Not all, however, left the spot.

Dick, Mark, Hugh Tracy, and Buttons remained behind with the captured cannon.

"They will be sure to treat us to a cannonade from the other side shortly," said Mark, "and as we must protect our retreat we will give them as good as we get."

In a trice these four brave boys commenced to work with picks and shovels in gallant style.

The trees were large, thick, and numerous on the top of the river bank.

Mark selected a place where two large oak trees stood about two yards apart.

In front of these for about three feet he and the other boys rapidly raised a breastwork of solid earth.

A place was cut out in the middle of this earth-work for the muzzle of their cannon to work in.

"Now, Buttons," said Mark, "where did you place the four horses?"

"Behind a clump of trees not far off, but out of danger. As we will have to gallop after the boys rather rapidly I placed eight instead of four horses, that I thought would be better."

"Just so; eight horses will gallop along with this light cannon like lightning; all four of us, however, must turn drivers. Load up the gun, lads!"

This was quickly done by Mark, Hugh, and Buttons, who put in a twelve-pound rifle shell.

"We shan't have to wait long before the Austrians begin to shell us, you'll find," said Mark.

Nor had they.

Those who managed to escape across the river from the combat, informed the general in command of all that had happened.

This defeat so enraged him that he opened fire across the stream upon what had but just been the boys' camp.

Shells came whizzing overhead and through the trees in quick succession, bursting luckily many yards from where the boys were.

"Hadn't we better return the compliment?" said Hugh, impatiently.

"Not yet," said Mark, spy-glass in hand. "Let them waste as much powder and shell as they like, they can't hurt us; we are well protected in front by the trees and our earth-work; they will get tired after a bit, and we shall be fresh, you know."

Still came the Austrians' shells screaming over-head, and bursting with great noisy explosion right on the ground where their tents had lately stood.

"They would have peppered us awfully, if we hadn't got out of the way," said Buttons; "Captain Frank was here to give 'em a dose of pills in re-turn."

"Don't be in any hurry, Buttons, my boy," said Mark; "our brave young commander will lead us on again, and I am only waiting for a good oppor-tunity; *you* can't see what they are up to, but *I* can."

The truth was that his spy-glass enabled Mark to perceive a group of mounted officers on the other side, standing near some ammunition waggons.

"Now," said Mark, "since they have nearly done, we'll give 'em a parting salute to remember us by; but, mark me, lads, directly the shot is fired, jump to your gun, ease it down the bank, and then pull away until we get to the thicket where our horses are."

"Just so, Mark; take good aim."

Buttons need not have said this, for Mark took deliberate aim at the group of officers standing near the ammunition waggons.

"Now I've covered them nicely," said he. "Dick and Hugh, take a wheel each to prevent too much recoil."

Saying this, he touched off the cannon.

A sudden roar.

A meteor-like object circled through the air, and descended plump among the waggons.

In a second a terrific explosion took place.

He had struck the ammunition waggons!

The very earth seemed to shake under their feet.

"Got 'em *that* time," said Buttons, with a chuckle, as they eased the cannon out of its place, and dragged it along towards the place where the horses were concealed.

It was well that they had been so quick, for the cannon had not been out of its place more than two minutes when the Austrians opened fire again from half-a-dozen guns, and tore up the little earth-work all to pieces.

Crash!—whiz!—bang! went their shells in all directions, smashing trees and shrubs with terrific force.

But in less than five minutes the four Boy Soldiers had harnessed their horses to their gun, and each acting as driver to two animals, they went tearing away after their retreating comrades, laugh-ing at their glorious action.

## CHAPTER XXVI.

THE MOUNTAIN CHIEF—ALARM OF THE BANDITTI —TREACHERY AT WORK—THE DEED OF BLOOD —THE ALARM OF AGNESE.

THE drug which Agnese had used proved powerful beyond expectation.

It was several hours before Basil the Bandit, and his swarthy band, recovered consciousness.

The first to do so was Basil himself.

He yawned, stretched himself, and then thoroughly awoke.

"Hillo!" said he, rubbing his eyes, "Hillo! how is this? Where are all the youngsters gone to, eh? Why, here are all my favourite men drunk. Ha! ha! Ah! I understand now, my chief man, Cavolti, has secured the young English strangers, put them in some place of safety, and then returned to finish the frolic among ourselves. Yet I didn't drink much," Basil mused; "but still my head aches fit to split in halves."

He struck the table heavily.

His daughter Agnese appeared.

"Bring me a draught of wine," said he, "and of the best, mind. My vitals are all on fire."

Agnese brought in and poured out for her father a goblet of the best wine, which he drank off at a single draught.

"Ah!" said he, "that's cooling and pleasant.

You can leave me—but stay. In what part of the cavern are the young strangers sleeping?"

"I know not, father."

"Did not Cavolti place them in a safe spot, then?"

"I know not, father; but suppose he did, for he always obeys your orders punctually."

"Of course."

"You and the strangers were singing loudly, and as you all appeared merry, and were all served with wine, I and Annette retired to rest."

"Quite right, quite right. You may go. Well, this has been a pretty bout, surely," said Basil, as he got up and walked about. "Why, here are all my men fast asleep around me, and snoring like young elephants. Ha! ha! It was lucky the Austrians did not attack us in this state last night."

With his foot he kicked several of his men, who awoke with staring eyes.

"Cavolti, come, rouse up! Awake! No more of this drunkenness. We must be up and doing. Cavolti, I say, awake!"

Basil's chief officer did awake, and was surprised to find that he, like many others, had rolled off his chair on to the floor, and there had lain huddled up like so many pigs in a pen.

"How is this?" said Cavolti, rubbing his eyes.

"Aye!" said Basil, laughing. "I suppose those young Englishmen must have been giving us a lesson in deep drinking, eh, Cavolti?"

"The English youths!" said Cavolti, rubbing his eyes, and looking around him wildly. "Oh! now I remember all; but where——"

"Ha!" said Basil, taking him aside; "that is the question I was about to ask you; where are they?"

"Where?" asked Cavolti, looking puzzled and fearful.

"Where, aye, where? Surely you must know something about them. If *I* was drunk and neglected them, surely *you* did not. Are they confined, or did you finish them all off at once with the cordial?"

"I know nothing of them," said Cavolti. "I have no more recollection of what took place last night than an idiot."

"What?" said Basil, with an angry oath, "a band of young desperate strangers among us, and you not know what has become of them?"

"I do not," said Cavolti; "but I dare say they are safe somewhere in the cave; they could not escape, for they could never find out the right path."

"That may be; but I very much doubt it," said Basil. "Am I to understand you know nothing of them?"

"I do not."

"Then you are no longer worthy to be my officer, Cavolti," said Basil. "Your life shall be the forfeit if they are not found."

"Be it so," was the calm reply. "You gave me no orders concerning them."

"Liar!" said Basil, fearfully angered, "liar!"

"Basil," said Cavolti, "you are my chief, and I should not reply; but, let me tell you, that no other man should call me liar and live."

"Ah! you threaten me, then, eh? What, treason and treachery at work! Men, sieze him!" said Basil.

Four men instantly obeyed.

"Now, Cavolti," said Basil, "your life is at stake, remember, if those youths are not found within an hour. Take him away and confine him in the strong room."

"Basil," said Cavolti, with a grinning lip, "you choose, then, to disgrace and degrade me before your own men, and for no cause. When next you wake up from a drunken sleep, you will think differently of me, and may repent."

"Take him away. Search for those youths in every hole and corner. Quick! Fly!" said he, waving his hand in angry command.

Cavolti was borne along by the four men, who took him along a wide stone passage towards the strong room.

Basil walked up and down the large banqueting hall, striking his forehead.

His whole band was now thoroughly aroused.

The caverns were searched far and wide, but not a trace could be found of the missing youths.

"Fled!" gasped Basil, white with rage, as reports were continually brought to him to that effect, "one of my men murdered before the main gate! Now, by heaven, deep, dark treachery is among us, and Cavolti shall suffer!"

Basil at that instant heard a slight noise in the adjoining passage that he could not understand.

In an instant after, the door was burst open right in front of where stood the bandit chief!

Cavolti dashed in, looking wild, haggard, and ferocious.

A blood-red sword was in his hand!

For a moment Basil looked stupefied, as if he beheld a ghastly spectre before him.

"What, Cavolti returned, and bloody!" he said, whipping out his sword, "and confronts me thus in defiance!"

"Four lifeless bodies lie in the passage," said Cavolti, bursting with rage, "and I come to add a *fifth* one. Your band is in revolt; I am King of the Mountains!"

"Fool!" said Basil, dashing at Cavolti; "you may have conquered four, but not *me*. Have at you, villain!"

In a trice Cavolti knocked the sword out of Basil's hand.

They clutched each other's throats, knives in hand.

The struggle was short and desperate.

They breathed hard, like two tigers in deadly embrace.

A dagger was uplifted, and flashed in the light.

In a second more all would be over.

Bang!

The report of a pistol was heard from behind the curtain.

## CHAPTER XXVII.

### NIGHT VULTURES.

Frank, however, was not alone on the battle-field.

Young Sam Bennet, who had also been wounded during the fight, was likewise left behind.

The Boy Soldiers had put Frank in a safe place during the latter part of the battle, but he crawled away towards a small spring to quench his thirst, and there remained.

Hence, when they came to look for him, he was nowhere to be found.

Supposing that he had been carried off by some of the party the boys retreated from the field, and did not discover their mistake until it was too late.

Thus the gallant young leader of the boy band was left through mistake, and in the darkness that overhung all with his young comrade Sam Bennet.

When morning began to break the clouds were thick and dark.

Lightning flashed through the murky skies, and thunders rolled.

Heavy, drenching rain began to fall, and it seemed as if the very heavens were about to deluge the earth.

This was greatly refreshing to the two wounded boys, who in different parts of the field lay huddled up, and perfectly unconscious of each other's presence there.

Frank, with a blood-stained brow, and a bullet wound in his left arm, was unable to move.

Sam Bennet had been hit in the thigh by a spent ball.

He also was unable to stir.

But, even during the drenching showers that fell all around him, Sam Bennet's quick ear detected the distant moaning of some wounded man.

Again and again he raised himself on his elbow, and looked about him to the right and left to see wherever it might proceed.

"Some wounded Austrian," thought Sam. "I'm glad our boys have left none of our party behind except me, for I have no doubt if these Austrian camp followers should happen to fall across any lads they would murder them on the spot."

He little thought that the moaning proceeded from Frank.

But it did.

Poor Frank was desperately hurt, and was almost if not entirely unconscious.

"Hang their stupid heads," said Sam, half aloud, "they have gone off and left me here alone; "it's through mistake, I know, but that don't make my situation any the less miserable and dangerous; but I dare say some of them will soon return when they miss me."

With such thoughts Sam Bennet tied up his wounded thigh, and tried again to scan the battle-field in order to discover who it might be that was groaning.

He raised himself on his elbow, but could discover nothing.

The truth was that a slight indentation of the ground concealed Frank from view.

"I wish I could only walk," thought Sam. "I dare say it's some poor devil of an Austrian, dying, perhaps, for a cup of water."

Towards the evening stars began to twinkle in the eastern sky long before the heavy clouds finally drifted from the scene.

Still at intervals he could hear the same distant moaning.

He listened again and again.

It sounds like the voice of a boy.

"What if it should turn out to be one of our band, though," he said. "I wonder who it can be. Surely they haven't left any one but me behind!"

These and such like thoughts puzzled and tormented the brave lad's mind.

Ere long, however, his eyes and thoughts were directed in another way.

In the distance he perceived an old, haggard woman, slowly looking about the battle-field.

She was followed at a short distance by a villanous-looking rascal, dressed and muffled up in a long, black cloak, and broad-brimmed slouching hat.

A cold sweat was on Sam's brow as he thought—

"They are 'Night Vultures,' come to rob and strip the dead—and the living, also, if they get the chance! I will be prepared for them."

Luckily, his rifle was close at hand.

He loaded very carefully and slyly, in order not to be perceived.

"They always come armed, I'm told; and if they fall across a half dying man, they make no scruple about giving him a taste of their daggers. But they shan't catch *me* asleep. I've heard too much about them long before this. Captain Frank has often spoken of this thing, and to be aware of drinking anything they offer; for if a fellow only happens to have a watch, a ring, or a few shillings in his pocket, they think nothing of poisoning him for it, the cursed wretches,—'Night Vultures' they are aptly called—but they must take care, or I'll do for one of 'em, if not for two, if they come near me!"

The old hag slowly moved to and fro about the battle-field, followed at a short distance by the unknown, murderous-looking villain.

They approached a spot about midway where Frank and Sam lay.

"Stop," said the villain, to the hag, "did you not hear distant moans? Listen again."

"I do," was the croaking reply; "and it sounds like the voice of a youth."

"Of a youth?" said the villain, with glistening eyes.

"Yes, I cannot be mistaken."

"If it should only be *him!*" was the quick, impassioned reply.

"Who?" asked the hag, with a low chuckle.

"It matters not. I dare say you would not feel very scrupulous about whoever it was, so he had a well-filled purse and a watch."

"Not I; no, not a bit," was the harsh reply. "I only wish I *could* stumble across such a one. But what makes you so anxious about these Boy Garibaldians?"

"That's my business," said the villain, gruffly. "But, hark! there are the groans again."

"I heard them plainly that time. Let us go and see."

"The bloodthirsty hounds!" said Sam. "They are bent on murder. I wonder who it can be that is moaning so? I'll watch them closely."

As he spoke he saw the old hag hobble across the field followed by her dark companion.

They did not go far ere she stopped and turned towards the villain.

"He moves, he breathes," she said, in a soft voice.

And so Frank did.

He was lying unconscious, with his head resting on a small mound of earth, and with his eyes closed.

Near him lay his cap and one of the Austrian drums that had been broken and left behind.

"'Tis he!" said the villain, with glittering eyes, pointing to the wounded youth, "'tis he!"

"What would ye have me do?" said the woman, with a croaking voice. and a dry, hurried laugh.

"Despatch him!" said the villain. "Strike him to the heart! No one sees us; you shall be well paid! Despatch him, I say!"

"Is he your enemy?"

"It matters not now to tell; no time must be lost. Despatch him, drive your long dagger through his throbbing heart! I hear the approach of distant horsemen. Quick, I say, quick! He is my worst enemy! let your dagger sink deep into his vile heart—he is my life-long foe!"

With upraised weapon the hag of the battle-field stood over the prostrate boy, in the act of dealing a death blow.

On the instant was heard the crack of a rifle.

With a loud scream, the woman threw up her hands, dropped the dagger, and fell to the earth—dead!

Sam Bennet had raised himself from the ground, and watched them.

He leaned against a waggon-wheel for support.

Directly he saw the upraised dagger about to descend, he fired.

The bullet struck her to the heart.

Sam fell to the earth again, prostrate from fatigue and pain. *

## CHAPTER XXVIII.

THE TREACHEROUS GUIDE—ADVENTURES IN THE MOUNTAINS IN SEARCH OF FRANK AND SAM BENNET—THE TRAITOR'S SHOT—THE TERRIBLE FALL INTO THE PRECIPICE.

THE unexpected shot, and the old hag's piercing scream as she fell dead, caused the cloaked villain to tremble with fear.

He hastily turned, and looked about him right and left.

No one was visible.

In terror he fled hastily away.

He would have stayed, perhaps, to accomplish his desperate purpose.

But at that moment several Austrian horsemen galloped on the field.

The craven-hearted scoundrel, whoever he was, seemed surprised at the sudden appearance of the Austrian horsemen upon the field, and he vanished in the darkness.

Several of the soldiers dismounted, and one proved to be a surgeon.

He looked here and there, and attended to more than one poor wounded fellow, who had been thus long neglected.

After a time, the moans of Frank arrested his attention.

He hastened to the spot, and was much struck by the handsome features of the disabled youth.

"Why, how comes this?" said the kind-hearted man. "Surely our men couldn't have been fighting with a band of boys last night?"

"Boys, eh, sir?" said one, grimly smiling; "if you'd only seen how they fought you wouldn't think them boys; they assailed us like young demons."

For some time the surgeon couldn't realise the fact that the Garibaldians were mere boys, and listened with amazement to the various adventurous stories told about them.

"And who can this youth be?" he asked.

"I should think that this youth must be some officer among them, judging by his appearance; perhaps it may be the young captain himself, for all we know."

"If so, you have made a lucky prize, then," said the surgeon. "There, bear him off the field, I have dressed his wound; a little rest and good hospital care will soon revive him."

Four men, with a portable stretcher of canvas, gently lifted Frank from the ground, and bore him away towards the river, where a boat was moored ready to bear him across.

In about half-an-hour, and after tending and carrying away a few of their own men who were disabled, the Austrians were about to depart.

Sam Bennet saw all that passed, but was not aware who the youth was he had seen carried away on the canvas stretcher.

He was afraid of being discovered himself.

He had more than once heard of the dreadful loathsome dungeons into which prisoners were cast.

But just when he thought they had missed him, a man stood by his side.

"Hullo, young 'un," said the gruff soldier; "we nearly missed you—hullo, comrades; hullo!" he shouted. "Here's another young Garabaldian here."

Sam was sadly disappointed at thus being discovered.

But there was no help for it.

It was useless to offer resistance, and in less than five minutes he was surrounded, and the surgeon very busy probing his thigh for the bullet.

This was a very painful operation, but Sam did not flinch.

He kept his countenance, and even smiled at some good-humoured remarks made by the docter.

"You stand all this probing manly, my lad," said the man of medicine, with a smile.

"Do I? La, that's nothing. I never felt it."

"Didn't you?"

"No, not a bit. We English boys can stand any amount of suffering without grumbling, when we like."

"I wish our soldiers could then; but I suppose you English are made of different stuff to other people?"

"Yes," said Sam; "made out of a mixture of leather, cast-iron, and gun-metal! Our captain is made up of solid steel."

The docter could not afford to be out-witted by such a mere youth, and so ordered him off to the boat, whither he was quickly carried.

Judge of his surprise when he discovered his young captain on board also.

* * * * * *

We will now follow the hasty footsteps of the villain who fled from the battle-field when the soldiers arrived.

He was foiled and defeated in his purpose.

He retired to a neighbouring wood.

A horse was tied up there.

In a few moments he was galloping away as hard as possible in the direction the boy band had taken when they retreated.

He had not gone far when he perceived in the distance the approach of two mounted youths, dressed like Garibaldians.

They were Hugh Tracy and Dick Fellows.

In a moment the black villain threw off his long cloak, and other disguises, and appeared in a red shirt, and in every way equipped like a true Garibaldian.

"Halt!" said he, to the two approaching youths, cocking a pistol.

"Who cries halt!" said Hugh and Dick, in a challenging tone. "Who and what are you, that you thus dare obstruct our pathway?"

"I am a Garibaldian, and have special business here."

"A Garibaldian! well, then, so are we."

"That remains to be proved, before I allow you to pass. I am on guard here."

"Well, then, we are two officers of the Boy Band, and are returning to the battle-field at the risk of our lives, to search for——"

"Your young captain, I suppose?"

"Yes; but how came you to know that?"

"Me? Ha! ha! my friends, you are but children yet in the art of war. I not only know him but can tell you more. He is in the hands of the Austrians—a prisoner!"

"A prisoner!"

"Yes; and is at this moment confined in a pass in the mountains yonder."

"Impossible! how came you to know this?"

"I have been to the battle-field since the fight, by the special orders of General Garibaldi, to see that none of you were left behind, and also to spy out the strength and position of the Austrian camp

* See Illustration No. 7.

across the river. While doing this I learned all about it."

"And where is this place in which he is confined?" they asked, quickly.

"It is useless to tell you, for it is so well-guarded at the mouth, that not a cat could pass without it was in Austrian uniform."

"You know, then, where he is confined?"

"I do. His wound, I heard, was but a slight one after all. It merely stunned him."

"I am sorry we made such a mistake as not to seek him before we left the field," said Hugh, sorrowfully.

"They will murder him by inches if the Austrians only find out who and what he is; I fear they will cast him into some loathsome dungeon there to die of starvation," said Dick, sorrowfully; "but we one and all, lose our lives or rescue our brave Frank."

The villain smiled, as he said,

"It is possible he may escape yet."

"Not without aid."

"But you can render that. You don't mind a little danger and expense?"

"No; neither. Our life for Frank Ford."

"Then I'll tell you what we'll do."

"What do you propose—to show me the mountain pass?"

"Yes; more than that."

"What then?"

"I will assist you."

"Brave," said Hugh, saking him warmly by the hand; "you are a true Garibaldian."

"Yes, and will prove myself such by assisting the escape of your bold brave English chief."

"But I must tell you," said the stranger, "before we proceed further in this desperate adventure, that it will not do for both of you to go."

"Not both of us! Why not?" asked Dick Fellows, quickly. "Why not both of us, pray?"

"Simply for this reason," said the dark stranger. "Two of us could well manage the business; but if three were discovered prowling about the mountain pass, it would excite suspicion."

The dark stranger's manner was so plausible that Hugh Tracy at once acceded to the proposition.

Dick, however, was much displeased.

"What, go alone on this terrible venture?" he said, half aloud, in English.

"Yes, why not?"

"I fear the stranger may deceive us both," said Dick. "His words and manner are plausible enough; but there is a something in his sparkling eye, and restless twitching of the mouth, that I do not like."

"Oh, fear not," said Hugh, gaily, "you haven't seen as much of these Italians as I have. What say you, shall I go?"

"No," said Dick, "not without me."

"Then will you go alone?"

"Not without you, Hugh!" said Dick.

"Three would excite suspicion, roaming about the mountains, and so near to the Austrian fort too."

"Well, as you please, Hugh," said Dick. "If you *will* go, of course there is no altering your determination; but, as to me, I fear the Italian. He may not be a Garibaldian after all."

"Think you he would expose himself to any stray shot by wearing the red shirt, then? Trust me, Dick, he *is* a Garibaldian, and a right good sturdy one also, if I'm not much mistaken."

So, after many words of warning, Hugh resolved to go alone with the guide, and "trust to luck."

"Never fear for me, Dick," said Hugh. "I am well armed, and if he does mean me any harm he will get more than he gives," said Hugh, in a whisper, aside.

The guide did not understand one word of English, so he listened to the conversation without profit.

But while they were talking apart, he narrowly scanned the features of the two youths in hopes of gleaning some information.

He was much mistaken, however.

Hugh and Dick were particular not to disclose their thoughts or intentions to the stranger by a single look or gesture.

Hugh Tracy and the guide departed.

Dick Fellows retraced his steps, and waved his hand in token of "good luck," but he had not gone far when he halted behind a ledge of rocks by the roadside.

"I do not like the looks of this new-found friend," said he, "and will follow at a distance; they shall not observe me, and if the guide does mean treachery he shall not live long to repent it, if there's any strength left in my good right hand to slay him."

Directly the guide and Hugh departed, Dick tied up his horse in the forest with a long rope so as to give the animal a good length of tether to feed, and he followed the two fast retreating figures.

"What does the black-looking devil want to be looking back so often for?" thought Dick, and this confirmed him all the more in his resolution to follow so as to be close at hand in case of danger.

"Where is this place where the Austrians have confined our young captain?" said Hugh. "Is it far?"

"No, not very far," said the guide; "we shall reach it in an hour or two."

"But in what direction?"

"Yonder," said the guide, pointing to a lofty group of mountains.

"Why, the highway to Vienna runs through them. I perceive even now the broad white tracks of the coach road.

"You are right," was the guide's reply. "It is one of the many military roads which the Austrians have cut through the mountains, and it saves a day's journey or more on the distance to Vienna."

"Yes, true; I have heard of these military roads before."

"The entrance is only fifty feet wide, and the outlet is not so broad. There is a large, strong party of soldiers always on guard at both entrances, night and day, and, as I have said before, not a cat would be permitted to pass by the house at either end without it was in Austrian uniform.

"Then how shall *we* manage to escape them?"

"Oh, leave that to me," said the guide, grinning; "there's more ways than one. I have often descended into that little valley before, and by a means the white coats little dream of."

"Ha! indeed, how is that?" said Hugh. "You must be a brave fellow."

"Well, as to that, there may be two opinions, you know. That I *am* brave, and well worthy of confidence is plain, or otherwise General Garibaldi wouldn't trust me with such important messages as he does."

"How did you manage to escape them? They would have shot you on the spot if you were discovered."

"I know that," was the dry reply, "but I never intend that they *shall* discover me. And yet I often go there for pleasure."

"For pleasure! and run the risk of being killed?"

"Pleasure! yes, why not?" said the guide, laughing. "Have you never heard of love?"

"Love! of course I have," said Hugh, laughing.

"Well, then, it is love which takes me there."

"Not of the Austrians, surely?"

"No; but love of a very pretty maiden who lives in that valley. Leander swam the Hellespont to see his sweetheart, and I, an humble imitator, often jeopardize my life to kneel for a moment at the feet of her I adore."

These words were uttered in a tone of so much genuine passion that Hugh was now more firmly convinced of the good faith of his guide than ever.

"They call the place Val Verde," said the guide, "or Green Valley. It is so healthy that the Austrians often send their wounded men here, your young captain is here also. When he is partially recovered they will send him on to Vienna, and cast him into some loathsome dungeon."

But, though Hugh and the guide were very chatty, the young soldier always kept himself on his guard against any treachery.

For this purpose he walked his horse several yards from his guide, and with his hand upon a pistol ready to draw and fire if need be.

This the guide perceived, but did not take any notice.

He smiled often, moreover, as he from time to time turned his head and always found Hugh a few yards behind him.

"How did you manage to elude the Austrian guards and see your sweetheart?" asked Hugh.

"Oh, simply enough, my brave young stranger; easily enough when you've tried it once."

On top of one of these lofty rocks, and near the edge of the precipice, stands an immense old oak."

"Well?"

"In times past, the mountaineers used to have a favourite sport of hunting for eagle nests."

"I understand."

"And for this purpose were wont to tie a long, thick rope to the old oak, and thus descend to the various ledges and shelvings of the rocks below."

"A good plan. I have heard of that method before."

"I discovered this rope, and often descended, and, when down as far as I could go, I found an excellent foothold, and thus descended by the goat track to the valley unperceived. Now you understand?"

"I do."

"And it is by this same means you and I will descend."

"Bravo!" said Hugh, delighted. "The idea is a capital one! If we only find out where poor Frank is, and rescue him, you shall have the biggest purse of money you ever had in your life!"

Chatting thus, Huch Tracy and his guide journeyed along for many miles.

The night was dark, and the moon's rising would not take place till long past midnight.

Cautiously and slowly they picked their way up the mountain side until it was no longer safe to ride.

The guide and Hugh now dismounted, and tied their horses to trees, and proceeded on their journey on foot.

They approached the entrance to the mountain gorge, and could see the Austrians on guard.

"I told you it would be impossible to think of passing in that way," said the guide.

Hugh was convinced of it.

On each side of the entrance to the gorge in the mountains Austrian watch fires and picket stations were placed, and the glimmer of their red logs sparkled in the darkness like so many stars.

Up the mountain they toiled until at last they reached the old oak tree spoken of by the guide.

The rope was there coiled up ready for use, and hidden from view by low brushwood and brambles.

It was stout and thick, but to all appearance had not been used for a long time, despite all the guide had said to the contrary.

They peeped over the side of the precipice, and in the valley below could see several small villages.

Hugh saw the place indicated, and was anxious to descend at once.

"Don't think of it yet for an hour or two; we are both weary and tired with climbing so far; let us have an hour's sleep; we will then be refreshed and ready for the descent; the ascent afterwards will try all your strength to the utmost."

Hugh did not object, but in his own mind he determined not to go to sleep at all.

"I don't know who nor what this fellow may prove to be," said he; "but in case he is treacherously inclined, as Dick imagines, I'll have a cat's sleep—with one eye open."

Throwing himself upon the ground the guide was soon fast asleep.

He began to snore loudly and heavily.

"Suppose I descend alone," thought Hugh.

Acting up to this idea Hugh Tracy rose from his seat very quietly, and, as he thought, unperceived.

He went to the edge of the precipice, and buckled up his sword and straps tightly.

"It isn't far to the first ledge of rocks," said he, "I see the goat track beyond, I will try it at once."

With a sword slung to his wrist he seized the rope and slowly descended.

"This isn't much after all," thought the gallant lad.

He had not gone far, however, when the guide appeared at the edge of the precipice.

His eyes glared wildly as he saw the youth quietly descending below.

In a moment he also seized the rope and followed.

His descent was much more rapid than young Hugh's.

"I was trying the rope, comrade," said Hugh. "It is strong enough for half a dozen men."

"I'm glad you think so," was the calm reply; "but I thought I might as well accompany you."

"Why?"

"Oh, nothing," said the guide; "mere fancy. Do you know who I am?" said he, with eyes twinkling with villany.

"A friend."

"As you please; I'm one of Basil's Band!"

"What! Basil the or——?"

"Just so."

"And what mean you? For heaven's sake, speak!"

"Life for life is our motto," said the ruffian, with a harsh laugh.

"You surely cannot mean to murder me?"

"I do, though," was the quick response.

In an instant he drew a pistol, and fired full into the youth's face.

With a loud shout of agony Hugh threw up his hands.

He fell from the rope headlong below.*

---

* See Engraving in No. 9.

# THE BOY SOLDIER;

## OR, GARIBALDI'S YOUNG CAPTAIN.

FRANK FORD CUTS OFF THE HEAD OF CAVO L 1I.

### CHAPTER XXIX.

TREACHERY—THE FATAL SHOT—VENGEANCE AT HAND—THE DEADLY DUEL.

At the instant he fired, although the ruffian did not perceive it, the figure of a second youth, sword in hand, was perceived some two hundred yards away on the edge of the precipice above.

"Ha! ha!" said the villain, "how nicely I entrapped this English youth; but they little dream of what an Italian's cunning is. Ha! ha! If he was not killed by my bullet, the fall would crush him to pieces. That's *one* of them—ha! ha! Would that I might finish my night's work by falling across the other lad."

With the nimbleness of a monkey he climbed the rope again.

He had scarcely pulled himself up to the edge of the rock, when he was startled to perceive the figure of a youth running towards him at full speed.

"Fortune favours me," the villain said. "I have been watched and dodged by this miserable boy."

In an instant he drew his heavy cavalry sword, and rushed at the youth approaching.

"Villain! bloodthirsty coward!" gasped Dick

Fellows, sword in hand. "I knew that your intentions were treacherous, but never dreamed you could have behaved so cruelly. I followed at a distance, and watched you. Oh! would to heaven I had been nearer to have saved poor Hugh's life!"

"Foolish boy!" said the ruffian, with a smile of scorn, "why throw yourself in the path of your direst foe? As your captain slew one of Basil's men, so have I one of young Ford's followers. 'Tis nought but life for life. Begone, I say! or I may dye my hands in your blood."

"Insolent knave!" said Dick Fellows, bravely, "Cowardly scoundrel! think you that an English boy heeds your poisoned words? Stand on guard, I say! I would not murder an unresisting man."

"You? A boy slay one of Basil's men? Ha! ha! Fool that you are. I have been well tried in battle ere now; but never, until this moment, have I ever allowed a youth to prate to me thus. Have at you, English whelp!"

"Thank heaven for this," said Dick, dashing at his tall opponent.

The bandit rushed at Dick, and had not the stroke been warded off, he would have been cut in twain.

With the nimbleness of a dancing master, however, young Dick stepped aside, avoided the blow, and next instant drew blood from the bandit's left arm.

With an awful oath, which hissed between his clenched teeth, the black-looking villain, with eyes flashing deadly fire, stood grinning like a hyena at his calm and handsome opponent.

Dick, with all the composure of an excellent swordsman, and without uttering a word, waited for the villain's rush.

It soon came.

With a mad bound like the sudden rush of an infuriated bull, the disguised bandit leaped upon his antagonist.

Again did he miss his aim.

Once more was his blow warded off by Dick with a smile of triumph.

It was an affair of life or death.

Each one felt this, and made up their minds for the worst.

Again their swords clashed, and sparks flew from their highly-tempered weapons.

The bandit tried to close, time after time, but as often as he attempted it, as often did young Fellows, with unerring aim, wound his black, villanous enemy.

The bandit's face was now a sorry sight to behold.

It was all covered with blood, and scarred in a dreadful manner.

He was hurt in the thigh, in the left arm, and upon the head and shoulders.

His hair was all wild about his furrowed brow, but all the while his dark eyes flashed a ferocious fire.

Dick, however, was also hurt.

His sword arm was bleeding dreadfully.

He was getting weaker and weaker.

His legs began to tremble under him.

The villain, however, seemed to be as strong upon his limbs as ever.

Dick felt that the struggle could not last much longer.

Again did their swords clash in deadly strife.

The bandit perceived Dick's increasing weakness, and laughed with bitter deadly hate and scorn.

"On your knees," the villain cried, "and sue for mercy."

"Never," was Dick's faint response.

At that moment his sword hilt broke from the blade!

He had dropped the blade upon the ground.

"All is over now with you," shouted the villain, as, with a hoarse laugh of triumph, he rushed upon Dick.

Young Fellows fell flat to the ground.

The bandit aimed his last stroke.

He stumbled and fell flat upon his face.

In a second Dick seized his sword blade from the ground, quickly wrapped his handkerchief round it for a firm hold, and resumed the fight.

Each moment was now fraught with life or death to one or both.

The crisis was at hand.

The bandit seized Dick by his collar with the left hand.

"Die! die!" he shrieked, in fiendish triumph.

A deadly haze came over his eyes.

He reeled, and made one feeble stroke for the last.

With a deep groan the villain dropped his sword.

He fell heavily to the ground.

The purple tide gushed from his side.

Dick Fellows had stabbed him with his last feeble and expiring strength.

The villain's eyes rolled in agony, awful to behold.

He gnashed his teeth, and writhed in pain.

With a last long-sounding sigh, he stretched himself out to his full length.

His head fell on one side.

He was dead!

## CHAPTER XXX.

HEROIC CONDUCT OF CAPT. TOM FORD IN THE "KAISER"—INTERCEPTED DISPATCHES—THE NIGHT SEA-FIGHT OFF TRIESTE HARBOUR—THE CUTTING-OUT EXPEDITION—TOM'S LETTER.

The consternation among the young volunteers when they discovered that their captain was missing may be more easily imagined than described.

They travelled fully fifteen miles ere they halted, and then it was that their faces became blanched at hearing that, in the hurry and confusion, their wounded chief was not among them.

Every one of the brave lads who were able volunteered to go back and search for him upon the battle-field, but this was not allowed by Hugh Tracy, who was then chief in command.

He and Dick Fellows, as we have seen, resolved to return, leaving the volunteers under the command of Mark Tilton, Frank's foster brother.

Every one was much pleased with Mark, and glad that he had been selected to govern them until Frank's return.

When Hugh and Dick had left the camp, Mark resolved to open the mail bags, and see what they contained.

This resolution was heartily seconded by Fatty and Buttons, who "were dying," as the saying is, to satisfy their curiosity.

When, therefore, the camps were all snugly arranged, and their fires brightly burning, Mark ordered the mail bags to be brought forth from the coach and opened.

Fatty and Buttons, staggering under the weight of a large bag each, threw their burden down among the anxious groups assembled.

Mr. Tony Waddleduck was very nervous, and desirous of opening one himself, and so was Buttons.

But this was not allowed; for all knew that Fatty was a bit of a thief "on the extreme quiet," and if he happened to fall across a small bag of gold coins he would have appropriated it to his own use in a very clever and mysterious manner.

The first bag which was opened contained letters and despatches from Vienna to the Archduke Albrecht, commanding the Austrians.

There were several lads, however, among them who well understood Italian.

Mark handed over a heavy letter to one of them, saying,

"There ought to be something of importance in such a big letter as this."

There *was* something important in it.

"Why, this letter speaks of nothing but sea-fights and night adventures," said one of the lads, looking through it.

"Does it? Oh, let's know all about it," said Fatty. "I like the sea, but the sea don't like me; let's hear what it says. Who does it talk about?"

"Why, about gallant Tom Ford—Frank's brother."

"You don't mean that?" said all, in chorus.

"I do, though. He's been whopping the Austrians awfully; these letters tell all about it."

"Read! read!"

"Bravo for Tom Ford!" shouted many, in one breath.

"Why, this despatch of the Austrian Minister of War speaks of their ships having run down an Italian mail steamer, and captured——"

"Not gallant Tom?" said all, in a breath.

"No, not Tom, but his letter."

"Oh!"

"The devil!"

"What has become of the letter?"

"The despatch says that this letter was written by Tom Ford on board the yacht "Kaiser," in Ancona Roads; but I don't see it anywhere among these papers. The general says it has been translated for the instruction of the Minister of Marine, and the original sent with it also."

"Where the deuce can it be?" said Fatty, rummaging among the papers.

"Oh, here it is," said Buttons. "I can tell the English writing. Yes, here it is; I'll read it for you."

"Good, Buttons, let's have it; no stuttering, mind."

Unfolding the letter, young Corporal Buttons read as follows:—

"Ancona, June—— 1866.

"On board the yacht 'Kaiser.'

"DEAR FRANK,—I know there is great difficulty in sending a letter to where you are, in Lombardy; but, although sick and tired with many strange adventures on the sea, and wounded, also, slightly, I thought I'd drop you a line to let you know that I am still in the land of the living; and, what is more than that, have been promoted to a captaincy in the Italian navy, for, as the papers say, 'gallant deeds.'"

"Bravo, for Tom."

"He always was a plucky chap."

"Go on, Buttons."

"Fire away, my brave corporal."

"Well," continued Buttons, reading the letter, "I'll narrate the particular affair which raised me to the rank of captain of an Italian man-of-war, and leave the rest for some other time.

"A squadron of Italian iron-clads and wooden frigates were ordered off from here to watch the Austrian fleet cruising off the mouth of Trieste harbour, and, hearing of it, I weighed anchor in the 'Kaiser,' and followed them.

"When we approached Trieste, the Austrians, fearing our numbers, and as their own fleet was not all there, only came out in the day-time, and cruised a few miles off the harbour, but always returned to port again at nightfall.

"There was an Austrian frigate, a wooden ship, called the 'Radetzki,' which always blocked up the entrance to the harbour, and acted as a guard ship for the others, to give warning at night of our approach, if too close in shore.

"In this position, the 'Radetzki' was considered by the Austrians to be as safe as if she was further away up the harbour.

"But they were much mistaken, for the Italians were burning for some chance to 'cut her out.'

"It was resolved by our admiral that this should be done, or at all events that the attempt should be made.

"Accordingly, the boats of the steam-frigate, 'Victor Emmanuel,' and the gun-boat, 'Novara,' manned entirely by volunteers, were put under the orders of Lieut. Capelli.

"A separation of the boats took place in the darkness, and the enterprise was abandoned for that night.

"Some of the boats, however, had penetrated to the mouth of the harbour, and lay on their oars until morning, in expectation of being joined by the rest, and before they could get back to their respective ships, two miles away, they were discovered by the 'Radetzki' and the batteries on shore.

"They removed the 'Radetzki' half a mile or more still further in the harbour, and made preparations for the future.

"They not only placed her near the shore batteries for protection under their many guns, but also put on board a hundred extra men. Arms and ammunition were brought on deck, and all their guns loaded up to the muzzle with grape shot.

"The batteries were also prepared for us, so we have since learned; and in order to guard against any further night surprise, they placed two boats at the harbour's mouth, to fire rockets and give the alarm.

"Having done this, they raised a large Austrian ensign on board the 'Radetzki,' with an Italian one under it, in token of defiance.

"Although every one knew that the Austrians intended to give us a warmer reception than we should have received at first, this only added to our ardour and impatience.

"After much pressing, Admiral Persano permitted me to man several boats with my own crew, and, as I understood him to say, take command of the night enterprise.

"Warned by the last failure, I resolved to keep my boats in close order together, and should the men from the 'Novara,' and 'Victor Emmanuel,' get separated, made up my mind to proceed alone with fifty men from my own yacht 'Kaiser.'

"This resolve I communicated to my brave lads during the day, and they sharpened their swords almost to the keenness of a razor's edge.

"At the last moment, however, I heard with greta annoyance that the admiral had altered his mind and would not let me take a chief command, for it was whispered that it would give offence to Italian officers much older than myself, and that I was too young for any such responsibility.

"I was resolved to go, however, and did so.

"Lieutenant Capelli took command, and about

midnight we all pulled off towards the harbour with muffled oars.

"During this time, however, the lieutenant commanding discovered two of the enemy's spy-boats, and gave chase to them.

"We waited some time for his return. I got impatient, and ordered all the boats to follow me.

"They did so without a murmur. We pulled in towards the harbour; and, to our surprise, saw the enemy exchanging signals from ship and shore. Delay now was dangerous.

"At this moment the wind, which had been behind us, suddenly changed, and blew right into our faces. This inspired me with a new idea. I gave orders to all my men that when we succeeded in getting on to the enemy's decks, the smartest of them should fly aloft and loosen the sails.

"One of the best men was to seize the rudder, while a second was to cut the cable. Having made these arrangements to cut the hip adrift, we pulled away at neck or nothing speed.

"At this instant the 'Radetzki' opened a heavy fire of musketry from every part of the ship, and showers of grape shot from the great guns.

"The effect of this hellish storm, let loose so suddenly upon us from both ship and shore, tore our men about in the most awful manner.

"Heads, and legs, and arms, were torn off.

"A boat or two was capsized, and a bullet whistled so close to my cheek as to wound it, and leave a scar behind.

"Still onward we pulled, and got under the enemy's bows.

"The attempt to board was gallantly and stoutly resisted by the Austrians, armed as they were at all points, and ready for us, with guns, pistols, sabres, pikes, and the like.

"But we fought our way up the ship's sides, and gained the enemy's decks.

"Those men who had been ordered to go aloft cut their way stoutly, and succeeded; but several of the poor fellows were killed on the spot, and others, desperately wounded, fell with an awful crash on deck again.

"Many of the brave English lads, bleeding from their wounds, scrambled out upon the yards, holding their cutlass between their teeth, and with wonderful quickness did their duty.

"In less than three minutes after the boats came alongside, down came the three top-sails.

"The prompt execution of these operations proved decisive.

"The moment the Austrians saw their sails fall, and found themselves under weigh and drifting out of harbour towards the open sea, they were greatly astonished.

"Some jumped overboard; others threw down their arms.

"My lads now soon got possession of the quarter-deck and forecastle; which, in five minutes after boarding, were nearly covered with dead bodies.

"The rest of the enemy having retreated below, kept up a heavy fire of musketry from the main-deck and up the hatchways.

"This obliged me to divide my men into two gangs.

"One party guarded the hatchways and gangways, and returned the fire of the enemy.

"The other party made sail, in order to clear the deck.

"To do this it was necessary for them to throw overboard two or three dozen of the poor devils who had fallen in the conflict, among whom were some of our own gallant companions.

"Scarcely was the 'Radetzki' clear of the point from which showers of musketry and grape were being played upon her, when the wind fell a dead calm.

"This calm left us exposed to the terrible fire of the batteries.

"The state of all our boats prevented us towing the captured vessel out to sea, for some of them were sunk, others were adrift with killed and wounded men.

"However, a light breeze soon springing up from the north-east, at length blew her out of further danger.

"The engagement had now lasted upwards of two hours, though during this time the enemy had kept up a constant fire from the main decks and shore, yet our lads managed to set every sail in the ship, and even got topgallant yards across.

"The ship being now quite clear of the batteries, and our men having twice threatened that they would give the enemy 'no quarter' if they continued their fire from below, they at last surrendered themselves prisoners of war.

"About this time some boats were perceived coming from the direction of the shore, which I suspected to be enemies; therefore, I immediately prepared for a new conflict, and had the sides of the ship manned with pikes and arms to defend her

"But on nearer approach we found them to be the crew of Lieut. Capelli, to whom, of course, I then resigned the chief command.

"The morning's dawn displayed a dreadful scene of carnage on board the frigate.

"Thus terminated an enterprise which, in this species of warfare, you will confess may safely be pronounced to be without parallel, and which, by mere accident, I had the honour to superintend, and successfully bring to a brilliant finish.

"The enemy were not taken by surprise.

"Not only the vessel but the batteries on shore which protected the 'Radetzki' were in readiness, and on their guard.

"The brave English boys under my command were exposed to a severe fire, both from the ship and from the shore, before they came alongside; we then fought our way up the sides of a vessel full of men, armed with every kind of weapon calculated to resist our gallant attempt.

"All this was done in the presence of the Austrian fleet not more than two miles away up the harbour, and by six boats.

"It was, moreover, accomplished under the order of your brother Tom, in the absence of Lieutenant Capelli.

"For this deed I am raised to the dignity of captain in the fleet of Victor Emmanuel, to the great pleasure and exaltation of my Boy Band in the 'Kaiser,' but to the annoyance of several others, particularly of Lieutenant Capelli.

"I may add that this officer and I have had a quarrel; we fight a duel to-morrow.

"But of this more another time. If I escape Capelli's bullets I'll write soon again.

"With love from my band of Boy Sailors to all the band of Boy Soldiers, believe me, Brother Frank, to be,

"Affectionately,

"TOM FORD."

The reading of this letter was interrupted now and then with repeated sounds of applause.

"Ho-o-ray!" roared Fatty, throwing up his cap. "British boys for ever! They can whop all the world!" said he, getting excited and red in the face.

It must be confessed, however, that his red face owed a great deal of its colour to a small bottle of wine he had "hooked."

"Three cheers for the gallant Tom!" said Mark. "He's as modest as he's brave."

"For all the world like me," said Fatty.

"Silence, Paunchey," Buttons remarked. "You wouldn't do for a sea-captain."

"Why not, eh, Master Impudence? why not?"

"It would take at least two ships to carry *you* anywhere," Buttons said.

Fatty made a slap at his young tormentor, but missed his mark as usual, and hit some one else instead.

A fight might have been the consequence, but Mark soon restored order by saying,

"Bring out a bottle of brandy, some one; we *must* drink Tom's health."

"Hear! hear!" was the unanimous response.

"Fill up, lads; fill up to the brim! Here's three times three, and a bumper to your noble companion and schoolmate, the gallant Captain Tom!"

"Ho-o-ray! ho-o-ray! hooray!" was the noisy response of all.

They had just done cheering, and were quiet once more, when one of their guards, placed some distance away from the camps, was heard to shout out,

"Halt! halt! Who goes there?"

"A friend," was the faint answer of some stranger approaching, muffled in a cloak.

"Advance, friend, and give the countersign," was the sentinel's response.

All was silent again.

"Who can that be?" asked one of another in surprise.

A moment of silence elapsed.

A stranger, escorted by two sentinels, slowly approached through the darkness.

All eyes were turned towards the stranger.

No one recognized him.

He threw off his cloak, more by accident than design.

All rose and raised an exclamation of surprise and astonishment.

The stranger's leg was bandaged, and his arm was in a sling.

His face was haggard and bloody.

It was Dick!

"What! Dick Fellows?" gasped each one in return.

Yes; it was the same brave lad, but so changed that his own comrades could scarcely recognize him!

"Where is Captain Frank? Where is Hugh?" asked one and another.

There was no response.

Poor Dick sank upon the ground, and had not strength enough to answer the questions, and could scarcely look any of his comrades in the face.

"Where is Captain Frank?"

"What has become of Hugh?" were questions still repeated.

"Give me a cup of wine," said Dick, faintly. "I am more dead than alive, and severely wounded. A cup of wine! quick, a cup of wine!"

## CHAPTER XXXI.

### THE BOY SOLDIERS, LED ON BY MARK, CHARGE THE BATTERIES IN THE MOUNTAIN GORGE.

As well as he was able Dick told the story of his strange adventure, of Hugh Tracy's fall from the precipice, and of the false guide's death.

All the Boy Soldiers listened with distended eyes to Dick's sorrowful tale.

The cheek of each one was flushed with anger, and they turned to rush to the rescue of their gallant young leaders, and avenge them.

"What, brother Frank and Hugh Tracy both gone!" said Mark, rising up. "Shall we sleep, lads, and not make any effort to save them?"

"No! no! no!" was the response of all.

"Let us away at once," said they.

"Lead us on, Mark."

"We will follow you anywhere."

"Then so be it. Prepare all of you for instant departure."

In a moment every one of the Boy Band jumped to his feet, and buckled on his knapsack and belts.

"Take plenty of ammunition, you will need it all."

This order was not necessary, for each one provided himself with at least two hundred rounds of ball cartridge, and in less than an hour the whole company were ready drawn up, and in marching order.

Mark tried to prevail upon Dick to remain behind in the camps.

But he would not.

Although weak and feeble he resolved to go out with the expedition in order to "pilot" them to the right spot.

The camp was left in charge of two youths, who pleaded sickness; the same two, it will be remembered, who remained on board the "Kaiser" when the Boy Band attacked the lighthouse fort, and fought their first battle with the Austrians in the ravine.

The two youths, who in reality were spies in the pay and in regular correspondence with Joel, were named Moss and Levi, and both of Hebrew extraction.

* * * * *

Directly Mark and Dick left the camp with their brave followers, Moss whispered,

"I say, Levi, what a capital chance we've got now."

"How do you mean?"

"Why, there is no one left behind but us, except half-a-dozen wounded young whelps, and that Austrian officer."

"Well, what of that? Speak softly. I don't understand you."

"Frank is wounded and done for; no doubt he is in a dungeon long before this; and as to Hugh Tracy, why, his neck is broken and his skull crushed to pieces by his fall down the precipice."

"Well, go on; but speak softly."

"Suppose we liberate the Austrian officer? He knows all about the strength of his comrades at the mouth of the gorge at Val Verde. If he were to get there before Mark and his boats, they would be prepared for these young Garibaldians, and perhaps extinguish the whole lot at one swoop."

"Not a bad idea. What say you, shall we sail?"

"Why not? I fear we are already suspected, and may be detected one of these fine mornings and shot."

"Rather an uncomfortable idea that," said Master Moss, rolling his small, dark eyes. "Have you heard anything of Joel to-day?"

"Yes; he's in the next village."

"How do you know?"

"Mark sent me out this morning to buy eggs at the village. There was one among them marked with red chalk. It was empty."

"Empty?"

"Yes; that is to say, the contents had been sucked out till quite dry, and a small bullet wrapped up in this slip of paper, put in instead," said Levi, producing a thin slip of tissue paper on which was writing.

"But why didn't he talk to you instead?"

"The truth is that the villagers like the young Garibaldians so well that Joel had to be very careful how he acted. I have called at the same house before for eggs and the like; but to day when I went I found Joel lodging there in disguise. He did not speak or even pretend to know me; but directly he had a chance he slipped an extra egg into my basket unobserved. I thought it meant something, and soon discovered that it was hollow.

"And what does the note say?"

"He says that he has found out that Frank has been captured by the Austrians, and was wounded. On their way to Vienna with him the Austrians were surprised in the mountains, many of them killed by a noted band of banditti, and Frank taken prisoner by them."

"Then he is *not* at Val Verde?" said Moss.

"No; no more than you or I."

"What a jolly lark! What a warm reception Mark and the boys will receive when they get there, and how awfully taken in, too! It's a miracle if a single one of them escapes."

"Not much odds to us, I think. We have our own game to play, and we must do it quickly."

"Then what do you propose?"

"Why, give the Austrian officer his liberty, mount him upon a horse, and let him deliver a message to Joel at the village for us."

"Capital! let's be quick."

No sooner said than done.

The officer was set at large, and mounted upon a horse.

"You say that no company of boys on foot could ever force their way through the gorge?" asked Moss of him.

"I do."

"Well, then, as we are masters here, we will set you free—on one condition."

"Name it," said the officer, delighted.

"Take this note to the principal inn in the village yonder, and bring back an answer to us. We will wait your return with all impatience. You will find us seated at the spring at the side of the road."

"Will you do this?"

"I will."

"And swear on your oath to fulfil it?"

"I do."

"Then depart, and good luck attend you."

The Austrian prisoner did as he was bidden, and galloped away.

* * * * * *

Mark's party had not gone more than a mile from their camps when it halted in a small wood.

A council of war was held there and then, at which it was decided between Dick and Mark that, in order to ensure success, all the boys should be mounted, whereas, as the case was, but few of them were provided with steeds, for many animals had died within the last few days from wounds and like casualties.

The innkeepers of the village, it was known, had many horses in their keeping.

These Mark and Dick resolved to possess without a moment's delay.

Several of the Boy Band went forth for this purpose, and what the villagers would not sell were stolen from them.

Some dozen or more had been thus secured and driven towards the wood where the company were staying under cover.

Most of the party, now well mounted and provided with saddles, were waiting for some stragglers to return ere setting out on their night expedition.

Fatty and Buttons were on guard a distance in advance of their comrades when they espied a horseman advancing from the village towards them.

The stranger looked about him from time to time, as if suspicious of being watched.

He came nearer and nearer to the wood without dreaming of danger.

Fatty and Buttons, on their hands and knees, watched him like a cat does a mouse.

"He looks very much like that Austrian officer we've got in camp," said Tony, in a whisper. "'Pon my word I do believe it *is* him, or else it's his ghost."

"Bosh!" said Buttons, "how can that be? Haven't we left Levi and Moss to mind the camp? It *can't* be him."

"Levi and Moss be hanged!" said Fatty, softly. "I don't think much of them; they've never been in any fight at all with us yet, and I've often thought they wouldn't mind betraying us. All they wish to do is to be cooks, and mind the camps when all of us are away."

"Oh, they're all right," said Buttons. "I dare say you only envy them for having the tit-bit out of every dish."

The single horseman approached still closer.

He entered the woods.

On his arm he carried a basket.

In an instant Fatty and Buttons rose up, one on each side of him, and seized his reins.

"It *is* the Austrian prisoner!" gasped Fatty, in surprise.

"What have you got there?" said Buttons, "and how came you here?"

"I was sent by the two youths in charge of the Garibaldian camps, and promised on my honour to return to them with a message they sent me with to yonder village."

"And where is the answer?"

"The only one I received at the principal inn was these eggs which a young English gentleman charged me to deliver in the camp of the Boy Soldiers."

"Eggs, eh?" said Fatty; "let's have one; I'm fond of sucking eggs. It clears the voice, you know, for singing."

He took one and shook it.

Something hard rattled inside.

He pressed it with his fingers, and it broke.

A bullet, wrapped up in tissue paper, rolled out.

"Hillo! what means this?" he said. "There's some strange affair in all this. Come, my brave and honourable man, for such you really are, dismount."

The Austrian, surprised at this unlooked-for adventure, did so.

Mark and Dick hurried to the spot and examined the words written on the tissue paper, which ran:—

"I have made all my plans. The latest news you sent me is worth any money. Fly on the instant you read this, and join me at the spot I have pointed out before. This night seals the fate of Frank Ford and the whole band.

"Your friend,
"JOEL."

"Dastard!" growled Mark.

"Vile treachery is at work all around us," said Dick. "How lucky we fell in with this messenger!"

In a few moments the Austrian prisoner was escorted back to the camp by two or three of the Boy Band, who had orders to handcuff Moss and Levi on the spot, and wait till the whole company returned!

* * * * *

"No time is to be lost, lads!" said Mark; "we must hasten to Val Verde, storm an entrance, and rescue Frank. There can be no doubt now that Joel has had paid spies among us, but they shall suffer for it when we return; we will hang them to the limb of a tree, and let vultures feed on their living bodies. Forward!"

This strange and startling episode only seemed to nerve the Boy Soldiers more and more, and each one swore to be revenged on Joel, and his confederates Levi and Moss.

Onwards they sped at dead of night and in profound darkness.

After several hours Dick led his brave companions to the mouth of the mountain gorge.

Instead of perceiving but a few soldiers on guard they discovered a half battalion drawn up, and guns loaded, ready for instant use.

How was this?

Joel had learned all about the intended movement from the note sent by Moss and Levi.

He galloped away on the instant towards Val Verde, and when the Boy Soldiers entered the village, and even called at his own inn in search of horses for the expedition, he had gone!

"They seem well prepared for us," said Mark, as, fully a mile off, he surveyed the spot with his glass.

"Have they any cavalry, I wonder?" said Dick.

The words were scarcely spoken, when a squadron of hussars were perceived galloping towards them at the charge.

In an instant Mark gave the order to counter charge.

The brave youths dug their spurs deep into the flanks of their horses, and, with a loud shout, galloped forward.

The two bodies of horsemen met.

The shock was awful.

A terrible fight ensued for a few moments; but the boys "peppered" them so vigorouly with their pistols and revolvers that the enemy retreated quickly and in the wildest confusion.

They were pursued some distance, even up to the cannons in the gorge.

This Mark did not desire.

"You have exposed your Garibaldian uniforms," said Dick; "and, I fear, if we attempt to approach them again they will know us, and we shall all be cut to pieces."

"Never mind," said Mark, "never mind, lads, we will play them a trick."

Each one was ordered to strip the dead and wounded hussars of their clothing and head gear.

This was quickly done.

"They won't know us now," said Mark. "We will approach the enemy at a walk, until we get close up to the guns, and then charge them like the devil!"

This trick proved an excellent one.

The Austrians were surprised that so few of their hussars had returned, and were on the look out for the stragglers.

When, therefore, Mark and his followers were perceived approaching the gorge in the darkness, and attired like their missing men, they took no notice.

The Boy Soldiers were about two hundred yards away, and, as it seemed, on the point of riding in unchallenged, when an English voice was heard to shout out among the Austrians,

"Fire, men, fire! They are Garibaldians! I know them well! It is all a trick to deceive you!"

The speaker was Joel Flint.

The words had scarce escaped his lips, when the Austrians prepared for a stubborn resistance, and fired rapidly from cannon and musket.

They had fired but one volley, however, when the English Boys raised a wild hurrah, and dashed into the mouth of the gorge, sword in hand.

Foremost of them all was the handsome form of Mark Tilton, the foster brother.*

---

## CHAPTER XXXII.

LOTS ARE CAST BY FOUR AUSTRIAN SOLDIERS FOR THE REWARD OFFERED FOR FRANK DEAD OR ALIVE—THE QUARREL—THE FIGHT—THE BANDIT'S GAME.

THE treacherous guide, as we have seen in another chapter, well deserved the fate which he met with at the hands of Dick Fellows.

What had become of Hugh Tracy in his terrible fall down the cliff side we shall shortly see; but, for the present, turn to the changing fortunes and adventurous straights in which Captain Frank Ford found himself.

It will be remembered that he had been captured on the battle field, wounded, and disabled.

His Austrian guards carried him away from the ground across the river, and did not bestow a moment's consideration on the dying old hag who was shot beside him, and lay weltering in her gore.

"This is a brave youth," said one of the Austrians, as they carried Frank away. "And the adventurous young devil has given us much trouble, but, from the look of the wound his in forehead, I doubt much if he'll be able to lead on his intrepid young band again in a hurry."

With much care, and great show of humanity, his captors bore him away.

They had not gone very far on their journey to head-quarters, when events took a sudden change, as we shall see.

Frank had been left in the care of four mounted men, their officer and the surgeon having gone to camp before them.

"There is a great reward offered for this youth," said one; "do you know it?"

"Of course we do," a second replied. "The Archduke, in his last order, spoke of this young man, which, from his description and appearance, I take to be the captain of the young Garibaldians."

"How much *is* the reward, then?"

"A thousand florins, I hear."

"Yes, and a fine day's work it has turned out for *me*," said the first.

"For *you*?"

---

* See Illustration in last week's Number.

"Yes, *me*."

"How do you make that out?"

"Why, I discovered him first."

"No, you didn't."

"But I say I *did*," was the angry response of the first speaker.

"And if you did, what of that?" asked the third.

"Ain't we going share and share alike?" the fourth inquired.

"Not a bit of it," said the first. "Grumble as much as you like; it won't benefit you much. Ask the surgeon if I didn't discover him first or not."

"Well, if you did, it don't matter much; we shall all have equal shares."

"I'm glad you think so," laughed the first; "but *I* don't, my lads."

"But, you can't help yourself," the second said, with an oath, and a flashing eye.

"Can't I? What do you mean by scowling at me in such a fierce style as that, eh? I tell you I can."

"Well, if we don't have shares, I don't see why we should trouble ourselves about carrying the youth any farther," said two at once.

"Oh, that's it, eh?" said the first speaker, with a fierce look. "Then lay him down beside this group of trees, and I'll soon tell you what *I* think about it. If you don't help to carry him into camp I'll *make* you."

"Come, comrades, come, let us have no more bloodshed; enough has been spilt already, I think."

"And more will follow if there are many words over it."

"I'll tell you what we'll do," said one. "Let us cast lots to see who shall have the largest share of the reward."

"Not me."

"Nor me."

"Well, then, let us cast dice for it."

"That's better."

"Do you agree?"

"Yes," said two.

"*I* don't," the first one snarled. "Whoever wins, matters little to me; I'll have the reward, aye, every florin of it, or the life of him who opposes me."

"You talk very bravely," said one, "and as if there were not three of us against you."

"I care not if there were a dozen," said the first one, curling his moustachoes in high anger.

During this altercation the four soldiers arrived at the edge of a small plantation.

They deposited the body beneath a tree, and walked some few yards away to throw dice to see who should have the reward of one thousand florins offered for the capture of Frank Ford.

At first they threw their dice in a very quiet manner, but in a few moments began to quarrel in a terrible style, heedless of the poor youth, who lay unconscious under the trees.

The first speaker, from his habitual good luck in dice throwing, was induced to join in, particularly as the highest score only reached twenty-four in three throws.

"I can always beat that number. Ha! ha!" he said, "so there ain't much hazard about it."

He did throw.

The total came to twenty-four.

It was a tie.

He bit his lip, and cursed at his disappointment.

"Never threw so low in all my life," said he. "Let's try again."

With a face flushed with anger the first one sat down by the roadside, and seized the dice-box.

"A tie was it?"

"Yes; the last was."

"Then I have the first chance?"

"Yes; you lead off."

The first throw was twelve, at which he grumbled.

The next time he had three fives up.

"Not bad that," said one.

"Oh! he's the perfect devil at dice," said another. "Look at that! look! there's luck!"

He had thrown two fives and a six.

"That's good play," said one of the two, who had lost. "Why, that makes a total of forty-three."

The player tossed the dice-box from him with an air of indifference to his antagonist, who smiled darkly as he rattled the box.

"Three fives that time," said one.

Not a bad beginning.

He threw again.

"Eighteen this time," said the player, with a triumphant laugh.

He turned up three sixes.

"That's not fair," said the first player.

"It is."

"It *was* fair," said one or two.

"Go on, then; let's see what he turns up this time."

The last throw counted eighteen.

"Bravo!"

"Well done."

"I've thrown fifty-one in all," said the player. "against forty-three. The reward is mine!"

"You lie!" said the thwarted gambler; "you didn't play fair."

"The lie stick in your throat, rascal!" said the successful one. "Take that!"

He struck his rival on the cheek with his heavy leathern gauntlet.

In a moment swords were drawn.

"Keep them asunder, comrades!" cried one.

"Stand aside till I cleave the skull of this dice-sharper!" said the loser.

It was a desperate encounter, and blood flowed on either side.

Even those two who were peacably inclined towards each other at first were now drawn into the brawl, and the whole four men were fiercely tilting and slashing at each other.

They might have continued fighting long and until they had scientifically cut each other's throats; but hostilities were suddenly brought to a close in an unlooked-for and very mysterious manner.

Loud shouts of derisive laughter suddenly burst upon the ears of the enraged duellists.

They drew back from each other, and listened.

"Ha, ha, ha!" echoed through the plantation.

"What means that?" gasped one and another, in surprise, each breathing hard for wind.

"Ha, ha, ha!" sounded again, in derisive triumph, through the dark, dense plantation.

The duellists looked at each other with staring eyes and open mouths, as they heard a rough voice in the distance, singing the refrain again and again of—

"Come fill up your bumpers, and our toast it shall be,
Here's health to all comrades on land and on sea;
Here's health to our captain, and 'tis our firm belief,
There's none half so good as bold Basil our chief."

"Basil the chief," said several, in half whispers.

"We are betrayed."

"The captain! the captain!"

"Secure the lad, and let us defend him like men, or we loose all reward."

With general accord they lowered their weapons, and hastened to the spot where they had laid the senseless form of young Frank Ford.

He was nowhere to be found!

"We have been tracked by Basil, the Bandit," said one.

"Curses on them!"

"We dare not follow."

"Let us hasten away. To pursue them is certain death."

Frank was again in the power of Basil, the fierce bandit.

How this came to pass the next chapter will show.

## CHAPTER XXXIII.

FRANK IN THE HANDS OF HIS FIERCEST FOE—HE IS CONDEMNED TO BE SHOT—DEVOTION OF LITTLE ANNETTE.

When Cavolti had seized Bazil by the throat in the fierce hand to hand conflict, which we have described in a previous number, the bandit chief was hurled to the ground with great violence, so much so, indeed, that his head resounded again on the stone pavement of the cave.

Just as Cavolti was in the act of piercing Basil to the heart, a pistol shot was fired by some one unseen behind the dark drapery that separated one vault from another.

This shot struck Cavolti in the right arm, and his dagger fell by his side.

This chance but fortunate shot saved Basil's life, who thereupon struggled hard with his mutinous follower, and would have killed him, but that Agnese, his beautiful daughter, rushed forward and stayed her father's murderous design.

But, like all bandit brawls and quarrels, they were soon forgotten, for exciting adventures that followed thick and fast upon one another, drove the memory of this, like many former incidents of the kind, out of their minds.

Nor did it much matter, in such a numerous band as Basil's was, if one or two men had fallen in mutual encounters, so that when it came to the chief's knowledge afterwards that Cavolti had slain four of his band in the long stone passage, as they were leading him to prison, he did not heed it at the moment, but waited for future events to give him opportunities for revenge.

"When Cavolti has served my purpose," mused Basil often to himself, "he shall be quietly dispatched, but not now; the band are divided. More than half, I find, would have revolted against me had I not spared his life. 'Tis well, I shall not wait long for some chance to kill him."

But the escape of the Boy Band from Basil's clutches filled that chieftain with great annoyance and vexation.

He raved and swore like a madman whenever he thought of it.

"To be outwitted by mere boys," he said often, with a bitter smile, "there must have been some treachery. But where?"

Aye! that was the question.

He little dreamed that Annette, and Agnese, his fair and only daughter, were the young culprits, or there cannot be a doubt he would have sacrificed them both in one of his drunken and half-crazy fits.

As it was he gave strict instructions to his band to be more vigilant than ever, and even promised the hand of fair Agnese, his daughter, to the one who should recapture Frank Ford.

Now Cavolti deemed this offer a slight upon himself.

He was the recognized second chief of the band, and had for a long time cast his eyes upon Agnese, but had never met with any mutual glance or friendly return.

This coldness of Agnese, and her positive dislike for him, as shown on all occasions, steeled the heart of Cavolti, who, though he smiled, had dark designs, and rejoiced in secret like a demon when thinking of their possible accomplishment.

"Basil has slighted me," he thought, "and insulted me, or why would he offer his daughter to any any one when he knows how much *I* love her? Well, no matter; time will work wonders. I know she hates me, and yet she saved my life when her father's dagger was at my throat; perhaps it was *her* bullet that wounded me. Who knows? 'Tis all past and gone; never mind. I have rude suspicions that Agnese planned the escape of our prisoners; and, if it be so, I'll wring her young heart until it bleeds again."

"What if *I* recapture this youth?" he thought at times, as he walked to and fro in the darkness of night, musing, and planning fresh villanies. "If fortune only so favours me, then will I triumph over her proud spirit; she shall—then she *must* be my wife."

Fortune favoured Cavolti.

He and a small party of brigands were prowling about, and on their way to the battle-field by night, to see what they could discover or secure, for intelligence had reached them in their mountain fastness of a recent fight between the Austrians and Boy Soldiers, and it was thought possible that they might fall across one or two of the wounded youths, and make them prisoners.

On their way they espied the four Austrian soldiers bearing the body of a wounded young Garibaldian.

They hid themselves in a roadside wood, in hopes that they might suddenly rush out and attack the four soldiers.

But, when the Austrians placed Frank beneath a tree, as we have seen, and began to gamble some few yards off, Cavolti perceived his opportunity, and crept through the high grass towards the wounded boy.

Judge of his astonishment to find it was none other than Frank Ford!

His small black eyes danced again with demoniacal joy, and every limb trembled with excitement.

Cavolti's companions were a short distance off awaiting his commands, therefore they were unaware of the great prize their leader had discovered.

With a sudden bound, like that of a fierce tiger in pouncing upon its sleeping prey, Cavolti seized the body of the half conscious and feeble youth, raised it on his stalwart shoulder, and hurried from the spot!

"The prize is mine!" he chuckled, in fierce triumph. "Agnese now belongs to me!"

He whistled thrice in a low bird-like manner.

In an instant he was surrounded by his followers, who, in wild joy, hurried through the dense wood towards a goat path which led to and up the mountains.

It was at this precise moment, when giving way

to their wild mirth and jollity, when far out of all harm's way, that the luckless Austrian soldiers heard the distant refrain which so startled them, and brought the four-handed duel to so sudden a conclusion.

With all the well practised agility of bold mountain robbers, Cavolti, followed by his men, sped along upward and onward over the mountains towards Basil's almost inaccessible and unknown retreat.

Long before they had reached the bandit's cave the shrill, long-sounding notes of their mountain horns could be heard reveberating among the lofty hills.

Basil, among the rest, heard the far-sounding horns, and hastened to the top of a high hill, to gain a distant view of his followers' approach.

In the far distance he saw Cavolti bearing something on his shoulders, and waving his hat.

After an hour or more, however, Cavolti's horn was again heard resounding, and its shrill notes fell like a funeral knell upon the heart of young Agnese, for something told her that the man she hated most had triumphed, and that the hour of her severest trial was fast approaching.

She trembled from head to foot, but why she could not tell.

Some dread mystery like a pall overweighed her heart.

She clasped Annette to her bosom, and burst into a flood of tears.

"As you love me, dear Annette, go and tell me what these shouts of triumph mean," she sobbed, "for my heart is filled with dread forebodings, and my soul sickens at the thought of ever becoming the bride of any one of my father's ruthless band. Go, Annette, go and learn all you can. Hasten to inform me. Give me death rather than a union with one my soul abhors."

So speaking, she sank upon her knees, and sobbed convulsively.

Annette left the cave stealthily, and went forth to see all that was going on.

As she hurried towards a group of trees to catch a glimpse of all that passed, she found that Basil and all the band had hurried forward to meet Cavolti, and were shouting in triumph at his approach.

She was almost paralyzed to see Frank Ford in the midst of the bandit band.

The rough usage he had received at the hands of his captives in some degree aroused Frank from the state of stupor in which he had been for a day or more.

His eyes gradually regained their wonted fire, though his face was deadly pale.

He could not well stand, for he was yet too weak, and he sat beneath a tree looking like one just awakening from a long and painful dream.

Basil and all his men, for the most part, were present.

Their angry words and fierce oaths thoroughly aroused the bold, brave youth.

"Shoot him!"

"Hang him!"

"Cut him limb from limb!" they shouted.

Young Annette felt the blood curdle in her veins as she listened.

She would have run to inform Agnese, but she trembled with excitement, and felt as if rooted to the spot.

"It *is* the handsome youth returned again," she sighed. "Oh! heaven preserve him! or he will be butchered in cold blood!"

"Hang him!"

"Shoot the saucy brat!" growled several of the band.

"Where am I?" gasped Frank, now, for the first time, recovering full consciousness. "Where am I? What! again in Basil's power?"

"Yes, in Basil's power, rash youth," said the fierce chief, with a laugh of bitter mockery and scorn. "Yes; in Basil's power once more, and not likely to give him the slip this time, eh, my bold lad?"

"No, captain."

"Shoot him!"

"Swing him up!"

"Basil," said Cavolti, approaching, "before we proceed with the execution of this bold spy, remember your promise—'Agnese shall be the bride of him who captures Frank Ford.' Do you recollect?"

"I do; and what of that?" said Basil, with a scornful look. "What of that? Think you I so soon forget my promises? 'Tis well, Agnese besought your life, and I granted it ['curses on her!' he said, softly], and 'tis well again she should marry the man she so much admires [confusion to her, the jade.] But, come, we must dispose of this youth, and at once; we can't afford to have spies about us any longer."

"I am *not* a spy, Basil," said Frank, in a faint voice. "And wherefore should you murder me in cold blood?"

"'Tis false," said Cavolti, frowning like a demon on the proud, pale, handsome face of the prisoner, "'tis false, and were it not contrary to Capt. Basil's orders, I'd cleave your vile English heart with one stroke of my stiletto."

"Brave, *very* brave," sighed Frank, with a smile of pity on the fierce villain.

"Who let you into the secrets of our cave?" said Cavolti, fiercely.

"Who conducted you in safety from my presence?" asked Basil, sternly.

"Who killed the guard, our comrade, at the main entrance?" growled several, in a breath.

He did not breathe a single word, but smiled.

"You smile, eh?" said Basil. "But do you know that in less than five minutes you will lie a helpless corpse at my feet unless you reveal who it was that rescued you?"

"I do," said Frank, faintly. "It will not take much to kill me; I am half-dead already."

"Oh, you do know, then, that certain death awaits you?" smiled Basil.

"I do."

"And still refuse to disclose the names of those who aided you?"

"I do," said Frank, with a look of scorn.

"Ah, would you scoff at Basil, the bandit chief, in the face of death?"

"I fear it not," said Frank, folding his arms. "Do your worst. I would scorn to call myself an English boy, and drag those into trouble who assisted me and my band to escape."

"Do you hear that?" said Cavolti, with a fierce glance. "Do you hear that, Basil?"

"I do, Cavolti," the chief replied; "there must be spies and traitors among us; and, by my wrath," said he, walking towards Frank, hastily, and in passion, "I will spare thy life if you do but tell me their names, or point them out. Once for all, will you do so?"

"No," said Frank, firmly; "do with me as you will, but I'll never turn traitor to a friend in need."

"Bind him to that tree," said Basil.

In an instant two men stepped forward and bound him.

"Blindfold him!"

They proceeded to do so.

"Hold!" said Frank, with a proud look of contempt, "take that handkerchief away. I have faced death before, and beg, as a dying favour, that you will not bind my eyes."

"Granted," said Basil. "Stand aside from him, men."

His orders were obeyed.

"Let three men load their carbines, and be ready for the word to fire!"

This was done.

One of them, the tallest and ugliest of the three, was Cavolti, who seemed to delight in the task before him.

"I will give you one more chance for life," said Basil. "Will you reveal the names of the traitors among us who played me false? Breathe their names, or point them out, and whoever they are they shall die in your stead."

"Right."

"Bravo, Captain Basil; they deserve it!"

"Will you?—once!"

"No," was the solemn answer; "not if I were about to sacrifice a hundred lives!"

"Will you?—twice!"

"I will not. Question me no farther, but fire!"

"Carbines! attention! ready! take aim! Will you, for the last time, tell me?"

"No!"

Basil was on the point of turning to give the command to fire, when Annette, with a piercing scream, rushed upon the scene, and fell between the victim and the executioners, exclaiming—

"'Twas I, Basil! 'twas I! Spare him! he is innocent! 'Twas I, Basil! 'twas I, Basil! Spare him! spare——" and fell prostrate to the earth. (*See Illustration.*)

## CHAPTER XXXIV.

THE PLANS OF CAVOLTI—THE SECRET MEETING OF FRANK AND AGNESE—THEY ARE DISCOVERED—THE INSULT—THE MEETING—FRANK'S GENEROSITY—AGNESE IS MYSTERIOUSLY STABBED—THE DEEP REVENGE.

THE sudden appearance of Annette among the brigand band, and just at that moment when Basil was about to give the order to fire, caused great commotion to all then present.

"Hold!" cried Basil, "hold!" he said, throwing up the carbines of the three villains. "How is this? What brings Annette here?"

"Spare him! spare him!" said the sobbing girl, with upraised hands and streaming eyes. "It was I, Basil, and I alone, who led him and his followers from the cave."

"You?" said the grim chief, in sudden surprise.

"What, Annette?" said Cavolti, in mute wonder.

"Yes; 'twas I, and I alone, believe me. Do not harm him, for the youth is innocent."

"Fire!" said Frank, bravely, but feebly. "Touch not a hair of that girl's head; I am to blame! she is innocent!"

"No! no! no!" gasped Annette, hurriedly, "do not belive him; he wishes to shield me and suffer death; but he is innocent, on my oath, I swear it! Let me die the traitor's death! Do not shed a drop of the brave boy's blood!"

"There is some deep, unravelled mystery here," Basil growled; "for the present we will defer the execution until more is known about it. Seize the girl, and 'ead her forth to a dungeon. Let us see what close confinement, cold water and bread can do."

In a whisper he addressed one of his men thus,

"Has the young English youth sent the money for Frank Ford's, head?"

"No, captain, not yet; he promised it."

"Promised it! Ha! ha! that will not do for us."

"He says the coin shall be forthcoming when his head is secured, but not till then."

"And then, perhaps, he will not pay at all, as the deed will then have been accomplished. No, no; this youth is a bold, brave fellow, and I would much like him to join our band."

"True, captain; there is no doubt as to his courage and intelligence, he has shown it on more than one occasion; but Cavolti, your chief officer, hates him."

"And that is one of the reasons why I like him all the more," said Basil, with a grim smile. "He shall not suffer, at least, at present; he shall live until we get the money, and, if that is not quickly done, we will force him in some way to join our band. Think you it could be done?"

"I have no doubt of it, if Cavolti could only be appeased."

"Leave that to me," he said; "we will get a head, but Frank Ford's is worth more to us than the reward offered for it."

"But beware of Cavolti," said the arch villain Basil was talking to.

"Never fear; I am as deep as he."

"Unbind the youth," said the bandit chief.

Taking Cavolti on one side, he whispered something in his ear which made the black-looking rascal grimly smile.

"We will use this youth like a decoy bird," said Basil; "his followers will never rest until they have found out his place of retreat. It will then be easy to entrap them all."

"'Tis well," said Cavolti, with a grim smile; "I never thought of that before."

"Leave it to me. We will give him partial parole."

"But he might escape our mountain bounds."

"No fear of that; our guards are numerous; he cannot escape their vigilance. Besides, if we keep him too closely confined he will not have any chance of holding out signals to those who are in search of him. We will give him the free range of our bounds near the cave, and he shall be well watched. Do you see my plans?"

"I do," said Cavolti; "but somehow I fear him."

"Fear him, and you a herculean man?" said Basil, with a smile.

Cavolti made no reply, but bit his lip.

Although he and Basil appeared thus for the moment on such friendly terms, they were, at heart, enemies, for Cavolti, in his advances to the fair Agnese, had only met with rebuff and scornful looks.

"Do as you please, Captain Basil," said he; "but, if you were to follow *my* advice, you would shoot the young English brat at once; there is something in his eye that bodes no good to you or the bandit band."

"I fear nought, and more than that, I will set watches around him. What say you if I prompt Agnese to coax him, and gain all the secrets she can out of him respecting his band. That would be a capital idea; he would never suspect her to be a female spy."

Basil's words were like wormwood to Cavolti, who smiled sardonically, and slowly left his chief.

"Agnese set to watch him, eh? Perhaps so; but

I will watch them both. I will bring her down to the dust; she *shall* own me her master. Revenge is sweet!"

* * * * *

For more than a week Frank remained a captive among the bandit band, and, greatly to his surprise, not only recovered from his wound, but fast regained his health and strength.

He was fed well, and comfortably lodged, but no one spoke to him save Basil, who more than once urged upon the brave Boy Soldier to join the Bandit Band.

But he would not, and treated the proposition with scorn.

He was allowed free range of the grounds in and around the cavern, and, after a few days, as fortune would have it, he met the fair Agnese.

He did not speak to her then, but, from her blush and timidity, he judged that the meeting was not altogether displeasing to her.

By private signals these two young lovers hit upon a pleasant rendezvous, in a shady grove, where evening after evening they met in secret.

The spot was a pleasant one, and no one ever dreamed of their secret nightly meetings.

And it was well that they thus supposed, for there were many of the band ready and willing to obey Cavolti in all his nefarious deeds.

But turn we for a moment to Cavolti and his plans.

* * * * *

It was here that the lovers would meet, and, unseen, as they thought, by mortal eye, breathe forth the sentiments of their hearts.

It was one of those delightful Italian evenings when not a cloud was to be seen in the heavens that Frank, proceeding to the well-known spot, a maiden of rare beauty rushed into his fond embrace.

For a few moments the lovers regarded each other with all the ardour of mutual affection.

"Oh, this is happiness indeed!" cried Frank, "to hold thee in these arms and call thee mine. But why that tear, fair Agnese? At such a time as this, joy alone ought to be the tenant of thy bosom."

"Alas! I know not why, brave Frank, but a mysterious dread rushes through my frame as though some dreadful calamity was about to happen."

"Nay, heed it not, love," said Frank, "'tis but imagination."

"It may be," said the beauteous maid; "but look! what is that?" at the same time directing his attention towards a dark object some short distance before her.

"Oh, it is but the shadow of some neighbouring tree," exclaimed Frank; "and yet it cannot be—no, 'tis some vile spy!"

Grasping his dagger he rushed to the spot.

The person quickly retreated, but not before he had a full view of his retiring figure.

"That form is Cavolti's, or I am much deceived."

"Cavolti!" responded Agnese in alarm to her lover; "gracious heavens! what does *he* here?"

"That I should have asked him," exclaimed Frank, "had he not like a craven fled; but why this agitation? what is coupled with his name to occasion this emotion? Tell me, Agnese, I implore you."

"Alas! you know not, brave youth; yet listen," cried the still trembling maid, "and I'll explain. You are, perhaps, not aware that Cavolti was an early suitor for my hand. On the plea of my extreme youth, and his hate of Cavolti, my father refused his proposals, and with joy I found myself freed from his hateful advances, and, as I hoped, for ever.

"In this I was deceived, for but a short time had elapsed ere he again proposed and renewed his pretensions with all his fierceness and former ardour, but he was again rejected.

"Vain were his efforts to conceal his rage at this my second refusal, which he averred arose from my love for some more favoured rival. This was soon after your escape from the cave.

"'I know the presumptuous villain,' growled Cavolti, 'who has dared to cross my path; but let him beware, for I will prove his deadly foe.'

"With these words he left me.

"From that time his conduct completely changed.

"The ardent expression which used to illumine his countenance when we met, is now supplanted by a heavy scowl, and he will fix his large, dark eyes upon my face with a fierce intensity that fills me with dismay.

"This morning I abruptly met him.

"Fire seemed to flash from his eyes.

"With difficulty could I suppress an ejaculation of horror, as I turned to avoid him.

"Seizing my arm, he exclaimed, in a bitter tone of warning,

"'The time will soon come when Agnese shall have bitter cause to repent the rejection of Cavolti. Think not, proud girl, ever to become the bride of him I suspect. No; I swear, by Heaven, rather than that, my dagger should stretch both him and thee lifeless at my feet.'

"Throwing my arm rudely from him, with the whispered word 'Remember,' he rushed from my sight.

"I am convinced that his heart is black enough to carry his threat into execution," said Agnese, trembling; "therefore, avoid him, dear youth, for should you meet I tremble for the consequences."

"Nay! fear it not, fair Agnese."

But while speaking the sound of distant footsteps broke upon the surrounding stillness.

Agnese heard her name called in loud, angry tones.

This was an unwelcome sound to the lovers, as it was a sure signal of her father's carousing and drunkenness.

"Farewell, Frank!" faintly escaped from her lips.

"Farewell, my love," returned he, folding her to his bosom; "to-morrow at twilight, at the same hour and place, we meet again. Till then, farewell!"

For a moment their lips met, then, sighing, they tore themselves from each other's embrace.

Frank followed her with his eyes until she was hid from his view, then, drawing his cloak around him, he proceeded on his lonely walk, musing on the threatening words uttered by Cavolti to the fair Agnese.

Lost in these reflections he walked, heedless of surrounding objects, until a sudden exclamation startled him.

When, looking towards the spot from whence the sound proceeded, he beheld the same figure he had seen before.

He was slowly preceding him, apparently unconscious of being observed.

The hot blood rushed to the cheeks of Frank.

His proud heart swelled to repay the insult offered to his fair Agnese.

Hastening forward the next moment beheld him by the side of the object of his resentment!

Cavolti seemed startled at Frank's sudden appearance.

But there was a storm gathering in the villain's dark eyes as he fixed them on the bold youth that would have appalled the heart of any one less brave than Frank, who, returning his scathing glance with one of scorn, proudly exclaimed,

"Nay, reserve thy fierce looks, Cavolti, for one who fears them. Methinks they sit but ill upon the features of a listener, and one who, on discovery, fled like a vile caitiff, as he was."

"'Tis false!" cried Cavolti, with fury, "'twas chance alone that led me to the spot; but," added he, with a galling sneer, "'twas not through fear of the English brat!"

"And was it chance that kept thee there until now?" returned Frank, proudly.

"Peace, babbler, as thou art!" interrupted Cavolti, "or not even thy immeasurable inferiority in age, size, or strength shall save thee from the chastisement you deserve."

"Nobly spoken," returned Frank, with cutting irony, "and well befits the man who would rather utter his threats in the the ear of a defenceless maid than face the object of his hatred as a man."

"Detested idiot! I'll hear no more!" cried Cavolti, frantically grasping his sword; "that falsehood shall be washed out in blood!"

"Now I understand thee," dauntingly exclaimed Frank, "and my answer is in my scabbard."

"Pluck it forth, then, and see if thou canst guard thy life, vile English dog!"

"Nay, look to thyself," returned Frank, as his bright blade gleamed in the air.

The cloaks of the combatants had fallen off, and the contrast in their appearance was strikingly different.

Frank stood a perfect model of youthful symmetry.

His opponent appeared a second Hercules, the gigantic proportions of his loins indicating strength nearly superhuman.

A look of defiance flashed from the eyes of each.

Cavolti rushed to the onset with the ferocity of a tiger.

Frank received him with unshrinking valour that bid defiance to his efforts.

Roused to madness by the coolness displayed by his youthful antagonist, Cavolti grasped his ponderous weapon.

With both hands he raised it high above his head; descending, it cleft the air, but Frank stepping aside avoided the stroke, and ere Cavolti could recover himself he, by a side blow, laid him prostrate on the earth.

Then placing a foot upon his broad chest Frank bade him beg his life.

"Never!" exclaimed Cavolti, in accents scarcely audible from passion. "Strike! the pangs of death are less bitter than those I now feel!"

Frank, taking his foot from his body, said, proudly,

"I give it thee, Cavolti; 'tis enough; I do not want thy life; take it, and endeavour to forget the occurrence of this evening, as I shall; but never dare dream of the fair Agnese."

Returning his steel to his scabbard he hastened towards the bandits' camp.

For a few moments Cavolti stood, seeming scarcely to believe his own senses.

Starting to his feet, revenge, like a demon raging in his breast, and crushing every nobler feeling.

"Forget my base defeat, and by a rival, too," he cried, in a voice hoarse and convulsed. "Never! 'Twere easier to forget myself. No; revenge is still within my power, and like lightning shall it fall on thy dastard head."

He rushed frantically from the spot.

The next evening, as the sun was fast sinking beneath the western horizon, Frank hastened to keep his appointment with Basil's fair daughter.

On reaching the well-known place, however, Agnese was not there.

This at first surprised him, as their usual time of meeting had long since passed.

Concluding something had happened to detain her he entered some old Roman ruins with the intention of waiting there, but scarcely had he seated himself for that purpose on one of the overthrown pillars, when a confused noise struck upon his ear.

He sprung upon his feet, and in doing so kicked against something on the ground, which, on taking up, proved to be a bracelet, which he instantly recognised, and exclaimed, in astonishment,

"'Tis *her* bracelet!"

Hardly had the words escaped his lips ere the noise was again repeated, and the words, "Save me! save me!" were faintly uttered by a distant voice, the first tones of which thrilled to his heart.

"Save thee!" thundered a voice, as Frank rushed forward. "No power on earth shall save thee!"

The shriek that followed curdled the blood in Frank's veins, and rooted him to the spot.

At that instant a dark figure glided past him.

Frank sprang forward and seized it.

The treacherous cloak alone remained in his grasp.

A low moan, and his own name, faintly repeated, now broke upon his ear.

"Ha! I come! I come!" exclaimed Frank, frantically rushing towards the spot.

But madness seized upon his brain as he beheld the horrid spectacle.

At his feet lay the body of Agnese, who loved him so well, the faithful maid who had jeopardized her life to save him from the poisoned goblet.

On her bosom was a gaping wound, from which the blood still flowed.

Her eyes were closed.

A smile played around her lips, from between which her breath was softly ejaculating the name of Frank, that frenzied being who now stood gazing on her.

He moved not; no sound escaped him.

A slight tremor afflicted his frame; his breast heaved convulsively.

"Agnese! Agnese!" burst in hysteric accents from his bursting heart.

His limbs refused their office, and, with a cry of agony, he fell by the side of the wounded maid.

* * * * *

The rosy beam of morn still found Frank stretched on the earth beside the wounded maid.

At length, being aroused from his lethargy, he started up as though awakened from some horrid dream, and he resumed his tender care of staunching the maiden's wounds.

At length his eyes became fixed upon the earth, and at that moment he beheld something on the ground.

He eagerly seized it.

It was a dagger encrusted with blood.

"'Tis her precious blood!" cried Frank, in a convulsed voice, and was about to dash the weapon to the ground when he observed some letters on the blade.

'Twas the name of his deadly rival!

"Oh, heartless villain! is this the reward for the life I gave thee?" exclaimed Frank, furiously. "Base scoundrel! but thou shalt not escape me for ever, Cavolti. I will search for and cleave thee to the dust!"

Thrusting the dagger between the folds of his garments, and casting a look of anguish and love on Agnese as he bore the maid away, he rushed from the spot.

With the wounded girl in his arms Frank rushed from the spot.

His passions were now wrought up to a state of madness.

He bent his steps towards the cave and entered.

The first person he saw was Basil himself.

"Halt!" said the bandit chief, as he observed Frank approaching his own apartment. "What brings thee here?"

"Urgent business."

"Of what nature?"

"Your daughter has been cruelly stabbed."

"Agnese stabbed?" said Basil. "Where is she?"

"I have placed her in one of your cavern rooms hard by. If you would but see her, follow me."

"Who has done this to my only daughter?" said Basil, for the first time realizing the feelings of a father. "Who has done this? Let me see her, and learn the name of the base villain."

Basil followed Frank to the room indicated.

Frank had well bound up the wound while in the garden with Agnese, but the blood still flowed.

Basil knelt beside the body of his unconscious daughter, and cold sweat oozed from his brow.

His bosom heaved, and he clenched his fists.

"Whose cursed blade did this?" he gasped.

"Cavolti's."

"Ha! say you so? What! he, my second in command, to thus outrage my daughter? No, no, he could not; I cannot believe it."

"You will believe your own eyes?"

"What mean you?"

"Why, this!" said Frank. "I found this dagger beside the spot where she lay bleeding and faint."

"'Tis Cavolti's!" Basil gasped. "It is one I myself gave him a year ago."

"I know not that," said Frank.

"Oh! the treacherous villain! that I might meet him face to face. To attempt to slay an innocent girl who begged his life from me!"

While Basil listened to the whole of Frank's story regarding his encounter with Cavolti—which, it must be confessed, greatly surprised the bandit chief—two of the mountain band came to the room door and knocked.

"What want ye?" said Basil, as they were admitted. "See you this horrid sight?"

"We do, Captain Basil, and have heard all about it; it is concerning this affair that we now come."

"And from whom?"

"From Cavolti."

"Why, he it was that did it!" Basil said. "Oh that I might grasp the villain once more by the throat and strangle him!"

"Cavolti, Captain Basil, did *not* do this," the two men replied, calmly.

"Did not?"

"No, he did not; he is too brave for that."

"Then who did?"

"The youth who now stands beside you."

"*I?*" said Frank, with the hot blood rushing to his face in anger. "*I* do such a dastardly deed? Who says so must answer for it with his life."

"Who says so?" Basil asked.

"Cavolti himself."

"But we have Cavolti's dagger, found near the girl."

"True, Basil; it was stolen from him while asleep, and by the youth who now looks so pale."

"Before heaven, I am innocent of this foul deed," said Frank, with upraised hand.

"This must be inquired into," said Basil.

"We have come to take away this youth, Captain Basil," said the messengers. "Cavolti waits for us."

"Where?"

"In the little dell between the mountains. The band for the most part have been summoned to witness the execution."

"The what?" gasped Frank.

"The execution," said the messengers.

"I am innocent."

"Who's to prove it?"

"*I* can," said a faint voice.

All turned and were greatly surprised to see the eyes of Agnese gently open and close again, as she sighed,

"Father, believe me, he is innocent."

"You hear that?" said Basil.

"The maid is raving," the messengers said; "she wishes to screen the young villain."

"I am not raving," Agnese replied, in a very faint voice. "Cavolti is the one who tried to assassinate me, and would have done so but for the timely interference of the brave youth now before you."

Frank, kneelt beside Agnese, and, affectionately kissing her hand, said,

"Thank Heaven for this denial, sweet girl. And now," he said, rising proudly, "now that this foul suspicion is lifted from my soul, I am strong enough to confront Cavolti and defy his base accusation, or those of any one in the wide world."

"You hear what my daughter says," said Basil; "the youth is innocent."

"Cavolti denies it," was the calm reply of the two messengers. "Our orders are imperative; we came to take this youth away."

"And murder me in cold blood," said Frank, with a mocking smile.

The messengers answered not.

"He must not go. Father, protect him from the fangs of the serpent Cavolti," said Agnese, faintly and imploringly.

"Fear not for me, Agnese," said Frank, boldly, "I dread him not. I *will* go, and alone."

"Nay," said Basil, "for a moment, stay. If you are innocent, as I firmly believe, on the words of my daughter here, I will protect you with the last drop of my blood; but there are rules and laws among us over which I have no controul, and one of them is that an accusation brought against any one of the band may be tried in two ways—either by judge and jury or by the ordeal of battle."

"Thank Heaven for that!" said Frank, aloud. "Then give me trial by battle! If I only meet my base accuser face to face in mortal combat, I have nothing to fear, for my cause is just."

"But, in this case, it cannot be," said Basil; "you are not one of our band; you must be tried."

"And sure to be condemned. But this shall not be," he said, approaching the door.

The two messengers opposed him.

Snatching up Basil's sword, which lay on the table, Frank, swift as lightning, struck one of the villains to the earth; in another moment the other's sword was flying through the air, and Frank's sword passed through his body, then, striding over their prostrate forms, disappeared before Basil could recover from his astonishment.

* * * * * *

"Now for vengeance," said Frank, as he issued from the cave, breathless with excitement, and rushed towards the trees, which on every side enclosed the mouth of the cave.

Once there he cared not for any who pursued him.

"I will seek out this black-hearted villain in the dell," said he, "and, ere sunset, his body or mine shall be food for vultures."

Frank had not gone far into the dense forest on the mountain side ere he heard the faint echoes of a horn!

He stopped to listen.

"I should know that sound," said he. "There it is again! It is not the bandits' call; nor is it any Austrian signal."

His face was flushed, and his eyes shot forth fire as he thought—

"It must be some of my boy band in search of me. I cannot be mistaken. They are searching the mountains for me. Oh, if they only knew where I am, how they would fly to my rescue. There it is again! Why, the sounds get nearer and nearer!"

Onward he went in search of Cavolti in the dell.

At this instant Frank was startled by hearing several horns of the Bandit Band now sounding all around him.

"It is an alarm," said he; "a general one, too!"

He had not long to wait in suspense.

He could hear the hasty tread of armed men in the forest.

"Haste--haste, comrade!" said one.

"What is the matter?" his companion asked. "Is it the Austrians?"

"No, worse than that."

"The Pope's soldiers?"

"No, no. They are of no account. It is the devil!"

"The devil, what do you mean?"

"Mean? why, two of our scouts have run in from their posts, all haste, to tell us that the English Boy Soldiers are prowling about the gorges in search of their missing comrades, particularly their young captain, Basil's prisoner."

"How many of them are there? This alarm is a general one; they must be numerous, or our horns wouldn't be sounding so loudly."

"They *are* numerous," was the reply; "three hundred or more, I hear. They have defeated the Austrians several times, and are so fierce a band of English boys that the best soldiers cannot stand before them. But we meet on the east ridge, just overlooking the small dell."

This was all that Frank could hear, for the men hurried away towards their rendezvous.

In a short time, however, he heard the distant rattle of muskets.

"That's Hugh Tracy or Dick Fellows," said Frank. "I wonder if it was Fatty who blew his horn just now; it sounded much like his blast?"

Again the reports of fire-arms could be heard, but not in a very great number.

"If it were the whole band," thought Frank, "they'd make more noise than that; and yet, if there are but few, these dark villains in the mountains will massacre them. But how did they find their way hither? and who could have told them of my rescue from the Austrians by Cavolti?"

"Who calls Cavolti?" said a distant voice.

Frank started.

It was Cavolti himself.

"You have escaped my messengers, I see," said the villain, with a grin of hate upon his dusky features; "but you shall not escape *me*."

"Nay, villain! you need not boast so early," said Frank; "I have come to meet you. A thing like you, who could waylay and stab a defenceless girl, has little cause to brag."

"I killed her! She is dead! Rather that a thousand times than see her in your embrace!"

"She lives, vile coward!" said Frank, "and I come to avenge her. Lead on towards the little dell; there, in sight of the whole brigand band, will I stuff thy loathsome lies down thy craven throat!"

"Vain idiot," said Cavolti, "follow me."

Frank did so.

Cavolti whistled as he approached the little dell.

The signal was repeated by some one.

"'Tis well," said Cavolti to himself; "I have two men in waiting at the dell, who shall seize and strangle this brat. They are concealed, and he knows it not."

They were now nearly out of the thick wood, and in view of the dell.

Frank cautiously followed his gigantic antagonist.

They were now on the edge of the wood, when Cavolti whistled again.

His signal was repeated.

"They are near at hand," said he, with a grim smile.

On the instant, however, and greatly to Frank's surprise, two youths dashed from their hiding-places, and pounced upon Cavolti.

They were two of the English Boys; one was Dick Fellows.

In an instant Cavolti was thrown to the ground, and with swords at his throat.

# THE BOY SOLDIER; OR, GARIBALDI'S YOUNG CAPTAIN.

ANNETTE SAVES THE LIFE OF FRANK FORD—SEE NO. 12.

## CHAPTER XXIX.

TREACHERY—THE FATAL SHOT—VENGEANCE AT HAND—THE DEADLY DUEL.

AT the instant he fired, although the ruffian did not perceive it, the figure of a second youth, sword in hand, was perceived some two hundred yards away on the edge of the precipice above.

"Ha! ha!" said the villain, "how nicely I entrapped this English youth; but they little dream of what an Italian's cunning is. Ha! ha! If he was not killed by my bullet, the fall would crush him to pieces. That's *one* of them—ha! ha! Would that I might finish my night's work by falling across the other lad."



With the nimbleness of a monkey he climbed the rope again.

He had scarcely pulled himself up to the edge of the rock, when he was startled to perceive the figure of a youth running towards him at full speed.

"Fortune favours me," the villain said. "I have been watched and dodged by this miserable boy."

In an instant he drew his heavy cavalry sword, and rushed at the youth approaching.

"Villain! bloodthirsty coward!" gasped Dick

"Yes, *me*."

"How do you make that out?"

"Why, I discovered him first."

"No, you didn't."

"But I say I *did*," was the angry response of the first speaker.

"And if you did, what of that?" asked the third.

"Ain't we going share and share alike?" the fourth inquired.

"Not a bit of it," said the first. "Grumble as much as you like; it won't benefit you much. Ask the surgeon if I didn't discover him first or not."

"Well, if you did, it don't matter much; we shall all have equal shares."

"I'm glad you think so," laughed the first; "but *I* don't, my lads."

"But, you can't help yourself," the second said, with an oath, and a flashing eye.

"Can't I? What do you mean by scowling at me in such a fierce style as that, eh? I tell you I can."

"Well, if we don't have shares, I don't see why we should trouble ourselves about carrying the youth any farther," said two at once.

"Oh, that's it, eh?" said the first speaker, with a fierce look. "Then lay him down beside this group of trees, and I'll soon tell you what *I* think about it. If you don't help to carry him into camp I'll *make* you."

"Come, comrades, come, let us have no more bloodshed; enough has been spilt already, I think."

"And more will follow if there are many words over it."

"I'll tell you what we'll do," said one. "Let us cast lots to see who shall have the largest share of the reward."

"Not me."

"Nor me."

"Well, then, let us cast dice for it."

"That's better."

"Do you agree?"

"Yes," said two.

"*I* don't," the first one snarled. "Whoever wins, matters little to me; I'll have the reward, aye, every florin of it, or the life of him who opposes me."

"You talk very bravely," said one, "and as if there were not three of us against you."

"I care not if there were a dozen," said the first one, curling his moustachoes in high anger.

During this altercation the four soldiers arrived at the edge of a small plantation.

They deposited the body beneath a tree, and walked some few yards away to throw dice to see who should have the reward of one thousand florins offered for the capture of Frank Ford.

At first they threw their dice in a very quiet manner, but in a few moments began to quarrel in a terrible style, heedless of the poor youth, who lay unconscious under the trees.

The first speaker, from his habitual good luck in dice throwing, was induced to join in, particularly as the highest score only reached twenty-four in three throws.

"I can always beat that number. Ha! ha!" he said, "so there ain't much hazard about it."

He did throw.

The total came to twenty-four.

It was a tie.

He bit his lip, and cursed at his disappointment.

"Never threw so low in all my life," said he. "Let's try again."

With a face flushed with anger the first one sat down by the roadside, and seized the dice-box.

"A tie was it?"

"Yes; the last was."

"Then I have the first chance?"

"Yes; you lead off."

The first throw was twelve, at which he grumbled.

The next time he had three fives up.

"Not bad that," said one.

"Oh! he's the perfect devil at dice," said another. "Look at that! look! there's luck!"

He had thrown two fives and a six.

"That's good play," said one of the two, who had lost. "Why, that makes a total of forty-three."

The player tossed the dice-box from him with an air of indifference to his antagonist, who smiled darkly as he rattled the box.

"Three fives that time," said one.

Not a bad beginning.

He threw again.

"Eighteen this time," said the player, with a triumphant laugh.

He turned up three sixes.

"That's not fair," said the first player.

"It is."

"It *was* fair," said one or two.

"Go on, then; let's see what he turns up this time."

The last throw counted eighteen.

"Bravo!"

"Well done."

"I've thrown fifty-one in all," said the player. "against forty-three. The reward is mine!"

"You lie!" said the thwarted gambler; "you didn't play fair."

"The lie stick in your throat, rascal!" said the successful one. "Take that!"

He struck his rival on the cheek with his heavy leathern gauntlet.

In a moment swords were drawn.

"Keep them asunder, comrades!" cried one.

"Stand aside till I cleave the skull of this dice-sharper!" said the loser.

---

# THE BOY SOLDIER; OR, GARIBALDI'S YOUNG CAPTAIN.

FRANK FORD CUTS OFF THE HEAD OF CAVOLTI.—SEE O. 13.

It was a desperate encounter, and blood flowed on either side.

Even those two who were peacably inclined towards each other at first were now drawn into the brawl, and the whole four men were fiercely tilting and slashing at each other.

They might have continued fighting long and until they had scientifically cut each other's throats; but hostilities were suddenly brought to a close in an unlooked-for and very mysterious manner.

Loud shouts of derisive laughter suddenly burst upon the ears of the enraged duellists.

They drew back from each other, and listened.

"Ha, ha, ha!" echoed through the plantation.

"What means that?" gasped one and another, in surprise, each breathing hard for wind.

"Ha, ha, ha!" sounded again, in derisive triumph, through the dark, dense plantation.

The duellists looked at each other with staring eyes and open mouths, as they heard a rough voice in the distance, singing the refrain again and again of—

"Come fill up your bumpers, and our toast it shall be,
Here's health to all comrades on land and on sea;
Here's health to our captain, and 'tis our firm belief,
There's none half so good as bold Basil our chief."

rushed towards the trees, which on every side enclosed the mouth of the cave.

Once there he cared not for any who pursued him.

"I will seek out this black-hearted villain in the dell," said he, "and, ere sunset, his body or mine shall be food for vultures."

Frank had not gone far into the dense forest on the mountain side ere he heard the faint echoes of a horn!

He stopped to listen.

"I should know that sound," said he. "There it is again! It is not the bandits' call; nor is it any Austrian signal."

His face was flushed, and his eyes shot forth fire as he thought—

"It must be some of my boy band in search of me. I cannot be mistaken. They are searching the mountains for me. Oh, if they only knew where I am, how they would fly to my rescue. There it is again! Why, the sounds get nearer and nearer!"

Onward he went in search of Cavolti in the dell.

At this instant Frank was startled by hearing several horns of the Bandit Band now sounding all around him.

"It is an alarm," said he; "a general one, too!"

He had not long to wait in suspense.

He could hear the hasty tread of armed men in the forest.

"Haste—haste, comrade!" said one.

"What is the matter?" his companion asked. "Is it the Austrians?"

"No, worse than that."

"The Pope's soldiers?"

"No, no. They are of no account. It is the devil!"

"The devil, what do you mean?"

"Mean? why, two of our scouts have run in from their posts, all haste, to tell us that the English Boy Soldiers are prowling about the gorges in search of their missing comrades, particularly their young captain, Basil's prisoner."

"How many of them are there? This alarm is a general one; they must be numerous, or our horns wouldn't be sounding so loudly."

"They *are* numerous," was the reply; "three hundred or more, I hear. They have defeated the Austrians several times, and are so fierce a band of English boys that the best soldiers cannot stand before them. But we meet on the east ridge, just overlooking the small dell."

This was all that Frank could hear, for the men hurried away towards their rendezvous.

In a short time, however, he heard the distant rattle of muskets.

"That's Hugh Tracy or Dick Fellows," said Frank. "I wonder if it was Fatty who blew his horn just now; it sounded much like his blast?"

Again the reports of fire-arms could be heard, but not in a very great number.

"If it were the whole band," thought Frank, "they'd make more noise than that; and yet, if there are but few, these dark villains in the mountains will massacre them. But how did they find their way hither? and who could have told them of my rescue from the Austrians by Cavolti?"

"Who calls Cavolti?" said a distant voice.

Frank started.

It was Cavolti himself.

"You have escaped my messengers, I see," said the villain, with a grin of hate upon his dusky features; "but you shall not escape *me*."

"Nay, villain! you need not boast so early," said Frank; "I have come to meet you. A thing like you, who could waylay and stab a defenceless girl, has little cause to brag."

"I killed her! She is dead! Rather that a thousand times than see her in your embrace!"

"She lives, vile coward!" said Frank, "and I come to avenge her. Lead on towards the little dell; there, in sight of the whole brigand band, will I stuff thy loathsome lies down thy craven throat!"

"Vain idiot," said Cavolti, "follow me."

Frank did so.

Cavolti whistled as he approached the little dell.

The signal was repeated by some one.

"'Tis well," said Cavolti to himself; "I have two men in waiting at the dell, who shall seize and strangle this brat. They are concealed, and he knows it not."

They were now nearly out of the thick wood, and in view of the dell.

Frank cautiously followed his gigantic antagonist.

They were now on the edge of the wood, when Cavolti whistled again.

His signal was repeated.

"They are near at hand," said he, with a grim smile.

On the instant, however, and greatly to Frank's surprise, two youths dashed from their hiding-places, and pounced upon Cavolti.

They were two of the English Boys; one was Dick Fellows.

In an instant Cavolti was thrown to the ground, and with swords at his throat.

# THE BOY SOLDIER; OR, GARIBALDI'S YOUNG CAPTAIN.

DREADFUL POSITION OF AGNES AND FRANK.—*See* No. 14.

"Hold!" said Frank. "How is this? How came you hither?"

"We know all, Captain Frank; we will speak of our adventures another time. This villain had two desperadoes waiting to despatch you, but we captured both, and learned much concerning you. Let us slay this cold-blooded scoundrel."

"No, lads, you must not kill that prostrate knave, neither will I fly."

"Not escape?"

"No lads, I am on my parole, and have given my word of honour not to trespass beyond certain bounds."

"Why keep faith with such knaves as these? They know not what honour is."

"That may be, but I do. No, I will not flee. Release the hound," said Frank.

Cavolti glared around him like a half-tamed wolf.

"Rise," said Frank, "and defend yourself in presence of these two youths, and in sight of your own band. You or I must die."

Throwing off his cloak Frank put himself in an attitude of defence.

The two Boy Soldiers were fearful of the result.

In the distance could be seen a great commotion among the banditti, who were perched on the ridge, but who could not descend to the aid of their second commander.

Cavolti, however, put on an air of fierce deter-

## CHAPTER XXXVI.

THE BANDIT COUNCIL — THE SURPRISE — THE DEFIANCE.

When introduced into the presence of the bandit chief, Frank found Basil smiling and happy instead of in a towering passion.

He could not understand this.

For some time Basil walked up and down, rubbing his hands, and bursting out into strange, wild laughter.

"Oh! you have returned, eh?" said the chief, at last, grinning, and showing his white, fang-like teeth, and rolling a pair of black, wicked-looking eyes. "You have returned I see!"

"Yes, Basil, I have. You, of course, know all?"

"I do, young man, and am sorry for you," said the chief, chuckling and rubbing his hands; adding in a whisper to himself, "Sorry, eh? Ha! ha! it's the best day's work ever happened to me; but he don't know it. This bold youth has rid me of the greatest villain that ever crossed my path or tried to circumvent me! and just when that comes to pass, a letter arrives from the Englishman, and a messenger, with the price of his head. The band don't know this, however, and never shall. I will stick to the golden coin myself. They will be none the wiser."

"So you have killed him?" said Basil, aloud.

"I have, and fairly, in sight of many of your men."

"Ah! that's another matter—we will have to decide all about that. The council sits to-night."

"For what purpose?"

"To decide what manner of death you shall die, so prepare yourself. This time to-morrow you will be dead."

"You are very consoling, Captain Basil," said Frank. "You talk of taking life just as coolly as if you did it regularly, like a butcher."

"I'm glad you think so; you'll die game I perceive. Ha! ha!" (No wonder that Englishman wants to get him out of the way. There is some mystery between them. What it is I can't find out. All I know is that he's flush of money, or he couldn't send so many bags of florins," thought Basil.)

"Am I to consider myself under arrest, then?" said Frank. "Am I allowed certain bounds as usual, or is it revoked?"

"It is revoked. Give up your arms and retire to your cell."

"How is this? Do you break faith with me then, Basil? You promised me certain bounds and the right to use my arms in self-defence."

"Circumstances alter cases—until your fight with Cavolti, it was all very well; but not now." ("I knew that they would quarrel," said Basil, aside. "Cavolti, I learned, had poisoned the tip of his sword. Perhaps for *my* breast; but I changed it! This youth, unknown to himself, has had Cavolti's weapon. A single scratch would have been sufficient for the purpose, but the lad did more, he beheaded him. Ha! ha! Their swords were alike, Cavolti never discovered the difference. What an excellent thought to change their weapons! The biter was bitten! Ha! ha!")

"If such be your decision, Basil, you have broken faith."

"No prattle, youth. You have heard my decision. Do not tempt me to enforce it."

He touched a bell.

Four men appeared, as if by magic.

Basil pointed to Frank.

"Nay, approach me no further. Put up your weapons, men; I fear ye not. No, not if you were twenty instead of four. Here is my sword, Basil," said Frank, proudly, throwing it upon the floor. "Take it. It is of no use to me now. If I die, it shall be as a man of honour."

"Send him away."

Frank was conducted from Basil's presence and cast into a dungeon.

"When does this young stranger arrive?" asked Basil, of one who entered on the summons of the chief.

"This evening, captain."

"You know our rules, of course?"

"The twelve masks and gowns are prepared fo the council, who will receive them."

"'Tis well; and what of Annette?"

"She is in close confinement, and awaits the decision of to-night's council."

"My daughter is too weak from her wound to appear, I fear."

"She is unwell, captain; but it strikes me, from all I hear of her nurse, the old hag, that if even she were well, nothing could be forced from her which would help to criminate this young Englishman."

"I do not understand you," said the chief. "Speak plainer."

"Her wound then, captain, is much better; whoever struck the blow missed his mark. If the dagger had penetrated one inch lower, it must have killed her instantly. She raves and rambles in her sleep, so the hag informs me, and is for ever calling on the young Englishman's name in the tenderest accents, and with the most loving words."

"Bah! love; stuff and nonsense. She is but a babbling girl; she must appear, and if she does not tell all she knows about this youth, why then she must suffer with Annette; we will have no spies among us."

"All you say is right and proper, Captain Basil," said the brigand, bowing, and about to retire.

"Stay," said Basil. "Now that Cavolti is dead, there is one of the council less."

"There is."

"You know that the position is one of great trust and secresy?"

"I do."

"Well, then, for your faithfulness, Ambrose," said Basil, "and for the devotedness you have shown to me and the band since you have been among us, I appoint you to the vacant maskhood and gown."

"Me!" said Ambrose, the brigand, in surprise.

"Yes, you. Will you take the oath?"

"I will."

"Then kneel."

Ambrose did so.

"Swear by this upraised sword to remain faithful and true; on your blood and life swear it."

"I do."

"Then rise. The vacant mask and gown is yours; disgrace it not.

"On my blood, I swear."

"'Tis well."

At that moment the brigands, who had taken Frank forth, returned.

"Have you caged him, men?"

"We have."

"You may retire."

They bowed, and left the apartment.

"Now, Ambrose, go you and see that this young captive is safely secured; he must not escape; his head is paid for; 'tis precious. Until the council meet to-night, farewell."

Ambrose left the room.

He directed his footsteps along a broad passage that had been cut out of the solid rock.

It was dark, winding, cold, and oppressive.

He reached the cell wherein Frank was confined, and was surprised to hear the captive singing as unconcernedly as if he had a lease of his life for a thousand years to come.

"This is a brave youngster," mused Ambrose, with a smile. "No wonder that Agnese loves and raves about him in her sleep. The bandit band would rejoice at having such a fearless, dare-devil for a leader, if it could only be brought about. Basil is brave, but he is getting too old now to lead on, and all he cares about is getting drunk and hoarding money. He has sacks upon sacks of gold and silver coin, besides an immense amount of booty stowed away somewhere in the cavern."

While thus he thought, Ambrose unlocked the cell door and entered.

Frank was surprised at this unexpected visit, but said not a word.

"You are to be tried to-night," said Ambrose, "and will be condemned."

"If my death is resolved upon by the bandit council, why go through the farce of pretending to try me?"

"It is the custom among us."

"Who is my accuser?"

"A fellow-countryman of yours; he has paid Basil a large price for your head."

"Indeed!"

"Yes, the money arrived in several large bags this morning. I brought it, and it has been safely stowed away by our chief."

"Then why came you thus to inform me of such a barbarous proceeding?"

"I *could* tell you," said Ambrose, in a whisper, "but I dare not."

"Dare not! why?"

"You are not rich."

"I know it."

"Then you cannot have many friends. Poor people," chuckled Ambrose, "never have many to assist them in the hour of need."

"I know that, also; but why came you here to taunt me?"

"No, I came as a friend, and will prove it."

"How?"

"I will soon show you; but, in the first place, you must answer my questions truly."

"I will; what are they?"

"Now don't be surprised at what I say. This fellow-countryman of yours, whose name I could never yet learn, lives not far from here, and seeks your life, by fair means or foul; he told me so."

"Indeed! why?"

"He told me this morning, when I took Basil's message to him, that he wishes it from a sense of justice: for he calls you a murderer!"

"A murderer!" gasped Frank.

"Yes, a murderer! Don't turn so pale; he has got an English detective officer with him, as I learn, who has come to capture you if he can for the murder of your uncle, Mr. Ford."

"Oh, heavens! *he* murdered!" said Frank, with choked utterance, "and *I* accused of that bloody deed!"

"He says so, and offers to prove it: but *I* don't believe it."

"*You* do not, Ambrose?"

"No, I do not. I have seen enough of you here to know that you would not, *could not*, do such a cold-blooded deed as that."

"Oh! thanks, Ambrose! thanks!" said Frank, shaking the brigand heartily by the hand.

"And to prove what friendship I have for you, I will run the risk of my own life to serve and save you."

"But, how?" said Frank, with a quivering voice. "Oh! that I had the base accuser face to face. *Me?* I kill my poor old uncle? No! heaven knows I did not. I could not. Alas! for the old man's untimely fate."

"There are not many hours ere the council will sit, Frank," said Ambrose, "and if I do something towards your release, you must promise secresy on your oath."

"I will, willingly, brave Ambrose."

"Then write me a note at once to your band in the mountains, and sign it with your own name and private mark, that they may not disbelieve me.'

"What would you have me say?"

"Only this—'The bearer is a friend, and perils his life to save me from an unjust and ignominious death; obey him as you would me, and place yourselves under his guidance.'"

"But this may be a snare to entrap my brave boys," replied Frank.

"Nay, have faith in me," said the young brigand, "you shall not be deceived."

"I will. There is the note," said Frank; "when shall I see you again?"

"Not before the council meet; but be not alarmed, trust to me: for the present farewell."

Ambrose closed the iron door and locked it.

He did not retrace his footsteps, but plunged farther along the winding stone passages, which at every yard became narrower and darker.

At length he issued out at the opposite side of the mountain by a large round hole, which was partly covered with ivy and concealed from the sight of any common observer.

Once he had gained the fresh air, he clambered down the mountain side and was soon lost to view on his way to the camp of the Boy Soldiers.

* * * *

This visit, and the disclosure made by Ambrose, the young brigand, filled Frank with amazement, and he sat in his lonely cell, pale, thoughtful, and sorrowful.

"My uncle murdered," he thought, "and I accused of the horrid deed! How could all this have come to pass? 'Tis most revolting, and I cannot believe it."

He paced up and down his dark dungeon, and sighed as he thought,

"Perhaps, after all, this Ambrose is an impostor, and has played this cruel trick upon me to entrap all my brave young band. I am sorry now I placed any confidence in him at all. What an idiot I was to be deceived by his plausible manner and smooth tongue."

Hours upon hours passed away.

He could hear the footfalls of men passing and re-passing his cell door with heavy tread.

Some doors were opened and others closed, with a harsh grating sound that fell upon his attentive ear like a death-knell.

Then all was profoundly quiet again.

Not a breath of air seemed to stir around him, and the close damp, fœtid atmosphere was almost suffocating.

"What a tale these dungeons could tell," mused Frank, "if they could only speak. Doubtless there is more than one poor wretch confined hereabouts, if the truth was only known. Poor little Annette, too, is confined somewhere near me—and all because she saved my life! Would that I could discover her prison house! or that she could hear me speak her name."

"Who calls upon Annette?" said a faint voice, in tones of sorrow.

Frank was startled.

"Whence comes that voice?" he whispered, half aloud. "Surely it was all imaginary. No one could have heard me."

"Who calls on the name of Annette?" said the voice again. "Think not of her. She is condemned, and will shortly suffer; but think well of what will to-night befall you. All hope, I fear, is lost! They are already preparing for your execution. The council chairs are already placed. In two hours your fate will be decreed. I have heard all. *I* am Annette. Hush! speak not, some one approaches."

Frank listened again, and all was a death-like calm.

"It must have been a dream, he thought," and walked to and fro deep in meditation.

Heavy footsteps were heard approaching.

The locks were turned.

A man, masked, with a hood over his head, and clothed from head to foot in a black cloak, was there, lantern in hand.

Four brigands conducted Frank, two on each side; the masked man led the way.

Not a word was spoken; not a sound was audible, save the echo of their own footfalls in the passage.

They approached the council chamber door.

Frank walked in, followed by the cloaked stranger.

The four brigands went their way.

When Frank entered the council chamber he was surprised to behold twelve figures, cloaked, hooded, and masked in black.

They sat in a very large circle, but with no table before them.

Frank felt that all were watching him as he entered, and could see their eyes through the eyelet holes of their masks glittering and sparkling.

No one spoke a word.

The apartment was very large, round, and lofty, and a single lamp hung from the centre of the roof.

The president's chair was empty.

Frank was placed in the centre of the figures, and stood proudly, like one conscious of his innocence.

The last to enter was Basil.

He was dressed like the rest, but from his unsteady gait it was plain that he had been drinking a great deal, as usual.

He staggered to the president's chair, and reclined at his ease.

After a long pause he said—

"The youngest member of the council (Ambrose) has already informed you of the charges against the prisoner?"

"He has," was the solemn and unanimous answer.

"Is he guilty of killing Cavolti?"

"He is," was the awful response of all.

Frank turned pale.

"He is accused of murdering his uncle also; you have heard the statement, made, as usual, by the youngest member of the council, before the prisoner was brought in?"

"We have."

"Are you satisfied as to his guilt?"

"No."

"What is your wish?"

"Let he and his prosecutor appear face to face."

"Is such your desire?"

"It is."

Basil appeared fretful and annoyed at this, but was apparently so tipsy that he could scarcely keep his eyes open.

"Bring in the accuser," said Basil.

Ambrose went forth, and soon returned.

He was quickly followed by a youthful-looking person, who cast down his eyes, and would not look at the prisoner fairly in the face.

Directly Frank saw him he staggered back a step or two in amazement.

"It is—it is Joel Flint disguised," he muttered, with astonishment.

At that moment one of the council put a small slip of paper into the hands of Ambrose.

Ambrose looked at it, and then addressed the accused thus—

"I am appointed to conduct this case, by the council's desire; you must answer a few questions."

The stranger bowed, and a sardonic smile lit up his features.

"Your name is——"

"Schmidt."

"And you know the prisoner?"

"I do. He is the one who murdered his uncle, old Mr. Ford."

"'Tis false!" said Frank, with a bitter oath. "'Tis false, craven-hearted knave! Thy name is not Schmidt. Basil, his name is Joel Flint. On my life I swear it!"

At the bare mention of his own name, Joel turned pale, and trembled as he said—

"Worthy Basil, believe not the unblushing scoundrel. I am *not* what he would represent me. Thou hast had ample proof of my trust in thee, and of my truth."

"What means the stranger?" said one of the twelve. "We are the judges in this case. Captain Basil is president only. He cannot decide a case like this without us."

Basil was half stupid with drink, and if he distinctly heard, he did not understand what had been said.

"What mean you by ample proof, stranger?" Ambrose asked.

"Why many," answered the stranger. "I knew not that all this ceremony was needed, or I would not have come. I demand the prisoner in the name of justice."

"Fear not," said Ambrose. "Justice shall be done, and to both. Brigands as we are, we know not what money is in a question of life or death, at least not in this case. What says Captain Basil?"

"I quite agree to that. There seems to be a dispute as to the truth or falsehood of each other's statements. I know not what he means by money."

"What!" gasped the stranger.

"I have not received a farthing from any one. If he persists in saying so," said Basil, "the stranger lies, that's all. Let them decide their question fairly by battle. There's nothing like it, is there lads?"

"No," said the council, as one man.

"Fight!" gasped the stranger. "I refuse to do anything of the sort."

"Why, an hour or two ago, you said nothing would give you greater pleasure than to cut his throat, didn't you?"

"I know nothing about what I did or did not say, but I refuse to draw weapons with this base fellow here."

"Then you are a coward," said Basil. "You were quite valorous until just now; and, by my wrath, since you swear I received money from *you*, which the brigand council well knows to be a lie, for I wouldn't do such a thing, you *shall* fight."

"Shall, Basil?"

"Aye. I'll make you. You must either fight the prisoner or me. What says the council?"

"Agreed!" was the response.

"I care not if both get killed," laughed Basil, to himself. "I have got the money, and as I am a little flushed with wine, I think an exciting combat would wake me up a bit. The sight of blood refreshes me at times. Ambrose! the swords!"

Frank smiled with confidence, as he seized the long weapon handed to him, and flourished it.

The stranger, however, trembled in every limb.

He turned ghastly pale, and his eyes rolled in horror.

"Come, prepare," said Basil, with a cruel laugh. "Put yourself into attitude, Mr. Schmidt. You told me you were an excellent swordsman. You've now got a chance of displaying your skill."

"I refuse to fight, Basil. This is all a cruel trick played upon me to dupe me out of my money."

"Fool!" said Basil, rising in anger, "mention money to me again, and I'll cleave your skull. Fight, I say; prove your accusation to be true at the sword's point, and then both I and the council will believe you; if you do not, then, by my wrath, you do not leave this place alive."

"Captain Basil, I thank you for this change in the order of your proceedings, for in the sight of heaven I am innocent of the cruel charges brought against me by this lying scoundrel, and as you will quickly see. I'll bring the rascal to his knees, and if he does not confess his villany before you all, then despatch me."

The stranger was now compelled to fight.

There was no hole through which to retreat, and his teeth shook and chattered in his jaws with fear.

"Here goes for a whisker," said Frank, in high glee.

After one or two passes, he cut off one of the stranger's false whiskers, which had been gummed to his cheeks for the purpose of disguising himself.

"Hillo!" said Basil, in surprise, as the whisker fell. "Hillo, that was pretty close shaving, and no mistake."

"A part of his moustache this time," said Frank, and, quick as thought, one of the stranger's false moustaches was knocked from his upper lip by the point of Frank's sword!

The accuser was now furious, and cut and slashed most viciously and wildly.

Had Frank desired it, there were many opportunities of killing his antagonist on the spot; but he only smiled, and warded off the stranger's cuts with extraordinary skill.

The remaining whisker and moustache soon followed suit with the others.

"Now that he is barefaced," said Frank, "little more remains to prove who and what the rascal is."

With a quick and clever cut, Frank took off the stranger's wig.

Basil, and the rest were thunderstruck at the sudden change in the accuser's appearance, and looked on with amazement.

"Now that we have got rid of the false hair, whisker, and moustaches, which made up the 'Mr. Schmidt,'" said Frank, gaily, "you shall see what stuff Joel Flint is really made of."

With the rapidity of lightning, Frank's sword flashed before the eyes of Joel.

The coward's sword fell from his hand, and he sprawled upon the floor.

In a second Frank's sword was at the villain's throat.

"Spare me! spare me!" he gasped. "Have mercy; pardon me; do what you will, but spare my life."

"Craven-hearted villain! I had my heel upon your throat once before at Bromley Hall, and after I spared you, you cursed me; you would follow me through the world like an evil genius, you said, and would never rest contented until I graced a gibbet. Do you remember?"

"I do, I do; but spare me."

All this was hurriedly spoken in English.

"What does he say? That he gave me money?"

"No, Basil, but you shall hear him. Now answer me. What is your name?"

"I have passed under that of Schmidt, lately."

"Was it your school name?"

"No, I was then called Joel Flint."

"Did I murder my poor old uncle?"

"I know not," gasped Joel."

"Swear, on your life."

"No, you did not."

"Was not all you have said regarding me false?"

"It was."

"Did you not pay two of my followers to act as spies on the movements of myself and the Boy Band?"

"I did."

"Where are they?"

"In a neighbouring village."

"With an English detective?"

"Yes."

"Captain Basil, do you hear all this?"

"I do. The impostor is worthy of death—kill him. What says the council?"

"Kill him. He is not fit to live."

"Spare me! oh, spare me!" gasped Joel, as he glanced with an agonized look at Frank's upraised sword. "Spare me, and I will be your slave!"

"Viper!" said Frank, "I could crush you under my heel; you rvile blood is worthless. Take your life, knave," continued he, spurning him with his foot, "take your wretched life. I give it you."

Joel's eyes danced wildly in his head, but when released from Frank's foot he crawled to a corner like a four-legged cur.

"If *you* think proper, Captain Frank Ford, to be so merciful towards this hypocrite *I* don't," said Basil. "Ambrose, seize the caitiff, and cast him into a dungeon."

Ambrose seized Joel very roughly by the collar, and, as he left the council chamber, Basil administered to his seat of honour such a vigorous kick that he sent "Mr. Schmidt" flying into the dark stone corridor.

"Now," said he, "we will proceed with the sentence. This youth has killed Cavolti, and, as you say, is worthy of death."

"We do," was the answer of the council.

"Then, as is customary, I deliver the blow," said Basil, rising and approaching the prisoner, who now was armless.

Frank folded his arms and looked Basil fairly in the face.

"Would you kill me?" he said, with a curling lip. "Know you where you are?"

"Where I am, rash youth? I do. Tremble, for your last hour is come!"

"Not yet. Behold!" said Frank, stamping his foot.

On the instant the masks, hoods, and cloaks fell from the persons of the grim councillors as if by magic.

Basil was surrounded by eleven of the Boy Soldiers!

As they had sat on chairs with big cushions

their size was not so noticeable before, but now that they jumped to their feet the trick was discovered.

Ambrose the Trusty had been as good as his word.

For a moment Basil's eyes rolled like balls of fire as Frank said,

"Captain Basil, listen to me. If you make any noise, or raise an alarm, I'll cut your throat, all our lives depend upon silence. Hark ye, when I entered this council chamber I knew nothing of this strange stratagem. It was not until you rose, dagger in hand, that I heard the councillors repeat the password of us Boy Soldiers. I then understood all. Blame not any of your band for this, for they are innocent. Teresa, Garibaldi's female spy, is my friend."

Turning to one of the boys he whispered a word or two in English.

Before Basil could utter a word, he was bound hand and foot, and gagged.

"Put out the lights, put on your cloaks again, and follow me," said Frank. "Make no noise; move about like mice. Hus-s-h! I hear some one coming!"

## CHAPTER XXXVII.

### THE RESCUE—THE PURSUIT—DREADFUL POSITION OF AGNESE AND FRANK.

For a moment Frank and his followers remained where they were in darkness and silence.

The person approaching walked on tiptoe, and groped his way through the darkness.

Each boy drew his sword, and waited with suspense for what might follow.

Frank took one step forward.

"Schmidt! Schmidt! where are you?" said a voice, in a whisper.

"Here I am," said Frank, imitating Joel's voice. "What do you want?"

"Ambrose sent me in. Is it all over?"

"Yes."

"Well, where is the young scoundrel, Frank Ford? You are all in darkness. I can't see you."

"No, but you can *feel* me," said Frank, in a rough, determined tone, seizing the intruder roughly by the collar.

"Oh, lors, mercy! spare me! Where the deuce am I? I always feared treachery all along. Oh! whoever you are, don't hurt me."

"What's your name?"

"Jenkins, servant to Mr. Schmidt."

"What brought you here?"

"My legs, sir."

"Sirrah," said Frank, shaking the stranger vigorously, "no joking with me. What brought you here?"

"I was hired by an English detective to come here with Mr. Schmidt to help him in securing a noted young prisoner."

"Oh, indeed. Why didn't the English detective come here himself?"

"He said it wasn't his business; he didn't like to poke his nose among brigands."

"But *you* did, I suppose? Well, my fine fellow, whoever you are, don't shake so much, and I'll introduce you to this Frank Ford."

"Will you, though? How kind! Is he very rough and violent?"

"Oh, no," said Frank, tittering in the darkness; "not much so. He has just finished killing one man, and, I dare say, would be happy to make your acquaintance. The brigand's watch-dogs are much in want of food; they relish and get fat on human flesh."

"Oh, lor!" groaned Jenkins. "What was the victim's name?"

"Schmidt," Frank answered, "your amiable master."

"Oh, horrible!" groaned Jenkins. "Just to think on it, to come so far away from merry old England to be made dog's meat of! What a horrible tale!"

"Yes; but it isn't all told yet, there is more to come!"

"Is there, though, more horrors?" Jenkins gasped.

"Yes; put your hand down there. Don't you feel something?"

"In course I does; I heard it snarl or growl, or summat. It's a man!"

"Just so, bound hand and foot. We are going to spit him in half an hour, and roast him before the fire!"

This was more than the heroic Jenkins could bear.

His teeth chattered so loudly that they sounded like dice rattling in a box.

"What must I do?—what must I do?" he groaned.

"I'll tell you. You must speak softer, or we'll kill you!"

"Consider me dumb, then," said Jenkins.

"Would you purchase your life?"

"Yes," sighed Jenkins.

"Will you serve me?"

"As faithful as a dog," sighed Jenkins. "If I don't, hang me!"

"Then follow me!" said Frank.

# THE BOY SOLDIER; OR, GARIBALDI'S YOUNG CAPTAIN.

THE FUNERAL OF A YOUNG GARIBALDIAN.

It was as much as the Boy Band could do to keep from laughing during the whole conversation, but they did so, for fear of awakening the suspicions of the numerous brigands in and around the cave.

They had all got into the broad, dark stone corridor, when Ambrose, who had been hitherto concealed, touched Frank upon the arm.

"So far we have succeeded. Teresa, the spy, met me in the mountains as I went to your camp; she had heard of your captivity, and made plans for your release. My good intentions were, therefore, forestalled. Everything is arranged for your flight; but I fear me there will be bloodshed ere all of you escape."



"Fear not," said Frank, "I have twelve followers with me, bold, brave youths!"

"But mark you, Frank," said Ambrose, "my life is in danger at every step I take."

"Then go you your own way; let us not bring ill-luck on your head after all you have done for us."

"It was all for love, Captain Frank."

"Love?"

"Yes; I adore Teresa, and have done so from the first moment I saw her in the mountains; it is for *her* sake that I have done all this."

"Then rely upon it, Ambrose, that whenever you need true and tried friends you will always find them in the Boy Band."

"I know it; but you would not depart empty handed?"

"How mean you?"

"Basil has immense treasures concealed in these caves."

"Let him keep them, then, for the present; we are rich enough without his ill-gotten coin. His daughter and Annette, however, must be rescued ere we depart."

"'Tis easily done. Let your followers make their way to the end of this long gallery, the same way Teresa pointed out to them unknown to me; let them wait at the end on the mountain side, concealed in the bushes until we return. Follow me!"

In a few hurried words Frank explained the position of affairs to his followers, and they obeyed his orders by making the best of their way along the gallery silently and swiftly.

Ambrose now dived down a side gallery, which was as dark as pitch.

He was followed by Frank.

After a time they came near to the spot where Frank had been confined.

"The next cell to yours is Annette's," said Ambrose.

"Then that accounts for the voice I heard."

"True, she was gagged and ironed by order of Basil and the council of twelve, which your followers have just now so well imitated. When I saw you this morning I unlocked her cell door, unchained and ungagged her. She is ready to fly, but knows not that you are still alive.

"But where is Agnese?" said Frank.

"Ah, that is a different matter. I fear that blood will have to be shed ere you carry her off."

"Why?"

"There is a guard placed at her chamber door night and day."

"By whose orders?"

"The council's."

"Cannot he be dispatched, 'tis easily done? The girl shall not suffer for my fault."

"Bravely said, Captain Frank, and like a true lover; but I have a better plan in view."

"What is it?"

"Give him wine."

"Poisoned wine?" said Frank.

"No, only drugged."

"That is better."

"Let us carry Annette away first, and leave her in charge of your followers, we will quickly return and do the rest."

Like two well-practised burglars Ambrose and Frank entered Annette's dark cell, and before the girl could recover from astonishment she was rapidly conveyed along the winding passages.

As they approached the further end, before described, the fitful gusts of pure fresh air revived her, and ere long she managed to crawl through the aperture, and was safe among the Boy Soldiers there in waiting.

All this had been quickly done, and without noise, for both Ambrose and Frank were in their stocking feet.

Ambrose, however, carried his boots in his hand, and when he approached the chamber in which Agnese was confined, he put them on again, so that his approach might be heard.

He motioned Frank to hide in a dark recess until called upon.

While secreted there, Ambrose went forward.

"Halt," said the gruff brigand at the chamber door, "who approaches?"

"Ambrose," was the reply.

"Advance, Ambrose, what want ye?"

"How long is it since you were placed on guard here?"

"Four hours."

"How is that?"

"The chief of the guard had warning that there were numerous armed strangers prowling about the hills, and he called off all the men he could muster to go and look after them."

"I know it. I myself gave that information to Captain Basil."

"That accounts then why the council will not sit to night."

"True; every available man has been sent off to the valley and gorge. Basil fears that the Boy Soldiers may even attack our stronghold here."

"No fear of that," laughed the sentinel; "no one knows the ins and outs of this place except ourselves."

"Quite true. You seem tired."

"So I am, standing here in the dark, and damp, and cold."

"Will you take a cup of wine? It will cheer you up."

"I don't mind, but you know it is quite against our orders; if a man is found drunk upon his post he is shot."

"No fear of that; who should speak of it? Not Ambrose, you may be sure; wait a moment. I am promoted to a councillor now, and can go anywhere in these caverns at my will."

In a few minutes Ambrose passed the spot where Frank was concealed.

As he went by he whispered, "In five minutes the guard will be senseless; wait till I give the word."

Ambrose procured the wine in a small apartment some distance away, and soon returned with a large goblet filled to the brim.

He stopped again, and spoke to Frank in a whisper.

"Drink," said he, "heartily, my lad; it will refresh you. I have not drugged it yet."

Frank took a draught, and with many thanks.

Ambrose now dropped a liquid drug into the wine, and walked on towards the sentinel.

"Here's health to you, Councillor Ambrose, and may you live to be chief of our band, instead of Basil, the drunken sot. Here's health to you."

He drank the wine with great avidity, and soon he became very talkative.

But Ambrose left him and went to Frank. In less than ten minutes both of them heard the distant sound of loud snoring.

"I told you so," said Ambrose. "The drug has done its work. He's fast asleep. Come, follow me."

In a few moments Frank and his faithful guide found themselves at the chamber-door of Agnese.

The tipsy, insensible guard lay flat on his face, snoring loudly, with his gun beside him.

They stepped over his body, and opened the chamber-door.

"I'll stay here until you return," said Ambrose. "No one knows what may happen. Her chamber is in the inner room.

Frank did not need to be told twice.

He quickly passed through the first apartment, and quietly opened a door which led into a second.

Within, and reposing on a small bed, lay the beautiful Agnese, her hair flowing over the pillow, and her breasts and arms all bare.

Beside her on a chair sat a wicked, cadaverous-looking old woman, whose eyes glared like two balls of fire.

She rose from her seat the instant Frank appeared and pulled out a pistol.

"Approach!" said she, in hissing tones, "and I fire! My life depends on it."

Not heeding her threat, Frank rushed towards her.

She snapped the pistol full in his face.

It missed fire.

The next moment she was struck a heavy blow in the face by Frank's clenched fist, and fell upon the floor.

The noise awoke Agnese.

In an instant she recognised her young deliverer, and with a faint cry of joy rose bolt upright in bed, and flung her arms around him.

There was no time for explanation now.

Haste was necessary, and caution.

He took the half-fainting maid upon his arms, and bore her away.

He had not got far along the passage when the old hag rose to her feet like a wild woman.

She tossed down the pillows on the bed.

Under them were concealed a pair of pistols.

She seized them, and ran after the fugitives.

She fired both weapons along the dark passage.

The balls could be heard rattling along the stone gallery.

They whistled close to Frank's head as he hurried along with his precious burden.

Not content with this the old hag began to scream and shout most horribly until the echoes of her cracked voice resounded in terrible tones of fright and alarm.

"Haste, Frank, haste!" said the faithful Ambrose, "or you will be pursued."

"Oh! that I had killed the witch," said Frank, "I had half a mind to do so; but I hate to shed a woman's blood."

"But she is *not* a woman," said Ambrose. "Wild cat is what I call her. A perfect she-devil."

Still the old hag's cries could be heard resounding, and still onward sped the fugitives.

Ere long, however, and when nearly exhausted with the burden, Frank heard the uproar and noise of many voices.

The clanging and slamming of doors, the sounds of heavy feet, curses and oaths were now audible behind him.

"Escaped! escaped!" were the shouts which now pursued him.

The old hag's cries had alarmed many of the bandit band, who were grouped under trees outside the cave.

Almost falling from sheer weakness, Frank at last reached the end of the gallery, and Agnese was passed through the large hole to his companions outside.

"Now that you are safe, farewell," said Ambrose.

He waived his hand as he said, "Descend the mountain; quick, for your lives; run along the gorge, and you are safe. We shall meet shortly again."

Frank and his followers did not need this good advice.

They descended the mountain-side as nimbly as monkeys, and soon reached the gorge.

In winter time this gorge was deep with water that flowed from the mountain range, and was impassible, thus making this side of the bandit's rendezvous impregnable.

Now, however, it was quite dry.

Mark, the strongest of the party, carried Annette.

But Frank would entrust none with Agnese; he carried her himself.

Love seemed to lighten his load, and he followed his companions at a rapid pace.

They had gone on some distance in safety and silence, and began to think that all danger was over.

When least expected, a wild shout assailed their ears!

Their flight had been discovered by several of the bandit band on the look-out on the mountain-side.

"Haste," said Frank; "haste, my lads, we are discovered and pursued. They are close upon us!"

This was true.

The bandit band on the mountain-side no sooner caught sight of the fugitives, than they hastened down towards the gorge, and began to fire rapidly.

Notwithstanding the danger, Frank refused to allow any one to help him.

He persisted in bringing up the rear, and manfully did he do it.

With a revolver, he frequently stopped, took deliberate aim, and shot down several of the dusky vagabonds.

But this was not all the danger.

The bandit band had now surrounded the Boy Soldiers, and in all directions were firing upon them!

The moment was critical and terrible.

It seemed as if every one of them would be cut down by the galling fire of the brigands.

"We are lost! we are lost!" cried several.

"Hope on, fight on," said Frank, bold as ever. "Do you hear that?" said he, with a face flushed with pleasure and triumph.

They listened.

It was the Boy Soldiers rushing to the rescue, led on by Fatty and Buttons, and directed in their course by Teresa, the spy.

## CHAPTER XXXVIII.

THE CONSPIRACY AGAINST MR. CASPAR—THE FALSE WITNESSES—MR. SCHMIDT MEETS WITH A VERY PLEASANT AND CHATTY COMPANION IN THE THEATRE—HE SITS FACE TO FACE WITH A DETECTIVE; BUT DOESN'T KNOW IT—THE WHOLE TRIAL READ AND EXPLAINED BY THE STRANGER, TO MR. SCHMIDT'S GREAT DELIGHT—THE MYSTERIOUS SERGEANT GALE—MISCHIEF BREWING.

WE return once more to the Detective!

Most people would naturally suppose that the very first thing Gale did when he discovered the whereabouts of old Flint, was to knock at the door, put his hand on the cunning old lawyer's shoulder, and say, "Mr. Flint, I am a detective, and you are wanted on the charge of wilful murder."

Nothing of the kind.

Detectives are not like other mortals, nor do they accomplish their ends in an ordinary manner.

When least expected they pounce down upon their unconscious prey, although they may hover around it for months ere doing so.

The first thing which Detective Gale did was to slip away from his companions—the negro minstrels.

As he strolled down the streets he espied a policeman.

He gave a peculiar sign by which they might know each other; but the constable looked, and stared, and looked again harder than ever at the black-faced fellow in astonishment.

"Don't you know me?" said Gale.

"Know you, of course I do. You're one of the street darkies."

"My name is Gale, and——"

"You don't mean that!" said the constable on the instant, in great surprise.

"I do, though."

"What's up, then?"

"Robbery, and a double murder."

"Who's the victim?"

"Old Ford, of the Red House, and the headless body found in Green Court."

"You don't mean that you've got both jobs on hand?"

"They are not two exactly," said Gale, with a peculiar smile. "If we are lucky both jobs may be traced to one and the same hand."

"What! and on the same night?"

"Yes."

"You haven't got on the track yet, have you? I heard there was so much mystery hanging around those affairs that they defied all Scotland Yard."

"Perhaps, so; but a week or two will explain all about it, or my name's not Gale."

"Any suspicious parties around here, then?"

"Yes. Do you know anything about a strange old gent, who has lately taken the parlours at No. 26 over the way?"

"What! that old cove as doesn't want the organ-grinders afore his door?"

"Yes."

"Why, of course I do. What of him?"

"Why, he seldom goes out in day time; but likes darkness to come on first. I noticed that last week when on night duty. What's his business?"

"Nothing as I know of."

"His name?"

"The servant girl says his name is Schmidt."

"Are you sure?"

"Quite sure."

"Keep a sharp eye on 26. Let me know if you see any strangers going in or out much. We must not lose sight of him night or day. I am just going now to report at Bow Street, and will put two plain clothes men on the look-out for this strange old gentleman."

And sure enough Gale *did* put two plain clothes policeman on duty there, who, unknown to the fugitive, watched him narrowly night and day.

For several days, however, nothing transpired worthy of notice.

Mr. Schmidt invariably came forth from his parlour-lodgings about nightfall, and with his over-coat buttoned up to the chin, and hat pressed over his eyes, walked rapidly through the streets.

He was followed to various places of amusement and never lost sight of.

Rather than mix with the throng in the pit or stalls, Flint, miserly as he was, always took a ticket for a private box.

He did not patronize the West End theatres much, it is true, for he was afraid of being noticed more than he cared to be by policemen both in and out of the theatre.

He, therefore, directed his footsteps to some East End house, and seemed to enjoy himself very much.

There was one theatre he was followed to more than any other, the name of which we shall not mention.

Why he liked to go to this one in preference to any other for some time puzzled the watchful officers, and they made up their minds to know the reasons.

Accordingly, one of the two officers dressed himself up very stylishly, paid his admission fee, and was ushered into the same box as old Flint.

The performance went on for some time without much marked attention on Flint's part, but when, in the third act, a murder was represented as having been committed and the victim robbed, Mr. Flint sat very uneasily in his chair, and turned his head.

"Horrible affair!" said Flint, half aloud, in disgust at the bloodthirsty character of the drama.

"It's too revolting."

"Oh, I don't know," said the detective, very coolly; "such things *do* happen in life sometimes. Now, for instance, I read a case in the paper a few days ago, in which a murder and robbery was committed just like that you've seen acted."

"You don't mean to say so?" old Flint replied, in tones of feigned horror and disgust.

"Yes, and the worst of it is, that circumstantial evidence was so strong against the *wrong* party that I thought he would be convicted and hung. I heard the whole case myself by mere accident."

"Lor!" said Flint, rolling his eyes. "Singular—*very* singular how some of these atrocious deeds are wrapped in mystery. What paper is it in?"

"The 'Daily Thunderer,'" the detective replied, coolly. "By-the-bye, I think I have the identical paper in my pocket. If you'd like to hear I'll read the account."

"Thanks," said Flint, with a choking sensation in the throat; "you are very kind."

The first piece was now over, and, as there were ten minutes intermission, the stranger took the newspaper, and, in substance read as follows, explaining as he went on:—

"MYSTERIOUS ROBBERY AND SUPPOSED MURDER.

"In our last issue we gave a report of the examination of the young man Caspar, late tutor at Bromley Hall Academy, on the charge of robbery.

"It was supposed, from certain circumstances lately brought to light through the indefatigable exertions of Detective Gale, that this young man might, in some manner, have connection with the late mysterious murder of Mr. Ford.

"It was even suggested, by some firm, strong, circumstantial evidence, that he might know something of the headless mystery that was dragged out of a room, during the conflagration in Green Court.

"Certain it is, however, rumour has been very busy during the past few days with various conjectures regarding this double murder; but, though he might not be charged with that horrible crime, many thought there could not be a doubt but that he had been guilty of the robbery at Bromley Hall, if any reliance could be placed on the evidence already adduced.

"Our report of yesterday brought the account of this important trial down to the close of the evidence for the prosecution.

"We now continue an account of the proceedings, and of the cross-examination of witnesses for the prosecution, which, strangely enough, refutes and disproves the charges.

"Mr. Shank recalled and cross-examined by Mr. Valentine.—'You said yesterday, Mr. Shanks, that you were a tutor at Bromley Hall for several years, that Mr. Jonathan was a man of refined temper, and of great goodness of heart?'

"'I did.'

"'You are not aware where Mr. Jonathan now is, or why he went so hurriedly away from the Hall?'

"'No.'

"'Could you not even guess?'

"'I could not. On private business connected with the school, I suppose.'

"'You are positive in what you said, yesterday, that the prisoner, Mr. Caspar, was the cause of the recent revolt at Bromley Hall? Very well. And you still persist in swearing that you were on the most intimate terms with the prisoner up to the time of his leaving, and that he swore to be revenged on Mr. Jonathan, somehow?'

"'I am.'

"'Is it not true that you and Madame Jonathan concocted a plan between you to ruin this young man? Is it not a fact that the night previous to the prisoner's departure you and your mistress were closeted together in the dark? Will you swear this is not true? Be careful, now, for you are on your oath.'"

'This question," said the detective, interpreting the printed evidence, "seemed to startle the witness, who got very red in the face, but he answered slowly—

"'It is not true.'

"'Very well, Mr. Shanks; now let me ask you whether it is not true that once or twice you and the prisoner fell out, and that Mr. Caspar threatened to publicly horsewhip you for your cruelty to the scholars?'

"'It is false.'

"'Is it not true—attend to me; do not be gazing around in that manner on the crowded court, for your liberty of person depends upon your answers—Is it not true, on your oath, mind, that the cause of Mr. Jonathan's continued absence arises from the unexpected flight of two poor little children he has had imprisoned for years and tried to starve to death?'

"This question startled the court as much so as the witness, who changed all manner of colours, as he stammered out—

"'There is not one word of truth in any of your questions; they are all false suppositions.'

"'Very well, we shall shortly see; but let me ask you again, did not Mr. Jonathan strike you fiercely, and swear at you when he discovered the two captives had been rescued by the young Garibaldians, as they called themselves, under Frank Ford?'

"'No, it is not.'

"'Stand down,' said Mr. Valentine, the lawyer. 'Stand down, sir; your face belies your words; we shall hear more of you presently. Your worship, I have particularly to request that this witness be detained in one of the ante-rooms of the court; he, himself, is charged with a very serious crime.'

"As Shanks descended from the witness-box, he was politely taken in charge by a policeman, who escorted him to a waiting room.

"The next witness called for cross-examination was Madame Jonathan, a person of very lady-like manners, elegantly attired in costly silks, and of rather pretty features.

"She looked at the prisoner for a moment with an air of triumph, and tossed her head in great contempt as Mr. Valentine began to cross-examine her

"'You swore, Madame Jonathan, in your yesterday's direct examination, that the trinkets found in the prisoner's trunks were stolen by him. Do you adhere to the statement *now*, madame.'

"'Yes, why not *now*?' said Madame, with a flashing eye; 'of course I do.'

"'Did you never make certain advances towards this young man; in fact, fall on your knees before him, and profess love? Did you not, in fine, urge him to fly from Bromley Hall with you, and that he spurned your proposals?' asked the clever lawyer, very calmly, and coolly watching the witness changing countenance.

"'What!' gasped Madame Jonathan, looking pale as death, 'What base tissue of calumnies is this I hear?'

"Mr. Valentine repeated the questions, slowly and distinctly, adding,

"'On your oath, mind, answer me.'

"'No,' said the witness, in a hissing tone; 'if the miserable prisoner before me says so he basely lies.'

"'Did you not leave your chamber and go to his for the purpose of secreting your property in his trunks in order that you might be revenged on him, and cause him to be arrested and convicted?'

"'I did not, on my oath.'

"'Have not you and Mr. Shanks, the last witness, had frequent conversations in the garden as to what you should or should not say on this trial? Have you not said that it was now impossible for your husband to return, and that you and Mr. Shanks would live as man and wife, and carry on the academy at Bromley Hall?'

"'*Me?*' gasped Madame, getting very red in the face; '*me?* I did not come here to be insulted, sir!' she said, with fierce looks, and a toss of her head. '*Me*, sir?'

"'Yes; *you*, madame,' said the lawyer, very coolly. 'Answer me?'

"'No!' she replied, in hissing tones.

"'You may stand down, madame; I have done with you for the present. I desire, your worship, that this witness may not be allowed to go beyond the precincts of the court, for certain reasons; at least, not until the conclusion of this case. Let Mr. Giles be called.'

"The old gardener with his white head, and tremulous with excitement, tottered forward through the crowd, and as Madame Jonathan saw him pass her eyes were suddenly lit up with a fierce and angry expression.

"'*He* here!' she said, in wonder, as he passed.

"'Yes, ma'am, *I am* here,' Giles answered coolly, 'and here for some purpose, as you will shortly discover.'

"He mounted the box, and was sworn as a witness for the defence.

"'You are and have been gardener at Bromley Hall for many years, and profess to know all about this robbery and mystery hanging about Bromley Hall?' said Mr. Valentine.

"'Yes, sir, I do; and more than any one here expects me to know. I am not what I seem to be,' said Giles, with a chuckle; 'sillly and old as they take me. In one word,' said Giles, colouring up, and raising his voice, 'all this prosecution is a foul and dirty conspiracy, gentlemen, and against one of the best and bravest young men as ever lived.'

"'How do you prove this, Mr. Giles? State fully all you know, but only as much as relates to this case, mind.'

"'Well, sir, these trinkets now produced were placed in Mr. Caspar's trunks by the last witness. I saw her do it myself, for I watched her as I have her husband, and the sneaking tutor Shanks, for years past.'

"'Have you heard the two last witnesses concocting plans, what to do, or what to say, in respect to this case?'

"'I have; they were in the garden together, and were talking French, so that I might not understand them, as I was working; but I *do* understand French, and have often heard Mr. Jonathan and Shanks talking about the two young prisoners who were released by Frank Ford and his brave companions. If it had not been for me they would have been slowly murdered for want of food, which I supplied to them. I know the day when they came, who brought them, and why; it is on account of their escape, and fear of his own punishment, that caused Jonathan, and old Flint, the lawyer, to fly.'"

When old "Mr. Schmidt" had heard this much he began to tremble in every limb, but did not betray it to his companion.

"Most extraordinary trial," said he, half aloud.

"Very," was the detective's answer; "I thought it would interest *you*."

"*Me?* Why *me?*" said, "Mr. Schmidt,' hastily. "Why *me?*"

"Oh! not particularly you; I meant it would interest any one who read it."

"Exactly."

"And allow me to say," the detective went on, "this trial promises to reveal some startling things, if these accusations against the schoolmaster Jonathan are only true."

"'He must have been a wretch indeed," said 'Mr. Schmidt,' as he again listened to the account read and commented upon by the stranger—:

"'But do you know, or have you any idea, Mr. Giles, why Madame Jonathan should entertain such wicked intentions towards the prisoner?'

"'Yes, sir; ever since Mr. Caspar has been at Bromley Hall he has been quietly persecuted by the attention of his mistress as often as she had secret opportunities for doing so. I often thought that her desires were wicked and unwomanly towards her husband, but never dreamed she would fall upon her knees, and almost force Mr. Casper to comply with her guilty wishes.'

"'When this occurred where were you?'

"'I was in the parlour hiding behind the screen, not for the purpose of watching her, but to ferret out something else that the officers of justice wished to know. I saw her fall on her knees before him, and, with tears in her eyes, beg of him to fly with her.'

"'And what was Mr. Caspar's answer?'

"He gently reproved her at first, and then, finding that she still persisted in her entreaty, he spurned her from him, and left the room. '

"'And what did she?"

"'For some few moments she remained as she had been, on her knees, but arose, walked up and down the apartment, and then resolved in firm, quiet tones to be revenged on the prisoner.'

"'What then followed, Mr. Giles?'

"'I watched her that night, and saw her distinctly come into Mr. Caspar's room, for I was hiding there. I saw her open his trunks with false keys, and secrete the trinkets now produced, each wrapped up in a piece of tissue paper. I swear all this most solemnly, and I would prove it on this instant if I were allowed to do so.'

"'How does the witness mean?' asked his worship.

"'I mean, sir, that she rummaged over all his papers, and abstracted certain things.'

"'What, the witness steal from the prisoner?'

"'Yes, sir; I could tell you what it was,' said Giles, "but do not like to do so in open court.'

"'Name it,' said his worship.

"'She stole several of his sweetheart's letters, and has them now in her reticule.'

"'Let the last witness be re-called,' said the lawyer.

"She again appeared in court.

"'In your journey to London, madame, did you lose anything?"

"'Yes; I missed my reticule at the railway station.'

"'Did it contain anything very valuable?"

"'Yes, letters of great importance.'

"'Is this it?' said the lawyer, producing the identical reticule. 'It was handed over to me this morning by a stranger: I have not examined it.'

"'Yes, that's it,' said Madame Jonathan, in a great hurry to it.

"'Does all it contains belong to you?"

"'Yes.'

"'No, sir,' said Giles; 'I saw her put some of the stolen letters into it half an hour before she left Bromley Hall.'

"''Tis false!' said Madame, turning out the contents with an indignant flourish; "you may examine all for yourself if you do not believe me,' she said, in full confidence that they would not do so.

"'Those three letters are the ones I allude to,' said Giles; 'I will swear to them.'

"'Why, these letters belong to the prisoner, Madame. How come they in your possession?' said Mr. Valentine.

"The witness was puzzled, confused, and surprised.

"She could not answer a word; but would have retired on the instant, and began to tremble, for it would seem as if a strange presentiment now came over her that in less than an hour, perhaps, she herself would be placed in the dock, and accused of robbery.

"Giles's evidence was continued, and through the well-put questions of Mr. Valentine (prisoner's counsel) the whole history of Bromley Hall was elicited amidst the breathless interest of the court."

"Suffice it to say," the detective observed "that through severely cross-examined, the prosecution failed to make old Giles contradict himself, and that the jury unanimously acquitted Mr. Caspar of the charge of robbery, amidst the great applause of a crowded court.

"Madame Jonathan and Shanks, who were in a waiting-room, heard the news with sinking hearts.

"They wished to depart on the instant; but a policeman politely said,

"'You must not go yet, if you please. Mr. Caspar is accused of being an accomplice in Mr. Ford's murder; the court is now hearing the case.'

"He left the room, and in about two hours returned.

"'Well, what news?' said Madame Jonathan, all flushed with excitement. 'Surely they have found sufficient evidence on that charge to remand him? The cloak, hat, and mask found by the detectives belonged to him. He owned it.'

"'All true, madame; but the witness Giles has cleared up all that,' said the policeman.

"'How do you mean?'

"'They were stolen from Mr. Caspar's trunks the same night the students left. Giles saw it done and knows all about it.'

"'By whom, pray?' asked Madame and Shanks both in a breath.

"'That I have not liberty to say. His evidence was given privately to Detective Gale, and there ends the matter. Mr. Caspar is acquitted of both charges, and this Giles is such a valuable witness in this abominable affair that he has been for the last two weeks the constant companion of Sergeant Gale.'

"The two witnesses heaved heavy sighs, and hung their heads in great dejection.

"'Then, why cannot we depart?' asked they with looks of doubt and apprehension.

"Simply, madame, for this reason. Mr. Caspar charges you with robbery, perjury, and conspiracy with the other witness, Mr. Shanks.'

"'Prisoner! *me* a prisoner?' gasped Shanks, in pale surprise.

"'Yes; both of you.'

"'But we can have bail?'

"'That depends; but not until after your hearing. This way, please.'

"In less than five minutes Madame Jonathan and the tutor Shanks stood side by side in the dock.

"Mr. Caspar and old Giles were the witnesses against them.

"They were remanded, and all bail refused.

"Madame Jonathan's lawyer was indignant that bail was refused; but it was all to no purpose.

"The reason of this was that a small note had been handed up to the judge by an inspector of police, on which were these words: 'Serious charges against the two prisoners. I would wish that bail be refused, or they may escape us.'"

"Lor! bless my soul! How extraordinary!" said Mr. Schmidt, when he had heard all about the mysterious affair. "It is astonishing to be sure! So the young tutor was acquitted, eh? But have they traced the real murderer yet?"

"Oh! yes," said the detective, coolly. "They have got on the track of one of them; but they don't want to disturb him until they have got the other."

"Oh! I see!" said 'Mr. Schmidt,' with a forced and uneasy smile. "What cunning dogs these detectives are! So you were in court and heard all about it? How strange!"

The ballet then commenced, and both gentlemen were silent; but "Mr. Schmidt" seemed to be very unhappy and uncomfortable, and eyed his companion from time to time in a very doubtful and suspicious manner.

## CHAPTER XXXIX.

OLD FLINT DOES NOT MUCH ENJOY THE BALLET OF THE "FAIRY BOWER"—JENNIE JACKSON, THE DANSEUSE, IS ENGAGED BY THE DETECTIVE—THE SUDDEN AND UNEXPECTED MEETING WITH OLD JONATHAN.

DURING the first part of the performance of the ballet called the "Fairy Bower," Mr. Schmidt seemed for the most part absent-minded, and cared but little for what was going on.

His companion, the detective, however, seemed to enjoy the spectacle immensely.

He laughed, and grinned, and applauded so much that it fairly made old Flint wretched and supremely miserable.

"How this talkative stranger does laugh and go on to be sure. Why is it that *I* can't laugh?" he thought. "This all comes of having companions in your box. Hang him! I wish he was far enough from me; his very hilarity makes my blood run cold. Who can he be, I wonder? Certainly not any one connected with the law; and yet he seems to know a great deal about police-officers. *Surely he can't be a police-officer himself?*"

This thought made old Flint very miserable.

He cast many inquiring side-long glances at his well-dressed, elegant-looking companion, as he thought,

"The devil! no, he's no policeman; he's got too much money for that. Look at his splendidly-fitting clothes! Why, his finger-rings and watch cost more than a policeman's salary comes to in a twelvemonth, aye, more than he gets in three years."

He looked at the ballet again and again, but did not seem to enjoy it.

Neither did he evince any inclination to leave the theatre.

"Capital piece, ain't it?" said the stranger, in high glee; "splendid performance. How well those girls dance to be sure—such legs! There, look at her! What a graceful thing she is!"

"Yes, she is, rather," said Flint, with a wicked smirk on his ugly old face.

"I shouldn't mind if I was introduced to her; she's the prettiest of them all," said the lawyer.

"'Tis the easiest thing in the world," said the stranger. "If you like, we'll go on the stage and get up a chat with her in the green-room."

"Go on the stage? It can't be done."

"Oh, yes, it can. My name is Frank Fairplay; and yours?"

"Schmidt."

"Just so. Well, then, Mr. Schmidt, we are somewhat strangers to each other as yet, but, if you don't object, what say you? Shall we go on the stage? Stay here a moment; I'll send in my card to the stage manager. He knows me."

So saying, Frank Fairplay, as he called himself, left the box, and went round to the stage entrance, spoke two or three magic words to the manager, and returned to his box again all radiant with smiles.

Arm in arm, he and Schmidt then left the box, and were soon on the stage.

This was the first time in all his life that old Flint gave way to such gallantry as to confront the whole corps de ballet of a theatre, great or small.

But the truth was Flint wanted excitement of some kind.

Sleeping or waking, the thought of old Ford's murder disturbed his soul.

Besides all this, he had in some sort fallen in love with a poor but pretty ballet girl, who nightly performed there, and he had given way so far to his amorous feelings as to throw her a bouquet every night he attended.

"I *must* have some excitement," he thought. "it doesn't matter how much money a man has, he can't eat it. I will enjoy myself in my old age, and have a jolly good spree before I go on the continent."

The pretty girl that old Flint's eyes fell upon, as it happened, was one of the sharpest and shrewdest creatures to be met with anywhere.

She was poor, it was true, but virtuous, and no man living could hold up his finger and say that Jennie Jackson was any man's sinful plaything.

She had good limbs, an excellent figure, and a handsome face.

This was all her fortune in the world, and it was not for choice so much as from necessity that made her thus exhibit herself nightly to the admiring gaze of an applauding audience.

When old Flint had sidled up to her she walked away with a proud, indignant air at his ogling and smirking, and again did the old lawyer try on his seductive scheme; but all to no purpose.

Jennie would not listen to his envenomed tongue, but treated him with the indifference she had always exhibited to wealthy strangers, who, as she knew, looked upon the green-room and the stage a market-places where virtue could be bought and sold.

The elegant Frank Fairplay, however, "had his eye," as he called it, on all the clumsy manœuvering of old Schmidt.

There was not an action that escaped his eagle eyes

When Jennie was alone, and old Schmidt out of sight, Frank Fairplay approached her, and whispered in her ear a few words.

The girl seemed astonished.

"None other, Jennie."

"What! can it be Mr. Alpin, who lives so near my mother's house?" she said, in surprise.

"And what do you here, dressed up so grandly?" she enquired, gaily. "Why, I took you for one of the finest gentlemen in the land."

"Aye, Jennie, but you are mistaken, you see. "Like you, we officers have to enact many parts in our time. You on the stage dress and act like village girls, or countesses at times. Fine feathers make fine birds."

"I see, I see," said Jennie, laughing. "So you are acting the 'gentleman' to-night?"

"Exactly."

"But for what purpose?"

"I cannot tell you precisely; but do you know that old fellow who spoke to you a minute ago?"

"How do *you* know I spoke to any gentleman just now?" said Jennie, with an arch smile.

"Because I was watching you."

"If you were, you did not see any harm."

"I am aware of that, my pretty little pert puss," said Alpin. "As luck would have it, I have known you too long to suppose anything of the kind, for, rough as I am, I would strike any man to the earth that I saw insulting you."

After a pause, he added,

"But do you know that old buck, on your word?"

"On my word I do not. All I know is, that he has been to this house very often, and every time he has thrown me a bouquet; that's all."

"Oh! he has, has he? Well, now, I'll tell you something; listen to me. He's not so innocent as he looks."

"Oh! I don't know," said Jennie, laughing; "he spoke to me very kindly, and offered me a situation in his house, if I'd accept it."

"Why didn't you?"

"He said he was sorry to see such a nice girl as I am treading the stage for a living, and, as I have said, offered to give me a situation in his own house."

"But, as it happens, he ain't got any house," said the detective. "Do you see, he's only a rich old humbug, after all."

"What!" said Jennie, indignantly. "Do you mean to say he meant me harm and deceit, then?"

"Of course he did, and I can prove it."

"How? I should like to have satisfaction out of him."

"Will you follow my advice?"

"In what way?"

"If you do as I tell you, you shall not only have good sport out of the old rat, but will be well paid beside. No harm can come to you; I'll take very good care of that, and, moreover, you will never regret following my advice," said Alpin, in earnest tones.

"When shall I see you again?" asked Jennie.

"To-morrow night at this time."

"Well, I will; I'm ripe for a bit of a lark with the old rascal," she said, gaily laughing.

The music now began to play again more noisily than before.

The "Fairy Bower" was coming to a close, and Jennie Jackson had to obey the call-boy's command, and be ready at the wings for the final tableau.

Standing at one of the wings, and looking on with eyes staring at, and absorbing the pretty Jennie in her graceful motions in the dance, was old Schmidt.

He sighed, and looked and looked, and sighed until he felt his old vile heart bumping against his sides with violent emotion, which he in his dotage mistook for love.

"Well, how did you get on, my fried?" said Mr. Fairplay. "By Jove! you have made a conquest of the prettiest girl in the whole ballet."

"*I?*" said Schmidt, in surprise.

"Yes; you."

"You are joking, my merry friend."

"By Jove, I'm not though. That girl you were talking to just now confessed in my hearing that you were the nicest gentleman she ever talked to in her life."

"Nonsense. Why, she turned her nose up at me."

"You are mistaken; it was only girlish bashfulness and timidity."

"If I thought so, begad, I'd address her at once; I've never seen such a pretty creature in my life before."

"And so clever!"

"Yes; and so voluptuous in her style."

"Virtuous as an angel, you can see that."

"I do. What a superb little beauty she'd make with silk dresses and plenty of money."

"True; but I wouldn't make advances too openly."

"How do you mean?"

"I would write to her."

"That wouldn't be a bad plan."

"The best in the world. Gammon her into thinking of matrimony; get her out, have a champagne supper, and——

"Just what I was thinking, Fairplay. No marriage in the matter, you know, only a——"

"Exactly; I know what you mean, make her a pleasant toy to beguile an hour or two away; dress her well, take apartments for her, and when you are tired cast her off upon the town, that's what we gentlemen always do; it's all a pretty ballet girl is fit for."

"You are a man of the world, I see," said old Schmidt, hideously grinning; "*you* know a thing or two, I perceive."

"And you, too, my gay old friend," said Fairplay, jocosely slapping Flint on the back.

"Well, by Jove, I think I *will* have a little bit of fun with this pretty wench. If I only knew her name and residence I would write."

"Do so; *I* will find out all that for you."

"Suppose we come again, then, to-morrow night?" said Schmidt.

"With all my heart."

The two friends had a bottle of wine together in the bar of the theatre, and left the temple of Thespis arm in arm together.

"I've got the old 'un tight this time," said the detective to himself. "Jennie Jackson shall worm all the secrets out of him, or my name is not Alpin. Where are you shoving to?" said he, to a tall, gaunt, half clerical-looking individual who came out of the theatre at the same moment as themselves.

"Where are you shoving to?" he said again, in a quick, angry manner.

Schmidt turned his head.

He looked deadly pale as he said, half aloud.

"Good heavens! that was Jonathan!"

"Who?" the detective asked, quickly.

"No one, my friend, it was only a passing word."

It *was* Jonathan!

The master of Bromley Hall was equally thunderstruck at the unlooked-for meeting.

He went on to the dark side of the street, and followed old Flint home with noiseless, wary steps!

# THE BOY SOLDIER; OR, GARIBALDI'S YOUNG CAPTAIN.

THE FIGHT WITH BRIGANDS.

## CHAPTER XL.

### THE COMPACT BETWEEN JONATHAN AND WARNER —THE HUNTED CRIMINALS.

It will be recollected that in a former chapter we described the strange meeting of Warner the Pug, and Jonathan, in old Flint's room.

When last we saw them they were all waiting for the old lawyer, who had so cleverly deceived them.

While there, with doors locked, the two policemen came again.

They tried the door, but could not get in.

Neither could Warner nor his companions get out.



"What is to be done?" said the Pug, in a whisper; "we ain't a goin' to be caught in here like rats, are we?"

"No," said Warner, biting his lip, "no fear of that; leave it all to me. How many of them are there?"

"Only two."

Jonathan was in a state of intense excitement, and watched his two companions with trembling lips, and a face of ashy paleness.

"Look you here, old 'un," said the Pug to Jonathan, "you wears a white choker, and all that sort of trick, but you are as big a rogue as any on us, for I can tell it by the twinkle of your codfish-looking eye, so listen to me. You don't want to fall into the hands of them coves on the landing, does yer? Well, then, you just do as we tells yer. Get hold on that poker, and stand bolt upright behind the door; when it's opened you slap him on the head, whoever he is; and you mind to do it; if yer don't, why then I shall do it to you, that's all."

"What do you mean?" said Jonathan, in a half-whisper.

"Vhot do I mean?" says Pug; "vhy I means that the 'slops' are on the stairs, and if they cotch us in here we shall get scragged, that's all—strung up like three whelps at Newgate, *that's* vhot I mean."

"Hu-s-s-h!" said Warner, "they are there again. "Silence, caution!"

Upon his hands and knees he crept towards the door, dagger in hand.

The Pug pulled a "jemmy" out of his large pocket.

Jonathan, poker in hand, stood behind the door.

All three were ready.

"They have got keys with them this time," said Warner.

"You open one door, and I'll open another," said the officers; "the rooms may be separate."

"D'ye hear that?" whispered the Pug in Warner's ear.

"I do," said the bold, determined villain. "You and this old chap stay here; *I* will go to the other door. If the stranger misses his blow, you make sure of yours."

"Never fear," said the Pug.

Warner crawled back again to the other door, and as noiselessly as an eel.

The two officers were now busy trying to open the doors with different keys.

At last they succeeded.

As one of them pushed the door open, he was struck a violent blow on the head by Jonathan, which felled him to the earth.

With a loud groan he fell.

The other officer would have rushed to the rescue; but before he knew what to do, Warner opened the door on one side, while the Pug and Jonathan took him in the rear.

Directly Warner saw him, he rushed at the policeman like an enraged tiger.

The officer was about to shout for help; but Warner seized him by the throat with a grip of iron.

The Pug now struck him a violent blow across the temples, which knocked the officer senseless.

"Fly! fly!" said Warner.

They all rushed down stairs.

A single officer was in the passage, and about to ascend.

Jonathan, all haste and fright, rushed forward, poker in hand, and struck him a terrible blow on the temple, which felled him.

"Bravo! parson!" said Warner. "I see you're up to this kind of work. We mustn't part with such a handy chap as you are in a hurry. Must we Puggy?"

"I should think not. His white choker is all a blind, you can bet on it. I shouldn't wonder if he turns out to be the cleverest cracksman in all London."

Thus they spoke as they rushed through the open door into the street.

"Down one street, across another, through dirty alley-ways and by-streets, the three men rapidly walked, Jonathan trying to lag behind, so as to escape.

After they had gone some distance, Warner called a cab, and shoved Jonathan into it.

Puggy got on the box, but Warner rode inside.

"It's of no use repenting *now*, old man," said Warner, "for you're as deep in the mess as any chap in London. You 'did' for that last bobby; he'll never kick again."

"Do you think so? I hope not."

"Hope not! Why not? It's better that he should die than all of us. You and I are sworn friends now. Give us your hand."

Jonathan was in a deadly fever of excitement, and trembled in every limb.

He had not dreamt that his adventure in old Flint's office would have ended in wilful bloodshed.

But, as we have seen, it had done so.

And this reflection, that he had dyed his hands in blood, alarmed him for the moment.

Not, indeed, through horror of the crime, but through fear of detection, apprehension, and punishment.

It is a true saying that a robber is a murderer in disguise.

Truly he goes to rob only; but in most cases he does not scruple to commit murder to save himself, if he can do so unseen.

The cab bowled along; but where he was going to Jonathan had not the remotest idea.

After some time, the cab drew up near the Seven Dials, and the party alighted.

The cabman was paid.

Puggy "tipped him" not to speak too loudly his suspicions to any one, and, ere many minutes, all three villains were drinking together at an obscure public-house.

Jonathan had not been used to strong drinks, and soon fell asleep on a long form in the parlour of the "Cat and Bagpipes," and while in this state Warner and Puggy rifled his pockets.

They didn't discover much of value, except a few private professional cards, prospectuses of Bromley Hall Academy, and the like.

But in rumaging still further among a bundle of his private letters, Warner discovered two fifty pound notes.

"This isn't so very bad," said he to Pug; "we might as well pay Bromley Hall a visit one of these dark nights. What say you?"

"With all my heart," said Pug. "Since we are now *obliged* to turn cracksmen, and keep out of sight as much as we can in the daytime, why, we might as well do the trick as genteel as possible."

"That's *my* opinion," said Warner. "And do you know, I think this old chap is not so innocent as he'd like people to believe, if he *does* wear a white choker."

"We mustn't part with the old cock," said Pug.

"Nor lose sight of him either; he knows too much of us already to let him go and blab all."

"What shall ve do vith him?"

"Why, force him to sign articles and join us."

"Couldn't he do the 'respectable old gentleman' well?"

"Just what *I* was thinking."

"He'll never leave us now he's stained his hands," said the Pug; "new beginners never get over that. Blood fastens 'em safe."

"Yes; but he's no 'innocent,' as you call it. Look at his face as he lies in sleep; where could you get a more hang-dog-looking countenance in all London?"

"True; at the best o' times, the old cove ain't much of a beauty—ha, ha! Well, old Calcraft ain't werry partic'lar; we might as well be hung for a sheep as a lamb."

So saying, Warner and the Pug drank each other's health, and long life to the triple partnership.

While they were thus merry together and oblivious of all care, the parlour door was suddenly opened.

A cabman showed his head inside, and, with a broad grin on his red face, said,

"Hillo, my covey! That you, Puggy, my boy? You didn't keep yer app'intment the day arter I druv that old bloke home on that stormy night, did yer? Well, no matter, better late than never. How are yer? My respects, sir," said he, bowing to Warner, and drinking off a large glass of gin, without even winking.

Then, whispering to Puggy, he said,

"A friend o' yourn?"

"Yes."

"Werry like that cove as bilked me out of my fare that night. D'yer recollect?"

"In course I does."

"Ever seen that old bloke since?"

"No; I should werry much like to though."

"What's all that fuss outside?" said Warner. "Why, the people are running as if the devil was after them."

"No vonder, sir, all respect to you. There's been some cracksmen as hev 'done for' three bobbies to-day near here; the people are running there to hev a look at 'em."

"Horrible!" said Warner.

"You don't mean that, Cabby," said Pug.

"I do, though, my tulip, and I knows who they was as done it."

"You do?"

"In course I does. Do you know this?" whispered Cabby, holding up the "jemmy."

It was all covered with blood.

"It's not mine," said the Pug.

"Gammon! Didn't I see yer on the box of Jim Jones's four wheeler, and didn't I find it on the seat and hide it, and follow you here to bring it, so as to get you out o' trouble? I'm allers a befriendin' o' you, and yet you never squares it."

The "Pug" was, no doubt, greatly surprised at the unexpected visit of "Cabby," but he only gave vent to a quiet, wicked smile, and said nothing for a few moments; at last he remarked,

"What are yer goin' to hev, Cabby? I ain't got much coin, but I dare say I can raise the price of a 'half a go.' What shall it be, a drop o' gin, or rum?"

"Vell, I doesn't much mind what it is, Puggy; but I *did* think as how you'd a kept your appointment, for, yer see, I might have made a quid (a sovereign) or two about that little affair at the Red House, but as you're a bit of a pal I wouldn't know nothin' about it."

"What little affair?" Puggy asked, in a half whisper, and with a look of great surprise. "You don't suppose as how *I* had anything to do with that scraggin' scrape at the Red House?"

"*Me!* lor bless yer, no!" said Cabby, tossing off his 'half go' of gin, and winking very mysteriously; "*me!* lor bless yer, no!"

"And as to these here gents, you can tell *they* ain't in the line," said Puggy. "Now, does they look like it?"

"No, in course not; but what's their little game then?"

"Vhy, they is country gents as come up to town to see a nice little 'mill,' but it didn't come off, so they are havin' a bit of a snooze arter bein' up all night."

"Zactly, Puggy; and now I comes to have a good look at 'em both, they *do* look like country gents. Are they pretty flush o' coin?"

"Not werry; but that's neither here nor there, they are friends o' mine, and that's enough."

While this little bit of chit-chat was going on between Cabby and the Pug, Warner looked very uneasy, and cast furtive glances at Cabby, which the latter understood.

"If that ain't the chap as was my first fare on that night when old Ford was murdered, may I be hanged," he thought, and sipped another "half go" with great complacency.

Cabby did not remain long, and soon retired to the bar, where he indulged in a pint of "cooper," and, with a new pipe, looked over the "Mornin' 'Tiser."

As soon as he was gone the Pug whispered a word or two to Warner.

In a moment afterwards Puggy entered the bar, and slipped two sovereigns into the cabman's hand.

The latter winked very slyly, took the coin in a back-handed way, and tossed off the dregs of his "cooper."

"Mum," said Puggy.

"O. K." said the cabman, and left the premises.

* * * * *

How little does any one know when thy start on a career of crime where all of it will end!

Little does the paltry thief think when, as a boy, he steals apples from a poor woman's stall, and laughs at the joke, that he is sowing seed that will perhaps one day lead him to the gallows.

Look at the "Pug."

As a lad he refused to work at any honest occupation, and loved to lounge about dirty pot-houses, and mix in the brawls which disgrace nearly every crowded street on a Saturday night.

Being strongly built, he had been often known to waylay poor mechanics, pick a quarrel with them, and then rob them of their dearly earned wages.

He had long been "spotted" by the police, but up to the present had escaped justice.

He next tried his hand in the prize ring, and got a sound thrashing.

Not caring for "hard knocks," he left the "ring" in disgust and returned to his old haunts, and was mixed up with burglars, smashers, and the like, and was liable at any moment to be arrested and transported for life, if not to grace the scaffold.

Warner also played for a large stake, and had been outwitted by the cunning lawyer, Flint, and placing all his hopes on a single cast of the dice, lost it, and was now penniless and friendless, hunted morning, noon and night by the bloodhounds of justice.

Jonathan also, from small beginnings, had now arrived at that pitch when murder no longer looked terrible in his eyes.

Here, then, were three scoundrels, each of them with an halter dangling before their eyes, afraid to move, or to speak above their breath, for fear of detection.

Wherever they went every honest man's hand was against them.

Where could they go?

What could they do?

Work they would not.

They feared to meet the gaze even of a child.

The whistling of the wind among a few dead leaves caused a fearful tremor to pass through their frames.

When each of them started on the high-road to ruin, they shuddered at the thought of bloodshed.

But not so now.

They had rapidly ripened in iniquity, and, as is nearly always the case,—

*Their days were numbered!*

* * * * *

When Jonathan woke from his sleep, and began to think of what he had done, or assisted in doing, he shuddered and turned deadly pale.

The "Pug," however, whose maxim always was that "it was much better to be hung for a sheep than a lamb," called for a large quantity of beer and spirits, and, though he did not pay for it, took great care to consume most of it himself.

"What shall we do?" said Warner; "we had better not show ourselves out in the daylight much."

"Do!" said Puggy, "vhy, nothin' is easier to do than this: let each on us go and take rooms over the vater, and commence business on our own account; if you've missed the coin in one job that's no reason vhy you should have the same ill-luck alvays."

"What do you mean?" said Jonathan.

"Mean, my joker! vhy this: I knows as nice a nest of cracksmen in the Borough as ever handled a 'jemmy.' I'll introduce yer; they knows me, well."

"And what then, turn housebreaker?" asked Jonathan, looking pale, and trembling.

"Cracksman, yes; why not? You needn't look so shivery, you know how to knock a 'slop' on the head as nicely as ever I seed it done in all my life; so you needn't feel squeamish about handling a wrench, screw-driver, or a nice little lever."

"But I object," said Jonathan.

"Does yer?" said Puggy, in an angry tone; "but *I* don't; and let me tell you, old 'un, it's too late for any backing out now you know, because if you don't join us, we shall know how to serve you; that's flat."

"Serve me; what do you mean?"

"Why, introduce you to Bow-street, to Sergeant Gale, a gentleman of very active habits. I dare say as how you've heard of him afore. Look at this will you?"

Thus speaking, Puggy handed over the "Mornin' 'Tiser" to him, in which was an account of young Caspar's trial.

Jonathan rapidly glanced over the column, and was thunderstruck.

"My wife act thus in my absence!"—"Two children discovered!"—"What, old Giles give evidence like this!—"The prisoner acquitted!"—"Shanks and my wife arrested for perjury!" he said, half aloud, but unaware that he had been heard.

Puggy and Warner were astonished at Jonathan's change of countenance, and heard all he said.

"I told you he was no novice," said Puggy, in a whisper. "Oh! he's a deep old file."

So firmly were the villains convinced that their new associate was the real owner of Bromley Hall Academy, that they taxed him with it, amid much bantering and rough joking.

Jonathan was so stupefied with what he had read, that he turned all manner of colours, as he said, in a firm, determined tone—

"All is lost! But I will have ample revenge. I will murder the wanton hussey, and Shanks also."

More drink and very little extra coaxing got Jonathan into such a maudling state, that he disclosed much of his past life, which fairly astonished both Warner and the Pug.

They were both delighted at Jonathan's open confessions, and slapped him heartily on the back, as they over and over again swore that he was a "brick."

During the day, as it was wet, foggy, and disagreeable, the Pug ventured out, and soon found the cabman, smoking his pipe upon the rank.

He had made a large hole into his two sovereigns, and from his flushed appearance it was evident he had been drinking heavily.

The Pug tipped him the wink, and they both retired into a tap-room.

"What's up now?" said Cabby, winking and blinking, in a half-drunken state. "Another partic'lar job, eh, Puggy?"

"Jest so. Does yer know much about the Borough?"

"Does I?" said Cabby, in disgust. "In coorse; vot part o' town is it I don't know? Vhy vot do you vant?"

"D'yer know where the 'Councillor' hangs out?"

"What, that long-headed cove as had seven-pen'orth once for getting into my uncle's in the Strand?"

"Yes."

"In coorse I does. I had a job o' his'n t'other night."

"Any swag?"

"Lots."

"What sort?"

"He lodged at a jeweller's one night, and took it into his head to leave about four in the morning," said Cabby, winking and shoving his red nose into a quart pot half filled with stout. "I happened to be near, yer see, and he gave me the job to drive him home."

"I twig," said Puggy. "Vell, I and them other parties vish to call on the Councillor to-day. Jest drive us there; it'll be all right."

In a few moments Puggy jumped into the four-wheeler, and, in less than half-an-hour, Warner, Jonathan, and the Pug, were in close conference with the Councillor.

And with the aid of spirits and malt liquors were soon as thick as thieves.

That night they all went to the theatre together, to drive off the blue devils and enjoy themselves.

It was while they were there that Jonathan thought he espied old Flint in one of the boxes.

How he went and dogged him home we have already seen.

Little did Flint imagine, however, that his night's pleasure would have such an unlooked-for ending.

## CHAPTER XLI.

### SEVERAL STRANGERS MEET UNEXPECTEDLY AT BROMLEY HALL—ARREST OF PUGGY.

With all his diligence and activity, Sergeant Gale was not yet able to trace the murder of old Ford to the right cause.

He had various surmises about it, but so undecided was the evidence and suspicions in his mind, that he feared to take any one person into custody until he had fully completed his chain of evidence against "other parties" he was in search of.

Old Flint, he thought, could not possibly escape, and yet what evidence was there against him?

Comparatively nothing.

Gale felt certain that the old lawyer, wicked as

he might be, was too shrewd and at the same time too timorous and weak to commit such a crime.

And where was the missing deeds and money?

Could they be traced?

This was merely a matter of surmise.

"Never mind," thought Gale, "I am in no hurry. If there are more than two mixed up in this affair, they are sure to fall out after a time, and split on each other; it's always the way."

Caspar's trial, however, served Gale very much, and from Jonathan's sudden flight from Bromley Hall, he felt convinced that he and Flint had something in common to do with both the murder and robbery.

"It strikes me," thought Gale, "that this Jonathan and the lawyer have had a hand in more than one job of this kind. I will visit and search this Bromley Hall; there is some mystery about the place I should much like to fathom."

But, as fortune would have it, there were other persons besides Sergeant Gale who desired much to do the very same thing.

These individuals were none other than Pug and Warner.

Puggy kept very close to Warner for many reasons, but the principal one was because Warner, he knew, was the wrong person to be out of money long if there was any earthly chance of getting it by fair means or foul.

"It would be a rare spree," said Puggy to Warner the night they all went to the theatre together, "it would be a rare old spree to go down and visit Bromley Hall. The master and mistress are both away now, there is no one there except a few old servants and his two daughters, and I'd lay my life there's something handsome to be picked up there."

It was resolved upon by Warner and Puggy to visit Bromley Hall within the next two days.

Puggy was very busy the next day collecting and borrowing "tools" from one professional gentleman or another.

On the morning of the second day he and Warner proceeded to the railway station, each carrying a small carpet bag.

As it happened, Detective Gale was going down to Bromley on that very morning, and arrived at the station just after Warner and the Pug.

He did not see them with the carpet bag in hand, or it might have gone wrong with them.

The bags were given in charge of the baggage master, and marked "Bromley."

As they stood on the platform, ready labelled, Gale passed, and directly he saw the bags he touched them in a careless manner with his foot.

"Hollo!" said he, "what's up now? Have we got any cracksmen in the train? That carpet bag looks very much like one the 'Councillor' had once."

He passed up and down the platform once or twice, and caught sight of Puggy in the train.

"What does *he* want here?" thought Gale. "Who is that other gentlemanly chap with him? He doesn't look much like one of Puggy's class; I must keep my eye on both of them."

As it happened, Puggy knew Gale well, but Warner did not; hence, when he saw the detective, he changed colour and turned his head.

"The werry cove as I didn't want to see, by all that's unlucky," said the Pug, with a curse. "Never mind, he didn't see me, so it's all right."

The train started, and in due time arrived at Bromley.

But Mr. Gale had got out at a station ten miles nearer London.

The Pug knew this, and was much pleased that it happened so.

"If he'd a only seen us with them ere 'tools,'" Puggy thought, "it would have been as good as ten penn'orth to both on us."

When they arrived at the village, and had refreshed themselves, Puggy took a stroll towards the Hall, "to see how the land laid," as he termed it.

As he approached the large building he pulled a small bundle of lace out of his pocket.

"This here's the fake for the sarvants," said he; "while I is argifying wi' 'em about a yard or two o' this here lace for their caps, I can take a good squint at the door-fastenings, and all about the outside o' the building."

With great boldness and perfect coolness the Pug advanced to the Hall door and rang.

The servants who answered the summons were shown the lace, and Puggy was directed to the back of the Hall near the kitchen entrance.

After much discussion several yards of lace were bought, and Puggy returned to the village.

"Right as a trivet," he chuckled, "there's nobody about, so that we can clear the place in about an hour."

Warner and the Pug fortified themselves with good suppers ere starting on their expedition.

About midnight they sallied forth, and in less than half an hour climbed the wall which surrounded the grounds of the Hall, and lay there in wait behind some bushes until such times as the last light should be extinguished.

So far all their plans had succeeded. There had not been a single baulk or hitch in anything, and both villains counted on complete success.

But there were two things which Puggy detested right heartily.

One was steel traps, and the other watch-dogs.

Now, as it happened, both these miseries were to befall him.

He had just jumped off the wall among the grass when his leg was caught in the steel trap.

With an oath he tried to disengage his bleeding leg, but had the misfortune to arouse the watch-dog by a bell which communicated with the kennel and the trap by a wire pully.

Hence Puggy had scarcely got out of the trap ere he was assailed by a couple of bull terriers, who snarled and rushed at him very viciously.

A vigorous blow of his "jemmy" laid one low.

Warner with a thick club, deliberately "brained" the other dog, so that they were now both free from further interruption.

When all was quiet, and as they lay hidden behind the bushes, the voice of one of the domestics was heard up at the Hall calling out.

"Tozer! Tozer! here Jip! here, lad! Good dorg."

"D—n Tozer and Jip too," snarled Puggy, with an angry oath, "if I'd a only knowed them dogs could a bit so hard, I'd a thought twice before giving Bromley Hall a friendly visit. Aye, call away my hearty, Tozer and Jip are both provided for; you can shout till all's blue, but you'll never wake 'em up again."

Now the plan which Puggy had made out in his own mind was this.

It was no use to think of forcing the Hall door, neither did he much care to pry open the parlour shutters, and thus gain admission; but he resolved to climb on to the immense water-butt in the kitchen-yard, swing on to the first-floor window-sill, and then get in.

Warner listened to all Puggy had to say, but remarked—

"Did you hear what old Whitechoker was talking about when asleep t'other day in the public-house parlour?"

"What, about some will in which two kids were concarned?"

"Yes—he little thought we heard him."

"The old cock seems to lay great wally on that ere dociment; and if ve comes across it, vhy, ve can make as much out on it as he."

"That's what I have been thinking."

"And that's vhy I vants to get into the old bloke's private room for," said Puggy, grinning. "I tumbled to it all; I dare say this night's vork 'll pay us tidy, if ve only does it clean."

Slowly and cautiously the two robbers approached the Hall.

They kept close in among the shrubbery, and then ran nimbly across the grassy lawn out of sight.

Once at the back of the building, they were safe.

Warner lifted Puggy up on to the immense water-butt near the kitchen door.

In a few moments he clambered cleverly on to the window-sill of the first floor.

The window was opened without difficulty, and Puggy was soon safe inside.

Warner followed suit, and, with the aid of a small stout rope, which Puggy threw down to him, soon clambered up and joined his companion.

They were both without boots, and walked about noiselessly.

It was arranged that one should search and rob in one direction, while the second did so in another.

They separated in the long dark gallery, and each went his way slowly.

With both hands groping against the walls, Puggy made his way towards old Jonathan's private study, and with false keys opened the door.

He entered, and looked about for a moment to see, as well as he could, what the place was like.

He was about to return to inform Warner of his success, but the door had been closed behind him.

This puzzled Pug for a moment, but he produced again his skeleton keys.

They were useless.

He could not re-open the door!

"How's this?" thought Puggy, "it's raytber strange."

He tried and tried again, but the door was firmly fastened.

In a few seconds he began to fume and sweat and inwardly rave, but it was all to no purpose.

"I can't be trapped," he thought, "the window is good enough. I have the coil of rope wound round my body, and can easily get out that way."

He walked across the room.

His foot pressed a secret spring in the floor.

A plank rose up slowly and noiselessly.

A phosphorescent glow issued from the aperture.

With staring eyes and trembling limbs his astonished gaze beheld the snow-white skeleton of the murdered girl, the same which old Giles had seen on a previous occasion.

Puggy was almost paralysed with fear, and shook in every limb.

He could not but look at the strange unearthly sight.

For some time he gazed; but the sight of precious stones glittering among the snow-white remains of silk and faded flounces roused his mean soul to energy again.

"Dead men tell no tales, I've heard," thought Puggy, "neither can they hurt a cove; but I never dreamed o' seein' sich a sight as this; and diamonds, too! lor, look at 'em shining there; but what makes the bones so bright all at once? it reminds a cove o' the 'Will-o'-the-Wisps' one sees in the Lincolnshire marshes. Here goes, I'll just see what these sparkling things are good for."

But first he opened the window and fastened the end of the rope to the cornice, so as to make his escape, if need be, at a moment's warning.

He hastily returned to where the bones lay buried.

The plank had descended again.

"That won't do for me," said Puggy; "I'll strike a light and have a good look; if it can be opened, I'll do it, for them 'ere stones seem to be worth no end o' money—any one on 'em's worth a Jew's eye."

He lit a small lantern he had brought with him, and sure enough trod on the secret spring again, but by mere accident.

Up rose the plank on its end, but this time so suddenly that it gave him a violent blow on the face, which almost knocked him down.

So eager, however, was the thief to desecrate the dead, that he heeded not the bump which instantly formed on his nose, and put forth his hand to take off a glittering jewel which sparkled on one of the bony fingers.

The small white fleshless hand suddenly clasped his own, and held him like a vice.

If he had been seized by the fangs of a rattlesnake, he could not have felt more pain.

It was not the pressure so much as an intolerable something which chilled his very marrow.

The bony fingers felt to him as if they were red-hot, and gradually burnt his own flesh.

With a groan of horror he started back.

His hand had upon it the impress of the bony fingers, and the outlines were as black as ink.

He started to his feet, like a man who had suddenly confronted and shaken hands with the devil.

His hair stood on end.

His eyes protruded out of their sockets, and he had scarcely strength to stand.

On the instant a heavy hand grasped him by the shoulder.

He had not power to resist.

His heart failed him, and he sank upon his knees trembling like a leaf.

Instinctively he turned his head.

His teeth began to chatter, and he felt half choked.

There stood beside him the headless spectre of Bromley Hall.

With a sudden bound, and electrified with horror, Puggy sprank to his feet with all the strength that remained in him.

He rushed to the window.

The headless spectre followed him.

Without a second thought, Puggy seized his rope and rapidly descended he scarce knew or cared whither.

He had not gone many feet when the rope slipped from above.

With a wild cry of agony and pain he fell upon a row of sharp spikes and broken bottles, which decorated the orchard walls.

Stunned, half dead with fright and pain, he had

not strength to extricate himself from the sharp spikes, but fell like a dead weight still further, some twelve feet below, through a sky-light, and into a large deep tank of water, which used to supply the bath-room of the students.

His shouts and noise attracted the attention of one who had been on the look-out.

This obliging person was Mr. Gale.

He and old Giles hurried to the spot, with several servants, and discovered Puggy, bleeding and bruised, struggling and floundering about in the immense water-tank without sufficient strength to extricate himself.

He was quickly dragged out, however, and to the surprise of all present Mr. Gale informed Jonathan's two daughters that he was a detective, and held in his possession a warrant to search the Hall.

Mr. Gale further observed that this same party, pointing to Puggy, had been long "wanted," and to save any further noise or trouble he firmly handcuffed the Pug before he could utter a word of surprise.

"Ladies," said Mr. Gale, very politely, and with an air of gallantry, "ladies, do not be in the least alarmed, for I assure you no possible harm can befall you; retire to your apartments again, and remain there. Let two of the male servants watch this half-drowned thief until my return; he has a companion concealed somewhere in the Hall: let no one make any noise or raise an alarm of any kind. I shall not be gone long. Come, Giles, arm yourself! you and I will find out the bold villain wherever he is."

The detective and old Giles left the spot, and went in search of Puggy's companion.

* * * * *

But what had become of Warner?

As we have before said, Bromley Hall was a very large place, in fact a perfect wilderness of bedrooms, school-rooms, and the like, so that it was possible that all this could have happened in one wing of the Hall, without Warner being at all aware of the rumpus in the other.

That this truly happened we shall presently see.

---

## CHAPTER XLII.

### WARNER MAKES STRANGE AND STARTLING DISCOVERIES—THE DEAD MAN'S HEAD SPEAKS—MYSTERY OF THE BRIDE AND BRIDEGROOM.

WITH a catlike step Warner crawled along the dark passage where Puggy left him, and began his solitary wanderings.

All was pitch dark, and he knew not whither he was going.

Up one flight of steps and down another he went, and the farther he proceeded the damper and more mouldy became the smell of everything around him.

"Where the devil can all this lead to?" thought Warner. "I was never in such a dismal hole in all my life. I have often heard that in some large old halls in England there are wings which are never used, and have been closed up for centuries. Perhaps Bromley Hall is one of these strange, wild, ghost-haunted places. But what have *I* to fear; *I* don't heed all the musty hobgoblin stories told by snuffy old crones and grandmothers in chimney corners. I rather like to explore such a wild, dreary place as this. What a place for a murder!" he thought.

He still went onwards and downwards.

The wind sighed dolefully, and the farther he went the more dense became the stifling atmosphere.

He produced his dark lantern and lighted it.

He discovered that he had got into a damp vault.

Rats ran hither and thither when they saw the light.

The walls were wet, slimy, and fungus-grown, and as he proceeded on his footsteps loudly echoed.

He stood before a huge, iron-bound doorway, which led he knew not whither.

While standing there, undecided what to do, he seized a large rusty knocker, and let it fall back again on the door.

The sound echoed, and Warner's blood became cold.

He knew not why, but by some strange circumstance he stood gazing at the old oak door.

It slowly opened before him.

He started back a pace or two, as if expecting to confront some horrible figure.

But none appeared.

"This is stranger still," thought Warner, but he boldly passed the open door and ascended the wet, moss-grown flight of stone steps.

"Where can this lead to?" he mused, as, lantern in hand, he ascended the stairs.

For a moment a sudden noise behind startled and caused him to stop.

It was the immense oak door which had closed upon him, and as it slammed to it awoke a thousand echoes in the vault and staircase.

Bent on adventure, and unconscious of the lapse of time, he went onward.

After a little, he came to a sort of landing, and at the side of it stood a small doorway, that apparently led into some apartment.

"Now I understand all," thought Warner; "this flight of stairs runs round all this wing of the building, and forms a secret communication to every room."

Such was the fact.

The original owner of Bromley Hall had so ordered the building of it that he could if it so pleased him gain admittance into each room of that wing without being seen or heard!

"How can I get in here?" thought Warner, prying about with his lantern.

He seized the knob of the door handle, and tried to shake it.

It was as firm as a rock.

In despair he pulled it.

The handle gave way and he fell against the wall.

He held in his hand the brass knob.

Attached to it, and forming a sort of key, was a dagger some twelve inches long, and of three equal sides.

But what astonished him more than all was that directly he had pulled out the dagger-handle, the door itself opened inwardly!

The apartment before him was large, empty, and dark as pitch.

To enter it Warner had to descend a flight of six steps.

Great and bold a villain as he was, Warner hesitated for a moment as he descended into the apartment.

"Who knows but that there may be treasures concealed here?"

This thought gave him extra courage.

With the lamp and dark lantern raised above his head, and pistol in hand, he descended into the apartment.

It was a large, round, vault-like room, and the only light in it was a feeble ray of pale moonlight, which streamed through long, narrow windows, barred with iron, and some six feet from the ground.

An ancient bedstead, of costly materials, dusty, and long disused, stood on one side.

A large bookcase, a wardrobe, couches, easy chair, and other furniture were there, the mouldy gilding on which looked dull and sombre in Warner's lamplight.

In the centre of the room stood a writing desk, and strewn upon it were piles of letters, reams of paper, and a small lamp, with matches, ready for immediate use.

"This place is old," thought Warner; "but for all that *some one* has been in the habit of using it, and lately also, for there must be some other entrance into this place besides that narrow door, or how could all this cumbersome furniture have been brought in?"

Lamp in hand he advanced to the writing-desk, and sat down.

To amuse himself he lit a cigar, for the dense, unwholesome atmosphere was almost overpowering.

He began to rummage among the papers, and at last eagerly seized one, the handwriting of which was peculiar.

"I ought to know *this* writing," he mused. "It's old Flint's, for a hundred! It can't be possible that the lawyer and old white-choker knew each other! But yet it might be."

He looked at the signature of the letter first, and dropped it in surprise.

"It *is* Flint's!" he gasped, in astonishment, and read the letter from beginning to end.

When he had finished, he exclaimed, half aloud—

"Oh! the damnable villany of the pair of rogues! Jonathan Gravestones is his name, eh? A pretty scandal to pretend to be a parson! Why, here is a compact between them for deliberate *murder!*"

He searched further among his papers, and the more he read the more he was astounded!

"What a treasure is here," Warner sighed, as he threw aside some of the papers, and put others into his pocket. "What a bloody career of villany this reverend gentleman has gone through to be sure, and yet when we proposed turning to housebreaking for a living, he turns up his eyes in horror! Oh! he's an artful old thief! When I return to London, I'll torment his life out; and in partnership with Flint, eh? No wonder this part of the Hall has been locked up for years!"

Full of curiosity, he rose from his seat, and approached the old bedstead.

It was dusty and moth-eaten.

On the bed lay a small axe.

The edge of it was exceedingly sharp.

Blood-stains were upon it, and the marks of some man's gory fingers were distinctly visible upon the white oak haft.

"Hillo, Mr. Jonathan, what means all this?" thought Warner.

He turned down the bed-clothes.

The sheets were all stained with what had once been blood.

The pillow, just on that part where the head should lie, was severed in two!

Warner measured the cut in the pillow with the edge of the axe, and both corresponded in size and length!

"There has been murder here!" he thought. "But where could he have concealed the body?"

In the room was an old iron chest of great size and strength.

At first it looked like an ottoman, for it was covered with drapery, nor would Warner have discovered his mistake, had not his foot accidentally kicked it.

It had a hollow sound, and he tried to open it. After much labour he managed to wrench it open by the aid of a "jemmy."

Inside he saw the remains of various old parchments.

A silver-hilted sword was there also, and a slouched hat, with drooping feather, such as might have been worn by some young noble in former days.

Underneath these he also found, carefully packed, a complete and costly suit of gentleman's wedding garments, all untouched, and wrapped up just as they had come from the tailors.

Beneath all these things, however, and covered up with empty money bags and costly jewel-cases, Warner's eye lighted upon a human skull.

It was evidently that of some young man, and was white and fleshless.

He took hold of it and placed it on the green-covered writing-desk, for the purpose of more closely examining it by the light of his dark lantern.

Warner sat in the old arm chair, gazing at this human skull, and wondering whose it might have been, and the possible history of the murder.

Judge of his astonishment, however, as he intently gazed at the eyeless sockets of the skull.

The jaws began to wag!

It spoke to him.

Full of horror, Warner listened, as the fleshless jaws moved, and a sepulchral voice issued forth in calm, solemn tones, and said—

# THE BOY SOLDIER; OR, GARIBALDI'S YOUNG CAPTAIN.

THE ATTEMPTED ASSASSINATION AT THE OPERA.

"You gaze at the head of a murdered bridegroom! Thirty years this very day I was to have been married to the once fair mistress of Bromley Hall. The night before marriage I slept in this room. How I came hither I knew not then. I know it now. When the marriage morning dawned I was missing. None knew whence I had fled! I was murdered! beheaded when sound asleep. My head was buried in lime. My body burnt!"

"Horrible!" Warner gasped.

"Yet, man with blood-stained hands, still listen more to me."

"Go on," sighed Warner.

"My bride, attired in gorgeous array, waited on the marriage day for my coming. I never came. She sat in her chamber lovely, pale, and beautiful as the dawn. When her bridesmaids entered, she was discovered murdered and—violated!"

"Nay, shudder not," the voice went on, "shudder not. I speak not this to you because I ask revenge, but because at certain times and seasons I walk my lonely round throughout the Hall, and am forced to tell my history to the first one I meet. Yet, hearken! The alarm was raised. The bridesmaids flew hither and thither in dread alarm. When they entered her chamber a second time, the body had disappeared!

"Both murders can be traced to two men, whose motives were lust and cupidity."

"Their names?" gasped Warner, in wonder.

"The fair orphan's tutor and my own lawyer."

What, Jonathan and Flint?"

"The very men."

"I will denounce them,"

"Nay, you cannot—you dare not. At this moment you are hunted down yourself—leave revenge and justice to the laws of heaven. Warner!—repent in time—adieu!"

The jaws closed again firmly, and with a loud click like that of a gun or spring trap.

"Am I dreaming? said Warner, after some time spent in thought.

"Not in the least," said a voice behind him. "You were never more wide awake in all your life."

Warner turned his head.

It was Detective Gale and old Giles the gardener.

* * * * *

With almost inconceivable agility, Warner fell from his chair upon the floor; and as Gale was about to fire his revolver, the bold robber knocked up his arm, and the bullet passed harmlessly overhead.

In a second Warner seized him by the pistol, and gave him such a terrible wrench that the revolver fell harmlessly from his grasp.

With a terrible blow of his clenched fist, he struck down old Giles, and was thus in a few seconds perfectly master of the position.

Gale in all his life had never met "with such an ugly customer," as he called him. And as Warner stood, revolver in hand, over him, too, the robber's eyes flashed with such deadly fire, that the detective knew very well, if he tried to push things to a conclusion, the roll of the police force would be minus the name of Serjeant Gale in the morning.

Like a clever officer, he wriggled and writhed on the floor apparently in much agony, but in reality was only "foxing," as it is termed, or in other words pretending.

If he had his revolver, he would have made a good and desperate fight with Warner; for it is a point of honor among policemen, and detectives especially, never to let a prisoner escape when once in custody.

But what could he do?

Some might say, why not fight and die, if need be, rather than let Warner escape?

But Gale did not.

"Discretion," he thought, "was the better part of valour; and, besides, who's to know that I did allow one of my prisoners to escape? Can't I get up a good story and have old Giles to corroborate it? Besides, I'm sure to fall across this chap again some day, and nab him at my ease. I'm not going to get a broken head, all for the sake of glory and two lines of flattery in a newspaper. No, not I."

Warner picked up the detective's pistol and cocked it.

He now had two weapons.

But with all his success over his two would-be captors, he had made one grand mistake.

He had allowed the detective to have a good look at his face.

If he travelled for twenty years, Gale could now identify him.

Warner did not think of this, but seeing a small secret door-like opening in the wall opposite to him, through which Gale and old Giles had entered, he dashed through it, and instantly slammed the door to again.

"It was a near shave," thought Warner, as he groped his way through a passage he knew nothing of, "but they haven't got me this time."

Revolver in one hand, and dark lantern in the other, he hurried along, feeling satisfied that neither of his late antagonists could pursue him for some time.

He had bolted them in!

## CHAPTER XLIII.

IN WHICH TWO FRIENDS ARE DELIGHTED TO MEET EACH OTHER, AND THE TABLES ARE SUDDENLY TURNED, TO THE GREAT SURPRISE OF BOTH PARTIES.

BUT let us, for a moment, return to old Flint, and to what he did on the night when accidentally discovered returning from the theatre.

When Flint arrived within a few doors of his own home, the detective bade him good night in a very jocular manner, and slapped him on the back familiarly, saying,

"Well, good night, old boy; when next we meet we'll make a night of it. But, mind how you act towards those pretty ballet-girls, or you may get into mischief, you old rascal; they might father their illegitimate children upon you, you know, eh? Ha! ha! that *would* be a lark."

Old Flint took all this as a very good joke, and, in his own mind, pronounced the stranger "a capital fellow, by Jove."

They parted.

Old Flint went to his own door with a very unsteady gait, for he had been drinking somewhat freely, and was the least bit "fuddled."

After much fumbling with his latch-key, and with great difficulty keeping on his legs, he let himself in.

Jonathan boldly walked up, and arrived just in time to prevent the door from closing.

When old Flint entered the parlour Jonathan passed the threshold with all the air of a man who had lodgings in the house, and had, of course, a right to be there.

All this had been perceived by the lynx-eyed detectives on duty in the street.

A very soft whistle was heard.

In a moment old Flint's companion at the theatre was seen to be in deep conversation with a policeman in plain clothes, who had heard the whistle, and, of course, answered the summons instantly.

"See that tall, classical-looking chap go in?"

"Yes."

"Don't live there, does he?"

"Don't know; at least, never seen him before."

"Think he has anything to do with Schmidt, the old cock I was out with to-night?"

"Perhaps so."

"Then keep an extra sharp eye on him; if he leaves the house get one of the lads to follow him and see where he hangs out."

Such were the detective's instructions to those under him, and he walked home to his wife and children, tired out with "playing the gentleman," but perfectly satisfied that old Schmidt and the new arrival would be watched like mice every moment of the night.

* * * * *

When Flint tottered into his parlour he stumbled about in the dark for some time, but soon managed to strike a light.

During this time Jonathan had ample opportunity to conceal himself in his friend's large wardrobe in the inner room.

The lawyer threw himself into a capacious old arm-chair, and began to yawn and stretch himself.

Several decanters of wine were on the table, and

he helped himself to the contents thereof very liberally, for the more a man drinks the more he wants.

He even went so far as to light a cigar, and, while puffing it, allowed his imagination to roam into the wild regions of fancy.

But the chief subject of his thoughts was of the pretty ballet dancer, Jennie Jackson.

"Lovely creature!" he sighed. "Superb limbs! such hair! *such* eyes! and *such* feet! Heigho! who wouldn't be a rich man to have it in his power to dandle and dawdle with such pretty playthings? Ha! who would not?"

And the old rascal, between the puffs of his fragrant Havannah, piously meditated on the misery and horror of being poor, and as he did so he chuckled to himself at the bare thought of how many thousands he himself had acquired by coolness and knavery.

With legs cocked up on a chair opposite to him, he blew clouds of cigar smoke, which curled round and round his head in light blue circles, until at last the room was half-filled with a narcotic atmosphere.

Immediately before him was a large mirror.

But the light of the candle being dim, and the clouds of smoke combined, prevented him from having a good look at himself as he sat grinning at the success of his own villany through life.

"Well, Mr. Flint," said he, chuckling, "you have been a very clever lawyer, very clever indeed, and can now retire from public life very handsomely. Here's success, and a long life of pleasure to you."

He raised a glass of wine to his lips, and was about to toss it off, when his astonished eyes caught sight of a reflection in the lengthy mirror before him.

The glass fell from his hand, and was smashed upon the floor.

"Great heavens!" he gasped.

It was the reflection of Jonathan as he stood behind the lawyer's chair.

"Great heavens!" said Flint, now thoroughly sobered. "Great heavens! where did *you* spring from? No; it cannot be. Do my eyes deceive me? No!—yes!—it *is* my old friend Jonathan!" said Flint, hastily rising, and confronting the stern features of the late master of Bromley Hall. "Why, as I live, it's you! Oh! how de-*light*-ed I am to see you. Give me your hand. How are you? Why, who'd ever a thought of seeing you here? Why, I've been looking for you all over the town for the past week or more; on my honour I have. I am de-*lighted* to see you."

"Indeed!" said Jonathan, very coolly taking a chair, and throwing himself into it. "Pass the bottle, I'm *very* thirsty, Flint."

Flint handed a bottle of port to his "dear friend," but with a forced smile upon his ugly, furrowed countenance, internally wishing that it might poison him.

"Here, my dear friend, help yourself. Oh! how pleased I am to see you. If you had been my own brother, this visit couldn't have given me greater pleasure; and you are looking so well too. Why, you look twenty years younger; on my honour you do."

"Do I?" said Jonathan, tossing off a bumper. "Really, how funny."

"No fun, my friend, it's the plain truth."

"Sorry I can't return the compliment, for I never, in all my life before, saw a man who looked so pale and grinned so ugly as you do. You look, Flint, as if Calcraft had acted valet to you, and decorated your neck with a stout bit of rope."

"H-u-s-s-s-h!" said the lawyer, in a confidential whisper. "I'm Flint no longer; at least, not so while here."

"What then?" said Jonathan. "To *my* knowledge you have gone under a dozen names in private life since I have known you. What's your alias now, then?"

"Schmidt, sir — Schmidt; don't forget. S-c-h-m-i-d-t," said the lawyer, spelling it, and counting off the letters on his thin long fingers.

"Well, it little matters to me," said Jonathan, "what you choose to call yourself. You know what *I* have come for, of course? The four days are past."

"Why, yes; so they have. I quite forgot all about that engagement."

"But *I* did not," said Jonathan, firmly, and with a grim smile. "I have gone through much trouble since last I saw you, and wish to come to a settlement at once."

"But the boy and girl?" said the lawyer, with a quivering lip. "Are they safely housed?"

"Of course they are."

"I intended to call at Bromley Hall in a day or two, but—"

"It's no use to go down there, at least for some time," was the reply; "for I must not be seen about Bromley."

"Indeed! Why?"

"Oh, nothing; it is simply a matter of keeping quiet for a little while, and taking another name, as you have done, that's all. The academy is broken up for the present, and all owing to those two young ruffians, Frank and Tom Ford."

After a pause, and some little explanation on Jonathan's part, old Flint remarked, drily,—

"Well, I'm sorry to think things have taken such a sudden turn for the worst, my dear friend, and if I could help you in any way I would do so with pleasure, but as it is I—"

"What!" said Jonathan, rising, and with an angry look, "What do you mean?"

"Mean, my friend; I simply mean this, that I have nothing more to do with your concern at Bromley Hall," said old Flint, trying to cow down and intimidate his long-legged companion; in truth, endeavouring to look and act as bravely as possible, although at the same time shivering in his shoes.

The possible consequences of any sudden outburst and display of physical force on Jonathan's part, caused Flint's heart to quail.

The lawyer met his companion's fixed gaze with a look of icy coldness, as he continued with a trembling lip: "I made a certain bargain with you concerning the boy and girl, with the promise that if they died within a certain time, you should receive a certain sum."

"Well, and have I not acted up to my share in this agreement, as I have in all others we have had together?"

"Perhaps not," said old Flint, rising and looking round the room as if in search of something.

The truth was that he began to tremble at Jonathan's vicious countenance, and for a moment walked into the inner parlor in search of a revolver he had there, lying by his bedside on a small table.

He found it and put it into his pocket, and returned to the front parlor.

Jonathan smiled viciously at the lawyer's remark, and took another copious draught of wine.

Flint, having the revolver in his pocket, now felt very valiant and resumed his seat in a very cool, careless, off-handed manner.

"So *that* is your opinion, eh?" said Jonathan, with a wicked chuckle.

"Yes, and I have no hesitation in saying that you have no more right to come here on account of those two brats, than I would have to go to you and ask money for my son, Joel, who is now travelling for health and pleasure in Italy."

"Indeed!"

"Yes, indeed! Why do you sit there and grin at me in that manner?" said old Flint, plucking up courage and actually sighing for some good excuse to blow Jonathan's brains out. "Indeed, yes indeed; a pretty thing for you to do, to gain admittance into my apartment like some midnight robber, and drink my wine, and take things free and easy with a man who does not owe you a farthing."

"How pious you are getting all at once," said Jonathan, with a sneer. "Do you think I am so stupid as not to know your kind intentions towards me, now you've got the brats off your hands?"

"And don't I know very well that the brats have been carried off by the young Garibaldians under Frank Ford?" said Flint, in triumph. "Can you deny it? And yet you have the effrontery to come here with a lie in your mouth to extort money," said the lawyer, indignantly striking the table.

A short pause ensued, when Jonathan responded in a very calm whisper,—

"And don't *I* know, Flint, that you are privy to—"

"What?" said the lawyer, quickly, and with a trembling lip.

"Nay, don't shake so much, my dear old friend," said the late master of Bromley Hall, with a sneer; "don't shake so much; you look as pale, and tremble just like you did on the night when old Ford was murdered and robbed."

"Liar!" growled Flint, clutching the revolver in his pocket, and getting it ready for instant use, unseen by Jonathan. "Liar!" he said, with flashing eyes; "I know nothing of what you say; it is all base insinuations."

"Do you owe anything to a gentleman of the name of Warner—Dr. Warner, mark me, who attended on your very *dear* friend Ford ——"

"Idiot! I——"

"Why do you keep out of the way of policemen, and change your name? You are very innocent, and I know feel 'de-*light*-ed' to see me."

Flint bit his lip.

"Shall I kill this fellow?" he thought. "Would that he might provoke or give me some good excuse for doing so; I'd send a bullet whistling through his cursed skull in no time."

"Satisfaction is what I want, Flint. I am a ruined man! blasted for life, and all through being led by the nose by such a viper as you. From one sin I have fallen into another and a greater one each time. I am a murderer, and so are you—the bride and bridegroom at the Hall, remember. Where is all the money? what has become of it? where has it gone to?"

"Into my pocket," Flint laughed, in triumph; "and will remain there, Jonathan."

He felt very courageous, because of his revolver, and especially because he knew that the long gentleman opposite was never known to carry weapons of any kind.

"Not if I have a hand to compel you," said Jonathan, rising in anger.

"Oh, would you use force to an unarmed, inoffensive man?" said Flint, in pretended alarm.

"Money, I say," said Jonathan. "Would you, for the sake of a few pounds, see me dragged by the law and hung like a dog, you who have thousands at your command? Money, I say, Flint, or, by heavens, there'll be murder committed here tonight. Money, I say, or blood!"

Flint now saw that Jonathan was thoroughly aroused, and he knew of old that he was a very desperate man.

"Unhappy wretch," said Flint, in tones of mock pity; "calm your insane mind; there are policemen in the street; remember, you are not in Bromley now."

"I know that, imp of the devil," Jonathan retorted; "but if there were a dozen here at this moment, they could not, they should not stay my just anger."

"Hold," said Flint, as Jonathan was about to rise, at the same time presenting the revolver at his visitor's head. "Hold, villain, you are in my power! move but an inch, and I'll blow the roof off your head!"

"Despicable hound!" said Jonathan; "you deserve to die; this is the end of all your professions, is it—you would kill me in your own room—you would 'silence' me for ever, as you call it, eh? Oh, you most consummate old villain."

"As you will," said Flint, grinning in triumph, like an old ape. "The game is over, my dear Jonathan; it has lasted for more than thirty years between us, and I have got the 'odd trick;' might is right."

Jonathan grasped at the weapon eagerly.

"Die!" said Flint, and he pulled the trigger six times in quick succession.

The caps snapped!

But the six charges missed fire.

"Damnation!" swore Flint, in pale surprise.

In an instant Jonathan seized him by the throat.

"Fool! idiot!" he said, in low, hissing tones; "think you I was not prepared for this? Ha, ha! I drew the charges for you—ha, ha!"

With a powerful effort he threw Flint upon the floor, and placed one knee heavily on his breast.

"This is better than your revolver," said Jonathan, brandishing a long knife before Flint's astonished eyes. "*This* makes no noise. Silence, fool," said Jonathan, almost squeezing the life out of Flint's body. "Silence, or I'll cut your heart in two."

"Me-r-cy!" groaned Flint.

"The money!"

"Mercy! and—oh, only let me rise! I'm suffocating. You shall have all I've got. Mur——"

Jonathan was on the point of cutting Flint's throat, when—

Some one knocked at the door!

"Who is there?" asked Jonathan, hoarsely.

No answer.

The knocks were repeated.

"Who is there, I ask?" said Jonathan, in a quick, angry manner.

For a third time the knocks were repeated.

"Curses on it," said Jonathan, in a whisper. "I am foiled again. Your promise," said he in Flint's ear, "you will not betray by word or sign ought that has now happened?"

"I will not," was the faint response. "Let me rise; I am almost dead."

"Another moment and you would have been," thought Jonathan, with a bitter smile, as he put up his long knife, and went towards the door.

He opened it.

A policeman entered the room.

In the passage were some half dozen others.

Neither Flint nor Jonathan had heard a single footfall until that moment.

As must be confessed, the feelings of the two

culprits can be more easily imagined than described.

Jonathan bit his lip, and stood erect as a post.

The lawyer sat in his arm-chair endeavouring to look calm and indifferent.

Both of them were almost crazed with fear and excitement.

What the officers came for, and did, will be seen in another chapter.

## CHAPTER XLIV.

### DICK'S DEATH-BED—SORROWFUL SCENE—AGNESE IS VISITED BY AN UNKNOWN FEMALE.

THE many scrapes and escapes of Frank Ford in the mountains among the treacherous brigands caused the Boy Band to look upon their young leader as if he possessed a charmed life.

The last adventure, however, in Basil's cave, and the abduction of the bold brigand's daughter Agnese, was looked upon as something almost miraculous.

For it will be remembered than when just upon the point of escaping scot free with the beautiful brave girl, he was attacked both in front and rear in the mountain-pass, and almost surrounded by the black, revengeful rascals.

The timely arrival of Hugh Tracy, with Fatty, Buttons, and other bold youths, broke the circle in which the daring young chief was surrounded, and, luckily for all parties, they made good their escape with but trifling loss.

But poor Agnese was much shaken both in body and mind, and her fair face became as pale as death.

She had suffered much from the brutality of her ignorant father; so much so, that but a few months more of such a life would have broken her young heart.

The only ray of hope that ever shone down upon her in her miserable mountain home among the cut-throats and robbers was the unexpected arrival of the bold, handsome, and dashing boy captain of the young Garabaldians.

From the first moment that their eyes met she had secretly loved Frank.

Yet she never told him the depth of her girlish affection, from motives of pure modesty.

Whenever she saw him she blushed deeply.

Her heart increased its beating, and her lips trembled with untold pleasure, as she often gazed upon him clambering the rocks with a firm fearless step.

She would have gone anywhere with Frank—aye, to the world's end, had he desired it.

There was nothing he might ask her to do but what she did it.

In truth she would have given her very life for her young preserver, and willingly sacrificed all her best hopes to gratify his least wish, except to stoop to dishonor.

And this she knew Frank was too much of a soldier and a gentleman even to imagine or desire.

She loved him as a friend, as a brother.

Yes, and something more than that.

In his society she was always happy, but sometimes tears flowed from her bright eyes, for she often caught Frank looking pale, thoughtful, and melancholy.

The reason she knew not, nor could she with all her ingenuity ascertain it.

She was safely placed in the care of a kind old innkeeper, in a small village some fifty miles from her father's mountain home, and far out of danger, where Frank often visited her.

The camps of the Boy Soldiers were now very near Garabaldi's head quarters, and beyond fear of being attacked or surprised by any superior force of the enemy.

They drilled now more arduously and regularly than ever, for it was the boast and pride of all the boys that they were the most soldierly company of volunteers under Garabaldi's command, as that old chief himself had often said, and with a smile of pleasure.

"Captain Ford, my dear young friend," old Garabaldi was often heard to say, as he rode down to the English Boys' camp to see them drill. "Captain Ford, I must compliment you, sir, upon the fine condition and excellent drill of your gallant lads; yours is the finest company among the whole volunteer force under my command; you have had some stirring adventures, I hear, among the mountains, and if I am not much mistaken, others are in store for you. I shall not forget to remember your services, and mention them to King Victor Emanuel."

This was no niggardly praise by any means; but though well deserved, caused much envy among other volunteer companies, and deadly rancour filled the hearts of more than one against young Captain Ford and his Boy Band of soldiers.

Of this we shall see and hear more anon.

In the afternoon it was Frank's habit to walk over the fields to the small village in sight to have a chat with and to console Agnese, who was still pale, thin, weakly, and very sick.

Agnese, propped up in bed with numerous pillows, always received Frank with beaming smiles, and her eyes were oft suffused with tears of tenderness.

But Frank's manner towards her had somewhat changed of late.

He was not so gay and lively and full of jokes and mad freaks as he had formerly been.

The death of several among his band had steeled his heart, and he regretted their loss as if they had been his own natural brothers.

But there was another cause for his silence and habitual thoughtfulness.

The mysterious death of his uncle had fallen upon him like a thunderbolt.

That awful barbarous murder stunned and shocked him.

And *he* was accused of it!

This thought almost drove him mad.

He sometimes made up his mind to leave the Boy Band, and return to England.

But this would appear like cowardice, he argued.

"Never mind, the war in Italy will soon be over," he consoled himself with thinking, "and then I'll return to London for a time, and face all my vile enemies. After that the band will go across the seas to Mexico, and seek fresh adventures and dangers. I don't like a life of idleness. Once a soldier always a soldier."

On one occasion, when he visited Agnese, he sat down beside her bed, and appeared very sad.

"What ails you, dear Frank?" whispered Agnese. "You look pale, careworn, and sorrowful; you are so changed of late. You do not appear like the same youth; all the colour has left your cheeks, your eyes are cast down, and you mope about like one half-witted at times."

Frank smiled, and tried to laugh.

It was a poor attempt.

He knew that what Agnese said was perfectly true.

"Have *I* occasioned this sad change, Frank?" she asked, in tones of sympathy and affection. "If

I have, let me return to my father, there to die, for I would not cause you a moment's pain for all the wealth in Italy."

"You, Agnese, you!" said Frank, with a flashing eye, and crimsoned cheeks. "No, dear girl, it is not you, believe me."

"Then who else?"

"Well, dear one, I have great cause to be thoughtful. One of my bravest boys is dead."

"Dead? Who is dead?"

"Dick Fellows," said Frank, sadly. "He died last night. As brave a lad as ever breathed."

"I'm sorry, very sorry to hear that, for you loved him as a brother. I have often heard you say so."

"I did, Agnese. If it had been my brother Tom I could not have felt more sorrow. Oh! it was hard to part with such a companion as he was."

"Last night he died?"

"Yes, and a sad, sad sight it was," said Frank. "He knew that death was drawing nigh, and he sent for me. I went into his tent. There he lay, looking calm, and pale, and resigned. He had been attended to daily by some kind old clergyman of the neighbouring town, and was quite resigned. When I entered the tent his eyes brightened up, and a faint flush mounted his pallid cheeks. I sat down upon the straw, and took his hand in mine. For several moments I could not speak; neither could he. I felt as if my very soul would burst, as I felt the faint pulsations of his heart. For there he lay wounded and dying, far away from relations and home, and in the land of strangers. I could—I would most willingly have exchanged my lot for his, for he was a dear, brave, and generous lad. For some moments he looked at me calmly and resigned. 'Frank,' he whispered, 'I shall not long be here.'

"I tried to rally him, but he faintly smiled and said,

"'Nay, 'tis useless to cheer me up. I know the whole truth, the doctor has told me all. I am going home fast, Frank, very fast; give my love to all the brave lads, and my dying blessing and love to father and mother. I know I did wrong in running away from home without asking them, but I wanted to be a soldier, Frank, like you.'

"'And you have been a brave one, Dick,' I answered.

"'Nay, Frank, I have done my duty, and that only. I lived like a true English volunteer, and I hope to die like one. Bury me like a soldier upon the battle field.'

"A long pause ensued here between us, Agnese," said Frank, "which was only disturbed by Fatty, who crept into the tent with his two eyes red and swollen with weeping.

"He was quickly followed by young Buttons, and at last the tent was crowded by the boys, who wished to surround Dick's death-bed, and do him honour to the last.

"Mark sat on one side, and I on the other.

"Poor Dick smiled on his young companions, one or two of whom, beside Fatty and Buttons, were silently weeping.

"He shook hands with all, and seemed resigned to his fate.

"The only words he said, beside the message for his father and mother, were these, 'My brave lads, follow Captain Frank, and obey him in all things!' and then he whispered in my ear, 'You will have much trouble and annoyance about your uncle's murder when you return to England, Frank, but recollect my words, you have not to go farther than to Jonathan and old Flint to have the whole matter cleared up, and your own honour vindicated.'

"Then addressing the boys, each by name, he said,

"'If I were rich, lads, I would leave you all some valuable memento of my friendship and dying love; but, soldier-like, I have nothing but what my kit contains.'

"His knapsack was brought to the bed-side and opened.

"He gave me his cloak, his photograph, and one of his revolvers.

"Mark had the other, and a valuable dirk also.

"He gave Buttons a pretty cigar case. Fatty was handed his sword.

"In truth, every one of the sorrowful lads received some small present from the dying boy, and knelt around him with sorrowful hearts.

"'When I am dead, Frank,' he whispered, 'undo my flannel shirt—you will find something there you will recognize: keep it, and let no one see it—let no one have it but the person who gave it to me—you understand!'

"I nodded and took his hand, Mark the other.

"He smiled upon us all, and while murmuring a sweet prayer, closed his eyes.

"His head fell back.

"He was dead!"

"Poor boy! brave youth! And what was it you found round his neck?" Agnese asked, while tears trickled down her fair face.

"The likeness of his sweetheart."

From the day he received it until the hour of his death he wore it like a sacred charm upon his heart.

"And who was she?"

"The only sister of our favourite tutor at Bromley Hall, Mr. Caspar."

While thus he spoke he suddenly rose to his feet.

The sounds of distant mournful music fell upon his ear.

It was a military band approaching and playing a solemn funeral dirge.

"It is poor Dick's funeral," said Frank. "I forgot the hour, and must away."

He hurried from the inn, and as he did so wiped a solitary tear from his eye, which, despite all his manhood and resolution, had involuntarily stolen down his sun-burnt cheeks.

As he dashed down stairs, he was met by a young girl dressed like a Sister of Charity.

He tried to look at her face.

But she avoided his gaze.

Yet, as he left the house, she looked after him and lingered on the stairs.

It was Nelly Lancaster in disguise! she was going to the sick girl's chamber.

## CHAPTER XLV.

### TERESA THE SPY—STRANGE STORY AND ADVENTURES—ESCAPE OF HUGH TRACY FROM PRISON.

SLOWLY and mournfully the funeral procession moved towards the spot where Dick's grave had been dug the night before by Fatty and Buttons.

Frank soon overtook the cortege, and now walked as chief mourner.

Next came the officers of the company.

Then a detachment of Boy Soldiers, who, with arms reversed, were to fire over the grave.

The rear was brought up by a large deputation of officers from different regiments, who thus came to do honour to the brave lad now dead.

The bier was borne on the shoulders of six strong youths.

Chief of these was Tony, who wept like a child all the way; but tried to hide his tears as best he could with the flowing pall.

When arrived at the grave, which had been dug beneath a cluster of old oak trees, one of the Boy Soldiers, habited like a clergyman, read the funeral service in a calm, solemn, and impressive manner (see Illustration in No. 14), while many shaded their eyes, which were moistened by tears.

The coffin was lowered into its last resting-place.

A parting volley was fired over the body.

All was over.

When all were about to depart Captain Frank stepped forward, and placed on the coffin a crown of flowers, and, in a stirring speech, recounted to all there assembled the daring deeds and many virtues of the deceased.

His oration was short, but feelingly delivered, and much pleased all who heard him.

He did not speak like a superior officer, but more like one who had lost a valued friend—in truth, a brother.

The grave was closed.

Each one of the Boy Band felt ambitious to throw a shovelful of earth, as a mark of respect, upon the dear departed, and, when all was over, a small wooden tablet of graceful design was placed at the head of the grave, on which was painted—

To the Memory of
Our brave companion in arms,
RICHARD FELLOWS,
Lieutenant in the Boy Band of English Garibaldians,
Who was mortally wounded in a skirmish
with Basil's Bandit Band, while
gallantly protecting his
Captain.
All honour to the young and brave.
May he rest in peace.

* * * * *

Captain Frank and his band had not long returned to the camps again, when their melancholy musings over poor Dick's fate were suddenly broken by intelligence which then reached them.

Teresa, the female spy, galloped up in all haste.

"The captain! the captain?" she cried. "Where is he? Let me see him instantly!"

She was soon ushered into Frank's tent.

"I have great news for you," she said, with an air of great reserve, and sitting in the deep shade.

"Of what?" said Frank.

"I will tell you presently; but first of all I have found out that there is going to be a great battle about here in a day or two—a bloody battle, as you will find."

"Indeed! how know you this?"

"I penetrated into the Austrian camp, and saw their preparations. The Archduke Albrecht is arranging his forces, and intends to fall upon the Italian lines when least expected."

"And does General Garibaldi know this?"

"Not yet; I am on my way to his head-quarters now; but I stopped here to tell you that your missing comrade is alive."

"What, the one that was so cruelly tossed down the precipice—Hugh Tracy?"

"The same."

"But how could he have escaped death?"

"Easily enough, when all is explained."

"How do you mean?"

"When the brigand villain (who was afterwards killed by Dick Fellows) descended the rope after your young comrade, he fired at the lad."

"And killed him, as we thought."

"Nothing of the sort. He was wounded, let go his hold on the rope, and fell among a dense growth of shrubbery that grew on the surface of the rocks."

"That accident saved him; it broke his fall."

"Well?"

"Thence he fell into a large pool. The shock as he plunged into the ice-cool water instantly revived him. He struggled manfully, and reached the bank and was saved."

"You astonish me!"

"Perhaps so; but truth is stranger than fiction, Captain Ford. He is now safe and well; but——"

Here Teresa paused.

"But what?" Frank asked, eagerly. "Speak, I beseech you!"

"He is now in the hands of some mountain robbers. They discovered him, and bore him away to their rock-bound caves, and there he is at this present moment."

"In the hands of a bandit band?"

"I am sorry to say so; in Captain Basil's power. If he had not been recognized as one of the Boy Soldiers he might have escaped; but as you ran away with his daughter Agnese he and the band swear most solemnly to have Hugh's life, and to torture him as no one was ever tortured before."

"Poor Hugh," Frank sighed; "but this must not be, Teresa; I cannot sit here in ease at peace and know this. He must be, he shall be rescued!"

"Take care," said Teresa, solemnly, "take care; once you get within their power again I fear all is lost!"

"I fear them not," Frank said, fiercely.

"But you have greater reason to fear Basil and his band now than ever; he has powerful friends."

"I do not understand you, Teresa."

"Then listen," said the spy. "You know Joel Flint?"

"I do. We have his servant among our band at this very moment."

"I am aware of it. If you had killed the imposter Joel when you had a fair chance in the duel you fought in the cave——"

"Teresa, I could not find it in my heart to kill such a miserable cur, such a worm as he proved to be. Had he been a brave man I might have been different."

"Foolish youth," said Teresa, with a curling lip, "he would have killed you as he killed——"

Teresa stopped.

Her eyes flashed fire, and her colour rose.

"Killed!" said Frank, in surprise. "Who could such a craven as he kill in fair combat?"

"Not in fair combat, perhaps," said Teresa, looking straight into Frank's eyes. "Not kill any one in fair honest fight truly, but he might murder a man if he had a chance."

"Murder?"

"Yes, murder!"

"Gracious heaven! you don't mean to insinuate that the scoundrel has murdered any one?"

"Ten chances to one that he has."

"Whom?"

"Your uncle, Frank Ford."

"Impossible!"

"Nay, it is very possible; he has an immense amount of money with him in notes and gold, that I know, and has all of Basil's band in his pay."

"If the wretch has done this, and I do but prove it," gasped Frank, "oh! I will drag him limb from limb!"

"If you can."

"If I can. What mean you? Think you I dare not do it?"

"Yes; if you can only get hold of him again," the female spy answered, with a smile. "He'll take good care never to come within sword's length of you again; he has been living with Basil for several weeks off and on, but I hear that he intends to depart in a day or two for parts unknown."

"Heaven grant that he may not do so ere I cross swords with him once more," said Frank, fervently. "But how know you all this?"

"I surmise as much only; I have no positive proof 'tis true; but circumstantial evidence points directly at this wretch, and yet to save his own neck, and to place the guilt upon your shoulders, he has employed numerous secret agents to track you out, and intends to be chief witness against you himself."

"But, good, kind Teresa, you do not believe me guilty of such an atrocious crime?"

"No, Frank, I do not; you are too brave for that. One who is truly brave can never be a murderer; but he is, I see it in his eyes."

"Much of all this must have been told to you, Teresa."

"It was. I found out where your comrade's prison-place was, and visited him: yes, and at the peril of my own life. He told me all he heard, and with what I could gather from other sources, have no doubt that Joel Flint is a blood-stained murderer."

"Hugh Tracy spoke of this, you say?"

"He did."

"How came it to pass?"

"You know that Teresa, the spy, as you Garabaldians call me, can change her disguise and penetrate anywhere."

"I do! we all know it."

"I found means to get to Hugh in prison."

"Ah!"

"Yes, and had conversation with Joel Flint himself!"

"Go on, I am all attention, Teresa; but why sit so far apart? I can scarcely see your face. Your voice, also, has much changed since last I saw you."

"It has, but I prefer to sit in the deep shadow; my eye-sight is not so good as it used to be, from long night-watching. But as I was about to say, I spoke to Joel Flint, who did not know me. He, in turn, spoke to Hugh, in prison. Whatever passed between them I know not, but next day the prisoner was allowed to take exercise out on the mountain side.

"This *I* perceived, and quickly took advantage of, as you may well imagine."

"But how could this sudden change have taken place? Surely Hugh Tracy did not enter into Joel's views against me!"

"He did though."

Frank's face was suddenly flushed in anger.

He darted a fierce look at Teresa, but immediately smiled and said cooly,

"Go on, I am all attention."

"Hugh Tracy must have promised to do something for Joel, or he would never again have seen the light of day, Captain Frank. But to continue.

"I watched Hugh, and resolved that I would use my utmost power to aid his escape. I slipped a note into his hand unobserved, and told him to meet me in the small ravine at the back of Basil's cave, where the banditti are wont to gather for pleasure, and to settle their differences in case of quarrel."

"I know the place well," said Frank. "Go on, I am all attention."

"He followed my advice, and went to the spot. I endeavoured to meet him there but was prevented, for I was watched. Hugh did not return at the proper time, for he was waiting for me. Search was made everywhere for him, but nowhere could he be found. The alarm was raised. Joel accused the two guards of having neglected their prisoner to Captain Basil. The old man was furious, and sent out armed men in all directions after the fugitive.

"Hugh waited and waited for me, but I came not. When he saw the commotion on all sides, and fierce men searching the mountain side, he knew that he was the object of their industrious hunting.

"He climbed up into a tree, and there waited still longer for me.

"When about to descend, he perceived half the bandit band approaching the fatal tree.

"In their midst were two of the band handcuffed.

"Basil and Joel were present.

"It had been decided at first to hang the two faulty gaolers, but as they were each accusing the other of having been bribed or remiss in duty, Basil swore that they should decide the question by wager of battle.

"Hugh told me it was an exciting sight, and one that would almost chill the blood to witness the sanguinary battle that then ensued.

"Up in the tree Hugh saw everything that passed, and heard every word, and was not discovered, for he concealed himself well.

"Dagger in hand the two bandits approached each other cautiously, like two tigers, and with flashing eyes.

"On the left arm of each they slung their short cloaks, to catch if they could any ill-timed blow in the thick folds, while all around were gathered their companions intently watching the deadly duel.*

* See Illustration in No. 15.

# THE BOY SOLDIER; OR, GARIBALDI'S YOUNG CAPTAIN.

A STORM AT SEA

Agnese burst into tears, ad could not make reply.

Had she been keen-sighted she would have perceived that the pretended Sister beside the bed turned away, and that, with a heaving bosom, she concealed her face.

Nelly Lancaster struggled to conceal her feelings, yet, as she left the sick girl's bedside, she kissed her hand, and left the room hastily.

When she had departed Agnese was surprised to see on her pillow a purse of English sovereigns, and the hand the Sister had kissed so affectionately had been moistened with the young visitor's tears!



## CHAPTER XLIX.

### THE ATTEMPTED ASSASSINATION AT THE OPERA —THE LOVERS MEET.

GARIBALDI'S success against the Austrian detachment before Crema had so elated the gay inhabitants of that town, that, after providing for the wounded, and burying the dead with all the honours of war, the citizens gave way to spontaneous merry-making.

Rich and poor, all vied with each other in celebrating the event with all due ceremony and pomp.

The town was illuminated for several nights.

Balls and parties were going on everywhere.

Among those who gave the most splendid balls and parties was Donna Julia Guilio, the wife of an Italian nobleman of great wealth and fame.

Among others invited to a grand ball and entertainment given by her in the opera house, hired for the occasion by Donna Julia, were the two young English volunteers, Captain Ford and Major Caspar.

Both of these gallant young men at first declined to accept the invitation, but they were so pressed on all sides that at last both got leave of absence for a few days, and went into Crema.

Frank and Caspar dressed themselves as neatly as could be expected for rough, hardy young soldiers, and, directly their names and rank were announced at the door of the reception-room by loud-mouthed officials, all eyes were turned upon them.

A buzz of admiration was heard on every side as these two gallant youths entered the opera-house, and neither of them had been there long ere they found themselves conversing with much spirit to two celebrated belles of the town.

Frank and Caspar were the envy of the men, and the idols of the fair sex, on that occasion.

The soft swell of lovely music fell upon their ears, and, as the entertainment was soon over, they whirled in the fascinating mazes of the waltz with charming signoritas, and thought but little of how things went in merrie England, the land of their birth.

The dance was at its height, and every one was merry.

Frank and Caspar loitered in the lobbies, partaking of refreshments and smoking, when who should pass close by but Nelly Lancaster, leaning on her father's arm!

If a thunderbolt had fallen at Frank's feet he could not have been more surprised.

He would have spoken, and was upon the point of moving towards her, when their eyes met.

Nelly's gaze was cold, hard, and cheerless.

She swept by him like a thing of marble.

There was even a slight curl upon her rose-bud lips, but slight as it was it sent the blood back to the young soldier's heart like an icy torrent.

He left Casper's side and walked rapidly towards her; but heard her conversing with an elegantly attired young Italian officer, and narrating a story she had heard about a certain young English volunteer officer who had abducted a bandit's daughter!

These few words fell like a death-knell upon Frank's ears, and he felt desperate.

"All is lost," he thought.

If he could but have five minutes' conversation with her, all things could be explained.

But this was impossible.

She was surrounded on all sides, and Frank had not the ghost of a chance of obtaining a stolen interview.

For the rest of the evening Frank was sorrowful and dumb.

Many a fair dame conversed with him, but he had no heart for frivolity or gaiety.

How long he remained sitting lonely and thoughtful he knew not, but was suddenly aroused from his reverie by Col. Medicci, who passed by arm in arm with a female wrapped up in a hooded cloak.

A sign from the colonel brought Frank to his feet, when De Medicci said, in a soft accent,

"I know the fair signorina will excuse me, but an urgent message has just reached me from Gen. Garibaldi, to which I must instantly attend; and therefore I commit you to the care of a young officer of great merit, who will conduct you to your carriage."

Frank took the young lady's arm, and as he did so Col. Medicci said, in an under tone,

"Come to me immediately; say nothing; but there is hot work in store for us."

By this time Frank arrived at the portico of the opera-house, outside which were ranged files of carriages.

"What carriage shall I ask for?" said Frank, for the first time speaking to his fair charge, whose face he could not see.

"Sir Edward Lancaster's carriage stops the way," said a loud voice.

In a moment Nelly stepped within it, and the vehicle drove off.

Frank stood there as if in a dream.

It was Nelly he had escorted, and he knew it not!

But as the carriage drove off he heard Nelly archly say,

"Capt. Ford will find all his old love letters returned to his camp by the time he returns—farewell!"

As he stood there dumb and unable to move, Caspar hurriedly approached him, saying,

"Frank, come this way; the police fear that some of Basil's band have intruded here. In that case they mean mischief to you; come this way."

"Oh! it cannot be possible!" said Frank, moodily, "that any of Basil's infamous band could have obtained admission here; but, if so, what of that, I fear them not, d—n the black villains."

"But come this way, I tell you. You stand in danger there, for how easy would it be for any cloaked rascal to approach you and deal a deathly blow."

After much persuasion, Frank followed Caspar's advice, and re-entered the opera-house.

As should have been explained before, the whole pit had been boarded over for the dancers; but in the programme two entertainments were announced, namely, an operetta to precede, and a divertisement to serve as an interlude, to the dancing.

This divertisement was in progress at the moment when Frank and Caspar re-entered, and stood near the great doorway smoking.

To the no small surprise of both these young officers they were now joined by several of the Boy Volunteers, who had received especial invitations and leave of absence from Colonel Medicci himself.

Among whom were Hugh Tracy, Mark, Fatty, Buttons, and others who had arrived in Crema that very night by coach, especially hired for the purpose; but all under promise to return to camp again upon the next day.

Fatty and Buttons amused themselves highly with eating and drinking at Donna Julia's expense, and almost made their heads ache with incessant dancing; Master Tony especially, who wheeled about just as nimbly and gracefully as a young elephant.

Frank was surprised but pleased at De Medicci's condescension to his brave young followers, and immediately left them in their glory to wait on the colonel.

"Don't let any one find out the secret, Captain Ford," said De Medicci; but the old general has got a plan in his head to storm the Austrian fort on the high road to Trent, as you know our volunteers have been battering at it for about a week with their cannon. They have already made a breach in the walls, and Garibaldi intends to assault it to-morrow night; in fact, he left Crema about an hour ago for the fort, and I should much like you and your friend the major to join us; in fact, it is the general's orders."

"General Garibaldi's wishes are always our commands," said Frank. "I thank you for the honour conferred upon me, and will be sure to be there. It is only about twelve hours' travel, I think?"

"Not more."

"You may rely on my punctuality, colonel."

Frank again sought his young comrades, and told them the secret, at which they were overjoyed.

"We must be the first to plant our flag on the walls, lads," said Frank. "So for a few hours enjoy yourselves. We will start ere daybreak."

While they were thus speaking to each other in confidential chat, with their backs to the stage, they had not noticed what was passing behind them.

Two Italians, dressed in long black cloaks, had crept behind Frank in a slow, cat-like manner, unheard and unseen.

They hovered for a moment around the young Garibaldians, as if uncertain which of the group before them was their especial object and victim.

Suddenly, however, the tallest of the two disguised rascals pointed to Frank with his long, lean finger.

The second in an instant obeyed the sign, and advanced towards Frank with an upraised dagger.

With an oath, low and guttural, he struck the blow.

But in a second Caspar turned his head, and perceived the villain's design before the blow had been given. *

Next moment his sword flashed through the air.

The dagger slightly pierced Frank's shoulder.

But the next moment the would-be assassin lay weltering in his gore.

He was cleaved through the skull.

The second rascal dropped his cloak and hat instantly, and fled amid the crowd, and could not again be recognised.

But the scene was so sudden and so tragical in its effect that cries and shouts were now heard all over the opera-house, and a great throng gathered around the Boy Soldiers, shouting and cursing loudly against the intended assassination.

Frank was carried forth instantly, and received medical aid, for

The rascal's dagger had been *poisoned!*

---

## CHAPTER L.

FRANK FORD, MAJOR CASPAR, HUGH TRACY, AND OTHERS, HAVE STIRRING ADVENTURES, DEADLY CONFLICTS—THE FORTRESS STORMED AT MIDNIGHT—FRANK LEADS THE VAN.

It was well for Frank Ford that he was immediately conveyed away from the gay and festive scene at the opera-house, and placed under medical care after he had received the wound at the hands of the cowardly hireling of Basil's band.

Had the gallant young fellow not been taken care of on the instant, he would have surely died, for—

*The point of the dagger had been poisoned!*

The commotion that ensued among all assembled in the opera-house, when they heard of the dastardly attempt at murder, was very great.

Gentlemen swore roundly, and endeavoured to discover the dead scoundrel's accomplice, but without success.

---

See Illustration, No. 16.

The performance was stopped.

The dancing and hilarity ceased.

All were intent on hearing the cause of the sudden attempted assassination.

But all was vain inquiry.

No one could tell why nor how this cowardly trick had been played upon so bold aud gallant a youth.

Under the skilful hands of an experienced doctor, Frank's wound was immediately attended to, and he took a draught which proved a powerful antidote against the poison which had been introduced into his system by the envenomed dagger point.

Crowds assembled round the house whither he had been conveyed, to inquire how the gallant young soldier was getting on.

Ladies left their cards, though late it was, and averred that they could not retire to rest until they had learned and felt satisfied that the youth's hurt was not mortal.

A few hours of medical care brought Frank round again, and though he bled a little from his wound, no serious consequences were apprehended, for the poison had been killed by the powerful antidote.

In a short time, therefore, and sooner than the medical attendants expected, Frank opened his eyes and began to commune freely and good-humouredly.

"So the poison is harmless, you say, doctor?" Frank asked, with a smile.

"It is, captain; and, thanks to your strong and healthy constitution, there is no danger. You have bled a little, but that is all the harm that has happened. You must remain quiet for a day or two, and all will turn out for the best."

"How long will it be then, doctor, before I am ready for active service?" Frank asked, fretfully. "If my wound's not dangerous, as you say, the sooner I am up and doing the better, for I hate to lie idle on a sick bed."

"Don't talk of active service," the doctor replied, with a smile. "You have seen as much of that as any one in the whole Volunteer army. But if you ask *my* opinion, I should say that you ought not to venture out under three or four days at least."

"And my companions?" said Frank, peevishly.

"Your comrades have started on the Tyrol road an hour ago."

"Gone!"

"Yes; surely you would not think of stirring out with such a wound as you now have in the left shoulder? It would be folly!"

"Have all of them gone?"

"No, I believe that one remains behind."

"One, eh! and do you know his name?"

"No. I saw him running hither and thither about the opera-house, in search of the second of the two rascals who set upon you, and threatened all manner of things to everybody because you were hurt."

"What kind of person was he?"

"A large, round face, fat-looking youth."

"Tony Waddleduck, for a hundred pounds."

"Now I come to think of it, his name is Tony. I heard your companions ask him if he was not going off in the coach with them, but he refused, and stood blubbering like a goose at the house-door, and swore he would not stir an inch until he felt satisfied that you were safe and out of all danger."

Frank smiled, and shortly after was left alone, the servants being told that he must not be disturbed, but remain quiet for several days.

Directly the doctor had gone, however, Frank,

who had pretended to be asleep, opened his eyes, and was surprised to find Fatty setting by his bedside.

"That you, Tony?"

"Yes, Frank, that's me, what's left of me, for I felt so knocked up when you were hurt, I thought I should have died. All I wanted was to find out that other chap as had a hand in this cowardly affair, but could not. If I had thought," said Fatty, with an oath, "I'd a' smashed him, and no mistake."

"And how did you manage to get into my room? Don't you know I'm not supposed to allow any one in to see me?"

"Yes, Captain Frank, I know all about it; but I wasn't going to let them Italian fellows wait on you while I was near."

"And Mark, Mr. Caspar, Hugh, Buttons, and the rest, what has become of them?"

"They have started off to assist in capturing the Austrian fort which stops the way of the Volunteers on their road into the Tyrol. They said, as you had promised your word to go, they felt in duty bound to be present."

"They were quite right," said Frank, "Colonel de Medicci expects them and me also."

"But, of course, you can't go?"

"But I *can* though," said Frank,

"You?"

"Yes, and you, too."

"I don't understand."

"It's very easily comprehended. Listen!—the doctors have extracted all the poison from my wound, and say that there is not any danger from that cause now, except a little loss of blood. I feel as strong and active as ever, and as I have the use of my right arm, I intend to go also."

"No, no, no, Captain Frank," said Fatty, "you must not go."

"But I tell you I *will*," said Frank. "I'm not going to lay here idle and do nothing, while the other lads are exposing their lives. I'm not one of that sort."

Fatty smiled, but said,

"If you go, I will also, Captain Frank. You ain't agoing to leave me behind."

"Well, then, get me a carriage and four horses immediately," said Frank. "You and I will start after Caspar and the rest immediately. We shall get there all in good time—the storming doesn't come off until to-morrow night."

Although he did not much relish the idea of his captain escaping from his sick-room with his wounded arm, there was nothing else for it but to order the carriage and four.

The vehicle was soon hired, and stood ready in the shadow of a by-street.

In less than an hour Frank escaped from his sick chamber, unperceived by any one in the house, and joined Fatty.

He flung himself into the carriage.

Fatty perched himself on the box seat.

The two postillions cracked their whips, and in less time than it takes to tell it, both were on the high road to Trent at a clipping rate.

* * * * *

It was in the afternoon of the following day that Frank and Fatty arrived in the plain that in part surrounded the Austrian fort, before which were gathered some five or six thousand gallant Italian volunteers.

Frank had heard the loud booming of artillery for several hours ere he reached the scene of action.

But the sight that he saw in the valley in front of the fort was something more than he ever expected to see. The air was calm and still.

A clear sky was overhead; but through the green valley volumes of sulphury smoke lazily rolled away from the brazen mouths of thundering artillery, and entirely concealed the lower part of the fortress, in the walls of which were visible three large rents.

A bright flash of flame would now and then burst from the walls; but the unceasing roar of the Italian volunteer artillery drowned all the other sounds, save when a loud ringing cheer would burst from the brave volunteers in the trenches, as now and then a well-directed shot brought some part of the heavy masonry of the fortress rattling down.

The utmost activity was visible on all sides.

Troops pressed forward here and there to the relief of their tired and powder-blackened comrades in the trenches.

Officers rode madly hither and thither, giving orders, and all betokened that the long-expected assault upon the grim fortress would soon take place.

While every volunteer in the army was anxiously expecting the final dicision of General Garibaldi, a general order was made known from head-quarters, in which, after briefly detailing the plan of assault, ended with these words:—

"The fortress must be carried by assault to-night, by orders of GENERAL GARIBALDI."

When the order was privately circulated among the principal officers, the activity on all sides seemed to increase ten-fold.

As the day drew to a close, the cannonade on either side was slackened.

A solitary gun would be heard at intervals, and its echoes would thunder through the valleys and the mountain gorges of the Tyrol.

But when night set in, even these sounds were not heard, and a death-like silence reigned on all sides.

In the trenches, which were crowded with anxious and well-armed soldiers, not a sound was audible, and even among that silent host the challenge of a solitary sentry could be distinctly heard.

The marine fortress loomed larger, as its dark shadow stood out in bold relief from the light blue sky, and was as silent as the grave, while now and then could be detected in the several trenches the sudden passing twinkling of a lamp, as the Austrian guards walked their rounds upon the lofty walls, and then suddenly disappear again, leaving all dark and gloomy as before.

Frank had not been long among the Italian officers when he learned that General Garibaldi had so much admired the bravery of Mr. Caspar, Hugh Tracy and Mark, that he had given to each of them the command of a storming party.

Garibaldi had heard of Frank's accident at the opera-house, and was much incensed with the cowardly trick played upon him.

He had given strict orders, moreover, that Captain Ford should refrain from further duty until his recovery was placed beyond all doubt; and Colonel de Medicci had even been heard to say that Frank had already rejoined his company of boy soldiers, and was then strictly under the doctor's hands, and would be unable to report for active duty for at least a month to come.

"This is fine news," thought Frank, laughing, "General Garibaldi fancies I'm in bed among my own lads, and here I am dying to have something to do, and take part in the grand assault to-night. And I dare not show myself to the old general either, or he will reprimand me, and have me under arrest. I am in a regular fix. But I wonder where Caspar,

Mark, Hugh, and the others are," he said, as he walked through the various camps, knowing not whither to direct his steps, and feeling like a fish out of water.

"How aggravating it is, each of them have been entrusted with the command of a storming party, and here am I walking about uselessly, and afraid to report myself at head quarters."

While thus he mused, he accidently met Major Caspar.

He sprang towards Frank, and grasping his hand said, hurriedly. "Glad to see you, Frank; but I heard the general say you were confined to your room."

"I might have been so," was the laughing reply, "but whether I offend or please the old general, I'm not going to be put on the sick list at such a time as this, at least while I've got a peg to stand on. What had I better do?"

"Why, retire to the rear, Frank, you are weakened too much with your two recent wounds to stand any further excitement and exertion."

"To the rear!" said Frank, "you would not insult me."

"Insult you, my lad, far from it," said Caspar, "I did not mean that; and, to prove how much I respect your valor, I want to beg a favour of you."

"What is it?"

"Why one of the young officers in the party I have to lead to the assault has just been wounded, and we want some one to lead his men. It is the young Count Volto, and although he is unconscious he still raves and insists upon leading his men."

"I'm your man," said Frank, laughing, "if I cannot lead on this occasion, why, then, I'll follow. Trust me, I shan't be far behind the foremost man who mounts that deadly breach to-night."

While he spoke, some one called out —

"Major Caspar, you are wanted this way."

"Follow me, Frank," said Caspar, as he dived down towards the trenches.

By the light of a lantern, two officers could be seen kneeling upon the ground.

Between them, on the grass, lay a third, upon whose features, as the pale light fell, the hand of death seemed rapidly stealing.

A slight froth, tinged with blood, rested on his lips, and the florid gore which stained his uniform, showed that his wound was through the lungs.

"He has fainted," said one of the officers, in a low tone.

"Are you certain it is fainting?" the other replied.

"You see how it is with the poor youth," Caspar whispered, "it is all up with him."

While he thus spoke, four soldiers of his regiment placed the wounded young officer in a blanket, and carried him out of the trenches.

A long sigh escaped him, and he muttered a few broken words.

"Poor fellow! it's his mother he is murmuring of," said Caspar, with a sigh. "I hear he only joined his regiment a month since, and is, as you are, a mere boy. But come, Frank, we must lose no time. By Jove, that's just what I expected! Did you see that rocket?"

"Yes."

"That's the signal for our assaulting column to form. In ten minutes more the stormers must fall in. What's the matter, there?" he asked of an officer, who had stopped the four soldiers with the wounded youth.

"I have been cutting the white band off his left arm, Major Caspar; for if poor Volto perceived it when he awoke to consciousness again, he would go mad to think he had not been one of the stormers; for the white band on the left arm is the sign by which the assaulters are to know each other.

"Just so—quite right—thoughtfully done," said Caspar, who was now every inch a soldier, and seemed to revel in that wild and daring life. "He was in the forlorn hope, Frank, as I said—"

"But you won't refuse me to take command of his men?"

"Refuse *you*, Frank!" said Caspar, grasping Frank's hand with both his own, "never, my lad; there's not another in the army I respect more than I do you; and if Garibaldi wasn't under the idea that you were confined to bed, and far away from here, I'd give up my command and follow you myself; but you must change your dress, Frank—that red shirt is too much of a mark for the Austrians, you would be shot down in a minute. You see, all of us here, in the 1st Regiment of Volunteers, wear blue—so must you.

"I can give your friend a cap, major.

"Here is a spare jacket for him," said another.

"And I," said a third, will give him a well-filled brandy-flask, which is by no means a thing to be despised when bound on such an errand as thie present one."

While Frank was making these necessary changes in his attire, so as not to prove too conspicuous an object to the Austrians, Caspar whispered to him,—

"I hope your sword and revolvers are in good order, for we shall have to fight like devils to-night. The town which this gloomy fortress defends have proved no friends to the cause of Italian independence; and I fear, that once our men get into it, there will be no stopping them: they will burn the place and pillage on every hand. But no matter; it is all death or glory with us."

While they thus spoke, Frank gave the care of his horse to Fatty, who wasn't positively aware what was about to take place, and Mr. Tony went to the rear grumbling very much; but swore he'd have a hand in the fight, cost what it might.

"This way, Frank!—this way, my boy; they are telling off the stormers of my party—quick!" said Caspar.

"Who commands the storming-party?" asked a rough voice, near by.

"I do," said Caspar.

"And who is second in charge?"

"Captain Count Volto," said Caspar, shoving Frank forward into his place.

"Very well, sir; keep your men together; be sparing of powder, and give the enemy plenty of cold steel."

So speaking, he shook Frank by the hand in the darkness, and moved away.

"Who was that, major?" Frank asked.

"Garibaldi's son; a brave officer, as you will soon find out."

* * * * *

Everything was now prepared for the assault.

The stillness of death reigned on all sides.

A deep-toned bell from the village, behind the fortress, tolled out the hour of midnight

Its echoes had not died away when through the darkness crept thousands of men towards the fortress, and advanced like shadows to the foot of the breach.

"Quietly, men; quietly," said Frank. "Don't crush—let not a word be spoken!"

He had scarcely uttered the words when a musket, belonging to one of the volunteers, went off accidentally.

The whizzing bullet could not have struck the walls of the fortress, when suddenly a bright flame burst from the ramparts, and shot upwards towards the sky!

For an instant the whole scene was as bright as noon-day.

Before them, on the fortress walls, and in every imaginable place, stood solid bodies of the Austrians.

Around the base of that towering pile were creeping the Italian volunteers with glistening bayonets!

A crashing discharge of musketry from Frank's party was the signal for the action to commence, while, with a loud shout of defiance, Frank and Caspar leaped into the deep ditch, sword in hand, followed by their men!

Suddenly a loud rumbling thunder crept along the earth!

A hissing, crackling noise followed, and from the dark ditch a forked, and livid lightning burst like the flame from a volcano!

A mine had exploded!

While this dreadful scene was going on on one side, Hugh Tracy's voice on the one hand, and Mark's on the other, could be heard cheering on their several detachments, and were foremost in the fight.

Frank knew their voices, and his heart leaped with joy as in the distance he perceived his two comrades, flag in hand, leading on the Volunteers.

The old fortress seemed girt about with fire.

From every part arose the shouts and yells of Italians and Austrians.

The rush on all sides was tremendous and awful.

For scarcely had Frank, at the larger breach, led on his men to the crumbling rampart, fighting and climbing up as best he could, when a large force, under Caspar, came after them, forcing the first ones right into the jaws of the enemy.

Then commenced a scene which it is almost impossible to describe.

The whole ground, covered as it was with combustibles of every deadly nature, was rent open with a crash.

Huge fragments of masonry flew into the air like feathers.

The deafening roar of cannon from the fortress—the shouts, yells, screams, and groans on every side—the bursting of powder magazines, the serpent-like hissing of shells—all was horrifying and hellish-like uproar.

Yet onward the gallant Frank, Hugh Tracy, and Mark, led their thinning ranks, at different points, and foremost in the deadly strife were they.

Each moment some well-known leader among the Italian Volunteers fell dead or mortally wounded; and his place was supplied by some brave officer, who, springing to the front, had scarcely shouted out words of encouragement to his men ere he also fell dead upon the spot.

For more than an hour the frightful carnage continued, and still but little was accomplished.

Frank, and a small party of brave fellows, clambered up the ramparts, and defended themselves there bravely, while fresh troops continually poured through the breach upon the Austrians, firing and bayoneting on every side.

The slaughter was most awful.

But above the dim, and while Frank and his brave fellows were battling against fearful odds on the ramparts, could be heard Caspar's voice as he rushed to Frank's assistance with a chosen body of desperate men.

"Officers to the front!" he shouted, as he leaped into the deep ditch and began to clamber up the broken masonry of the walls.

His men bravely followed him.

"See there, lads, see there!" said Caspar, shouting in triumph, as he pointed to Frank Ford, who, with the Italian colors in one hand, and his sword in the other, stood upon the highest part of the granite rampart. "See there, lads, see there!" said he again, waving his cap in triumph.

A loud shout answered Caspar, and they fought their way up the breach with the impetuosity of bloodhounds.

The Austrian garrison, however, fought like heroes.

Man to man was now the combat.

No cry for quarter was heard.

No supplicating look for mercy.

It was the death-struggle for vengeance and despair.

At this instant an explosion, louder than the loudest thunder, shook the air.

Italians and Austrians were alike the victims.

The great magazine of the fortress had been ignited by a scoundrel in bandit uniform, whom Frank recognised as one of Basil's band.

The walls and forts tottered and fell.

Black smoke, with a lurid flame, hung above the dead and dying.

The artillery and murderous musketry were for a moment stilled, as if paralyzed by the ruin and devastation all around.

Both friend and foe for a moment paused in the dreadful work of slaughter.

But the pause was for a moment only.

Loud shouts from Frank, Caspar, Hugh and Mark were heard cheering on their men, and the cries of the dying steeled every Italian's heart.

A fierce burst of vengeance rent the air.

The fiery volunteers closed on the Austrian ranks.

For an instant the shock was dreadful.

The next moment a host of Italian bayonets gleamed on the walls and ramparts.

Their colours, in Frank Ford's hand, were thrown out to the night breeze in triumph.

The battle was over—the fort was captured!

## CHAPTER LI.

### THE DESPERATE PERIL OF FRANK—THE TRAITOR'S DOOM—REPRIMANDS AND PRAISE.

When the long, loud shouts of victory reached his ears, Frank suddenly felt like one in a trance.

He leaned against an angle of the parapet, overpowered and exhausted.

His old wounds pained him much.

His uniform was torn into shreds.

His head was bare, and of his sword blade there remained but four inches to the hilt, while in his left hand he firmly grasped an Austrian's flag-staff he had captured on the ramparts, but with only a few yards of tattered silk attached to it.

As thus he stood, fresh troops came pouring through the trenches into the fortress and town, trampling alike on the dead and wounded in their path.

Weak, exhausted, and overcome, he sank among the crumbling ruin.

Loud shouts and screams from the fortress and town told that the work of slaughter and robbery was going on, and still, in the far distance could be heard the pattering of musketry, as the Austrians were still fighting hard to protect their retreat.

Thus passed the long night, more terrible from horrors of lying among the dead and wounded than all the dangers and hellish excitement of the assault.

While thus Frank lay in the ruins of the breach, among the ghastly bodies of the slain, he was aroused by the distant sound of several English voices, the chief of whom said,

"Bring him this way, lads! Over the breach with the rascal into the fosse!"

"He shall die no soldier's death, by Heaven!" said one.

"Oh, mercy, as you hope for mercy!"

"Traitor! scoundrel! don't dare to mutter to us of mercy."

As the last words were spoken, Frank, in some degree, recovered consciousness, and turned to look whence the sounds proceeded.

He saw, not far from him, four of his own band —Fatty, Buttons, Mark and Hugh Tracy—dragging forward a pale and haggard wretch, whose limbs trailed behind him like as if he had the palsy.

His uniform was that of some Austrian regiment, but his voice was English.

"Kneel down there, and die like a man, Moss," said Hugh, with a lip trembling in rage.

"No, no! have mercy. Pardon me," said the voice, whiningly.

"There is no pardon for such scoundrels as you," said Mark.

"Didn't you try all sorts of plans to get Captain Frank into Joel Flint's clutches?" said Fatty, with an oath.

"Wasn't he in league with Basil's men?" said Buttons.

"Didn't you desert from our camps, you and your pal, and go over to the Austrians like a traitor?" said Hugh.

"I saw him firing at us for fully an hour," said Mark; "and, I verily believe, the villain has shot Captain Frank, for we can find him nowhere, high nor low."

"Have mercy!" said Moss, imploringly. "Have pity on me!"

"Fix bayonets, lads," said Hugh. "There is no possible doubt of his knavery, for we discovered him concealed behind a broken embrasure, and caught him with his Austrian uniform on."

"Forgive me! for the love of heaven, forgive me!" screamed the voice of the victim, Moss, the one who, as we have seen in previous chapters, had deserted.

But his last accents ended in a death-cry.

For as he spoke the bayonets flashed for an instant in the air, and the next were plunged through his body!

Frank saw all this take place, but was unable to speak.

Nor did his companions perceive him, as, dusty, powder-blackened, and exhausted, he lay hidden among the rubbish and ruins of the rampart.

What was worse, Hugh Tracy and the others left the spot, and did not for a moment dream that their young captain, for whom they were searching, was at that instant within twenty yards of them, and had seen all that took place.

He lay there helpless for more than an hour, when a party of the 1st Volunteers, four in number, commenced to search among the ruins near by, but did not perceive him.

"Was he killed, think you?" said one.

"There cannot be a doubt about it," another replied. "Did you see him fighting for the Austrian flag upon the wall, single handed?"

"Yes; and a right good rousing cheer we gave him for his valor. These English are very brave and no mistake."

"Captain Ford's conduct, and that of his young companions, is the talk of the whole army."

"When did you see the young captain last alive?"

"At the top of this breach."

"Then if he fell we must surely find him somewhere hereabouts."

While they spoke thus, and searched for the body of the brave youth who had led them, one of the party caught sight of a fragment of the Austrian banner which Frank held in his hand.

"Curses on him," said he; "why here is an Austrian ensign still alive, and with the colours in his hand."

A short and fervent prayer burst from Frank's lips as he thought,

"They mistake me for an enemy, and are about to shoot!"

The leader of the party called out, "Make ready! aim! one! two!"

"Ground arms! ground arms!" the leader suddenly roared out, "don't fire! ground arms!—'tis the young English Captain himself!"

Down went the muskets with a crash.

Springing towards Frank, the sunburnt Italians changed their scowling revengeful looks for smiles, caught the brave lad in their arms, and with a jerk mounted him on their shoulders.

The shout they gave when this was done sounded like the wild yell of maniacs.

"Ha, ha, ha! we have him now," sang their wild voices, as with blood-stained hands, and powder-blackened features, they bore him down the rampart towards the town.

In this manner, on the shoulders of four volunteers, Frank was borne towards the market-place, where several hundred men of different regiments were bivouacked.

A shout of recognition welcomed their arrival, when suddenly three or four youths springing from the ground rushed forward with drawn bayonets, calling out in angry tones,—

"Give him up!—give him up to us this minute! or, by heavens, we'll make short work of you!"

The order was made by youths who seemed well destined to execute it, and accordingly Captain Frank was grounded with a sudden shock, that thoroughly aroused him to consciousness.

As he sat passively on the ground, looking wildly about, he perceived that Fatty, Buttons, and Mark were beside him.

About him also were encircled scores of volunteers, who gazed upon the pallid youth with looks of admiration as they whispered to each other the many deeds of daring done by him during the assault.

"Where is Major Caspar?" Frank faintly asked.

"In the church, captain," many answered.

"But why there?"

"There's one of your generals badly wounded."

"Did you hear his name?"

"No, sir; all I know is, that he was one of the storming party."

"Where is the church then?" asked Frank faintly, and for the first time trying to walk.

"I'll show you," said Hugh.

Leaning on Hugh's and Mark's arm, Frank slowly moved towards the church, and as he did so, all the straggling soldiers rose to their feet, and gave him the salute.

After they had turned down a small narrow street, they came very near the private door of the church, before which a sentry paced up and down.

Hugh and Mark, by his own desire, now left

Frank alone, and returned to the market-place, while he walked slowly towards the church entrance.

"Halt there! and give the countersign," said the sentry, in a gruff voice, at the same time levelling his musket at him.

"I am an officer," said Frank, endeavouring to pass in.

"Stand back! stand back!" said the sentry, more gruffly than before.

"Is Major Caspar in the church?"

"I don't know."

"Who is the officer so badly wounded?"

"I don't know," he answered, while with an oath he muttered, "Stand back, I tell you, sir; don't you see the general and his staff approaching?"

Frank turned round hastily, and at the same instant several officers, who had dismounted at the edge of the street, were seen approaching.

They came hurriedly forward, but without speaking.

He who was in advance of the party wore a red shirt, and carried a heavy sabre only.

The rest were in full regimentals.

Frank, dusty, dirty, pale, and in ragged uniform, had scarcely time to get out of the way, when Garibaldi stepped and said, in a stern voice,—

"Who are you, sir?"

Frank startled for a moment at the harsh sound, but at last said feebly,—

"Captain Ford, of the English Boy Volunteers."

"What brings you here, sir? Your company is far beyond Crema; and, besides, you have been reported unfit for duty a week ago."

"True, general; but I did not wish to remain idle while so much was doing."

"It matters not, sir, you should obey orders. You have done wrong. You have been wounded at Crema, and at the opera-house the other night; you should have remained in your quarters until further orders."

"Dam'me, now I come to look at him, that's the young Englishman who led the storming party of the 1st Volunteers. Yes, that's him, general, the person I spoke to you about. Is it not so, Captain Ford?"

"Yes, sir, I led a party of the 1st Volunteers."

"And right gallantly you did it. Why, general, I saw him spring on to a rock and attack some powerful brigand who was picking off all our officers. The leap was a desperate one, for it was just at the edge of the fortifications, and a deep precipice was yawning beneath them both. It was truly a death struggle. But after a fierce encounter the young captain here, with one blow cleaved the scoundrel's skull, which broke the captain's sword blade off to the hilt, but the next moment the villanous brigand was hurled down the precipice (see illustration in No. 17). When this was done, and that dangerous sharp-shooter had been disposed of, the young captain leaped back again right amidst the Austrian ranks, and seized one of their standards. He snatched a sword from an enemy, and fought for the flag like a hero! By Jove!" said the speaker, with a laugh, "why, that's the remnant of the flag he has now—there's the flag-staff still tightly clutched in his left hand!"

While Colonel de Medicci—for such was the speaker's name—went on narrating all he had heard or seen of the young captain, those around looked upon Frank with eyes of admiration.

Not so General Garibaldi, who smiled calmly, and said,

"Orders must be obeyed, young sir. Did you obtain the doctor's leave to quit your apartment?"

"No, general."

"Then report yourself at your own quarters under arrest for disobeying orders."

"But, general," Colonel de Medicci began.

Garibaldi did not stop to listen; but entered the church, and the others followed him.

"Confound the luck!" thought Frank. "I'm always getting into scrapes of same kind; instead of having praise for what I've done I only receive blame and a sharp reprimand besides. Hang the fortune!"

As thus he thought, he heard the sharp click of the sentry's musket again, and Colonel de Medicci came forth from the church.

"Ha! Captain Ford, still here, I see. I didn't expect to hear of you taking any part in this storming after your accident at the opera-house; but you love the smell of gunpowder, I see."

"Yes, colonel; but who is wounded in the church?"

"A general, and your friend Caspar, very severely through the arm, and, I fear, the lung also. He has spoken to all of us about you, and your gallant conduct deserves all praise. The major takes all the blame for allowing you to command Count Volto's men; in fact, if you are able, you are to have the distinguished honour of carrying General Garibaldi's despatches about this affair to King Victor Emmanuel".

"Could I not see my friend Caspar before I go?"

"No; General Garibaldi supposes you are on the way to your own company half an hour ago."

Not knowing the fate of poor Caspar, Frank returned to the market-place, and there found his four young companions, who were waiting for him, mounted, and ready to start for his own camps again beyond the town of Crema.

# THE BOY SOLDIER; OR, GARIBALDI'S YOUNG CAPTAIN.

THE BOY SOLDIER'S REVENGE—*See* No. 20.

## CHAPTER LII.

### FRANK ENTRUSTEL WITH DESPATCHES TO VICTOR EMMANUEL—BUTTONS AND THE REPORTER.

THE next morning, after Frank had reached his Boy Soldiers again, he sat in the upper room of an old farm-house, round which the company were camped, and was buried in deep thought about the news he had heard about affairs in England from Caspar, respecting his uncle's death, the sudden disappearance of Jonathan from Bromley Hall, Caspar's apprehension and acquittal, and old Flint's mysterious flight.

"I should dearly like to return to England



for a few weeks," Frank thought, "if only to investigate the foul charges which have been made against me; but I fear I would not get leave at such a time as this; besides, these Italian fellows might think I wanted to shirk duty, and get out of danger. No; that will never do; nevertheless, if I *could* get leave for a few weeks, it would greatly relieve my mind, for there cannot be a doubt but that I am surrounded by enemies who will not be over nice in anything they attempt against me."

These were Frank's thoughts, when his attention was withdrawn to a conversation going on beneath his window between young Buttons and an Italian lancer.

"I say, my lad, are you Captain Ford's servant?" said the lancer to Buttons.

"Well, suppose I am?" said Buttons, going on with the brushing of Frank's boots.

"Because, if you are, take these letters to your master; there are important despatches among them. Be alive. I will wait for a written receipt. Come, be quick, I'm in haste."

"Oh! don't be in such a hurry, life is short," said Buttons, looking at the letters very leisurely. "Oh! there's nothing but invitations to dinner, or something of that sort. Our captain is bothered with them every day in his life; but tell me, my friend, didn't any of the generals send *me* an invitation, or a letter? I don't see my name among them."

"Come, come," said the lancer. "No joking, my time is short."

"Then all I can say is, your nose isn't," Buttons replied, as he ran up stairs, and delivered the letters.

In a moment Frank wrote an acknowledgment of the letters, and so much pleased was he that he handed it to the lancer, and therewith a sovereign for his pains.

"In less than an hour, Buttons," said he, "we must start for Florence to deliver those despatches to the king."

Buttons was overjoyed at the prospect of the journey, and, according to Frank's orders, he put on his old livery as a page—the hat and all—so as to make out his young captain—in the eyes of the world—a greater and a richer man than he really was; and also to show the Italians that he really could afford servants in his own country, however much he might do without them in time of war.

He left Hugh Tracy in command of the company, and, with Buttons as servant, he started off within two hours for Florence.

Even in these days, Italy is not furnished with too many railways, and in consequence Frank and Buttons were obliged to make most of their way by means of a coach and four, as best they could. Wherever they went, however, by some strange circumstance which Captain Frank could not understand, the people turned out to welcome him; and when they stopped to change horses at a village, all the inhabitants shouted and cheered like madmen.

This cordial reception on the route astonished Frank very much, for he could not conceive how any one had found out the object of his journey.

Master Buttons, however, might have been able to inform him, for, perched on the roof of the coach, he amused himself with dancing, and singing, and playing wild, discordant solos on a brass trumpet he had captured from some stray Austrian during the assault.

All Frank's attempts to keep Buttons quiet on the road were useless.

He had pledged Frank's health so often during the day—had drunk so many toasts to the Boy Soldiers—so many to Garibaldi, and so many to himself on the route, that when, in the evening, the coach rolled into Modena and stopped at the principal hotel, Master Buttons was obliged to be put to bed.

It was then, to his great surprise, that Captain Frank found out the cause of so much rejoicing on the road, for Master Buttons had placed at the back of the coach a large placard, which, in immense letters, caught the eye of the astonished Italians,—

"Terrific and Bloody News!<br>Capture of an Austrian Fortress!<br>5,000 Prisoners!<br>100 Cannon captured!"

When Frank had somewhat refreshed himself, he took a walk through some of the principal streets; and on returning to his hotel was astonished to see hung up in the reading room an immense poster, round which a large number of persons were gathered reading.

Frank walked up to it, and almost laughed right out as he read,—

"The Battle of Crema!<br>Bloody Details!<br>Capture of an Austrian Fortress!<br>Great deeds of Valor! Hundreds of Prisoners!<br>and<br>Scores of cannon captured!<br>With a full account, and all particulars.<br>By Captain Buttons,<br>of the English Boy Volunteers."

Leaving those around to puzzle themselves as much as they liked, as to who Captain Buttons might be, Frank took a waiter on one side, and asked,

"What is the meaning of that placard over the fire-place? where did it come from?"

"Most important news, sir, to appear exclusively in the 'Modena Post', to-morrow morning; the young captain has just arrived."

"Who, pray? What gentleman?"

"Captain Buttons, sir; large bed-room, blue damask, supper for two, six dozen oysters, champagne, and so forth, sir."

Frank laughed right out as he said,

"I am an Englishman also, and a volunteer, I should much like to make the acquaintance of this Captain Buttons; show me to his room."

The waiter bowed.

"Follow me, sir, if you please; this way. What name shall I say, sir?"

"You need not announce me. I am a fellow countryman of his. Show me his room."

"I beg pardon, sir," said the waiter, "the reporter of the 'Modena Post' is deeply engaged with him, and the captain has given positive orders not to be disturbed by any one."

Frank smiled.

"Leave the matter to me," he said, at the same time placing a gold coin in the servant's hand.

Frank opened the door.

His entrance was unseen, on account of a large screen which stood before the door.

Seated in a large arm-chair, with his heels cocked on the table, was Master Buttons, dressed in new regimentals Frank had bought on the road, in order to present a favourable appearance before the king.

Buttons had a cigar in his mouth; lots of oyster shells were scattered up and down the room.

Champagne bottles had been broken off at the neck; and, with Frank's sword by his side, Master Buttons looked a strange compound of fun and sleepiness.

Opposite to him, sat a round-bellied, pock-marked old gentleman, pen in hand, who seemed very much vexed that the "captain" would not go on with his interesting narration instead of drinking and smoking.

"You must remember, captain, time is pressing, the placards are out, and it's now nearly twelve o'clock; unless we make haste, we shall not be able to have the account in the morning edition, so let us proceed once more. You were at the great ditch, I think, before the fortress."

"Hang me, if I know, or care, where I was," said Buttons, hiccupping. "Just ring that bell; them oysters were beautiful; just order in five dozen more, and plenty of wine and cigars."

"But, captain, pray proceed; you sent for me, and according to your desire, I came, and have paid you well beforehand for the information you promised."

"Just so; but don't hurry yourself. See how I'll knock that bust off the mantel-piece with this shell."

So saying, Master Buttons commenced throwing the shells about the room, and making a "cock-shy" of everything.

He next commenced performing on his trumpet until the reporter almost became deaf.

Signor Dando tried to smile at the capers Buttons was making.

But he saw there was no prospect of getting any information, so was about to depart.

But this Buttons would not allow, so compelled the poor unlucky Dando to take off his coat, and dance a hornpipe to the abominable music of the brass trumpet.

In truth, old Dando was compelled to jump about like a performing bear for the amusement of Buttons; and as often as he left off, the captain gave him gentle taps over the shins with a walking-stick.

In truth, Master Buttons was very nearly intoxicated, and so was old Dando.

But this did not end the performance by any means.

Buttons commenced to play all kinds of tricks with the unfortunate man.

He made him stand on his head.

Next, with Frank's sword drawn, he threatened to cut off Dando's head, unless he stood on one leg and held the other one up with his right hand for five minutes.

Next he got some soot, and painted whiskers and moustachois on his visitor's face, to show him how much he resembled Colonel de Medicci.

All these tricks and antics lasted for more than an hour, but still the incorrigible Buttons would not let the man go until he had tried him with the boxing gloves, a set of which were in Frank's trunks.

"I'll give you a lesson or two," said the captain, capering round his victim; "it's excellent sport."

But poor Dando didn't think so.

"You are no hand at the 'mittens,'" said Buttons, laughing.

And at it they went tooth and nail.

Dando was dying to get away, but could not; and, although Buttons laughed whenever he gave his antagonist a good punch in the ribs, Dando was getting savage in the extreme.

At last he waited for a good opportunity, and gave Buttons such a tremendous thwack on the jaw, as laid the captain sprawling on the floor.

Next moment Dando, puffing and blowing, flew down stairs, much like a man who has suddenly escaped from Bedlam.

## CHAPTER LIII.

### THE PUG TURNS INFORMER.

THE mishap which befel the Pug in falling on the sharp spikes of the garden wall at Bromley Hall, and his subsequent apprehension by Gale, the detective, did not by any means improve his temper or his language.

He cursed and swore like a true blackguard; but that only he was able to do, for he was strictly guarded by the domestics of Bromley Hall, who, with thick clubs in their hands, stood over him, ready to administer a sound thrashing to him should he at all prove refractory or troublesome.

Meanwhile, Gale and the old gardener, Giles, went in search of Warner.

They searched high and low for him, but nowhere could he be fouud.

Intending to renew their search at some other time, Gale returned to the Pug, and conveyed him to the railway station.

The Pug was very low spirited, and did not appear to be at all inclined to open his mouth.

Gale, however, laughed and joked in such a merry style, and he was all at once so very polite and kind in giving his prisoner a pipe of tobacco, and a good stiff glass of brandy, that the Pug began to think that "'the slop' wasn't sich a bad sort o' chap arter all."

They had a separate compartment in the railway carriage to themselves, and, on the way up to London, Gale became very chatty.

"Bad job for you, Puggy," Gale began.

"Yes, it were a nasty fall on to them ere spikes, and I feel werry sore about the thighs."

"I dare say you do. But what took you to Bromley Hall at all, Puggy?"

"Nothing."

"Of course not. A man of your professional abilities don't travel from London for nothing. Ha, ha! you don't gammon *me* in that way, Puggy," said the detective, with a broad grin. "What brought you in the first floor, then?"

"I were only curious to see how the place was built, that's all."

"And curious to see what you could lay your hands on also, I suppose?"

"Me? Lor' bless yer, I hadn't the slightest notion of nicking anything."

"You hadn't time, that's all; but I can tell you one thing, it is a very bad job for you."

"What, being caught in the house?"

"No, not that."

"What then?" said Puggy, opening his eyes very widely at the detective's solemn manner.

"Oh, you know; it's no use of you looking so innocent; you know all about it."

"Know all about what?" persisted Puggy, with well-feigned innocence.

"About that affair of old Ford, the miser."

"Me? Upon my soul I'm as innocent as a kid."

"I dare say. I never knew a thief or a rogue as wasn't, at least in his own mind. If you go to Newgate, and ask every one of the prisoners there, they'll all tell you they're innocent, but that won't do for me. I have 'wanted' you for this job some time, Puggy."

"Who told you as how I were in it?" asked Puggy; at the same time thinking of, and mentally cursing the cabman.

"It doesn't matter who told me, Puggy; but I know all about it," said Gale, with the air of a man who is cognizant of everything in life.

But the truth was he did not know all about it.

He was "pumping" and "bouncing" Puggy, who, Gale knew, was an arrant coward in his heart.

"Look here, Puggy," said Gale, breaking silence; "you have got into a very nasty mess, and it is your own fault if you don't get out of it."

"I'm as innocent as a kid o' that ere job," Puggy persisted.

"Innocent or not, it matters little, but you wouldn't like to have a 'lifer' or 'fourteen-penn'orth across the herring-pond' for it, would you?"

"No, not me."

"Well, then, you had better make a clean breast of it."

"Yes, you. I watched him like a cat would a mouse."

"Oh, Heaven? I cannot believe it."

"But *I* can. Come, come this way; pull off your boots and follow *me.*"

"I *will* not."

"But you *must;* we are linked in life or death, Flint."

As he said this there was a terrible meaning in his words, and a fierce fire in his eye, which the old lawyer knew meant mischief.

With their shoes off, Jonathan and Flint left the parlour, first having blown out the light.

Jonathan next bolted the street-door, and double locked it.

All this was done noiselessly and quietly, so much so that no one in the house could possibly hear him.

"Follow me," said he to the old lawyer.

Quickly he mounted the silent staircase, followed by the panting lawyer.

Flight after flight was ascended.

They had now arrived at the fourth floor, when a sudden noise startled Jonathan.

He paused, breathed hard, and listened.

Some one knocked loudly at the street-door.

"What can that mean?" Flint sighed.

"The officers have discovered their mistake, and are just returned."

"Impossible."

"Hold your prate, old fool as you are," said Jonathan, grasping Flint firmly by the coat collar. "Mount that ladder."

"What for?"

"Why, we must escape over the roofs of the houses."

"I cannot; I shall surely fall into the street, and dash my brains out."

"I wish he would," Jonathan thought. "If I only knew where the old villain secreted his money."

Bang! bang! bang! went the door knocker.

"Quick," said Jonathan; "up the ladder you go."

Flint was half-way up the ladder when the door of a chamber on the same floor opened.

"Who is there?" inquired a voice.

There was no response.

Jonathan and Flint dared not move.

They held their breath in the darkness.

They knew not whence the voice proceeded.

"Who's there?" was the repeated question. "Speak, or I will raise the alarm of thieves, robbers!"

"'Tis a female voice," thought Jonathan.

He approached the door.

Biddy, the cook and housemaid, stood shivering and alarmed at her chamber door, half-dressed, and trembling with agitation.

Jonathan seized her by the throat.

Before she could struggle or articulate a sound, he said,

"Breathe another word, and you die."

"Oh, spare me! Oh, mercy! thieves——"

"Hu-s-s-sh!" said Jonathan.

His grip upon her throat was more persuasive than his words.

The poor servant-maid trembled, and fell to the floor.

"Speak again, and I will kill you! Do not stir out of your room on any account."

Bang! bang! bang! again went the street-door knocker.

Jonathan closed and locked the servant's door, and mounted the ladder on to the roof with the agility of a lamp-lighter.

"Keep out of sight," he whispered to Flint, "or they will perceive us from below."

So cautioned, Flint crept along the roof near to the gutters, behind the heavy stacks of chimney-pots and had crossed the roof of a house or two, when he stopped from sheer exhaustion.

"Go on, go on," growled Jonathan.

But Flint refused.

Jonathan, however, with his dirk-knife, pricked the old lawyer several times in the leg.

This made Flint wince with pain, and he crawled on faster and farther than ever.

The noise below now convinced the two fugitives that the officers had burst into the house.

"Quick, quick! for your life," said Jonathan.

By this time they had crossed over more than a dozen houses, unperceived by any one below, and had reached the corner of the street.

They were now on the roof of a large warehouse.

Jonathan and Flint were completely concealed by an immense stack of chimney-pots.

Yet in the distance they could perceive the bull's-eyes of the officers' lanterns.

They were now on the roof also, but far away.

The little gleam of light caught old Flint's eyes, and his heart sank within him.

"This way," said Jonathan, who had discovered a trap-door. "This way."

He opened it hastily, and in a great hurry old Flint descended the ladder.

"Are you down?" asked Jonathan.

A deep groan of agony was the only answer.

Flint's leg had been caught by a watch-dog.

In a moment Jonathan descended.

"Help! help!" groaned Flint, "or I shall be worried to death."

Jonathan, however, thought it of more consequence to secure the trap-door than look after Flint, and, therefore, barred it from the inside so that the officers could not follow, and should be thrown off the scent.

When this was done, during which time the watch-dog had been gnawing at old Flint's leg, Jonathan descended to the staircase, and, with one thrust, stabbed the watch-dog to the heart.

With a terrible growl in its death-agony, and a final bite at the unfortunate lawyer's legs, the animal died.

Jonathan seized it, and in the dark was about to throw it downstairs, when he violently struck some unknown person to the floor.

A curse and a groan was the only reply.

It was the watchman of the warehouse, who had noiselessly approached.

He was alone.

Flint, in his hurry and flight, stumbled over the prostrate watchman, and tumbled head over heels downstairs, and with a loud smash fell through a sky-light all of a heap into a room on the ground-floor.

Jonathan was more lucky.

He delivered a series of such violent kicks and cuffs to the unlucky watchman, as left that unfortunate man more dead than alive, and afraid to raise any alarm.

With much difficulty, he found out Flint, and released him from his place of confinement.

Flint wished to be left behind.

But this Jonathan would not think of.

"The old villain wishes to get rid of me," he thought; "but that must not be. If I lose sight of him *this* time, I shall never set eyes on him again; besides," thought Jonathan, "he might turn round and prove an informer."

More dead than alive, Flint was dragged out from his place of concealment.

The door was broken open, and both villains were safe in the passage.

The front door was only barred.

Jonathan forced back the bolts and listened.

There was the sounds of many voices in the streets of persons hurrying to where Flint had lived.

Jonathan looked out, and found the coast clear.

"Quick! quick!" he said.

He and Flint hurried away as fast as possible, and turned into another street.

They had scarcely done so, when several policemen turned the corner, and were enticed to join the chase which now ensued by the night-watchmen of the warehouse and others running after Jonathan and Flint, shouting,

"Stop thief! stop thief! Burglars! murderers! Stop thief! stop thief!"

## CHAPTER LV.

### FRANK'S HEROISM—THE LIFE-BOAT AND RAFT.

When Frank arrived at Modena it was his determination to proceed to Florence by land.

But he was informed that King Victor Emmanuel was then at Leghorn, in Tuscany, superintending both military and naval affairs in that province.

This was a sore disappointment to the young soldier, for he was in a great hurry to join his Boy Band again.

Besides, it obliged him to go to the sea coast, and perform the rest of his journey by water, a prospect which did not, by any means, agree with the wishes of Master Buttons, who heartily hated the tossing and buffetings of the sea at all times.

But there was no help for it.

If the despatches from Garibaldi were to be delivered at all it must be done quickly.

Frank, therefore, directed his course towards the nearest seaport, where a frigate, several troop ships, and a valuable envoy were waiting to set sail.

When Frank learned that his brother, Tom Ford, was at Leghorn, his heart felt rejoiced at the unexpected change in his journey, for it was now a long time since he had heard or seen anything of the gallant lad.

The prospect of soon meeting Tom, cheered both Frank and Master Buttons, who went on board the Italian frigate, "Carlo Alberto," with light hearts and joyful anticipations of a short and pleasant journey along the beautiful coasts of Tuscany.

The "Carlo Alberto," the troop ships, and others, however, had not left port more than twenty-four hours, with a fair, fresh breeze in their favour, when a terrible gale arose.

It was the first time that either Frank or Buttons had beheld the sea in such a wild commotion, and the sight was terrible in its grandeur.

The noble frigate was borne like a weed upon the ocean, at the mercy of the mighty tempest, which howled through the rigging so as to deaden the shouts of the brave seamen while furling the sails.

Billow after billow beat over them, and, as the foamy waves dashed up their snow-white crests to heaven, roaring in the wildness of their fury, Frank stood calmly on the quarter-deck, with a proud smile on his handsome face.

The troop ships and others were now scattered far and wide upon the broad, storm-crested surface of the waters.

But, now and then, some of them could be distinguished as they appeared for a moment on the surging foam like dim specks on the verge of the horizon.

Night came on, and with it ten thousand horrors.

A pitchy darkness, which seemed almost palpable to the touch, hung with a funeral gloom above.

The waves, lashed by the fury of the tempest, sparkled with diamond-like foam.

All this seemed but to render the heavens above more dense and horrible.

The wind now changed favourably.

The "Carlo Alberto" dashed through the liquid element with astonishing swiftness.

But the shifting of the gale and sudden change in the whistling, howling winds, produced a still wilder commotion in the waves, which seemed to be struggling for the mastery, and threatening instant destruction on every hand.

Wave after wave, and billow after billow, came raging after the devoted frigate, and threatened to engulf it.

But, like a bird upon the wing, the gallant vessel lifted and rose to the swell, and rushed down the steep and yawning abyss, tracking her path with brillancy and light.

The terrors and horrors of that fearful night were appalling.

Buttons was more dead than alive.

But Captain Frank, with that real bravery for which he has been always noted, was here, there, and everywhere, performing feats of daring that astonished and delighted all on board.

Morning dawned at length.

But if the gale of the preceding night had been furious, it now became doubly so, and the "Carlo Alberto," which before had steered her course with majesty and pride, now lay groaning beneath the foaming and angry billows.

Things were now getting desperate.

Orders were given to furl the foresails.

Sixty seamen sprang aloft to execute the order.

They had already extended themselves upon the yards, and were in the act of gathering up the folds of the sail, when a heavy sea like an Alpine mountain came rushing upon them.

Their situation was most awful.

No human voice could warn them of their danger in time, nor any hand be stretched to help them.

All was now dreadful suspense.

Still onward rolled the mighty waves.

It struck the vessel fair upon the bows, and the decks were deluged with water (see cut in No. 18).

A crash, with a wild, tumultuous yell ensued.

When the spray had cleared away it was found that the foremast had been swept away, and over fifty of the seamen buried beneath the yawning waves.

Some few remained entangled in the rigging, but man after man was washed away.

One alone was left!

That one was the gallant Frank Ford!

He had, without being asked, led on the gallant seamen in that perilous duty.

When discovered that it was none other than the gallant young captain of the Boy Soldiers who was thus clinging to the rigging, and suspended between life or death, a shout of horror and pain was raised on every hand.

"Save him! save him!"

"The gallant youth is lost!" were the cries of all.

There he was and no one could save him.

He struggled boldly and manfully against the winds and waves, and his strong limbs writhed round the shattered mast.

But no fear was depicted on his noble face.

Every one thought that each moment would be Frank's last.

Not so, however.

The gallant lad did not seem to take any heed of himself.

All he was intent upon was to clear the foremast of the wreck which still clung to it.

"An axe! an axe!" cried Frank, in a cheery voice.

With great agility Frank still clung to the wreck with one arm and his legs.

With the other arm he collected and threw down a thin long rope upon the deck.

"An axe! an axe!" he shouted.

This was fastened to the end of the rope, which Frank quickly hauled up.

By exerting all his strength, he cut asunder the tangled rigging which still fouled the fore part of the vessel, and in less than ten minutes the top part of the broken mast fell with a loud splash into the foaming water.

This bold and daring act saved the frigate from certain destruction, for the fouling of the mast as it hung over the ship's side made it keel over, and had it long remained in that state must have swamped the vessel.

The storm after some hours greatly abated, but still Frank would not leave his post on the cross trees of the broken foremast.

He tied himself to the mast and swept the angry ocean with his eagle eye.

In all directions he could perceive ships, like black specks upon the water, tossing and heaving and rolling in the most frightful manner.

Amongst those who laboured in the terrific storm were several troop ships, filled with soldiers bound, like himself, to Leghorn.

From his high position Frank could plainly discern in the distance the decks of several ships covered with parts of wreck and broken spars.

Some of the ships appeared to be water-logged, but on the decks and in the rigging of each were discernible crowds of soldiers, sailors, and others clinging as if for dear life.

Not far away, and nearest of all was a dismasted brig, which rolled and pitched most frightfully.

It seemed as if this doomed ship would each moment be sent to the bottom by the immense weight and power of the dashing waves.

In an instant there flashed from her dark sides a streak of fire.

Presently came booming over the deep a long, heavy reverberating sound.

It was a signal gun, a token of sore distress!

"Man the boats! the vessel is sinking to leeward of us. Man the life-boats! man the life-boats!"

Frank's voice was clearly heard above the whistling of the wind and the splashing of the angry billows.

"Man the life-boats! man the life-boats!" Frank still shouted, in stentorian tones.

"'Tis madness! the boats cannot live in such a sea," was the response. "Do not unlash the boats, men; 'tis folly."

Enraged beyond measure, Frank slipped down a rope on to the deck, and spoke to the commander.

"There are women and children on board that vessel, captain; I saw them waving their handkerchiefs as signals of distress."

"I cannot help it," was the cold reply. "I cannot send either men or boats away from my ship in such weather as this, it is certain destruction; we must look to ourselves."

"I care not if I perish," said Frank; "these poor creatures must be saved."

"I cannot allow my men to lose their lives uselessly."

"Give *me* a boat, then. I will go alone."

"You may have one of the boats if you choose; but, take my advice, do not venture out to sea in such frightful weather."

"But I *will*," said Frank, firmly; "and will go alone if no one else will volunteer."

"You shall *not* go alone Frank," said Buttons, summoning up all his courage. "If you sink we must perish together."

"Bravo Buttons!" said Frank, slapping his young companion on the back. "Bravo, my lad, unlash the ropes, and let's lower the life-boat at once. Who will volunteer?"

"I will."

"So will I," said half-a-dozen brave sailors, in a breath.

In a moment the boat was lowered to leeward.

Buttons was at the tiller.

Frank had the bow oar, and a boat-hook ready for instant use.

Before the gallant crew of the life-boat had pulled away many cables' length, loud shouts were heard on board the "Carlo Alberto."

"She's gone down!"

"All is lost!"

"The vessel has foundered!"

"Return! return!"

Frank heard these dismal tidings, but they only tended to nerve his heart with fresh courage.

"Return! never!" said he. "Pull away, my merry merry men; pull away, we must surely pick up some of the unfortunates."

---

## THE BOY SOLDIER; OR, GARIBALDI'S YOUNG CAPTAIN.

THE MURDER OF THE OFFICER.

"It is the great thing, as you say, Mr. Jonathan; but some people don't get along as fast as others. How some people make large fortunes is very mysterious sometimes."

"Yes. Who'd have thought, Carrington, my boy, that old Flint would ever have been able to boast of such a bank account as you say he has? I knew him thirty years ago, and then he was almost picking rags in the street, and was scarcely better than a bundle of rags himself.

"Not that I say so to his disparagement, you know," said Jonathan, with mock charity; "it is to his credit rather that, from nothing, he should have gradually risen up to be among the wealthiest.

No. 21

"It shows, Carrington, as you are yet quite a young man, what can be effected by untiring industry and prudence.

"Instead of being otherwise, I should feel buoyant at your age; with education, talent, good address, and winning exterior. I would not give your chances of success for the oldest and richest in the world.

"And let me tell you, also, something in confidence, which your father told me. The bank directors are very much pleased with you, and propose raising your salary. What do you think of that? And again, you may imagine the confidence they have in you, from the fact that, although, from all other clerks, even from directors' sons, they demand rich connections as securities, nothing of the kind has ever been exacted from you or your worthy parent. That shows what an excellent and sound education you must have received under me at dear old Bromley Hall; for, from almost nothing in the bank, you and your father have gradually risen to what you now are, and, in time, I have no doubt he will be president of the establishment."

Shaking hands, "kind old Mr. Jonathan" left his young friend in the bank parlour, and ascended the stairs to converse for a short time with Mr. Carrington, senior.

"Old Jonathan can preach as well as any of them. Not a bad sort of old fellow, though, but mighty stingy. He's all right, and don't care much for anybody, so that he gets a fat salary for doing nothing at Bromley Hall, while all the work falls to the poor tutors. Never mind, Rome wasn't built in a day; my turn will come one of these fine mornings. Who knows? I may have a bank of my own. They are going to increase my salary, eh? Well, they are very long-winded about the business, and should have done so long ago. What's three hundred a year to a fellow like me, in times like these? Why, I could spend that amount in less than a week, if I only 'let loose' a little."

Thus thought young Carrington, while old Jonathan was upstairs, conversing with his father.

But while Jonathan's pupil was in a deep reverie about the large sum which old Flint had to his name in the bank from time to time, and reflecting upon the many scenes in which he and Joel Flint had taken part at Bromley Hall, Jonathan himself was detailing to Mr. Carrington, senior, the whole history of the terrible school riots at Bromley Hall.

But, it must be remarked, the servant who let Jonathan in had not gone up more than two flights of stairs, when Jonathan turned and left the street-door ajar.

While he was conversing, therefore, with his former pupil, Bill, Jack, and Alf, the burglars, entered the establishment, and hid themselves.

After a long time spent in conversation with the old master of Bromley Hall, Mr. Carrington and his son persuaded the old tutor to remain all night.

This was exactly what Jonathan wanted.

Hour after hour passed in pleasant conversation, about all manner of subjects, and at last bedtime arrived.

Jonathan was shown to his room, and retired to rest.

In another hour the whole house and the bank were as quiet as the grave.

The night watchman went his rounds.

All was safe and still.

But little did the watchman dream that three determined villains were then in the bank, hid away.

Neither did he suspect that old Jonathan was likewise awake, and moving about the house in his stocking-feet.

He was about to descend the stairs, to assist in the robbery, when his quick ear caught the faint sounds of—

"Help, help!" and of a quick, violent scuffle going on in the bank below.

Again all was still.

"Have they killed the watchman, I wonder?" thought Jonathan, with bated breath.

He descended the stairs cautiously and slowly.

"I will go and assist them," thought he, "or I shall have nothing for my share. In the morning I shall be found fast asleep in bed. No one will ever suspect me of having done anything—besides, I shall leave the house long before the bank opens on Monday morning."

He had descended two flights of stairs, and was about to go down the third, and last, when a door opened, and a hand was laid roughly upon his shoulder.

"Who are you?" said some one, in the dark, and in a whisper.

"Who is he? what brings him here?"

The whispered tones of the unknown men were so harsh, quick, and decisive, that they made Jonathan tremble.

"Who and what are you?"

"I am a visitor, a friend of Mr. Carrington, the resident director."

"What brought you down from your chamber, then, at this time of night?"

"I heard a mysterious noise, and faint cries for help, as if of some one in distress."

"Indeed—and you came to his assistance, I suppose?"

"I did, or to ascertain the cause of the noise ere alarming the household."

"You did well, then. You may go to your apartment again, and leave the rest to us. Had you alarmed the house, you would have spoiled everything."

"Why, what is the matter?"

"Oh, nothing in particular—there are three professional burglars in the bank—that's all!"

"Burglars in the bank! impossible—and you are—"

"Police officers."

"But the cry of help I heard, then, arose from—"

"The night watchman. He was seized, bound, and gagged; but no harm will befall him."

"But how did you know of this affair?"

"From information we received, we entered the house just half an hour after the burglars. We have been watching them several hours. When they have done their work below, we shall collar 'em, and transport 'em for life."

"But how could you watch them?"

"We bored a hole with an auger through the first floor ceiling. Have a peep?"

Jonathan did have a peep, and through the hole could plainly see the three burglars hard at work trying to prize open the safe.

"Now are you satisfied?" said one of the officers.

"Yes, I am. Oh! the villains! see how hard they are working. Why, Alf and Bill are actually perspiring. If they only worked half so hard in any honest labour, they'd make their fortunes."

"I dare say they would; but who told you that those two men trying to prize open the safe were called Alf and Bill?"

This question took Jonathan fairly aback, and for a moment he felt his heart in his mouth.

"I heard them whisper their names just now," said Jonathan, telling a lie.

"The very men we suspected," said one of the officers, who was Josey's friend Radfen. "I thought they were concocting some villany or they wouldn't have kept so quiet as they have done for the past week or two."

"The third party as is guarding the door must be Jack, then," whispered another officer.

"Yes; that's him."

"But why don't you go and arrest them at once?"

"We are waiting for a fourth party," said Radfen.

"Two more, I think you said, Radfen?"

"There were two strangers with them in the den, but I don't know whether they are all pals or not."

"Who told you, Joey?"

"No; I can't get anything out of him," said Radfen; "but I found it out in a curious sort of way."

"How was that?"

"Why, this morning they sent to the public for a quart of gin. Any other morning they only have a pint between them. So I knew that there must be one or two extra people there."

This conversation was carried on in whispers, and yet they watched the robbers at work below with hawk-like eyes.

"Now's our time," said Radfen; "we can't wait any longer. If we stop for the other two, we may loose these three. To work, my men, each one to his post."

Jonathan was glad enough to creep out of the way, yet he seemed charmed, and fixed to the spot.

He dearly wanted to see how the officers would effect the capture of his late associates; and these four knelt down, and looked through the hole in the flooring.

The officers, in their bare feet, left the room.

For five minutes nothing was heard or seen of them.

Bill, Jack, and Alf were still very busy with the safe, and were upon the point of forcing it open, when they dropped their tools, and looked around sharply.

In the distance Jonathan could see that Radfen and two others had got into the bank by a side door.

They were there crouched low down in front of the counter.

No noise had been heard.

Yet by instinct, the three burglars knew that some one was within pistol shot.

They listened.

But no sounds were heard.

Bill, now upon tiptoe, approached the counter, to look over.

A loud oath escaped from Bill.

He drew his revolver, and fired at Radfen.

The poor detective staggered and fell.

"I told yer last time you should have it Radfen, and now you've got more nor you want."

The other two detectives jumped across the counter.

By a well-directed blow Bill levelled one to the ground with a small "jemmy."

Jack and Alf now rushed forward, bent on murdering the remaining officer.

On the instant, the door leading into the entrance hall was forced open by half-a-dozen officers.

The fight now was desperate.

Pistol shots were fired quickly by the three desperate men, who fought with the desperation of savages.

Radfen, faint from loss of blood, still persisted in attempting to arrest Bill, but was unable.

He staggered forward, and grasped the burglar firmly by the throat.

The struggle was brief.

Bill threw Radfen to the ground, and fell heavily upon him.

A knife was at the detective's throat.

"I always said I'd 'do' for you, Radfen; and so I will if I 'swing' for it.

He raised his dirk knife, prepared to plunge it into the brave detective's heart—

When a truncheon blow laid him speechless upon the floor.

As faint and weak as he was, Radfen immediately pulled out a pair of irons, and handcuffed Bill ere he was conscious of it.

Jack and Alf fought most desperately to get away.

"It is liberty or transportation for life for us," they thought, and struggled most savagely to get away.

Knives, pistols, crowbars, "jemmies," everything had been used by the three desperate robbers, who fought like fiends.

Many of the officers were fearfully cut and wounded about the head and face, and blood flowed freely on either side.

Yet during the entire conflict, the brave detectives used no weapons at all, except their stout truncheons.

But they laid about them so vigorously and earnestly, that in less than ten minutes, Bill, Jack and Alf were cut and bumped and bruised in a most terrible manner, and their faces were red with blood.

But it was not until fairly exhausted and unable to stand, that the burglars gave in.

And even when they lay prostrate upon the floor, Jack and Alf resisted all attempts to handcuff them, until at last they were forced to submit, and were tightly bound both hand and foot.

A cab was called, and the three prisoners driven off to the nearest station house.

All this exciting and terrible scene old Jonathan saw through the hole in the ceiling.

But when it was over, he began to think of his own safety.

The whole house and neighbourhood were of course alarmed.

Mr. Carrington and his son, revolvers in hand, rushed downstairs, but it was all over ere they arrived.

Old Jonathan perceived them among the officers and servants, and took the opportunity to go into the chambers of both father and son, and helped himself to whatever he could find of value.

Then mixing with the motley crowd of officers, servants, and others, he greatly condoled with Mr. Carrington, and felt so much interest in the "barbarous attempt at burglary," as he termed it, "that he would go forthwith towards the police station to see if the three rascals were like some thieves who a year before had robbed Bromley Hall."

It need not be added that Mr. Jonathan never went to the station house at all, for——

No sooner had the old villain placed his foot in the streets once more, than he called a cab, and was driven to the outskirts of London out of harm's way.

In less than an hour after Jonathan had left the house, the three burglars—knowing there was no hope for themselves—divulged everything.

"And where is this friend of yours, Mr. Carrington, the old master of Bromley Hall?" Radfen asked.

"Why, officer?"

"Oh, nothing in particular, sir; only there's £200 reward offered for him and two others, on the charge of wilful murder."

"Impossible, officer!"

"The three burglars have confessed all."

"Indeed!"

"Yes; do you know a person who was a lawyer of the name of Flint?"

"Yes, well," said young Carrington; "his son and I were schoolfellows at Bromley Hall."

"Has he any account at your bank?"

"He had at times a very heavy account, and also other deposits which he managed for his clients. The last sum he drew was £500 to day, and closed his account. Why do you ask?" asked young Carrington.

"He is the second of the three for whom the reward is offered."

This news fell like a thunderclap upon the bank director and his son, who raised their hands in horror.

"They are both at large," said Radfen, "but still in London. They must be tracked at once."

So saying, the active detective, wounded as he was, went forth in search of the two criminal fugitives.

## CHAPTER LXI.

### JEALOUSY AND LOVE—THE CHALLENGE.

The gallant behaviour of Captain Frank during the terrible storm was the subject of universal approbation among both sailors and soldiers.

Frank himself was doubly rejoiced at his own good fortune in saving the lives of so many poor creatures.

But that Nelly Lancaster and her father should have been among the number filled him with astonishment.

Both Nelly and her father were tenderly cared for by the officers of the frigate, and, strange to say, not one of those who volunteered to go in the boats with the gallant Frank were either injured in any way or drowned.

When they reached Leghorn the news was spread far and wide about the heroism of the young Englishman both upon land and sea, and the king, who, from his youth, always delighted in acts of daring and heroism, and never forgot those who in any way distinguished themselves in flood or field, received Captain Frank with marked favor, and gave him several medals, which the young volunteer wore with great modesty and becoming dignity.

But no one succeeds to fame or power without making enemies for himself.

And so it was with Frank.

There were several young Italian officers, though much older than himself, who took every opportunity to laugh at and detract from the brave deeds performed by the gallant band of English Boy Soldiers.

These tales were told to Frank by Master Buttons, who, though willing enough, was much too young to think of taking up the vindication of his brave companions.

Not so Frank, however.

For several days he enquired at the hotel regarding the health of Miss Lancaster.

Each time he was told that she was no better, but that her father was up and well again.

The servant said that Mr. Lancaster was sorry he could not see Captain Ford then, but would at some future time when Nelly was better.

Now it came to the ears of Frank that Nelly *was* better.

More than this it was known that Mr. Lancaster had often invited Italian officers to dine with him, who seemed enraptured with Nelly's beauty and accomplishments.

But, perhaps, more than all charmed with the reputed wealth of her father, the banker.

It came to Frank's ears, by some mysterious means, that among these young officers there was one, named Marquis de Sangri, who aspired to Nelly's hand in marriage, and never allowed any occasion to pass in which Frank's name was mentioned to jeer at the young soldier, and sneer at his reputation.

This pleased Mr. Lancaster.

His daughter's likings or dislikings never gave him a thought.

He wished to see Nelly surrounded by counts, marquises, barons, and the like, never asking himself the question whether they were worthy of his daughter's notice.

All he wanted was "men of title" about him.

"Count" sounded well in his ears; "Baron" still better; and the style of Marquis de Sangri threw him into raptures.

If De Sangri had only been a "duke" now, although not worth a stiver, and with no more brains than a cabbage, old Lancaster would almost have adored him.

He had heard much of Frank, and of his attachment to Nelly.

But bravery, honour, honesty, virtue, and qualities of that kind, in a young and gallant English soldier, were not remarkable enough for the silly old banker.

He wanted Nelly to marry no man who was without a grand, high-sounding title, although he lived in private on nothing better than German sausage, or sour krout.

Frank met Mr. Lancaster one day by accident.

After thanking the youth for saving his own and his daughter's life, he offered Frank a £100 note "for his services!"

Young Ford spurned the offer with disdain.

Had any one else so affronted him, he would have knocked them down on the spot.

"I did not expect an insult, Mr. Lancaster," said Frank, sorrowfully.

"Insult! Is it an insult to offer you payment for your services to me and my daughter? What else could you expect?"

"I expected the pleasure of once more seeing and conversing with one—if only for a moment—who has ever held possession of my heart."

"Heart!" said old Lancaster, getting red, and jingling money in his pockets; "the lad must be mad! Have pretensions to my daughter! Why, sir, you must be crazy!"

"I have known Miss Lancaster a long time, sir."

"More's the pity. Good-day to you. But let me tell you this, young Ford. I have heard of this attachment before, but have broken it off; if we ever meet again, it must be as strangers."

Mr. Lancaster went his way, leaving Frank Ford standing like a statue.

He knew not what to think or say.

As he thus mused, and felt sorrowful at heart, a fine English carriage and horses passed him.

The vehicle was open.

To his astonishment, Frank saw Nelly Lancaster and De Sangri sitting in it, side by side.

His eye caught Frank's.

De Sangri twirled his moustachios in triumph.

Nelly hung her head.

Frank returned De Sangri's look with one of scorn and defiance.

And he shook with passion.

"That is the scoundrel who has been circulating all manner of false stories about me. I will call him out, and have satisfaction. He is an accomplished duellist, I am told; but no matter; one of us must fall. I care not now to live, since Nelly has proved false. She must be false, or why insult me by riding out side by side with that conceited fop?"

* * * * * * *

When Frank returned to his hotel, Master Buttons said that a fierce-looking, podgy, military man had called, and left his card and a note.

On the card was—

COUNT BODZO,
Capt. of Artillery,
Hotel Victor.

The note ran thus—

CAPT. FRANK FORD,

SIR,—Your hasty and ungentlemanly conversation with Mr. Lancaster, as reported to me to-day, requires an instant apology, or otherwise, as a gentleman, I demand that satisfaction which a soldier expects of any one, and condescends to ask from such an impostor as Capt. Frank Ford.

I remain,
DE SANGRI,
Marquis de Novolo, &c.

P.S.—Any answer to this, addressed to my friend Count Bodzo, will receive instant attention. S.

"A challenge, eh? Why, what an old fool Lancaster must have been! I never insulted him. I have too much love for his daughter, and respect for his own old age for that.

"I suppose he has magnified the matter over his wine, and this De Sangri, who has longed for a duel with me, has considered it a peg on which to hang a quarrel.

"Well, so be it, I am not at all averse to the meeting, but will answer De Sangri's challenge at once."

Frank sat down and wrote.

Hotel de Londres.

To the MARQUIS DE SANGRI,

MARQUIS,—I have never yet given utterance to any word of which I have felt ashamed to acknowledge, and I can assure you no single sentence of mine could have given offence to Mr. Lancaster, a gentleman whose life, under Providence, I lately saved.

As your insulting language, however, leaves no doubt that on any pretext, however slight, you desire a hostile meeting, I should not be an English Volunteer if I declined, although you are perfectly well aware that recent wounds, received in battle, are still unhealed. I will say no more, but leave further argument until our meeting. In the meantime, I refer your friend, Count Bodzo, to confer with my brother, Captain Tom Ford, of the King's Navy, who is staying with me for a few days.

I am, Marquis,
Yours, &c.,
FRANK FORD,
Capt. (Brevet Major) of English Volunteers.

"There," said Frank, "this upstart marquis has long desired this meeting, and much good may it do him."

So saying, he attired himself in his best uniform ate a hearty dinner, and went to the opera with his brother Tom.

## CHAPTER LXII.

DETECTIVES ON THE TRAIL—THE FATAL SHOT—THE ENCOUNTER AND DEATH.

RADFEN was much too weak to think of starting in pursuit of Jonathan.

He, therefore, by the inspector's advice, entrusted "the job" to Sergeant Gamble, a "plain clothes" man, who was very expert and bold.

Gamble first enquired at all the cab ranks near the bank if any one had been called off within the hour.

He found out from the waterman that a Hansom cab had been called off by a long-legged, clerical-looking person.

"Where did he want to go?"

"Epping Forest."

"Did you hear him say so?"

"No, but the driver told me."

"Get me a cab, then—the best on the rank. Did you see the party yourself?"

"Yes,"

"And could identify him?"

"In course I could."

"Hi, cabby!" said Gamble, to the driver of a Hansom, "how's your horse—fresh?"

"As a daisy!" was the reply.

Cab horses are always "fresh," although out all night, and most part of the day very often.

"Then drive like the devil to Epping Forest. Come along, waterman; you must go also, I can't do without you, for I never saw the chap as I'm after in all my life."

Gamble and the waterman jumped into the cab, the driver cracked his whip, and off they went to Epping Forest.

Through the dark and silent streets they clattered at a fearful pace, until the horse was all afoam.

From time to time Gamble peered out upon any passing vehicle.

But cabby did not stop for anything, although he drove so near to the curb occasionally that there was great fear of his "spilling" his fare into the road, or smashing the cab.

When they fairly got a mile or two into the country road, Gamble stopped the cab, and asked one of the mounted rural police,

"Seen a cab along the road to-night?"

"Yes."

"How long since?"

"An hour, and going like the devil. Why?"

"Murderer wanted, that's all."

And on the Hansom cab rattled along, mile after mile, until in the distance they espied Epping Forest.

Beside the roadside stopped Jonathan's cab.

## CHAPTER LXIII.

THE PURSUIT—WHAT CAME OF IT—THE SAD END—THE CONCEALED VILLAIN—THE FATAL SHOT.

"Is that the cab, waterman?" asked Gardner, the detective, as his own conveyance bowled along at a sharp pace towards Epping Forest.

"Jest so, Mister Gardner."

"Who drives it?"

"Old Job Perkins."

"I know him well enough; he used to drive a four-wheeler."

"Yes, but he's got up in the world lately."

"How do you mean?"

"I can't explain it, for, as you see, Job is an artful old devil, and has more ways than one of making money these hard times."

"I don't understand you, waterman."

"Well, what I mean, Mister Gardner, is this here; you see, one rainy night when Job was driving a four-wheeler, he was called off his rank in a great hurry by a very suspicious-looking party, but as he drove along he heard some one calling out for him to stop; he did so, and the party who called out for him to stop was no other than Puggy."

"Puggy, eh," said Gardner, with a smile; "and where was this?"

"Well, I heard Job say once it were in the next street to where old Ford was murdered in the Red House."

"Oh, the Red House, eh, and on that very night, too? What brought Puggy so far from home, I wonder, on that particular night?" said Gardner.

"That I don't know; but this I *do* know, old Job said that Puggy was minding an old gent as fell down in a fit, and wanted Job to take him up; he refused at first, but when he discovered that the chap who called him off the rank had hooked it in a very queer way, without going his journey and paying his fare, why he takes up the old gentleman and drives him home. Job saw Puggy some time ago, and as he was flush, 'Here, Job,' says Puggy; 'I met that old cove as you drove home, and he told me to give you this,' so saying he put ten twenty-pound notes in Job's hand, and tells him that the old gent wants him to start a Hansom, so that's how old Job got such a sudden rise in the world."

"Yes, yes; but how did Puggy get so much money?"

"The old gent gave it to him."

"Nonsense," said Gardner; "if even he had, Puggy isn't such a fool, or rather such an honest fool as to hand it over to old Job; not he, he's more likely to stick to all he gets. *I* know Puggy this long time."

"So do I," says the waterman; "and how he came by that money quite 'licks' me."

"I dare say I could explain it all," said Gardner. "The deepest mysteries are unravelled at times."

"It would puzzle the devil, I'm thinking, to know all that the Pug has been up to in his life."

By this time the detective and the waterman came up to Job's cab, which was standing by the side of the road, near a small inn.

Gardner jumped out, and walked into the tavern tap-room.

Before a blazing fire, old Job sat smoking a long pipe, and at his elbow stood a mug of hot spiced ale.

When he saw Gardner and the waterman enter, he took the pipe out of his mouth, and stared as if he had seen an apparition.

"Am I a dreaming?" said Job, "or has the Strand keb rank shifted to Epping forest?"

"No, you are not dreaming, Job," said Gardner. "You know me?"

"I should think as how I did; but what's yer little game? What are yer arter?"

"I'll tell you presently."

The waterman took "a long pull" at Job's spiced ale, which that worthy did not at all relish, as he said,

"'Old 'ard, there, vatercock, it ain't kimmon stuff as you're gulping."

After a few moments of ordinary conversation, the waterman left Gardner and Job to themselves in the tap-room.

The detective shut the door, and locked it.

He then sat close beside old Job before the fire.

"And vhat's yer little game?" said Job, looking very wise. "What's yer hup to?"

"Where is that party you brought down here in your cab, Job?"

"Can't tell from Adam."

"What do you mean?"

"Mean? Vhy, I mean that I drew him to the edge o' the forest, he got out, paid me two quid, and then hooked it."

"Went into the bare forest?"

"Yes; jest so."

"Was there no house in view?"

"No; net even a pigsty."

"What sort of a person was he? Did you ever see him before?"

"Yes; once."

"When?"

"Well, I called to hev a pipe and a pint one day at a house I uses, and I sees this chap in the parlour with two others."

"Who were they?"

"I can't say."

"Now look here, Job," said Gardner, "let's have no nonsense. You do know who they were."

"So help me never I——"

"No swearing, Job; you *do* know. One of them was Puggy. You needn't look so surprised; you and he are great friends."

"How d'yer mean?"

"He brought some money to you from an old party you drove home one night."

"Who told you?"

"Puggy himself."

"Never!" said Job, in greater surprise than ever.

"He did, though."

"Blowed the gaff, eh? Well, they can't touch me," said Job, drawing a long breath. "*I* hadn't any hand in it."

"In what?"

"Why, in smashing them two bobbies in the old lawyer's office."

"Oh, ho!" thought Gardner; "this is something fresh."

With a few well-put questions, in which he drew from Job all he knew, heard, or had seen of Jonathan, Flint, Warner, and the Pug, the detective rose.

"Yes; it were the same party as you described, Mr. Gardner," said Job; "nobody who has seen that long gent once would ever forget *his* ugly mug."

Job drove the detective to that part of the forest where Jonathan had alighted.

Gardner examined the ground, and, for a few minutes, proceeded among the trees in the direction Jonathan had taken.

There were no marks or footprints to be seen.

All was cold, bleak, wild, desolate and quiet.

Beyond the whistling of the winds no sounds were heard.

"You are sure that this is the correct spot he got out at?"

"Positive," said Job.

"You didn't know there was a heavy reward out for him, did you?"

"You don't mean that?"

"I do, though."

"Has any o' their pals split, then?"

"Puggy has turned approver."

"You don't mean it?"

"Fact; keep dark, though, Job. If you aid me in this affair I'll make it all right with you."

"All right, Mister Gardner, I'm your man, then; but what must I do first?"

"I'll give you a note to take to Scotland Yard. We must have a score of men to beat up the forest in all quarters before many hours. If he is concealed anywhere hereabouts we shall find him."

"Beat up in all directions at once, eh?" said Job; well, then, there's small chance of *him* escaping; but you'd better look sharp, Mr. Gardner, or else the bird will have taken wing."

"True," said Gardner, "time is precious. I'm bound to take the villian, if it costs me my life; he has hitherto foiled all the 'force,' but now that *I* am on his track, I'll follow it up to the death."

So saying, he got into the cab and hastily wrote a note to Scotland Yard.

"Here, Job, take this to our head-quarters. Drive like the devil; you'll get well paid."

"But ain't you a coming?"

"No."

"What, are yer going to stay here all shivering in the cold?"

"I am."

"You must have a queer taste," said Job, grinning. "You ain't like most o' the detectives; they'd rather go into the public for an hour or two, and have a pipe and some good old ale."

"Never mind, Job, there is two hundred pounds reward if I catch the rascal."

"Oh, Moses and Son!" exclaimed Job, "jest think on it—two hundred pounds!"

He cracked his whip, and drove away towards London.

Gardner, the detective, stood against a tree by the roadside, muffled up and deep in thought.

All this time, Jonathan, the fugitive, was not more than twenty yards off.

He had heard every word of the conversation, and was concealed in an old tree.

Thus, then, were standing, near each other, two deadly enemies.

Gardner had sworn to capture him, dead or alive.

Jonathan had resolved to kill the officer!

"He could not have gone far," thought Gardner, "for, after all, his cab didn't have such a long start of mine, but Job says he was ordered to drive like lightning itself.

"But what on earth could have prompted the fugitive to come to such an out-of-the-way place as this?

"He would have been much safer in London.

"If I could only track him by his footprints, how easily would the reward drop into my ready hand."

While he thus stood behind a tree thinking what he had better do and what course to pursue, Jonathan crawled out of the large, old, hollow trunk of a giant oak tree, and cautiously peered about.

He could not see Gardner, but he knew instinctively that the officer was very near.

He retreated to his hiding-place again, and examined his revolver very carefully.

It was all right.

"I have got six shots for him if he comes within reach," thought Jonathan, with a fiendish smile.

Now, as chance would have it, Gardner was doing exactly the same thing.

"It will not do for me to enter the forest, unprepared," he said, and so minutely examined every chamber of his "six shooter."

"Now for it," thought Gardner, as he left the road. "If this long-legged rascal is anywhere concealed, and sees me, it is all up with me; he may shoot before me."

With a stealthy step Gardner crept rather than walked along.

His eyes were like those of a ferret, and he peered in every direction in hopes of discovering some traces of the fugitive.

"He may have hidden in some old tree; there are lots of rotten hollow trunks hereabouts. I must give them a wide berth.

"What was that?" he thought, as he heard a sudden rustling noise as of some one stirring.

He stopped and listened.

His quick bright eye looked in every direction.

"That's a very large old trunk," he thought, as he approached the tree wherein Jonathan was concealed.

"I must not approach too near," he mused; "who knows, he might be hidden in it. Good thought," said Gardner, "I'll hide in that old tree myself. The fugitive may retrace his steps, and then I can suddenly pounce upon him."

Again he heard the rustling sound.

"I wish I could get on the other side of that old trunk," he said, "for I'm sure it is hollow; and yet I don't see any opening."

Prompted by some instinct, he levelled his revolver full at the old trunk and fired.

The bullet passed through the trunk and grazed Jonathan's cheek.

As may be supposed, he was greatly surprised.

He did not stir out, however.

"He couldn't have seen me, neither could any one have told him that I intended to stay on the borders of the forest for the night. It is only his suspicions. He won't fire again."

Jonathan wiped the blood from his cheek, and crouched down to the bottom of the trunk.

"He surely will not fire again," thought the fugitive. "I did not make any noise. This silence will disarm the officer's suspicions. I do not hear his stealthy footsteps in the dry leaves. Had I made the slightest noise it would have proved my ruin."

But Jonathan had made a noise, but unknown to himself.

When the officer's bullet grazed his cheek he started suddenly.

"Hullo!" said Gardner, as he heard the slight noise. "What could that have been? Some squirrel, perhaps. It wasn't a man, I'll wager for £100, or else he would have bawled out; mortal men can't stand a bullet through 'em without wincing with pain."

In order to satisfy himself of the truth of his suspicion, Gardner fired again at the old trunk.

Twice, in quick succession, he fired.

The bullets on this occasion did not merely graze the hidden fugitive, but, as low as he crouched, one of them almost scalped him; and the other striking lower, hit Jonathan in the ankle.

For a moment or two persons who are wounded do not feel any pain, but a certain sort of numbness.

When they *do* feel the pain, however, it is thrice more excruciating than anything the imagination can fancy.

And so it was with Jonathan.

The scratch on his head, which, had it been but an inch lower, would have killed him, and the bleeding ankle, caused Jonathan to writhe again in agony.

Yet he made not the slightest noise.

"It is a case of life or death," he thought. "He has fired off three of his charges, and has but three remaining. I am three charges the better of him, therefore. If it comes to a hand-to-hand combat, I am more prepared."

He bit his tongue in agony, and listened for the officer's footsteps.

He heard nothing.

But through the bullet-holes he could see Gardner standing about ten yards away, peering about.

He did not advance or retreat.

From some unknown cause he paused, and seemed fastened to the spot.

"There cannot be anything or anybody concealed in that tree," he thought, "or if there was I should have heard some moan or groan, for I must have hit him in some part."

So thinking, he cautiously advanced to examine it.

"Now is my time," thought Jonathan.

He peeped through the bullet-holes, and saw Gardner advancing.

He cautiously turned, and crept out of his hiding-place, yet concealed by its bulk.

A fiendish smile of triumph was upon his features.

"He is a dead man, and I am free," thought he.

In a trice he stepped out of his hiding-place.

"Ha!" exclaimed Gardner, as he saw the figure of Jonathan.

The exclamation had scarcely passed his lips, when Jonathan discharged the charges of his revolver at the officer.

Gardner threw up his hands, and fell to the earth half dead.

Jonathan ran towards him, as best he could, considering his wounded ankle, and knelt over him.

The officer was unconscious.

He was bleeding to death.

Jonathan's aim had been too true.

He was dying.

A smile of bitter scorn played round the murderer's features as he limped off.

"I must make the best of my way from this place," he thought. "Old Flint told me he had part of his treasure concealed in that old inn. I know he sometimes goes there, and has a bed-room always at his disposal; that is the reason I came here; but he knows not that I am aware of all this. If I could only meet him, and have my revenge on him, like I have had with that officer, I should feel content."

At that moment, and while he limped along the road, he heard, in the distance, the sounds of a horse galloping hard.

In the distance he could perceive the muffled figure of some one approaching.

He got behind some bushes, and awaited the horseman's approach.

"Who can it be?" he thought. "I want a good horse now, and if I can only stop the stranger and rob him of it, I can make my escape; if not, this wounded ankle will cause me to be arrested and hung. It is better I should, for my own sake, steal a horse than be swung up at Newgate."

The horseman had now approached within a hundred yards of Jonathan's hiding place behind the bushes, and checked his horse into a leisurely walk.

## CHAPTER LXIV.

### HOW JOEY, THE COSTERMONGER, SERVED OUT PUGGY.

JOEY, the reformed thief, though he now disliked robbery and all such villany, yet felt a kind of old liking for Bill, Jack, and Alf, for in sickness and other distresses they had helped him along.

When, therefore, Joey went into a public-house to have his dinner, he took up the newspaper—the "*'Tizer*" was his favourite journal—and was astonished to read an account of the arrest of several persons charged with breaking into a bank.

"It's Jack and t'others for a quid," said Joey, "and that all come of Mr. Puggy; if they *will* go robbing for a living instead of sticking to hard work like any honest man, why it sarves 'em right.. But still, that don't excuse Puggy—he has turned informer, and is paid for his pains: he won't work, and is afraid to steal, so he takes a kind of middle course, and gets an easy crust by informing on those who do steal.

"And he 'fancies' himself too, and thinks he can fight, but I never heard of him holding up his hands to any one who wasn't a deal the weaker man. I should dearly like to have a shy at him one o' these times on the quiet."

Joey had not long to wait for an opportunity of meeting Puggy "on the quiet."

There was to be a ratting match for £10, at "The Clippers," and as usual, on Monday night, Joey "did himself up" rather sprucely and went there.

For Joey was very fond of "sport" of any kind, and would much rather spend "his tanner" in looking at a ratting or a boxing match, than stand "boosing" about beer-house bars.

On the night in question, Joey went early, and after the ratting match was over, "boxing" commenced.

Among the "gents" in the "shilling place," Joey espied Puggy in the company of a sprucely-dressed detective.

"Puggy seems well up," thought Joey. "It ain't half-a-pint, and a ha'porth o' tobacco now with him; and ain't he conceited in his new togs?"

After a few rounds by several indifferent amateurs, Puggy went into a side room, pulled off his things, and put on the boxing gloves.

He felt very anxious to exhibit his knowledge of "the noble art."

But though he had been in the ring several minutes no one among the non-fighting men present seemed anxious to meet him.

Puggy smiled, and was about to throw off the gloves again, when Joey stepped forward.

"Don't pull 'em off, Puggy," said Joe, "*I'll* give you a turn."

"*You?*" said Puggy, in disgust; "why I'm a stone heavier than you."

"I knows it," said Joey, pulling off his shirt, and tightening his belt. "That's why yer head is so big."

This rather nettled Puggy, who, in truth, had a very large and ugly head.

The numerous bystanders laughed at Joey's retort, and when they saw what a trim-built, sturdy little fellow he was, with not an ounce of useless flesh about him, and his muscles standing out from his arms and shoulders like a mass of steel, they could not but contrast him with his big and bloated opponent.

Joey fastened on his gloves, and stood in the middle of the ring ready for action.

"Play light, Puggy," said Joe, with a confident smile.

"Make it as hard as you like," said Puggy, with an oath; "for I mean to smash yer smeller afore I've done."

"All right," said Joe, and they began to spar.

Every one was silent, for they could see that the two sparrers had no love for each other.

"Close the door, Weazle," said the sporting landlord to one of his "stud," on the sly. "Let no one come up, 'cept swells, for this here's going to be a reg'lar slogging match, I can plainly see."

"Puggy is too much for t'other," said Weazle; "he's two stone heaviest."

"No matter, the little 'un's got game, you'll see."

During the first round Puggy smiled like a man who has a very short and easy job before him.

He advanced, and feinted, and jumped back in very clever style, which caused some applause.

Puggy was very vain, and wished to show those present, and his detective friend in particular, "what he *could* do if he liked."

Joey did not make any show whatever, nor did he hop and skip about like a tom-cat on hot bricks, like Puggy.

He waited for an opening.

It soon came.

"Stop sparring, and go in, Puggy," said the detective.

Puggy *did* go in.

He made a feint with his right, and then reached Joey's nose with the left.

The same instant, however, he was knocked clean off his legs.

For Joey had waited, and then cross-countered Puggy's left with his own right.

THE IMPORTANT COMMUNICATION.

Such a spank it was that it took all by surprise and no one more so than Puggy himself, who got up, attempted to smile, but looked daggers at Joey.

"Time," said Weazle, the master of the ceremonies. "Time, my men; make it quick and merry."

And then he whispered to several professionals,

"They've got an old grudge against each other. You'll see some capital 'give and take,' shortly."

The boxers met again.

"That was the first ewent for me, Puggy," said Joey, smiling, and getting confidence.

Puggy did not answer, but seemed bent on "cutting down" his opponent in "no time."

He capered around the coster for a minute or two, saying, "the second ewent will be scored to me," and then let drive a terrific hit at Joey's head.

The coster ducked his head cleverly.

Puggy's fist struck the wall with great violence, and Joey, turning quickly round, gave Puggy "one, two," on the mouth with such effect that it made his nose bleed, and his teeth to chatter like a dice-box.



Great applause followed this display in favour of Joey, who had not yet been hit at all.

Puggy was in a terrible rage, and pulled off the gloves to fight it out with his fists.

"No, no, no!"

"Take him away!"

"He's too big for the little 'un!"

"It ain't fair play!" cried many, when they perceived Puggy's intentions.

"I can't allow this," said the sporting publican, "in my house. Besides, Puggy is big enough to eat him."

"Let him alone," said Joey, pulling off his gloves, "I ain't afraid on him, if he was as big as St. Paul's; he's nothing else but a slop's pup—an informer!"

Puggy heard this and his face was red with rage.

He swung his bare arms about in a ferocious manner, and rushed at Joey.

But again and again the Coster met his rush with a tremendous smash on the nose, which made the blood spurt out in all directions.

"The big 'un's caught a reg'lar Tartar," said several in high glee.

"Go it, little 'un!"

"Give it him, big 'un!"

Puggy now rushed to close with Joey.

A fearful struggle ensued for the first fall.

For a moment it was any odds against the Coster, for Puggy was so big and strong that he caught up Joey in his arms, and seemed bent on splitting his head against one of the stakes of the ring.

But, as Joey termed it, "it was all a bit of kid" on the Coster's part.

He wished Puggy to waste all his strength, which he did do.

And then Joey wriggled like an eel, and, when least expected, gave his opponent "the leg," and Puggy came to grief with a "buster" on the floor.

"The three events to me," said Joey, grinning.

"Bravo!" cried all assembled.

"Capitally done!"

"I back the little 'un for a tenner," said a sporting gentleman present.

"I think you'd better chuck it up," said the publican who was a fighting-man himself.

"I think you'd better chuck it up Puggy, or else the Coster 'ull eat yer afore he's done."

But this was only said to rile Puggy.

The "sport" had now assumed a very serious aspect.

But the doors were locked, and several hangers-on of the establishment were round about the corners ready to give the alarm if any of the "slops" were near.

More than a score of gentlemen from Regent street, and the Haymarket, hearing of the fight, "going on on the extreme quiet," at the Clippers, hastened to witness it.

And when they got into the room, and saw a round or two, bets ran high.

"Make up a purse of ten pounds, gentlemen," said the landlord, "and the sport shall go on."

"Done," said several.

"It's a capital mill."

"I'll back the Coster."

"The big 'un *must* win," said the publican, who wished to get all the bets he could on the other side.

The fight continued.

Four fighting-men were found among those assembled, who, for a dollar each, were willing to second the men.

When Puggy next came up for the third round his face had been wiped, and he looked fresh and confident.

He advanced boldly, and hit Joey in the ribs with his right; the Coster repaid it with a smack on Puggy's right eye, which made it blink again, and grow black almost instantly.

Blow now followed blow in quick succession.

Puggy began to look very serious.

Joey was as lively as a cricket.

The Coster received all Puggy's blows on the chest and ribs.

But Joey invariably "landed" with the left and right on Puggy's face, nose, and eyes, until his countenance was cut and bruised and bumped in a shocking manner.

Puggy's heart began to fail him.

He had always looked upon Joey as an easy conquest.

But he had reckoned without his host.

Because Joey had always been a very quiet and civil fellow, and averse to fighting, Puggy looked upon him as a bit of a coward.

Now, however, the tables were turned.

Puggy looked more serious than ever.

His heart began to fail him.

He was also weak in the knees; but Joey was as strong as ever, and, except a few bruises on the body, was untouched.

Puggy began to think of crying "a go."

But he knew not in what way to do it without appearing to lose the battle and the purse.

He resorted to the old game.

First he complained of his knee being hurt, then of his thumbs being swollen; his boots hurt him, he was not "in condition," but had been very sick, &c.

But it was of no use.

The publican knew Puggy of old, and was well aware that he was a great coward at heart, though one of the greatest bullies that ever lived.

"Fight on! fight on!"

"There's nothing the matter."

"Finish him, little one."

"Use both your hands, my lad," said the publican to Joey, on the sly, "and you can sew him up in ten minutes. A pound a minute for you, recollect, if you win."

"Win! I mean to win!" said Joey, as he sat on his second's knee.

"I don't care a straw about the money, although I'm poor; but I do care about giving that sneaking rascal a good hiding. He's nothing else but a thief, and a liar. And now I've got him, I'll pay him off for getting three of my old pals lagged."

So saying Joey advanced to the scratch for the last round.

Seeing that Puggy began to show the "white feather," Joey made up his mind "to go in and win."

Amid great confusion and applause, he advanced and met Puggy in the middle of the ring.

A regular "slogging" match ensued.

Joey was all life and bustle.

He smashed Puggy's nose, and made it almost level with his face.

He knocked out several of his teeth, blackened both his eyes, and almost split open his jaw, and finished the battle, amid great applause, by knocking Master Puggy all of a heap upon the floor, where he lay senseless and immovable.

Amid great enthusiasm, Joey was carried out into an adjoining room in the arms of his admirers.

That was how Joey "served Puggy out."

## CHAPTER LXV.

### FRANK AND TOM MEET A VERY OBLIGING FRIEND IN THE HOUR OF NEED—WHAT HE DID.

WHILE Frank and Tom were at the opera enjoying themselves, and thinking but little of the duel that was to take place on the morrow, they made the acquaintance of a fine old military officer, named Count Cellini, who had served in all the previous battles of Italy, from 1848, when the brave Piedmontese were so gallantly led by Carlo Alberto.

The Count had heard much of the boy soldiers, and seemed delighted to make the acquaintance of two such gallant youths as Tom and Frank Ford.

After the performance at the opera, the Count accepted an invitation to sup with the two young Englishmen at their hotel.

Supper passed off with great good spirit, but as Frank sat at table over his wine, a servant handed him a letter.

An answer is required immediately.

Frank opened the note, which read:—

"Capt. FRANK FORD,

"DEAR SIR,—I received your acceptance of the Marquis de Sangri's challenge, and although most happy to do all I can in an amicable manner, I must, as his second, decline the presence of your brother as second on your part.

"There is no objection to his presence on the ground, but we would much prefer your selection of some Italian gentleman who would perform the office as second. If you would send an immediate answer, naming place, time, and weapon, it would much oblige."

Frank threw down the note in great annoyance. He knew not what to do.

Among all his acquaintance he knew no one who could, or perhaps would, perform the dangerous office of second.

"You look put out, my boy, about something," said the Count, in a good-humoured manner. "Are you ordered off to your company?"

"No, Count, something worse than that. I paid my final visit to the King this afternoon, but my own and my brother's success in war has created many enemies. This is the consequence," said he, shoving over the note for the Count to read.

"Oh, that's it, eh? my young fighting cock, eh? —began to duel already, eh?

"Yes, but what am I to do? I have no second; 'tis now past midnight, and I have nearly all the preliminaries to settle."

"'Tis a great pity," said the Count, "that any Italian soldier should try to pick any quarrel with one who has done so much good in the cause of Italian liberty; but although I don't like the office, and as you are young in the business, why, if you don't object, *I* will be your second. I have been 'called out' very often myself."

"Thank you—many thanks, Count," said Frank, in high glee. "Will you settle this little affair for me at once?"

"Certainly, my boy," said the Count, with as much coolness and good humour as if he were about to write out a check for £1,000 or more for Frank. "Give me pen, ink, and paper. I'll soon write the Major a line—he's a regular fire-eater. I know him well."

Within a few minutes the Count wrote a letter, stating that the Marquis de Sangri would be accommodated either with pistols or swords on the morrow, and to come to the ground provided with both weapons. The place selected was a small island in the narrow river, not more than a mile from the Marquis's estate.

All the necessary writing having been done, the letter was despatched, and Frank felt very easy in his mind.

"But in case anything in our little arrangement should miscarry, Frank, my boy," said the Count, good-humouredly, "I'll go over and settle this little affair personally for you with the Major. You must stay quiet in your hotel until I come back, and not go out of your apartments on any account. I've got a case of broad-barrelled pistols that will answer your purpose beautifully. If you were anything of a shot," said he, smiling, "I'd lend you my own pair of little favourites, with the ivory cross on them; they are beauties."

"I can hit the stem of a wine glass, at fifteen paces," said Frank, rather nettled at the tone in which the Count spoke.

"I don't care about that, Frank, my boy, you are too young to understand this barbarous practice of duelling which is forced upon us. You, and a great many more, can do fine things with the target in a pistol gallery, but, then you see, my boy, as neither the target nor the wine glass can hold a pistol levelled at you, you see that makes all the difference. Take your own pistols, then; look at me, hold your pistols, thus; no finger on the guard, these two on the trigger, they are not hair triggers, drop the muzzle a bit, bend your elbow a trifle more, sight your man outside your arm, outside mind, and pop the bullet right into his hip, if any higher so much the better."

The Count went forth, and soon returned. He threw himself on a sofa, and had a gentle doze for a couple of hours.

So did Frank and Tom.

At five o'clock they were called, and soon completed their toilet for the eventful meeting.

The old Count placed under his arm a small mahogany box which contained what he called his "peace makers," and led the way towards the hotel stables.

When the Count, Frank, and Tom reached the stable yard, no one was visible but Buttons.

He sat upon a stone step in a half-dreamy state, and seemed the very picture of misery.

As they approached, he suddenly rose, and giving them all a quick, searching look, seemed staggered at the small mahogany box the Count so affectionately handled.

"I see it all," gasped poor Buttons. "I heard of it before, but would not believe it; they are bent on murdering Captain Frank in a duel. I'll run off and inform the gendarmes."

But ere he had gone a few yards, Tom seized him by the collar.

"It won't do, Master Buttons. I know what you intend to do; but you shan't spoil sport, my brother *must* fight, his honour is staked."

"Oh, don't, don't go out to fight this duel, Master Frank; I am certain those black-looking villains want to kill you."

"Hold your tongue, or I'll cut off your head, Buttons," said Tom. "Do you want to alarm all the hotel and have us arrested for a breach of the peace?"

"So I will, so I will, but don't, don't do it."

"Do what, you whimpering donkey?" said Frank, vexed with Buttons.

"I'll soon stop his blubbering," said the Count, opening the mahogany box.

Taking out one of "the beauties," he cocked it leisurely, and pointed it at the head of poor Buttons.

"Speak another word, shed another tear, my lad, and I'll blow your brains out."

"Do it if you like," blubbered out poor Buttons. "Do it if you like, I'd rather have my brains blow nout than his."

He had scarcely spoken these words, when Tom and Frank, both laughing, took hold of Buttons and shoved him into a stable.

The Count, Frank, and Tom, soon got out a two-horse trap, and harnessed the horses.

"It's about an hour's smart drive where we have to go to," said the count, as he jumped into the trap and seized the reins, "but if we leave that young follower of yours—Buttons I mean—in the stable, he is sure to get out somehow, and spread the news all over the town."

"So he will," said Frank, "and instead of us meeting with De Sangri and his friends, we may fall into the arms of a company of soldiers."

So saying, he opened the stable door, let Buttons out, and gave him a seat in the trap.

They had travelled on some time in silence, when the old Count remarked,

"We are to cross the river on to the island. They won the choice of ground, and the marquis seems to like the spot very much. He shot a friend of mine there some two years ago; but he's got worse luck now, you know, my boy, for by all the rules of chance he can't do the same trick twice in succession."

The Count still went on conversing in a merry tone and talked of duelling much like as if it were only an innocent pastime.

"What are you thinking of, Frank, my lad?" said he after another pause, as he whipped up the horses into a brisker pace.

"I was just thinking if, after all, I should happen to kill the Marquis."

"Quite right, my lad, I don't think there is much danger in you doing more than wounding him, but if you only had the good fortune to do so, you know, I'll guarantee to settle everything for you. You are not a very great hand at pistols, I think, are you?"

"No, nothing to boast of; I am much better with the sword."

"Well, never mind if I lose the toss; I know De Sangri will select pistols, he's a great shot and he knows it, but never mind that; you've got a good eye, never take it off him after you're on the ground, follow him everywhere. De Sangri's father, that's now dead and gone, always killed his man in that manner; he had a way of looking without winking that was very fatal at a short distance, a sort of killing look, as one might say. But, by the bye, here we are at the river bank," said the Count, throwing the reins to Buttons, and jumping out upon the sand, very gaily.

"Yes, here we are," said Tom, slapping his brother Frank on the back, "here we are, the boat is in readiness for us. Now for the honour of old England."

"No fear of me not defending it," said Frank, "it is a case of life or death for one, if not both of us, Tom."

Tom Ford smiled bitterly, as he muttered between his teeth, but unheard by any one,

"If there is any foul play they shall pay dearly for it. If Frank falls he shall be bitterly revenged. I will never leave the island alive; both of us shall be buried in one grave!"

## CHAPTER LXVI.

### THE BOY BAND OUT ON A NIGHT ADVENTURE UNDER MAJOR CASPAR.

Major Caspar and the brave Boy Soldiers were not destined to remain long idle.

Captain Frank and Buttons had not started off to the king's head quarters more than a day or two, when an orderly officer rode up to Caspar's tent with a letter.

Caspar opened it, and read,

"Major Caspar must report at General Garibaldi's head quarters without delay on most urgent business."

"What can this mean, I wonder?" he said. "I have no sooner done one thing than they give me another. I wonder what's up this time? I hope none of Captain Frank's lads have got into any scrapes now that he is away. But my arm pains me dreadfully from the wounds I received when storming that fort."

He had not to remain long in doubt.

He went to Garibaldi's head quarters, and was immediately introduced to the old general.

"Major Caspar, I have sent for you on most important business, which brooks no delay."

"May I ask what it is, general?"

"Yes, I want you and a party of well-mounted volunteers to penetrate into the enemy's lines, ride round the country, and report to me all you see as to their strength, position, number of guns, and such like, for I believe, in a few days, we shall receive orders for a general advance upon the enemy, and it is necessary, therefore, to know as much about them as possible."

"From what regiment or corps am I to select my volunteers, general? It is a very dangerous expedition, and requires not only very brave and well-tried soldiers, but also expert and very light riders."

"True; well, then, select your own men, and I will take good care they shall be well mounted."

"I think I could pitch upon a company that would delight in the task, general."

"What company, major?"

"The English Boy Volunteers; they are all good horsemen, light riders, and as to their gallant bearing——"

"There is no question about that," said the general, with a smile. "Well, then, think over it; but in two days report yourself at my quarters ready for the expedition."

"We shall want some guns from the flying artillery."

"True; I will myself select two guns and have them doubly horsed and manned. Prepare yourself as soon as possible."

Caspar was delighted with the confidence which Garibaldi reposed in him, and went to his tent happy.

"What a treat this will be for the Boy Band," he thought; "all of them can ride like jockeys, and are as true as steel."

He wrote off immediately to Lieutenant Hugh Tracy, and, within half-an-hour after the receipt of the order, the Boy Soldiers were on their way, rejoicing at the prospect of what was before them; Fatty being the noisiest of all.

In less than two days Caspar had the pleasure of seeing all his plans arranged, and he called on the old general for his final orders.

"I have come to the conclusion, major," said the old general, "that, as the Austrians are very strong in cavalry, you had better take with you three companies of you own dragoons, besides the English Boy Volunteers; and, instead of two, have four pieces of flying artillery, so that if you are attacked you can make a stand, and give battle to the enemy."

This was all the instruction Caspar received from the old general, yet ere he started, the chief of the engineers gave Caspar a well-made and accurate map of the country he was going to ride through, with all the lanes and roads marked in red ink.

All being prepared, and the force paraded, Major Caspar started out late in the afternoon, and towards evening camped in a forest very near to the enemy's pickets.

Rising early in the morning, and before the heavy mist had cleared off the roads, Caspar with his four companies of volunteers, and his light cannon, dashed along the road, and as the Austrian pickets were unable to tell what the cloud of dust which they saw rising in the distance could mean Caspar's men rode through several small Austrian camps.

Some few prisoners were secured, and placed upon stolen horses, and onward went Caspar's men again.

They had not gone far, however, when they discovered several companies of Austrian hussars drawn up ready to receive them.

Caspar sounded a halt, prepared his men, and then dashed at the enemy sword in hand,

They did not stand, for the shock was too great' and they hurriedly dispersed in all directions, their officers being the last to leave the ground where their men had so disgraced themselves.

Pistols, swords, and other trophies were here picked up, and onward went the volunteers again

They had not progressed more than two miles, when another body of Austrians were discovered.

One company was sent on, to entice the enemy forward.

This had the desired effect.

The Austrians did not know that Caspar's main force was over the hill.

On came the Austrians full tilt up the hill.

But they had not got more than half way up, when Caspar and Hugh Tracy's men came over the hill, and rushed upon them with loud shouts.

The Austrians were unable to withstand the shock, and were broken up in a few minutes, and scattered like chaff before the wind.

Thus progressed Major Caspar's expedition through the enemy's country; wherever they met the foe, the brave lads soundly thrashed them, even when three to one against them.

But now Major Caspar played a clever trick upon the enemy.

As night was coming on, he halted his command in a forest, and called for Hugh Tracy.

"Hugh," said he, "I have over a hundred Austrian uniforms, perfect in all particulars, what shall I do with them?"

Hugh laughed.

"I see, your idea is like mine."

"Suppose I dress all my lads up in them, and let us go into the nearest village, and levy contributions from all who will not swear to be loyal to the Italian cause."

"That was just my idea," said Caspar. "Bring up the lads, let us transform them into Austrians at once."

Hugh Tracy told his brave lads of the intended trick, and his proposition was received with great joy.

Fatty rubbed his hands in great glee in anticipation of all the good things he and the rest were to enjoy.

Towards midnight they sallied forth to the nearest village, and from information furnished by an Italian sympathiser they found out the names of all who were true to the cause.

But while they were levying contributions right and left alarming news reached them.

They heard the sounds of distant firing.

Caspar's camp had been surrounded by a strong Austrian force.

Hugh Tracy collected his men on the instant, and prepared to returned to camp and to Caspar's assistance.

While on their way thither a messenger dashed forward to meet them.

"Quick! quick, Hugh! or we shall all be lost! Quick! quick! I say, or we shall all be butchered!"

With a loud hurrah! Hugh Tracy and his gallant lads galloped back to the rescue.

How they succeeded and what they did will quickly appear.

## CHAPTER LXVII.

### A COLD-BLOODED VILLAIN—FRANK'S DUEL.

As the boatmen pulled in towards the island all perceived, a few hundred yards off, a group of persons standing, whom they soon recognised as their opponents.

"Frank," said the count, grasping his arm tightly, as he stood up to spring on land, "Frank, although you are only a boy, I may say I have no fear for your courage; but, still, more than that is needful here.

"This De Sangri is a noted duellist, and will try to shake your nerve.

"Now, mind that you take everything that happens quite with an air of indifference.

"Don't let him think that he has any advantage over you, and you will see how the tables will be turned in your favour."

"Trust to me, count," said Frank; "I'll not disgrace my name or country."

He pressed Frank's hand tightly, and Frank thought that he discerned something like a slight twitch about the corners of the count's grim mouth, as if some sudden and painful thought had shot across his mind; but in a moment he was calm and stern-looking as ever.

"Twenty minutes late, count," said the short, red-faced little major, with a military frock, and foraging cap, as he held out his watch in evidence.

"I can only say, major, that we lost no time since we started; we had some difficulty in finding a boat; but in any case we are here now, and that I opine is the important part of the matter."

"Quite right; very just indeed. Will you present me to your young friend? Very proud to make your acquaintance, sir; a countryman of yours and I myself met more than once in this kind of way. His name was Beresford; I was out with him when he shot old De Sangri, who, by-the-bye, was called the crack shot of our city; but, begad, your countryman knocked his pistol hand to shivers, saying, in a dry way, 'he must try the left hand this morning.' Go out a little this side, please."

While the count and the major walked a few paces apart from where Frank stood, he had leisure to observe his antagonist, who stood among a group of his friends, talking and laughing away in great spirits.

As the tone they spoke in was not of the lowest, Frank could catch much of their conversation.

They were discussing the last occasion that the Marquis de Sangri had visited this spot, and talking of the fatal event that happened there.

"Poor devil," said De Sangri, "it wasn't his fault; but you see some officers of his regiment, it had been said, had been showing the white feather before that, and he was obliged to go out and fight.'

"In fact, the colonel said, 'fight or leave the corps.'

"When called out he came.

"It was a cold morning in February, with a frost the night before going off, with a thin rain.

"Well, it seems he had consumption or something of that sort, with a great cough and spitting of blood, and this weather made him worse, and he was very weak when he came to the duelling ground.

"Now," said the vain marquis, laughing, "the moment I caught a glimpse of him, I said to myself, 'he's got pluck enough, but is as nervous as a lady,' for his eye wandered all about, and his mouth was always twitching.

"'Take off your great coat,' said one of his friends, when they were going to put him up, 'take it off, man.'

"He seemed to hesitate for an instant, when one of my friends remarked, laughing, 'ah, let him alone, it's his mother makes him wear it for the cold he has.'

"They all began to laugh at this, but I kept my eye upon him. And I saw that his cheek grew quite livid and a kind of grey colour, and his eyes filled up.

"'I have you now,' said I to myself," and, said the Marquis de Sangri, with the laugh of a demon, "*I shot him through the lungs.*"

"And this poor fellow," thought Frank, "was the only son of a widowed mother."

Frank walked from the spot to avoid hearing further, and felt, as he did so, something like a spirit of fiery vengeance rising within him for the fate of one so entirely cut off.

"Here we are, all ready," cried the major, springing over a fence into the adjoining field, "take your ground, gentlemen, we have tossed for weapons, De Sangri has won—pistols must decide it."

The count took Frank's arm, and walked forward.

"Frank," said he, "I am to give the signal. I'll drop my glove when you are to fire, but don't look at me at all. I'll manage to catch De Sangri's eye, and do you watch him steadily—and fire when he does."

"I think that the ground we are leaving behind us is rather better," said some one.

"So it is," said De Sangri, "but it may be troublesome to carry the young Englishman down that way, after I have killed him—here it is all easy."

The next instant they were placed before each other, and Frank long and well remembered that the first thought that struck him was, that there could be no chance of either of them escaping.

"Now, then," said the count, "I'll walk twelve paces, turn, and drop this glove, at which signal both of you fire—and together, mind.

"The man who reserves his shot falls by *my* hand."

This very summary denunciation seemed to meet general approbation, and the count strutted forth.

Notwithstanding the advice of his friend, Frank could not help turning his eyes from De Sangri to watch the tall retiring figure of the count.

At length he stopped.

A second or two elapsed.

He wheeled rapidly round and let fall the glove.

Frank's eyes glanced toward his opponent.

He raised his pistol and fired! His hat turned half round on his head, and De Sangri fell motionless to the earth.

Frank saw the people rush forward, and caught two or three glances thrown at him with an expression of revengeful passion.

Frank felt some one grasp him round the waist and hurried him from the spot, and it was at least ten minutes after, as they were skimming the surface of the river, before Frank could well collect his scattered faculties to remember all that was passing.

The count, pointing to the two bullet holes in Frank's hat, remarked,

"Sharp practice, my brave lad. It was the overcharge that saved you."

"Is he killed?" Frank asked.

"Not quite, I believe, but as good as killed. You took him just above the hip."

"Can he recover?" said Frank, with a tremulous voice, which he vainly endeavoured to conceal from Tom.

"Not if the doctor can help it," said the count, smiling, "for the fool keeps poking about for the ball; but now let's think of the next step. You'll have to leave this part of the country, and at once too."

Little more then passed between them.

As they neared the land a strange spectacle caught their eyes.

For a considerable distance along the shore, crowds of country people, De Sangri's tenants, were assembled, who, forming in groups, had evidently been watching with great anxiety what had taken place on the little island.

Now the distance was at least one mile, therefore any part of the transactions which had been enacting there must have been quite beyond their view.

While Frank was wondering at this, the count cried out suddenly,

"Too infamous! By Jove, we're murdered men!"

"What do you mean?" said Frank.

"Don't you see that?" said the count, pointing to something black which floated from a pole at the opposite side of the river, on the island.

"Yes; what is it?"

"It's De Sangri's coat they've put upon an oar, to show the people, his tenants, that he's killed, that's all. Every man here, on the river bank, is his tenant, and look there! They're not giving us much doubt as to their intention, the villains."

Here a tremendous yell burst from the mass of people along the river bank, which, rising to a terrific cry, sank gradually to a low wailing, then rose and fell again several times, as the death-cry filled the air and rose to heaven, as if imploring vengeance upon a murderer.

The appalling influence of these "death-cries," as they are called, had been familiar to Frank from the time of his first arrival in Italy, but it needed the awful situation he was placed in to consummate its horrors.

He knew well, none better, the vengeful character of the peasants of the country, and that his death was certain he had no doubt.

## CHAPTER LXVIII.

THE EXCITING CHASE—THE ROCKY CHANNEL—THE SUDDEN SQUALL—THE GREAT PERIL OF ALL ON BOARD—THE ESCAPE.

As the boatmen looked from him toward the shore' and again at Frank's face, they, as if instinctively' lay upon their oars, and waited for the Count's decision as to what course to pursue.

"Rig the sprit-sail, my boys," said Tom, "and let her head be up the river, and be alive, for I see they are baling a boat below the reef, there, and will be after us in no time."

The poor fellows, who, although strangers to Frank and the Count, sympathising in what they perceived to be Frank's imminent danger, righted the light spar which acted as mast, and shook out their scanty rag of canvas in a minute.

Tom, meanwhile, went aft, and, steadying the boat's head with an oar, held the small craft up to the wind till she lay completely over, and, as she rushed through the water, ran dipping her gunwale through the white foam.

"Where can we make to without tacking, my lads?" asked the gallant Tom.

"If it blows on as fresh as it does now, sir," said the boatmen, recognizing a thorough sailor in Tom, "we shall run ashore within half a mile of the new battery."

"Put out an oar to leeward," said Tom in a cheery tone, "and keep her more up to the wind, and I promise you, my lads, you shall be well paid for your trouble if you land us near the new battery."

"Here they come," said one of the boatmen, in mortal terror as he pointed back with his finger to a large yawl which shot out suddenly from the shore, with six sturdy fellows pulling at their oars.

Three or four others on board of her were endeavouring to get up their rigging, which appeared tangled and confused at the bottom of their boat.

The white splash of water, which each moment fell beside the pursuing vessel, showed that the process of baling her out was still continued.

"Then the devil admire me, but it's the old 'Dolphin' the villains have launched to pursue us," said one of Frank's boatmen.

"What's the 'Dolphin,' then?" asked Tom, smiling.

"An old boat that belongs to the Marquis de Sangri, that hasn't seen water except when it rained these four years or more, and is sun-cracked from stem to stern."

"She can sail, however," said Tom, who was looking intently at the pursuing craft, and was not at all pleased with her rapid progress through the water.

"No mistake about that, sir; they say she was once a smuggler's boat, and she's well used to sailing. But see, sir, how hard the crew are pulling after us."

"Lay out upon your oars, my merry men," said Tom, "the wind is failing us."

The sailors now began to flag lazily, and the wind to die away.

"It's no use, your honour; we shall only break our hearts in trying to escape from the 'Dolphin;' they are sure to overtake us," said one of the boatmen surlily.

"Do as I bid you," said Tom, in an angry tone, and looking daggers at the boatmen. "Do as I tell you. What is that I see ahead of us?"

"It is called the Oat Rock, sir. A vessel with grain was coming up the river, and struck there, and went down with all hands on board three years ago."

"There's no channel between it and the shore," said another. "It's all hidden rock, every inch of it."

"Good," said Tom; "here comes a fresh breeze, my lads."

The sail fell over as he spoke, and the little craft lay close to it until the foaming waters bubbled over her lee bow.

"Keep her head up, sir; higher, still higher, sir," said one of the boatmen in fear.

But Tom, at the helm, little heeded what they said, but steered straight for the dangerous channel spoken of between the Oat Rock and the shore.

"Heaven preserve us," said the terrified boatmen, in a breath. "The Englishman is steering straight in among the rocks. Death is certain; we shall all be drowned."

"Sacristi," said one, in a fierce tone to Tom; "why don't you keep her head away from the fatal channel? I shan't be drowned for any of your mad English whims."

As he spoke, he rose up, looking black as thunder, and drew a dirk, muttering curses between his teeth.

"Sit down, sit down there and be still," said Tom in a determined tone. "Sit down, I tell you. Don't I know more about a boat than such a thick-head as you are?"

To show what he really meant to do if the boatman did not obey him, Tom drew out a revolver from his breast.

"Sit down, I say, and don't stir for your lives until I order you," he said, with an angry oath; "unless you want some leaden ballast to make you do so."

"Here, Frank," said he, coolly handing over his revolver; "take this, and if those ugly-looking rascals dare do anything contrary to my orders hile I am steering, pull trigger and let 'em have it. You understand me?"

The boatmen sat down sulkily, muttering all manner of strange things, and with flashing eyes.

The small craft was now actually flying through the water.

Tom's object was a clear one to the Count and Frank.

They saw that sailing as they did, their craft was no match for the "Dolphin" pursuing them.

Their only chance for life and safety lay in reaching the narrow and dangerous channel between the sunk rock and the shore.

By doing this they could very greatly distance their pursuers.

Nothing but the great danger behind them could warrant such rash daring.

The whole channel was dotted with patches of white and breaking foam, the sure evidence of the dangers beneath.

Here and there a dash of spurting spray flew up from the dark waters where some cleft rock lay hidden beneath.

Escape, however, seemed impossible.

But who would not have preferred even so slender a chance of escape, with so frightful an alternative behind them, of falling into the hands of De Sangri's infuriated tenantry?

As if to add terrors to the scene, Tom had scarcely turned the boat ahead of the channel when an ominous blackness spread over all around.

Thunders pealed forth, and, amid the pattering of hail and the bright, almost blinding flashes of lightning,

A squall struck them!

The squall struck the little craft suddenly with great violence, and laid them nearly keel uppermost for several minutes.

The little craft righted herself, however, and rushed through the dark and blackening flood almost half filled with water.

All on board were obliged to kneel down, and hold tight to the gunwales for safety.

Roll after roll of thunder, loud and deafening broke right over head.

In the swift, hissing, dashing rain around them every object was hidden.

The other boat was now lost to view.

The terrified boatmen looked more dead than alive.

They were livid pale.

Each moment they expected to find a watery grave.

They knelt down, and began to pray.

Tom and Frank were the only two persons who seemed careless, and indifferent to all dangers.

Even the Count felt fearful, and as he looked first at Frank, and then at Tom, those two gallant youths chatted and laughed.

"These English are sea-devils," he muttered, "they don't know what peril is, they laugh during this horrid storm, as if it were only child's play."

As Tom, still at the rudder, guided the craft, he could not help but smile at the frightened boatmen, and was about to give them a word of comfort when—

A second squall, more terrible than the first, struck the little craft.

The small mast bent over under it, and snapped asunder with a sharp report like that of a pistol shot.

It tumbled over the stern, and trailed the sail along the milky sea.

Meanwhile the water rushed clean over them, and the boat seemed to be settling down in the current.

At this dreadful moment the boatmen turned their eyes upon Frank, and in horror muttered,

"This all comes of helping a murderer to escape! A murderer he is, for he has killed the Marquis."

Had it not been for Frank's revolver, which he held ready cocked, it is more than likely that the terrified and superstitious boatmen would have seized both of the brothers and pitched them overboard.

There was so much firmness about the two young Englishmen, however, that they dared not move.

Tom at the rudder was as calm and cold as ice.

He seemed to rollick in the dangers of the deep, as much so as Frank did in those of a soldier's life.

The Count, however, did not know what to make of these repeated squalls, and looked pale and resigned.

Meanwhile, the boat flew through the darkness and the hissing waters, and Tom seizing a favourable moment, he and Frank unshipped what remained of the little mast, and threw it overboard.

The storm now began to abate.

The black mass of clouds broke up, and in a short time it was sufficiently clear to perceive the pursuing vessel in the distance.

All on board of her seemed to be engaged in baling the boat out.

The 'Dolphin' seemed to be sinking!

The mist which had hidden the two vessels no sooner dispersed than those on board the 'Dolphin' ceased baling out the sinking vessel, and looking towards Frank's boat, burst forth into a yell, so wild savage, and so dreadful in its meaning, that it was enough to make the stoutest heart quail again, as the shouts fell upon Frank's ear.

The boatmen huddled together, and prayed.

When they heard the dreadful shout of their pursuers they turned paler than ever.

They crossed themselves, and muttered.

"Heaven help us this day, if the 'Dolphin' with the dead Marquis's tenants overtake us, we shall all be murdered in cold blood."

Tom and Frank, however, no sooner heard the yell than they raised a shout of defiance, and waved their hats in triumph.

Onwards dashed this gallant little craft through the dangerous channel.

"We are safe now," said Tom, in high glee, just as they had cleared the last group of sunken rocks, over which the waters foamed. "We are safe now, Count," said he, "the storm and all peril is over."

"The 'Dolphin' can't follow us through that channel," said Frank, "she is too large, and draws too much water."

"True, brother," Tom replied, "they will have to go right round, and thus we have gained a mile of ground; the river makes a long winding sweep just at that point."

"Here we are near the new battery," said the Count, "and right glad am I that we have escaped these bloodthirsty pursuers, for as sure as life, all of us would have been butchered, if De Sangri's people had laid hands on us."

"Yes, but what are *we* to do," asked the boatmen, "we must flee as well as yourselves, and what is to become of the boat."

"We'll look after all that," said Frank cheerily. Run the craft ashore, Tom."

"Yes, ground her anywhere," said the Count, "so that we get on land again."

"You English are as fond as ducks of water, but I hate it.

Tom laughed, and ere many minutes, grounded the vessel.

In doing so, the boat struck heavily upon a small rock close in to shore.

The bows were stove in with the shock.

All on board jumped on shore hurriedly.

In a moment after, the little craft which had so gallantly braved all dangers and perils of that exciting trip, split into halves.

It was a perfect wreck.

"Make haste, make haste," said one of the boatmen, "the 'Dolphin' is flying through the water; they are going to ground her higher up; if they land they may cut off our retreat."

Tom, Frank, and the Count, turned to look.

Sure enough, those on board the 'Dolphin,' perceiving that ere long she must sink, were running her aground, just ahead of the Oat Rock channel.

So intent were all in watching this manœuvre, that they thought not of flying, and of their own danger.

"They have grounded," said Tom.

All looked in the direction indicated, and could perceive those on board the stranded vessel leaping on shore wildly.

They could see Frank and the others, lower down on the river bank, and as they did so, raised loud shouts of vengeance, brandished their weapons, and hurried off to gain possession of the road, before Frank and his party could do so.

"There will be a bloody fight, I'm thinking," said Tom.

"It is a race for life," said the Count; "if they gain the high road before we do, I fear blood will freely flow."

"Fly! fly!" said the terrified boatmen.

"I scorn to fly before such a rabble as that," said Frank.

"But, my boy, take advice, be advised by me, we *must* fly."

"I will not fly for any one," said Tom, in a surly tone. "Englishmen scorn to do such a thing; they are only three to one."

"*Only*," said the Count.

"Yes, only," said Frank; "I have fought against greater odds than that many a time."

"Come, come," said the Count. "Be advised by me. Let us try to gain the high road first; but if the villains are there before us, and are bent on killing us, why, then, we'll make short work of them, that's all."

"Agreed!" said Tom. "They can only kill us."

"Only kill us, eh?" growled the boatmen, and looked astonished.

They wished to walk behind, and began to mutter among themselves in a very threatening manner.

But Frank and Tom soon put a stop to that.

The boatmen were forced to walk in front.

The Count, Frank, and Tom, followed, each with pistols in their hands.

"You don't know these rascals as well as I do," said the Count. "They would kill you in a moment if they got half a chance."

# THE BOY SOLDIER; OR, GARIBALDI'S YOUNG CAPTAIN.

BUTTONS IS STARTLED BY THE SKELETON IN THE BOX.—*See next Number.*

Just while he spoke a squadron of dragoons was seen approaching at a hard gallop.

"What can this mean?" said Frank.

"I don't know; without it is they come to arrest us."

"And why?"

"De Sangri is in some way related to the royal family."

"What!" said Frank, astonished.

"He is, though not so vastly wealthy, you know; but he's got title, that's everything in Italy, and if he's dead you have rid the world of one of the greatest villains that ever lived. He has ruined many daughters of the best families in Italy, and



afterwards vindicated his own honour, as it is called, by killing their brothers and other relations in duels."

"And that was his intention towards Nelly Lancaster," said Frank, with an angry and flushed cheek.

"Without a doubt. He would have borrowed all the money he possibly could from her silly old father, under the pretence of marrying his daughter, and then when he had got all he could, would have dishonoured the girl, if he could, then left her, and afterwards laugh in old Lancaster's face."

"The villain!" said Frank.

While he spoke the dragoons drew near.

## CHAPTER LXIX.

### TOM'S GALLANT TARS GO ON A SPREE—WHAT THEY DID AT THE PLAY.

But while Tom Ford is away duelling with his brother Frank, let us take a glance at what his crew did.

Tom's fame upon the waters had spread far and wide.

Among the first to hear of his exploits were numerous English sailors.

Now as Tom had lost nearly all his original crew of Italian seamen, he determined, if possible, to make up the required number by enlisting Englishmen at the different ports he called at.

The prospects of "plenty of fun and lots of prize money," acted like a charm upon numbers of English seamen, who ran away from their ships, and joined the Italian cause, under the leadership of gallant Tom.

With a first-class crew of hardy English volunteers, Tom was able to do much more against the Austrians than he had been able to do with his former Italian crew.

"For brave as they might be," Tom said, "they can't come up in anything to our own gallant British tars."

In a short time many prizes were sent into port, and lots of money was the consequence.

The number of Austrian merchant ships that Tom captured and sold was considerable.

When, therefore, Tom returned to Leghorn with his gallant craft, each man had a large amount of money to receive.

Wherever they went they were well received, and soon picked up sufficient knowledge of the Italian language not only to speak on ordinary topics; but could enjoy themselves at theatres and the like.

But the British tar doesn't like operas.

He rather rejoices in a bloody five-act play, wherein there is any amount of fighting.

In order to please the gallant British tars who had rendered such good service in the cause of Italian liberty, the good-natured people of Leghorn puzzled their brains in all manner of ways to get up various amusements for them.

Among other things, and that which pleased Tom's English crew most was, that the mayor had promised that a large portion of a small theatre should be given up to them free on a certain night, and the performance selected for their amusement was the tragedy of "Othello."

The gallant tars were delighted at the prospect of seeing an English tragedy, and when the theatre opened, the sailors were not slow to seize good places.

In fact, the small theatre was crammed with people.

Some came to see for the first time an English tragedy, and others more especially to have a good look at Tom Ford's brave blue-jackets.

The tragedy progressed, but brandy, wine, and other drinks had got into the sailor's heads, and they were very noisy, and made great fun of the chief character, Othello, because he was, they said,

"A big, ugly, black nigger, and nothing shorter."

When Othello came to the passage where he says,

"And this—and this—the greatest discords be" (kissing the fair Desdemona) "that e'er our hearts shall make—"

"I'll bet a week's grog," roars out one of the tars, "that their first young 'un 'll be a creole!"

"Aye, sink 'em!" said another "there's the luck o' them black devils. Why, 'twas only t'other day I twigs the young captain's steward in tow with one o' the freshest, rosy-cheeked little craft as you'd see in a day's sail through Leghorn!"

Cassio's silly speech, where he reels about, and sings,

"Do not think I am drunk, &c.——"

"No, not you," roared out another at the top of his voice. "Why not walk the plank, and prove yourself sober, mate? That's what we do."

These interruptions caused much laughter on the part of all present, for any one could see that the sailors took the tragedy in too serious a light.

But whatever excitement the sailors had shown during the first part of the play was nothing compared to the noise, tumult, and din that existed on all sides when the jealous Moor of Venice approaches Desdemona's bed to murder her.

The shouts at this particular part became alarming.

Volleys of oaths were hurled at Othello's head; "his eyes and limbs" were cursed until they couldn't swear any more.

"What!" shouted out one of the loudest of the crew, "can the black brute cut her life-lines, eh, Bill? She's a reg'lar-built angel, and as like my Bet as two peas in a pod!"

"Aye," said another, striking the box front vigorously; "it all comes of being jealous, messmates, and that's all as one as being mad. But if he does kill her, why in course he'll get scragged, Harry, my boy."

When Othello seizes Desdemona by the throat in bed, she shrieks for permission to say but one short prayer, and he will not grant it.

The gallant blue-jackets were worked up to a fearful pitch of excitement.

They could endure it no longer, and gave the most alarming indication of their determination to mix in the murderous scene below.

"I'm hanged, Dick, if I can stand it any longer," shouts out one in the boxes.

"You are no men if you sit quietly there, and see the poor gal murdered," said several, in reply.

"Hands off, you bloodthirsty black villain!" roared out another.

In the twinkling of an eye, a lot of sailors clambered out of the boxes, the pit and the gallery, and scrambled over every one in their way till they reached the noisy boatswain's mate, who was struggling to get on the stage.

Many persons now became seriously alarmed, and rushed from the house in terror.

The musicians had their instruments broken, and fought like mad-men to beat back the English tars.

Fiddles, drums, trombones and the like were smashed on every side.

The fight became general.

"Now's our time, lads," roared the sailors.

"Pipe the boarders away, all hands, if you're a man as loves a woman."

"Now for it! Go it, you cripples, wooden legs are cheap!"

The sailors, hearing their boatswain's pipe, dashed furiously over all obstacles.

Smash went the footlights.

The feeling became general, and the sailors, led on by the boatswain, swept all before them.

Out poured all the actors from the side scenes to assist Othello.

It was all to no purpose.

The sailors fought right and left like young bears.

Desdemona was carried away in triumph by the tars.

Othello slipped behind the scenes out of the way

of a broken head, and ran wild through the street in full costume.

But the rumpus did not end here.

Some unlucky person, in excitement, turned off nearly all the gaslights!

This added to the intense confusion.

Shouts and yells and screams were heard on every hand.

Almost in total darkness the sailors hit right and left.

Some were knocked into the pit.

A fat Italian actor lost his footing, and fell into a broken drum, and rolled all about the orchestra.

The benches were torn up in the pit.

The box curtains were all pulled to pieces.

The side scenes were all rent and torn.

It was a perfect Babel of noise, confusion and discord.

Oaths and yells, and shouts and screams were heard on every hand.

Everybody imagined that the English sailors had gone mad every one of them.

The police were called in.

But these got so roughly handled by the gallant tars that they were only too happy to get out of the scrape.

They made a rush upon the stage it is true.

But it is a notable fact that in a moment afterwards they rushed off again in an alarming hurry, chased by the Jack tars all through the streets, until they reached their own ship again, safe and sound, gloriously tight, singing, shouting, and dancing like so many escaped lunatics.

Such had been the havoc made by Tom's men, that the little theatre was a perfect wreck, and a wilderness of broken benches.

## CHAPTER XX.

IMPORTANT DISCLOSURES—A FRIEND IN NEED—THE ITALIAN DETECTIVE—THE FLIGHT.

THE appearance of the dragoons, it must be confessed, did not look very re-assuring either to Frank, Tom, or the count.

But still they met their gaze fixedly and proudly, nor did they betray the slightest fear.

The whole party proceeded quietly to the town of Leghorn, and escaped the attacks of the infuriated peasantry of the Marquis de Sangri.

The boatmen, greatly to their pleasure and surprise, were well paid for their trouble, and departed with many expressions of thanks for the generosity of the "gallant young Englishman," although a little before that they had been very loud in their denunciations of him.

When the dragoons reached the town, the commandant approached Frank, and said,

"Signor, my orders are that you must remain in your hotel until you receive an important communication from the War Office."

Neither Frank, Tom, nor the count could make out what all this meant, but still they obeyed orders, and indulged themselves freely in wine and conversation.

"Lor' bless you, my gallant lads, *I* wouldn't be cast down by anything that dragoon officer said."

"But, what important information can they send to *us?*" said Tom, who was very impatient to join his ship once more.

"We haven't done anything of consequence," said Frank.

"No, you have only shot a man, that's all," said the count.

"Well, and what of that? Didn't he insult and challenge brother Frank?"

"Quite true, my bold young English tar," said the count, tossing off a bumper. "Killing a man isn't so very great a crime in this Italy of ours, where nearly every one carries knives and pistols, but——"

"But what?"

"This De Sangri is no ordinary fellow, you know, and, it may be, that some enemy of yours has sent some information to the government, which may cause them alarm."

"True," said Frank, "that is possible. But who could have done so?"

"We have no enemies that I know of," said Tom, indignantly.

"Are you sure?" said the count, thoughtfully.

"Yes."

"*Quite* sure?"

"Yes; why do you ask so seriously?"

"Nothing, my brave lad, but I think you have enemies about."

"Indeed!"

"Yes. Come, now, don't be offended with an old soldier like me; but think again. Haven't you any enemy you can think of?"

After a moment's reflection, Frank said,

"I have had a cur at my heels all my life, but cannot think he would be base enough to turn an open enemy when I spared his life in Basil the Bandit's cave."

"But I do," said the count; "you shouldn't have dealt so mercifully with him, for when a cur attempts to bite, kick him well—he will fight shy afterwards. What's the fellow's name?"

"Joel Flint."

"What! it cannot be," said the count, in surprise, "are you sure that that is his name?"

"I am."

"Does he not go under any other sometimes?"

"Yes, I have heard that he calls himself Schmidt."

"The very man," said the count, slapping the table until the wine bottles danced again; "by Jove! how lucky."

"What do you mean?"

"I mean, my lad, that this same fellow, to my own positive knowledge, has been dogging your footsteps from the very hour when those two ruffians attempted to take your life in the opera house."

"You do not mean that?"

"I do."

"Explain."

"This same rascal, under various names, and in all sorts of disguises, has managed to get into society he has no right or title to. At one of Mr. Lancaster's parties, I perceived he paid particular attention to De Sangri, who, from some chance expression he heard, made him believe that the marquis hated your very name."

"Now I begin to see into it all," said Frank, biting his lip. "He it was, then, who, by cunning words, loans of money, and anonymous letters, urged him on to violent measures against me."

"Yes, you have hit the right nail on the head this time," said the count. "I never thought of mentioning this to you before, but now I see it all; everything is as plain as noonday."

"But why should the dragoons have been on the look-out for us?"

"That is explained very quickly. Had you been killed all would have gone right with this rascal Flint; but as you killed his friend, I have no doubt in the world that he received a hasty message, and on the instant lodged false information against you, either with the prefect of police or at the war office."

"Oh! the remorseless villain!"

"But how can he prove anything against me?" asked Tom, indignantly.

"Easily enough. He has plenty of money, and that can do anything. For a thousand or two of pounds he could buy up a dozen false witnesses, aye, two or three dozen; for the lower order of our Italians are knaves at heart."

"But what had we better do?" asked Frank.

"Go up stairs, pack up your things, and make ready for an instant start."

"But we cannot do so."

"Yes you can; you have not been put under arrest, nor have either of you given your words of honour as officers and gentlemen not to leave this place."

"True, we have not."

"Then why stand upon ceremony; make good your escape; it will be much better than to lay rotting in a gaol until the war is over, at the mere false information given against you by this rascal, Joel Flint. I know these Italians better than you do."

Acting upon the count's advice, Frank and Tom hastened up to their apartments, and began to pack up.

They left the count alone discussing his wine and smoking cigars.

He had not been very long so engaged, however, when a young stranger, neatly attired as a civilian, hastily entered the room in which he was.

"Count," said he, "where are the two young Englishmen?"

"Why do you ask?"

"I have information which must reach their ears at once."

"Indeed! then who are you, pray?"

"I am one of the secret police."

"Oh, oh! and what business have you with them?"

"I have an important communication to make to them." (See cut in No. 22.)

"I cannot see how that can be, seeing that you are one of the secret police."

"It is easily explained. They have befriended me and mine—saved them from death."

"Who, pray?"

"Teresa, Garibaldi's female spy."

"And because they did that——"

"I have waited for an opportunity of repaying their great kindness and bravery, by disclosing to them the plot which is laid for their very lives."

"Go on. I am surprised. How came all this about?"

"It all followed from Captain Frank's duel with the Marquis de Sangri."

"I know it."

"But, for a long time, this young English wretch, Flint, or Schmidt—whatever his right name is—has been bribing all sorts of people to give false information against the two gallant brothers, Frank Jude in particular."

"As I supposed, and spent large sums, I have no doubt."

"Yes, very large sums."

"And you accepted a bribe?"

"I did, but never intended to hurt them."

"As the brother of Teresa, you could not have done so, without proving a great scoundrel."

The detective laughed, as he said,

"I threw myself in the way of this false Englishman, Flint, and, while I took his money, I got all the information I could out of him."

"Very wisely done," smiled the count. "And what charges has this English rascal made against them?"

"He gave information this morning that the Boy Band of young Garibaldians intended to turn traitors, go over to the Austrians, and tell the Archduke Albrecht all our plans."

"The villain!"

"This was all the more villanous, because it is already known in influential circles that the whole Italian army under the king's command intends to march against the Austrians in four days at the furthest."

"I never heard this before."

"But I did. More than this. Flint has sworn that the two brothers are concerned in a most horrible murder committed on their poor old uncle some time ago in England."

"I cannot believe such a monstrous charge."

"Nor I either; but this Flint has gone so far as to swear that Major Caspar and all the rest have had dealings and correspondence with that pest of the mountains known as Basil the Bandit."

"These are strong charges."

"But the last and worst charge is, that he offers to prove their cowardice before the enemy, notwithstanding all the gallant deeds they have performed."

"The imp of the devil!" said the count, with a fierce oath. "Why, braver lads never drew a sword!"

"Every one knows it, count, but the prefect of police has given orders to have them arrested."

"But it shall not be!" said the count; "I will stand their friend through thick and thin, if I die for it!"

"And so will I," said Tomasso, the detective, "and already I have proved my fidelity to them."

"In what manner?"

"As soon as I got positive information of what this Flint intended to do, I wrote off to Major Caspar, Hugh Tracy, and the rest, telling them of the storm that was approaching, and begged of them to hold themselves in readiness to fly at an hour's notice."

"But that cannot be done. Where is the ship to convey them?"

"I have it in readiness. Last night, I went on board Captain Tom Ford's vessel, and informed the officer in command of everything."

"And what did the English lieutenant say?"

"He swore he would blow Leghorn to atoms if the authorities dared to lay a hand on their gallant captain and his brother."

"Bravo! Bravo!" said the count; "that's just like those English tars; they don't care about the very devil himself when their blood is up."

"The two brave lads must be informed of this at once," said the detective.

"Very right and proper; but if we do get away, we'll teach these Austrians that we are not cowards. The Boy Band shall fight one more battle, and then Captain Frank can do as he pleases—stand his trial, retire from the service, or remain in it, just as he pleases."

"There is one piece of advice I would give, then," said the detective.

"And what is that?"

"Why, do not persuade them to return to England yet."

"And why, pray? Are two brave boys to be accused of atrocious crimes, and not endeavour to sustain their untarnished honour?"

"No, I do not mean that; nothing in the world would please me more than that they should do so."

"Then why advise them otherwise?"

"'From information I have received,' as the English detectives say, I have reason to believe that Sergeant Gale is already on the track of the true culprits, and if Frank or Tom appear upon the scene at an improper moment, it might cause fresh complications, and, perhaps, thwart the ends of justice."

"But how could *you* get to know all this?"

"Why, with Joel Flint's own money."

"I cannot see that, for, from what I have heard, the English police *cannot* be bribed to give information."

The Italian detective laughed, as he said—

"Policemen all over the world are alike in many things, and I can tell you that a few florins in Italy, like a few pounds in England, have a wonderful effect on constables, and they will swear white is black, if they only have a chance. The reason of this is they are over worked, and very badly paid. It is true, if you wish a detective to get you out of a scrape, you must 'palm' him far more heavily than a man in uniform—for you must know this much, detectives themselves are watched by detectives, as constables are by constables, for in the police force no one would trust another further than they can see him, and, in most cases, they look upon every man, woman, and child as born thieves and vagabonds."

"Not a very flattering description, certainly," said the count, laughing,

"No; but it is true, though, count; and the way I got my information is easily told, for the King of Italy has Italian detectives in England like he has in Leghorn, and everywhere else; these know the English ones, so they are well informed of all that's going on, whether it concerns them individually or not."

"You are a clever——"

"Rogue you would have said, count," the detective remarked, laughing. "Well, as you please; I have only done my duty to two trusty, gallant friends in this instance, for they deserve all that one true man can do for another. I have fulfilled my mission, and am satisfied. I must leave the rest to themselves."

"You are very kind," said the count, "and to reward you, here is my purse," said he, offering it to Tomasso.

The Italian detective shook his head, and looked grave.

"No money between friends," said he, with a look of annoyance.

Taking up his hat, he was about to depart, and said,

"Captain Frank will find his Boy Band on the road towards Verona. The Italian army is ready to advance on Verona, leaving Peschiera on the left about ten miles. The army will not move for four or five days."

So speaking, he bowed himself out, and left.

"This is a bold fellow," thought the count; "but who knows but what he may be a spy, after all? I must advise my young friends to depart at once, in case the detective's plausible tale might prove nought else but a trap to secure them."

When informed of this conversation, both Frank and Tom were much amazed.

Buttons was astonished, and swore very loudly for a youth of his inches that—

"He wouldn't stay in Leghorn, to be clapped into a loathsome gaol for six months, on a trumpery charge made up by Joel Flint, or any one else."

He was dying to rejoin Fatty and the Boy Band, and when the count, Frank, and Tom, after a short council of war, decided to depart that very night, he danced and kicked up his heels in such a wild, extravagant manner, that the Italian cooks and chambermaids thought the droll English boy had taken leave of his senses.

That same night, when no one expected it, Frank, Tom, the count, and Buttons boldly walked out of their hotel towards Tom's ship.

As they approached the landing, they were recognised, and surrounded by a large posse of police.

"That's your man—seize him!" said the chief pointing to Frank.

In an instant Frank, Tom, and the count drew their swords, and fought their way through bravely.

They must have soon been overpowered, however, but, just as the police were gathering stronger and stronger each moment, a loud shout was heard from the waterside.

A loud, ringing English cheer resounded in the air.

In an instant Frank's party were joined by a strong boat's crew from Tom's ship, who, cutlass and pistol in hand, dispersed the Italian police force like chaff before the wind.

In an instant two brawny sailors seized Frank, and carried him in triumph to their boat, and in a few minutes another loud cheer told the Italian officers that the English youths were then safely and triumphantly on their way towards Tom's gallant barque.

In less than half an hour Tom stood on the quarter deck of his gallant craft, and she sailed from Leghorn with every inch of canvas set, and dashed through the sparkling waves like a thing of life.

"Ho-o-ray! ho-o-ray!" shouted young Buttons, with all his might; "ho-o-ray, we shall soon join the Boy Band again."

"Yes," said Frank, in his ear, "but before we leave Italy, we must join in the first battle that takes place, to show these lying rascals that we are not cowards, but made of sterling English steel; and when that is over, we'll all seek adventures in another clime before we return to England."

"Where to?" asked Buttons, with breathless curiosity.

"Why, in—Mexico; to help the people this time, and not tyrannical upstarts who call themselves kings."

## CHAPTER LXXI.

THE COUNT NARRATES THE EXPERIENCE OF AN OLD SOLDIER—CADET'S LIFE—THE BATTLE OF NOVARA—TERRIBLE SLAUGHTER.

FRANK, and everybody on board, imagined that the vessel could not possibly be more than three or four days at most in reaching the port they desired to land at.

But they were all very much mistaken.

The winds were so contrary and boisterous, that they drove the noble vessel off its course, and they lay more than a week buffeting about in the tempestuous seas, and many times were in great danger of being wrecked.

It was a sad disappointment to Frank, the old count, and all the crew, that they could not be able to land in time to take part in the expeditions of the land forces.

But there they were tossing and rolling, and pitching and plunging about without any help for it.

In consequence they had to make a virtue of necessity, and arrange things on board as comfortable as possible.

The evenings were devoted to story-telling and like amusements; and the old count, being a perfect mine of adventure, the time passed quickly and pleasantly by.

"You have had many long years of soldiering, count," said Frank, one evening as they lingered over supper.

"Many years, my lad, aye, fully a quarter of a century off and on."

"You see," said the count, "I was an orphan, and being brought up by cold-hearted relations, I got more kicks than half-pence.

"But there was plenty of 'blood' in me, my brave lads, and blood, you know, will tell one of these days.

"They sent me to the village school when I was about eight years old, but the old master soon wanted to get rid of me.

"They wanted to stuff a lot of Greek and Latin into me, but after long trying, much thrashing, and great patience, I found the only thing anyone could stuff me with to my own liking was good eating. In that department I always excelled.

"I did not stay long at the village school.

"And for a good reason why.

"We formed a club and raised a conspiracy against the master.

"He found it out, and mounted me on a boy's back for the purpose of soundly thrashing me with rather a heavy cane.

"I knocked the big boy over with a sound smack on the jaw, and then having got possession of the cane, I laid about me right and left until I cleared out the whole school, and remained the only one in possession.

"I finished my performance by smashing the desks and everything I possibly could, and then returned home.

"When I reached my uncle's house, he looked and frowned like a thunder cloud.

"'All he is fit for is to be a soldier,' said the old schoolmaster.

"'That's just what I should like to be,' I answered joyfully.

"It was then decided that I should be sent to a preparatory seminary in order to fit me, in a few years, for the Cadet's College, at Padua.

"I worked very hard at the seminary for three or four years, and longed for the time when I should have learned sufficient to enter as a cadet.

"Now I had heard a great deal of these cadets, and knew them to be violent, frolicsome fellows, fond of a spree, and of kicking up a row with the quiet, easy going tavern keepers and others, and always ready to 'go out' when called upon to fight a duel.

"In fact, their reputation was that of perfect fire-eaters.

"The time came, and I started for the Cadet Academy.

"On my first entering the lodge gate, I was met by a posse of these gentlemen.

"One asked my name.

"Another where I came from.

"And a third knocked my new hat over my eyes, because, he said,

"'I looked cool.'

"Fortunately, further attentions were spared me by a new comer, and I escaped.

"The head of my room told me my principal business was to wait upon him, brush and mend his clothes, and make myself generally useful.

"For I found the other two young cadets were favourites of his, whom he had applied for, one being a personal friend, and the other a particularly clever fellow, engaged to coach him in mathematics.

"I remember the first morning, on coming out after breakfast, being struck with astonishment at seeing a pair of legs sticking out of the large mortar opposite the dining-hall, the owner evidently occupying the bore of that weapon, and making frantic efforts to extricate himself from his uncomfortable position.

"He was with difficulty released.

"He was a wretched 'last-joined,' still in plain clothes, who had ventured to appear on parade in a cap with anchor buttons.

"Besides my regular duties, I had to fag out at cricket, and never see an innings.

"And often for an hour or so to work the treadle of one of the lathes, as my master was fond of turning, and we had no steam power then as we have now.

"Picking up ninepins was another pursuit I took no delight in.

"And conveying cooked chicken, jellies, and other luxuries in my coat-pockets for my master when under 'arrest,' was anything but a pleasant employment.

"My greatest difficulty was in procuring fresh eggs for tea (which in those days we partook of in our rooms), no easy task when you have neither money nor credit.

"Yet I generally managed it, cooking them afterwards in a nightcap tied to a long string, and lowered for three minutes into the copper of boiling water with which we made our tea.

"Woe me if the eggs were boiled too hard, or found to contain young chickens.

"My neckties and other superfluities were bartered away to a wandering vendor of fish for stale crabs, pickled mackerel, shrimps or lobsters.

"My master, being a bit of a gourmand, was never satisfied with the plain bread and butter, which was all that we were allowed.

"So, when every supply was exhausted, I used to pay a slight visit of a morning to the general store (where parcels and goods were deposited when they arrived) to try and discover whether any kind parent had sent a hamper of good things to their affectionate son.

"And when visiting other rooms, I always kept one eye open, looking out for 'straws' lying about, evident tokens of recent unpacking.

"Was I successful in any discovery, I boldly entered the happy room at tea-time, with my roommate's compliments, in the hope that they would kindly ask me to partake of what they had.

"But it was a very different affair when we received a hamper from any sympathising relative. How carefully we brought it over to our room, when few were about, hiding it away out of sight, and allowing only a very little to remain on our table at a time, so as not to rouse the expectations of any casual visitor.

"In less than a week we 'last-joined' were introduced to a new functionary of stern and sober mien, a sergeant of artillery, who was to be our drill-instructor.

"He was evidently a Tartar, and always prefixed his orders or remarks with 'Last-jined.'

"He first placed us in two ranks, a little apart

from one another, and then gave us a lecture on 'setting-up' drill.

"How our chests were to be expanded, and the body leaning a little forward, standing well upon the ball of the foot, with our hands extended, our little fingers touching the seam of our trousers, heads well up, eyes firmly fixed in front, and so on.

"His 'style' was too much for me, I began to laugh.

"But a voice behind soon sobered me.

"'You will turn out to drill to-morrow morning, sir, for unsteadiness in the ranks.'

"It came from the officer on duty.

"This sentence had a good effect upon us all, and the sergeant having finished his harangue, set to work to try and reduce our round shoulders, and make us hold up our heads.

"First we were to move our arms round and round like windmills.

"Then to place both of our fists under our chins, and jerk our arms backwards, as if to try and put them out of joint; then stretch over without bending our knees till we touched our toes with the tips of our gloves, causing our tunics to creep up under our arms, and buttons to fly, and seams to crack, in every direction.

"At last we all looked as if we were going to break a blood-vessel, or have a fit of apoplexy.

"So our instructor had pity upon us, and gave the order to 'stand at ease.'

"It seemed to me a most uneasy attitude, one foot behind the other, and our hands clasped in front, as if we were all struck with pensive thought at something he had said to us.

"Take it all together, my brave lads, the life of a cadet is one of labour, love and frolic.

"If you are not studying hard you are making love hard to some pretty damsel, and may get a bullet through you next morning for your pains.

"*My* friends and relations never gave me too much money to spend, you may depend upon it.

"Yet, what little they did send, I had the good sense to make a proper use of.

"So that when I had passed four years or more in hard work, I passed my examination rather creditably, and was appointed a year after to a lieutenancy in the army of Charles Albert, King of Piedmont, the brave father of the present King Victor Emanuel.

"I received several wounds, though, in duels with my fellow students, through love affairs, and I can tell you more than one sound thrashing at fisticuffs from long-armed rustics, whose sweethearts I have attempted to dance with at fairs and the like."

"But what matter," said the old count, laughing, "war always accompanies love, and always will, I suppose."

"But what was the severest battle you were ever in," asked Frank.

"Well, that's hard to say, because one battle is much like another, as far as soldiers are individually concerned, for whether the battle be big or little in its results, you are fired at all the same."

"And *I* have learned that bullets thrown at one's head are not very nice compliments," said Tom.

"True, my lad. It's all very fine being dressed up in fine clothes, and marching behind splendid bands, but that is not the thing.

"It is when one regiment stands before another, firing five thousand shots a minute at each other, or when you are marching to the point of an enemy's bayonet, that's the time when the real duty of a soldier takes place."

"But about the battle of Novara, count," said Tom. "I have always heard that it was the severest fight ever fought by the Italians against the Austrians."

"So it was, my brave lads, and for this reason,

"King Charles Albert was the only one of the Italian kings or powers who had the courage to throw defiance in the face of Austria, and strike for liberty.

"When his army first marched out against Marshal Radetzki, the Austrian leader, they carried everything before them.

"But no other state came to his assistance, and the result was, that instead of marching on to Vienna we had to fall back towards Novara.

"During our retreat, the fighting between our rear guard and the Austrian advanced guard became very hot and sanguinary.

"In truth, long after we had taken up our position to fight on the morrow, our pickets fired incessantly, and drove the Austrians some distance back, through a long field of standing corn.

"As morning approached, many of our men sallied forth beyond the standing corn, to despoil the Austrian dead, and this being perceived, brought out the enemy's pickets, who opened a brisk and lively fire.

"It must be confessed the audacity of our men in this proceeding was beyond all precedent, for, n the hills immediately beyond, the enemy were in imposing force, and certainly flushed with their success of the previous day.

"A constant picket-firing on our left gave warning that the action would soon open.

"Our troops rose long before day, and the most provident cooked them..lves breakfast; and, smoking their pipes, sat in groups, chatting sociably, not knowing at what moment all would be summoned to 'fall in.'

"Soon, simple picket-firing was succeeded by the roar of musketry.

"Whole volleys continually broke upon the ear at different points of the line, which, together with the occasional roar of howitzers and rifled pieces, was more than enough to rouse the entire army.

"Commanders were busily engaged, and rode from place to place with a business-like manner.

"No hurry or confusion was visible.

"All seemed to look upon the matter with indifference and cheerfulness.

"Our troops had smelt powder long before, and they simply said, 'Another day's work is before us,' and tightly buckled their straps and belts, as if bound for a march, or a long, fatiguing drill.

"Fighting on our left now commenced in earnest. Troops which had been prowling about fields fronting the standing corn, were seen to hasten their movements, and on came the Austrian line-of-battle in good order.

"Observing our clouds of skirmishers rapidly withdrawing from their front, and disappearing in the corn fields, they gave loud cheers, and thought that little resistance would be offered until they had arrived at the top of the hill, where some of our troops were posted, or had found shelter in the woods.

"Their mistake was a grievous one.

"As the Austrian line-of-battle reached the fence up rose our men from their place of concealment among the corn, and delivered several volleys right in the faces of their foes, who, surprised and staggering with loss, retreated over the open ground, and were cut up fearfully by our batteries, which now opened with rapidity from our rear.

"So accurate was the artillery fire that whole

files of Austrian soldiers lay dead parallel with the fence, behind which we were.

"Hundreds of shell from the enemy now dropped in all directions, making our position in the standing corn very unpleasant.

"And although we disputed their advance stubbornly, they gradually forced us back, until they penetrated into the corn-fields, which their heavy line-of-battle beat and broke as they came sweeping onward with loud cheers.

"Supposing us to be beaten at this point, their commander lost no time, but seemed determined to push forward rapidly, and smash our left wing.

"As brigade after brigade rushed gallantly forward they were subjected to a continuous and galling fire.

"But no token was given of our strength in the dense timber to which our men now fell back in skirmishing order.

"When the enemy had traversed the corn-fields, and reached the summit of the rising ground, the ground slightly 'dipped,' so that our commanders in the woods had full view of the Austrian force as it advanced.

"Every fence and every tree was made available by our sharpshooters, who constantly poured into their heavy masses a galling fire.

"Still onwards they came impetuously, and, from their hurried movements, were apparently breathless.

"Down went every fence in their paths, as they rapidly crossed the road towards the woods; and lustily they cheered as the last of our skirmishers disappeared from their front and were lost in the dark, thick forest.

"All was silence within our lines.

"Regiments were lying flat on their faces, with rifles cocked, and the men cautiously peered at the enemy as they came rushing into the woods in great masses and with much noise.

"Suddenly, up rose our left line of battle.

"The enemy halted.

"A moment of silence ensued.

"No man stirred.

"And then deafening, quick, accurate, and numerous volleys broke from our lines.

"The enemy were too numerous to be missed; and, amid frightful loss and confusion, they broke and rushed forth from the woods, trembling like beings who had seen some dreadful apparition.

"Soon as these fugitive masses had gained open ground our batteries in rapid succession broke loose, belching forth grape and canister in such profusion that the infernal storm could be heard raining upon them with a hissing noise, and it literally ploughed furrows in the confused masses, so that daylight could be seen through them at every discharge.

"Round shot bounded and bounced.

"Shells, after whizzing overhead, dropped with loud explosions, in the groups rushing through the corn fields and dotting the landscape.

"The carnage was frightful.

"Through these fields the enemy (exulting in their success the previous day) had come cheering in dense lines.

"But a few moments before they had swept from their front every man opposed to them, and had entered the woods with deafening shouts.

"They had not been lost to view many minutes ere they rushed back in confused, bleeding, staggering masses of human beings, without officers, without order, pursued by our lines of battle.

"Rapidly our brave fellows pushed over the well-fought fields, and, amid showers of shell, kept close to the flying foe, and incessantly poured into their shattered ranks murderous volleys, which whistled through the corn and peopled every acre with scores of dead.

"Field officers of the enemy gallantly rode to the front, and endeavoured to rally their brigades.

"Reinforcements were seen approaching to their relief through open fields beyond; but onward pressed our victorious men, and did not halt until the foe was safely screened in their original position of the morning.

"Fighting on the left had now lasted several hours.

"Our men were thoroughly exhausted, and unable to advance further upon the enemy.

"In truth, it would not have been wise to do so, for our position for defence was preferable ground to any we could win.

"Cannonading now opened with great fury on both sides, and it was soon ascertained that the foe was largely reinforced, and beginning another advance.

"This they did in gallant style, but were met again by such a determined, withering fire, and their loss was so great, that no impression could be made upon our position.

"Not only were they loth to follow us into the woods, but they were quickly beaten and demoralised in open ground.

"Constant volleys were now exchanged by both sides; and as reinforcements arrived to succour us, they were immediately thrown in front to withstand the third attack, then organizing along the enemy's right, which was to be composed of all the commands there present.

"The new line of the enemy seemed to be of immense strength.

"But as they came fully into view, our artillery opened upon them with such rapidity and accuracy that great confusion and disorder began to reign ere they became sufficiently close to exchange shots with our infantry.

"Long and constant volleys resounded along our whole wing.

"Both combatants were stationary.

"Sometimes we slightly gave ground, and again recovered it, until at last our fire began to tell among the enemy, and it seemed that little was now required to drive them completely from the field.

"While indecision seemed to reign among the Austrian commanders ours were unanimous for an advance, and when the order was received, loud cheers and yells burst forth from our troops, and the cannonade re-opened with redoubled fury.

# THE BOY SOLDIER; OR, GARIBALDI'S YOUNG CAPTAIN.

THE MANIAC.—SEE NEXT NUMBER.

"The onset was furious; nothing seemed to withstand the impetuosity of our men.

"The enemy gradually withdrew from the open ground in much confusion.

"Fresh divisions were hurried to the front to check our advance.

"The meeting was terrible, but the shock of short duration.

"Beaten again and again, they were at last driven beyond the position originally occupied.

"Through woods and copse, across corn-fields and ploughed fields, grassy slopes and meadows, over gullies, ditches, brooks and hedges, the combatants in this wing had contended since early morning, and their lines had advanced or retreated again and again, until it seemed that every acre of the landscape was strewn with dead.



"Tokens of carnage were visible on every hand.

"The woods were torn and shattered.

"The corn and grass were trodden under foot; outhouses and farmhouses were heaps of blazing ruins, while, for miles, long lines of smoke ascended over the fertile valley, and numerous batteries uninterruptedly belched forth showers of shot and shell.

"Still the contending lines swayed and advanced, or broke and retreated, so that, to civilised beings, it seemed like some ghostly panorama of things transpiring in a nether world. Charles Albert's impetuous advance at length halted.

"His men had far surpassed their olden fame; but it soon became apparent that weakness was enfeebling our efforts, and that without reinforcements, we could not maintain the conquered ground, should any fresh body of the enemy assail us.

"Indications were not wanting to prove the enemy's activity, and the signal corps soon gave warning that fresh and heavy masses of Austrians were concentrating and forming, to make a final effort to dislodge us from our advanced position.

"Soon the enemy appeared to our front again, and advanced with a steadiness which plainly indicated they had never yet pulled trigger during the day.

"The meeting was fierce, vindictive, and bitter.

"Volleys were given, and returned incessantly.

"Their artillery slowly moved up to the front, and one line began to fall back, with regularity and coolness.

"We would again retrace our steps, we thought, and invite them into the woods where their first attacking corps had so suddenly melted away.

"Slowly, we fell back, and still more cautiously did the enemy pursue.

"For some time the fight was maintained by us in open ground, and our superior fire inflicted great loss among them.

"Through the corn-fields once more we enticed the enemy onwards, and boldly they advanced to try there again the fortune of war.

"Once within the forest, our generals quickly prepared for their coming, and fell back some distance.

"Forward still the enemy came over the numerous dead of their own army; but ere they entered the woods they opened a long and fierce cannonade, throwing hundreds of shells and round shot on those spots which we were supposed to occupy.

"Our men, however, having re-formed much further back than at first, these missiles fell short.

"Not a man of our lines was touched, but all lay quietly on their faces until daylight was shut out from our front by the dark, massive lines of the enemy, who, slowly approaching, made the woods echo with their cheers.

"Cautiously they advanced, and single shots of sharpshooters resounded through the forest, as of solitary hunters in search of game.

"Moving forward up a gentle rise, their long lines came full in view, and instantly our artillery and infantry opened upon them with a deafening roar.

"Branches of trees showered down upon friend and foe alike.

"Trees cracked, and bowed, or toppled over, and fell with a crash among the enemy in the ground, and still volleys upon volleys whistled through the cover, until it seemed as if the clouds had opened, and rained down showers of bullets.

"The smoke, confusion, dust, and noise was indescribable, and how long the fierce conflict lasted I know not, but it seemed an age.

"Bravely had the enemy assailed us, and gallantly were they repulsed; King Charles Albert could not be moved, but held his ground, and, taking advantage of apparent indecision and mystification, gave the word to advance, and this, the fifth corps sent against him, was hurled bleeding, staggering and defeated from his front, and retreated from the forest, with great loss; but Charles Albert was too weak to attempt another advance, and was content to hold the enemy in check until positive information could be ascertained of their operations on other parts of our lines.

"Thus the battle continued all day long.

"It was a terrible conflict, for in the balance hung the great question of Italian independence, and, as might be expected, our men fought with the ferocity of demons.

"Austrian cuirassiers charged our squares in vain.

"Our batteries belched forth upon them showers of deadly missiles, and the cries of the wounded and dying rent the air.

"Thus it continued all the live long day.

"But as night set in we all found, that though we were not beaten and driven off the field, the Austrians were too strong for us.

"To add to the horrors and dangers of the situation, we learned that the cunning Austrian commander, Marshal Radetski, was endeavouring to get a large force in our rear, and thus cut off our retreat from Alexandra.

"What must be done?

"Mortal men could not have done more than we had done.

"The king, Charles Albert, and his brave son, the present king, Victor Emmanuel, galloped into the thickest of the fight during the day, and we all thought that they sought death.

"At midnight, and when all was still, we silently and sullenly retreated, nor did the Austrians dare to pursue, for our misfortunes and disasters had wrought us up to the pitch of madness.

"The carnage of that day I shall never forget," said the old count, with a heavy sigh.

"I was wounded twice; once in the head with a sabre cut, and the second was a bullet in the thigh.

"Three horses were killed under me, yet I so distinguished myself that one of the first things the old king did was to promote me, and raised me to the dignity of count, a title which my forefathers had won centuries before.

"This was the severest and bloodiest engagement I was ever in," said the old soldier; "and I never hope to witness such a sight again."

Just as the old count had finished his story, one of the sailors came down into the cabin, and, doffing his cap respectfully, said,

"A sail in sight, Captain Tom. Bearing right down upon us."

"What does she look like? an Austrian?"

"Can't tell, captain; we have signalled her, but she shows no colours."

"Then prepare for action; it may be an Austrian cruiser, and, if so, we must be ready to give her a warm reception."

In a few minutes after Captain Tom had given this order all was bustle and excitement on board.

Every one was busy in making the ship ready for action, and each moment the strange, suspicious craft approached nearer and nearer, but did not show her colours.

## CHAPTER LXXII.

### THE CHASE—THE UNEXPECTED MEETING.

THE excitement of the moment was very great.

The strange sail was now not further than a mile away.

Yet not a man could be seen upon her decks.

Captain Tom and Frank went aloft with their glasses to "look into her," but it was all to no purpose.

Not a soul could be seen on board.

It looked like a well-rigged craft which had been abandoned, and was now drifting about on the lone ocean without officers or men.

Tom and Frank were puzzled; they knew not what to think or make of the suspicious-looking craft.

Judge of their astonishment, then, when they were within three quarters of a mile from her, she changed her course, and bore away at a clipping rate, as if afraid "to speak," or encounter Tom Ford's vessel.

Away she went like a bird upon the wing.

"Hillo! What's the meaning of all that?" asked the count, in astonishment.

"It means this, count," said Tom; "I take her for some Austrian privateer. She came close enough to see that we were too much for her, and is now going before the wind to get out of the way."

"But you will not permit her to do so?"

"No; trust me," said Tom, laughing; "she must pay for peeping. Set every stitch of sail, my merry men; we'll soon overhaul the rascals, and if they don't heave to, and show colours, we'll send her to Davy Jones's locker."

The sudden movement of the stranger in changing her course was very suspicious, to say the least.

But this only heightened the curiosity of Tom's English crew, who cheered lustily, fired a gun after the stranger, and danced among the rigging as nimbly as monkeys, and spread out every inch of canvas the ship could carry.

The more Captain Tom's gallant fellows strained every nerve to increase the speed of the chase the more the stranger did likewise.

For more than an hour the two vessels kept on their course full sail.

The breeze was equally fair for both.

Yet neither gained a single cable's length on each other.

"She's a regular clipper," said Tom, "and no mistake; see how she sails—how beautifully she is handled."

"She's no Austrian vessel, sir," said several to Tom.

"That's what I've been thinking."

"She's beautifully handled," said Frank.

"Yes," said the count; "but we are going off our course at a devil of a rate. Instead of steering for the Italian coast, we are going towards the Atlantic."

"Never mind, count, we'll keep the chase up all night; at all events, we mustn't let them beat us."

"What flag are you flying?" asked Frank.

"The Italian flag, as usual."

"Then change it. Hoist the English flag, and see if she'll acknowledge it."

"A good thought," said Tom.

In a few minutes the English flag was raised above that of Italy.

On the instant the stranger ahead eased all sail, and boldly hoisted the English colours also.

"This looks strange," said Tom; "they hoist colours and ease sail quickly enough; but I can't make out a single soul on board."

"Nor I, sir," said several.

"It must be the 'Phantom Ship,'" said one, who was an old sailor; "I've often heard that, like the Wandering Jew on shore, there is a Phantom Ship roaming over the whole world in full sail. No one can catch her; she's a Will-o'-the-wisp, like, and is sure to lead us on to rocks or reefs."

Tom laughed; but as the stranger eased her sails his vessel was quickly gaining on her.

In half-an-hour they were abeam, or, as might be said, breast to breast, but yet some quarter of a mile north and south.

"Take every precaution, brother Tom," said Frank; "we must not be led into any snare."

Tom was not one of those who was at all likely to be led into any snare, for he had prepared his ship for instant action.

His men stood to their guns, and were ready for the word of command.

Nearer and nearer the two ships approached each other, like two wary giants.

"Stand by, my men," said Tom, quietly, glass in hand, as he mounted on the poop.

"Aye, aye, sir."

"Ship ahoy!" he shouted, through his speaking trumpet; "ship ahoy!"

"Ship ahoy!" was the anwser.

"Your name, and whither bound?"

"Are you English?"

"Yes; from Leghorn."

Tom's answer was scarcely given when the stranger's decks were suddenly crowded with soldiers, as the captain asked—

"Have you heard anything of Captain Frank Ford, of the Boy Volunteers?"

"Yes; he is on board here, now. I am his brother, and command this craft."

On the instant the stranger's rattlings were swarmed by a great number of nimble youths.

With three cheers they hailed and saluted Tom's vessel.

"It is Hugh Tracy and the Boy Volunteers for a thousand pounds!" said Captain Frank, greatly excited. "I cannot be mistaken!"

It *was* Hugh Tracy and the Boy Soldiers, and foremost among them all was the gallant Caspar!

In a short time the two vessels came to, side by side, and the meeting between the captain and his brave young companions in arms baffles all description, for on all sides reigned merriment, noise, and confusion.

"Sail away for Mexico, Captain Tom," said Frank. "We have done with Italy, and will go to the land of the Montezumas—the land of love, war, and adventure!"

This announcement was received with loud applause by all.

Fatty and Buttons were in ecstacies.

They danced and capered about like two lunatics; Fatty with a huge piece of bread and meat in one hand, Buttons with a bottle of wine in the other.

"To Mexico! To Mexico!" resounded on all sides, and ere long the two ships set sail again in company along the Mediterranean, gambolling over the bright blue water like things of air.

---

## CHAPTER LXXIII.

JOEL FLINT IS "DONE" ON BOTH SIDES—TOMASSO, THE ITALIAN DETECTIVE, PROFESSES TO BE ASTONISHED AT THE COURSE OF EVENTS.

TOMASSO, the Italian detective, had not left the court more than an hour, when he well knew that the prefect of police was making preparations to capture both Tom, Frank, and Buttons that very night.

For your Continental police seldom make a descent upon any place in the daytime, but always manage to make their captures at night, when the unsuspecting victims are in bed and sound asleep.

This Tomasso well knew.

When night-time came Frank's hotel was surrounded by police; but, greatly to their chagrin and disappointment, they found that, with all their cunning, the English bird could not be caught with chaff, and had taken wing!

The prefect was in a frightful rage.

He walked up and down his office stamping and swearing and could not make it out.

"To be fooled by two such youths as they are!" he exclaimed. "Why, it is a perfect disgrace! Where is Tomasso?" he asked, repeatedly.

"He is without, in waiting on your honour," said an attendant.

"Call him in at once," said the prefect, seating himself in an arm chair, and looking the picture of wrath.

Tomasso entered, and politely bowed.

The prefect ordered him to be seated.

"How is this, sir?" he began.

"What, sir?" asked Tomasso, innocently, although he knew all about it.

"Why, they tell me those English youths have escaped."

"Indeed—impossible!"

"No, sir, it is not impossible. They have gone, bag and baggage. How they managed to do so is a mystery."

"So it is, signor prefect, but I did my duty. I watched the place, but I did not see them depart."

"Strange, sir, strange; they could not have flown away."

"No, truly, signor prefect; but if they have gone, they must have done so in a very mysterious way."

"No doubt. I have no hesitation in my mind but that they have been tampering with some of our detectives."

"Impossible, signor. It cannot surely be that any of our honourable body have so disgraced themselves as to be bought over," said Tomasso.

Although, at the same time, he very well knew that the prefect himself was "to be bought over" as easily as any one, if a good chance offered.

"It is shocking, sir," continued the prefect, "that the culprits should have escaped us after all the time and money spent in their apprehension by the young Englishman, Signor Flint."

"Quite true, signor prefect, quite true. As you say, Signor Flint, or Schmidt, or whatever his name may be, is, no doubt, an open-hearted, free-handed young gentleman, and deserves that success should crown his efforts."

"Perfectly right, Tomasso, perfectly right; but though they have escaped, I do not in any way blame you, for I am certain we have not another officer in the force who is more faithful and true than yourself."

Tomasso smiled, and bowed to his superior in a very respectful manner.

"You know this young Englishman, Flint, well, Tomasso?"

"I do, signor prefect."

"And are aware where he lives?"

"Yes."

"Then go to him, tell him all that has happened, and confer with him as to the very best measures to be taken for the capture of these daring young Englishmen."

"I obey," said Tomasso, and he left the prefect's office, smiling archly.

He was on his way to the hotel where Mr. Flint resided, when he was unexpectedly met by Joel himself, whose face was radiant with smiles.

"Have you heard the news?" said Joel.

"No."

"We have got 'em."

"Who?"

"Why, Frank and Tom Ford."

"Who told you?"

"The prefect, this morning."

"Oh, indeed."

"Yes, and I am now on my way to the prefect's office, to accompany the officers who are ordered to surround the hotel and capture them."

Tomasso laughed loudly.

"What are you laughing about?" asked Joel, in disgust.

"Why, I was just on my way to your hotel to tell you some important news."

"Indeed! What was it? Have you got them already?"

"No; you would never guess."

"What is it, then?"

"Why, they have escaped."

"Escaped!" gasped Joel, biting his lips in vexation.

"Yes; they got away unknown to any one, and are now sailing in Captain Tom Ford's vessel as fast as the wind can carry them."

"The devil!"

"'Tis true."

"And where are they bound for?"

"Why, to join the Boy Band of Volunteers, in Lombardy."

"Excellent!" said Joel, plucking up courage again. "Then, we may recapture them after all."

"Yes, if——"

"If what?"

"If we have money enough to do it."

"Oh, as to money, I have enough for that. My worthy father in England is very wealthy, and he would give anything to have those two villains safe in the hands of the law."

"Very considerate on his part," said Tomasso, smiling.

"Yes; but you know," said Joel, "I have spent a large sum already."

"I know you have."

"I loaned poor De Sangri a large sum."

"Which you will never get back again, for he is dead."

"I know it, and am sorry. I should have jumped for joy had he brained Frank Ford."

"But he didn't do it, though, you see."

"No," said Joel, with a fierce look; "the boot was on the other leg that time."

"True; and yet the marquis was a professed duellist. He was never known to have been hit before. He was 'a dead shot.'"

"I know he was. Poor fellow, he's a 'dead' shot now, and no mistake."

"You are witty," said the detective, laughing.

"No, I am not. But what plan do you propose? How are we to get these two young villains in our hands again?"

"'Tis easy enough."

"How?"

"You have plenty of money, and *that* can do everything."

"True; but what have you done with that two hundred pounds I gave you a month ago?"

"I spent it in hiring men to watch them. I did not keep a penny for myself; I entered into your case for love only."

"I thank you, Tomasso," said Joel, putting his hands into his pockets. "But I also gave you one hundred pounds last week."

"Which was also spent in bribing their young companion, Buttons."

"Impossible!"

"'Tis true, or how could I have gained all the private information I did?"

"In that case, if Master Buttons is leagued with us, all will go well; but I can tell you," said Joel, sorrowfully, "that my money is getting very, very low; all I have left is two hundred pounds, and when that is gone, if we do not succeed in capturing these two expert young villains, I fear I must return to England again."

"Oh, nonsense!" said Tomasso. "We cannot fail this time."

"I'm glad you think so; but in any case if money is wanted, I suppose I must give it."

"You wouldn't expect me to do it, would you? For see how long and faithful I have laboured for you from pure friendship alone; been out night and day looking after and hunting up these two enemies of yours."

"Well, how much do you want?"

"How much have you got?"

"Only two hundred pounds."

"Well, say you give me one hundred and eighty pounds, and in less than a week they shall be secured and in gaol."

"But that would only leave me with twenty pounds."

"Suppose so. Wouldn't you rather succeed than fail? Of course you would; and, besides, see the number of spies I shall have to employ both in and out of the army."

"True, true," said Joel, handing over the one hundred and eighty pounds. "And when shall I see or hear from you?"

"In a week at most. Good-night; consider they are captured already."

"I will; good-night, dear Tomasso, good-night."

"Good-night, fool!" said Tomasso quietly to himself, putting the money in his pocket and walking away.

---

## CHAPTER LXXIV.

### TWO "VERY DEAR" FRIENDS MEET.

THE unexpected meeting of old Flint with Jonathan, on the road near Epping Forest, was startling alike to both those cunning worthies.

Flint at first tried to spur his horse onward.

But Jonathan's ferocious aspect, and his levelled revolver, struck terror into the craven heart of the old money-grubbing lawyer.

Seeing there was no earthly chance to escape, he pulled up his horse, and appeared timid, as if just meeting with some highwayman or other he had never heard of before.

"Halt!" said Jonathan, advancing into the middle of the muddy road.

"Halt, I say, or die!"

"What!" gasped old Flint, who was muffled up to the very eyes in comforters and the like, "What did the man say?"

"Halt, or die!" said Jonathan, seizing his bridle rein.

"Who are you, my good man? What do you want with me?"

"Want with you? Why, I want a good deal."

"Some money, perhaps?"

"Yes, that is one thing I stand much in need of."

"Well, then, let go my horse, my good man; let me pursue my way, and I will well reward you."

"Don't 'good man' me," said Jonathan, with a growl of passion.

"I don't know you."

"Don't you, though? How very innocent you are, all at once!"

"No; upon my word I don't!"

"You don't want to know me,, perhaps; but I know you."

"Indeed!"

"Indeed!" laughed Jonathan, with a mocking echo; "Indeed! you old rat! Come, get off your horse at once, or I'll pull you off, Flint."

Jonathan's words and gestures were so full of meaning, that old Flint saw it was not of the slightest use for him to try and deceive him.

He therefore gave a little start, as of surprise, and said—

"What! is that my dear friend Jonathan?"

"Yes, it is your 'dear friend' Jonathan," the other chuckled.

"Why, who would have expected to see you here?"

"You didn't, at all events, I am very certain; and, if the truth were known, I have no doubt you would rather have encountered the very devil himself instead of me. Ha! ha!"

So Mr. Flint would, had he had the choice, particularly as the devil was never known to carry a six-barrelled revolver.

The old lawyer smiled in a ghastly manner, however, as he said—

"Well, really, this meeting is delightful—such a pleasure is beyond all my expectations!"

"I dare say it is; but I have no time to waste in talking to you here upon the public road."

"Why can't we talk here as well as anywhere else?"

"For a good many reasons."

"For a good many reasons, eh?" said Flint, thoughtfully, knowing not what to do.

At last he said—

"That's a very nice, pretty-looking revolver you've got, Jonathan; let me have a look at it."

"How very simple you are, Flint! Ha, ha! What should I be able to do—what would become of me—in less than a minute, if I did, eh, old fox?"

"Oh, upon my word I didn't mean any harm, or intend any treachery."

"Oh, of course you didn't! I wouldn't suspect you for all the world, Flint! Ha, ha! You didn't mean treachery, I suppose, when you bribed Bill to let you go after you went to the bank, eh? I heard all about it. But if you managed to trick him, you won't do so with me. I'm too old a bird for that now, Flint!"

"Well, well, friend Jonathan, there is no use of us growling together about that little affair. It is true, I *did* trick Bill, as you say; but it was my intention to use my freedom in getting you released out of the hands of those housebreakers."

"I dare say you did! Words are only wind, Flint; I don't believe anything you say. But, as you observed just now, this *is* a very pretty revolver I've got, isn't it?"

"Quite so."

"And what do you think I have just done with it?"

"Can't tell; you are an excellent shot, I have heard. You have been amusing yourself with rabbit shooting, I suppose, in the forest."

"Yes; two-legged rabbits."

"What!" said Flint, turning red; "it cannot be. Surely you have not——"

"Yes, I have, though; it was a case of life or death with me. I shot the officer who came after me."

"Oh, heavens! murder again!"

"Murder again? Yes, and why not? What are you whining about? Do you think I have made up my mind to be hung, then, like a cat for *your* sake?"

"My sake?"

"Yes, *your* sake," said Jonathan, with flashing eyes. "Has not all my misery and crime arisen from you?"

"No."

"Liar!" said Jonathan, firmly seizing the horse by the bridle. "Liar, Flint! you know it has. Ever since I knew you I have had my hands steeped in villany and crime."

There was such a terrible look of vengeance in Jonathan's countenance that Flint quaked for fear.

"What do you mean to do?" gasped Flint, in alarm. "Put down that revolver. Don't point it at my head, for heaven's sake! Put it down, Jonathan; I see a devil in your eye."

"Yes, a dozen devils, Flint. Ha, ha! I have longed to meet you, I even prayed for it."

"And why?"

"That I might have vengeance on you."

"Do not speak in that threatening manner," said Flint, in a beseeching tone.

"But I do, though, and will. I have six chambers of this revolver loaded, and every bullet shall be discharged through your old heart, unless——"

"Unless what?" said Flint, with a faint ray of hope dawning in his mind. "Unless what, Jonathan? Speak. For mercy's sake take that revolver out of my face."

"My terms are—divide the booty."

"But I haven't got it."

"But you know where it is."

"True; but the chest is far from here."

"No matter; I must have some money at once; get it how or where you can, or otherwise you die!"

"But what gratification could it be to you to kill *me?*" whined old Flint. "I am willing to give you money, plenty of it; but, for Heaven' ssake, put down your revolver; your hand might slip, and then it would be all up with me."

Jonathan, still holding on to Flint's horse, led it back towards the inn.

"What are you about to do, Jonathan?"

"Why make you wait until I hire a horse also."

"But suppose they have none."

"Why, then both of us will ride together on one. Don't think for a moment that I intend to lose sight of you this time, for you are too slippery to catch again in a hurry."

Now, as it chanced, the landlord of the inn had a very good saddle horse of his own in the stable.

After a little negotiation it was hired, at a high price, and after drinking a glass of brandy, and filling their travelling flasks, the two horsemen put spurs to their horses, and galloped away.

## CHAPTER LXXV.

THE VILLAINS ARE NOT YET CAUGHT—THE PUBLICAN'S HORSE WILL NEVER RETURN—THE PURSUIT—THE POOR PEDLAR'S JEOPARDY—THE DEAD BODY.

"THAT stranger paid a tremendous price for the loan of my horse," said the old landlord, jingling Flint's gold in his pockets. "I wouldn't mind hiring out my horse every day at that price. Just fancy a man paying five sovereigns for a twenty miles' ride. He will return to-morrow morning, he says."

"I'm not so sure of that, husband," said the old landlady, shaking her head; "I didn't like the looks of either on 'em."

"Stuff and nonsense, wife. You like the appearance of no one, to hear *you* talk. It was very wonderful you ever took a liking to *me* then. I tell you they are both gentlemen, wife, or how could they afford to sport their money in that way?"

The wife shook her head, and the innkeeper filled out for himself some rum and milk, muttering as he smoked,

"My wife is a simple woman. What does *she* know of this ere world of ourn? Not she, poor creature! When she's lived and knocked about, as I have, this six-and-fifty year or more, she'll know that these gentlefolk are queer fish when they are bent on a spree. Didn't the Marquis of Waterford sell real guineas in the streets for a farthing each for a wager? and what's giving five pounds for hiring a good horse to that?—why nothing. I made a great mistake, though. I should have charged him a ten pound note; he'd have thought more of me."

While he thus thought, and smoked his pipe, the rain began to descend in torrents.

Black, lowering clouds quickly encompassed all the earth.

Vivid lightning flashed across the scene.

Thunder crashed over head, until it made the rafters of the inn shake again.

The rain came down incessantly.

Such a tremendous storm, and one so sudden, had never been known before, for the torrents of rain came down with such violence and fury that the roads were soon naught else but pools of water.

"My eye!" said the old innkeeper to one or two who had dropped in out of the rain; "my eye, mates! it do come down, don't it?"

"Yes, in buckets full," was the rejoinder, as the two wet and dripping strangers walked into the taproom, looking like half-drowned rats.

"And so sudden too," said the landlord, smoking, and poking up the fire into a merry blaze.

"It's playing the very devil with the forest," said one.

"How so?"

"Why, the lightning is blasting the trees in every direction."

"You don't mean that?"

"I do, though; and more than that, master—if I didn't hear somebody groan as I passed, you can hang me."

"Groan, man?"

"Aye, groan."

"You must have been dreaming."

"No, I wasn't, master. I was so wide awake that I ran away hither as fast as my legs could carry me. It was like the last gasp of a man who was dying."

"The deuce!"

"There has been a murder committed there, or I'm not a sane man," said the stranger.

The publican eyed the man with a look of fear and suspicion, but said not a word.

"A murder, eh?" thought mine host. "Well, this chap is a pedlar; who knows but what he may have done it? I'll keep my eye upon him."

While the publican and his two customers were roasting their shins before the fire, several horsemen rode up to the door in great haste, and dismounted.

The noise of the storm was still so great without that no one had heard their approach.

They entered the tap-room so suddenly that the innkeeper and his customers were taken by surprise, and rose from their seats.

They were seven mounted policemen.

For a few moments no one spoke.

Indeed, the publican's breath was fairly taken out of his body at the appearance of the men in blue.

He changed all manner of colours, put the pipe on one side, and looked like a man who was "wanted" for something or other.

"Has any officer in plain clothes been here this morning, landlord?" asked the chief of the policemen.

"Why, yes, gentlemen, I think there *was* one, who came in a cab. He didn't stay here long, though; but said he'd take a walk in the forest for an hour or two. He paid his cab, ordered breakfast, and such like; but he hasn't returned yet. Won't you sit down, officers, and take something?"

"As it's a cold, wet, stormy morning, I don't think a little drop would hurt any one," said the red-faced sergeant. "Let's have some hot spiced ale, landlord, as quick as you like; we must be off again directly."

"In all this pouring rain?"

"Yes; our business is important. Will you take care of our horses until we return?"

"Yes; but surely you are not going forth on foot, gentlemen?"

"Yes we are; but we shan't be long."

They drank their hot spiced ale, and went forth towards the forest.

The landlord took care of their horses, and comfortably stabled them.

Yet still the rain continued, and still the two strangers crouched beside the fire, loth to go forth into the drenching storm.

In less than an hour the heavy, regular tread of men was heard approaching the inn door.

"Here they come," said the old landlord, as he went to the front door to open it.

He had scarcely lifted the latch when he fell back into the passage again with a cry of surprise and horror.

The six policemen carried between them, on some limbs of trees, the lifeless and blood-stained body of Gardner, the detective.

"This is bloody work, master," said the pedlar, as he stood aghast, looking at the horrid spectacle; "this is horrid work, master," said he. "I told you," addressing the publican, "that a murder had been committed, didn't I?"

"So you did, so you did. Alas! poor gentleman, he left my house not four hours ago, smiling, to take a walk; but look at him now; look at him now!"

"I told you there was a murder committed," repeated the pedlar, with the air of a man who has prophecied truly.

"Indeed!" said the sergeant. "You seem to know so much about it that I shall detain you until we inquire into this bloody affair."

"*Me?*" said the pedlar, "detain *me?* Why, what have *I* done? I've done nothing."

"We don't know that," said the sergeant. "Scroggins, take charge of the pedlar, and search him."

The pedlar now began to tremble in every limb.

"Hullo, what's this?" said Scroggins, pulling a revolver out of the pedlar's pocket.

"It's what I found when skirting the forest," said the pedlar, all pale.

"When?"

"This morning."

"It's one of yours, sergeant," said Scroggins, showing the revolver to his officer.

"Yes, I know it; it belonged to poor Gardner. This pedlar knows more about it than he likes to confess," said the sergeant. "Handcuff him, Scroggins, and don't let him go out of your sight. Any one else been here this morning, landlord?" asked the sergeant.

"Why, yes, sir; two gentlemen have been here; one came on horseback, the other on foot. The latter hired a horse from me, and paid a good price for it."

"Oh, indeed! And what sort of persons were they?"

"Well, the one as hired the horse was a tall, long-legged, dark-looking fellow, and——"

"That's quite correct."

"What did you please to observe?"

"Go on, we are listening; and the other was——"

"Quite the reverse."

"Just so; and did they appear to be in any hurry?"

"Oh! a terrible hurry, I couldn't make it out."

"And which way did they come?"

"From the direction of the forest."

"All right, they are the men we are after," said the sergeant; "but I didn't expect we should find them both together hereabouts. So much the better. Did you hear which way they were going, or intended to go?"

"Well, no; but I heard 'em whisper something about 'express train,' 'Southampton,' 'Germany,' and such words."

"As I expected," said the sergeant, "here is a murder committed, and the culprit has fled by express train."

"And my horse," said the publican, in a flurry.

"Oh! hang your horse," said the sergeant. "Never mind that."

"Yes; but I *do* mind it," said the innkeeper, storming and raving. "It was the only one I ever had. Worth £20 of anybody's money. Such fine action, such splendid——"

"Yes, I dare say," the sergeant coolly observed. "A very grand animal, no doubt; but you'll never have him back again."

"What!" gasped Boniface, striking an attitude with the poker, just as he was about to stir up the fire. "What! my horse gone, and never to return?"

"Just so. The 'gentleman,' as you called him, who hired it, was a murderer. He was the one who must have killed poor Gardner. Old Jonathan is a desperate villain."

"We had better haste away," said one of the officers. "If they have gone to the station we may overtake them by sharp riding."

"Too late," said the sergeant, looking at his watch. "Too late. The express is due at 9. 'Tis long past that now."

"But then we can telegraph."

"True; if the wires are not all blown down."

"If that be so, then, sergeant, I fear these two rascals have escaped us again."

"D—n them!" said the publican, red with passion. "Why, I took them for gentlemen."

The sergeant smiled, as he said,

"Yes; and so have a great number of people; but your worst of scoundrels are usually dressed the best, and have the politest manners."

"Why, they seemed to have *lots* of money," said the publican; "at least, the smaller of the two had his purse full of coin and notes—filled, indeed, almost to bursting; it made my eyes water to look at it."

"That's all right enough; they have lots of money; at least, the lawyer has; but where he keeps it is a secret. In one word, landlord, these people we speak of are the greatest and most cunning scoundrels in all the world. We have been a long time after 'em, and each time, when we thought we had got 'em, they slip through our fingers like slimy eels. Never mind, we'll have another try. Come along, my men, let me take care of the pedlar, and another look after the body of poor Gardner, and we will be off to the railway station. All hope is not yet lost."

So saying, the sergeant and his six comrades mounted their strong horses, and galloped away to the nearest railway station.

---

## CHAPTER LXXVI.

### THE RIDE FOR LIFE—THE "VULCAN," AND ITS DRIVER—THE SERGEANT'S FEARS.

THEY were not very long ere they reached the station.

They galloped so fast and furious, that when they arrived there, their steeds fairly trembled again, and were covered with foam.

They made all sorts of inquiries of the porters, ticket-takers, and the like, and were much pleased to find that the two strangers described had been there, and had taken tickets for the express train to Southampton.

"How are the telegraph lines?" asked the sergeant.

"All right, I believe, sir," said the operator; "but I will try them. I shouldn't wonder, though, if some of them have not been blown down by the storm."

The operator went to the instrument, and worked at it for several seconds without any reply.

At last, the signal bell rang, and an answer came.

"Express train passed here half an hour ago—the line is broken down beyond this."

"Hang the luck," said the sergeant.

"What had you better do?" asked the station-master.

"Is it possible to overtake the express train?"

"With an engine and tender, you mean?"

"I do."

"Yes, it is possible, but *only* possible; but it will be a tight race if you *do* overtake the express, for it has got a long start."

"No matter. Can we have an engine and tender?"

"Certainly, if you demand it. There is the 'Vulcan,' a splendid locomotive, just steaming out of the shed, and the line is all clear."

"Then let us have it—no expense is to be spared. These two villains must be captured at all cost."

In a moment or two, the sergeant and his men gave their horses into the charge of a stableman at the station.

The officers jumped on to the tender of the "Vulcan," and the engine-driver received his orders from the station-master.

"All right, sir; leave it to me," said the driver, with a smiling look, "it will be quick and dangerous work to overtake the express, but as it stops several times before reaching Southampton, I have little doubt I shall overtake it, or, at all events, be in as quick as they will."

He gave a shrill whistle.

"Hold on tight, gentlemen," said he, "and keep your backs to the wind, for it blows hard enough to take one's head off."

In less than one minute after leaving the station the "Vulcan," like a high mettled steed, had got into its "full stride."

Away they went, at almost lightning speed.

Through meadows they glided like a thing of air.

Deep "cuttings" in the hills were run through with a scream and a yell.

Steam streamed forth, and the fires glowed.

The machinery worked with almost countless velocity.

The piston was almost noiseless, and trees and woods and streams and villages darted by like specks in a dream.

Past one station and through another they flew.

The porters and others had scarcely time to turn their heads to watch its approach, when the "Vulcan," with a scream of triumph, tore by at a giddy speed, and was quickly lost in the far distance like a small black object in the fog, and sleet, and rain.

Bravely did the "Vulcan" try its highest speed.

It seemed to bid defiance to wind and rain, and laughed at mile posts as they vanished by like white spectres in the hazy morning.

"Twenty miles," said the driver, smiling, as he rattled through a small country station at his top speed, "twenty miles. What time have I made?"

"Fifteen minutes," shouted the sergeant, as he held on with both hands tightly to the tender.

"Good work," said the oily, black-faced stoker, in a loud voice (for the rattle and noise of the engine was very great). "Good work, that," he repeated, as he shovelled in more coke; "but the old 'Vulcan' can do better still if it likes; can't it, Joe (addressing the driver)?"

"All right, Bill; so it can," said the driver, shouting, with one hand to his mouth, in the fashion of costermongers. "Shake her up, Bill."

Bill, the black-faced stoker, did give her a shake up in earnest.

He piled up the fire afresh, examined the state of the water, and, seeing that that was all right, shouted,

"All square, Joe; let her have it!"

"Hold on, gentlemen," said the driver, smiling. "We're coming to a long and level bit of running ground—a clear fifteen or twenty mile spin. Look at your watch and time us."

With increased speed, and like a race-horse who is winning, and is let loose towards the finish, the "Vulcan" dashed forward.

The speed was now frightful.

The officers, though brave men enough, were not prepared for this dangerous exhibition.

They literally flew through the air.

Hats were blown off.

Coat tails for a moment flapped in the wind, and next moment were in rags.

The sergeant and his men looked like birds whose wings had been clipped too short.

They pulled out their brandy flask, and tried to hold it to their mouths, but could not, for the jolting made their teeth chatter again.

"Joe" the driver and his demon-looking companion, "Bill," grinned with delight at the anxious, serious-looking features of the "bobbies," and drank off the brandy without even winking.

# THE BOY SOLDIER; OR, GARIBALDI'S YOUNG CAPTAIN.

A DELIVERANCE—SEE NEXT NUMBER.

The sergeant and his men tried to smile, but they could not.

This trial was too much for their nerves.

They expected a "smash" to take place every minute.

This catastrophe was rendered almost certain when "Bill" the demon stoker received the wink from "Joe" the driver as he shouted in the sergeant's ear,

"You ain't afraid?"

The sergeant looked blue all over, but with a faint smile shook his head, as much as to say,

"No; none of the force are ever afraid of anything."

"I'm glad o' that," said Joe, "because I'm going to carry a little more steam. Shake her up, Bill."

Bill gave her (that is to say, "Vulcan") a "good shake up," and seemed much pleased, as he winked at Joe, and said,

"The safety-valve's all right, ain't it, Joe?"

"Yes, I think so; it's a little shaky, but it don't much matter; if the 'bobbies' ain't scared, I don't know why we should be. Give her another good shake up, Bill!"



The sergeant now began to look very serious, for he heard something about the safety-valve being "rather shaky," and he firmly resolved if he should only escape that time, he'd never trust his life and limbs on a "fast engine" again—no, not for the chief inspector himself.

There was no knowing how much Joe "could get out of her" (Vulcan) in speed, but at all events he had gone at a terrific rate, but that while passing through a station the danger signal was up, and the signal-man waved the danger flag in a wild, excited manner.

Joe perceived the long arms working, and the flags waving.

"I thought so, Bill," said he, with a grin; "we ain't far behind, I think."

"Ease her, Joe," said Bill, "we might have a smash up."

Joe eased "Vulcan" into a twenty-mile-an-hour trot, and had not gone far, when he espied the express turning a corner in the track, and enter a tunnel.

"All right, Bill, the 'Vulcan' has done its duty

this morning; we've beat the express, and given it forty minutes start; that ain't bad going."

"No," said the sergeant, who now tried to smile, and look like himself again. "No; you have gone at a devil of a rate."

"Oh, it's nothing when you're use to it."

"But I should never get use to it," said one and another; "I have been dizzy for more than an hour."

"My hat is lost."

"My coat tails are blown to ribbons."

"And my teeth ache, and are almost loosened out of my jaw."

Joe and Bill laughed like two oily, black-faced demons, as Joe observed,

"We went at sixty, sixty-five, and seventy. We could have got more out of her (Vulcan), if we had only given her another good shake up."

The sergeant and his party were heartily glad that the "Vulcan" had not another good shake up, and began to enquire how far it was to the nearest stopping place.

"Only thirty mile," said Bill, "and I'm glad on it, for we can give you, gentlemen, another specimen of what we can do before we can reach the terminus. I know you like it."

"Lor', bless yer," said Joe, with a smile, "I've driven this here engine three years or more, off and on, and if they were to insure my life, I would warrant to run eighty miles an hour, or ninety even, for two or three hours together."

"How long is the tunnel?" asked the sergeant, as they approached it.

"Oh, not long," said Bill, smiling; "two mile and a half, or thereabouts. I don't know to a mile or two; do you, Joe?"

"No; I think it's about five mile or thereabouts."

"Vulcan" gave a loud whistle, and proceeded at a moderate rate after the "Express."

But they had not gone very far, when every one was startled at the sounds they heard.

The "Express" had run into an ordinary train in the long tunnel!

"Stop her!" shouted Bill.

In an instant Joe turned off the steam.

But it was too late.

The "Express" had run into the train before it by some unaccountable means.

And the "Vulcan," at the rate of at least twenty miles per hour, went with a terrific crash into the "Express!"

The noise, confusion, shouts, cries, hissing of steam, and general uproar was indescribable.

In a second, the driver, stoker, and the police-officers were jerked off the tender and engine.

There was a double collision in the tunnel!

All was darkness, haste, uproar, and the mingling of many voices.

Some wounded, some dying, and some shouting out commands, made up a fearful Babel, which it defies the powers of description to portray.

## CHAPTER LXXVII.

### FRANK'S FAREWELL TO NELLY LANCASTER.

Tomasso, the Italian detective, had so played his cards that he had not only deceived the prefect of police, but, among the rest, Joel Flint also.

He had made "a very good thing" out of Joel.

For Mr. Flint had been so over anxious in some way or other to encompass the destruction of Frank or Tom Ford that he did not seem to care about what the expense might be.

Hence it was that Tomassa, while being able to help his friends, had so beautifully fleeced Joel that when it at last came to the final pinch, Joel had not a copper to spend or spare.

Worst of all for Joel was that, though up to the present he had been in constant and regular correspondence with his father—from whom, from time to time, he had received frequent and large sums—the troubles at home with Jonathan and others had been such that, for more than three months, he had heard nothing of the doings of old Flint.

What Joel was to do he knew not.

Up to the present he had had "lots" of money, but now he could hardly find sufficient to buy a cigar.

His position was certainly not enviable.

He applied to Mr. Lancaster, the old banker, to lend him a sum sufficient to take him back again to England.

But, although that rich, hard-fisted old man could smile upon any one who heartily hated the young Fords, he was too much of a miser to part with one stiver to any one who could not give in exchange unquestionable notes of hand, which, it must be confessed, Joel could not.

Young Flint, therefore, under the circumstances, knew not what to do.

He was at Leghorn, and there he must stay, for all anybody cared, and scarcely one among those who had formerly known him would condescend even to bow to him in the public streets.

Among those, however, to whom old Lancaster was at all liberal must be mentioned Tomasso, the well-known detective.

Young Joel had told him so many stories about the villany of the two youths, Tom and Frank, that the old banker made up his mind to spare no expense on his own part which might tend to bring them to justice.

When, therefore, he heard of the duel between Frank and the Marquis de Sangri, and of its unexpected termination, he raved and swore like a lunatic.

He had fully made up his mind that De Sangri would kill young Frank, and he felt delighted.

For it must be confessed that he had his suspicions, and strong ones, also, for supposing that his charming daughter Nelly not only liked, but loved, the Captain of the Boy Volunteers.

He had given Tomasso large sums to assist him in bringing Frank and Tom to justice regarding the duel, but Tomasso quietly put the money into his own pocket, and winked slyly.

When Frank and his brother Tom, therefore, had made good their escape from Leghorn, Tomasso sought an opportunity to speak with old Mr. Lancaster at his own hotel.

But the old banker was out when the detective called.

"This," Tomasso said, "was a sad disappointment to him;" and he pulled such a very long face that the servants at the hotel thought Mr. Lancaster's absence at the moment was a great misfortune.

But Tomasso thought otherwise.

He knew that the father was out before he called.

In truth, he had patiently waited until the old gentleman *had* gone out, and then he boldly went up to the hotel; and, since he could not see the father, he asked to see the daughter.

Nelly, beautiful as ever, but looking rather pale, melancholy, and thoughtful, received the message for her father, and, as the detective was descending the stairs, she discovered on her own writing-desk a letter, which was directed—

"MISS ELLEN LANCASTER.

"Personal and Private."

"What can this mean?" thought the blushing maid, as she toyed with it. "Oh, I suppose it is a billet from some love-sick count, marquis, or duke, as usual. All they admire me for is my father's money."

She was about to toss it into the fire, when a second thought struck her.

"The handwriting seems familiar," she mused. "I have seen it before, somewhere—yes, but where? The hand seems somewhat disguised. Who can it be from?"

She seated herself in an arm chair, and opened the letter.

Directly she saw the interior of the note, her face became deadly pale, as she whispered to herself—

"It is from Frank!"

For some minutes she could not—she dared not attempt to read it.

She tried, but the tears flowed to her eyes freely, and blinded her vision.

With haste she went to her own chamber, and there, in strict privacy, she locked the door, kissed the letter times and times again, and read it through and through.

It ran thus:—

"DEAR NELLY,—Ere you read this, I shall be many miles away upon the briny ocean, bent on seeking fame and fortune in a land far more distant, and filled with more dangers and adventure than the sunny clime of Italy.

"You have heard of that sad occurrence between myself and the late Marquis de Sangri.

"Believe me, Nelly, the quarrel was not of my own seeking. It was the doing of your father in the first instance; and, although I went forth to do battle for my own honour, it was no less the love I bear you that steeled my hand and heart to do that dreadful deed.

"Nelly, you know not how much I have loved you throughout my whole life; whether in school at Bromley Hall, or in the tented field, you have ever been my guiding star of, love and hope.

"Your father hates me because I am poor; but, Nelly, gold does not make the heart, or control its longings and beatings. Were you poor, and I rich, I should love you all the same, and far more intensely than even I do now.

"But the world tells me, Nelly, that you, too, have grown cold and heartless, and that the name of 'Frank,' no longer escapes your lips.

"Be it so, fair one!

"May honour and happiness accompany you! is my earnest prayer. But, remember! the time may come, and that, perhaps, at no distant day, when you may learn to love and prize the heart you now so coldly despise.

"Your faithful lover, and always

"FRANK FORD."

Had a dagger pierced young Nelly's heart it could not have caused her more intense and acute agony than did the perusal of the brave young soldier's letter.

"He loves me still," sighed Nelly, with streaming eyes. "Oh, Frank, did you know me as I know myself, you would never accuse me of forgetting or despising you.

"Then, all the stories I have heard from the lips of Joel Flint and De Sangri about Agnese, the bandit's daughter, are untrue," she thought, at last, as she sighed heavily. "My heart told me that those rumours were false. I knew they were; his face, look, actions, words, all told me so, and yet I would not believe it. Oh, poor heart, how hast thou been deceived—aye, cruelly deceived."

As thus she spoke, she dried her tears, and a red, angry flush mantled her beautiful cheeks.

"They have played upon me," Nelly sighed. "I must be a woman, and no longer a girl. I will play upon them in return."

Surrounded as Nelly Lancaster had always been (since she started on her travels with her father, the old banker) by persons of title only, she knew and heard but little of what was really taking place in the great world around her.

Old Lancaster was a plebian, and had raised himself from nothing; but now that he was rich he had "great designs" for his daughter.

In other words, he, when young, had married from love, but he had made up his mind that young girls with fortunes had no right to look after such an article as love in matrimony.

If Nelly could only marry a duke, or a lord, or a marquis, all would be well, but that she could and should actually cast her eyes upon a friendless youth like Frank Ford seemed madness in his mind, and he could not entertain the thought for a single moment.

But we are not made as others would wish us.

We have hearts and minds of our own.

And if *he* had married for love alone in *his* hey-day of youth, it was more than possible that Nelly would make up her mind to do the same.

"For what are all the titled persons around me?" she often thought. "They are called counts and barons and dukes, and such like, but they are all like painted dolls; they do not like me for myself, they only covet my father's wealth, and, in exchange, would give me a faithless, worthless heart, and a lifetime of misery."

Such, however, was a destiny that Nelly Lancaster little cared about or feared.

"I would rather be a farmer's wife," she thought, "if he loved me, than all these painted, decorated, heartless people around me."

And the more she thus thought, the more her heart yearned to meet Frank once more.

But he loved another, she was told.

She could not—she would not believe it.

Did not his manly letter give the lie direct to all the falsehoods she had heard about him?

Was he not young, handsome, brave and talented?

And more than all, had he not loved her all his life?

This thought was too much for her feelings.

She sunk her head upon her heaving bosom and wept.

"He is now far away on the ocean," she thought; "it is impossible for me to meet him again, perhaps for years. Cruel, cruel youth!" she sobbed. "Why not have told me the whole truth before?"

## CHAPTER LXXVIII.

IN WHICH MATRIMONY IS SPOKEN OF—PROPOSALS FOR NELLY LANCASTER'S HAND—NELLY, LIKE A TRUE YOUNG WOMAN, CHOOSES FOR HERSELF.

WHILE the daughter thus wept in her chamber a curious scene was going on in the drawing-room, of which Nelly never dreamed.

Mr. Lancaster was talking to a dandily-dressed Italian fop, who, to his family name, had appended half a dozen titles.

He was a young insipid ape; yet he wore upon his breast the ribbons and insignia of many orders.

Orders, truly, which Mr. Lancaster was not aware could be *bought* from five pounds upwards.

This important, self-inflated, padded, walking advertisement of a tailor's bill he had never paid, and, moreover, never intended to pay, had been a frequent visitor during the old banker's sojourn in Leghorn, and rejoiced in the princely income of about £200 a year.

In truth, so attracted had he been by Nelly's reputed wealth, that he had followed her about from city to city, and would have proposed for her hand long before only the Marquis de Sangri had stood in the way.

And as De Sangri, as we have seen, was a great bully and duellist, this timid "nobleman" very wisely stood aloof until he had been "put out of the way" by Frank's well-directed bullet.

"Well, Baron Vermicelli," said old Lancaster, with a look of fatherly importance, "I have heard your proposal for my daughter's hand; but, you know, no one but the son of the best family in Italy could ever hope to obtain it."

The baron smiled and bowed.

He was able if need be, he said, to show Mr. Lancaster that he was the lineal descendant of Cæsar Augustus.

Which he could easily do, he knew, by procuring at one sovereign's expense some heraldist to trace his genealogical tree as far back as he liked even up to Noah, or Adam himself.

"But there are more considerations than title, even," said the banker; "I should not like my daughter to marry against her will."

"Oh, not for worlds," said the baron, twirling his moustaches.

"In the meantime, baron," said the old man, "I will think over the matter, and, as you seem to have been on very good terms with my daughter, I have no doubt but that the issue will prove favourable to your suit, and that the illustrious house of Vermicelli will not be in any way lowered by an alliance with the equally distinguished family of Lancaster."

The baron bowed himself out, and in a few moments Nelly found herself in the presence of her pompous father.

"Nelly, my darling," he began, "do you know the Baron Vermicelli?"

"Yes, father."

"Well, my dear, he has proposed for your hand in marriage."

"*My* hand, father?" said Nelly, laughing.

"Yes, *your* hand; he is of noble family, and can trace back to the time of the Cæsars."

"Really, father, you cannot be serious in this matter," said Nelly, biting her lip in annoyance.

"But *I* am, though," said old Lancaster, with a look of displeasure; "I have riches, and he has title, a very good exchange, I think. Think how it would sound in English society—'the charming young Baroness de Vermicelli.'"

Nelly laughed right out at her father's pompous manner, and afterwards said, calmly, but with an arch smile,

"I think the 'Countess de Maccaroni' would sound much better."

"I do not like your girlish whims," said old Lancaster, with a frown. "I have made up my mind on this match, and it must be as I wish."

"Would you have me marry a man I could never love?"

"Love? Fiddlesticks! What's love? It's all moonshine and shilly-shally, baby, girlish twaddle. Position is everything. He seems to be a nice young nobleman, and his attire——"

"Proves him to be a brainless ape," said Nelly, in scorn. "He is well enough in a drawing-room, and can be as namby-pamby as any one; but he will never be *my* husband!"

"Daughter."

"Father."

"I do not understand this foolish mood of yours."

"Nor I, father, understand why you should wish me to become the wife of the man I could never love."

There was a majesty in Nelly's manner that took her foolish parent by surprise.

He opened his eyes still wider, as she went on—

"Marriage, father, is not for a day, but for a life. When I marry, it must be to a gentleman of my own choice. Give me virtue in preference to wealth; love I would exchange for rank, and riches I would freely fling to the winds for an honest man—such an one I already love. Not all the world will change me, and, whether I be rich or poor, my affection will remain still the same—yes, as unaltered as *his* affection is for me."

"You love already, you say?"

"I do."

"And who may be the person, Nell? I think I guess who it once was—De Sangri!"

"De Sangri? Never!"

"Who then, Nell?" said old Lancaster, relenting. "Whoever it be, I know he must be noble, handsome, talented and brave."

He is all that, my father, and more," said Nell, falling on her knees before him, at the same time tears flowed from her eyes. "He is all you describe, father dear, and more."

"I do not understand you."

"He is *poor*," said Nelly; "but I love him all the more for that."

Old Lancaster frowned, as he said,

"His name?"

"Frank Ford."

"What!"

"Frank Ford."

Old Lancaster hastily rose from his seat.

He was red with vexation and passion.

"Mention not his name again, as you are my daughter."

"Why not, father? What harm has he ever done?"

"I *hate* him," said old Lancaster.

As he spoke, he disengaged his hand from those of his daughter, and thrust her from him.

As he left the apartment, he turned round, cast a look of withering scorn upon Nelly, as he muttered,

"Frank Ford! I *hate* the very name, and would rather see you dead at my feet, Nell, than ever consent to such an unequal match."

---

## CHAPTER LXXIX.

### FATTY FIGHTS WITH THE BLACK SPECTRE OF THE RUINS, AND DANCES WITH A SKELETON.

"And how have all the lads behaved themselves since I have been away, Hugh," said Frank, one evening, as they were sailing merrily and gaily across the Atlantic, on their way to the sunny land of Mexico.

"Oh, nothing could have been better," replied Hugh, "they acted on all occasions worthy of their name and nation, and were the pride and admiration of all with whom they came in contact."

"And Fatty, how has he been?" asked Buttons, with a grin. "Has he got into any scrapes?"

"A few, I'll warrant," said Frank, "for the fat old rascal is always up to some nonsense or other. But here he comes. Don't say a word. I'll question him, and pump out of him all that has happened."

"Why Fatty," said Frank, "you don't seem as stout as usual. What has happened?"

"Oh, he swears that one night he saw a ghost."

"A what?" asked the count, laughing.

"A ghost, count," said Hugh, laughing.

This announcement was received with roars of laughter by all present in the cabin.

The loudest of all in their merriment was Master Buttons, who laughed till the tears ran out of his eyes again.

"What are you laughing at, eh!" growled Tony at Buttons. "You are always laughing at me. I won't stand it any longer."

"No, I wouldn't," said Frank, tittering, "but you see, Fatty, it is very hard to believe in ghosts."

"I don't think so," Fatty replied, moodily, "for *I* have seen one, and more than that, I have played cards with a ghost. What do you think of that?"

"Played cards with a ghost," said the count, in surprise, "why, what next, I wonder."

"But it's true, though," said Fatty, "and no mistake."

"Tell us all about it, Fatty," said the general voice.

"Well, I don't mind, but you must keep all your laughing to yourself, for to me it was anything but a laughing matter."

"Well go on—we are all attention."

"Fill up the glasses, first," said Tony, "and pass a cigar this way."

This was done, and after a moment or two of profound silence and expectation, Tony began thus:—

"I see Master Buttons grinning already, but before I'm done I have no doubt he will shiver in his shoes.

"You see," said Fatty, "that the chaplain of the 12th Garibaldian Volunteers, who were encamped next to us, died rather suddenly, and as he requested to be buried in the churchyard of his own native village his last wishes were complied with.

"The old man was much beloved by all the volunteers, and as a mark of respect, one man was detailed from each company around us to do him honour.

"Hugh Tracy detailed me to represent the Boy Volunteers, and as I much wanted a little spree of some kind, I felt very glad of the opportunity thus afforded me.

"There were twenty-four volunteers attending the funeral, and as I was fond of driving, and knew more about horses than the Italian fellows, they appointed me to drive the four-horsed hearse.

"Now the village we had to go to was just in front of our 'lines,' and very near the Austrians, altogether about ten miles from our camp.

"We did not, from one cause or another, stir on our journey until about four o'clock in the afternoon.

"Now the men of the village we were going to had heard of the old clergyman's death, so that when we marched slowly along towards our destination, we were met by crowds of men, women and children, who had come forth to do honour to the worthy old man.

"Such crying, howling, and lamentation you could never conceive; for among those then present, some had lost sons, and fathers, and husbands in the war, and they cried out vengefully against the Austrians, and their iron rule over the Italians.

"We had not gone far, however, and were mounting the side of a lofty and steep hill, in slow, solemn procession, when it came on to rain.

"The clouds lowered, and all soon became inky darkness around us.

"We toiled along until we came to the top of the hill, when it was decided to halt the procession until next morning.

"This was agreed to willingly by me, for I was almost soaked to the very marrow with rain.

"At the top of the hill stood the ruins of an old church, which had been destroyed by cannon shot during a recent battle, and as it afforded a good place of shelter for the night, I unhitched my four horses, and tied them up out of the rain in a good shed.

"The next thing to do was to place the coffin in a place of safety.

"The vestry of the old church was in good order, and our men placed the body there upon tressels for the night.

"Some of the volunteers went into the village, and some to farm houses.

"Before I was aware of it I found myself alone, deserted, and miserable in that old ruin, with no one to talk to but the dead body of the old chaplain.

"More than that, the country folk said the place was haunted.

"I didn't like to make a noise about it, so tried to arrange things as comfortably as I could for the night.

"I collected a large heap of wood, and soon had a fire crackling and roaring up the chimney.

"I next took several of the mourners' cloaks, and hung them up before the window to keep out the wind.

"I closed the door, and drew an old stool up to the fire, and leaned my head on the ruins of a three-legged table I found there, and made myself as cosy as possible.

"When on the road, I appeared to be in such grief about the old chaplain, that the good country folk, to comfort me, made me presents of bottles of wine, pork pies, and such like, until at last I had a basketful before we had reached the ruin.

"With this basket and its contents I soon made acquaintance, for I was terribly hungry."

"As you always are," whispered Buttons.

"Silence!" said Frank. "Go on, Fatty."

"When I had demolished three large pork pies, and washed them down with a bottle of wine, I began to feel dozy.

"But to keep myself awake, I drank more and more of the wine, and pulling out a pack of cards, tried to amuse myself, until at last I tumbled off the stool, and fell fast asleep before the roaring fire.

"How long I remained there I can't tell.

"It could not have been very long, perhaps, but when I awoke the fire was burning dim and low, the candle was almost out, and what should I see sitting on his haunches opposite to me but a thin, long-legged stranger, dressed in black from head to foot.

"My blood curdled in my veins, for, thought I, this is the ghost they spoke of.

"I slowly raised myself up, and sat on the stool, eyeing the mysterious stranger.

"But he moved not, no, not a muscle; not a wink was visible; and his coal-black eyes stared at me, and glowed fiercely in the fire-light.

"I am a soldier," said Fatty, "and don't fear any man; but when a fellow falls in with a ghost, no wonder his legs tremble, as mine did.

"We sat facing each other for fully five minutes, and my heart was beating violently.

"I filled out a goblet of wine, and took a long drink, to keep up my courage.

"'It's very warm to-night,' said I, trying to commence a conversation.

"'It is,' said the ghost, in sepulchral tones; 'it's always warm where I come from.'

"'And where did you come from?' said I.

"'From below.'

"The devil! thought I; this is a ghost, and no mistake, and my hair began to creep on my head. I'm certain it stood on end.

"'Will you have a drink?' said I, handing the ghost a goblet of wine.

"'Thanks,' said the man in black, taking the wine from my trembling hand, and looking right through me with his glowing eyes.

"'Thanks,' said he, in that same sad, sepulchral tone. 'I'm very thirsty; it's very dry where I come from.'

"He drank the wine with a sour-looking face, as if the liquid was gall.

"We did not speak for some time.

"He was watching me, and I was watching him, like two cats in the dark, just before they spring at each other's throats.

"His fingers were long, bony, white, with sharp nails, and as he spread them out on his knees and grinned at me, I could see two rows of teeth, which looked more like the fangs of a serpent than anything else.

"Besides all this, his face was thin, narrow, and of a tallow colour.

"His nose was hooked, and his eyebrows widely arched, and above them, his temples looked all bare, and there was little hair on his head, except on the top.

"The more I looked at him, the more I hated him, but what was to be done? I did not like to run away, but looked at the vestry door very anxiously.

"'The door is locked,' said the man in black, with glittering eyes.

"I knew not what to do, but at last I trimmed up the candle, and taking up the pack,

"'Will you have a game of cards?' said I.

"'Not the least objection,' was the answer.

"In an instant he rose to his feet with a sudden spring that startled me, and sat on the edge of the table.

"I could scarcely breathe, but still I said,

"'What shall we play for?'

"'Anything you like,' was the answer.

"I shuffled the pack, but this did not suit him.

"He took the cards, and played with them for a second or two, and it seemed to me the cards flew about and around him as if they were enchanted.

"He dealt, and I led.

"But, lor! it was no use of me attempting to play with him.

"He won every game, and I drank deeply of the wine.

"I had lost all my money. In fact, I played him for the very clothes on my back, aye, down to the boots I wore.

"He won all—everything.

"Each game he won made him more anxious to play again.

"But I had nothing to play for now, and was getting so drunk I could scarcely see.

"But I saw plainly enough that while his long, bony fingers shuffled the cards, he was grinning most hideously at me, and his eyes seemed to penetrate my very heart.

"'Is there anything else you will play for?' said he, in a solemn way, which made my blood run cold.

"Oh, the devil! thought I, this monster has won everything I've got in the world, and now he asks me if I've got anything else I'd like to play for.

"Perhaps it's my soul he's driving at, thought I.

"The blood rushed to my face, and my hand trembled, as I seized an empty wine bottle and flourished it over my head.

"'Devil, avaunt!' I cried, staggering about. 'Angels and ministers of grace defend us; be ye a spirit of health, or goblin damned. Avaunt! quit my sight, my name is Danger.'

"But the ghost did not stir.

"He laughed loudly, till the old ruins shook again, and the clock struck twelve!

"''Tis the witching hour of night, when churchyards yawn,' said he, with a ghastly smile.

"I stopped to hear no more.

"With one blow I closed with the ghostly stranger, and broke the bottle over his head.

"The fight that then took place between us was terrible, and deadly.

"I was sobered in a minute, but he clutched me in his arms, and would have borne me away, but my legs caught the tressels which supported the dead man's coffin, and down it came with a crash, broke the coffin, and out rolled the dead body!

"Here was an awful sight.

"Beyond this I remember nothing. I have some recollection of having hit right and left, but the last thing I can recall was the ghost laid me low, as flat as a pancake, with the three-legged stool, and,

"With a horrible laugh, he vanished through the window, shouting '*we shall meet again!*'

"Next morning I found myself lying down across the dead body of the chaplain, with my head all cut and bruised.

"I had a couple of black eyes, and every tooth in my jaws was loose.

"Large bumps had risen on my cheek bones, and my lips were swollen to the size of those of an African negro.

"When discovered I was moaning and groaning.

"I told my story to all the villagers and peasantry about, and they believed firmly, as I did and do now, that I had encountered the Black Spectre of the Ruins, about which there has been so much talk in those parts."

"Well if *they* believed it was a ghost, *I* don't," laughed the Count.

"Nor I."

"I do," said Buttons, whose eyes were starting out of their sockets with the story.

"But I haven't finished yet," said Fatty, tossing off a bumper of wine.

"Well, what happened afterwards?" said Frank.

"Not much, we buried the old chaplain next day, and, strange to say, the village clerk had his right eye bandaged, and a large white cloth round his head, for he, too, it seems, had met with the Black Spectre somewhere in his travels on that same night, and had been served out just as I had been.

"I should not have noticed this strange adventure but for one thing," said Fatty, solemnly, "and that one thing proved to me that I had seen a real ghost and no mistake."

"What was it?"

"Why, when he vanished through the window, he screamed out,

"'*We shall meet again.*'

"And did you?"

"Yes."

"How did it happen?"

"When?"

"Well, I'll tell you.

"Several weeks after that, when I had got rid of my black eyes, and the bumps on my head had disappeared, I felt as gay as a lark, for all the ladies around Crema sent me presents, because they said I must be very brave, and good, for I had fought with the devil himself, and had come off victorious.

"Presents of all kinds came flowing in upon me, and as there was a grand bal masque to come off in a few days, I was invited by an old nobleman who had heard my story.

"'You need not provide yourself with any dress,' said the old Italian, 'for I have many suits which will prove suitable.'

"All life and joy, I went to his house, where the masque was to take place, and, as dancing did not commence in earnest until about ten o'clock, I sat at dinner longer than usual, and amused them very much with stories about the Boy Volunteers, and particularly with my terrible adventure with the Black Spectre of the Ruins.

"'I'm glad to hear you are such a brave fellow,' said the old noble, with a smile, and, in a confidential whisper, added, 'There is an old room in this mansion which is haunted.'

"'Is there?' said I, by no means relishing the idea of meeting with any more ghosts or spectres.

"'Yes,' said he, 'and, as you seem to have the power of expelling evil spirits, I should much like that you would try and find out all about this mystery in the house; if you succeed, I will bestow upon you anything you name.'

"Now, as he was rich, and had very pretty daughters, I made up my mind to face the devil himself in order to marry one of them.

"But, just as I had made up my mind, I could hear a dismal echo, which said more than once,

"'We shall meet again.'

"I drank deeply of wine, and about half-past nine the old noble conducted me to a room where I could exchange my soldier's dress for a masquerade suit.

"He opened the door, and I entered.

"'You will find plenty of clothes in that box,' said he. 'Help yourself, and do not be long ere you join in the dance.'

"'But about this haunted room?' said I.

"'There will be plenty of time to see into that little matter after supper,' said he, and left me.

"Directly he had gone the door closed with a sharp crack as if a spring had snapped.

"I did not take any notice of this at the time, and began to prepare myself for the bal masque.

"The old oak chest the nobleman pointed out to me contained splendid suits of all kinds, sizes and colour.

"I selected the gayest-looking, and dressed myself with great care, for, as I was the 'lion' of the evening, I wished to make as great an impression as I could upon the fair dames present.

"I never did so before, but on this occasion I powdered and brushed, and did everything I could to make myself good-looking."

"A very difficult task, I should think," said Master Buttons, grinning.

Fatty looked fierce for a moment, and then proceeded.

"I had been fully an hour over my toilet, and as I stood before the glass admiring myself, I came to the conclusion that there could not be a finer fellow anywhere than I should prove to be in the ball-room.

"I danced about the room, trying all my best 'steps' and 'graces,' and yet something said loudly in my ear—

"'We shall meet again!'

"I laughed off this thought, and was about to look into the old chest again for a splendid silken scarf I wished to wear, when, judge of my horror and amazement, there sprung out of the box a living skeleton! (See Cut in No. 23.)

"I would have shouted with horror, but could not.

"My tongue was dumb, and my knees shook almost from under me.

"'We have met again!' laughed the skeleton.

"And in an instant he was beside me, and whirled me round and round the room in a fast and furious waltz.

"What to do or what to say I knew not.

"Judge of my intense horror to be dancing madly round and round in the embrace of a skeleton!

"I was more dead than alive.

"I should like to have fainted, but I could not.

"Before I could recover my senses, the skeleton whipped a long red cloak out of the chest, and put it on.

"He next found a plumed hat and a black mask.

"This he also put on, and, suddenly seizing me by the arm, touched a secret spring.

"The door opened, and we both went forth from the apartment arm-in-arm.

"It seemed to me that I was dreaming.

"But it was not so; for, whenever I felt weak in the legs, the skeleton gave me such a pinch in the arm or thigh with his long, bony fingers, as made me wince again with pain.

"Arm-in-arm we went down the grand staircase.

The band was playing delicious music.

"The servants flung wide the the folding-doors, as, with a loud tone, they announced, 'Signor Toni Waddledooki!'

"At any other time, I should have felt proud, but at that moment I would have given worlds not to have heard the sound of my own name.

"The skeleton, disguised as he was, still clung to my arm until we got into the centre of the room, where we were met by the old nobleman and a large crowd of ladies.

"'Allow me to introduce to you, ladies,' said the old nobleman, smiling blandly, 'allow me to introduce to you the brave hero of the Black Spectre of the Ruins.'

"I bowed sadly, and would have said something; but the bony gentleman beside me gave me such a pinch that I fairly groaned with agony.

"'And who is your friend in the red cloak?' said the old nobleman.

"Before I could answer him, the skeleton stranger threw off all disguise, and appeared in his true form before them.

"Loud screams from the ladies followed.

"Some fainted; others dashed madly from the room.

"The musicians jumped out of the orchestra, trampling on each other, and breaking all their instruments in the wild confusion.

"The gas was turned off.

"All was pitch darkness.

"The mansion was in a terrible uproar from top to bottom.

"Old ladies and gentlemen tumbled over each other in getting down stairs.

"The footmen, cooks, and other servants rushed about madly hither and thither.

"Such a terrific noise, confusion, bustle, cursing, and swearing, and general babble you could never conceive.

"The whole town was soon alarmed, and the house was besieged by an angry, excited mob.

"What came of it all I didn't stop to see, so hurried down stairs into the street, and, dressed as I was, never stopped running until I got to our camps again.

"If *that* wasn't a ghost or a spectre," said Fatty, out of breath, "there never was one."

"An excellent story," said several, in a breath.

"Yes; rather an exciting one," said Frank.

"But it only lacks one thing to complete it," said Hugh, laughing.

"Then there is some secret about it," said the Count.

"Yes."

"What is it?"

"Why," said Hugh, "the truth is that the Black Spectre of the Ruins that Fatty saw was none other than the clerk of the next village, who had called to pay Fatty a visit."

"I won't believe it," said Tony.

"It is true, though; but you were so tight you could not distinguish anything that night."

"Well, but it was a real skeleton, anyhow," said Fatty, "no one can dispute that."

"Yes, *I* can," said Hugh, laughing. "I had heard so much nonsense about our bravery in fighting ghosts, that, when I was informed of your going to the bal masque, I got into the mansion, hid myself in the old chest, where I knew the old nobleman kept his masque suits, and, with the aid of a few human bones, and a skull, I attired myself as a skeleton, and almost frightened Tony out of his wits.

"I know the affair created a great noise at the time, but now that we are far away from Italy, the truth does no harm."

Hugh's explanations were received with much merriment and laughter.

## CHAPTER LXXX.

WARNER STILL GROPES HIS WAY IN THE LEFT WING OF BROMLEY HALL—THE PLACE IS HAUNTED.

THE position of Warner in the deserted wing of Bromley Hall was not by any means an enviable one.

He would have given a thousand pounds to have got out of the mouldy and damp place, for wherever he went he only encountered fresh horrors.

What had become of his companion Puggy he knew not.

Time seemed to have no change.

All was darkness and perpetual night.

"Am I to *die* here?" thought Warner, as he sat down, prostrated with weakness and fatigue.

"This place is filled with horrors.

"Whichever way I turn I encounter some strange and supernatural spectacle.

"What brought me here at all?

"What has become of my companion, Barney?"

Thus he thought, and on whichever hand he endeavoured to grope his way in the darkness, he found no possible outlet for escape.

"I am entombed alive!" he gasped.

The memories of all the villanies he had committed in his whole life flitted through his mind in a ghastly, dismal procession.

These recollections were worse than death itself to Warner.

He could have torn his hair in madness.

The ghost of old Ford, and the spirits of the murdered policemen darted across his staring eyes.

Each hole and corner seemed peopled with devils, who on every hand were shouting out—

"Murder! murder! murder!"

Days passed, and yet he could find no way to escape.

He retraced his steps as best he could, without a lamp, and he only wandered about in the inky darkness to find himself still more puzzled and baffled.

The position of Warner was terrible indeed.

Had he not fortunately discovered a few dozen bottles of choice old wine, he must have died from sheer starvation.

The nutritious juice of the grape, however, sustained his tottering limbs.

A week passed, and yet he could not liberate himself.

He had, in this time, grown haggard and old-looking.

His hair, and brow, and limbs, were bathed in a clammy sweat, and his knees shook from under him.

Now he would grope about like a feeble child.

Again he would sit down as if to die.

He tried to resign himself to his awful fate, and resolved to hang himself if possible.

Anything was better than the agony he was suffering.

Sleep forsook his eyes.

His brain was almost reeling.

He fell upon the stone pavement of a dark chamber, and his head knocked against it with so much force that the sound re-echoed again.

"I must die at last!" he gasped. "I have no further strength; my brain is all on fire!"

As he thought thus, he distinctly heard two voices conversing outside the door.

He started like a man in a terrible dream.

"I tell you he cannot escape," said the faltering voice of an old man.

It was Giles, the gardener.

"I tell you he cannot escape, Mr. Gale, if he has once got into this old deserted wing, for it has been shut up for half a century or more, and has never been opened as far as I could ever find out."

"But I tell you that he *will* escape, if there is but a rat-hole through which he can crawl."

"Gale!" thought Warner. "Why, that is the celebrated detective. What brings *him* here?"

"It is doubtful if he *is* here," said the old man. "It is more than a week since we captured the other one."

# THE BOY SOLDIER; OR, GARIBALDI'S YOUNG CAPTAIN.

THE MYSTERY.—*See Number 28.*

"After long observation Pedro, our guide, rode up, shouting 'stampede,' 'stampede.'

"And quicker than may be imagined, our waggons were halted and formed into squares, and our horses secured therein against the possibility of their being tempted to run away with any of the wild companions approaching.

"Within a short time we saw a long black line in the far distance, and as the dull and increasing roar of thousands of hoofs came galloping towards us, we distinctly saw immense herds of these wild horses plunging along, tossing their heads and manes and tails high in the air, and kicking up their heels in utter wildness.

"Nearer and nearer they came towards us.

"Pedro and many others of us anticipating some sport and profit were busy with lassos and ropes.

"Our cattle being safely tethered to the waggons, we awaited the coming charge of these wild horses with composure.

"Following Pedro's example, I and others turned Spaniard for once, and coiled up our horse-hair lassos, designing to cast them at the coming herd, and try our fortune in catching wild horses.

"On they came nearer and nearer, the noise increasing every instant.

"They perceived our waggon train, and swerved to the right and left of it, sweeping along at a tremendous gallop.

"We waited upon their flanks.

"The horses we rode were excited to very great nervousness and quivering in every limb with excitement, until at last they sweep past us amidst a vast cloud of dust like a mighty rushing wind.

"We approached and galloped near them, and then threw the lassos.

"But all in vain.

"The dust prevented us seeing whether we had secured anything or not.

"But my lasso being loose convinced me I had not at all events.

"In the confusion and dusk, some stray wild horse 'cannoned' against poor 'Dando,' and rolled both him and me in the grass; the last horse in the wild herd jumped over me very unceremoniously, and gave more than one kick in passing to the prostrate 'Dando.'

"From the shouting of Pedro and the others, and the tautness of the lassos at their saddle bows, and objects rolling helplessly in the dust, some yards from each, convinced me that many of our brave lads had succeeded much better than myself, and were each leisurely securing a horse.

"Meanwhile the track of the flying herd was plainly seen.

"For their passage through the grass was like a well-trodden, well-rolled road, and the dusty cloud in their rear, broken by the passing breeze, revealed in the distance many animals straggling far behind.

"Among the dozen wild horses secured by the lads of our train was a very fine stallion, who broke the rope that bound him, and starting up with great fury charged right through the circle of his captors, and dashed after the herd with headlong speed.

"The other captures being mares and yearlings, offered but little opposition after the first desperate attempt at liberation, and followed our train among some tame horses with but slight indications of rebellion.

"This episode delayed our journey for some time, and as nightfall drew near, I could see that Pedro was hurrying on the train as fast as possible, so as to cross the river before sunset.

"We were yet several miles from it, and dismounting, he sent one of the Mexicans ahead so as to find the best ford and select good grazing and camping grounds.

"As we gradually approached the stream, Pedro looked often very anxiously towards that part of the horizon whence the wild horses had come.

"For the whole atmosphere in the west looked gloomy and smoky, and the clouds for many miles wore a dark, dull red colour.

"The last waggon had entered the forest, and had passed to the other side of the river.

"Teamsters were 'hobbling' their animals before going to graze, while pots and pans were busily employed around the many camp fires sparkling under the dark shade of the richly grassed forest.

"Until everything had been safely landed on the southern bank of the river, Pedro was frightfully nervous and excited, and frequently looked towards the smoky, blood-coloured clouds which hid the fast-setting sun.

"But as soon as all were safely landed he resumed his usual gaiety, smoked cigarettes, and lay stretched on his blanket, apparently oblivious of every trouble in the world.

"While some were parching, or grinding, or making coffee, and others were concocting nameless savoury dishes of 'chili con carni,' I questioned Pedro, and he coolly observed that—

"*The prairie was on fire!*

"At first he did not think so, although the 'stampede' of horses suggested it, and careful subsequent observation had confirmed it.

"This fact so startled me, that it seemed strange such an idea had not presented itself before.

"We were perfectly safe, however, for the flames could not cross the river, and in all probability would not even touch within a considerable space of the woods opposite, for the pastures were green, and would not ignite.

"While sipping my coffee, I begged Pedro to recross the river, so that I might witness this novel sight; and after giving our horses an excellent feed of 'mice' (Indian maize corn), we went forth into the darkness, and recrossed the river, leaving our many fires sparkling against the dense darkness of the background, reflecting their light on the swarthy features of our teamsters and servants, and our merry band of boys, smoking, chattering, grinning, and card-playing, in groups of twos and threes.

"As we approached the edge of the forest, I could occasionally hear a dull roar, which came and went with each gust of wind.

"And when we trotted out of the forest into the open prairie, these sounds were explained.

"To the westward stretched, as far as the eye could see, a black line of smoke rolling against the blue and starless sky. Beneath it another, of flames, fanned into red, and orange, and white by the fitful breeze.

"Whenever the flames were red, the line was thin and low, and seemed not more than an air line on the landscape, advancing slowly.

"But when sudden blasts fanned it into white and yellow flames, they rose many feet in view, and swept along rapidly, destroying every blade of parched vegetation.

"The wind, beginning to blow freshly from the west, fanned the conflagration, and we could distinctly hear the crackling of reeds and underbush.

"It did not approach the green pastures bordering the forest nearer than within five hundred yards, and as it came towards us, our horses became exceedingly restive, and could scarcely be restrained from 'bolting.'

"In a few moments the fiery body advanced and passed us, and sped rapidly onward, leaving the prairie in a dull red heat, glowing or dying, while here and there a solitary tree, in bright silvery flame, stood out in bold relief against the blue of the sky and the glowing blood-colour of the plain.

"Such sights were not strange to Pedro, who puffed his cigarette with great composure, and looked on the smoking scene with Spanish indifference, simply thanking his holy Mother that they had got to camp in time.

"On the way back to camp, he told me many alarming and frightful stories of the ravages sometimes effected by these conflagrations; but as in the present instance the country was not populated, it could not get into the settlements before encountering some stream, which would effectually retard its progress.

* * * * * *

"At midnight, nearly all in camp were fast asleep, save Pedro and myself, who guaranteed to keep watch. Most of the fires were fitfully burning, and our men lay stretched under the waggons or beside the embers, snoring loudly and inharmoniously.

"Pedro, with back against a tree, was yawning, and as now cigarettes had no charm for him, I felt certain I should be the only one awake.

"No sounds were heard in this grand old forest,

save the owl, with its sudden flight and ceaseless challenge of 'teewit, teewit, teewho!' echoing from distant parts, and the moaning winds sighing among gigantic chestnuts, birches, and patriarchal oak trees.

"The moon began to peep from amid the clouds, and from where I lay beside its osiered bank, could see the deep dark waters of the river floating, winding on swiftly and silently, until lost in the labyrinthine mass of dark timber bending in lofty arches above, while rays of moonlight stealing through the leafy roof, discovered flocks of water fowl sleeping on its banks.

"The white crane stood sentry in the shade.

"Herons fluttered in the marsh.

"Startled birds would dart across the stream, where silver-backed fish were rolling and disporting on the surface.

"The scream of the wild cat and sudden flight of birds; the long howling of the wolf, the cry of the panther, and scream of the wild hog; these were the sounds that occasionally broke upon the ear in the quiet of the night as I lay absorbing the beauty and contemplating the magnificence of the scene, feeling dwarfed and full of awe at the prodigality of nature, and the magnitude and colossal proportions of this temple of nature, rising in island-like grandeur amid a sea-like expanse of prairie.

"If the dust-begrimed and careworn denizens of European cities knew but a tithe of the peace, beauty, plenty, and prodigality of nature strewn with lavish hands in the prairie islands of the west—if the pallid and weary man of thought could but escape for a time to enjoy the unearthly quiet and repose of these priceless retreats, to hunt in its woods, and bathe in its streams, to inhale the bracing breeze, and by manly sport to feel himself hourly growing robust and strong, with his dogs and gun and trusty horse tethered and waiting beneath the wide-spreading beech; it would solace his soul with a calm and peace unknown before, and for ever wed him to a closer communion with, and an instructive contemplation of, the wonders and magnificence of nature.

"But while I thus thought and dreamed of far-off England, I was suddenly aroused by a fierce and terrible growl behind me.

"I turned my head, and was horrified at what I there saw."

## CHAPTER LXXXIII.

TOM FORD AND HIS GALLANT CREW ONCE MORE PUT TO SEA—THE COMBAT—A HAPPY DELIVERANCE.

WHEN the old count had departed with Frank on their overland journey towards Mexico, Tom Ford and his gallant lads were left alone in the port of Galveston.

The Americans there knew very well that the Boy Soldiers were bent on joining the people against the French, and they rejoiced at it, for nothing could ever displease them so much as the idea that an emperor should install himself so near them on the great continent.

When Tom bade adieu to his brother, therefore, the Americans loudly cheered the Boy Soldiers, and escorted them for a long distance on their way with bands, banners, and much cheering.

But the Americans had no idea that Captain Tom Ford was also on the side of the Mexicans, for his two vessels were much too small to cope with the French men-of-war in those waters.

They were much deceived if they, for a moment, thought that Tom would remain idle, for such was not his nature.

There were several French spies, however, who had narrowly watched Captain Tom's manœuvres, and they were not slow in sending on their information and suspicions to the French and Mexican admirals at Vera Cruz.

Tom didn't suspect this until quietly informed of it by an American friend.

"What!" said Tom, to the American, "do you mean to say that any cowardly lubber has sent word to the French admiral, and that ships of war are on the way to watch us?"

"I guess that's the fact," said the long-legged American, chewing his quid, with a smile, "and although I don't wish any kind o' harm to any o' the sons of old Johnny Bull, I'd give you a piece of advice, and that is, skedaddle as fast as you kin, until sich times as you air strong enough to return to these diggings, and give the Frenchers an etarnal whipping."

Tom could not but smile at the American's advice; but before he acted he consulted the wishes of his crew.

That same night, at midnight, he was about to weigh anchor and depart, when the long-legged American again made his appearance, and, mounting the ship's side, he whispered in Captain Tom's ear,

"I calculate I've got a bit o' news as will suit you roving Britishers."

"What is it?" asked Tom, with a smile.

"Just awhile ago the Americans in town received word by pony express across the plains, that the French are driving all out of Mexico at the point of the bayonet who don't take the oath of allegiance to old Maximilian; there's a whole ship-load on their way to prison now, I hear."

"You don't mean that?"

"I do, though, and some mighty fine ladies on board, too; and if you could just chance to fall across that craft and capture it, I'd bet my bottom dollar you'd not repent the adventure."

"Perhaps not, my friend; but what sort of craft is it, and what's it's name?"

"It is called the 'Austrian Eagle,' and is a fast-sailing, ten-gun brig. You're sure to fall in with her if you go as far south as Zambia or Vera Cruz.

"All right, my friend," said Tom, and heartily thanked the long-legged American for his information.

The Yankee "liquored up," that is to say he drank a good draught of brandy with Captain Tom ere he left the ship, and went ashore rather "mellow."

That night, and about an hour after the American's visit, Tom signalled both ships to prepare to sail, and ere morning both vessels were far out at sea, with all canvas set, sailing for the south.

* * * * *

Tom had been two days at sea when the man on the look-out at the mast-head shouted, and hailed the deck.

"A sail! a sail!"

"In what quarter?"

"On the port bow."

"How far?"

"About twenty miles."

"Can you make her out?" shouted Tom, through his trumpet.

"Not much, captain."

"What is she like?"

"A fast-sailing brig, sir."

"Any guns?"

"Can't make them out, sir."

"Go aloft, lad," said Captain Tom; "and take my telescope to the look-out man at the mast-head."

"Aye, aye, sir," said the boy; and, with a smile, clambered up the rigging, and was at the mast-head in no time.

"Make her out now?" said Tom, through his trumpet. "See her ports?"

"Yes, captain; she's a ten-gun brig, and as pretty a craft as I ever saw," was the answer.

These words sent a thrill of joy to the hearts of all, both officers and men.

"Signal our companion," said Tom; "do you see her, look-out?"

"No, captain; she is obeying orders, and crossing to the eastward."

"Isn't she in sight?"

"No, captain. She was out of sight an hour ago."

"Fire a gun, captain," said another; "that will bring her closer."

"No, no guns, my lads, that would spoil all the sport. We mustn't let this Austrian brig know that we carry any guns at all, without she strikes her flag, and if she don't, why then we must sink her, that's all."

In a few minutes, all was prepared on board the fast-sailing, trim-looking vessel "Kaiser."

The guns were double shotted, and every man was at his post.

"Let every man jack of you hide himself as best he can," said Tom; "for the Austrians will be very curious to know who and what we are, but we must take care to deceive them."

In a few hours the two ships approached each other, and came almost within gun-shot.

Tom pretended not to notice the flag of the "Austrian Eagle," as it floated out in the breeze.

He made it appear as if he wished to pass the enemy without showing his own colours.

But he was soon forced to change his mind.

The Austrian commander fired a gun, and the shot ploughed up the water just athwart the "Kaiser's" bows.

"Rather cheeky, that," said an old salt, turning the "quid" in his mouth. "Rather cheeky, that,' of the stranger; I hope Captain Tom will return the compliment."

But, instead of "returning t... compliment," Tom backed his sails, and made ready to speak to the stranger.

"Ship, ahoy!" said the captain of the "Austrian Eagle," with his speaking trumpet, in stentorian tones.

"Ship, ahoy!" answered Tom.

"What vessel is that—where do you come from —and whither bound?"

"More cheeky still," said the old salt, in disgust.

"Answer that same question yourself," said Tom, in defiance.

"Are you for the emperor or the people?" asked the Austrian.

"The people, of course, always," said Tom, defiantly. "D——n Maximilian, say I, and all despots."

At the same time he said aside to his crew,

"Stand by, my merry men; be ready to run out your guns, and give the Austrian 'pepper.'"

He had scarcely spoken, when the Austrian captain, looking with contempt at the little craft, shouted out,

"I have seen your craft before."

"I dare say you have," laughed Tom, "and now you see it again, my hearty, I hope it will do your sore eyes good."

"Haul down your flag," said the Austrian; "that craft was captured by a band of English boys in the Adriatic some time ago. It formerly belonged to the Austrian admiral. Haul down your republican colours, or I'll sink you. Surrender, I say, surrender!"

"Come and take us, then, my brave fellow," said Tom, laughing; "you talk loudly enough, but I don't think you can do much when it comes to the 'pinch.'"

"Haul down your colours, you buccaneering rebels!" roared the Austrian captain, white with rage. "Haul them down this instant, or I'll sink you."

Instead of doing so, however, Captain Tom hauled up the British ensign over the Mexican flag, amid the cheers of his crew.

At that moment the Austrian fired a broadside at the "Kaiser."

But all the shots flew wide of their mark.

Shouts of derision resounded from the "Kaiser," and in a second the little craft discharged her guns in return.

The shots were well aimed, and tore the Austrian fore and aft.

The action now between the two vessels was desperate and quick.

The "Kaiser," however, always managed by Tom's superior seamanship to take the wind out of her enemy's sails, and he brought up his vessel so close that his crew could almost climb on the decks of the big Austrian.

"Quick and devilish, my merry men," said Tom; "don't waste much powder and shot at 'long taw.' Haul the 'Kaiser' closer still, rake her fore and aft once more, and then board her, sword in hand."

This resolve was received with loud cheers by Tom's English crew.

The Austrian, however, although the fight had lasted only ten minutes, was so damaged, that she wanted to get away, and sneak out of the fight, if possible.

Tom's quick eye saw this, but he only laughed, and shouted out, amid the din of battle,

"Keep close to her, lads; don't let her haul off an inch. Close with her, my lads, and show the Austrian and Mexican traitors what men can do who fight for liberty."

Dressed as he was in a splendid Mexican uniform, Captain Tom looked more handsome and brave than ever, as, sword in hand, and bare-headed, he rushed at the head of his men to board the stranger.

"They have got a lot of women and children on board, Captain Tom," said several. "I heard them scream, and beg the Austrian commander to surrender."

"I know that, my lads," said Tom, with an oath, "and that's the reason why I wish to board her at once, so as to spare the lives of the innocent."

When it became generally known on board the "Kaiser," that there were many women and children on board the Austrian, Tom's followers were mad with rage, and begged to be led on at once to board her.

"This way, then, lads—this way! I'll lead you."

"No, captain, you stay behind; you might get hurt or killed," said many brave tars.

"Let us go first, captain, and clear the way."

"No, you won't," said Tom, laughing; "I have always been first in danger, and will be first now. Follow me!"

With a loud shout, Tom's men followed their young and gallant leader.

They clambered up the sides of the Austrian ship like monkeys, and in an instant rushed on board, sword and pistol in hand.

Tom was first on the enemy's decks, and at one blow struck down two or three of the enemy.

The combat, for at least five minutes, was desperate in the extreme.

But the fiercenes of Tom's followers was so great, and the weight of their blows struck such terror into all who opposed them, that ere long a joyful shout from his men told too well that the fight was over and that the ship was captured.

The last to surrender was the first lieutenant of the Austrians.

He was a big, burly, ferocious-looking man, and he rushed at Tom with a frightful oath of vengeance.

Tom parried his blow, and the next instant the Austrian lieutenant was cleaved to the deck.

At that moment, and while the old commander, on one knee, begged for his life at Tom's hands, great cries were heard from below.

A number of fair ladies rushed on deck in a frantic manner, and, falling on their knees, hailed their deliverance with joy, kissing Tom's hand, and blessing him as their deliverer. (See Cut in No. 25.)

## CHAPTER LXXXIV.

THE CAUSE OF ALARM—FATTY IN TROUBLE—HE IS RATHER FOND OF HIS MEDICINE—BUTTONS WISHES THAT HE HAD PLENTY OF SUCH STUFF TO CHEER HIM — FRANK CONTINUES HIS JOURNAL, AND RELATES ALL HE SAW OF FIELD, FOREST, RIVERS, BIRDS, "VARMINT," AND THE LIKE, WHICH HE OCCASIONALLY READS TO HIS COMPANIONS.

THE cause of Frank's surprise and horror can be easily explained.

He had been so absorbed in the wild beauties around him, that he took no heed of the fact that nearly all of his boy followers were fast asleep.

He had heard all sorts of noises from wild animals in the forest, but he took no notice of them.

He had also heard a peculiar noise very near him like that of a baby's rattle.

He did not know what it meant.

Twice he heard it, at short intervals.

The third time it sounded, he was startled by a sudden cry of pain from one of the lads.

A rattle-snake had given its usual warning, but master Fatty and Buttons were so intent upon finishing a pigeon pie, which Pedro the guide had made, that they took no notice of anything, until, with a scream of agony, master Fatty found himself in the folds of a large-sized rattle-snake.

In an instant, his cries aroused the whole camp.

The Mexican teamsters ran off on the instant, but Frank at once saw what ought to be done.

The rattle-snake's tail was coiled round a small tree, and the remainder of its powerful body would have crushed Fatty to death.

Frank seized his sword, and bounded down the rock with fearlessness.

With two strokes, he cut the rattle-snake into halves, and then, with another blow, severed off its head.

Fatty's speedy deliverance from the folds of the snake saved his life.

But all was not yet over.

The venom of the reptile had entered Fatty's veins.

How was it to be eradicated?

No one knew.

At that moment, Pedro the guide, came forward with a cup of whisky.

"Drink, drink," said he, in haste, "it is the only cure we know of here in these parts."

Fatty did not refuse, but drank down the whisky until it almost choked him.

"My eye," said Buttons; "talk about medicine being nasty stuff, I wish I had Fatty's complaint, that's all."

"Drink, drink, I say," repeated Pedro, "it's your only chance for life, you must get blind drunk, or it's all of no use."

Tony's fat body was somewhat bruised, and he felt so sore all over, that he could not refuse anything, and not only drank one cup of whisky before he was blind drunk, but, as Buttons observed, "made a very large hole and signed his name pretty legibly in a second cup."

Fatty continued taking his medicine regularly for more than an hour, about which time he began to reel about and to hiccup, to sing, to dance, and make himself generally ridiculous to all assembled in camp.

As Pedro said, it was the only medicine for deadly, poisonous, snake-bites known in that wild region, and, true enough, it saved the life of Fatty, although he rolled about and tumbled over everything that came in his way, and at last fell down beside a roaring camp-fire and was soon fast asleep, snoring loudly.

This incident, which at first caused so much fear and alarm among the travellers, was duly recorded in captain Frank's journal.

But, unlike the rest, it did not cause him any uneasiness.

He again went forth into the moon-lit forest, and amused himself.

Everything he saw was so unlike anything he had heard or read of in England, that he did not fail to make remarks thereon in his note-book, some of which he thought might be amusing or interesting to those who might ever chance to read his journal.

We will not in this place attempt to describe his thoughts or note his observations, but the best thing we can do for those who have followed in these pages the fortunes and adventures of the Boy Soldiers, is to give the young captain's ideas in his own exact words.

Therefore, we continue the journal where it left off in a previous chapter, which reads as follows:—

"Unconscious of the flight of time, I sat gazing on the view around me, beneath the shade of a towering chesnut, puffing volumes of smoke, and full of pleasant imaginings.

"No description could paint the scene, and I sighed for power to reproduce, in any form, the mass of wild beauty abounding on every side.

"The moon was high in the heaven, and its light was so brilliant and entrancing that one could read the smallest print with ease.

"I distinctly saw animals moving about the undergrowth, and many cautiously approached the river edge to drink.

"Terrapins on logs occasionally flapped and splashed in the water.

"Groups of geese and ducks would cackle and quack in sudden alarm and rush to the river, and, where they had been but a moment before undisturbed, foxes or wolves stealthily approached to reconnoitre.

"The solemn crane and stately turkey took sudden wing, and again silence reigned over all.

"The hard-breathing, ungainly bear was heard in the distant cane-break, trampling down the cane, which cracked like the explosion of numberless crackers.

"The king-fisher and fish-hawk would suddenly dive, and emerge from the surface with one of the finny tribe hopelessly gyrating in their bills or talons, and fly off into the darkness.

"And even as I turned and stirred the dying embers of the fire, its light disclosed a splendid buck, who had quietly approached, and, with head proudly erect, was looking at the intruders of his domain stretched in sleep.

* * * * *

"The camp was astir early in the morning.

"But the sun had arisen, and the forest was alive with the song of birds.

"The water and pasture being of excellent character, and as the animals required rest after toiling through heavy sands, Pedro resolved to camp there for one or two days.

"This determination of our head man was received with acclamation, and each began to prepare for the chase.

"Guns were plentiful, and all had revolvers and hunting knives, and when Antonio (second in command) returned before breakfast with a string of squirrels thrown over his shoulder, and threw them to the cook, with orders to fry immediately for our meal, our swarthy, large-eyed attendants were in surprise, and anxious to go forth immediately in search of 'potstuff.'

"After appointing camp guards, Pedro, Antonio, and myself, with many others, went forth with shot guns and rifles in search of game.

"But others of our train were already blazing away in all directions, and, from their shouts, there could be no doubt of their success.

"My companions were excellent hunters, and, although having but few dogs, and those untrained, made good use of their time, and reported success.

"I did not relish being incommoded by any excitements of the chase, but rather enjoyed my solitary walk through the forest, for at every step there was novelty.

"The strange herbage, birds unknown, of varied plumage, and wild flowers never seen before, attracted me more than hunting, and I strolled through tangled under-brush in pleasant reverie, the sunlight pouring in golden columns through leafy apertures—the sudden glance of variously-plumed birds through these streams of light into the deep, densely-wooded shade.

"The rapping of red-topped wood-peckers on blasted trees—the shiver and rustle of the tender ivy, and the gay festoons of wild vines and honeysuckles arching from the trees and forming picturesque colonnades of shade.

"The song of the matchless mocking-bird—the flitting of squirrels, and flight of wild canaries, made this ramble in an untrodden forest a joy and pleasure never experienced or dreamed of before.

"I trod, perhaps, where mortal never trod before, and everything told of a wild, primeval beauty in which nature revels, and the slowly moving, gentle shaking of gigantic oaks and elms—the mammoth trunks of cypress and chestnuts, spoke of their existence in centuries wrapt in the history and mystery of the past.

"But though the density of the undergrowth prevented easy progress, there were here and there well-defined paths running through it, and so devoid of every vestige of vegetation as to look more like ordinary footpaths than cattle tracks, and I could not divine their origin or use.

"It seemed impossible that man could penetrate such dense shade, and by constant traffic thus form such roads.

"And I might have long remained in total ignorance of their meaning but from an accident.

"Observing, at intervals, on these footpaths, tumuli from two to four feet high, I sat upon one, and, lolling upon another, went fast asleep.

"But I had not long been thus, when I was stung on all parts of my person by a swarm of large-sized ants, both black and red.

"Suffering intolerable torture, I hurried away as fast as possible.

"For it was not only the needle-like sting that pained, but the hot and venomous nature of it that tingled the flesh long after.

"Beating my person violently in all directions, I must have destroyed hundreds, but I was literally covered with them, and the attraction of a few crumbs in my pockets had filled them.

"Such torment I never experienced before, and would have divested myself of everything immediately, only that the path on every side was beset with thorns.

"Hurrying to the river, I laid my rifle down and plunged in, clothes and all.

"For the first minute I suffered indescribable torture, for in their dying agonies they stung me with tenfold fury; but ere long they were killed, and the relief was indescribable.

"I remained submerged to my neck in water for many minutes, for it soothed me unspeakably, and I returned to camp a wetter and wiser man.

"These 'well-defined paths,' which attracted me so much, were naught else than grand highways of ants, occasionally extending for miles and with junctions here and there, leading to their various colonies. There is not a particle of anything growing on them, and, for a foot wide, are as well beaten as a garden walk or footpath through the meadows.

"They are used indiscriminately by ants of any size or colour; but there are frequent fierce battles between various tribes for pride of place; but I have often taken notice that the very small blacks ants always proved victorious, for they usually go forth in greater numbers, and attack the large red ones with much skill and success, not forgeting to carry off the carcase in triumph to their own colony.

"Unless there had been ocular proof, I could never have imagined that their numbers were so vast in these deserts.

"Yet, after rain, there is not two square inches of earth but what is literally moving with them.

"What office they may perform in the order of nature it is difficult to conceive; but they till the earth most indefatigably, and, doubtless, add to its fecundity, even as infinitesimal coral lay the foundation of islands in the south seas.

"My compulsory bath much relieved and refreshed me, but, on returning to camp, to change clothing and hang my leathern suit to dry, I found the place deserted by all but two lazy teamsters, who, under the shade of the waggons, were fast asleep, and perfectly oblivious of the depredations done by wild hogs or wolves, which, from the sudden rush through the bush and an occasional grunt, I knew had been there, feeding luxuriously on our various stores.

"As best I could, I made my way to Pedro and Antonio, and met two of the party returning with venison, ams, and skins.

"As we beat through the forest, Pedro suddenly halted, and pointed to a distant tree, up which a fine young bear had climbed some fifteen feet, and, unconscious of our presence, was scooping out honey from a knot-hole, which formed an entrance to the hive.

"A sudden gleam of sunshine gave a better view of Bruin, industriously engaged in robbery.

"His head was perfectly smothered with a swarm of bees, buzzing and stinging him in every part.

"Heedless of the busy creatures, Mr. Bear continued to scoop out and eat the honey, while a stream of the golden syrup ran to the ground.

"A shot was followed by a sudden roar, and, quickly descending, the bear disappeared in the tangle-wood.

"The excitement of a bear-hunt I never before experienced, and resolved to follow the grim Bruin.

"'You had better stay in camp with us, captain,' said Pedro, in a warning manner. 'You English are too rash. Bear-hunting isn't as easy as fox-hunting, you must know.'

"Thinking that there was a great deal of sarcasm in Pedro's remark, and to show him that English boys fear no danger, I grasped my rifle tightly and dashed off into the thicket after the enormous bear, with what success will be seen in another place."

## CHAPTER LXXXV.

### WARNER'S FLIGHT—THE CHASE—THE FRIENDLY RUSTIC—THE HIDING-PLACE.

THE intense sufferings which Warner had undergone in his place of confinement had reduced him almost to a skeleton, but now that he had a chance for freedom within his reach he felt a little stronger.

His wounded foot caused him much pain, and, as he stood shivering at the edge of the water, he knew not what to do for the best.

The hounds and dogs were barking and howling on the other side in a most inharmonious manner, but the servants of the Hall were clamouring and shouting like madmen.

"He has escaped!"

"I saw him get out on the other side!"

"I see him! I see him!"

"Let us run towards the bridge and stop him before he gets to the village."

Such were the cries which reached Warner's ears, as, almost fainting from fatigue, he hid behind a tree.

He had no weapon with him save the poker which he had stolen out of the parlour of the Hall.

But he seized it now more than ever with the energy of desperation.

For some time he remained behind the tree shivering and shaking.

He dared not go to the village, for he thought detective Gale might still be there.

To go to a farm-house and ask for shelter would have been equally unwise he considered.

For his appearance was so ragged, haggard, and his face so black and grimy that he would have been detected and informed upon immediately.

While he thus stood considering what to do, a man approached and touched him on the shoulder.

"Hullo, mate!" said the new comer; "you seem wet, and cold, and hungry."

"Yes, I am all that," said Warner, looking in astonishment upon the stranger.

"But what do you want here?" said the escaped villain, grasping his poker in a threatening manner.

"Oh, nothing, mate, in particular. I heard the hounds and dogs barking close by, and it seems the folks at the Hall are chasing somebody."

"So they are," said Warner, coolly. "A thief has been discovered on the premises, but he escaped."

"La! you don't say so?"

"I do, though. I was staying at the Hall myself with Mr. Gale, the detective officer, and hunted the villain all through the mansion, but couldn't catch him."

"Not up the chimney, sure-ly?" said the countryman. "For now I comes to look at you, it seems you are all smothered with soot."

"That's true enough. But where do you live?" said Warner.

"Just down here abit, in that small cottage."

"Will you let me stay there for half an hour. I'm too tired to think of going back to the Hall yet."

"I've no objection in the world, seeing as how you have been living at the Hall; for I used to be a labourer there myself once, before old Jonathan left so suddenly."

"Indeed," said Warner, who, though he spoke in a firm, but husky tone, still kept his ears open for the distant sounds of the dogs and the shouts of his pursuers.

"Oh, yes," said the rustic, "I have worked off and on at the Hall for this ten year or more. This way, mate. We haven't far to go."

Warner felt rejoiced at this news, and followed the rustic with hurried steps.

In a short time both of them reached the cottage and entered it.

A bright fire was glowing on the hearth, but there was no one there to greet him.

Warner had not been in the house more than ten minutes, when the sounds of the dogs could be heard more plainly than ever.

"They are on my scent," thought Warner, "and will be here in less than five minutes."

Warner now knew not what to do or how to act.

To fly would have been madness, for he was thoroughly unstrung, and was now as weak as a kitten.

The rustic smoked his pipe, and spoke not for some time; but he eyed Warner in a strange manner.

"You look rather shaky, my friend," said the rustic, smiling.

"Yes, I do, rather."

"The sounds of the dogs don't please you, I think?"

"What do you mean?" said Warner, fiercely.

"Oh, nothing, my hearty, only I saw your eyes looking rather wild, that's all."

"*Do* they look wild?"

"Yes, for all the world like those of a man who has just escaped from a lunatic asylum, or who has had a sharp run for his life, ha, ha."

"What do you mean?"

"I mean this," said the rustic, quietly. "You are the chap the detective has been after for some time past. *That's* what I mean."

And as he spoke, he smiled, and winked.

"What?" said Warner, seizing his poker.

"Nay, nay, friend; put that bit of iron down, there's no occasion for it now. Not here, at all events."

"What *do* you mean?"

"I only wish to ask you one question, that's all."

"What is it?"

"Will you tell me the truth if I swear to act your friend through thick and thin?"

"I will."

"Then your name is——"

"Smith," said Warner.

"Ha, ha; Smith, eh; well that's good and no mistake."

"It's the truth, though."

"No it ain't."

"How do *you* know?"

"I have good reasons for knowing it. Your name is Warner."

At the bare mention of his own name the villain's lips trembled.

He raised the poker in an instant.

"No, no, none of that here, Mr. Doctor," said the rustic; "for two can play at that game, you see."

And, as he spoke, he suddenly displayed a six-barrelled revolver.

"Now listen to me," said the rustic, coolly, "you don't know me, but I do know you. Ha, ha, strange, ain't it?"

"Why did you call me doctor for, then?"

"Because you are very clever in attending on sick people who have got lots of money to leave their nephews; look at Ford, the old chap as you——"

"H-u-s-h!" said Warner, sinking in a chair, hu-s-s-h; I perceive you know all. I am undone."

"No you ain't, if you promise me one thing."

"And what is that?"

"Go up-stairs, wash yourself, and have a shave; you'll find everything at hand ready for use, and more than that, look into the cupboard and you'll see plenty of clothes of all sorts and sizes, help yourself, and don't come down again until I whistle."

"I will."

"Then do it quick. Bolt the door after you, and if you should hear any men snoring in bed, don't mind them, they are pals of mine."

"But the light?"

"No one can see you; the room is formed right under the roof. You'll find a dark lantern burning. Up that ladder with you; quick, I say. Let the trap-door down gently again. Quick, I hear your pursuers approaching."

Warner did not wait to be told a second time.

He ran up the ladder and disappeared.

Directly he had done so, the rustic took away the ladder, and, opening a cellar-door, dropped it in, and closed the aperture.

"I hear them coming," said the rustic. "The dogs are howling awfully; but Warner is safe this time; he's a clever rascal, and will serve me after this as faithfully as a dog. If he don't *I'll kill him!*"

As the rustic thus thought, loud raps were heard at his cottage door.

Dogs were growling and sniffing outside; but the rustic did not speak.

Again the knocks were repeated, and more loudly than ever.

"Come in," said the rustic, gruffly.

"Open the door!"

"It *is* open."

"It is *not*. Open the door at once, Zoe, or we'll burst it open."

"Oh! you will, eh? Then burst away, you can't do much harm."

True to their word, the servants from the Hall, and others, broke open the door, and tumbled headlong into the cabin, dogs and all.

## CHAPTER LXXXVI.

FRANK CONTINUES HIS JOURNAL—THE BEAR FIGHT—HOW THE GALLANT YOUTH FOUGHT WITH BRUIN—THE VICTORY—THE BOYS CONTINUE THEIR JOURNEY THROUGH THE WILDERNESS—THE WAGGON TRAIN STOPS AT A VILLAGE ON THE SAN FERNANDO RIVER TO RECRUIT THEIR HORSES, OXEN, AND MULES—A GREAT PIGEON HUNT.

"WHEN the bear rushed away into the thick undergrowth in the forest, prudence would have taught me not to follow him.

"But Pedro's taunts aroused me, and rifle in hand, I darted after the beast.

"For some time I could not track him; but could plainly hear the huge monster trampling down the herbage and small shrubs.

"I wanted to get a good look at him; but could not.

"I was so much excited that I had no notion of how the time was passing, and less idea of how far I had gone from our camp.

"At last I caught sight of the bear.

"He was facing me, and his eyes glared most savagely.

"I leaned against a tree, and took deliberate aim.

"I discharged my rifle, and saw the bear fall, and give a most horrible growl.

"'I knocked him over that time,' thought I, and pulling my empty rifle against a tree, ran forward.

"But judge of my horror.

"The bear had been wounded, and the blood was flowing from him.

"But unexpectedly he rose on his hind legs, and with his fore legs was sparring at me like a fighting man.

"I was so surprised for a moment that I knew not what to do.

"I was then only about five feet from the monster.

"I dare not turn back, or he would have been upon me in an instant.

"His eyes rolled savagely.

"His jaws were clotted with blood from his wound in the head, and his white teeth glistened like ivory.

"He was snorting, and each instant approached me still nearer and nearer.

"My situation was most critical.

"I had nothing with me but my hunting knife and my revolver, all the chambers of which were empty save *one!*

"More than all, I was far away from all my companions.

"It was a case of life or death for one or both of us.

# THE BOY SOLDIER; OR, GARIBALDI'S YOUNG CAPTAIN.

THE FIGHT WITH THE INDIANS.

"I did not for a moment take my eyes off the monster.

"For I had often heard that directly you do so the 'varmint' will be sure to take advantage of it, and pounce upon you.

"Nearer and nearer the bear approached me.

"His long fore-paws almost scratched my arm.

"No time was now to be lost.

"I drew my revolver and took deliberate aim at his heart.

"At the same time I clutched my long hunting knife firmly in the other hand.

"I fired.

"My aim was good.

"But I missed the monster's heart.

"With a growl like distant thunder he rushed upon me.

"His fore paws enclosed me.

"He had me now in his embrace.

"The squeeze was terrible.

"I almost fancied I could hear my ribs crack.

"Struggle as I would it was of no use.

"I could not wriggle out of his embrace.

"My eyes and brain began to reel.

"I saw his white teeth close to my face and neck.

"Like a madman I drew my knife, and plunged it several times in quick succession into the monster's side.

"Blood spurted out in torrents and almost blinded me.

"The last plunge I gave I heard a terrible growl, and then I knew not what happened, for I lost all consciousness.



"When I awoke I found myself lying on the ground covered in blood.

"The bear and I were still in a tight embrace.

"As I turned my eyes wildly about me I was rejoiced to find that the monster was stone dead.

"My last stroke of the knife had found his heart.

"That last slash had killed him.

"But even when dying he did not let go his hold, but we both fell together.

"My escape was most miraculous.

"I got out from the dead bear's tight hold as best I could, and looked at myself from head to foot.

"I was literally covered with blood all over, and a painful sensation in the left arm told me that the beast had bitten me.

"I was very weak, and leaned against a tree for support.

"In the distance I could hear Pedro, the count, Caspar, with Fatty and others searching for and calling me, but I could not reply for they were still too far away.

"I rested for more than half an hour, and then commenced to skin the bear, for his hide was a splendid one.

"This job lasted more than one hour, but at last I secured the skin.

"In order not to take cold I put the skin around me like a cloak, and walked towards the spot where my companions were waiting about for me.

"I had not gone far when I discovered the Count and Fatty some distance off.

"I could not shout, but heard Fatty cry out with all his lungs.

"'Fire, count, fire, there's an immense bear walking towards us.'

"'Where?' said the Count.

"'There,' said Fatty, pointing towards me, and then ran away towards the camp as fast as his legs would take him.

"I had just time to jump behind a tree out of the way when the count fired.

"His rifle shot glanced against the bearskin, and then throwing it off my shoulder I discovered myself, and was received with loud cheers by all the party.

"'Brave lad,' said the old count, almost in tears.

"Hurrah!' said Caspar, 'we have found him.'

"'But, where's the bear?' said Pedro.

"I showed the way back, and we cut off the hams, and returned to the camp. Some of the lads forcing me to ride on their shoulders.

"Fatty was not aware of what had happened, and when I got in camp, I found him eating a huge lump of pudding, and telling most wonderful lies to the Mexican teamsters about the bear fight he had had in the morning.

"To cure Master Tony of his boasting I threw the bear skin around me, and muddy and bloody as I was, suddenly placed myself before him in the dim firelight.

"He dropped his pudding on the instant, and scampered off like mad, shouting and yelling to the great delight of all in the secret.

"Buttons was wild with joy, and capered about like a half wild young monkey as he always proved to be.

* * * * *

"We started again on the following morning, and after three or four days hard travelling through the parched prairie grass, were all glad when, one morning, we came in sight of the dense forest bordering the Sans Fernando river.

"As our horses, oxen, mules, and men required a few days of rest, Pedro piloted us to a large village in the wilderness, called Las Angalos.

"This large village was a half-way place between Mexico and the town of Galveston in the United States.

"The pastures were excellent, the water splendid, and the wild sports of the forest were more than sufficient for the most enthusiastic hunter.

"Our lads, and, in fact, all our train, were comfortably provided for, and camped out in the green forest with tents and fires.

"We made up our minds to stay in that part for a week, at least, in order to strengthen and fatten our horses for the other half of the long journey.

"The Count, Caspar, Hugh Tracy, and all the rest, made many friends among the Mexican villagers, and the longer we stayed the more they seemed to take to us.

"Unable to resist the invigorating air and beauty of a spring-time morning in this lovely climate, I often rose with the sun and galloped along the red, sandy roads until my chest expanded, and the blood bounded through my veins with unwonted power.

"The dew-moist verdure of field and wood; the ever-fresh half-wild aspect of its forests, all passed before my delighted, unaccustomed eyes, until an unbidden abandon came over me.

"I laughed in the saddle, and rollicked in the freshness of the scene, as even my horse, who, with swishing tail, wide spread nostrils, and steaming flanks, snorted and shook his head, and cantered along the wood-fringed road in juvenile hilarity and freedom.

"The smoking chimneys of huts; the crowing of cocks, and barking of dogs; the plantation bell, and the shouts of teams a-field, recurred on every hand.

"Nature seemed to revel in its youth and beauty.

"One thing had particularly struck me.

"In my morning rides at sun-rise the air was literally darkened with the rapid flight of pigeons, which continued for hours.

"Their return at evening shut out from view the sinking sun.

"While watching these immense clouds of pigeons, one fine morning, an old darkie, with a spade over his shoulder, observed my curiosity, and dryly said,

"'Dats true, massa; dere's no end on 'em down these parts, rader hab dem away, do. De corn'll be none de better arter *deir* visits—sure! De Lor' help de crops whar deys goin'; won't be much left, for dey digs up de young shoots, massa, mighty clean-like, and takes de seed.'

"Some friends informed me that there were immense pigeon roosts some few miles in the interior, and so many stories were told of their vastness, and the heavy losses occasioned by them, that I determined to have ocular proof ere crediting the marvellous stories heard on every hand.

"Some said they knew of roosts twenty-five miles long, and ten wide.

"Others went farther than this, until I began to imagine they were dealing in the marvellous, since one would suppose that a forest area of thirty miles by twelve, would more than suffice for all the pigeons in creation.

"I resolved to examine the statements.

"Towards evening, I saw several of my acquaintance leaving the village with light waggons, who were going to a roost, and I accompanied them.

"They were bent upon a 'spree' I could judge, for all were laughing and singing.

"And by a frequent gurgling sound, I arrived at the conclusion that plenty of whisky was on board.

"The negro teamsters cracked their whips and smoked their pipes.

"Some walked while others lay stretched in their straw-bedded waggons, spinning tough yarns of hunting, &c.

"There were but few weapons in the party, and those who had them were having occasional shots at the number of squirrels jumping about in all directions.

"The sun had sunk two or three hours when we arrived at the dark, heavy mass of timber constituting the roost.

"The moon was peeping over the distant forest, giving sufficient light to discern the configuration of the scene of our intended battue.

"The waggons were halted in the hollow of a neighbouring copse.

"Approaching the roost, we could distinctly hear a sea-like murmur, and the scarcely audible twitter and flutter of millions of birds in swarms upon its swaying branches.

"As the moon-beams chanced to play through the less wooded spaces, we could distinctly see the inconceivable mass of birds clustered like bees.

"A few would occasionally flutter to a new branch and cause disturbance.

"Small trees, crackling here and there, caused occasional commotion.

"While some, bolder than the rest, flew out into the unclouded moon-light, and, after a short flight, would re-enter the timber again.

"The whole forest was a living mass of birds, and a single accidental shot would cause the uprising of thousands.

"None were foolish enough to enter the 'roost,' nor were there any dogs that might disturb it.

"For had accident affrighted such vast numbers, they would have flown out into the open grounds, and possibly knocked us down and smothered us.

"For if such numberless creatures bend and break down huge limbs of trees, and leave their roost a mass of broken timber, with a thick layer of feathers, manure, and débris, few persons would have the temerity to go within dangerous proximity, for fear of personal harm.

"Having, therefore, previously provided some dozens of thin deal boarding, and fixed them firmly against a fence in the form of a hoarding, and then placed a large mass of pine wood several feet in front, we ignited it, and immediately retired to a respectful distance, to watch and await the result.

"The smoke soon ascended in columns, and the flames began to crackle and send forth a lurid glow, which lit the face of the woods.

"As soon as the light brightened, the roost appeared to be in an uneasy state of rustle and flutter, and occasionally a few birds took wing, flew towards the fire, skimmed round it, and retired.

"Presently, however, as the pine wood shot forth a mass of light, the birds flew about in hundreds, and fast increased to thousands, sweeping hither and thither, until the moonbeams streaming through the forest were completely darkened.

"Their numbers increased every moment.

"Flying directly at the blaze, hundreds dashed against the boards, and lay fluttering on the ground.

"Thus the 'sport,' if it may so be called, continued, until large heaps of birds almost covered the hoarding against which they had been stunned, smothered, and killed.

"It was wise that we had retired a considerable distance from their line of flight, for had any one dared to approach such masses, they must assuredly have been killed, for nothing could scarcely resist their weight and numbers.

"When the fire had burned out, and the birds once more returned to roost, we ventured forth, and filled two waggons with the spoil, leaving several waggon loads behind.

"The depredations of such immense flocks upon neighbouring plantations are very grievous; and I am assured that they are almost like locusts, for coming at spring time, they despoil thousands of acres of their seedlings, causing sad havoc, and entirely destroying prospective crops.

"Occasionally their stay is but short, but sometimes they choose to remain weeks and months, and there seems to be no method of being rid of them.

"To one who watches the flight of a few pigeons in a city, they seem to be the most harmless creatures in creation; but even the dove, emblematic as it is of innocence and purity, is one of the most destructive of the feathered tribe, and causes much mischief at spring time in the south, where they assail the seed already in the ground, and follow the sower with great diligence and pertinacity.

"The effect of such numbers is best seen in whatever forest they may have used as their 'roost.'

"I once visited one, and could scarcely credit the havoc there visible.

"The earth was covered with large branches, and everywhere a thick layer of manure and feather-down.

"Hogs, wild or domestic, are great patrons of such spots, and grow amazingly fat, for, from some cause, dead birds lie as thickly as fallen fruit in autumn.

"Towards morning, our party of pigeon hunters returned.

"Among our number were Fatty and Buttons.

"The former danced about like a maniac, and was for ever talking of 'roast pigeon,' 'boiled pigeon,' 'pigeon soup,' and 'pigeon pies,' until his merriment almost made our heads ache.

"True enough, we had now sufficient pigeons to last us for a long time.

"But, to my surprise, Fatty and Buttons showed us all an example by which to profit.

"They plucked the feathers, and made feather-beds, and the first sleep which Fatty had thereon lasted for twenty-four hours or more.

"In fact, his bed was such a huge one, that he was almost hidden among the feathers, and could not be induced to show himself in public, except at dinner-time, and at that particular hour, to use his own words—

"'He was always on hand!'

---

## CHAPTER LXXXVI.

### TOMASSO THE DETECTIVE AND JOEL FLINT.

THE position of Joel Flint in Leghorn, deprived as he was of all communication with his father in England, was not by any means very pleasant.

He was without money.

And more than that, he was without a single friend.

That he must do something shortly he very well knew, but what to do he knew not.

Tomasso, the detective, instead of proving a friend, now turned round upon Joel, and watched him both night and day as if he had been a thief, if not something worse, wherever he went; whether to the parks, to the theatres, or for a walk, he was sure to meet with Tomasso.

This, at last, became so painful to Joel, that he felt as if he were haunted by some dreadful gnome.

One day, when Joel was walking alone by the sea-side pondering on what he had better do, Tomasso touched him on the shoulder rather unexpectedly and suddenly.

The movement, though slight in itself, made Joel turn deadly pale.

He trembled, and for a moment could not speak.

Tomasso's black eyes glistened again as he watched the sudden pallor of the English youth.

"You are quite a stranger," said Joel; "how do you do, Tomasso?"

"Nay, I am very well, I thank you; but how are you, Mr. Schmidt?"

He laid such peculiar stress on the Mr. Schmidt, that Joel felt more uneasy than ever.

"Nay, how are *you*, my friend?" said Tomasso, again. "I heard you were about to leave for England?"

"So I was, but——"

"But what?" said Tomasso. "I hope there is nothing unpleasant going on at home."

"Unpleasant? I do not understand you," said Joel.

"Well, I meant that I hope your worthy father had not met with any reverse in fortune or anything of that sort, you know."

"Oh, no," said Joel, with a well-assumed air of pride. "No misfortunes of that nature could overtake our family; for my father's wealth is immense."

"I'm glad to hear you say so. But, if that be so, how the devil is it that he doesn't send you some money to pay all your debts at the hotel and other places?"

"Well, you see," said Joel, with the air of a young man who had thousands at his command, "you see, my friend Tomasso, affairs of this kind are beyond your comprehension. My father may be busy, his letters may have miscarried, or even the mail robbed."

"Ah, I dare say. Very unlikely, I think; but you have delayed paying *me* so long that I——"

"Pay you? Why, what in the name of Heaven do I owe you?"

"Owe me, eh? Ha, ha! well, that *is* good, upon my word."

"Yes, owe *you?*" said Joel, with a slight flush across his face. "I owe *you* nothing."

"Don't you, though. Not so fast; just you listen to me."

"Nay, you just listen to me *instead*," said Joel. angrily. "I have given you hundreds upon hundreds to capture and convict that young rascal, Frank Ford, but instead of doing that you let him escape."

"Oh, indeed; go on. I am listening. Proceed, I am all attention."

"And let me tell you," said Joel, "you have acted very shabbily towards me, for you have not only robbed me——"

"Robbed? Nay, nay, stop, stop, young man; don't you use such words so freely. My honour and reputation are beyond all suspicion."

"Beyond all suspicion, eh? Fiddle-de-dee, Signor Tomasso! You are like all of your trade, and will receive money from both the innocent and the guilty at the same time."

"I received it from the *guilty* when I took the money from *you*," said Tomasso, with an air of triumph.

"Me guilty?" said Joel, astounded. "Guilty of what? How dare you, sir, insinuate such foul charges against a person of my standing! Go your way, sir; for two pins I'd give you in charge for swindling!"

"Would you indeed?" said Tomasso, grinning. "How very polite you are all at once. Give me in charge for swindling, eh? Ha! ha! By Jove! that is good, and no mistake."

"It would not be very good or pleasant to you, I think, if I were to expose all your rascality to the prefect of police."

"I dare say not, in *your* opinion; and in *my* opinion it would not be pleasant if I were to have you up before the same prefect, and tell him all about your——"

"My what?'

"Why, all you've done in connection with your father in robbing old Ford, and depriving the young Fords of their fortune."

"Robbing—old Ford—the young Fords! What do you mean?" stammered Joel.

"Oh! nothing; but you see robbery was not the worst part of the business—*murder* was done, Mr. Schmidt."

Tomasso said these few words in such a low, earnest tone that made Joel's blood run cold again.

He answered not a word, but for a second looked the Italian fairly in the face, pale with astonishment.

"Murder!" Joel mechanically answered.

"Yes, murder," said Tomasso, with glittering eyes.

Joel tried to speak, but could not.

"Look you here, Mr. Joel Flint, Mr. Schmidt, or whatever your name is," said the detective. "I have had my eye on you for a very long time."

"For what?"

"Why, for taking part in the robbery and murder of old Ford. A mere trifle, ain't it?"

"But I am innocent."

"Of course you are. What scoundrel is there living who is *not* innocent if you believe them, ha! ha!"

"But surely you cannot for a moment think that I'd do such a foul thing as that?"

"That depends."

"How do you mean?"

"Why, if you have plenty of money——"

"But I have not a five-pound note in the world."

"You didn't hear me out, don't be in such a hurry, but listen. If you have plenty of money, or can get it by any means, why, then, you are innocent; but if you are poor, and can't raise a stiver, why, then, you are guilty."

For some time Joel nor Tomasso spoke.

Joel was deep in thought.

He felt as if he had been clutched by some desperate, cruel-handed demon.

"Come this way," said Tomasso. "Let us go into this cafe and have a quiet chat, this one near the steam-boat pier. I have much to say to you."

Joel followed his companion, and ere long they were seated in a small private room.

Tomasso locked the door, and finding everything safe and snug around him, helped himself to wine, threw himself into an arm chair, and pulled out of his pocket a bundle of official and private papers.

"There," said Tomasso, "if you only knew the contents of those letters, it would turn your hair gray."

"Indeed! Why all this mystery?"

"I will soon explain. The very night of old Ford's murder you did not sleep at Bromley Hall Academy."

"How do you know that?"

"By private information."

"Well, what of that? According to the newspaper accounts the murder must have taken place on the night of the very day on which occurred the riot at Bromley Hall."

"You are right; your recollection is not at fault."

"But there were many who did not sleep in the Hall that night. The young Garibaldians had left, and many others; Caspar, for instance."

"I know it; but can you tell me where you slept on that particular night?"

"Y-e-e-s," said Joel, "of course I can."

"Where, pray?"

"Why, in the village."

"But, of course, you can prove that?"

"I can."

"You can *not*," said Tomasso, with a smile. "You did not sleep in the village at all."

"What! would you make me out a liar?" said Joel, in great anger.

"Yes; you are not only a liar, but one of the greatest that ever lived. Sit down."

Joel sat down, for escape was impossible.

He was now in the lion's den, from which there was no chance of running.

"Now, of course you don't know that Mr. Caspar was tried and acquitted of robbery?"

"I heard it by chance."

"Jonathan's wife and Shanks, the tutor, were punished for perjury."

"I also heard that."

"But you did *not* hear, I suppose, that Jonathan himself was hunted night and day by the police?"

"Impossible!"

"No, not at all. He also had a hand in old Ford's murder."

"The scoundrel," said Joel, with well assumed indignation.

"Yes, wasn't he? And his partner in that business is even a still greater vagabond."

"No doubt. What's his name?"

"The same as yours, exactly."

"It can't be."

"It is though; your father, Joel, is as deep in the mud as old Jonathan is in the mire."

"You are joking," said Joel, "and try to act upon my fears."

I do not," said Tomasso. "Here is the best of proof."

So speaking, he read the following letter:—

"SIGNOR TOMASSO, DETECTIVE POLICE, LEGHORN.

"DEAR SIR,—In answer to your letter, I have to inform you that, up to the present moment, the detectives of Scotland Yard have not been able to capture the two old villains, Jonathan and old Flint, the lawyer.

"The officers have not the slightest doubt of their guilt in the matter of old Ford's murder; but the old rascals are so cunning that they have eluded the vigilance of the whole detective force for the present.

"The old lawyer has a son somewhere abroad; but where cannot be discovered.

"If we could only unearth old Flint's son, it is more than likely that we could fasten upon him also some share in the bloody tragedy.

"Before the old lawyer made his escape, it has been ascertained that a large iron safe was packed in a box, and sent to Southampton for transmission abroad; but whether it did or did not go on the continent is a matter of doubt.

"That the safe contained many things of value there cannot be a doubt, for it has been ascertained that a day or two previous to old Ford's murder, old Flint the lawyer had deeds and documents in trust for the two nephews, Tom and Frank Ford, besides a very large sum in ready money.

"If you can trace either his son or the large packing case, we have no doubt but it would tend to clear up this mystery very speedily, for nine chances out of ten the son knows where the treasure is, and, perhaps, may be living on part of it.

"If you discover the son, track him, and intercept his letters, for there can be no doubt but that they (the father and son) correspond with each other. Hoping to hear from you soon,

"I remain, yours, &c.

"GALE, Detective."

Tomasso finished reading the letter, and Joel stared at him like one who was half demented.

"You see," said the Italian, "I have you in my clutches."

"So it seems," said Joel, and he breathed very hard, and was flushed in the face. "And what do you intend to do with me? You cannot arrest me on mere suspicion."

"But I have more than suspicion of *your* share in the murder," said Tomasso.

"How?"

"Why, a pocket-book was discovered in Caspar's room the night *you* stole his cloak and mask."

"*Me* steal his cloak and mask?"

"Yes, *you*, Joel; it could not have been any one else, or why should Gale inform me of finding your pocket-book in his room?"

Joel was nonplussed at the amount of evidence Tomasso seemed to have against him; but he made no other remark than to say,

"Oh, all this kind of reasoning is trumpery; no doubt I did loose my pocket-book in Caspar's room during the riot, but I did not steal the cloak and mask."

"That remains to be seen; but perhaps you will explain the meaning of several mysterious notes which we found in the pocket-book, coming from your father, and all speaking of Mr. Ford's affairs, and what he thought of the boys. There are several very broad hints in them to the effect that if Frank and Tom could only be *accidentally* drowned while bathing, it would be a matter of thousands in his, your father's, pocket as well as your own."

"Who told you all this nonsense?" said Joel, rising from his seat. "Do you suppose for one moment that I believe anything of all this you have told me? No, not one word."

"It is a matter of very little importance to me whether you believe it or not. I have got copies of the letters to which I allude, and that is sufficient for your apprehension."

"And do you mean to do that?"

"Yes, unless you buy my silence."

"But suppose I were to do so, what then?"

"Why, you could pay me a handsome price. I should retire from the 'force,' and then——"

"I might go to the devil, I suppose?"

"Exactly. Come, what do you say?"

"I say this much, that I have not a five-pound note in all the world."

"But you know where the iron safe is; there is plenty of money in it."

"I don't know where it is, or I should not allow myself to be in such poverty as I am at present," said Joel.

"Oh, that's all nonsense," Tomasso replied. "You know where it is well enough, but you can't get at it, perhaps, eh, that's more likely?"

"You seem to know more about the affairs of my father than I do myself," said Joel.

"I do," said Tomasso, "and, if you will be guided by me, I will get you out of the scrape you are now in."

"In what way?"

"*I* know where the safe is."

"You?"

"Yes, and more than that, it is not a mile away from here, as you know very well."

"I tell you again and again I do *not* know where it is."

"And I tell you again and again that you *do*. Listen to me, Joel. I have your life in my hands; but, as I perceive a good chance to make my fortune out of you, I am going to do so."

Joel bit his lip.

"I know that your father sent that safe to Southampton, and there it remained until, by his letters to you, he advised you to send for it."

"I never received those letters," said Joel, in surprise.

"I dare say not, but I did, and sent for the safe. It is now lying in the custom-house, and remains there for you to call for it."

"Are you serious?"

"I was never more so in my whole life."

"This is a trap you have laid for me, Tomasso," said Joel, with a quivering lip. "I knew that the safe was there, and that it was guarded both night and day by two men, who have been sent from England for that purpose. I have no right to go and demand the safe, and therefore shall let it remain where it is."

"Then I shall this instant ring the bell, call in a couple of officers, and cast you into prison."

Acting up to his word, Tomasso rose to ring the bell.

"Stay!" said Joel, with a flushed face. "I am in your power, although I am innocent. Do not ring that bell, Tomasso, on your life!"

"What?"

"Do not touch it, on your peril! I am desperate, and mean all I say."

So saying, Joel pulled a revolver out of his breast pocket.

"You see this," said Joel. "I have always carried it about with me since I have known you, for I knew that the time would come when it would be necessary to use it."

Tomasso, for once, was foiled.

With a sudden spring, he leaped upon Joel, and grasped the revolver.

For a moment they wrestled for the possession of the weapon, and at last Tomasso wrenched it from his grasp.

With a blow of his clenched fist, he knocked Joel down, and he crouched beneath the Italian's feet like a cur.

"Now who is master?" said Tomasso, with a fiendish grin. "Rise, dog, rise, and do my bidding, or in less than a week you shall dangle from the gallows!"

Joel rose very humbly, and looked haggard and chapfallen.

"Go, take this order to the custom-house," said Tomasso, "and demand the safe. I will go and see that no harm befalls you."

"But those two men who are guarding it will recognise me."

"Change your attire and disguise yourself. But why need even that, when you are innocent? Come, come with me—I will see you through this adventure. In an hour I shall be rich."

So speaking, and like a lamb being led to slaughter, Joel followed the Italian detective with trembling limbs.

## CHAPTER LXXXVII.

### IN WHICH THE LOST TREASURE IS FOUND.

The safe really was, as Tomasso described, awaiting a claimant at the custom-house.

According to orders given them, two Englishmen were hired to watch and mind it. Not that such a heavy package could be well purloined out of the well-guarded government storehouse, but in order to see who and what the person or persons might be who called to inquire for or claim it.

Necessity is the mother of invention, it has been said, and so it was in the case of Joel.

He swore, in his heart of hearts, to "be even" with Tomasso.

And so he was; for it is generally found to be true that cunning men can outwit the bravest people, though timid and cowardly themselves.

Joel thought of a great many plans and expedients by which to entrap Tomasso.

He received the order from the Italian detective to go and receive the safe.

To the custom-house therefore he went, but did not go near where he knew the safe to be safely stored.

He lounged about for some time, and then leisurely strolled to the sea side of the custom-house, where a number of boats were plying to and fro.

He hailed one.

"Do you want a job to-night, boatman?" said Joel.

"To do what?"

"Why, to row me up and down the harbour. I am in search of a great thief to-night."

"Certainly, sir. When and where shall I meet you?"

"At this spot, about nine o'clock. Don't fail, and I will pay you well."

The bargain was made, and Joel retraced his steps towards the warehouses again.

Into one of these he stepped, without being perceived, and hid himself among the merchandise.

From his place of concealment he commanded a good view of where the safe was, and of the men who constantly guarded it, both day and night.

Joel had not been more than an hour concealed in his hiding-place, when Tomasso, becoming impatient at the long delay, entered the custom-house yard, and began to make enquiries concerning Joel.

Among others, he particularly questioned the two Englishmen who were minding the safe and its treasure.

"Have you had any one here enquiring about this large package, my men?" said Tomasso.

"No," was the answer, "and I don't think there is any likelihood of it."

"My mate here begins to think that there can't be anything of value in it, or somebody would have called long ago."

"And so I do," was the response. "Here have we been a month or more minding this big ugly package both night and day, and nobody comes for it. I suppose we shall have a twelvemonth's work yet."

"I wonder if they've got serpents inside——"

"Or mummies, or what?"

"No, my friends," said Tomasso, "but I'll tell you a great secret."

"What is it, master?" said the men, anxiously.

"Why, that big package has a large iron safe inside, and," said he, in a soft voice, that Joel could scarcely hear, "inside of that safe is a tremendous lot of gold and Bank of England notes."

"The devil there is! I never heard of that afore, master," said the two men, in great surprise.

"It is crammed with money, I tell you, so you must not let it out of your sight for a moment."

"No fear of our neglecting our duty."

"I hope not; but now listen to me. You know me well enough?"

"Yes."

"Well, then, there will be a young man who will call and claim this package."

"Yes; we have been on the watch for him a long time. His name is Flint."

"Yes, that's the name, my men; but the treasure doesn't belong to him. The real owners are named Tom and Frank Ford."

"We have heard of both of them before, and brave lads they are, on sea and land."

"Yes; but they get into all manner of scrapes wherever they go. They are gallant, hardy young fellows, though, for all that," said Tomasso.

"I don't think it possible that either of the brothers will call at any time for it, for I have heard they left Italy several days ago."

"But since our orders are not to deliver up the case to any one but the young Fords, it is more than likely we shall have this job of watching it for some time to come."

"You are right, without you receive a government order to do otherwise."

"That's right enough, master, we'll attend to all you say. I suppose you are after this young scoundrel Flint yourself?"

"Oh, yes; I have been hunting for him in all directions, but can't discover his hiding-place.'

"And do you think it likely that Government will send down an order for it, master?"

"I don't know for certain; it was spoken of the other evening by the Prefect of Police, who begins to think that, perhaps, there is no money in the package after all, but some dead man's body."

"Oh, horrible!"

"It might be so, you know, my lads."

"No telling, master—we live in awful cut-throat times; but let it contain what it may, there is no chance of young Flint coming to claim it, for each of us have got his photograph, and would know him in a minute."

"Just as I supposed," thought Tomasso to himsels. "It was a wise plan of mine to disguise Joel beforehand."

"I suppose you know the prefect's chief messenger when you see him, don't you?"

"No."

"Well, here is his likeness," said Tomasso, giving the watchers a description. "He is about five feet six inches high, wears black whiskers and moustache, dressed in police uniform, but without side arms. If he should call and bring an order, you will not fail to obey all he tells you."

"The document will, of course, have the prefect's seal upon it?"

"Certainly; such an amount of treasure could not be removed from the customs' yard without it."

"All right, sir; if he comes we will attend to all you say."

"If he comes at all, it will be by boat; he will land at the custom-house stairs."

"Not to-night, I hope," said one, "for I want to have a good sleep while my mate is keeping watch."

Tomasso went away from the men, and, as he was known to all the officials in the custom-house yard, his prying about was not noticed."

"Where the devil can that young wretch have got to?" he thought. "I gave him a first-rate disguise—a bran new police uniform, false hair, whiskers, and moustache. Surely he has not fallen into any mischief! Where can he be? I gave him the order—one I counterfeited—with the prefect's seal; it ought to have been arranged long ago. What if he plays me false!"

This thought made Tomasso bite his lips in anger, but he made his way to the café where he had promised to meet Joel and hear how he had succeeded.

Joel, of course, was not there.

Tomasso waited hour after hour, but Flint did not keep his appointment.

In a hurry Tomasso went back again to the gate of the custom-house.

It was locked for the night.

The Italian cursed and swore right roundly at his ill-luck, and slowly walked back to the cafe once more in hopes of meeting Joel.

But young Flint was still in his hiding-place, and intently watching the manœuvres of the two men who were guarding the safe.

Yet he was not aware that the doors had been locked upon him.

And there he was, hidden among boxes, and bales, and sacks, peeping out of the first-floor window, and with his ear cocked for whatever he might hear from those below.

"I say, Jimmy," said one of the men, "are you going to have that snooze you spoke of, or what?"

"No, mate," was the reply, "sleep won't know me for the next twenty-four hours."

"Why not?"

"I've got an idea."

"So have I."

"I should very much like to see what there really is in this immense packing-case, for, hang me! if I don't begin to think as how there's some mystery going on here, or they wouldn't be so very particular about giving orders, and so on."

"That's just what I were a thinking on," the other replied.

"Well, what say you? There ain't many guards about here during the night. We could easily open it and help ourselves without any one being the wiser."

"That's what I were a thinking; and, if you like to go shares and shares, why I'm your man."

"Done!" said the other; "but where can we get tools from?"

"I know," said the other, and without another word he went his way, and got the necessary tools.

"You keep watch while I am at work, and when I'm tired, do you take a turn."

"Agreed."

In a moment, one of the men sauntered away to keep a good look-out for the sentries which patrolled the custom-house yard, so as to give his companion warning.

The other with hammer, chisels, and a small crow-bar, commenced to work vigorously at the packing-case, and as it stood under a shed in the shade, he was unperceived by any one save Joel Flint.

With a few vigorous and silent efforts with the chisel and crowbar, he soon cut open the thick planking of the packing-case, and commenced to work at the door of the safe.

While so engaged, his companion whistled in a warning manner, and the work ceased.

Presently a patrol passed the spot; but seeing nothing that attracted particular attention, the man passed on, and the robber began to work in darkness again.

"This won't do," thought Joel, from his hiding-place, "they are bent on breaking open the safe. If they succeed all will be lost."

He, therefore, climbed out of window, and at the risk of breaking his neck, slipped down the water-pipe, and reached the ground.

He crept close to the warehouse wall out of the moonlight, and in a few minutes reached the street.

His step was so cat-like that the dishonest watchman "operating" on the chest did not hear him approach.

In fact, Joel actually tapped the man upon the shoulder ere he was aware of any one being present.

He started to his feet, and would have fled, but Joel presented a revolver at his head.

"Stir," said Joel, with the air of a very brave man, "stir, and I will not only kill you but raise an alarm, and have you and your companion hung."

"You know all, then?"

"I do. I have heard every word you said, and have been watching you both for more than an hour."

"You are one of the police, from your dress."

"I am not, but your friend, if you like."

"My friend?" gasped the astonished thief, in much surprise.

"Yes, your friend. I have had my eye upon this safe for the past month, and intended to do exactly what you have begun; what say you, shall we be friends and share the prize?"

"With all my heart."

"Then let me tell you that there is a boat waiting for me just off the custom-house stairs. I have simply to hail it, and we are safe, then, with our prize."

"Then you intended to prize it open to-night, eh?"

"I did, or else carry it away by main force, which is much better, for I have friends in the boat."

"An excellent idea," said the rough fellow in reply. "If we could only get it away in a boat, all the rest would be easy; but how is it to be done, there are too many guards about?"

"I'll tell you how," said Joel, "there are three of us."

"Well."

"Let each go and set fire to one of the warehouses. When they blaze up all will be confusion, hurry, and bustle; during the hubbub, we will haul off the safe to our boat."

The robber seemed appalled at the boldness of the proposition, but he knew that now was not the time to mince matters, so, therefore, after a little more persuasion, he consented to the diabolical scheme and signalled to his mate, who was still on the look-out.

When this fellow perceived Joel he recoiled, and would have run away in fright.

When things were explained to him, however, he stoutly refused to set fire to anything.

It was not until threats of personal violence had been used that he consented to join in the devilish business.

Each went his way, and, for some time, nothing was heard or seen of them.

In less than half an hour, however, red flames burst forth from no less than half-a-dozen warehouses.

The appalling grandeur of the conflagration came so unexpectedly upon the view, that the town and harbour were instantly and beautifully illuminated by the light.

"Fire! fire! fire!" was the dreadful cry which now resounded from the custom-house guards.

"Fire! fire! fire!" was re-echoed far and wide.

The gates were thrown open, and in poured a multitude of excited people, all intent upon saving the government property or bent upon petty peculation.

"Keep back! keep back!" shouted the guards at the gates, as, with levelled bayonets, they tried to resist the maddened rush of an excited populace.

But it was all to no purpose. The guards were knocked down and trampled under foot.

On rushed the excited people, shouting and clamouring.

In less than five minutes the engines arrived, one after another, in rapid succession.

Through the tall iron gates they dashed at headlong speed, with foaming horses, amid the shouts of a half wild, hat-waving people.

It was too late. Everywhere the flames had got the mastery.

The red glare was oppressive. The black clouds were lit up with a glow like that of a thousand furnaces.

Timber cracked, beams fell, roofs tumbled in, and on every hand the sparks flew up to heaven in bright red showers.

"Mind the powder! swamp the powder magazine!" shouted a thousand voices; but still the crowds got thicker and denser, and on every hand could be seen workmen and policemen and firemen saving valuable property from destruction.

Much brandy was destroyed, hundreds of wine barrels had their heads knocked in, and all who worked the engines and handed buckets about, refreshed their thirsty throats, while hundreds who did not and would not work did the same.

Boxes, barrels, cases, bales of goods, and other property, were wheeled or carried away by the devouring element.

On every hand confusion, noise and tumult reigned.

And above the dull roar of thousands of voices could be heard the regular clank clank of the hand engines, and the shrill whistle of steam machines.

Amidst all this hubbub, however, there was one particular individual who was looking after his own particular interests.

That individual was none other than Joel Flint.

When a large number of persons had run into the great yard, Joel issued from his place of concealment, and mingled among them.

In the undress uniform of prefect's messenger he was looked upon as an official, and every one made way for him.

He rushed about hither and thither as if intent upon saving property instead of stealing it.

He soon encountered one of his accomplices, as he approached the much-coveted safe.

"Where is your mate?" asked Joel, in a hoarse whisper. "We have not a moment to loose; this must be conveyed away at once. Where is your mate?" he again asked.

The pale incendiary trembled, and as he looked at Joel, gasped out,

"Oh, what have we done this wretched night? Would that I had never seen you, or that I had died ere doing what I have done."

"Why, what is the matter? Is there not a mine of silver and gold in the safe to reward us?"

"Reward? reward?" the man gasped. "What reward can compensate for what we have done—a wife and her children have been burned to ashes?"

"What of that, dolt?" said Joel. "What is that to us? Where is your mate?"

"He went into a warehouse, and after he had set fire to the goods he tried to escape but could not."

"Is that true?"

"As true as Heaven's above us; he too had a wife and children in England. Now he is no more —he is dead."

"Dead?"

"Yes; the smoke and flames overpowered him. He tried to escape over the roof; I saw him with my own eyes; but, just as he was about to leap on to the top of a house near by, the roof fell in with a crash! He threw up his hands in wild despair, gave a shout of anguish, next moment he disappeared."

"Horrible?" said Joel. "But, nevertheless, we must get to work, or it may be too late."

Finding that his companions in crime were too much shocked by the terrible judgment which had fallen on his mate, Joel gathered around him a dozen idlers, and in the confusion that reigned on every hand, managed to drag away the safe from under the shed towards the boat landing-stairs.

While this was going on, Joel ran towards the sea-wall, and hailed the boat which he knew would be in waiting for him.

"Boat ahoy!" he shouted.

"Boat ahoy!" was the response, and in a few moments a swift four-oared craft shot under the sea-wall, and was moored at the foot of the boat stairs.

"You have come at last, signor?" said the coxswain. "And, as your excellency wanted swift rowers, I have brought three beside myself."

"Right," said Joel. "Fasten your boat, and come on shore. I must not look after harbour thieves tonight, but try and save as much of the Government property as I can; therefore, come on shore, all four of you, and assist me to bear away a large packing-case."

# THE BOY SOLDIER; OR, GARIBALDI'S YOUNG CAPTAIN.

THE THREAT.—*See No.* 30.

With the prospect and promise of extra pay, the four boatmen leaped on shore, and in a few moments were working very hard in getting the large packing case towards the boat.

This was soon done, however, and all were seated at their oars again, ready to pull away from the shore, when Joel was suddenly startled by hearing some one in the crowd shouting out,

"This is one of the watchmen; this is one of them, I can swear to it. Where is the safe? Tell quickly, man. Where is your mate?"

It was the voice of Tomasso.

Upon the first alarm of fire at the custom-house he had hurried thither.

Had he been here five minutes sooner, he would have seen and saved the safe; but it had been got into the boat.

The Italian detective was furious.

He seized Joel's sole companion in crime by the throat, and would have strangled him in passion.

"The safe, I say! the safe!" he cried.

The now half-demented man struggled, but all to no purpose.



He could not escape from the vice-like grip of the officer.

"Unloose your hold, and I will tell you all. The safe is there in that boat yonder!" he shouted, pointing to Joel, who was busily engaged in loosening the mooring ropes.

With the bound of a wounded tiger, Tomasso pressed through the crowd, and ran towards the boat.

"Pull away, men! pull away!" said Joel, in a terrible state of alarm. "Pull away, men, I will handsomely reward you. There is great treasure in this safe. Pull away! pull away!"

The boat had not got more than four feet from the landing, when Tomasso dashed towards it down the stone steps.

"Stop! stop!" he said, in tones of passion, and his eyes flashed like those of a demon. "Stop! stop! on your lives!"

"Pull away, men! pull away!" said Joel, in great fear.

One moment more, and Tomasso would have leaped on board; but as he tried to do so his foot slipped, he fell into deep water, and Joel struck him a heavy blow on the head with an oar.

An oath from Tomasso, as he struggled in the water, and a laugh of triumph from Joel, was all that passed between them at that fearful moment.

---

## CHAPTER LXXXVIII.

### ATTACK OF THE INDIANS UPON THE ENCAMPMENT OF THE BOY SOLDIERS.

As is always the custom among those who are travelling through the vast prairies, Frank Ford followed the count's advice, and established a strong guard which should protect the camps at night.

On one occasion when they had travelled a long distance during the day, Frank camped rather earlier than usual.

The waggons were formed into squares, the horses and mules were allowed sufficient length of rope to graze by, and the oxen were all hobbled so that they could not stray too far away.

Fires were lighted, the sentinels were put on their various posts, and all was snug and comfortable.

Nearly every one who had nothing in particular to do were already stretched in their blankets and rugs before the fires or under the waggons.

Frank, however, with Caspar, the Count, Hugh Tracy, Pedro the guide, and several of the Boy Soldiers, were chatting and smoking and listening to various accounts which one and another had to relate of Mexico, and the war then raging.

While thus pleasantly engaged with pipes, cigars, and the like, Frank said,

"Pedro, you didn't seem in good spirits to-day."

"No, captain, I did not."

"And why not?—what was the cause?"

"Why, gentlemen, if you *must* know the cause, I will simply say that I feared some attack from the Indians."

"Indians!" said Frank.

"*I* couldn't see any," said the count.

"No, gentlemen, I dare say not, nor could I see them, but I have no doubt in the world but that they were not far off."

"Indeed, what makes you think so?"

"Well, you see, gentlemen, I have travelled these prairies many a year, and was never mistaken once yet. This morning, when we struck camps, and continued our march, I saw certain signs in the grass to convince me that some Indian or other had paid us a visit the night before, unknown to any one."

"Can it be possible? Why, we had our guards out as usual."

"Yes, gentlemen, I know all about that; but an Indian will creep through the grass as quietly as a mouse, and within three feet of any one who is not well acquainted with their manners and customs."

"Why, he might have cut all our throats," said Fatty, indignantly.

"No, not that exactly. Whoever it was that came, he must have been some big brave, as they call them. He came to see what we had of value among us, and I haven't the least doubt but that the villanous Blackfeet know by this time as well as we do ourselves how many men and rifles and horses and mules we have among us as we do ourselves."

"I heard the wolves howling and barking all night," said Hugh.

"So did I," said Caspar, "and saw them too, for one came very close to our provision waggon, and began smelling about, but when I rose to fire my gun, he darted off into the long grass again."

"Are you sure that everything that moved about during the night *was* a wolf?" asked Pedro. "I fancy you are very much mistaken. These Indians can and do imitate all sorts of animals when they like; but this spy, whoever he was, came on horseback."

"Then some of our party *must* have seen him?"

"No, they didn't," said Pedro. "The Indian must have ridden close up to us before the moon rose. He then lassoed his horse, threw it upon its side, and tied its legs with cord, thus hiding it in the long grass. After this performance, I dare say he covered his head and body with the skin of some wild animal, and then crept close up to us. That is the way they do it. I know 'em well, the red-skinned villains."

"I wish I had known it," said Buttons. "I'd have sent a bullet through his hide."

"You think so, perhaps, but these Indians have sharper eyes than you give them credit for. He would have sent a bullet through *your* hide more likely," said Pedro, laughing.

"Well, and what do you expect will result from this visit?" asked Frank. "Seriously, do you suppose they will attack us?"

"I have no doubt of it."

"The devil!" said Caspar, "then we had better prepare for them."

"Don't fear, major. I have done that already; every gun, pistol, revolver, and rifle in all our company is already cocked and ready, but they won't come to disturb us to-night, I think."

"I'm glad of that," said Fatty. "I want a good sleep to-night, and shouldn't like to be disturbed by the beggarly Indians."

"Have you not noticed a slight cloud of dust to the westward, which has followed our march for the last three or four days, Capt. Frank?" Pedro asked.

"I have."

"So have I," said Caspar.

"I didn't think you knew the meaning of it, so therefore didn't like to disturb you until there was some real occasion for it."

"What was it, then?"

"It was a party of Blackfeet who have been following us; but were waiting for a favorable opportunity to attack us."

"You don't mean it."

"I do. They were the ones who set the prairie on fire. They thought of burning up all the grass around us, so as to starve our horses, and leave us helpless."

"The cunning devils!"

"I, myself, have had very little rest for the last three or four nights, and last night I so arranged the guards that should any spy visit our camps, he would be sure to tell his companions that we were careless, and not on the look-out for them."

"I never dreamed of such trickery," said Hugh; "but if they do come, we'll give them a rare welcome."

"Yes, and no mistake," said several.

"What I fear is," said Pedro, "that they will suddenly dart upon us when we are travelling through some wood, and try to cut off the waggons."

"But we have no forest to pass through yet," said Frank.

"Yes we have, captain," said Pedro. "To-morrow morning we shall enter one about ten miles from this spot; and, mind me, every one must be on the look-out for them."

"Never fear," said all; "if they try to entrap us, we must do the same with them."

"All right," said the count, "so the villains don't disturb us in our rest to-night, I don't mind; so, good night, Pedro."

"Good night, gentlemen," said Pedro, the guide, and he left Frank's tent.

All was still, and every one feeling safe and secure, went to sleep.

They had not been slumbering more than an hour, when Pedro, ever watchful, went out to see that the camp guards were all awake, and doing their duty properly.

One or two he found fast asleep in the grass, and these he kicked so vigorously that they jumped to their feet in great alarm and astonishment.

"What the devil are you all about, eh?" swore Pedro. "Do you want us all butchered in cold blood by the Blackfeet? Get up, and if you dose off again, I'll have you whipped right soundly."

He went further, and found young Buttons on guard.

At first Pedro could not see him, for Buttons was crouched down upon the ground, intently watching something in the distance.

"What do you see?" Pedro asked.

"I can't tell what it is," was the whispered reply, "but for the last half-hour I have seen a great way off something dancing among the high grass, like a man on horseback."

"Where? In what direction?"

"Why, yonder," said Buttons, pointing in the direction meant.

"Do you see it now?" said the quick-eyed young volunteer.

"Yes I do."

"What can it be?"

"I can't tell yet; but will soon find out whether it be a man or a buffalo."

So speaking, Pedro went to one of the camp fires and seized a burning brand.

This he twirled around his head thrice, and then threw it into the fire again.

"If you see any object approach our camp at full gallop, don't fire," said he, to Buttons; "it may be some trapper who has lost his way, or escaped from the Indians."

"And will he know what you meant by that signal?"

"Yes, if he's trapper, he will; but if it's an Indian, he'll think I was breaking up a faggot—listen!"

They did listen, and in a short time both could distinctly hear the rapid approach of some horseman.

In five minutes the outlines of the stranger approaching could be plainly seen.

He came nearer and nearer.

"It is a trapper," said Pedro, "don't fire or alarm the camp."

Buttons did not fire, and shortly the trapper galloped towards them.

"Halt!" said Buttons.

And on the instant the mounted man stopped.

Pedro went out to meet him, and conducted him into the camp.

He was a tall, rough, ragged-looking fellow, without arms or weapons of any kind, save a long, dirk knife.

His hair was hanging all over his face and shoulders.

Blood was upon his hands, and his face was discoloured with gore which ran down from a bullet-wound in his cheek.

"Water, water!" he faintly asked for, and seemed to be so weak that he could hardly speak or keep his seat in the saddle.

The horse he rode was an Indian mustang, and foam was on every part of him.

"Saved! saved!" he said, and slipped off his horse. "Are you Mexicans, or Americans?"

"Neither," said Buttons, proudly. "We are English volunteers, on our way to Mexico."

"Good!" said the trapper. "I heard as much, but could scarcely believe it. The Indians are on the war trail, and will be upon you before many hours."

"How do you know that?" said Pedro.

"I have just escaped from the Blackfeet, and know all."

"Come this way," said Pedro, and he led the trapper to Frank's tent.

Frank, Hugh, Caspar, and the Count, were fast asleep at the time.

When they were awakened, Fatty looked astonished at the grisly, blood-stained appearance of the stranger.

Pedro soon explained all to Frank.

"Escaped from the Blackfeet?" said the Count.

"Yes, sir, and the truth of the whole matter is this Captain Tom Ford and his two ships have been playing the very devil with Maximilian's shipping down in the Gulf of Mexico, and the liberals heard that you were on your way to join Juarez in fighting against the French."

"Quite true."

"Juarez knew me to be a well-know trapper and gave me a dispatch for you."

"Where is it?"

"I have destroyed it, but know its contents very well, word for word.

"When the French heard of your coming they acquainted Maximilian of it, and he communicated the fact to his minister.

"This minister, who is a renegade Mexican, sent word to Eagle-wing, chief of the Blackfeet, to intercept you on the plains, cut off your cattle, and then destroy you in the wilderness.

"Juarez heard of this and sent a despatch by me to warn you in time.

"But, unfortunately, I had not been more than four days on my journey to meet you, when I was surrounded by the Blackfeet, and, after a terrible running fight which lasted half the day, my horse was shot from under me, and there I was among them wounded and helpless.

"I tore up the message Juarez had given me, and thus, if even they knew how to read it, they were unble to get any information about my journey.

"I remained among them for more than a week, and suffered all sorts of insults and ill-treatment.

"They had made up their minds to kill me, but were so occupied in looking after your trail that they put off roasting me until some other day, for I could see they knew my real character.

"They could not speak any language but their own, which I understood well enough, but did not pretend to do so.

"From their joyful jabbering I knew they had got on your trail, and last night one of their numbers even penetrated into your camps——"

"I told you so," said Pedro.

"And got back safely to his comrades, and reported you to be very few and careless; but that you had lots of horses and provisions.

"They held a grand council, and resolved to attack you and destroy your train.

"I heard all about it, and tried to plan some means of making my escape.

"I was tied both hands and feet, however, and could not move.

"An Indian watched me both night and day, and I could not stir but his dark eyes were upon me.

"In order to have plenty of rest before they tracked you, they all went to sleep at sunset last night.

"I pretended to slumber myself; but it was all sham.

"My guard, however, dosed off beside me, and lay down quite close to me.

"In turning over, his hunting knife fell from his belt.

"With great difficulty I picked it up with my teeth, and managed to cut the tight things around my right arm.

"This done, I quickly cut the rest, and was about to get up when my guard awoke.

"I seized him by the throat, so that he would not cause any alarm, and in an instant killed him.

"In a moment I crept out among the horses.

"Vaulting on to one, I galloped away.

"But just as I did so, some villain espied me, and fired.

"I knew that I should be pursued, and so I was for several miles; but I rode in quite a different direction to where your camp fires lit up the sky, so as to throw the Redskins off the scent; but a stray bullet, the last they fired at me, struck me on the cheek, and glanced off, otherwise I should have been a dead man long ago.

"And now that I have told you the truth, the whole truth, and nothing but the truth, give me a drink of whisky, and let me have a sleep."

The trapper's account of his adventures and sufferings was so true in all particulars that no one doubted hin for a moment.

"And when do you think they intend to attack us?" Frank asked.

"To-morrow morning, I think, but they may change their mind before that," said the trapper, groaning and wiping the blood off his face.

"Then let all prepare at once for them," said Frank.

"Yes, that's right," said the trapper, "be prepared for them, but make no noise or bustle, if you do you will be seen, for I have no doubt they have a spy or two out in the high grass watching all your movements.

Frank, the Count, Pedro, Hugh, Casper, and every one began to prepare for the coming conflict; but night passed on and no Indians were visible anywhere.

When the sun rose the company started on their journey again, very carefully and close together.

Some of the party rode far out into the prairie, to the right and left of the waggon train to look out for the enemy.

But nowhere was a single Indian visible; not the slightest trace of any one or anything could be seen.

Noon was passed, and Frank began to think that the Indians might have changed their minds and gone off without attempting to harm him or his friends.

Towards evening, according to Pedro's word, they were approaching a thick forest, and soon after entered it.

The waggons were well guarded, and in front no one ever for a moment thought of danger, and began to imagine that in less than an hour all would be snugly encamped and resting for the night.

They were all mistaken.

For while they were just entering and passing through an open space in the forest, a numerous band of Indians, mounted and on foot, rushed upon the waggon train with ear-piercing yells.

They were armed with pistols, knives, bows and arrows, rifles, tomahawks, and heavy spike-headed bludgeons.

They rushed upon the volunteers with great fury, and for a few moments all was uproar and confusion. (See cut in No. 28).

Eagle-wing, the chief, was foremost in the fray.

Mounted on a strong young horse, he galloped about, dealing blows to the right and left with his ponderous war club.

The fight which now ensued between the Boy Band and the Indians was of the most fierce and sanguinary description.

Rifle shots and deadly arrows were flying about in all directions.

Frank Ford, with the greatest coolness, commanded during the entire combat, and gave his orders in a loud, cheery voice, which could not be mistaken by any one.

For some time the shouts, yells, and screams of the Redskins was something dreadful to hear.

Fatty and Buttons, not having any horses, were compelled for some time to fight on foot.

But the danger was very great, and each moment they were well nigh trampled under foot both by friend and foe.

Fatty and Buttons therefore climbed into one of the waggons, and kept up such a lively fire with their rifles and revolvers, that in a very short time more than a dozen Indians were knocked over and bit the dust.

The Count, sword in hand, accompanied by Caspar, Hugh Tracy, and others, dashed right into the midst of the terrible Redskins, and cut down all before them like as if they were dry reeds.

Eagle-wing, the chief, seeing his men fast falling all around him, and with no hopes of final success, became desperate, and rushed hither and thither, with his immense war-club and tomahawk, and dispersed the Mexican drivers, who cared more to save their lives than to protect the waggon train.

It was in vain that Frank and others called upon them to act like men.

They would not.

They had been hired to drive the teams, they said, and not to fight; and therefore hid out of the way under the waggons, or even climbed up trees.

Frank threatened to shoot the rascals like dogs if they did not fight.

But all these threats they did not care for, and began swearing and growling about their ill luck in pitiable tones.

Eagle-wing roused up his Indians for a last attempt.

They retreated for some little distance, and then turned back again with greater fury than ever.

Eagle-wing espied the escaped trapper among the Boy Soldiers, and made a dash at him.

The trapper was much too weak to encounter such a powerful man as Eagle-wing single-handed.

He therefore dodged the terrific and deadly blow which was aimed at him, when Frank Ford galloped up to his rescue.

The meeting of Frank and Eagle-wing was one which few of the oldest Indian hunters have ever witnessed, or even heard of, for bravery and obstinacy.

With a loud laugh of scorn, Eagle-wing rode up to Frank, and made a terrific stroke at the brave youth's head.

Frank smiled, and warded off the blow.

Next instant Eagle-wing gave a sharp cry of pain.

Frank had wounded him in the right arm with a sabre cut.

Again and again they met and exchanged deadly strokes.

Caspar, Hugh Tracy, and others, would have assisted Frank in the combat.

But this the brave young soldier would not listen to.

"Leave this grisly chief to me, lads," said Frank, gaily; "I will soon finish him. Attend to the others; disperse or kill them; the victory is almost gained."

With terrible curses on his lips, the Indian chief rode down upon Frank, and seized him by the throat.

Next instant both combatants were on the ground, wrestling in a death struggle.

It was now a case of life or death for one or both.

Frank was becoming exhausted, and the Indian perceived it. With a cry of triumph, he was about to throw Frank to the ground and kill him, when Frank, with great cleverness, tripped up his grim antagonist.

With a heavy sound Eagle-wing fell to the earth.

In an instant Frank placed one knee upon his breast.

Eagle-wing writhed in agony and torture.

It was impossible for him to move, however, yet he managed to free one of his hands.

Frank perceived this.

Eagle-wing raised his knife, and would have stabbed Frank to the heart.

It was the last time, however, that he raised that bloody scalping knife.

In a second Frank put the revolver to his head.

A sharp report followed.

Eagle-Wing gave a last shrill cry.

He was no more.

Frank knelt upon the prostrate body of his foe.

Eagle-wing's cry, however, had been heard by his followers, and filled them with consternation.

With loud shouts they fled from the scene of action on all sides, leaving their dead and wounded behind them.

"Pursue! pursue!" shouted Caspar, and followed by every one who was able, the Boy Soldiers sallied forth with three hearty cheers after the galloping figures of their bloodthirsty Indian foes.

"Hurray! hurray!"

"England for ever!"

Such were the shouts heard on all sides, as the gallant boys, now joined by Fatty and Buttons on horseback, dashed away through the forest after the villanous Blackfeet.

---

## CHAPTER LXXXIX.

### THE BLACKFEET INDIANS ARE ROUTED—THE VICTORY GAINED—THE TRAPPER'S TERRIBLE STORY.

"THANK heaven, we have proved victorious!" said Frank, as he stood looking at the grim, blood-stained body of the gigantic Indian chief, Eagle-wing. "Thank heaven we have come off conquerors, or else——"

"Or else," said the trapper, who stood by his side, laughing, "or else, my friend, the Blackfeet would have made soup of all of us before the week was out."

Frank smiled as he pointed to the dead chief near his feet," and said,

"Trapper, it was a fair fight between us, wasn't it?"

"Oh! yes," was the careless reply, "it was all fair and square, and you served him out beautifully; but if I had been only a little stronger on my legs, *I* should have had the honour of doing for Eagle-wing here. Oh, yes, you English boys fight splendidly, and no mistake; but you must never stand on 'honour and fairness' when you are in a scrimmage with the darned Redskins—the Blackfeet in particular, for they are such treacherous, cowardly fiends. Why, look at Eagle-wing here, with blood streaming all down his face, why, he has killed—nay, murdered, that's the way to call it—many a white man in his time; and look you here, Captain Frank, if the old settlers on the borders were only to know this minute that you and your gallant lads had 'done for' over a dozen of these rascally Redskins, they'd dance for joy, for Eagle-wing has been the terror of the plain for over twenty years; yes, ever since I could remember. A murdering villain he was, and no mistake. You deserve a medal for doing this little job, and no gammon. Won't the newspapers give you a long puff for all this? Mark me, if your hands ain't almost wrung off with shaking pretty girls. I'd give a thousand dollars to have had Eagle-wing's scalp-lock. And so I will!" he added, with an oath.

In an instant, and before Frank could prevent it, the trapper knelt down beside the dead chief, whipped out his long knife, and cut off Eagle-wing's scalp-lock.

Frank was astonished and disgusted, as the trapper, in triumph, held up the gory trophy, and turned away towards a waggon to procure some refreshment.

"You hate the Indians most intensely, trapper?" said he.

"I do, Captain Frank, and so would you if you had suffered so much from 'em as I have done."

"Have you suffered much, then?"

"Yes, all my life."

"Indeed!"

"From the time I was a boy, I can remember nothing else but bad blood between us whites and the Indians."

"But I suppose the white settlers were the first to begin the quarrels and fights?"

"I don't know that. That's what all you English people say; but I remember when a boy, these same Blackfeet came down upon a small settlement, and butchered all the white people they could find—my father and mother among them—burnt all the houses to the ground, ran away with the cattle, and violated and scalped all the young girls they could find."

"Those were terrible times, trapper."

"Yes, they were, Captain Frank, and many a gallant man has lost his life since through the cunning and knavery of those same Indians you fought so well to day."

"Eagle-wing, yonder, dead and cold, could tell a terrible tale if he could speak."

The trapper for a moment seemed in deep thought; but said at last, very gravely,

"It is not so bad now as it used to be, when a fellow was obliged to sleep with only one eye open, and often woke up in the morning and felt in vain for his scalp.

"No! they are golden times now compared with formerly: no, I meant to say they were formerly golden compared with now.

"At that time a good beaver-skin was worth from seven to ten dollars, and now a fellow is glad to get rid of it for two or three.

"It was certainly not altogether right among the Redskins; but, to make up for that, you had a jolly little fight now and then.

"The devil! fights still more delicious than ever take place now.

"No; the world is much too spoiled for such excitement.

"There is no life now, and the Indians have become just such sleepy heads as the whites.

"You should have been here ten years ago; there were men to be found then—thunder and lightning!—men who fought when they hadn't as much skin left on their heads as would cover a finger-nail!

"Men who made faces at their foes long after they were dead!

"Aye! those were the times!

"Only think, not far from here—we shall probably pass the spot to-morrow—there is a heap of stones, and under it one of my best friends.

"He was generally known by the name of Jolly Baptiste, for never did a white hunter put a bullet into the eye of a stag or into the brain of an Indian with a merrier face than Jolly Baptiste did.

"He might be a year or two older than I, but you must not forget that many years have passed since then.

"Good, then; he and I, and half a dozen hearty beaver-trappers, were going to the Guadaloupe River to hunt as free trappers with friendly Indians, and were camping in a ravine not far from the heap of stones which, as I said, we shall probably pass to-morrow.

"It was an evening just as fine as this one.

"The spider-webs were floating just as slowly through the air, and the prairie wolves were howling and barking just as sweetly as to-day.

"Ah, poor Baptiste! it was his last Indian summer—his last evening!

"Confound the thing, I would give my rifle and horse for him to be still alive!

"But no matter, he died like a man—like a warrior.

"Well, we had made our camp, were smoking tobacco, and chewing dried meat.

"We had not been lucky in hunting during the last few days, so says Jolly Baptiste,

"'Hang me, if I will blunt my teeth any longer on this stuff; I *must* have fresh meat.'

"So he takes his rifle, and goes down into the plain.

"We were all satisfied with this, wished him luck, and advised him not to return empty-handed.

"We thought of anything less than Indians, for we had not seen the fresh print of a mocassin for at least ten days.

"A good half-hour may have passed, the sun was about as low as now, when we suddenly heard in the distance the crack of Baptiste's rifle.

"I knew its voice as certainly as my own mother's: I mean years ago, when she was still alive, and I was a boy.

"We guessed from the sharp crack that the shot had been fired on the plain and not in a gully, and went up to learn the result.

"What do you think we saw? Oh, Jupiter! I felt the blood stand in my veins, for I was at that time quite a young fellow, to whom such a thing might happen—I saw my friend, Jolly Baptiste, fighting with no less than four accursed villains of the Blackfeet.

"One of the dogs lay already on the ground, for Baptiste's bullet had passed through his brain.

"But the three others attacked him at the same time, firing arrow after arrow at him.

"I began to think that they were too much for Baptiste, for at the moment when he became visible to us he fell down on the grass.

"But it was only his cunning.

"For when we scaled the hill again to hasten to his help—we had merely run back to fetch our rifles—he was on his legs again.

"The merry lad only wanted to get the villains nearer to him, and lost no time.

"He swung the heavy rifle round his head as if it were a twig, and the second of his foes fell to the ground with a fractured skull.

"But now the two last were upon him: we saw them struggle with him for a little while, and then all three fell.

"We could not distinguish anything further.

"We ran as quickly as we could set one foot before the other, and yelled and implored him to hold out a few minutes longer.

"But it was too late, and poor Baptiste's fighting was over.

"We had not arrived within rifle-shot, when one of the Indians suddenly rose, uttered his fierce war-yell, and shook Jolly Baptiste's bloody scalp at us.

"Yes, I still see him before me.

"I would have given ten years of my life if I had been within gunshot.

"But what was the use?

"The dog bounded away like an antelope, and I shed tears of fury.

"The scene we witnessed on reaching the battle-field was, although bloody, most truly consoling.

"There lay our brave friend in the midst of his defeated foes.

"At about a rifle-shot off was the man he first killed.

"Two paces from him was the one whose brains he had dashed out with his clubbed rifle.

"And close to him the third, whom he had throttled with his right hand in the fullest sense of the term.

"He held the fellow so tight, that we were obliged to cut his neck muscles to free Baptiste's hand.

"In spite of the four or five arrows which stuck deep in his body, Jolly Baptiste had succeeded in settling two of the prairie villains.

"He would have given the last one his dose if the throttled man had not driven his knife up to the hilt in his chest, and the runaway split his skull with his tomahawk.

"The dog had also stripped off his scalp with such cleverness that not a single hair was left behind.

"Only a thorough old hunter could have given such a circular cut.

"It is, at any rate, a consolation that he was not scalped by a boy.

"And Jolly Baptiste, what do you think he did after he was dead?

"He looked wildly after the flying Indian, and thrust out his tongue at him.

"Yes, such a man was Baptiste.

"A doctor at the military station, to whom I mentioned this fact, said that the Indian must have knelt on the dying man's throat, which produced such a strange performance.

"But that is a lie.

"I have run about the prairie long enough to be a judge of such things.

"It was pure impudence on his part to make faces.

"He would have shook his fist, too, only he did not like to let loose his victim's throat.

"We buried my good friend, I may say my best friend, Jolly Baptiste, at the spot where he fell.

"We buried him like a great warrior, and then piled a heap of stones over his grave, as you will see when we pass it to-morrow.

"Eagle-wing, that you just now 'finished,' Captain Frank, was the very rascal who scalped poor Baptiste, and I swore then to have the rascal's scalp-lock for a trophy, sooner or later, and so I have. Here it is; and I wouldn't take any money for it."

## CHAPTER XC.

### WARNER AND THE "CRACKSMAN."

THE cottage in which Warner had hidden out of the way of his pursuers did not present any strange or suspicious appearance to those who had burst in the door, so that after having satisfied their curiosity, they came to the conclusion that the occupant must have been a fool not to have unfastened the door before, and allowed them to make their visit without damage to his premises.

First in one corner and then in another, they looked; but so well were the trap-doors in the ceiling and in the floor concealed, that they soon came to the conclusion that the dogs had got upon the wrong scent.

When they had gone, however, the rustic owner of the place knocked at the ceiling three times, and Warner appeared at the aperture.

"Come down, stranger," said he.

"Yes; but where's the ladder?"

"Oh, never mind that, it won't break your neck, I think."

"But I am wounded in the heel."

"Are you? Then so much the better; that will be a guarantee of your not running away in a hurry."

In a moment, however, the rustic produced the ladder, and Warner descended.

"Well, you weren't frightened, I hope?"

"No, not in the least; but it appears to me there is some mystery here," said Warner.

"Well, and suppose there is; you have been saved from the gallows, so ask no questions, and I'll tell you no lies."

"I cannot thank you too much for your protection."

"No thanks; honour among thieves, you know."

"Just so."

"And now I want to speak to you on business," said the rough-looking rustic; "and listen to me attentively."

"I am ready; speak on; but is it not possible there may be some one outside on the watch listening to us."

"No fear of that, I have got one or two on the look out. No one can come here or go away again without I know it."

"Indeed!"

"Yes; I was told by one of my look out men that you were half drowned, so I went out to have a good look at you, to see what kind of article you were."

"Very kind of you."

"And seeing you were a fellow craftsman out of luck, why, I took compassion on you."

"Many thanks again," said Warner; "but what is this business you spoke of?"

"You know the cabby you bilked out of his fare, the night of old Ford's murder?"

"Me?"

"Yes, you; you needn't look so surprised, I know all about it."

"Well, yes, now that I come to think of it, I should recognise him again."

"I dare say you would, and so would *I*," said the man, with a wicked twinkle in his eye.

"Have you, then, had any unpleasant dealings with him?"

"Perhaps I have, and perhaps I haven't; but *you* have at all events."

"Well, I'm listening."

"Do you know anything about the old lawyer who ran away with all old Ford's money?"

"No; I have heard of him, and was once in his office——"

"With Barney and Jonathan?"

"Yes."

"Well, of course, you know that old Flint the lawyer, and Jonathan are fast friends, and are now together."

"No, I did not know it before."

"Well, they are, then, and have got a chest full of valuables with them."

"The old hypocrites."

"Now what I want you to do—in fact you *must* do it—is to go up to London, and look out for this Mr. Barney, and his friend the cabby; and after you have found out their abode let me know."

"I am perfectly willing, but am short of money."

"Oh, that's nothing; I've got plenty of tin."

"Then you are the very man I want to be friendly with," said Warner, smiling.

"Well, it matters nothing whether you do so or not. All I've got to say is this—you must swear to do my bidding on pain of death!" said the rustic-looking fellow, very solemnly; "I am not the sort of man my rough looks and shabby dress would indicate. Now, what name do you wish to go under?"

"I have only one name."

"Gammon!" said the stranger, laughing; "when you were a doctor, you had different names for different lodgings."

"Well, then, call me Warner, when among friends."

"Very well; and when in the company of those we don't well know, we will pronounce Warner backwards, and call you Renraw?"

"That will do."

"Give me your hand, and with it your oath."

"I will; here it is," said Warner; and they shook hands.

"Well, that is all right; and now to business. You would like to know who and what I and my companions are, of course?"

"I would."

"We are 'cracksmen.'"

"I thought so."

"None of your common fellows, but gentlemen."

"I am glad to hear it."

"Break into banks, and such like, and make enough in one or two jobs to keep in fine feather all the year."

"That's the sort for me. But why are you here?"

"We have done a little business not many miles away from here."

"And got the quad here also?"

"Not likely; but, as I was about to say, the 'slops' are off the scent, and several of us are supposed to be over in France at this moment horse-racing and betting."

"That's the blind, I suppose?"

"No; my brother and I own two or three."

"The devil you do! And support it out of your craft?"

"Of course. Who'd suspect us?"

"Well, no one, I should suppose."

"That's the real trick, my lad," said the rustic; "we are gentlemen abroad, and cut as fine a dash about the Haymarket as any nob in London."

For a moment Warner seemed astonished.

The rustic laughed as he continued:

"You know enough of us, then, for the present; and now what I want you to do is to make your way by railway as fast as you can to Weedon, and at the station call for a leather trunk with 'S. T. S.' painted on the side. It is quite new, and has two brass locks. If they want to know your name, give any you like. There will be no difficulty about the matter, for it is directed to be left until called for."

"I suppose it is 'swag'?" said Warner, smiling.

"It is."

"And what am I to do with it?"

"Are you well acquainted with the 'Lane'?"

"Well, yes—a little—not much," said Warner, with an air of dignity.

"Oh, you needn't feel too proud," said the rustic, with a smile; "there's much better men than you or I who have visited that place."

"It may be. But why do you ask?"

"Take the trunk with you in a cab, and be at Aldgate church to-morrow night as the clock strikes nine. If you are punctual to time an old gentleman will poke his head into the cab, and say, S. T. S.; your answer will be, O. K. The person I speak of will then conduct you to a neat, genteel fence; the money he gives you, you will bring back to me."

"And what kind of a person is he?"

"An old Jew. We call him Moss, for short; a clever old fellow, and has been out with a ticket of leave for the last four years. His hair is long and grey; his whiskers, beard, and moustache, long and untrimmed. He is rather shabbily dressed, but wears a costly diamond ring on the little finger of his right hand. If he doesn't wear the ring, don't leave the trunk, for it is a sign how the wind blows."

With these directions Warner prepared to go.

But ere he went he was introduced to several of the gang who had been concealed in various underground apartments, and, after having had his wound roughly dressed, he left the cottage provided with money and all things necessary for his journey.

He was accompanied by the chief of the gang for a long distance until they came to a village several miles nearer to London than Bromley.

"You are now togged up," said his guide; "good-night. Go and hire a trap, and get to the nearest station as fast as you can. In four days at the farthest let me see you back again."

"All right," said Warner.

They shook hands and parted.

Warner procured a trap at the village, and, after driving about ten miles at a rapid rate, he arrived at a small country station.

He wished to take a first-class ticket for the express train, but, as that did not stop there, he had to wait an hour and got into the mail for London.

Now, this was the very railroad line upon which Jonathan and Flint had met with the terrible accident recorded in another chapter.

But of this Warner knew no more than the railway officials, for all the telegraph wires had been blown down by that storm.

Into the train Warner hobbled as best he could with his wounded leg, and ere long was whizzing along at a rapid rate towards London.

For miles they dashed along, but, ere many minutes, they reached a curve in the line just before they came to the long tunnel.

As they were rattling along, unconsious of any harm or danger, they suddenly saw in the far distance many lights and lanterns flitting to and fro.

This unusual sight in the darkness and fog alarmed the engine-driver, who instanly shut off the steam and put on the breaks.

The nearer they approached the tunnel the more discordant and noisy became the sounds.

Shouts of warning were heard on every side, and men, half frantic, waved their arms and hats like lunatics.

Fortunately the engine stopped just at the edge of the tunnel, when a number of excited persons rushed forward and told the sad tale of the collision.

Traffic was stopped at both ends of the tunnel, but inside of it all was noise and lamentation.

Those who had not been injured were assisting those who had, and dead bodies were being brought out one after another, in dismal procession.

All along the bankside of the railway lay maimed persons groaning and moaning.

The train in which Warner had come was soon emptied of its travellers, and filled with the dead and wounded.

All this had occurred because the telegraph wires had been rendered useless by the storm.

"Hillo, what does all this mean?" said Warner, to a bystander.

"Mean," was the reply, "why the express has run into a train in the tunnel and smashed it. A 'despatch' engine coming close afterwards, ran into the express, and there are scores of passengers killed and wounded."

Warner did not at first recognise the speaker, but in a moment afterwards saw he was a policeman.

He hastily moved away, and mingled with the crowd, for in his guilty soul he hated an officer of justice.

"Here comes another," said a bystander.

"What another bobby?" was the answer.

"Yes, that makes two dead 'uns as have been dragged out."

"How comes it so many policemen have been killed?" asked Warner of a workman.

"They say the 'despatch' engine was sent after the express to overtake it, in order to capture two noted villains, who were running away."

"Oh, I see; and did you hear their names?"

"No, sir; but I heard one of the officers who escaped say that one of them was an old lawyer, and t'other a schoolmaster, or something of that sort."

"It must be Jonathan and Flint," thought Warner, "I wonder if the two old villains have been killed."

He had not long to remain in doubt.

As he moved about in the darkness, he suddenly espied the tall, lanky form of Jonathan, who was limping away as if shunning the look of every one he met.

Behind him crawled the bent-up figure of Flint, who tottered as if shaken in every limb.

They slunk away in the darkness, and, as best they could, clambered over the railings into an adjacent field, and sat down under a hedge.

"How lucky," thought Warner; "I'll follow and listen to what they have got to say."

While intending to act thus, he was suddenly slapped on the shoulder by a constable, who said to another close by—

"This is the man, sergeant."

# THE BOY SOLDIER; OR, GARIBALDI'S YOUNG CAPTAIN.

THE OATH—(*See No.* 34).

He was impatient for night to approach, that he might gloat over and delight his bleary eyes with contemplating the rich store of stolen plate which Warner was to bring to him.

For Moss, as it will be perceived, kept a well guarded "fence," and was known to the best of thieves and housebreakers throughout the United Kingdom.

It was by buying stolen property that he had accumulated riches so very fast, and at the time of which we now speak, he was worth tens of thousands, although but a few years before that he was not worth a shilling.

Besides his rag and bone and bottle shop, old Moss had large warehouses, in which all sorts of goods were stowed away.

It was locked and bolted and barred more like a prison than a goods warehouse, and at night time, the old Jew was wont to unchain a fierce bulldog, which ran at large in the warehouse, and was a good guarantee for the safety of his master's property.

By certain signs and pass-words old Moss well knew his friends and customers; hence, when he went to Aldgate church, and found the Hansom cab in waiting, he spoke but a word or two as he passed, and was instantly recognised by Warner.

Moss jumped into the cab, and both were driven to a very respectable coffee-shop, where Warner



proposed to hire a room for the night, or, at least, for as long as it would require to settle the business with the Jew.

When they retired to the comfortable room, Warner ordered supper for two, for which he made old Moss pay, and in less than fifteen minutes they were "as thick as two thieves."

But the Jew would not eat, he was too anxious about Warner's errand.

Warner warmed himself with several glasses of brandy; but the Jew, with a keen eye to business, refused to take anything of the sort, until he had come to some settlement about the price to be paid for the stolen property.

"Well," said Warner, "and now to business."

He opened the trunk, and old Moss was delighted.

It contained various things of great value, such as gold watches, diamond rings, brooches, necklaces, bracelets, gold and silver ware, coffee and tea pots of silver, which had been smashed up or broken, and other things of great value.

Old Moss was pleased beyond measure.

He sucked his lips and rolled his eyes.

But he spoke not a word for all that.

"There," said Warner, "what do you think of your Bromley friends now, eh, Moss, old fellow?"

"Is dish all?" answered the Jew, with a curling lip.

PUBLISHER'S NOTE.

PP. 234-257 AND PP. 291-297 ARE MISSING.

"A-l-l!" Warner replied, in disgust. "How much did you expect they'd send at once, eh? Perhaps you'd like a cart-load?"

"It ish not much," old Moss replied, stroking his chin, and trying to appear very much disappointed. "It ain't vort much, my fren."

"Oh, isn't it though."

"No, not mush, I say; dem diamonds are paste, dat plate is not goot, it ish only vashed mit shilver."

"The devil it is!" said Warner. "Do you think I can't tell what is good metal as well as you? No matter, if you don't want to buy it why there's no harm done; I'll go to old Isaacs, your neighbour, he'll buy it, I know."

"Shtop! shtop!" said old Moss, "don't pe in such a hurry; I did not shay I vill not puy."

"Then be quick about it," said Warner; "let's have no higgling over such things as these."

"How mush you vant for dem?"

"How much will you give?"

"Dat is not what I ask."

"What are they worth, then?"

"Ah! dat ish ferry differant," said the old Jew; "to me dey ain't vort notting."

"Ain't they, though?" said Warner, with a malicious grin. "How very clever you are, Moss."

"Vell, not vort mush, I mean. How mush you vant for dem?"

"Well, your friends at Bromley told me to receive nothing less than £300."

"Vhat!" exclaimed the Jew, in horror, "tree huntred pounce? Vhat you mean? Are you mat? You must pe shoking; I vill go, they ain't vort it."

"£300 is the price," said Warner.

"Ha! ha! ha! my goot frendt, you mak von pig mishtake; I go hom."

"Good night," said Warner.

"Goot night," said old Moss, going to the door.

He had his hand upon the door handle, when he suddenly turned round, and said,

"I'll tell you vat I vill do."

"Well, name it."

"I gif you £200 for de lot."

"Not a penny less than £300."

"Vhy, my tear frendt, £300 is von fortune!"

"I can't help that. Will you give it or not?"

"No; I haf not as mush."

"Then the affair is settled. I'll call on old Isaacs and sell the lot to him."

The old Jew's eyes glistened with anger when he heard Isaac's name mentioned, for they were deadly rivals in business, and kept opposition "fences" in the Lane.

"Vell, vell, den, ve vill shay no more; you shall haf tree huntred, put I haf not got it vit me."

"I can stay here until you return."

"Well, I shuphose I can take de goots vit me?" said old Moss, with a twinkling eye.

"No, not one," said Warner, grinning; "I'm not so soft as that."

"I meant no wrong, my frendt."

"I dare say not; all right, Moss; go and get the chink, and all the lot is yours."

Moss went down the stairs, and the cab was still standing at the door.

He got into it, and was rapidly driven down to the Lane.

He was in a very great hurry, and bustled into his shop puffing and blowing.

He told his wife the full particulars of what had occurred, and she in turn was jubilant.

"Put you tink, vife, de prish, de prish. Tree huntred pounce—it ish von fortune."

For a few moments the husband and wife were engaged in a deep conversation carried on in whispers.

"Yah, yah, if ve couldt do dat, vife, it vould pe fine—perry fine; put who vould do it for me?"

"That rough fellow who, as I told you, called to-night."

"Vhat Parney?"

"Yes; he is a fighting man," replied the wife, "and exactly the kind of person who would do it."

"If I couldt ony findt him," sighed old Moss.

He had not to sigh long, for Barney had been watching for the Jew's return home, and entered the shop.

The tinkling bell gave old Moss warning of somebody's entrance, and Pug was astonished to find how glad the old Israelite was at the meeting.

He did not explain his business to Barney then, but asked him if he would meet him outside the Great Eastern Coffee House, Whitechapel Road, in half-an-hour.

Barney said he would be only too happy, for upon meeting the Jew there depended the arrears then due to him for the stolen articles.

After much trouble old Moss and his wife managed to rake and scrape together £300 in gold and notes.

He placed the money in a leather bag, and carried it under his coat.

The cab was still in waiting, and he was soon driven back again to where Warner was in waiting.

As Moss got out of the cab, he was much surprised to find that Barney was already waiting outside the Great Eastern Coffee House.

He slipped a crown into the Pug's hand as he passed in at the door, saying, "Stay here for half-an-hour;" and thinking—

"He will go and get something to drink, and by the time I want him, he will be right and ripe for anything."

Barney did not belie the old Jew's supposition.

The first thing he did was to have some rum and hot water, and the taste so much agreed with him, that he frequently called for more, and in less than fifteen minutes his round pox-marked face was all aglow, and his eyes unnaturally bright.

At the appointed time old Moss re-appeared at the door, and two waiters were lugging out the trunk towards the cab.

It was placed inside the vehicle, and off the cab went to old Moss's "fence," Barney and all.

The cab had scarcely stopped, and that very suddenly, before old Moss's shop, when three long-nosed Jewish-looking fellows appeared, and the trunk disappeared into the shop in the twinkling of an eye.

All this seemed a mystery to Barney; but still he kept his seat inside the cab, and he and old Moss returned to the coffee-house, conversing together all the way in a very animated manner.

"Vhat do you shay, frendt Parney, vill you do it?"

"Yes," said Barney, "I will, if you stand my friend in case of any difficulty."

"'Pon my shoul I vill, Parney; dere ish mine handt on it."

"Agreed," said the Pug.

"I tell you what you do, Parney," said the cunning Jew, "if you get in and get de pag of money, you gif it to me on de sly, and I vill make it all right vith you, my tear poy."

"Very well, we shall see," the Pug replied, "but mind and leave the door on ajar."

"I vill not forget, trust me," said the Jew, entering the coffee-house once more.

Old Moss went up to the room in which Warner

was, and found him, with cigars and a bottle of brandy, enjoying himself.

He had counted the money during the old Jew's absence, and, as he expected, found it to be a pound or two short of the amount agreed upon.

He did not say anything about it, however, for he knew full well that if a Jew were dealing with the devil himself he would endeavour to cheat his Satanic majesty.

Old Moss pretended to be very happy, and poured out for himself a glass of brandy, and was soon occupied with a huge cigar.

He left the room door ajar, in order to let out the tobacco smoke, he said.

And he so arranged his own seat, that he could very well see all that took place in the room.

But Warner could not, for he sat with his back to the door.

The bag of money was still on the table, and placed a little behind Warner's right elbow, in a very careless manner.

But this pleased Moss all the more.

"For," thought the cunning Jew, "Parney can creep in on his hands and knees, and steal the coin unobserved."

But the wily Israelite had miscalculated his chances.

On the mantelpiece there was a small mirror, and by turning his eyes to it Warner could perceive any one approaching from behind.

This old Moss never thought of until it was too late.

Both these worthies drank often, but the Jew, as he thought, unobserved by Warner, took but a small portion at a time, and spat it out again.

This, however, did not occur without Warner perceiving it, but he smiled as he thought,

"The brandy costs him nothing, and yet he spits it out again. He must have some object in view, and I will keep my weather eye open."

In less than an hour Warner appeared to get very groggy, but he could drink much more without becoming affected than Moss ever dreamed of.

Hence, when they had been sitting together for about two hours or more, Warner proposed a song, and began to sing.

The Jew joined in with a very loud, discordant voice, and occasionally looked very anxiously towards the door.

Warner lay back in his arm-chair, winking and blinking as if in more than a half state of intoxication, when Moss, unobserved, coughed three times in a very peculiar manner, and lowered the lamp until the light became very dim.

Still he sang and smoked, and thumped the table in applause of Warner's songs, and appeared to be enjoying himself immensely.

While all this was taking place, Barney had crept upstairs unobserved and unheard.

On his hands and knees he crawled into the room, and hid behind the bedstead.

Still Warner and Moss sang on, and the former drank more deeply than ever.

Perceiving this, and having received a signal from old Moss, Barney crawled behind Warner's chair.

The old Jew now became intensely excited.

He could perceive Barney's eyes glistening in the deep shade.

Still Warner sang on loudly, and drank his brandy as carelessly as ever.

Old Moss was almost choking with expectation.

He endeavoured to accompany Warner in his song, but could not, for he perceived Barney's hand upraised, and approaching the table.

Next moment he could see the big, fat, puffy hand of the Pug upon the table.

It was ready to grasp the bag of gold.

His hand was on it.

"Careful, Barney, be careful, now; make no noise, or all is lost," thought the Jew, as he trembled with doubt and fear.

In a moment, however—for Warner had perceived all through the mirror on the mantel—and, with the quickness of thought, Warner plucked the dagger from his belt.

The next instant it was plunged right through Barney's hand.

The Pug was pinned to the table!

With a shout of horror and pain Barney rose to his feet.

But Warner pulled the weapon from the wound, and brandished it before him.

"Make any more noise, traitor, or attempt to stir, and I will plunge this through your vile, black heart," he said, savagely.

Old Moss rose suddenly, and would have rushed to the door.

But, with a powerful blow in the face, Warner knocked the cunning Jew all of a heap on the floor, where he lay, sprawling and bleeding.

Warner looked with triumph first at one and then at the other of his unfortunate victims.

He locked the door, and put the key into his pocket, as, with a laugh of contempt and scorn, he said,

"This was a prettily-arranged plan of your's to rob me, wasn't it, Moss?"

"Oh, 'pon my shoul, I hat not de shlightest intention to rop you," the Jew groaned; "let me go, let me go!"

"So you bargained with that traitor, then, Barney, eh, to do this while I was drunk as you supposed? But I saw through your plans, my cunning Jew, and you shall have to pay dearly for it."

"I don't know him; on my vort as a shentleman I do not," old Moss replied. "You just ask him?"

"Liar!" said Warner, kicking the Jew in the ribs; "liar! didn't I watch all your movements? Didn't I see you talk to the Pug there, and arrange about the time? Liar as you are, you shall pay dearly for this!"

"How do you mean?" the Jew whined.

"What do I mean, old fool! I mean that this night's work shall cost you all you possess in the world, if, indeed, you do not suffer all your whole life for it. Think you I can ever forget or forgive such treachery as you would have played upon me?"

Turning to Barney, who was suffering great agony with his wounded hand, and bleeding profusely,

"And you, villain!" hissed Warner, as their eyes met; "so you have turned informer, eh?"

Barney averted his eyes, and made no reply.

"We have met sooner than I expected, cur!" said Warner, his eyes flashing deadly hate, "but not too soon for my keen revenge. If it were not to gratify my passion still more than I have done—were it not that I wish you to suffer additional torture, I would despatch you on the spot!"

At that instant, and unobserved, old Moss pulled out a revolver, and, taking deliberate aim at Warner, he fired thrice in quick succession!

---

## CHAPTER XCIX.

### JONATHAN AND GALE HAVE A VERY CONFIDENTIAL CHAT.

HAD a thunderbolt fallen into the room, old Jonathan could not have felt more stunned and surprised than he did when the detective entered in such a good-tempered off-handed manner.

Tom Ford, for a moment or two, could scarcely refrain from downright merriment, for the old master at Bromley turned so pale and red, and red and pale by turns, that at last he fairly looked blue.

He turned first towards one and then towards the other, knowing not what to think or how to act.

Gale looked the old man firmly in the face, and the officer's gaze was so firm that old Jonathan quailed before him.

"Don't you know me?" said Gale.

"Know you, sir? How should *I* know who or what you are?" said Jonathan, with a well-assumed air of offended dignity.

"Oh, you don't, eh?—then I must explain myself," said Gale, with a merry twinkle in his eye. "I dare say we shall be on more intimate terms ere long."

"How do you mean, sir? I cannot understand your inuendos."

Turning to Captain Tom Ford, who was smoking very complacently, old Jonathan said,

"Do *you* know this person, or is he an intruder?"

"Know him, of course I do; and so will you shortly."

"Oh, he knows me well enough," said Gale; "but he doesn't want to do so, that's all. It's always the way, you know."

Although Jonathan was endeavouring to keep up his courage, he felt as if he could sink to the floor with weakness.

"Do you read the newspapers, sir?" asked the detective.

"Yes; that is, sometimes I do."

"Did you ever hear of the name of Gale?"

"Gale, Gale," mused Jonathan; "no, I think not."

"Not Gale, the detective?" said the officer.

"No. Why or how should *I* know any person of that profession? What have *I* done to require the assistance or services of such a person?"

"Well, 'pon my soul, he keeps it up well," said Gale, to Tom; "don't he?"

"Sir, I demand an explanation!" said Jonathan, stammering.

"Then you shall have it; but first answer me a few questions. If you do so honestly, it may be of great service to me and to yourself. Mind, I don't say and promise that it *will*, but that it *may*."

Jonathan felt like a man whose time has come at last.

He sank into a chair and breathed very hard.

Yet, up to the very last, he played his part to perfection, and acted "injured innocence" to a nicety.

He did not speak for a moment or two, but watched the officer who, with pencil and pocket-book, was making ready to jot down the old man's answers.

"As I have said before," Gale began, "if you answer my questions in a straightforward manner, it *may* be of great use both to you and to me. To begin, then, do you know where your wife is?"

"I do not."

"Nor Shanks, your former tutor?"

"No, hang him! Why do you bother me with such questions?"

"Because I wish to show you that I mean to act squarely."

"Well, then, what of my wife and Shanks?"

"They have been in prison for perjury; but are now out, and are living together as man and wife."

"No, you don't mean that!" said Jonathan, jumping from his seat in a towering passion. "No, you don't mean that; she could not be so wicked and brazen!"

"I am telling you the plain truth, Jonathan."

"Oh, that I had both of them within my power this instant," said Jonathan, grinding his teeth in a great rage, and stamping his heel heavily on the ground. "I would murder them," said he with a savage oath.

"Your two daughters ——"

"Yes! what of them," said the old man, trembling.

"They are still at Bromley Hall. We will not disturb them yet awhile, for we intend to explore the old mansion from top to bottom, shortly."

"Indeed," said Jonathan, with a glistening eye, "and why, pray?"

"It is filled with mystery," said the detective, with a knowing wink, "and Giles says ——"

"What has that old villain to say about me?" Jonathan snarled.

"He is not an old villain," Gale replied, "but, on the contrary, a most respectable old man."

"He is not; he is an old good-for-nothing liar."

"He is not, Jonathan, but *you* are, if you persist in saying so. He has rendered me great assistance already, and I should never have found out as much about the ins and outs of Bromley Hall if it had not been for him."

"I dare say not, the old scoundrel," said Jonathan, with an oath. "I wish I was only down there again for twenty-four hours, I'd soon teach old Giles a different tale."

"I dare say you would," said Gale, and in the *dark*, no doubt."

"In the 'dark,' what mean you?"

"Oh, nothing at present. But to come to real business, Jonathan, tell me truly, do you know a person of the name of Flint."

"Flint! Flint! Flint!" mused the cunning old rogue, as if he had never heard the name before in all his life.

"Yes, Flint, an old lawyer, who once had apartments in Green Court?"

"Oh, an old lawyer," said Jonathan, looking up with a smile, "yes, oh, yes, now I come to think of it, I do; that is to say, I *did* know such a person."

"Indeed," said Gale, with a quiet smile. "You don't know where he is *now*, of course you don't?"

"No, why should I?"

"Oh, nothing, but I thought perhaps that you might know, you see."

"Me, lor bless you, I know nothing of him."

"No, I suppose not, for you see this old Flint, wherever he may be hiding, is accused of being an accomplice in the robbery and murder of his friend and client, old Ford, Captain Tom Ford's uncle."

"Monstrous!" said the old hypocrite, holding up his hands in mock horror, "Monstrous!"

"You don't know anything of that foul affair, I suppose?" said Tom, for the first time speaking.

"Me, lor bless the handsome youth! I know no more about it than the child unborn," said Jonathan.

"People may differ about that," said Gale; "now I, for one, think you know a great deal regarding old Ford's murder, and not only that, but the murder in Green Court, also, and many other villanies which have not yet seen the light in Bromley Hall."

Jonathan shivered, but still he maintained a bold front as Gale went on.

"It is nonsense of you to say that you do not know anything of this Flint, for you do; from information received I am certain that you do know; and, more than that, 'Doctor' Warner is mixed up with both of you deeper than you think or would like to confess. But listen to me, Jonathan," said Gale, in a very earnest manner, "if you cannot do any further harm, at least do some good."

"I am always willing to do that," said the old schoolmaster, in a very meek and humble manner. "In what manner can I serve you?"

"In this way," said Gale. "Old Flint suddenly left his apartments after the mysterious murder, and carried with him the numerous deeds and documents which of right belong to this young gentleman, Captain Tom Ford, and his brother Frank."

"Indeed!" said Jonathan, elevating his eyebrows; "it is the first time I have heard of it."

"And the property stolen amounts to many, many thousands; nay, hundreds of thousands of pounds!"

"You astonish me," said the old schoolmaster. "Hundreds of thousands, eh?"

And as he spoke he rubbed his hands in a frenzied manner, as much as to say—

"Oh, would that I had been behind old Flint when he left town the first time, wouldn't I have settled with the old rascal once and for ever."

He could not but inwardly groan as he reflected how clumsily old Flint had managed matters generally, and how they might have lived in wealth and secresy only for the bungling of the lawyer.

"If you do know anything of old Flint or this missing treasure you would confer a great favour on me, and I have no doubt it would redound to your credit before a jury of your own country-men."

"A jury of my own country-men?" gasped Jonathan, in horror, for in imagination he already saw himself standing in a felon's dock and receiving sentence.

"Before a jury of my country-men?" he repeated, mechanically, and as he did so he loosened his cravat, for a certain unpleasant choking sensation came over him as if his toilet at that moment had been superintended by that world-famed valet for great criminals—Mr. Calcraft.

"Before a jury of my countrymen!" he repeat ed for the third time. "Why, what have I done?"

"Oh, nothing, of course," said Gale; "I never knew a rogue yet but was always 'innocent' if asked why sentence should not be pronounced upon him. Oh! nothing, of course," said Gale, laughing.

But he sidled up to Jonathan, and whispered so that Captain Tom couldn't hear him.

"Where you ever at Epping Forest?"

"Epping Forest!" said Jonathan, with bloodshot eyes.

"Do you know anything of the bank robbery?"

Jonathan hung his head.

"You had better make me a friend than a foe," said Gale, very solemnly.

"What will you promise?" asked Jonathan, in a hoarse whisper.

"I can't promise anything," was the reply; "but I will do the best I can for you."

"On your honour?"

"On my honour as an officer."

"We need not stay here, then?"

"No, we can go now, if you like; a cab is standing at the door."

"You will not degrade me by putting handcuffs on me?" said Jonathan.

"No, if you promise to go quietly."

"That I will do, of course, for what could an old man like me do against such a powerful individual as you are? But, don't let this Captain Ford know anything of what we are about to do."

"No, I will not."

With a low bow, Jonathan advanced to Captain Tom Ford, and extended his hand.

But Captain Tom refused to shake hands with him, and turned away from the old hypocrite with looks of contempt and scorn.

"You would not refuse to shake hands with me if you only knew how much you may be indebted to me," said old Jonathan. "But I am not disappointed; the world is full of ingratitude."

He and Detective Gale left the captain's apartments arm in arm, as if nothing had happened.

But, as the detective sallied forth, he cast one quick glance at the young captain, as much as to say,

"All right. I shall soon return. I have got one of the rascals at last, and terror will make him reveal all he knows about the others, as you will quickly find."

"What a perfect old villain Jonathan is," thought Captain Tom, when his visitors had left the room. "I always thought he was a close-fisted hypocrite when he was master at Bromley Hall, but I never dreamed he could play the part of an oily vagabond so well."

As he thought thus, he took up the latest edition of an evening newspaper, and, with a sailor's turn for all things nautical, his eye was soon riveted by a small paragraph, which read as follows:—

"Shipwreck on the Cornish Coast.

"Another disaster has occurred on our coast. The brig 'Dolphin,' from Leghorn, which had been signalled for several days beating about in very rough weather, without sails, masts, or rudder, drifted ashore on the sands of Redruth early this morning. We are happy to state that all who survived the terrific storm were safely landed through the heavy surf by means of a rope, which, through the gallantry of the captain, was made fast to the wreck and rocks. All, save one, were rescued in this manner, and he, it appears, from some insane idea, remained on board; his name is unknown. The tide floated the wreck into a small creek, and there she lies high and dry upon the sands, but is rapidly falling to pieces, for all her timbers can scarcely hold together any longer. The wreckers are hard at work, endeavouring to save as much of the cargo as possible."

"Poor devils!" thought Captain Tom, as, in a line or two below, he read on—

"Among the passengers were Mr. Lancaster, the well-known banker, and Miss Ellen Lancaster, his daughter."

"What!" said Tom, in surprise. "It surely cannot be Nelly Lancaster and her father—yet, it is very likely; indeed it must be, for they were at Leghorn when Frank and I left there. Here's a bit of news to send off to Mexico, and no mistake. Poor brother Frank! He dearly loves Nelly Lancaster, and she him, but I fear it will never come to anything between them.

"But who could this poor fellow have been who refused to leave the ship, I wonder? I daresay his sufferings made him half crazy."

Little did kind-hearted Captain Tom Ford imagine that the "poor fellow" was none other than his worst enemy, Joel Flint.

## CHAPTER C.

### JOEL FLINT IS MASTER OF THE WRECK.

"There," said Joel Flint, when the last man had left the "Dolphin," "there! they have all got safely to land; but I'll stay here. No, no, I shan't be such a fool as to leave my treasure behind. No, no, one might as well be dead as without riches."

So thinking, he loosened the end of the rope which was on board.

"Poor devil!" said the captain on shore. "The rope is loose, he must have fallen into the sea and perished."

With a sigh, the captain, and those who had been saved, left the painful scene, and clambered up the rocks.

They made the best of their way towards the nearest town, which was Redruth, fifteen miles away, intending to procure assistance, and return to the wreck as soon as the weather had moderated a little.

But what did Joel Flint do?

With a cunning, for which few would give him credit under such trying circumstances, he rushed about hither and thither, gathering together everything of value which he could lay his hands upon.

"The vessel is firmly imbedded in the sand," he thought, "and if it moves at all the tide will carry it still further in shore into that snug creek yonder. If I could only get my treasure on shore, I would snap my finger at all the world."

With these thoughts he went into the cabin and forecastle, and rummaged about in all directions.

He broke open the captain's private desk and drawers, ransacked the luggage of Mr. and Miss Lancaster, and found many things of value, such as watches, rings, purses, bank-notes, and the like.

"This was well worth staying for," thought he, in great glee. "The storm is fast abating, and in a few hours the water around will be smooth and unruffled."

Whatever he could lay hands upon of value, did Joel Flint purloin.

He emptied a trunk, and put all his plunder into it.

This he well corded, and placed on the deck ready to drop into any boat or fishing vessel that might come to his assistance.

All day long he worked very hard in tugging at the safe, and, after great labour, managed to tie stout cords around it.

As night advanced again, Joel began to feel very uneasy, for the storm threatened to commence again.

"And if it does so," he thought, "I shall be lost."

To cheer up his courage, Joel broke open the spirit-room and helped himself to a plentiful supply of bread and meat and wine.

He also found a box of cigars, and began to smoke.

The next thing to be done was to raise some sort of signal; but he was too timid to mount up the masts and hang out a white sheet.

For some time he knew not what to do.

At last a happy thought occurred to him.

"It is getting devilish cold," said Joel. "I dare not go to sleep, and yet I am so tired, I could fall to sleep standing; but that I must not think of doing, in case the wreck shifts from its position.

He next gathered a few broken boxes, and made a small fire on the forecastle of the brig, and sat down to warm himself.

The winds increased from seaward, and soon the small fire gave forth a strong blaze, so much so that in a short time it caught the deck of the forecastle, and would have destroyed the brig if it had once fairly caught.

Joel did not at first notice this, but laid him down before the cheerful blaze, and intended to keep wide awake.

Nature, however, was thoroughly exhausted, and Joel dropped off to sleep near the fire.

How long he slept he knew not; but was suddenly aroused from his uneasy slumber by his clothes catching fire.

He jumped to his feet instantly, for the blaze was threatening more and more each instant.

To save himself and his treasure from certain destruction, he seized a bucket, and drew up water from the sea, with which he ultimately managed to extinguish the flames.

On this occasion, Joel was obliged to work with all his might, for had the forecastle once got into full blaze, the ship must have burned to the water's edge.

While he was dancing about, throwing buckets of water upon the fire, he suddenly perceived a fishing boat looming up in the misty distance, which had been drawn to the spot by the glare of the flame.

"Ship ahoy!" came the fisherman's welcome sound; "ship ahoy!"

"Ship ahoy!" answered Joel, with all his strength, and, in less than five minutes, the fishing smack changed her tack, and, rounding under the brig's stern, lowered her mainsail and made fast.

Joel ran to the stern like a wild man.

"What ship is that?" asked the fishermen, from below.

"The 'Dolphin' of London, from Leghorn, grounded in a gale."

"That's very plain," answered the rough voice of the fishing master. "How many have you got on board?"

"I'm the only one."

"The devil you are!"

"'Tis true. Come on board, some of you. Be quick, my men, I will pay you well."

"Thank you for nothing, my man," said the rough skipper, "we'll pay ourselves, without asking any questions. It's a wreck, and our lawful prize."

"Not quite so fast, my friends; I'm the supercargo, and must look after the interests of my employers."

"Do you want us to work for nothing, then, mate?"

"No," said Joel, "I do not; all I want you to do for me is to help me land the ship's books and papers, and then you may do what you like with the sinking craft."

"Well, that's talking in reason," said the fishermen, cheering up.

"How far is the nearest town from this point?"

"Fifteen mile, or more."

"And what's the name of the place?"

"Redruth."

"Is there no town nearer to a railway station than that?"

"No; but the nearest station is only ten miles off."

"Then land me and the ship's books and papers as soon as you like, my brave men; meanwhile I'll telegraph to the owners, and leave you in full charge of the wreck."

"What's her cargo?"

This question, for a moment, puzzled the self-styled supercargo, who, as such, should have known to a hundredweight what the cargo was.

However, Joel stammered out,

"Cargo, eh? Oh! ah! Yes; it's a general cargo, and very valuable."

"To stave off any further questions which might have proved very annoying and embarrassing to him, Joel introduced the fishermen to the spirit-room, and helped the rough-looking fellows very liberally to whatever they wished.

But all this time Joel seemed to be sitting on thorns in case the strangers might prove to be too inquisitive about the iron safe.

However, after much drinking, and swearing and smoking, the men hauled out the safe and several trunks, and lowered them with stout ropes into the fishing smack.

He himself got on board, and, leaving several of the men in charge of the wreck, he and two others hoisted sails and rounded a small headland, and soon lost sight of the unfortunate "Dolphin."

## CHAPTER CI.

### MOSS HAS TO PAY THE FIDDLER.

ALTHOUGH the cunning old Jew, Moss, had not shown his weapon before, he fired, and it must be acknowledged that he took good aim, for one of the shots took effect in Warner's hip.

But it was "a glance shot."

Had it not in the first instance struck against some hard substance in his pocket (money), it would have smashed his hip. As it was it so stunned Warner, that when he awoke to consciousness he was surrounded by the master and mistress of the coffee-house, and several alarmed servants.

He looked around him wildly, in hopes of seeing Moss or Barney, but neither of those treacherous rascals were in the room.

Both had vanished the instant they heard the approach of the servants, thinking, or at least hoping, that Warner had been killed.

So great had been their hurry, that they forgot the bag of gold which was on the table, and left it behind.

"This way, Barney, this way," said the old Jew, as he lightly tripped downstairs, followed by the Pug, "this way, follow me."

Into the yard went the Jew, followed by his companion, and as it was intensely dark, they escaped the servants, who were hurrying upstairs.

Old Moss, with more activity than any one would have given him credit for, climbed on to the roof of a large dust-hole.

From this he was within easy reach of a wall, on which he clambered, followed by the Pug.

The descent into the next yard was easy, and as the back premises belonged to a public-house, they soon made their way into the bar, and thus escaped to the next street unseen or unheard.

"It was lucky I had a revolver with me," said Moss; "I very seldom carry one; but something told me that this stranger would prove too cunning for us, and so I brought it."

"D—n him!" growled Barney, who was suffering intense agony from the wound in his hand, "d—n him! I only hope you have killed him, that's all."

"I did it in self-defence, you know," said the Jew; "there's no knowing what he might have done to us."

"He's done more than enough for me," said the Pug, with an oath; "and if ever I meet him again, one or both of us shall die."

"You know him, then?"

"Yes, too well. And," thought Barney, "if the old Jew had only told me the stranger's name, he would not have caught me in such a trap; but I'll be even with old Moss yet, as sure as I live."

Thus speaking, the worthy pair made their way to the Lane in a stealthy manner.

But the Jew's thoughts were ever on the money which Warner had.

"And we didn't get the bag after all," sighed old Moss! "oh! what a misfortune. I'd have given you half if you had collared it," said the old Jew, sighing.

"I dare say you would," thought the Pug; "but I was too intent upon escaping to think of money, for I saw 'murder' plainly written in Warner's eye. He meant it, but was thwarted."

As old Moss had now no more occasion for Barney's services, he bid him good night, and didn't so much as give him a crown-piece.

"Well," said Barney, as he walked off towards a surgery near by to have his hand dressed, "well, of all the hard-fisted old vagabonds I ever came across, Moss is the greatest. Just to think on it; here he gets me face to face with my greatest enemy, who stabs me, and yet, for all, he never says, 'here, Barney, here's a quid for you.' Never mind, I'll serve him out, see if I don't."

He went to a surgeon, who dressed his hand very skilfully and carefully, but he expressed his decided opinion that it would be almost a miracle if he didn't lose the use of the limb for ever.

It had been bleeding fearfully for some time, and the Pug felt very weak; in fact, he staggered from loss of blood, and at last fell right down in the surgery.

"Send for old Moss," said Barney, feeling very faint. "Send for old Moss, doctor; you know him very well, or, at all events, he knows you, it's all the same. He will pay you for your trouble."

"Never mind paying me for my trouble," said the kind-hearted surgeon; "but you want taking care of. I will send round for old Moss at once."

A messenger went for the Hebrew, who, however, denied all knowledge of Barney, and cursed and swore roundly at being disturbed in his supper, and wouldn't send the man a single shilling.

"Never mind, my poor fellow," said the good surgeon, "you are not fit to move about with such a hand as that, you must go to the hospital at once."

With more than ordinary kindness to his fellow man the surgeon called for a cab, and took the Pug to the hospital, where he was admitted immediately, and the desperate wound in his hand was again seen to, and ere long the unlucky Pug found himself nice and snug and warm in one of the hospital beds with kind nurses around him.

"This is the style for me," said Barney, when he had somewhat recovered from the weakness and faintness. "This is the style for me; nice beds, clean clothes, the best of everything, and all for nothing. Good luck to the man who first invented hospitals, say I."

The Pug, with all his cowardice, cunning, and revengeful feelings, could not help feeling grateful for the stroke of good fortune which had thrown him into such good quarters.

"For," thought he, "I hadn't a 'brown' in my pocket, and where I should have slept to-night is a mystery to me. But won't I serve Warner and Moss and Matty out when I get well, though?" he mused. "Never mind, every dog has his day they say, and I suppose I shall have mine. I should like to have 'copped' that bag of shiners, though, and no mistake; it would have set me up for a twelvemonth to come; but Warner was too sharp for me. Lor! what a look he gave me, eh? I made sure he would have murdered me."

Thus ran the current of Barney's thoughts, as beneath the clean sheets of his hospital bed, and his hand bound up in a sling, he lay wide awake, and thinking of the present and the past.

"So the 'doctor' has turned 'cracksman,' eh? Well, who'd a thought it? and a nice haul he and his pals must have made, and no mistake, else old Moss wouldn't have forked over so many 'yellow boys' for the swag. I wonder what gang he belongs to, some of the 'swell mob," of course. Well, Warner was always very clever, but not quite clever enough for old Flint, though; the old lawyer hooked it with all the lot when Warner did that trick for old Ford in the Red House. He's got his knife deep into me, though, and I must take care."

Whatever Barney thought of things in general, one thing is very certain, he felt very happy and very glad that he was in the hospital, for, said he,

"I shall stay here for a month or two, so that if Gale or any on 'em want me they will have to hunt a long time before they find out my hiding-place."

* * * * *

But to return to Warner.

The kindness of the coffee-house-keeper, and the prompt surgical aid that was brought to him, soon made things very comfortable for Warner.

The wound was found not to be a very desperate one, and the ball was extracted without much pain.

To all questions he replied that he had called there to have dealings with an old friend of his in the city, and that some villains or other must have found out he had a large sum of money to lay out; and he, Warner, added that while dozing in his chair, with his money on the table, two ruffians must have entered unobserved; but he caught them in the act of stealing, and before he could offer any resistance, or call for aid, one of the miscreants fired at him.

The landlord, as might be supposed, was indignant at the outrage perpetrated on his lodger, and advised him to consult the police immediately.

But this was the very thing Warner wanted to avoid.

He said, however, that he would do so in the morning when he was more collected and calm.

What surprised the worthy landlord more than all, however, was that after the surgeon had left him, he resolved to leave the coffee-house that same night.

They endeavoured to dissuade him, but it was all to no purpose; he *would* go, "for," as he rightly imagined, "if the police get wind of this affair, they will, whether I like it or not, come and institute inquiries, and ten chances to one I shall be recognised, and arrested for that little affair at the Red House."

Therefore, notwithstanding his painful hurt, Warner ordered a cab, and, with the assistance of two stout waiters, he was put into it.

But he did not tell the driver the right direction until they had been some time on the road, when he suddenly thrust his head out of window, and ordered cabby to drive in quite a contrary way.

"As I am flush of money now, I might as well do the grand," thought Warner, and, therefore, he was driven to a private hotel, not beyond a hundred yards from where he, Flint and Jonathan lived.

He gave such a plausible account of how his wound was received to the proprietor of the hotel that that gentleman looked upon the new arrival as some military officer, perhaps, who had had "an affair of honour," and wished to live "in strict seclusion" for a week or two, and then resume his duties without the outside world being any the wiser.

The first thing that Warner did, however, when he had retired for the night, was to sit up in bed, and write a long account of the whole matter to his friends near Bromley Hall, in which he detailed all the particulars of his transaction with Moss, and the unexpected meeting with Barney.

This letter was posted, and in less than twenty hours was not only read by the Bromley gang, but four of them started off for London at once.

One of them dressed himself up like a doctor, that is to say, in black from top to toe, gold spectacles, and gold-headed walking-cane. His "make-up" was perfect; for if he had to enact the part on any stage, the picture could not have been carried out more life-like.

He sent up his "card" to Warner, who was astonished when the would-be medical man was ushered into his sick chamber.

In truth, for a few moments Warner himself did not know who the stranger was, until at last the doctor changed his tone of voice, and made himself known as the leader of the Bromley gang.

"Hush!" said he, as Warner was about to express surprise, "hush! speak in whispers, for walls have ears."

"You surely couldn't have got my letter in such quick time?"

"I did. I have had a man hanging about the village post-office for several days. Some of the gang thought you would prove false, and stick to the lot; but I didn't. Where's the money?"

"All but a few pounds are in my trunk there in the corner."

The pretended doctor went to the trunk and took the bag of gold.

He did not take it all, but left one-third for Warner's use, that is to say, nearly £100.

"You'll want some to carry you along; but you needn't fear, old boy; this old Moss has been having a merry dance with us all for some time past; but 'he'll have to pay the fiddler' you'll find, and very heavily, too, for this bit of treachery. And so you met Barney, eh? Why didn't you kill him? he don't deserve any better fate at our hands, and sooner or later will get all he deserves."

"But what brought you up from Bromley?"

"We held a meeting directly your letter was received, and resolved to fleece old Moss of what you sold him, besides all else we can lay our hands on."

"But how? he doesn't keep his 'metal' in the house."

"I know that, my lad; but I know where he does keep it—stowed away among old rags and bottles, and bones and rubbish in his warehouse."

"And you know where it is?"

"Better than I know you."

"But he has a terrific bull-dog chained up there all night."

"What of that?"

"And do you intend to break into his warehouse, then?"

"I don't intend to do so; some pals of mine have already done so."

"How do you mean? I don't understand."

"One of our London chaps has been looking after your goings and comings ever since you have been in town.

"Dogging me?" said Warner, in surprise.

"Yes, you; and why not? we were not sure you would act on the square, so determined to keep watch on all your movements. He also wrote to us, and gave information by telegraph, that you had got the money. In turn we telegraphed back that he should hit upon some plan for serving out old Moss, and he has done so."

"But how?"

"The warehouse and stable up the mews, next to that of old Moss, is unoccupied."

# THE BOY SOLDIER; OR, GARIBALDI'S YOUNG CAPTAIN.

A SUDDEN ATTACK—*(See No. 35)*.

"I never knew that before."

"I dare say not, but we did; so he and two of his pals hid themselves in this empty stable, and removed part of the brick partition wall between the two places."

"Now I see it all," said Warner.

"Besides all that, we have made arrangements to carry off a great deal of the old rascal's property to-night, and thus punish him for his treachery and cunning."

"But do you think you can accomplish all this successfully?"

"I haven't any doubt of it. As to the dog, we will poison him during the night with a bit of beef, and when old Moss goes to his warehouse to-morrow morning, he will discover all, and moan, and groan, and tear his hair in despair."

"But are you certain that he has got much of a 'swag' there?"

"One of my men has been on the watch for a long time, and reports that last night he saw the old Jew take a large trunkful of things. Therefore keep yourself quiet, my lad, and ere the morning dawns you will have had ample revenge on the old rascal, for if he is robbed it will break his heart."

"But what of the villain Barney?"

"I will keep a sharp look out for that oily rascal, and once he gets into my clutches you may be sure he wont have much mercy shown to him."

"When will you call again, then?"

"To-morrow morning, and then I will tell you all, for I know that my men are very busy about this time, and are determined to make a good haul. Take care of yourself, my lad; you have proved faithful to us, and you may rely upon it that we will prove true to you."

So saying, the pretended "Doctor" left Warner, and went his way towards the East end of the town.

"So, Mr. Moss," thought Warner, "if I am not very much mistaken, you have got the wrong pig by the tail this time, and will have to pay dearly for it; by to-morrow you are a ruined man."

## CHAPTER CII.

### MR. MOSS IS IN GREAT AFFLICTION.

THE next morning after this conversation between the chief of the "Bromley gang" and Warner, old Moss sat at his breakfast table congratulating himself upon all the great bargains he had of late made with notorious thieves and rogues both in town and country, when his wife stopped his meditation by saying sharply,

"Moss, you have often talked of retiring from business like an honest man, and living in peace and comfort in your old days."

"Old days, eh!" said Moss, "what do you mean by old, eh? Do you call a person of fifty years an old man, eh?"

"Well, you have made quite enough money to retire on, at all events," said the wife, "and you know the game we have been playing for the last few years is a very dangerous one."

"Nonsense! wife, nonsense! what do you know about it? There's no more danger in keeping a 'dropping shop' (fence) than any other sort of business, if you know how to conduct it, as I do."

"Ah, well, do as you please," said the wife. "I have had terrible dreams lately, and I'm sure they mean no good."

"Dreams! Nonsense, wife, what do I care for dreams? See how much I made last night. Why, what Barney brought was worth two 'quid,' and you gave him half a dollar for it! Think of that."

"But you laid out £300 last night.

"I think I did, and should like to lay out as much more every night. See my profit!"

"How much, Moss?"

"Why, that lot from the country will clear me £500 when it's put into the pot. Think of that, wife; and you croak about retiring from business!"

"But I fear the 'beaks' have their eyes on us, Moss."

"Let 'em go to the devil, for all I care," said the old Jew, with an oath, "they ain't half clever enough for me."

"I don't know, Moss," said the wife, brooding over her dreams, "it's a very long lane that has no turning."

"Ah! very well, woman. You mind your own business, and I will mind mine. I'm not going to retire yet awhile to please you or any one, when I can make five or six hundred pounds in the week."

"Oh, Mister Moss!" said the little urchin, Isaacs, running in, "didn't you go to your warehouse last night?"

"Yes; why?" said the old Jew, cocking his ears.

"Did you leave the door unlocked?"

"Unlocked, no. What do you mean?" said Moss, in great alarm. "Is it unlocked?"

"Yes. Some other little boys and me were playing in the yard this morning, and the dog didn't growl as usual."

"Well."

"So I goes and peeps in through the door which was ajar, and what d'yer think I see?"

"What?"

"The bull-dog was dead and cold."

"No, no, Isaacs, you don't mean that?" said old Moss, jumping up from his chair in dread alarm. "You cannot mean that?"

"I do, though," said the little urchin, with bright cunning eyes.

"Oh, then I am robbed! I am ruined! I am lost!" said the old Jew.

In a moment he seized his hat, and rushed off towards his warehouse, in great haste.

Little Isaacs was so much pleased with the discovery, that he went at once to inform his own father, whom he knew would be overjoyed to hear of any calamity that might befall his rival, old Moss.

Moss ran breathlessly towards his warehouse, and as young Isaacs had said, he found the place unlocked, the door ajar, and the watch-dog dead.

He swore and raved, and tore his hair like a madman, for he quickly discovered that the trunk, containing all he had bought from Warner, was missing.

The place had been tumbled about, and was in the greatest disorder.

He soon found out how the thieves had entered from the next stables, and cried like a child when he perceived the broken brick-work, and a large hole in the wall.

He knew not what to do or what to say.

He was more insane than otherwise, and cursed and swore, and he moaned his losses like an idiot.

The neighbours, among others, old Issacs, hearing of the robbery, gathered around old Moss, and condoled with him.

But it must be confessed that old Isaacs was delighted at what had befallen his rival; but concealed his true feelings with a great deal of cunning and hypocrisy.

"What shall I do? what shall I do?" said Moss, in great grief. "I am ruined, and must go to the workhouse. I am not worth a penny—I, who am so honest, just and good to all my neighbours, eh, Mr. Isaacs?"

"Yes," said Isaacs, "it is very sorrowful just to think that any one should rob a poor old honest man like you."

"What shall I do? what shall I do?" said Moss, wringing his hands, and sitting down on a bag of rags.

The Jew had not long to think what he should do, for two policemen in plain clothes mixed among his neighbours, and attentively listened to all that passed.

"You had better go and report the affair at once to the police," said they.

"So I will—so I will," Moss replied, jumping up. "I would give a hundred pounds if I knew who robbed me."

Off he went to the police-station, and, in a long, rambling account, stated his losses.

The inspector detailed two officers to go and inquire into the whole matter, and take such steps as might lead to the apprehension and punishment of the thieves.

"Leave the matter in our hands, Mr. Moss," said the polite inspector. "If there is any chance of tracing the burglars, you may be sure we won't leave a stone unturned."

"Just to think," said Moss, "that I have been an honest tradesman down the Lane for the last ten years, and now to be robbed in this way. Why, it will break my heart."

Away went Moss and the two detectives to his warehouse, and at once they began to examine the premises very minutely and carefully.

To all appearance, the place contained nothing but bales and bags of rags, piles of old cording, rusty iron, and such like; but the two officers winked knowingly at each other as they entered the warehouse.

Old Moss accompanied the officers to and fro very anxiously.

"This is the way they got in," said one, creeping through the hole in the wall; "but they took the goods out through the front door after the dog was poisoned."

"Hullo," said one of them, as he picked up a valuable brooch from a pile of brickdust, "hullo, what is this, eh, Moss?"

"Oh, nothing," said old Moss, trying to get possession of it. "That is only a brooch my wife lost here the other day when she was sorting rags, that's all."

"Oh, indeed," said the officer, putting the valuable into his pocket.

"You need not search any further," said old Moss, very nervously. "They have left nothing behind; there is nothing here but rags and old iron."

"Do you call *this* old iron?" said the second officer, holding up a coffee-pot he had discovered under some dirty sacking. "Why, this is solid silver."

"Any name on it," asked his companion.

"Yes, Ford, the Red House."

"Ford, the Red House," said the other, thinking for a moment. "Surely it cannot be any of the plate which was stolen from that murdered gentleman's premises a little while ago?"

"Have you got a description of the missing property?"

"Yes, somewhere in my note-book. Gale got the description from the murdered man's old servant. Here it is," said the officer, reading over a long list.

"Why, it corresponds exactly," said the first officer.

"So it does. Where did you get this, Moss?"

"Don't know anything about it."

This was a lie, for it was one of the articles which he had bought from Barney.

"But you must know something about it, or how did it get here?"

"Somebody must have planted it, so as to ruin me," said old Moss, trembling.

"Oh, that is a very unlikely tale," said the officers, laughing. "We must search the whole place now."

"No, don't; there's no occasion. I'm sure you'll find nothing."

"We don't know that. We must take you into custody for having stolen property in your possession, Moss."

"Me?" gasped the Jew.

"Yes; you."

The Jew sank upon a bag of rags.

He felt that his course was run, and that he was in the hands of the law, from which there was now no possible hope of escape.

He offered bribes to the two officers.

But those worthy men indignantly refused his tempting offers.

One of them stood by guarding Moss.

The other prosecuted his search thoroughly, and, in less than half-an-hour, found a number of valuable articles in precious metals.

Before they took the old Jew down to the station one of them called two constables, and took possession of his shop in the Lane.

Amid a gaping crowd two other officers conducted old Moss to prison, and, so weak was he, that he almost fell upon the way.

He was not searched, but charged with having stolen goods upon his premises, and all bail refused.

He was cast into a cell, and there left to his dismal meditations, and, ere long, the old rogue wept like a child; not out of sorrow for years of crime, but because he felt that he was now utterly powerless to have any revenge on his enemies, whoever they were.

"Who could have done all this?" he mused, as, with his head between his hands, he thought for hours on the events of that unlucky day.

He took out of his pocket an old red tattered rag of a handkerchief to wipe his eyes, and a letter fell upon the floor.

"This came this morning, but I was so low-spirited I could not open it."

However, to divert his thoughts, old Moss tore the envelope and read as follows:—

"MOSS.—You have played the old villain long enough; you are not content to buy swag and make hundreds out of it, but you must needs try and get your money back again by robbing.

"Now I and my pals have had our eyes on you for a long time, and played the same trick that you would have played on us; that is to say, we have stolen our 'metal' again, besides other valuables, and have kindly informed the police of the event by letter. When you are lagged, and enjoying your lifer, think of this, and your old pal, "IKEY."

"The devil seize and choke him!" gasped Moss, and he raved and swore in such a terrible rage for more than half an hour, that he foamed at the mouth like a madman, and tried to destroy himself in his cell.

But the gaolers soon put a stop to his wild pranks, for they handcuffed him and tied him down.

"Wish I was dead! I wish I was dead!" groaned the Jew, in great agony.

The tight grip of the law was on him.

He wriggled and writhed like a wounded worm as he was.

Hundreds had suffered for his sake, and now he had to suffer for theirs.

He had been making money and dancing to pleasant music all his life.

The moment was fast approaching when he had to pay the fiddler.

## CHAPTER CIII.

EXTRACT FROM FRANK FORD'S JOURNAL IN MEXICO ABOUT BIRDS, WILD FOWL, AND THE LIKE, WHICH HE AND HIS BOY SOLDIERS OFTEN MET WITH, AND SHOT AND STUFFED FOR THE PURPOSE OF FORMING A MUSEUM FOR THE BOYS IN ENGLAND.

"DEAR BROTHER TOM,—

"I received a letter from you before you sailed towards England, and I hasten to answer it.

"I shall, according to your directions, send this to the Grosvenor Hotel, London, where you intend to stay should you land in England.

"I have much to tell you about our military affairs here in Mexico; but before I speak of those things, I shall continue my journal, and, as you and the boys wish it, will describe what else I saw upon the broad prairies, and then continue my narrative of our Mexican campaign.

"In the first place, then, cranes and herons of all kinds—black, white, and gray, crested and without crest—are common here. Pelicans but rarely are seen in the laguns. One immense bird, called a Borignon, is common enough: it has a body bigger than a swan, and moderately long legs, but with almost no neck, and an immense beak projecting from a small head, set deep between his shoulders.

"This bird is white, and has his wings edged with black, his legs, head, and beak being also black.

"Bitterns are very common, and beautiful birds they are.

"Curlews and snipes, great, small, and jack, abound.

"These last are absurdly tame. They never fly over twenty yards; and, dropping in the open plain, even after being fired at and missed, feed without any fear of being again molested.

"Divers and water-rails frequent all the lakes and streams in myriads: some of the former are very graceful and elegant birds.

"Flamingoes, spoonbills, and birds of that kind

I met with occasionally, but seldom shot at any save ducks and snipes.

"I think the most curious of the aquatic birds I saw was a large diver, with a neck almost as long as a swan, and short legs, which sat in grass, by the waterside, and when frightened took to the water in great haste.

"This bird—which, I think, is called the black-bellied Darter—always chose a high and quite naked tree, and, before starting, moved his neck backwards and forwards in a very curious style.

"I often tried to procure a specimen, but ineffectually, as they were very wary, and their feathers too close set to admit of a long shot taking effect.

"A very pretty little bird, called Madrugador, or early riser, of a brilliant yellow, was very common, as were also kingfishers of all sizes and colours.

"The land birds are as various as the water, and I was puzzled to find names for most of them. The commonest and most domestic is a handsome black fellow, with a magnificent tail, and considerably larger than an English black-bird, called Sanati. He frequents all houses, and is even more impudent and self-sufficient than our common sparrow.

"Starlings exist in immense tribes, some entirely black, others with brilliant yellow and crimson heads.

"I used to observe that these birds always roosted in the same spot, and retired to rest at the same time, till at last, when out with my gun, I saw the starlings coming, I never required to look at my watch to know that it was also time for me to be jogging homeward.

"These flocks, containing immense numbers, had been all day scattered over the plains, picking up the vermin which fell from the cattle and mules, each of these animals being always surrounded by some hundreds of these little birds.

"They were now returning to their homes, the main body always preceded and flanked by detached parties.

"This army extended often a quarter of a mile, and occupied two or three minutes in passing me, casting a distant shadow on the ground as they flew.

"Occasionally the whole body made a sharp curve in their flight, always an indication that a hawk was looking out for stragglers.

"The most beautiful of all the birds is, I think, the Cardinal, which is met with everywhere; it is of a bright crimson, and beautifully crested.

"Wild turkeys are also seen among the mountains, but I had never the good luck to fall in with any.

"Hawks of all kinds are very common, and I have seen eagles, but rarely. Caspar one day killed one when out with me.

"There are some peculiar birds of the hawk species, called "Bone-crushers," large and powerfully made, with beautiful red crests and eyes.

"These sit motionless upon stones and trees, never touching the carcase of any animal till the zopilotes have done with it, when they proceed to remove whatever flesh still adheres to the bones, and get the marrow out of the bones themselves.

"I have also seen them attack small birds.

"Many of the hawk tribe are most useful, from their destruction of snakes and other reptiles.

"I have often seen one soaring away with a snake a yard long wriggling in his claws.

"One of these birds once dropped his prey at sight of me.

"I found, on inspection, that the snake was not dead, but nearly so, his skull being laid entirely open with a severe peck.

"The Count told me one day that, the day before that, he had seen a hawk attack a snake too large for him, and, that whilst he was carrying him off in mid air, the snake wreathed himself round the wings of the hawk or eagle (as my friend called him), and both came to the ground together.

"Although this is both an old and poetical story, I will answer for it that my friend, the Count, was never in the way of hearing it, and have no doubt whatever that he saw what he described.

"There are plenty of owls, but one does not often meet with them in daylight, even in Mexico.

"Pigeons and doves of all kinds abound, and when my ducks and snipes failed me, I had capital sport among the former in a thicket by the side of the laguna.

"There is a small sort of dove very beautiful and very tame, no bigger than a thrush, of which numbers used to build in the orange trees in the garden.

"They appeared to live mostly on the ground and ran very nimbly; half a dozen of these little birds made as much noise in rising as a large covey of partrides.

"Now let me turn to soldiering and tell you all that has happened since last I saw you, for believe me, Caspar, Hugh Tracy, Buttons, Fatty, and all the rest have had plenty of stirring adventures in this strange, but delightful and far-off country.

"As you may be sure, dear Tom, when our gallant lads heard of the capture of the brave old count, and of the severe wounds he received in the encounter between the renegade Mexicans and French, we all felt deeply sorry at the mishap, and immediately arranged an expedition in order to rescue him from his state of captivity.

"Among all my teamsters and guides, I had not half as much affection for any one as the American trapper, and Pedro, the half-bred.

"Without consulting any of the Boy Soldiers, I called the trapper to my tent, and had a long chat with him, for I made up my mind, cost what it would, to leave no stone unturned until I had secured the release of the brave old count.

"'Could you find out whereabouts the count is, do you think?' I asked Pedro.

"'Yes, captain. I could do so without any difficulty in the world; but I am a half-bred, and would be suspected immediately if they saw me prowling about their "lines."'

"'Then, what had best be done?" I asked

"'I should say that no one was more fitted to undertake such a duty as the tall American trapper here,' said Pedro.

"'Oh, as to me,' said the American, with a broad grin, 'I don't mind what I do so as I can be of any sarvice to you, and the brave English Boys.'

"'You are not afraid?' I asked.

"'Afraid!' said the American, with a look of disgust, 'I ain't afeard of the devil himself, if I only has a good horse and plenty of money.'

"After much chat with the trapper, I at last agreed that he should be the one to send.

"I was particularly anxious to get the good old count out of the hands of the enemy, for, from information that I could get, it was very likely we should have to fight a hard battle in less than a week, and the old count's advice and assistance was of great help to us on all occasions.

"I therefore mounted the tall trapper on one of the fleetest horses I ever rode, gave him a purse of gold pieces, and made him change his dress for something better than the skin jacket and trousers he always wore.

"He started off that same night, and for three or four days I heard nothing of him.

"I told Caspar and Hugh Tracy of all I had done, and they heartily approved of all I thought proper to do; but each of them gave it as their opinion that the tall brave fellow must have met with some fatal accident, or he would have returned long ago.

"I could not help thinking as much myself, but said nothing to my fellow officers and friends, in case it might dishearten them, for the old count was a great favorite with all of us.

"At the end of the fifth day, and when all hope was given up of the brave trapper's return, I was surprised to see the tall American ride into our camp, looking care-worn, dirty, pale and bloody.

"He had found out the hiding-place in which the Mexicans and French had placed the old soldier.

"He represented to all that he was an American citizen, travelling for pleasure and pastime, and thus threw dust into the eyes of all with whom he came in contact.

"They took him round all their batteries and camps, and as the trapper was flush of funds and treated everybody to whatever they liked to eat and drink, they all unanimously pronounced him to be 'a fine fellow.'

"They even took him to see the hospitals, and in one of these he discovered the old count, who, though pale and weak from loss of blood from his wounds, was fast recovering from his injuries.

"The old count, he says, instantly recognized him, but did not let any one see it.

"The trapper even went so far as to curse and swear at the count and all the Boy Soldiers, in a very hearty manner, so as to throw the Mexicans and French off their guard.

"The old count smiled and swore back again.

"This pleased the bold trapper, who saw at a moment that the old count saw 'his little game,' and fully understood it.

"Now, as the ex-trapper was dressed much like a middle-aged gentleman of property (thanks to the wig, false whiskers, and clothes which I had given him) neither the Mexican nor French had the least suspicion that he was a spy, and treated him with every respect.

"The trapper thought that no one would discover him, but he was greatly mistaken.

"He went to a first-class hotel in a small neighbouring town, and lived like a lord of the land for two or three days.

"He had dressed himself up much like a well-to-do banker or private gentleman of means, and carried his imposition so far that he actually invited several French and Mexican officers to dine with him.

"The time fixed for dinner was about six.

"The trapper entered the dining-room to see that everything was in perfect order for his friends and found several ladies of the hotel (whom he had also invited to dine with him) already seated at the table, but the officers had not yet arrived.

"The trapper could not understand their want of punctuality, and sat down to dine with his lady friends without a thought why or wherefore the officers were absent.

"But a servant explained that both the French and Mexican officers had at the latest moment been forced to decline the trapper's kind invitation as the French general in command had heard that I and a strong reinforcement of English volunteers had entered the service of the Republican army, and were all likely to attack their position before the besieged town, and in consequence they must be on the alert night and day.

"The trapper did not relish this information; but he put a good face upon matters, and sat down to dine with all that careless stoicism peculiar to our American cousins.

"While he was at dinner, however, and solely in company of the ladies, and an American gentleman he had invited to meet the French and Mexican officers, a beautiful but half-wild-looking girl dashed into the room, pushed by the waiters, and confronted the disguised trapper face to face.

"With extended arm, and a shrill voice, she pointed to the American, and said aloud—

"'Traitor, I have been on the watch for you! Seize him, seize him! he is a spy and an informer from the camp of the Boy Soldiers; he is not a gentleman; he is a trapper—an informer, and is in the pay of Frank Ford, the captain of the English Boy Volunteers.'

"This announcement, as might be expected, astonished every one present. (See cut in No. 32).

"The brave American trapper rose to his feet astounded.

"For a moment he knew not what to do.

"As quick as lightning, however, he rushed towards the girl, pushed her aside, and left the room in great haste.

"The girl followed him, screaming at the top of her voice, and in a moment the hotel was all agog with excitement.

"To go to the stables and mount his gallant horse was the work of but a few moments.

"Yet still these few moments were more than sufficient to arouse all in the hotel.

"The townspeople also (at least such of them as were favourable to the French and the usurper, Maximilian) raised a great outcry.

"The brave trapper fled away with the speed of lightning, but he was hotly pursued.

"Shots were freely exchanged on both sides; but luckily for the trapper, he was not seriously hurt, although wounded in several places.

"As might be expected, he did not fail to fire back, and one of his shots (by mere accident be it observed) not only passed through one of his pursuers, but also wounded the girl who had informed upon him.

"This the trapper did not know at the time, for he was galloping through the town at the top of his speed; but I afterwards ascertained all the facts, and was very sorry.

"But in the hurry, uproar, and confusion this accident could not be well avoided, for at the moment he fired the fatal shot, he was opposed to, and almost surrounded by, a hundred or more of excited citizens, who were thirsting for his blood.

"The trapper came safely into our camp, but, as might have been expected, he did not get off scot free.

"He was wounded in several places, and much fatigued; but the information he brought to us was worth more than gold, for from subsequent information we ascertained that the old count, and a few of the better sort of his comrades, were instantly taken from the hospital, and sent far to the rear, among the mountains, for protection.

"Now, instead of the French authorities sending the dear old count to a place of greater safety, they placed him in a locality which was of easy access to us, as will be hereafter seen.

"Suffice it, therefore, in this letter, to say that we made instant preparations for his rescue, and that, had it not been for the bold trapper, the old count might have been forced to linger and die in a state of captivity, instead of being, as he is now, well and hearty among us.

"But this I will explain presently.

"To return to the trapper's unexpected and hasty flight.

"The shot which he fired ultimately killed the girl, who, at first, had been only slightly wounded.

"But her death arose more from the surgeon's want of skill than otherwise, for, from all I can learn, the danger was not at first very great; so little indeed did any one apprehend death would ensue, that even her friends and father made light of it.

"This girl, strange to say, was the youngest daughter of a rich gentleman of the town, who, seized with a wild mania to serve the French, had gone forth and amused herself with acting the part of a female spy upon the Republicans.

"She was young, beautiful, and accomplished, and when her death became known, the whole town, or most part of it, at least, went into mourning for her.

"A coroner's inquest was held over her, and the jury was made up of the most wealthy and influential of the townspeople, who, after brief consultation (but opposed to the evidence) returned a verdict of wilful murder against the trapper.

"The poor girl was laid out before the jury in a very becoming manner, and attired in white.

"But the most impressive part of the whole proceedings was when her only sister threw herself upon the dead body, and wept bitterly; while the aged father advanced towards his young daughter, and, laying his hand upon her cold forehead, swore that 'he would never rest until he had slain with his own hand the American spy who had shot his daughter.' (See cut in Number 33.)

"All these particulars of our doings, dear Tom, I know will interest you, and all our boy friends in England; but, for the present, I must postpone writing to you of our several hard-fought battles here, and of the extraordinary doings of our gallant young English Volunteers under my command.

"In my next letter, or through the newspaper, you will learn all particulars of our exploits.

"Caspar, Tracy, Buttons, Fatty, and the count, have covered themselves with glory.

"I hear the drums now beating. We expect another attack from the French every moment; so I must hastily conclude this letter, and remain,

"Your loving Brother,

"FRANK.

"P. S.—If you are in England, I hope you will lose no time in unravelling the mystery of our Uncle Ford's murder.

"I have faint hopes that you will ever meet with old Jonathan Flint, or that young scoundrel Joel; but if you do, let us hear all particulars from you at the earliest moment.

"The drums are still beating. Our Boy Soldiers are now falling in to repel a second assault of the French and renegade Mexicans.

"In haste,

"FRANK."

---

## CHAPTER CIV.

### LIFEBOATMEN SEARCH THE WRECK FOR JOEL FLINT.

THE very first thing which the two English detectives did, when they reached the shore from the shipwrecked "Dolphin," was to see if Master Joel would come on shore, for all along they had shrewd suspicions that he was the very youth they were in search of, although they had not, for a moment, given him any ground for supposing so.

But finding that he did not come ashore as he might have done, they felt doubly certain that he was the person they wanted.

They, therefore, at the earliest possible moment aroused the coastguard and lifeboatmen on the shore, and told the chiefs what their suspicions were.

Hearing that there was, and had been, a very large reward offered for the capture of the young culprit who was still on board, two picked crews volunteered to man their boats and go out to the wreck; but this could not be done till long after nightfall.

With this object they got two boats and launched them in the little harbour, and they could plainly see in the distance the smoke on the wreck, which arose from the half-extinguished and now smouldering fire which Joel had made to warm himself, and serve as a signal of distress.

Within the harbour all was comparatively smooth, but the gale outside was so strong that the boats made headway with great difficulty, the wind sometimes driving the oars out of the rowlocks up over the men's heads in spite of their utmost efforts to keep them down.

Slow progress was thus made outside.

Here the sea was running mountains high, and it became evident that no boat of any description could live long under it.

One of the detectives, however, being still determined to try the boats even under these circumstances, made his final arrangement for a bold experiment.

He directed the boat which accompanied him to lie in comparative shelter under a small grassy island 78 feet high, over which the sea was making a full breach, so that she might watch the fate of her consort, and render assistance if possible.

Then, with his own coastguard crew, he dashed out into the bay, watching each tremendous roller, and rounding her to meet it.

About a quarter of an hour passed in this struggle, when a great tidal wave was observed by the spectators on shore gathering itself about a mile to seaward.

Distinguishable by lookers-on far inland, like a mighty Andes towering above the lesser mountains, this Atlantic giant swept in, extending right across the bay, and leaping far up the cliffs on either side.

In the opinion of experienced seamen who observed it, this sea would have swept the decks of the stoutest vessel.

As it neared the devoted boat, its appearance became more terrific.

The water shoaled there from ten to seven fathoms, and, changing its shape with the conformation of the ground below, that which had been a rolling mountain rose into a rushing cliff of water.

Never were six men in more desperate circumstances.

Yet what men could do was done boldly and steadily.

The rule laid down for meeting a desperate sea is to pull against it with the utmost speed.

But for meeting such a sea as this no rule was ever made.

Cheering his men forward, the steersman put his boat right at it, calculating nicely to meet the sea at a right angle.

Steadily, as if spurting in a race, the men strained

at their oars, and gliding, on even keel, like an arrow, the boat entered the roaring avalanche, its crest towering twenty-five feet above her, and overhanging.

The officer, who was steering, and the chief boatman, who was pulling stroke oar, were hurled headlong over the boat's stern by the falling sea.

Had she not been of extraordinary strength, owing to her peculiar double-sided construction, she must have been shivered like a bandbox.

Crushing her bodily fathoms down, the sea bore her astern at lightning speed, tearing away her rudder-irons and steering-crutch by the pressure.

The steersman was caught head downwards as she passed, by some projecting hook or spur rowlock, and dragged thus for a few seconds, then found himself suddenly freed and rising rapidly.

On reaching the surface he met his chief boatman already afloat, but looking very much confused.

The latter afterwards described himself as having been conscious of receiving some tremendous impetus, which caused him, as he imagined, to turn a series of somersaults under water.

Though cased in heavy water-proof boots, thick pea-jackets, and oil-cloth overcoats, the life-belts supported them with perfect ease.

The sea which had hurled them out of the boat had beaten the rest of the crew down as they bent over their oars in a stooping posture, each man on the thwart before him.

The bowman alone was stunned.

The remaining three retained perfect consciousness.

They had their eyes open, but all around was total darkness.

They described their sensation as like that of being whirled in an express train through a railway tunnel.

But whether they were in the boat or in the sea they could not distinguish at the time.

At length a faint dawn of light reached their eyes, increasing rapidly, and they were conscious of rising through the green water, and at last they emerged through the broken foam, sitting each man in his place.

The first object that met their eyes as the boat rose to the surface was the buoy of the little harbour close alongside of them.

This place is by measurement over 400 yards from the place where the sea had struck their boat.

She had been shot about a quarter of a mile under water, and had risen in the exact position in which she had entered the sea, at right angles to it

A spare rowlock and a pair of boots were lying loose in the bottom of the boat, giving clear evidence that she had not once turned over during her extraordinary submarine passage.

The oars had all been lost but one, and with this the men managed to keep her head to the seas, though she was drifting fast upon the rocks astern.

In the meantime, the crew of the other boat had watched the whole occurrence.

But so appalled were these hardy fishermen by the appearance of the sea, and by the sight which they had witnessed, that they refused at first to pull out to the rescue in the face of what appeared to be certain death.

The brave man who commanded her, however, the second detective, was determined to save his comrades or share their fate.

By dint of entreaty and command he got them to pull out into the bay.

Skilfully watching his time, sometimes putting his boat away before the breakers, sometimes driving her over them, shipping seas forward and on both sides, he succeeded in picking up the officer and chief boatman, after they had been near half an hour in the water.

They then pulled away for the other boat, and reached her as she was fast drifting on the rocky shore, over which the sea was breaking furiously.

A very few minutes later and boat and men would have been pounded to fragments on the sharp ledges that were rising black at intervals through the foaming waters.

They supplied the drifting boat with the oars which they had picked up from the water, and both crews worked their way back into harbour without loss of life or even the slightest injury.

The time during which the boat remained submerged is difficult to arrive at.

Under such circumstances seconds seem like minutes both to actors and spectators; but, as far as can be judged from pretty fair data, she must have been about two minutes under water.

The brave efforts of these two boats' crews to reach the "Dolphin" were unavailing.

Time and time again the two detectives, one in each boat, encouraged their men to attempt to reach the wreck; but the brave coasters were appalled at the danger they had already undergone, and thought that it would be useless and madness.

In truth, the storm, instead of abating, increased furiously, and the rough mountainous seas washed over the decks of the doomed "Dolphin," each moment threatening to break it into pieces.

"Oh, the young rascal is sure to be lost!" said the detective. "In less than an hour one plank will not remain of the gallant brig."

They gave up all hope as lost.

But while they stood on shore with telescopes in hand, little did they imagine that Joel Flint had escaped in the fishing-smack, and that the only persons on board were innocent men.

At the moment when this exciting and gallant effort had been made to seize the young scoundrel, Mr. Joel Flint was safely landed on shore several miles from where they stood.

Joel was safe, and his treasure on shore also.

More than this, he was rattling away in a train towards London, whither we must follow him.

---

## CHAPTER CV.

### JONATHAN MISSES HIS OLD FRIEND FLINT.

THE arrest of Jonathan in the rooms of the Grosvenor Hotel was a matter of great rejoicing among the detectives, and particularly so to Sergeant Gale, who had long been on the look-out for him and the others.

On the way to the police station Gale was very chatty to old Jonathan, who protested his innocence all the way in the most vehement manner.

"Well," said Gale, "if you hadn't anything to do with old Ford's murder, you know more about it than any one else; and it might serve you a great deal before a jury of your countrymen if you were to divulge whatever might assist us officers in tracking and apprehending the right parties."

"Oh! no doubt of that," said Jonathan, thoughtfully; "but you know I am as innocent as a child."

"I dare say you are; but appearances are very much against you for all that."

"How can that be?"

"Well, at all events, you know who killed the officer in Epping Forest."

"I could make a shrewd guess."

"Was it yourself?"

"Me! lor bless you, no."

"Who was it, then?"

"I think, from all I've heard him say, that it was Warner."

"But, I dare say, if Warner were in your situation he would say quite to the contrary."

"But that cannot be, for old Flint would bear witness."

"So Flint knows all about it, eh?"

"Why of course he does."

"But who did the deed in Green Court?"

"Why, Warner, of course."

"How was that?"

"Why, it appears that after the murder of old Ford, Flint ran away with the old gentleman's title-deeds and money. Warner thought he might be in Green Court, and so pounced down upon him, or somebody else; but it was a mistake."

"A great mistake, I think, for the poor clerk."

"Yes, wasn't it?"

"So you say that Warner did all this?"

"Yes, I am sure of it."

"And where is he?"

"He was living with me and Flint—no, I mean that he found out where old Flint and I lived together, and used to call sometimes."

"Oh, indeed!" said Gale, with a dry laugh; "you were intimate, then?"

"Oh dear, no; that is to say, he and Flint had dealings with each other, more or less, but not with me. I wouldn't be seen in such company."

"No, I suppose not; you are too good and clever a man to have any such associates."

This was said with such a dry laugh that Jonathan quaked again with fear.

"And where was this house where you and old Flint used to live?"

"I will show you."

"Very well, I have no objection; tell the cabby to drive to this direction," said Jonathan, handing a card.

The cabby cracked his whip, and, ere long, they both arrived at old Flint's residence.

Jonathan knocked at the door, which was quickly opened by Matty, who was blubbering.

"Oh, master, master," she began, wiping her eyes, and talking to Jonathan in the passage; "oh, master, master, there has been such a row and such a shine in the house."

"How? who? what?" said Jonathan.

"Oh, such a row, master!"

"Has Mr. Warner returned?" asked Jonathan, in great haste.

"Mr. Warner, sir? No, sir; nor do I think he ever will return."

"But Mr. Flint," said Jonathan, in great haste; "*he* is here?"

"No, sir; nor him either. I found him lying on the floor, bound hand and foot with cords, and he was struggling hard to get out of them. I thought he was mad; but, at last, after much begging and praying, I cut the cords and let him loose."

"And what did Flint do then?"

"He took out of the room some of the most valuable articles, such as the marble time-piece and other things, and pawned them. I asked for some dinner, and he slapped me in the face and knocked me down. I screamed, and in came the landlord and landlady in great haste, and demanded their rent; Mr. Flint said he had let the house to you, and must look forward to you for the rent."

"Very kind, indeed," groaned Jonathan. "And where is he now?"

"I haven't the slightest idea; but, before he went, several tradespeople came for their money, and wouldn't go without it, and there was such a row—a regular fight, it was. Such cursing and swearing, and stamping of feet you never heard before in your whole lives."

"And did he get away?"

"Yes, sir; he promised to pay them all to-night, and they went away; but about half-an-hour ago they all returned, such a troop of them."

"And where are they?"

"In the front parlor, sir; and a pretty noise they have been making to be sure."

"Oh, it's no use of me staying here," said Jonathan, "if that is the case; they will tear me in pieces."

"But, sir, the landlord is going to send me to prison for stealing the clock, and ornaments, and all sorts of things. What shall I do? Oh, Mr. Gale, what shall I do? *I* didn't steal the things."

"Never mind, Matty," said the detective, "they can't touch you, my girl; I know you well enough. It is old Flint who is to blame; he is the thief, not you."

"And he was the one who rented the lodgings also," said Jonathan; "*I* hadn't anything to do with it."

"Oh, here he is."

"That's him."

"This is the old scoundrel," said one and another of the creditors, coming out of the parlour, and surrounding Jonathan like a pack of hungry wolves.

"Where's my money?"

"Yes, and where's mine?"

"Give him in charge!"

"Have him up for obtaining goods under false pretences."

"Transport the old rascal!"

Thus, on all sides, clammered the infuriated creditors, cursing and swearing.

"Black his eyes!"

"Punch his head!"

"Tear the coat off his back!"

"Break his long, ugly nose!"

These were the discordant cries heard on every hand, and highest and loudest among them all were the landlord and landlady, the latter with a big broom in her hand, each moment threatening to break Jonathan's head.

"Preserve me! save me!" gasped Jonathan, who was fairly out of breath with excitement and the many kicks and blows he had received in the stomach, face and back.

"Preserve me! save me!" he roared.

"Hands off! hands off!" said Gale. "He is my prisoner."

"No, he isn't. Tear the old scoundrel from him! He's a sham policeman."

And then began a fierce fight in the passage to see who should secure the unlucky Jonathan.

# THE BOY SOLDIER; OR, GARIBALDI'S YOUNG CAPTAIN.

A PIC-NIC PARTY—(*See No.* 36.)

## CHAPTER CVI.

COUNT SCHMIDT ARRIVES IN LONDON, AND CALLS ON NELLY LANCASTER—JOEL VOWS TO HAVE REVENGE.

THE escape of Joel from the wreck, as detailed in another chapter, was almost miraculous; for it has been seen that the life-boats and boats of the coast-guard were unable to reach the "Dolphin."

But on board the "Dolphin" were several of the crew of the fishing-smack which had taken Joel off safe to shore.

These brave men fully expected that the weather would hold good, and that in a few hours their smack would return again to release them, and take off much of the valuables they had gathered together in the wreck.

But these men were doomed.

The storm set in again.

Their cries and signals were neither heard nor seen.

The fishing-smack did not return.

Heavy foaming seas towered over the stranded brig, and in less than three hours, on that frightful night, the "Dolphin" went to pieces, and the dead bodies of several unknown fishermen were washed ashore



"The young rascal, then, has met his just deserts after all," said the detectives one to another.

"How well he maintained his disguise, though," said one.

"Yes; but I knew him in a moment, but did not want to let him see it."

"Well, he's only cheated Calcraft, that's all; he would have been hung, as sure as eggs are eggs," said the other. "How unlucky it was, though, that the storm set in again so violently."

"True; for it cheated us out of the £200 reward offered for him."

"Never mind; better luck next time, comrade; but it was rather hard, as you say, to miss the young devil after we had been on the look out for him so long."

"Well, he's dead, that's one comfort.

"Yes; and his treasure is at the bottom of the ocean."

"Those young lords, then, will be no better off than ever."

"Just so; it's rather annoying, though, that things should have taken such an unfavourable turn, at the moment, too, when we expected all things to work cleverly into our own hands."

"Well, we've had a long trip through Italy, if that's any comfort · so we had better hasten up to

London and report all we know of the drowned man."

The two detectives took conveyance to the nearest railway station, and early next day found themselves at Scotland Yard.

They detailed all that had happened, and Detective Gale bit his lips with passion.

"Dead!" said he.

"Yes, dead as a door-nail; he was drowned in the wreck."

"How unfortunate; for I have got one of the old scoundrels in custody already, and have good hopes of securing the others in a few days. It was rather clever of you, though, not to pretend to know the young rascal on the voyage."

"Yes; but you see we have not been successful after all, though we deserved to be so."

"I received information from Leghorn of all that has happened," said Gale; "it was sent to me by Tomasso, signed by the prefect of police, and came by the mail steamer a week in advance of you, and I had good hopes of seeing the young rascal safe in your hands; for I have no doubt he had much to do with setting fire to the Custom House and storehouses in the harbour. He almost killed Tomasso with a blow from his oar. Tomasso is getting better, however, but vows vengeance against young Flint, and swears he'll come to London, and never rest until he captures him."

"He'll be very smart, then, I think," said one of the detectives, laughing, "considering that this young Flint is down among the fishes."

But, luckily for himself, Joel was not "down among the fishes," but was up to his eyes in pleasure and debauchery.

For when he arrived in London, Joel lost no time in decorating himself with all that money could buy, and hired lodgings in several directions, so that, in case of suspicion or flight, he could find a place of temporary refuge.

It will not be wondered at, therefore, that he purchased and wore all manner of disguises, which so well suited him, that his most intimate friends would have been deceived.

So well did he manage matters, that he frequently saw in the streets the two detectives who had been on board the "Dolphin," but they did not recognise him.

This gave Joel fresh courage, and he resolved to find out the whereabouts of his father, if possible.

But this seemed to be a work of impossibility, for he had long left his old haunts, neither could any one give the least information, except the police; and those gentlemen, as may be supposed, were the very last Joel wished to make acquaintance with.

He was dressed splendidly on all occasions, and took frequent exercise on horseback.

He cantered and galloped about Rotten Row like some grandee or prince, and went by the name of "Count."

While out one day galloping about, he espied the carriage of Mr. Lancaster, and in it sat Nelly, looking more beautiful than ever, but still sad, melancholy, and deadly pale.

Her father, the old banker, was with her, and, as the vehicle passed along, Joel bit his lip in anger.

"I've got a grudge against old Lancaster," he thought, "and now that no one knows me, I will have revenge on the old man for the very scurvy manner in which he served me in Italy. If I could only frame a good excuse to speak to speak to him, the thing would be easy enough; for once I am introduced to Nelly again, it will not take me long to elope with her, for I know she is beginning to hate her cross-grained, tuft-hunting father."

For several days Joel dressed out in the grandest style of fashion, sought those promenades and drives where the rich are wont to go, and saw Nelly and her father as usual.

He followed the old banker home, and noting the house and number, resolved to call there when the evening had fairly set in.

"For," thought Joel, "although my disguise is faultless, I don't want to throw any chance away, for the old miser's eyes are wonderfully sharp and piercing."

When night came, therefore, Joel boldly walked up to the banker's house, and rang the visitor's bell loudly.

A tall footman opened the door.

Joel handed his card, which was placed on a silver salver, and taken up to old Lancaster.

"Count Schmidt," mused the old banker, looking at the card, "Count Schmidt! I don't know any such person."

"Perhaps you may have forgotten, papa, this particular person, for when abroad you were introduced to so many persons of title," said Nelly.

"Just so, daughter, just so. You see, in Italy and Germany, one meets with so many titled personages, that really I have forgotten the names of two thirds or more. Show the gentleman up," said old Lancaster.

In a few moments, Joel Flint, as bold as brass, ascended the marble staircase, and entered the drawing-room.

Nelly Lancaster rose from the piano, and her father bowed to the stranger.

"Count Schmidt, I believe," said the old banker.

"Your humble servant," Joel replied, with a well-feigned foreign accent, bowing profoundly.

"You come from Leghorn, I believe?"

"I do; although that is not my residence, or place of birth."

"And might I ask the reasons or motives for this visit, sir?"

"With pleasure, sir," said Joel, smiling, and taking a seat.

"You did not know me, I believe, in Leghorn?" said the old banker.

"No, sir, I had not that honour, for I was not then in Leghorn; but I have the satisfaction of knowing that the hospitality and urbanity of Mr. Lancaster, together with the beauty and accomplishments of Miss Nelly, your daughter, caused the most favourable, nay, profound impressions among a large circle of my noble relations and friends in Italy."

This compliment seemed to please the vain old man, who smiled graciously, and bowed.

"You have relations there, then, Count?"

"Oh, yes, many, very many, indeed; some of them near of kin to royalty."

This information pleased old Lancaster still more, who felt very grand indeed.

"But, sir, I do not come to compliment you only," said Joel, still imitating a foreigner speaking broken English; "but am desirous of asking your advice, for I have £10,000, if, indeed, not more, to which I desire to lay out to the best advantage, and my noble friends in Leghorn have spoken in such glowing terms of your ability and wisdom that I——"

"I feel flattered," said old Lancaster, "and shall be delighted, of course, to have the disposition of so large a sum."

"I dare say you would," thought Joel; "but I am not going to let you have it for all that, you old rogue. But I also came on another errand," said Joel, "and one that concerns you deeply."

"Indeed!"

"Yes; but I hope you will not be surprised or annoyed?"

"Oh, certainly not."

"Did you ever know in Leghorn an English youth named Joel Flint?"

"Yes, certainly I did."

"What was his general character?"

"An impostor, sir! a rascal! if not more: one who for a time played on my good nature, and actually had the audacity to make half proposals to my only daughter."

"Indeed!"

"Yes, and more than that; I am sorry to say that he took passage, under an assumed name, in the same vessel I did."

"What was the name of the vessel?"

"The barque 'Dolphin;' it was wrecked on the Cornish coast, and we were saved by a miracle, and lost all our valuables and baggage."

"You say you were sorry he sailed in the same vessel with you? Was he saved likewise?"

"No; thank goodness, the young rascal was drowned. Unknown to me we had two detectives on board, who discovered what he was, and would have had him hung at Newgate only that he perished with the wreck in the storm."

"A most happy deliverance for society," said Joel, "for I have information from Tomasso, an officer at Leghorn, that the same Joel Flint was suspected of murder."

"Horrible! horrible!" said the old man.

"But my business on the present occasion, Mr. Lancaster, is not so much to speak of this young rascal Flint as to restore what he has from time to time stolen from you."

"Indeed, sir!"

"Yes, truly. Did you not miss articles of value, such as diamonds and the like, during his visits to you at Leghorn?"

"We did, papa," said Nelly; "but I never suspected that he could have stolen them."

"He did so, and some of my noble friends traced them to several old Jews, who purchased them for a small amount."

"You astonish me!"

"I have brought one or two of the articles with me," said the would-be count, presenting a likeness of Nelly Lancaster to her father, the borders of which were set with diamonds.

"I never saw this before, Nelly," said old Lancaster, looking in astonishment at his daughter. "Who gave you this?"

"By touching that small spring you will see, sir," said the count, with a fiendish grin.

Old Lancaster touched the spring, and beheld the likenesses of Captain Frank Ford and Nelly Lancaster sitting lovingly side by side with their hands locked.

Under the portraits were the words—

"Wear this for me, Nelly, and let not our hearts be ever sundered."

Old Lancaster turned all manner of colours, and would have broken out into a terrible rage, except for the presence of the Count, whom he wished to please.

Two diamond rings and a bracelet were also handed over to old Lancaster by the Count, all of which the enraged father knew, from certain marks and mottoes on them, came from the generous hand of the Boy Captain he hated so much.

Nelly was astounded at the recovery of her lost presents, and would have claimed them on the spot but an angry look from old Lancaster caused deep blushes to suffuse her cheeks, and she left the drawing-room endeavouring to conceal the tear drops which trickled down her cheeks.

"I have the game in my own hands now," thought Joel, "and will persecute them both by every means that cunning and money can devise."

For some time the pretended "Count" continued to converse with the banker, and so far won upon the old man's good opinion, that he was invited to call again, and it was hoped that he would make himself at home on all occasions, and consider himself a frequent and welcome guest; for, from his mode of speaking, the Count left the impression that he was not only immensely rich, but one of the leaders of fashion, and a person who might prove of great weight in political and banking circles.

When he left the house, Joel could not but chuckle at the success of his deceit, and as he went home, thought again and again,

"I will work upon both father and daughter, and if I am not much mistaken, I shall be able to make Nelly my wife."

He had not gone far down the street, however, before he perceived two suspicious-looking persons approaching him.

They were well dressed, but evidently not gentlemen; and when they came within a few feet, one of them inquired the number of Mr. Lancaster's house.

Joel told them, and they went hurriedly towards the banker's residence, and knocked loudly.

"Who can they be, and what business can take them to the old banker's at this unseasonable hour?"

He thought thus, and when turning the corner of the street, he heard one policeman say to another—

"What's up now, I wonder?"

"Why, sergeant?"

"I saw Gale and another plain clothes man go into old Lancaster's house."

A cold thrill passed through Joel.

He shuddered, and hurried away through the dark and silent streets.

---

## CHAPTER CVII.

CAPTAIN FRANK WRITES TO HIS BROTHER TOM AND HIS BOY FRIENDS SOME ACCOUNT OF THE FRENCH INVASION OF MEXICO AND OF THE SIEGE OF PUEBLA — AWFUL AND STIRRING SCENES.

"DEAR BROTHER,—In my last letter I promised to give some account of our doings with the Mexican army, which promise I now proceed to comply with.

"You know that, in the first place, the French had really no just cause for making war upon the Mexicans, but because the republic owed them some large sums of money, and, as a great war was raging in the United States, they thought it was a favourable time to carry out their long-designed project for conquest.

"The poor Mexicans were very badly prepared for the visit of their plundering visitors, but, nevertheless, they were fully aroused to the danger which threatened them, and resolved to leave no stone unturned to prevent the French marshal and his army from marching on to the capital city of Mexico.

"The chief town which lay in the proposed French route to Mexico city was Puebla.

"The Mexican forces, poorly clad, badly armed, and, for the most part, raw conscripts, made very little show against the well-drilled forces which the French could oppose to them.

"Therefore, having felt the want of it in several encounters in the open plains, the Mexicans held a council of war, and resolved to retreat back to Puebla, and there resist the enemy's progress as long as they could, in order to gain time to raise both men and money in the interim.

"The disasters to the Mexican army, however, so far from shaking the resolution of Juarez, the President of the Republic, or his brave Mexican followers, appeared only to stimulate them all to still greater exertions in the service of their country.

"Although proclamations were issued commanding all old men, women and children to quit Puebla, none of them did so; they preferred to remain and participate in the dangers and glory of a stout resistance to taking flight.

"Every able-bodied inhabitant was called upon to contribute all he could in money and labour to the common cause, and nearly all the population turned out to assist in strengthening the defences of the city.

"The rapid approach of the French, however, did not give the inhabitants time to complete their fortifications as well as they wished to do, although they had been labouring at them both night and day for weeks.

"The utmost efforts were made by one and all to strengthen their feeble fortifications, and young and old laboured at them without distinction of rank or station.

"A continued line of outer defensive earth-works had been erected as far as time and circumstances allowed.

"The old walls, which had not been built to resist anything stronger or fiercer than the inroads of Indians, were now bristling with cannon.

"Large stores of provisions had been formed; arms and ammunition were in abundance, and the town contained something near twenty thousand Mexican troops, regular and irregular, besides a numerous body of armed rustics and townspeople.

"But not only did the Mexicans doubly strengthen their walls to keep the enemy out, but they also made provision for a stout defence if the French should succeed in getting into the town, for every house of any importance or strength was barricaded and stored with arms and provisions, ready for a siege, so that if the French really got into the town, they would have been obliged to fight from street to street.

"For a week the grand citizens of Puebla were working like bees, preparing for the enemy.

"All strangers were told to leave the city within twenty-four hours under pain of punishment and enrolment among their troops.

"At last, however, the French came, and swarmod on two sides of the town like bees. They consisted of about forty thousand men of all arms, with an immense park of artillery, and everything necessary to destroy whatever opposed them.

"During the first night, the French engineers erected a number of heavy batteries opposite the eastern gate, and in the morning gave warning that if the city did not surrender in twenty-four hours the bombardment would commence. An indignant refusal was sent to this unjust demand by Juarez; and, true to his word, at the expiration of the time, General Bazaine opened his guns upon the devoted city. A large shell, one of the first that had been fired, accidentally exploded in a half-finished Mexican battery near the east gate, and unfortunately a large amount of ammunition was blown up, which, for a short time, caused much confusion among the gallant garrison.

"The French took advantage of the temporary disorder.

"A column crossed the canal by an old aqueduct which the French had possessed themselves of the night previous, and entering the east gate battery, managed to sustain themselves against the efforts of the garrison.

"This advantage, however, was only for a time, for the Mexicans, led on by skilful leaders, dashed headlong at the French, and drove them out of the battery with great loss.

"When they were in possession of the east gate battery, the French were so confident that the game was all over with the Mexicans, that they sent a flag of truce to President Juarez again demanding the surrender of the city.

"'Talk of surrender when I am dead,' was the bold answer.

"Soldiers and citizens were alike worthy of so bold a leader.

"A distinguished countess had formed a sisterhood among the ladies of the town, which numbered over three hundred members, whose business it was to carry provisions, ammunitions, and other things to the brave men who manned the batteries, and to succour the wounded.

"Nuns, wives, widows, all alike were engaged in this noble work, and all throughout the terrible bombardment never flinched from their duty day or night.

"Even boys were inspired with the feelings of heroes.

"One lad, twelve years of age, offered himself as a volunteer; but was not allowed to enroll himself, on account of his age.

"Nevertheless, he mixed with the soldiery, and performed prodigies of valour, for when the French had entered into the east gate battery, he himself led on a valiant company against them, and, with his own hand, bore off in triumph a stand of French colours, amidst the almost frantic enthusiasm of his countrymen.

"This gallant youth, throughout all the siege, was the most fearless of any one engaged in either army.

"He exposed himself continually to danger, but escaped death in an almost miraculous manner a dozen times.

"The name of this young hero is Don Fernandez Rivero, and I know you will feel delighted to learn that he is now one of the officers in our Boy Band of English Volunteers, and much beloved by all.

"On the other side of the river, seven regiments of French infantry, with a large body of horse, attempted, in the night, to win the suburb of the east gate.

"The command on this side had been entrusted to General Mendez, who, after an action of five hours, repulsed the French.

"They renewed the attack with their reserve, and their fire was so hot, and the attack so fierce, that the patriots were somewhat disordered.

"Mendez, followed by Juarez, hastened to the spot, put himself, sword in hand, at the head of his countrymen, rallied them, encouraged them by his voice and example, and the French were at length defeated and driven back, leaving thousands of killed and wounded upon the field.

"On the next day Marshal Bazaine advanced against the suburbs on the left of the river.

"He was encountered by about four thousand of the garrison posted in the woods and gardens, from which, after a warm contest, he succeeded in dislodging them.

"He then attempted to carry the suburb by a coup-de-main.

"In this he failed.

"Repulsed in all his efforts, after a long and fruitless contention, he at length, withdrew his troops, pursued by the garrison, with the loss of nearly one thousand men.

"The French now regularly invested the place, and the besieged on their part endeavoured to complete the work of defence.

"A few days afterwards, Marshal Bazaine, who had now fixed his head quarters at a village two miles from Puebla, addressed a letter to Mendez, assuring him that Mexico city had capitulated, and that any further resistance on the part of the Pueblans could only produce the total and inevitable destruction of the town.

"He also spoke of his earnest wish to spare the effusion of blood, and to preserve so fine a city.

"The Emperor, he said, had given him power to put a stop to all further evil; and his heart as well as his duty, made him urge the city to accept the peace which was proposed.

"Juarez replied, 'that if the capital had indeed capitulated, it must have been betrayed. The second of May,' said he, 'is a day which has no parallel in history, for either that city defends itself, or it has been sold. But what if it has been sold! The capital is but a single town. What avails it to talk of danger to men who know how to die? We, in Peubla, are not to be intimidated by horrors of a siege—that has been tried and failed. And for the effusion of blood which the French marshal is so desirous of sparing, it is as honorable for the Mexicans to shed blood in such a cause as it is ignominious for the French to be instruments in shedding it.'

"President Juarez also addressed a proclamation to the people of the capital.

"'The dogs by whom they were beset,' he said, 'scarcely gave them time to clean the blood from their swords. But they still found their graves at Peubla. The defenders of that city may be destroyed, but compelled to surrender they could not be. We know,' he added, 'that we were born for posterity not for ourselves.'

"And he promised as soon as he was at liberty, to hasten to the deliverance of the capital.

"On the last day of the month a sally was made, which brought on a sharp action.

"The French suffered considerable loss, and Juarez ordered every man who had signalized himself in this affair to wear a red ribbon of distinction on his breast.

"The ladies and nuns admirably seconded Mendez, the general, and were animated by every feeling of honour, enthusiasm and duty.

"If the most heroic and devoted courage could have ensured success, the confidence which Juarez had expressed would not have been frustrated; that is to say, had there been only the enemy to contend with—but an infectious disease broke out in the city, and pestilence accomplished for the besiegers what they might else, with all their mighty means of destruction, have been unable to effect.

"At the beginning of the investment of Puebla, the French appeared to think that a few hours of sharp cannonading would have been sufficient to frighten the brave Mexicans out of the city; but they were much mistaken if they thought so seriously. On the 12th, the terrible bombardment began in earnest.

"The main fire was directed towards the head-quarters of Juarez and Mendez, adjoining which was the cathedral; and this precious monument of antiquity was consumed, with everything it contained. The bombardment was so violent that the clergy suspended the administration of the sacraments.

"The magnificent convent of St. Joseph and the bridge of Don Pedro were won by the superior numbers of the enemy.

"Don Miguel, the brother of General Mendez, and a member of the National Assembly, left the city in hopes of effecting a diversion in its favour.

"He embarked at night in a little boat, and descending the river, established himself at a village, called Castello, and instantly organized the peasantry, and, by his active measures in concert with others, harrassed the communications of the besieging army, so that they began to be distressed for provisions.

"The movements of bodies of armed peasantry in the surrounding country occasioned considerable annoyance to the besiegers.

"Bands were formed on all hands, which, though unable to resist the attack of disciplined troops, yet were sufficiently formidable to require perpetual vigilance, and numerous enough to narrow the supplies of the besieging army in a very important degree.

"The emperor became impatient at the slow progress of the siege, and sent a special messenger to Marshal Bazaine, ordering him to assume the command himself in all departments, and accelerate the operations.

"This annoyed the French marshal, who directed General Noel to leave Puebla, and to act on the river and other parts.

"This general attacked the force of Don Miguel, and succeeded in dispersing it with considerable loss.

"Marshal Bazaine, in order to depress the hopes of the garrison of all external assistance, addressed a letter to Juarez communicating the circumstance, and detailing all the other disasters which had befallen the Mexican detachments.

"But the mortifying intelligence did not shake the firmness of the undaunted leader.

"He rejected all compromise, and continued, with undiminished vigour, to oppose every possible obstacle to the progress of the enemy.

"A breach was soon made in the mud walls, and, then, as in former sieges, the fight was carried on in the streets and houses.

"The only means of conquering Puebla was to destroy it house by house and street by street, and upon this sytem of destruction the French proceeded.

"Three companies of miners and eight companies of sappers were incessantly at work, and the Mexicans, being quite unused to this species of warfare, vainly endeavoured to oppose them by countermines.

"Meantime the bombardment was unnecessarily kept up.

"'Within this last forty-eight hours,' said Juarez, in a letter addressed to a friend, 'six thousand shells have been thrown in, two-thirds of the town are in ruins; but we shall perish under the ruins of the remaining third rather than surrender.'

"In the course of the siege about seventeen thousand bombs were thrown at the town.

"The stock of powder with which Puebla had been stored was exhausted.

"They had none at last but what they manufactured day by day, and no other cannon balls than those which were shot into the town, and which they collected and fired back upon the enemy.

"It was on the 20th that the besiegers effected their first lodgment within the walls.

"Every house was defended most heroically, and every day houses were blown up.

"On the 21st, sixty were thus destroyed.

"This mode of war occasioned the loss of a great number of lives to the French, for every inch of ground was purchased dearly.

"Noel, their commander, was killed.

"The bombardment continued two and forty days, but still within the walls the contest was carried on as unshrinkingly as at first.

"The inhabitants of the part of the city most injured by the bombardment were driven into the other quarters, where many of them took up their abode in cellars, which afforded comparative seclusion from the shells.

"The consequence was that these dark and miserable receptacles became the focus of infectious fevers.

"The Plazza was crowded with soldiers from all parts of the town, and one night, when the besiegers received a severe defeat, part of the troops were under arms in the Plazza for two or three hours while heavy showers were falling, which was succeeded by intensely hot weather on the morrow.

"This produced an infectious catarrh, which was soon followed by all the alarming and dreadful symptoms of camp contagion.

"To these causes may be added scantiness of food, crowded quarters, unusual exertion of body and anxiety of mind, and the impossibility of recruiting their exhausted strength by needful rest in a city which was almost incessantly bombarded, and where every hour their sleep was broken by the tremendous explosion of mines.

"It was impossible to check the ravages of the pestilence, or confine it to one quarter of the city.

"Above thirty hospitals were immediately established, and as soon as one was destroyed by the bombardment, the patients were removed to another.

"And thus the infection was carried to every part of Puebla.

"Famine aggravated the evil.

"The city had, probably, not been provided at the commencement of the siege, and, of the provisions which it contained, much was destroyed in the daily ruin which the mines and bombs effected.

"The misfortunes of the Mexicans were hourly accumulating.

"The number of dead per day amounted to hundreds from the fever alone.

"The hospitals were too small to contain the vast number of patients, and the necessary medicines were exhausted.

"The burying grounds were choked with corpses, and large pits were dug in the streets, into which the dead were tossed indiscriminately.

"Heaps of bodies were piled before the churches, where they were often struck by the shells, and the maimed and ghastly carcases lay dispersed along the streets, a frightful spectacle of horror.

"Even under such evils the courage of the Mexicans did not fail.

"The city was soon open to the invaders, but not one inch of the ground was yielded without a strugg'e.

"Juarez, however, did not limit his efforts to obstructing the progress of the enemy.

"He made vigorous efforts to recover the ground already lost, and drive the assailants from their stations.

"The nuns and ladies bore part in these operations.

"The former carried munitions, and gave succour to the dying, animating the soldiers at once by their words and their example.

"The latter carried refreshments to their sons or husbands, or fathers, and, sometimes, when one dear relative fell by their side, they seized his arms, determined to revenge his death or perish by his side in the same glorious cause.

"Notwithstanding the utmost efforts of the garrison, the French gained ground on the left.

"They obtained possession of two monasteries, which adjoined each other; two of the strongest, and most defensible places left.

"Having been repelled in assaulting the breaches, the assailants sprung a mine, and by that means effected an entrance.

"A desperate and determined struggle was long maintained in the church.

"Every column, every chapel, every altar became a point of defence.

"The pavements were stained with blood, and the aisles and body of the church strewn with the dead or dying.

"In the midst of this scene of horror, the roof of the edifice, shattered by balls and bombs, suddenly fell in with a terrible crash upon friend and foe alike.

"The boldest held their breath for a time; but those who escaped renewed the fight.

"Fresh parties of the French poured in; men, women and children rushed to the defence, and the contest was continued amid the ruins, and above the mangled, writhing bodies of the dead or dying.

"As day after day passed on, the situation of things for the brave Mexicans looked so desperate that persons of rank and unquestionable patriotism begged Juarez Mendez, Don Miguel, and other brave leaders to resist no longer, but surrender.

"But, with proud, undaunted hearts, these brave leaders of the people refused to listen to any such advice; but, instead, they addressed the citizens in stirring speeches, and roused up all to fresh exertions and deeds of daring.

"For several days longer they continued the defence.

"At last the French made a fierce attack on the suburb nearest the cathedral, and, after two unsuccessful trials, carried it by assault.

"A tremendous fire from fifty guns soon cleared this suburb of all obstructions, and made a clear road for the assaulting columns.

"By mid-day a breach was effected in the stout walls of the convent of San Jerome, which commanded a bridge over the river, and, after fiercely fighting, the Mexicans were driven from the old building.

"All communication between the suburb and the city proper was now cut off, and the French, intercepting Mexican reinforcements, captured 200 prisoners, who were too feeble from disease and suffering to make any stout resistance to the numbers who opposed them on all sides.

"The capture of the convent of San Jerome involved that of the suburb round it, which was without ammunition or provisions, yet many of the people continued to wage a fierce but hopeless war in the streets.

"Some scores crossed the broken bridge under a shower of bullets, and effected their escape to the city.

"Others crossed the river by swimming or in boats.

"In the meantime, Mendez, who had been the life and soul of the defence, was attacked by fever, and, as he lay writhing on a bed of suffering in an old vault, was compelled to give up his command.

"A council of war was immediately assembled to deliberate on the condition of the city, and the measures most proper to be adopted.

"At this meeting it was stated by a cavalry officer that only 100 horses were now alive, the rest having died from want, or been slaughtered for the use of the famished troops.

"Of the infantry, not one-third were fit for duty, nearly all the ammunition was exhausted, and if a stray shell now struck the only magazine, their last cartridge would be destroyed.

"The engineers stated that the walls and fortifications were almost demolished.

"There were neither men nor materials for repairing them, and bags of earth could no longer be made for want of material.

"In order to ascertain the chances of external succour, Mendez, the commander, was sent for; but the fever had seized upon his brain, and he could communicate nothing.

"His papers were examined; but these only tended to increase the conviction that no relief could reasonably be expected from without.

"With regard to the measures to be adopted, the council were divided in opinion.

"Twenty-six voted for capitulation, and eight (amongst whom was the president) against it.

"The latter urged that there was a possibility of being succoured.

"With a lofty gallantry of spirit which has not its parallel in modern history, the opinion of the minority was adopted.

"For they who had voted for surrendering had done so for the sake of others.

"For themselves, there was not one among them who would not rather have died than have capitulated.

"A flag of truce was sent to the enemy, proposing a suspension of hostilities for three days, with the view of ascertaining the situation of the capital; it being understood that should no immediate succour be at hand, the council should then treat for a surrender.

"This proposal was declined by the French commander, and the bombardment recommenced.

"On the next day the garrison made a last and unsuccessful attempt to recover two guns which the enemy had captured on the preceding day.

"Affairs were now desperate.

"The fifty guns which had been employed in the attack of the suburbs, opened fire on the city, and the streets in the neighbourhood of the old cathedral were completely destroyed.

"The council now deemed it necessary to order that measures should be taken to ascertain the sentiments of the people with regard to the state of the city.

"Two-thirds of it were in ruins.

"Thousands of the inhabitants had perished, and from three to four score persons were dying daily from the pestilence.

"Under such circumstances the council declared they had fulfilled their oath of fidelity, and that Puebla was destroyed.

"A flag of truce was despatched to the French head-quarters, followed by a deputation from the council to arrange the terms of capitulation.

"The French were at first disposed to listen to nought but unconditional surrrender.

"The proposal was indignantly refused by the deputies, and Don Miguel declared that rather than submit to it the garrison should die beneath the ruins of their city.

"'I and my companion,' said the noble patriot, 'will return there and defend what remains to us as best we may.

"'We have yet arms and ammunition, and if these fail we have daggers.

"'War is never without its chances, and should the Pueblans be driven to despair, it yet remains to be proved who are to be victorious.'

"This answer convinced the French commander that the sooner the siege was concluded the better for the honour of their arms.

"It was accordingly conceded that the troops should march out with the honours of war, that the herioc Mendez should be suffered to retire to any place where he might think proper to fix for his residence, and that all persons not included in the garrison should be suffered to quit the city in order to avoid contagion.

"Next day the posts of the city were delivered up to the French, who began immediately, as was their custom, to pillage.

"And thus ended one of the most strenuous and extraordinary struggles of which history bears record.

"By their own account the French threw above 17,000 bombs into the city, and expended above 160,000 lbs. of powder.

"More than 3,000 men and 500 officers lay buried beneath the ruins of Puebla, exclusive of a vast number of women and children who perished, the victims of fire, pestilence, and famine.

"The loss of the French must have been very great, but it was studiously concealed.

"The contemplated operations of the besieging army on other points were in consequence prevented.

"When the French took possession of the city, only 2,400 men were capable of bearing arms.

"The rest were in the hospitals.

"On the March to Vera Cruz, 270 of these men, weakened by famine and disease, were unable to proceed with the rapidity with which their conductors considered necessary.

"They were left on the road to perish, and to serve as a spectacle and a warning to the succeeding divisions.

"Among the prisoners was Ponquita Isabella, who had distinguished herself in the former encounters with the French.

"At the commencement of the siege she took her station, at the East Gate, by a gun, which she served constantly through the siege.

"'See, general,' said she, with a cheerful countenance, pointing to the gun, 'I am again with my old friend.'

"Once, when her wounded husband lay bleeding at her feet, she discharged the cannon at the enemy in order to avenge his fall.

"Though exposed during the whole siege to the most imminent danger, Isabella always escaped without a wound.

"On the surrender of the city she was too well known to escape notice, and was made prisoner.

"But she had already caught the contagious fever, and being taken to the hospital she subsequently made her escape.

"Another heroine, named Juanita, was shot through the heart.

"Her sister, who headed one of the female corps which had been formed to carry provisions, bear away the wounded, and fight in the streets, escaped the hourly dangers to which she exposed herself, only to die of grief upon hearing that her only child, an infant, had been killed.

"During the siege not less than 600 women and children perished by the bayonets or bullets of the enemy, and sickness or fever.

"Now that I have given you some brief account of the doings of the French in this far-off land, and of the Spartan heroism displayed by a people who despise and hate Maximilian and his kingly rule more than anything else on earth, it is time that I now turn to say something about my own particular doings with the Boy Soldiers, and of the many individual adventures and scrapes which have befallen Fatty, young Buttons, and others of those whom I know you feel interest in.

"I find, however, that the length of this letter has far exceeded my original intention, and therefore, until next week, will reserve what I have to say about myself, Caspar, Hugh Tracy, and many of our young Mexican recruits, who have greatly distinguished themselves of late.

"I and all the lads are impatiently waiting to hear news from you about what has become of old Flint, Jonathan, Shanks, and, last of all, regarding the doings of Joel.

"From English newspapers which have reached us, I learn that Sergeant Gale expresses his firm conviction that ere long he will be able to arrest and perhaps convict all the scoundrels who had anything to do with uncle's cruel murder.

"I hope this may prove true, and in hopes of hearing from you quickly, give my love to all the boys, and believe me to remain,

"Your brother, FRANK FORD."

## CHAPTER CVIII.

### JOEL FLINT MEETS SOME ONE HE DOES NOT WISH TO KNOW, BUT CANNOT SHUN.

FOR any one who has a large income, and nothing to do, London presents numberless attractions, and there are a thousand and one opportunities hourly and daily offered for killing time.

Thus thought Joel Flint as he strutted about in the finest broad cloth, bedizened with rings and jewellery of all sorts and sizes.

From morning until night he had now nothing to think of but the best means of enjoying himself, and this he endeavoured to do on all occasions.

If the best living, almost unlimited cash and impudence, could make any one happy, Joel should have been so. But he was not.

Whichever way he went, he felt as if some demon stalked behind him.

He could obtain no real or substantial pleasure in anything.

He appeared almost afraid of his own shadow.

A dark, lonely, and unfrequented street struck terror into his soul.

He once had courage enough to pass the "Red House" in a cab, but as it rolled by, he dared not look at it, for in imagination, he perceived a ghastly head at each window, which shrieked out loudly in his ears, "Murder! Murder!"

Such is the lot of the wicked, and those who live by the proceeds of crime.

The thief, wherever he is, is in momentary dread of being "collared" or "wanted" by some officer.

Every man's eye seems to be upon him, and in nine cases out of ten, he cannot look fixedly at any one without betraying a certain restlessness which says more loudly than words.

"I am not a man, but a paltry thief, too lazy to work, and a burden alike to myself and society."

But what must be the feelings of a murderer!

The rustling of a single leaf startles him, his knees tremble at the sound of thunder, and each moment he expects to be struck blind by avenging lightning.

Both day and night, in society or out of it, waking or in dreams, a red hand points to him with a gesture of everlasting vengeance.

He cannot look at the bright blue heavens without being abashed—the fields and flowers and warbling birds have nought of beauty or music to his soul—for human blood has extinguished in his soul every, yea the most latent spark of sensibility, and he stalks through society, with the outward show of manhood, but with heart and soul petrified and inhuman.

Thus it was with Joel.

Whatever money could obtain, he had, and every sensual desire was gratified.

But though he drank deeply, and could dress elegantly, though the ribald joke could cause a laugh, and the flattery of worthless ones cause a smile of gratified vanity, his heart was bursting and the cancer of despair was eating away his very life inch by inch and hour by hour.

Such is the curse of ill-gotten wealth.

When morning broke upon his troubled slumber, he wished it were night, for the light of day was too pure and blinding.

When dark night came on, the air seemed peopled with haunting spirits, and the distant sigh of each passing wind thrilled every sense.

Though young, he was very, very old; and though rich, he would, perhaps, have exchanged his lot with any one for the peace of mind enjoyed by the poorest of the poor.

Three or four nights after his visit to Mr. Lancaster he was reeling along the streets intoxicated, and, imitating others, he too would appear to be gay, and hummed a popular tune of the times, but each word seemed to stick in his throat, and his own shadow in the moonlight appeared hideous and revolting.

It had an hour or two before been raining hard, but the clouds no longer obscured the silvery moon, and homeward staggered the dandily-dressed Joel Flint.

He had not gone far, however, when a poorly-dressed old man, wet to the skin, with tattered hat and shoes down at heel, accosted him, and begged for the price of a bit of bread.

Joel, who had never known what want or the keen pangs of hunger were, insulted the houseless wanderer.

Again did the man in rags beg, for the love of Heaven, to be relieved.

"Out upon you, rascal!" was the brutal answer, "out upon you, rascal! Don't speak of heaven to me; but get out of my path!"

With a fiendish laugh he raised his walking-stick and struck the beggar man full in the face and severly cut it.

The blow knocked the old man's hat off, and he fell on his knees from faintness and hunger.

"Oh, God, have mercy on me!" he whined, and looked up into Joel's face like a poor half-famished dog.

The moonlight fell upon his face.

Joel started back in mute surprise, and gazed on the ragged stranger like one demented.

"What!" he exclaimed, suddenly sobered and filled with astonishment, "what! it cannot be!"

The old man hung his head, and wiped his bleeding face.

It was the meeting of father and son!

It was Lawyer Flint and his son Joel!

# THE BOY SOLDIER; OR, GARIBALDI'S YOUNG CAPTAIN.

THE ESCAPE.

## CHAPTER CIX.

### THE MEETING BETWEEN JOEL FLINT AND HIS FATHER.

THE accidental meeting of Joel with his father for a moment stunned him.

He knew very well who it was; but the old man was so shabbily dressed, and presented such a picture of misery, that the young gentleman did not deem it proper or wise to stop for any explanations, well knowing that, under the peculiar circumstances under which each of them were placed in the eyes of the law, his father would not dare to make any disclosures in the public streets.

Joel, therefore, made the best of his way from the spot.

He crossed the road, and observed all that took place afterwards.

In a short time, old Flint, staggering from weakness and from want, rose to his feet, and hobbled away as best he could; and to shun the chance of being interriogated by the police, he preffered to go by the back streets, for they were more lonely, dark, and least frequented.



He had not gone far, however, when Joel followed him.

The rain now began to fall again; and, to secure himself from the storm, old Flint crouched in a spacious doorway in one of the squares.

Joel, as we have said, followed, and also stood under the same doorway.

"Filthy night, old man," said Joel.

"Yes sir, a very nasty night; but more than nasty for those who have got no home to go to."

"Is that the case with you, then?" asked Joel, with an assumed foreign accent.

"I am sorry to say it is," the old man replied.

"But your address is not that of such a very poor man?"

"That may be, sir," was old Flint's reply, with a sigh. "I know that appearances are against me, or, otherwise, I should succeed much better as a beggar than I do."

"Why, from the tone of your conversation, I should judge you were once a gentleman."

"So I have been, and a rich one also."

"And what reduced you so low?"

"The knavery of friends."

"Indeed! How?"

"My only son proved a villain."

"How?"

"I entrusted a large amount to his keeping, and since then I have not seen him."

"Monstrous ingratitude! And so you are reduced to beggary, eh?"

"Quite so; and if I could only find out the whereabouts of that young rascal, my son, I would have him transported."

"Say if you could," Joel observed, dryly.

"Could? Why, what is there to prevent me?"

"A great deal, perhaps, old man. What might your name be, pray?"

"I decline to answer your questions, or to have anything more to say to you. I have not put myself under any obligations to you, and, therefore, I decline to have any more conversation with you."

"Ha! ha!" laughed Joel. "You are proud as well as poor, I perceive."

"And intend to remain so, sir. Take your hands off my shoulder! Let me go! I fear you! You make my limbs tremble!"

"Your name, old man?" said Joel, still keeping up his disguise.

"I refuse to answer your question."

"It matters not, however, for I already know it."

"Indeed!"

"You need not be surprised. I am better acquainted with you than you imagine."

The night, as we have said, had turned dark and stormy.

Old Flint turned his face to look at the speaker, but could not detect who he was.

At first, old Flint thought it impossible that any one could or did know him, and, therefore, he answered boldly,

"It matters not to *me*, sir, whether you know me or not. All that I can say is that I am only a poor gentleman."

"A poor thief," answered Joel, with a dry laugh.

"A what?"

"A poor thief. Didn't you hear what I said?"

"You are an insulting fellow!" said the old lawyer.

"If I am, why not give me in charge of the police then?"

"I would, only——"

"Only you are afraid."

"Afraid of what?" said old Flint, with chattering teeth.

"Why, afraid of becoming known to the authorities, that's all," said Joel, laughing.

"You are a strange person, sir, whoever you are."

"But you are much stranger. Do you know me?"

"No, I do not. Who are you that thus dares interrogate me?"

"A detective officer," said Joel, calmly.

"A what?" said old Flint, in surprise.

"A detective officer."

"And what can you want with me?"

"More than you suppose. I have been following you about all night. Your name is Flint."

"No, it is not."

"Then Schmidt, if you like,"

"No, nor that either."

"What have you done with all the money and valuables you stole from old Ford?"

This last question almost knocked the breath out of old Flint, who fairly winced again.

"Old Ford? I never knew any one of that name."

"Oh, yes you did: and old Jonathan, how is he? And Warner, and the Pug? How are all you friends?"

This last question was a poser for the old lawyer, who knew not how to answer.

He trembled violently, as well he might at the thought of falling into the hands of the law.

"If I run away," thought he, "this fellow will give the alarm, and I shall be hunted through the streets like a mad dog. But what must I do? What *can* I do under the circumstances? I have no money, nor a place wherein to lay my head to-night. What had I better say to this fellow? He is muffled up to the eyes, and I cannot get a full look at him. If I had a good knife, now," thought the lawyer, "I should feel much more comfortable than I do, for then I could defend myself if he attempted to seize me."

"You tremble, old man," said Joel.

"Do I? I think you must be mistaken."

"No, I am not."

"Why should I tremble? I have never done any harm in all my life."

"A jury would not say so, though," laughed Joel. "Here, old man," said he, "I don't want to frighten you, for I am *not* a detective after all."

"I thought you were not. You have the manners of a gentleman too much for that."

"Thanks," said Joel, bowing.

"You are a foreigner, are you not?" said old Flint. "I should judge so, from your voice and manner."

"I am," said Joel; "and it may surprise you to hear that I very well know your son."

"My son, Joel!" said the lawyer, in surprise.

This seemed to startle the old man very much, who said—

"Do you know where my son Joel is?"

"Yes, without doubt," was the reply. "But surely you would not like to see him?"

"I should, indeed. If I could but have half an hour's conversation with him I would give the world!"

"Well, then, you will not have to give anything if you'll take my advice."

"And what is that?"

"You are ragged and poor."

"But what of that?"

"He is quite a dandy and rich."

"Ah!" said the old man, with a deep-drawn sigh, "*I* know where his riches come from."

"That doesn't matter now," said the stranger; "if you'll promise to follow my advice you will do well."

"And what is it, young man?"

"Take this purse; it doesn't contain much, but there is sufficient for your purpose. Buy a new suit of clothes, and call at the residence printed on this card," said Joel, presenting a card to his father.

In a moment afterwards Joel left the old man, and, calling a cab, was soon out of sight.

Old Flint went and stood under a lamp-post and looked at the card which had been given to him.

"Count Schmidt!" said he, in a rage. "Why, the fellow is living on the proceeds of what I stole," and as thus he thought, he trudged along through the rain and entered a public-house.

Before he did so, however, he looked into the purse which had been given to him, and perceived that it contained eight sovereigns.

"Eight sovereigns," he said, half wild with joy. "Why, this is a little fortune to me, and no mistake. Who'd a thought of ever meeting with such a kind young gentleman? Ah, he knows Joel, that's it."

Old Flint went into the public-house, changed one of the coins, had six pennyworth of brandy and water, and then directed his footsteps to a ham and beef shop, where he remained for a good hour gorging himself, and devouring many plates full of all manner of delicacies.

After this he strolled about, and went to a coffee shop and got a shilling lodging, and popped his money under the mattress for fear of being robbed during the night.

In the morning he went to Moses and Son's large tailoring warehouse in the City, and bought a suit of clothes, and sold his old ones to a rag merchant for half-a-crown.

He patronised a barber, and told him that he was an actor at one of the theatres, and required several false wigs, whiskers, and moustaches—second-hand would do. These he also purchased, and when he got on one of the wigs and a pair of whiskers, he looked so strange that no one would have known him.

When night came on he went to the residence of Count Schmidt, and knocked at the door.

## CHAPTER CX.

### BARNEY LEAVES THE HOSPITAL.

For some time Gale and other officers were very desirous of finding out the whereabouts of Barney, but they could not.

The wound which he had received in his hand proved a very serious one, and he lingered in the hospital for many weeks.

Owing to great skill and care, the hand was almost cured and restored to its former usefulness, but still he felt great pain occasionally, and would groan aloud.

He was a very cunning fellow, for Barney thought to himself, "It don't matter how soon they cure me, I ain't going to leave such snug quarters as these yet a while, trust me if I am. No, no; I must keep out of the way until these affairs blow over, and then all will be serene and jolly.

"But I wonder what's become of old Moss and Warner and the rest of them. I suppose half of them have got lagged before this for something or other."

Now, the surgeon and nurses, after tending on Barney for several weeks, thought he might be well enough to leave the hospital, and attend as an out-patient.

But this didn't suit the views of Barney.

"No, no," thought he, "you don't catch me leaving if I can help it, leastways not yet awhile."

So whenever they came round to his bedside and asked him how he was, Barney always pulled a long face and swore that he suffered awful agonies at times.

"How's your appetite?"

"Werry bad," said Barney; "werry bad indeed."

"What's his diet?"

"Beef-steaks, porter, vegetables, and so forth," said the nurse.

"Oh, just so; and does he eat regularly?"

"No, sir, not werry regular," said Barney; "I tries to, but I has to force the grub down. If it weren't for that ere small drop of porter which you allows me, I don't know what I should do, that I don't; I should fairly choke, that I would."

"True, true," said the doctor, feeling his pulse; "now that you are getting better we must give you a full diet, such as you usually had before you came here."

"Thank'ee, sir."

"You have been a pugilist, I think?" said the doctor.

"Yes, sir."

"And fought often."

"Oh, yes, werry often, and licked I don't know how many," said Barney, grinning.

"Ah, so you've said before. You pugilists live uncommonly well when you are training, I have heard."

"Yes, sir, unkimmon well; chops, steaks, port wine, dry toast, and sich like," said Barney. "I was in training when I came here, and for a day or two I thought the grub would have choked me."

"Well, we must prescribe a more generous diet," said the surgeon; and he wrote on the board over Barney's head, "port wine, beef-tea, stout and cocoa."

"That's the ticket," said Barney, when the nurse told him what had been ordered. "That's the ticket," said he, in high glee, and he rolled himself up in the blankets, making up his mind not to leave the hospital for a month to come.

"Who's to know the difference," said Barney, "if I can kid 'em into thinking as how my nerves are shook, why I can come in and go out just as I pleases, and take up my quarters here for a month or two."

Thus Barney thought, and was indulging himself with the hope that, by the time he got out, Warner and all the rest would have left London, when some strangers entered the ward in which Barney lay, and went from bed to bed consoling the patients.

One of them was dressed up like a parson, and as Barney saw him approaching, he pretended to be asleep.

"That's the worst of it," thought Barney; "it would be all very well if they'd let a cove alone, but they sends around them track distributers, and bible-readers, and they do give a cove so much jaw, I hate 'em."

Now the clerical person who entered on this occasion was a jolly-looking individual, with red cheeks, coal-black whiskers, and curly hair.

He approached Barney's bed, and looked at the board on which his daily diet was prescribed.

"Not bad, that," said the cleric to Barney, with a wink. "A good many lads in London would not mind having a cut hand if they could get port wine, beef-tea, and chops every day, would they?"

Barney "wouldn't tumble," as he called it, to the stranger.

He wanted to make believe that the diet didn't agree with him by any means.

"How long have you been here, my good man?" said the parson.

"Oh, about three weeks, I think."

"And have you ever thought about leaving?"

"Leaving, no, not me!" said Barney, in anger. "Why do you ask? Is it likely I should leave, with such a hand as this?"

"Perhaps not; but have you ever thought of spiritual affairs since you have been confined?"

"Oh, yes, werry often," said Barney, thinking of the gin-shops and favourite taps he was wont to patronise.

"Because you, as a fighting man, my friend, have been leading a very bad life."

"I know it," said the hypocrite.

"And are very sorry, of course?"

"In course I am," whined Barney.

"You have mixed with many bad characters in your time," said the clergyman.

Barney turned up his eyes as much as to say "to my sorrow."

"Ah!" continued the reverend gentleman, "they

may have a long turn; but their end is sure to come some day."

"Quite true," ejaculated Barney,

"Now, only yesterday," the clergyman went on, "there was one tried at the Old Bailey, a Jew, named Moss, who was one of the most notorious receivers of stolen goods in London; though suspected by the police he has always managed to escape detection, but now proofs are clear against him, and he is sentenced to twenty years' transportation."

"Je-ru-sa-lem!" said Barney, "ain't that 'ere a jolly lark? Old Moss got 20 penn'orth! They've cooked *his* goose pretty nicely, I think."

"You seem to rejoice over the news."

"And so I do, and so would you, if you knew as much about him as I do."

"Oh, indeed! Ah, then, that accounts for it," said the clergyman, with a bland smile. "But you should not rejoice over another's misfortune."

"Shouldn't I, and why not? Harn't old Moss rejoiced hisself many a good year over the misfortin of others, eh?"

"I'm sure I don't know anything about it," said the cleric.

"Well, but then, you see, *I* do," Barney replied.

"You know this old Moss?"

"Yes—that is——"

"You have had dealings with him?"

"Yes—no—I mean that I know parties as *have* had dealin's with him, that's all."

"Oh, indeed; not thieves, I hope?"

"Is it likely?" said Barney. "Oh, not quite so bad as that."

"But still you know him by reputation?"

"Yes, and a fine old rascal he was, and no mistake. He made all his money by dealin' in stolen goods."

"Horrible!"

"No mistake about it. They say he was worth £20,000."

"And through robbery?"

"Yes, every penny. He had quite a school round him, but I suppose some of his clever lads must have rounded on him. Well, now he's transported, I feels comfortable," said Barney.

The clergyman smiled as Barney went on dilating on the awful enormities and sin of the Jews generally, but for some time he said nothing.

At last Barney said,

"And how did it all happen?"

"They broke into his warehouse."

"'Fence' is the right name for it."

"Well, 'fence,' then; and he called in the police to see if they could detect who the thieves were."

"The worst thing he could a'done," said Barney; "the very worst. He might a'known as how the 'beaks' would discover more than he wanted 'em. Well, whoever heard o' sich a lunatic—go and call in two 'bobbies' to search a reg'lar 'fence.' Well, such a cove as him deserves to get lagged."

"But I understand that none of his friends have been arrested as yet."

"As *yet*," said Barney. "Why, what do you mean?—are they after any of them?"

"Why, yes; the police are after several fellows who have deposited stolen property with him."

"Did you hear any of their names?"

"Well, the newspapers say that the police have discovered so many valuable articles relating to certain celebrated robberies and murders of late, that they have no doubt but that the persons whom old Moss named to the police must have had some hand in all these affairs."

"Hang old Moss for a thief," said Barney, red in the face.

"You seem displeased."

"No, I ain't; but I should like to hear that he got scragged, for all that."

"You are very un-Christian in your feelings."

"Christianity don't extend to Jews," said the Pug, red with rage; "and what were the names of the parties he informed on?"

"Why, one goes by the name of Warner."

"Warner, eh?"

"Do you know him?"

"Me! no; how should I know him? That's the same chap as they say is mixed up in old Ford's murder at the Red House."

"I believe it is. You seem to know all about it."

"No; only what I've heern," said Barney.

"So they is arter Warner, eh," he thought, "and I hopes they may catch him, that's all. They will be sure to drop on him one o' these fine mornings. Any more?"

"Yes," said the clergyman; "there is another rascal they are looking after."

"And what's his name?"

"'Barney, the Pug,' they call him."

"You don't mean that," said the Pug, rising in bed; "you don't mean that?"

"Well, that is what the newspapers say of it. Do you know him?"

"No; but I've seen him."

"You have met him out in sporting circles, I suppose?"

"Yes, just so."

"Let me see; they have admitted you here under the name of James Tompson, stone-mason?"

"Yes."

"But that isn't your sporting name; the name under which you have appeared in the prize ring?"

"Oh, no; when I appear in the 'magic circle,'" said Barney, "I goes under the name of 'Young Ruffian, or the Terror of the Dials.'"

"A very pretty name, indeed," said the clergyman, smiling.

"Yes, ain't it?"

"Quite classic."

"No mistake about it."

"But you are quite sure that that *is* your name?"

"Why, in course it is. Why?"

"Because there is an advertisement which appeared in this morning's papers, advertising for a Mr. Barney, who was supposed to be ill in some hospital."

"Gammon," said the Pug, incredulously.

"No; quite true, my friend. A reward of £50 is offered to any one who can give his direction or any information concerning him."

"What a rare chance for somebody. I wish I knowed where he was, I'd earn the £50 like a shot. But what do they want him for?"

"He has been left a large sum of money."

"What!"

"That is what the advertisement says, at all events."

"All gammon, sir; all gammon," said Barney; "it's only a catch—a bit o' cheese in the trap, that's all. I suppose Mr. Barney has been up to some game or other, and the bobbies want him. That's it, you may be sure. I'm up to their little games, long ago."

"Oh, I suppose he is hiding somewhere," said the clergyman.

"And I don't blame him, either. Wouldn't you?"

"I don't think he'll be able to hide long, considering that Gale, the detective, is after him."

"You don't mean that."

"Certain of it; he's got Jonathan in custody already."

"The devil!"

"He is securing them one by one—slowly, but surely."

"Well, but what has this all to do with me?" said Barney, at length, after a few moments of thought; "what has all this to do with me?"

"A very great deal I should judge," said the clergyman.

"How? in what way?"

"Well, to put you out of your misery, I might as well tell you all."

"All what?"

"Why this: we have been on the look out for you for a week or two, but should never have discovered you, perhaps, had not Moss told us about the wound in your hand."

"You ain't a parson, then?" said Barney, in surprise and turning pale.

"No! I am not."

"Then who or what the devil are you then?"

"An officer from Bow Street."

"What!" said Barney, in surprise jumping up in bed.

"I dare say you know me now," said the officer, pulling off the white neckerchief and his wig.

"I dare say I does," answered Barney.

It was Mr. Gale!

"What does yer want o'me now, this time, Mr. Gale?" said Barney, chapfallen.

"Well, not much, perhaps, Barney."

"You are always getting me into hot water," said Barney.

"Then you should behave yourself. Why don't you go to work, instead of skulking about the streets doing nothing but thieving?"

"I don't thieve now, Mr. Gale," said Barney.

"Where did you get that silver coffee-pot from?"

"Which one?"

"Which one; have you stolen so many then that you cannot recollect? Why, that one you sold to old Moss the night you met with that accident to your hand."

"I didn't sell him anything o' the sort," said Barney, in a terrible passion; "the old scoundrel lies if he says I did."

"No, he doesn't, Barney, for you were watched, and every action that you or old Moss did on that night was noted down."

"I didn't sell him that one," said Barney.

"Oh yes you did, and you know where it came from."

"Not me."

"Yes you do! It belonged to old Ford, and was one article among many which you stole on the night of the murder, Barney."

"You are pinching a fellow very tight, Mr. Gale."

"Calcraft will pinch you tighter, I'm fancying."

Barney winced at this thought.

"I am werry ill, Mr. Gale, and feel awful queer," he said, very meekly.

"No doubt; but the law don't consider that. Come, get up, and dress yourself at once; I've been looking after you too long already."

"Get up! no I'll be hung if I do."

"If you don't I must be obliged to use force, that's all, and take you dressed or undressed."

"Ah! I little thought as how it were you," said Barney, "when you come to the bedside talking o' religion, and all that kid."

"Well, never mind, you must make up your mind for the worst, for we've been long enough over this murder job, I think, and all we want is to get Warner to complete the evidence."

Barney was forced to get up, and in less than half an hour he bade adieu to his snug quarters in the hospital, and was walked off to Bow Street, and placed in the same cell with Jonathan.

## CHAPTER CXI.

### WARNER IN SEARCH OF JOEL FLINT.

Now there was a reason and a very good one why Gale thought proper to direct that Barney and Jonathan should be placed in one cell.

Gale made certain that when these two rascals got together, they would commence conversing about their past doings.

"Holloa! here, who are you?" said Barney, with an oath, as he looked at the haggard and careworn face of the late master of Bromley. "Holloa! here, who are you?" he repeated; "get up, don't lay sprawling on that bench—somebody wants to sit down as well as you."

Jonathan was unwilling to get up from his sleeping posture, but Barney soon made him, for he administered such a punch to Jonathan's ribs that he rose instantly, and in great surprise.

"Don't do that again," said Jonathan, "or else——"

"Or else what?" said Barney. "Are you inclined for anything?" and as he spoke, he "put up his hands," and threatened all manner of things.

"Holloa, there, holloa!" said Gale, peeping through the iron bars. "Holloa, there, holloa!" he repeated. "What are you up to now, eh, Barney?—fighting already? Why I thought you had a bad hand."

"So I have," Barney replied, sulkily; "but I can lick this cove with one hand any time."

"You'd better keep quiet, though, if you'll take my advice, for the other party is an old pal of yours."

"Pal o' mine!" said Barney, "nonsense."

"Yes, he is—that's old Jonathan, of Bromley Hall."

"What, Jonathan!—never!" exclaimed Barney, recovering his good temper on the instant. "Why, how are you, old pal? Give us your flipper."

"Don't talk to me," said Jonathan, in disgust; "I don't know you, nor do I want to know you."

"Oh, that's it, eh, old chum! You're getting more stuck up the lower you are coming down. There's nothing like it, old man—keep your pecker up, and die game."

"Die," said Jonathan, "who talks of dying?" he said, shivering.

"Why, I do, in course; it's a plain case against you, and no mistake—you're a great hand at killing, I hear."

"What do you mean, you babbling fool?" said Jonathan, in a hoarse whisper; "don't you know we are overheard? If you *do* know me, there's no occasion to let every one know it."

"Ah, now, I tumble to you," said Barney; "it's a sad case for both on us, I'm thinking; but you're worse off than me."

"Why?"

"There's old Ford's affair."

"I hadn't anything to do with it."

"You can say so, of course; but that don't make any one believe it for all that; and then there's that ere affair in Green Court—that's No. 2."

"I know nothing of it."

"Then, there's the job with them bobbies in old

Flint's office; you remember all about that, of course—that's No. 3."

Jonathan was bursting with passion, and could have knocked Barney senseless.

"And then," continued the Pug, "there's that little job with the detective in Epping Forest, which makes No. 4. And —— "

"If you don't hold your tongue," said Jonathan, with a bitter oath, "I'll strangle you."

"Which would make job No. 5," said the Pug, laughing.

For some time Barney and Jonathan communed together in whispers; and though Gale with another officer listened with the greatest attention, they could not catch a single word that passed between them.

"When did they catch you?"

"In the hospital," said Barney, cursing his own ill luck.

He explained all the circumstances of his meeting with Warner, and of the wounds he received.

Jonathan was greatly surprised when he heard all this, and bit his lips in anger.

"I wouldn't care what I suffered," said he, "if those old devils, Flint and Warner, were also here."

"Nor I," said Barney; "it ain't fair nohow that two should suffer and not all; but did you hear the news?"

"What news?"

"About Bromley Hall."

"No; what was it?"

"Why, they are going to search the place from top to bottom—for old Giles, the gardener, swears the place is haunted."

"Old Giles ought to be put into a lunatic asylum," said Jonathan, "he has been at Bromley Hall many, many years, and should have died long ago, for all the good he has been to any one."

"He claims to be master of Bromley Hall," said Barney.

"He cannot be, for I bought it."

"Let that be as it may, he says he can prove that you are a murderer, and if you escape the charges that are now preferred against you, there are many others that he can well prove."

"Speak lower," said Jonathan; "it is bad enough for us to be here on one charge, without letting every one know all our secrets."

"But what had we better do?"

"Escape is impossible," Barney whispered.

"Nothing is impossible to determined men," said Jonathan in Barney's ear.

"How do you mean?"

"Won't money do any good?"

"I haven't any."

"Nor I."

"But we might bribe the gaolers in some other way; by promises, or the like."

"I fear there is no chance; but at all events I'll try."

"How?"

"Oh, leave that to me, and if I get off you may be sure I'll endeavour to set you free also, if you promise to do the right thing with me afterwards."

"How do you mean?"

"Why, old Flint must have plenty of coin hid away somewhere."

"No, he has not, the treasure is lost."

"No matter; they can but hang us once," said Barney in a whisper. "If I get ten yards start of any of them, the devil himself will not catch me."

Barney did not say anything more to his friend at that moment, but next morning, when he was about to be removed to the van which was to take him to the House of Detention, he walked along the stone corridors meekly and humbly.

But directly he got into the street, he tripped up the officer who held him, gave a sudden and vicious kick at another which almost lamed the man, and made his escape before any one had the slightest notion whither he had fled or how.

Jonathan was not so fortunate, for two officers conducted him to the van, and they held him so tight by the coat collar that he was almost suffocated.

When Barney made his escape he ran like a deer.

He did not go into the public streets, but ran through numberless lanes and alley ways round about Drury Lane, until at last he was completely exhausted.

He had not a farthing of money wherewith to buy a loaf, and he sat crouching on the step of a coffee-house door.

While thus he sat meditating what to do, who should come out but old Flint.

"The very man I wanted," said Barney. "But lor, ain't the old 'un togged out to the nines and no mistake."

"Hullo, old man," said he, touching Flint upon the shoulder. "Hullo, old man; haven't yer got an odd copper to give a poor cove?"

Flint perceived who it was that addressed him, but did not wish to be recognised.

In his hurry then he turned away his head, and put a hand into his pocket, and felt for a farthing.

He gave it to Barney, and passed out.

"Oh, crikey," said the Pug; "here's a jolly go; the old man has gone and give me a 'quid' by mistake."

It was certainly a great mistake on Flint's part.

He did not at first wish to give Barney anything; but fearful of being recognised, and in order to get rid of his ugly acquaintance, he had given a sovereign away in mistake for a farthing.

The old man did not realize his mistake and loss, but hurried away.

"I'll follow the old bloke; he's well up, now, and can stand a 'tenner' without much grumbling."

Now old Flint was afraid that Barney would follow him, and, therefore, the first thing he did when he got out of the street was to call a cab.

But Barney, to use his own words, "was all there," and was not going to be "humbugged" any longer.

"If there is any money floating I must have part," thought he, "or I'll know the reason why."

He, therefore, followed the four wheeler, and got up behind.

When it arrived at the residence of Count Schmidt he got down and went on the other side of the way.

"Oh, that's the house, eh, is it?" thought the Pug; "and a nobby place it looks, too. I wonder who the devil this Count Schmidt is?" he thought; "old Flint ain't related to the aristocracy, as I ever heerd on. There must be some little game on hand here. I'll stop and watch."

He went and bought himself a pipe and some tobacco, and, after having several "goes" of gin near by, he stood looking through the tap-room window watching the cab, which still remained in the street waiting for old Flint.

But while the Pug is waiting and drinking a large amount of gin and water in the tap-room, let us follow old Flint into the presence of "Count Schmidt."

A servant introduced the old lawyer into the drawing-room.

But no one was there.

He looked about at the elegant apartment for some time, and was wondering who or what Count Schmidt might really be, when he turned sharply around and confronted his own son.

"What! Joel!" shouted the old man, in tones of triumph.

"Silence!" said Joel. "I am your son no longer. Mind, while here, I am the Count——"

"I see! I see it!"

"See what?"

"You have robbed me, Joel! You have secured all the treasure!"

"And why not? Who has a better or a greater right?"

"But you have not killed those boys, Joel."

"No, nor is there any chance of doing so. I have gone through a world of adventures since I saw you last; but both Tom and Frank escaped me. They are in Mexico."

"May the sea swallow them!" said the old man, fiercely. "If you had only managed to poison them!"

"I tried, but without success."

"Why not insult and quarrel with them, fight a duel and kill them that way?"

"It is all very well for you to talk in that manner. Frank Ford is not such a fool as you imagine him to be. He has killed one man in a duel to my knowledge—the most famous duellist in all Italy; how many more beside I cannot say. He and his brother are perfect fire-eaters! No, no, you don't catch me picking quarrels with such fellows as those."

"But could you not have procured their death in some way?"

"I endeavoured to do so a dozen times. He was in the hands of the brigands once or twice, but instead of them doing what I bargained for, the captain's daughter fell in love with him, and he played the devil with the band."

"You got the treasure safely?"

"I did."

"And have not expended much, I hope?"

"If I have, what's that to do with you? I can do what I like with my own."

"Your own? Why, you young villain, it's all mine."

"Possession is nine points of the law. As a lawyer, you should know that well enough."

"Where is it, I say? Where is it? Have you safely secreted it, or is it all squandered?"

"That is my business. I did not ask you to come to me that you might quarrel. I might never have made myself known to you as your son had I been so minded, for Count Schmidt I might have remained to the day of my death, and you would not have been any the wiser; but it was to lift you up out of your misery that I spoke to you. And now that you discover who and what I really am, you are not content to take a share of the spoil; but must fain want all. Oh, no, old man, I am no longer your dutiful son in such respects. I shall look after myself first, and you afterwards."

"True, Joel, true. I might never have discovered you had you not made yourself known."

"Be content, then, with receiving a part," said Joel, "and let us leave England at once. At least you must do so, for from all I can hear, the hounds of the law are after you, and never will they rest until they have shed your blood."

"Ah! me!" said the old lawyer, "it was a cursed hour in which I fell across old Jonathan.

"'Tis no use repining about the past, the present is what we have to look to. Time flies—each moment is precious. Will you start for Holland at once—to-night?"

"But why this hurry, my son?"

"Because I know more of this world than you do, old as you are. And am convinced that if you remain forty-eight hours more in England, you will be arrested and cast into prison.

"And you? What are you going to do?"

"Stay here until I have tidings of Tom or Frank Ford. I shall never rest until I have had revenge!"

"Well said, Joel; well said. That Frank was always a tyrant, I hear."

"Yes, he was; but I will punish him, and hurt him in the tenderest spot of all."

"How do you mean?"

"Why, marry Nelly Lancaster."

"Impossible!" said the old man, in high glee. "What! my Joel to marry the rich banker's daughter?"

"There are more unlikely things than that," said Joel, with the air of a man who thinks very highly of himself.

"Why, my son, you astonish me!" said the old man.

He sat down in deep thought for a few moments, and trembled violently—so much so, that Joel was alarmed.

"What is the matter?" said he.

"Nothing, nothing, Joel, nothing."

"Why turn so pale?"

"For *your* sake."

"My sake?"

"Aye; for yours, my son."

"Explain yourself."

"You have heard me speak of Warner?"

"Yes I have, but I do not wish to make his acquaintance for all that."

"Never fear," said the old man, still trembling; "I should never introduce you to such a villain as Warner; he is a murderer, at least, in heart he is so."

At the word murderer, Joel also turned pale, and bit his lip.

At that moment, it seemed as if both father and son could have torn out each other's heart, so inflamed were both with hellish passion.

"What makes you look so pale, Joel?" asked the trembling, old man.

"Nothing, it was merely a passing qualm."

"You would not feel offended if I ask you a question, would you?"

"Ask as many as you like, only be quick; I can't be dawdling away my time here with you."

"Do you know what this same Warner says of you."

"Of me? What can such a fellow know of me?"

"He pretends to know much more than I ever did."

"Indeed."

"Yes, and when speaking of old Ford's murder, he accuses——"

"Whom?" said Joel, suddenly.

"You."

"Me?"

"Aye, you."

"He lies in his heart, the base scoundrel. Where are his proofs?"

"He will swear to it."

"What, old man, are you, too, turned idiot?"

"No, Joel, I am not turned idiot. Warner says, and swears most solemnly that he would recognise you again, and the clothes you then wore, even the disguise of Caspar's cloak and mask."

"Caspar's cloak and mask," said Joel, turning pale. "Were they found?"

"They were."

"By whom?"

"By Warner, I believe, in the first instance, for he says he found a letter in a side-pocket of the cloak."

"D——n!" said Joel, in a hot rage. "You must be raving, old man."

"No, Joel, I am not; I fear me that the officers are more after you than me."

"You are an old dolt," said Joel; "and, if it is only to whine and snivel that you come here, why, you had better depart at once."

"Pity a father's feelings, my son."

"Better attend to your own, I think," said the young man, with a coarse laugh; "it would do you much more good. Will you leave England if I give you sufficient money to do so?" said Joel. "I ask you for the last time; if you do not accept my offer I must leave you to your fate."

"You would banish and transport me then?"

"Would it not be better than to be dogged night and day by the police?"

"I confess it would."

"Then, you agree?"

"I do."

"Then, sit down, and let us talk over matters calmly and quietly," said Joel.

"A gentleman below wishes to speak to you, Count Schmidt," said the servant, entering.

"What sort of a gentleman?"

"An oldish-lookish person, sir."

"Show him into the small drawing room."

The servant did so, and went below to the regions of the kitchen again.

While he was gone this gentleman boldly walked upstairs, and listened at the door to what was going forward.

Joel and his father were quarrelling and using very high words.

"They are talking about money matters, I hear, so it is about time I think to have something to say in the same matter."

Without knocking, he entered Joel's apartment, to the great astonishment both of father and son.

"Who and what are you, sir?" asked Joel, in an angry tone.

"Your friend or enemy, as the case may be."

Old Flint trembled in every limb, for he had a suspicion that the intruder was disguised, and not in his natural appearance.

"How dare you, sir, make use of such language in my place," said Joel.

"Dare, eh?" grinned the stranger.

"Yes, dare! Speak, quickly, or I will have you arrested; the police shall be made acquainted with you."

"And you also," said the stranger, "if you don't keep a civil tongue in your cheek."

"Me, sir? What does the impudent fellow mean? Have *me* arrested? Why, know you who and what I am?"

"Oh, yes, I know all about you," said the stranger, "and perhaps better than yourself."

Joel Flint, in a passion, would have attempted to use violence on his strange visitor.

But the old man begged of him to be calm.

"You came lately from Italy, I believe?" said the stranger.

"I did. And what of that?"

"Your present name is that of the Count Schmidt?"

"My name, sir, has always been the same. I have never had cause to disown or change it."

"Perhaps not," said the stranger, chuckling. "Who is that old man there, who looks so pale and trembles so much?"

"A visitor on business, if you will pry into my affairs."

"Why don't you say your father, at once," the stranger laughed; "the resemblance in ugliness is so great that no one would be mistaken in taking you for what you are."

"It is not my father, sir!"

"You are labouring under a mistake; it *is* your father, but you are ashamed to own him, and he is or was a lawyer, and his name is Flint."

Father and son looked at each other in astonishment; but at last Joel, mustering up all his courage, said,

"And pray what is your errand here?"

"To get some money."

"From whom?"

"Why, both of you."

"And why? For what, pray?"

"Because I have earned it, long ago."

"This man must be an escaped lunatic," said Joel; "I will soon rid the room of his disagreeable presence."

He walked up to the mantel-piece, and took down a revolver, and was about to turn round, when the stranger pulled out two pistols, and levelled them at the heads of both father and son.

"Stir," said he, "and I will blow your brains out, both of you."

Joel put down the revolver, and turned pale, for he was a braggart, and not a brave man.

"Do you know me now?" said the stranger, throwing off his wig and false whiskers.

It was Warner!

## CHAPTER CXII.

A SANGUINARY BATTLE IN MEXICO—THE FRENCH SLAUGHTER THE MEXICAN IRREGULAR SOLDIERY—FRANK FORD'S ACCOUNT TO HIS BROTHER TOM.

"DEAR TOM,—Since my last letter I am sorry to say that squabbles have entered into the council of the Mexican leaders, and, as might be expected, disasters have befallen them.

"I gave my counsel honestly to them, and advised them not to force or accept a pitched battle with the French, for it cannot be expected that raw levies like those we have here can cope with the disciplined forces under Marshal Bazaine.

"All my good advice, however, has been thrown away.

"Fight the French they would in the open plain, and dearly they have paid for their temerity.

"The Mexican forces, under the leadership of Juarez, moved out of Monterey to encounter the French force, and were thoroughly beaten.

"I was not there myself, but have learned all the particulars from a French officer, who was taken prisoner by a scouting party of our Boy Soldiers some six days after the battle.

"I cannot do better, then, than to give you in substance the Frenchman's account of it, leaving you to deduct a little on account of his lively imagination.

"During the night of the 27th the whole army was in motion to march against the Mexicans.

"For several days General Juarez had waited for us in the plains before Medellin, having previously surveyed, with the help of engineers, the advantageous position where his army way stationed.

"The Mexicans, to whom pitched battles had

# THE BOY SOLDIER; OR, GARIBALDI'S YOUNG CAPTAIN.

A LITTLE BIT OF FRIENDLY ADVICE.

"P-o-o-r fellow!" sighed Morris, shaking his head. "And so you are to be married to-morrow?"

"Yes."

"And your father is to give you a very large dowry, I hear?"

"Quite true."

"But, Lady Emma, for the sake of that friendship which my lord, your father, entertains for me, let me ask, do you know quite enough of this man you are going to marry?"

"Mr. Morris, I do not understand you."

"I mean, have you known him quite long enough?"

"I have been acquainted with him for three months; but he has known *me* for over a year, he says, and followed me about like a shadow."

"So *he* says, I suppose."

"Yes; but, then, you know the family of Duncoff is very ancient and noble, and is of great renown in Russia."

"So *he* says. But what does my lord say?"

"Nothing."

"Well, then, Lady Emma, let me ask one question. Have I not, in a thousand ways, served your father?"

"You have."

"And do you suppose that I could for a moment entertain any wish or desire that would willingly give him pain or displeasure?"

"No, Mr. Morris, I do not; except for your great sagacity and intelligence my father would have been a ruined man long ago. But why look so serious, Mr. Morris?"

"Because, my lady, I have serious matters to talk about."

"Indeed! Any which personally concern me?"

"Exactly so."

"And what, pray?"

"You must *not* marry this Russo-Dutch baron."

"Must not?"

"No, you must not; he would cause your ruin and unhappiness."

There was something in the manner of Morris which the lady did not admire.

And, feeling offended at what seemed to her to be his over officiousness, she abruptly left the room.

"Well," said Morris, "and now the game begins

in earnest. Who is this Baron Duncoff? Do I know him or not?"

"He is here, if you wish to ascertain that fact for yourself," said the baron, proudly, as he entered the room in a lofty manner.

Morris, for a moment, was very much confused, and scarcely knew what to say.

But, recollecting himself again, he rose and bowed politely.

"You seem to be a very great friend of the family," said the baron, "and assume the airs of one who pretends to have authority in the household."

"No more authority, believe me, than what my lord freely accords me."

"Oh, indeed! And does he consult you, then, on his most important affairs?"

"That is my business, and not yours."

"I don't know that," was the baron's proud answer. "Do you know that I am about to marry Lady Emma?"

"I do."

"And you have been speaking to her about the eligibility of the match?"

"I know not what authority you have for saying so, sir," Morris replied, getting red in the face.

"I heard as much.'

"Perhaps *over* heard as much," said Morris.

"Sir, I am no eavesdropper."

"How otherwise could you have heard what I did or did not say concerning you, then?"

"From the lady herself."

"Indeed," said Morris, annoyed.

"Yes, from the lady's own lips. And now let me tell you, sir, that, had you not been a particular friend of the family, I should have kicked you out of doors."

"You are very obliging, truly."

"You laugh, sir."

"I do, Baron Duncoff."

"And why, pray? Do you know who and what I am?"

"Yes, certainly I do; you are a man, that's all, and so am I. But before you begin to kick anybody out of the house, you should remember that Englishmen can play at that game as well as fortune-hunting Dutchmen and Germans."

"Why, the fellow is absolutely insulting me!"

"I always answer people according to their true merits, baron."

"And my merits, sir, you appear to think lightly of?"

"You speak the truth; I do."

"Know you not that my family is noble, rich and ancient?"

"That may all be; but a family crest, baron, does not make a man noble. It is his actions; and from what I should judge of your actions, I doubt very much if you ever did a really good one in all your life," said Morris, laughing.

"Come, come, you must be joking," said the baron, attempting to laugh.

"No, I am not."

"And why should you judge so?"

"From your face."

"My face? Why, I am reputed to be a very handsome man!"

"'Fine feathers make fine birds.'"

"And what is it you see in my face you do not like? Come, now, I am disposed to be amused."

"And perhaps annoyed, baron."

"How so?"

"If I told you what I really think, you would be very much annoyed."

"I cannot see the force of your remark."

"Well, then," said Morris, "I will explain. "Your eyes are deep and cunning."

"So, so. Go on; I am all attention."

"Your mouth is thin-lipped and revengeful."

"What next?"

"Your forehead is low and receding."

"Which indicates what?"

"That you have not much brain."

"But what little I have got is of a good sort, I suppose?"

"Yes, baron, good—nay, very good of its kind."

"And what kind, pray!"

"A very bad kind."

"Come, come, you are *provokingly* absurd, but yet very amusing. And so you think these points are not in my favour?"

"I do not."

"And where did you study physiology, my friend? You seem to depend much upon it."

"I do, and always have done so; and never was mistaken in the looks of an honest man yet."

"This time excepted."

"No, baron, not even on this occasion. You ask for my opinion, and I freely give it."

"And what is it, in one word?"

"That you are a very bad man—nay, even a rogue!"

The baron began to laugh quite heartily at Morris's opinions, and, while doing so, my Lord Rattletrap came in.

"You are merry, baron," said he.

"Yes, and who could be otherwise, my lord, with such an amusing person as this Mr. Morris, your old friend?"

"Why, what is the subject of conversation, then?"

"Why, the fellow has been reading my character, and pronounces me—what do you think?"

"I know not; something very distinguished, no doubt."

"A rogue, sir—a vagabond, sir. And not a whit less."

And the baron laughed very heartily at what had been said.

Yet Morris looked stern and serious.

"Come, come, friend Morris," said my lord, when the baron had retired, "you have been making rather too free observations on my intended son-in-law."

"Do you think so?"

"I am sure of it. I saw his flushed cheek when he left the room."

"He would not be flushed at all, then, my lord, if I had not spoken something near the truth."

"You ought to apologise."

"I never will, and, more than that, I would advise you to break off the match."

"Why, the wedding takes place this very day by license!"

"Then I, for one, don't like it."

"What objections can you have? Is he not rich and handsome? Is not his family very great? And does not Emma love him dearly?"

"That may be all true, and it may not. Had Lady Emma loved Harry Steinbeck, her old and faithful lover, instead of this baron, her happiness would have been certain."

"Oh! Harry Steinbeck! don't mention his name, my friend. He is not only very poor, but a great radical, I hear; besides, I want to add lustre to my house in this marriage."

"If Harry is poor he jeopardised his life more than once to save Emma; and if he is now a bit of a radical, as you call him, whose fault is it? Who was more exemplary than he before you denied him the house, my lord? If Harry had not riches, he had talents; if he had not an ancient family crest, he is of good blood, and noble natured."

"That may all be, Morris; but speak no more of such a matter, he is forgotten."

"Not by Lady Emma, I think, my lord."

"Yes, I think so; and even if the recollection is not quite gone, why the giddy whirl of high life will drive it from her head."

"Never," said Morris.

"Never?"

"No, never, my lord. She may say she forgets him; but she cannot. No woman could ever forget such a gallant fellow as Harry Steinbeck."

At this moment a servant entered, and announced that the little magistrate was desirous of speaking a word or two on very important business."

"Admit him," said my lord.

He was glad that the conversation about Harry Steinbeck was interrupted.

Emma and Harry at one time had loved each other very greatly.

But my lord broke off the acquaintance, simply because Harry was not of a titled family.

He had had his own suspicions that his daughter even now had a liking for the handsome youth, but her marriage, he thought, would put an end to that romantic idea.

In a moment the little magistrate entered the apartment in great haste and flurry.

"What is the matter?"

"Matter! my lord, matter! no end of matter."

"Then explain yourself."

"I have this moment received a despatch, post haste from London, informing me that there is every reason to believe that the notorious Jack Dingles is at this moment in Windermere."

"Impossible!" said my lord.

"Nay, very, very possible indeed," said Morris, smiling.

"Where is the despatch?"

"Here, my lord, read it."

"Who brought it?"

"A young gentleman of handsome exterior."

"And his name?"

"Harry Steinbeck."

"I am surprised."

"And so am I, my lord."

"And have you conferred with the local constables?"

"It is no use I fear, my lord."

"They are too stupid to be of any use in this case," said Morris, with a dry laugh. "It would take the rural police a whole year to get on the scent of such a rascal as Jack."

"This is very unfortunate," said my lord. "The marriage ceremony must not be postponed on account of this news, however."

Some directions were given in writing, by my lord, to the little magistrate, and he left the apartment to superintend all that was necessary about the marriage ceremony.

"Let me look at that," said Morris, snatching the instructions out of the magistrate's hand. "Let *me* look at it," he added, in a laughing manner.

"Well I never! Who ever heard of such impudence in all their lives? Why, this fellow must be mad."

"No I am not mad," said Morris, laughing; "and to show you that I have got my wits about me, look here."

At the same time he tore up my lord's written instructions into a hundred fragments.

"The devil!" said the little magistrate, turning pale in astonishment; "the devil!"

"Come my friend," said Morris; "leave this matter in *my* hands."

"Your hands!"

"Yes, mine."

"It strikes me, my fine fellow, that you know more about this famous rascal than you'd like to be known."

"So I do."

"I thought so; and, perhaps, then, you are the very identical person?"

"Silence," said Morris, in such a sudden manner that it startled the little man considerably. "Silence! and be guided by me."

"And who the devil *are* you, I want to know?" said the little man, in great surprise.

"In less than an hour you shall know. Come this way; let us be present at the marriage ceremony."

Morris and the little man sauntered into the drawing room.

When they arrived they found the attorneys busy with their papers, and arranging them on the table.

A minister was there also, ready robed, to perform the ceremony of marriage.

The baron and Lady Emma stood side by side.

"Now, my dear baron," my lord began, "we will first sign the marriage settlements, and immediately afterwards his reverence here will perform the religious ceremony."

"I am quite ready and willing, my noble father," said the baron, "for this is the happiest moment of my whole life."

"I am very glad to hear it," growled Morris.

"What did you say, Morris?"

"Nothing, my lord."

"Why, yes you did; I heard you myself," said the little magistrate. "I never saw such a man in all my life; he's always saying or doing something he ought not."

"You look frowning, my friend," said the baron, to Morris.

"Do I?"

"Yes. And why, pray?"

"Because, to tell you the truth, baron, I am right sorry to see such a lamb united to such a wolf as you are."

"The man is mad, baron, quite mad, I assure you, baron," said the little man, in confidence.

Duncoff had no time to make a reply, for at that moment my lord said,

"Now, baron, we will begin business. Here are notes to the value of £50,000, which I give you as my daughter's dowry, and I hope that, by your prudence and sagacity, they may get in time treble their value."

"Thanks, my lord, thanks," said the baron, as he pocketed the bundle of notes in a very careful manner.

"See how the devil grins at the money," said Morris, half aloud; "I thought his eyes would start out of his head."

"Now, my dear daughter," said my lord, here is the pen; sign the marriage contract."

For a moment or two Lady Emma seemed very much confused, and hesitated.

She seemed to be very faint.

While my lord and the baron were talking apart, Morris approached Lady Emma, and whispered—

"If you don't love him, do not sign the contract."

"I must."

"You can refuse; it is not too late even now."

"I dare not; it would be worse than death to my father."

"Never mind that; consult your own happiness. Think of Harry Steinbeck."

For a moment Emma seemed irresolute.

But at last she rose, and, approaching the table, signed the contract and then sank into a chair.

The baron's turn now came, and he was about to sign his name, when Morris said, in a loud tone,

"I forbid this marriage!"

"You, sir?" said my lord, in a great passion.

"Yes, *I* do, my lord; this is not the Baron Duncoff—I do not believe it is he."

"Can you prove what you say, insolent fool?" said the baron. "Beware how you speak in your madness."

"I don't believe you are the baron at all," repeated Morris, in an indignant manner.

"Were you not in the presence of ladies, sir," the baron replied, "I would strike you to the earth."

"These interruptions, Mr. Morris, are unaccountable," said my lord.

"Quite so, sir, most rascally and impudent," said the little magistrate; "that's what I have told the fellow a dozen times to-day."

"I care not what you say, my lord, and I care not what people may think, I still assert that this person cannot be the true baron."

"Cannot, stupid fool?" said the baron, red with rage, "cannot? Would you have proof?"

"I would."

"Can you read?"

"Yes."

"Then read *that*," said he, placing a document in Morris's hands. "That, you impudent, vulgar fellow, is my name, title, and pedigree, written and signed by myself, and, as you see, if you are not blind, is counter-signed and sealed in half-a-dozen different places by the various foreign consuls in Holland, who have known me and my family for years."

"Quite true," said my lord, "quite true, baron. "I have read the document through and through, and am perfectly satisfied of its authenticity."

The baron bowed.

"And my daughter also. Is it not so, Emma?"

"It is, my noble father," Lady Emma replied; "I have read the document, and am perfectly satisfied with its authenticity."

Morris hung his head like a man who had committed some grave fault.

"Are *you* satisfied, my inquisitive friend?" said the baron, advancing towards Morris, with a supercilious smile upon his countenance; "are you satisfied, my friend?"

"No, nor shall I ever be," said Morris, proudly. "I know that both my lord and his daughter are infatuated with you, but I am not. I know in my heart that you are an impostor, and nothing in the world shall make me think otherwise."

These words were spoken in a low tone of voice.

No one heard them save the baron himself.

From that moment there was a deadly hatred between Morris and Duncoff.

Any judge of human nature would have seen in the eyes of each a revengeful fiery glow.

"Come, baron, sign the marriage settlements," said my lord.

Duncoff went to the table and signed the contract.

As he did so Morris glanced over the baron's shoulder, and then burst out into an uproarious fit of laughter which astonished every one.

"He has signed the document truly," said Morris, "but *not in the same handwriting as his family deeds!* He is an impostor; it is not Baron Duncoff, he is Jack Dingles! I know his handwriting. To become possessed of this family deed he must have been the man who murdered the true baron on the road to Windermere!"

"What!" exclaimed my lord; "not the same writing?"

And he looked first at the signature in the marriage settlement, and compared it with the record of the Duncoff family.

"It is not the same writing," said my lord.

"Not by a long deal," said the little magistrate, in great excitement. "There is some mystery here."

The would-be baron turned all manner of colours and would have dashed out of the room, carrying with him Lady Emma's dowry, which he had in notes in his pocket.

But on the instant he was seized by the little magistrate, Harry Steinbeck, and Morris, and firmly held.

"You have got the odd trick, Morris," said Jack; "it is no use of denying it. I am not the Baron Duncoff."

"I knew it," said Morris. "No one else but Jack Dingles?"

"The same."

"Then I arrest you on the charge of murdering the real Baron Duncoff," said Morris.

"As you like," said Jack, crestfallen and annoyed. "I have all along been playing for a very heavy stake, but lost. I came very near doing the trick; but you out-played me. I am tired of life; do with me whatever you please."

Jack Dingles was led forth, handcuffed, cast into gaol, tried, sentenced, and soon after hung at York Castle.

"But what became of the daughter, Lady Emma?" said Tom Ford.

"She ultimately married Harry Steinbeck," said Gale, "and my lord, through his influence at court, managed to have the title and estates revert to Harry Steinbeck upon his own demise."

"And it was proved, then, that this desperate fellow actually did murder the true Baron Duncoff?"

"Yes; Jack Dingles stopped at the same road-side inn one night whereat the baron was putting up. He learned everything he could about him, and waylaid him, stopped the carriage, drove off the coachman and footman, killed the owner, and appropriated all his goods and valuables."

"What an audacious scoundrel!" said Tom. "But what did my lord do for Mr. Morris?"

"He gave him a very handsome pension for life, and so did the government, and, as you will say, he richly deserved it."

## CHAPTER CIV.

### GALE RELATES ANOTHER OF THE DETECTIVE'S STORIES.

"BRAVO!" said Tom, when Sergeant Gale had finished his narration, "bravo, for the clever fellow Morris. Let us drink his health in a bumper, Mr. Gale."

"With all my heart, Captain Tom," the officer replied.

"And is he living now, Gale?"

"Yes, and doing well."

"Not in the 'force,' I suppose?" said Tom.

"No, he has retired many years ago."

"Well, good luck to him, say I, wherever he is."

"And so say I also. Most people, perhaps, might look upon what I have now told you as a bit of fiction; but it is not, for truth is stranger than fiction."

"And so I believe," said Tom, "for I have had experience of many things of a like nature, which, if told to the many, would not be believed; but I know of facts which have come under my own knowledge equally as new and strange as the story you have now told."

"I have no doubt of it," Gale replied. "But, I have not told you the best story yet. There is another one which Morris related far superior to that."

"Indeed!"

"Yes."

"And what is that about?"

"Why, he saved a young nobleman from ruin, and even from death."

"You don't mean that?"

"I do, though."

"How?"

"I'll tell you if you'll only listen patiently; and, after this story, we'll both go out together, and see if we can fall across this Warner or old Flint."

"Agreed."

THE YOUNG NOBLEMAN AND THE DETECTIVE.

Well, then, one night Morris and I were sitting in Bow Street, warming our toes before a roaring fire.

The night outside in the streets was filthy dirty, and the rain fell in torrents.

I didn't have much to do with detective cases then, for I was much too young, and hadn't been in the force very long.

But, I liked Morris, for he was a quiet, shrewd, brave fellow, very gentlemanly in his manner, and few would have taken him to be a detective, and one of the best in all the world.

He was, in truth, a gentleman, who had become suddenly reduced in circumstances, and all through the knavery of a gang of sharps, who had ruined him.

He could speak and write French and Italian almost as well as he could English.

Well, while he was sitting before the fire on the night in question, the inspector called him into his private office, and—

"Morris," said he, "I have got a very particular job for you."

"What is it?" said Morris.

"Well," said the inspector, "I can't explain it very well, but here is a card; you see the direction upon it; go to the address, and you will there learn all particulars."

Morris took the card.

It was a beautifully enamelled bit of pasteboard, and on it was engraved a coat of arms.

The name on it was the "Countess Frimley, No. 190, Grosvenor Square."

"A countess," thought Morris; "what the deuce do they want a detective in Grosvenor Square for?"

A moment's reflection might have convinced Morris that rich people are sometimes as great rogues as poor ones, and require the services of the "force" occasionally on matters of great importance.

But, then, in the case of the rich, these affairs are so "hushed up," that the common people and the newspapers seldom or ever hear of their evil doings.

Morris went home and dressed himself in his very best.

It was past nine o'clock when he got to Grosvenor Square, and he rang the servants' bell, rather too loudly, for "Jeames," the footman, looked amazingly angry, and puffed out his cheeks and breast with any amount of pride as he opened the door, and said—

"Well, and what do you want? who are you?"

"What is that to do with you?" said Morris, "and how dare you ask me?"

"Jeames" was slightly taken aback by Morris's cool manner, and eyed the detective very carefully from head to foot.

"Well, sir, and what is your name?" said Jeames, bursting with curiosity.

"Find out," said Morris. "Take this note up to her ladyship instantly; I will wait here for an answer."

"I have no doubt you will," said Jeames. "Did you expect to be asked into the drawing-room, then, eh? ha, ha!"

The footman went upstairs with the note.

Presently he came down, all smiles, and began to bow to the detective as if he had been the Sultan of Egypt.

"Will you please to walk upstairs, sir?" said the flunkey, blandly; "her ladyship will see you in the small drawing-room."

"Will she?" said Morris, with a comical grin that almost abashed the footman. "Then show the way, fellow; I will follow."

"Fellow, sir, fellow," the footman began.

"There, don't stand there chattering and bobbing like a parrot; show the way, I say."

Jeames showed the way.

His pride was hurt.

Directly the drawing-room door had closed on Morris, "Jeames" shook his fist, as much as to say, "I only wish you'd call me a 'fellow' out of doors, that's all." And he struck an attitude outside on the landing, as if he were about the pleasant operation of punching the stranger's head.

"The Countess Frimley, I believe," said Morris, bowing.

"The same, sir; and your name is ——"

"Morris."

"The same person who is mentioned in this note?"

"Yes, madam."

"There is no mistake, I hope?"

"Not the least, madam, I assure you."

For a moment the countess looked sideways at the visitor, as if she could not believe that such a well-spoken, well-dressed person really could be a detective officer.

For a few moments she seemed to hesitate and knew not what to say.

She endeavoured once or twice to begin the conversation, but did not exactly know how.

"I suppose that the inspector, sir, has told you everything?"

"No, my lady, not a word."

"Well, then, as you are an officer, I might as well say that I have sent for you to speak regarding my only son, Charles."

Morris bowed.

"He is not quite twenty years of age yet, and I fear he has fallen into the hands of — the snares of ——"

"Very wicked people, I have no doubt," said Morris, quickly, "and, as a mother, you would like to see him rescued."

"That is just what I was about to remark," the countess observed.

"Oh, that is nothing new; I can assure your ladyship such cases come under our notice continually; therefore, my dear lady, you need not have any fear or reservation in speaking to me fully on the subject, for such communications are always inviolable secrets.

"So I have heard," the countess remarked, coldly.

But she did not at that moment imagine it possible that "inviolable secresy" was one of the virtues possessed by the detective force as a body.

"He is an only son, sir," the countess went on, "and during the last twelve months has squandered a great deal of property—property which really is not his own as yet, and will not be until he arrives at the age of twenty-one."

"I understand, my lady; he may have got into the hands of the Jews, and you, perhaps, desire to recover some of the money which they have in polite terms fleeced him of?"

"No, sir, I do not think he has been borrowing much. I fear my son's case is worse than that."

"Indeed, my lady!" said the detective, in surprise, but with a smile, added, "I think, my lady, there are few things which could befal a young gentleman of fashion much worse than falling into the hands of grasping money-lenders."

"I fear, sir, that Charles has been seduced into the company of gamblers."

"Oh, indeed!"

"It is not so much to recover what he has lost, sir, that I care, but I am naturally desirous to see my only son rid of such company."

"Very natural, my lady; very natural indeed."

"I am certain that within the past year he must have lost £10,000 in gambling."

Morris shook his head.

"He has spent this amount, as he thinks, unknown to me, and were it not for a mere accident, I might never have come to the knowledge of it.

"I am very sorry to hear this, my lady, for I fear we shall never be able to recover a tenth part of this loss."

"I do not care for the money," the countess repeated; "if he had spent twice that sum I should not have minded his ways, if such an amount had only been spent in some legitimate way. It is for his honour and standing as a gentleman that I am concerned, Mr. Morris, for I have reason to believe that he has, at times, when in want of money, actually taken certain family jewels of great value, and made away with them."

For a moment the countess did not speak, and could scarcely refrain from tears.

She handed a photographic likeness of the young man to Morris.

"And you have not, of course, the slightest idea of where your son goes to?"

"No, not in the least."

"He is out very late, you say?"

"Yes, he comes in at all hours of the morning."

"Does he often go to the opera, my lady?"

"Yes, he is very partial to music, and always was."

"That is all I want to ask, my lady, for since you have given me his portrait, I could find him out among a thousand."

"And do you think you have any hopes of reclaiming him, sir?"

"Yes, my lady; at least, let me hope so."

"I would go to any expense, you know, in order that he might be rescued from these wicked men."

"It will not cost much, my lady."

"But your expenses will amount to something, and of course, as this case is strictly of a private and confidential nature, I will provide for every necessary outlay."

Morris bowed.

The lady went to a writing-desk, and gave him some thirty sovereigns in gold, and some half-dozen five-pound notes.

"This, perhaps, may be sufficient for the present," said the countess.

"Thanks, my lady," said Morris, bowing; "and now that you have told me all, there is one thing I would particularly impress upon your ladyship."

"Name it, sir."

"Do not, by any means—no, not to your most intimate friends—ever whisper a word about this transaction; it must remain a dead secret between us."

"Very well, sir."

"And no matter what I do—when I come to this house, with your son, my lady, which I perhaps may sometimes do, as his friend—do not, I say, even by look, intimate that you have ever seen me before."

"I will not; good night."

Morris bowed and retired, saying,

"I will communicate by letter, my lady."

Directly he reached the hall door, he said, in a loud tone, to "Jeames,"

"When do you expect Charles to return, fellow?"

"Charles?" said "Jeames," in astonishment at the stranger's freedom of manner, "Charles, sir? The Hon. Charles, I suppose you mean?"

"I mean what I say, fellow. Charles, I repeat; my friend Charles, when do you expect him to return?"

"Very early, sir; very early."

"Tell no lies! You do *not* expect him very early, and you know it."

"Sir."

"Don't stand there sir-ing me," said the officer; "you know he seldom ever returns before daylight."

"Upon my honour, sir——"

"There, that will do, don't tell any more lies. Of course you always tell my lady that he returns early—it is your policy to do so, but you know he does not for all that."

Morris looked "Jeames" strait in the eyes, and the footman was abashed.

"Does it rain?" asked Morris.

"It pours."

"Then go and call a cab."

"Me, sir?"

"Yes, you, do you hear? Go and call a cab instantly."

"Me, sir, in all this rain? Why, it would spoil all my livery."

"Better so that than lose your situation, I think," said Morris. "Go this instant, I repeat, or I will return to the drawing-room and inform the countess of your insolence."

The flunkey was amazed.

He knew not what to do for a moment.

But he looked at the determined face of the officer, and did as he was told.

Through the pouring rain he went, and soon returned with a Hansom cab.

Morris jumped into it.

"Jeames" tried to listen to the directions given to the driver, but could not hear a word.

"No doubt the young radical has gone to the opera," thought Morris. "I'll go and change my dress and drop in for half an hour at Her Majesty's Opera House."

Morris was driven home, and in less than half an hour he came forth from his own house dressed in the approved manner, and alighted from his cab as gaily as any nobleman in the land.

He did not appear to take much interest in the performance, but gazed round the house.

He could not see any one in any way like the Hon. Charles Frimley.

He was thinking what might be the best thing to do next when laughter from one of the boxes attracted his attention.

He turned round, and, at a single glance, perceived there were two persons in the box.

One was none other than the young gentleman he was in search of.

"But who's the other, I wonder?" thought Morris.

He levelled his opera-glass at the other person, and in a moment felt satisfied.

It was "Con" Williams, or, as he was generally called, "Captain" Williams, one of the most unscrupulous gamblers and cheats in all the world.

"So, that's it, eh, Con?" thought Morris. "You are plucking the 'pigeon' very nicely, I perceive, and the Honourable Charles has no notion of your real character.

"I must be very careful how I proceed in this matter," thought Morris. "This Con belongs to a desperate band of scoundrels, and might murder me if they knew who and really what I was.

"But, then, they don't," thought he. "It is many a good year since he and his friends 'plucked' me out of a hundred or two, and they'll never expect I am other than a gentleman of means from my dress and conversation."

For a moment a red flush came over the face of Morris as he remembered how, long ago, this same Con Williams cheated him out of his money at cards, and afterwards turned round and laughed at him.

"Never mind," thought Morris, "I always imagined that I should have revenge out of him in the long run, and now I am in a fair way of getting it; but if they only suspect, if they have the very shadow of a doubt about me, I am a gone man, therefore, I had better arm myself with a revolver against all emergencies, for I have no desire to be stabbed in the dark by any of his French or German friends."

So thinking, Morris left the opera-house, and went to his lodgings for a revolver, and soon returned again.

But, this time, he did not go into the pit, but walked boldly round to the box wherein he had seen the Honourable Charles Frimley in company with this so-called "Captain Con Williams."

As luck would have it, the door of the box was on ajar, and he could hear the "Captain" and Charles Frimley conversing.

"You were very successful last night," said Charles.

"Well, yes, perhaps so; but to no great extent. See how *you* have won occasionally; why, you are the very devil at cards; but you can't expect to win always, though."

"No, certainly not; but, I have had a fearful run of bad luck lately."

"Oh, never mind, better fortune next time. I'll give you revenge to-night, if you like."

"No, I don't think I shall play at all to-night."

"Why not? Why, come, man, you are not going to desert us in that way, I hope? Who knows *I* may be the loser to-night?"

"Well, I don't mind having a game or two; but for a small stake, mind. I can't afford to lose any more thousands, you know."

"Certainly not; but it was all perfectly fair and honourable, you will admit?"

"Yes, oh, yes."

"It was luck, my boy, mere luck."

"Was it?" thought Morris, as he listened, and a fiendish grin flitted across his face. "Was it all luck though?" thought the officer, "I don't know so much about that; we shall see."

He entered the box, to the no small surprise of the "captain," who, after a quick look, recognised the new comer.

"Beg pardon, sir," said Morris, bowing to the Honourable Charles, "I beg pardon for intruding; but I recognised in your companion an old friend I have not seen for years."

"Why, Morris, my dear fellow, how are you?" said the "captain" shaking the new comer by the hand. "I heard you were dead."

"Dead! no; I'm better than ten thousand dead men."

"Glad to see you, my friend, very glad," said the "captain," introducing Morris to the Honourable Charles Frimley. "I had not the least idea of ever seeing you again. When did you come up from the country?"

"To-day."

"Oh! indeed!"

"The old gentleman died lately."

"What! your rich uncle you used to speak of?"

"Yes; and left me £30,000."

"Well done; come, that isn't very bad news, is it, Charley?" said the captain, thus familiarly addressing the young nobleman.

"No, by Jove! quite the contrary. I wish some one would leave me half that amount, I shouldn't grumble."

"Nor me neither," said the captain, laughing. "You are married, I suppose, Morris?"

"Oh, yes, and steady, very steady; no more larks bout town for me, you know."

"Oh! of course not!" said the captain, laughing heartily. "A man with £30,000 can't afford a night or two in frolic; but you shall, my boy, shan't he, Charley?"

"I should not object to your friend's company, by any means," said the Honourable Charles, yawning. "Anything you like; I'll make one."

"Well said," Williams replied. "Let's leave this dull affair, and go over to some snug coffee-room I know of. We'll have a jolly good feed, and afterwards—why, anything, or anywhere you like."

Captain Williams left the house, followed by Morris and Charles Frimley.

They went to the supper-room, and the "captain" ordered a very fine and savoury supper, which Morris partook of with great relish.

He had not enjoyed such a repast for many a long day, and, therefore, did ample justice to it.

The only excess he guarded against was that of drinking, or mixing his wine.

"And so fortune has turned up 'trumps' once again, eh, Morris?" said the "captain," picking his teeth. "Well, I'm deuced glad to hear it, my boy."

"I dare say you are," thought Morris, who, from the captain's sparkling eye, imagined, and truly, that the sharper was planning some game to ruin him, as he had done years before.

"It is a very long time since I have seen my old friend, Morris," said the captain to the Hon. Charles, "but I can assure you there wasn't a gayer fellow about town at one time than he was. He threw his money about like sand," said Williams; "and as to fast horses, and the like, there wasn't one to compare to him."

"So much the worse for me," thought Morris; "but I hadn't the sense I have now, as the captain will soon find. I was totally ruined through this same cool-handed villain, and myself and poor wife reduced to the utmost and most abject poverty;

and all through card-playing and drugged wine. But my hour of revenge is drawing nigh."

After supper, the captain proposed a "cosy little game" of cards.

"Only one game you know," said he.

"Well, just as you like," said young Frimley; "but only one game, mind."

"Oh, of course, only one."

"Well, I shall go home," said Morris.

"Oh, don't say that, my friend," Charles remarked. "If *you* don't have a game *I* won't."

"I never play now."

"Oh yes, you do," said the captain, with a sly wink at Morris, as much as to say, "Come, have a game or two, I'll take care you don't lose anything."

After much persuasion, Morris went with them to a noted gambling-hell, in one of the by-streets near the Strand.

The captain stopped before a dark-looking house, and gently knocked twice.

There was not a light to be seen in any of the windows, but Morris carefully noted the number of the house.

After a moment the door was opened.

All three gentlemen entered the passage.

The captain and Hon. Charles Frimley were quickly recognised by the servant.

"But who is this gentleman?" said he, approaching Morris. "What does he do here?"

"He," said the captain, "is an old friend of mine."

"Indeed; oh, then, I beg pardon. I thought he was an intruder, you know. I know the gentleman's face well, somewhere, but cannot call to mind how, or when, or where."

"The devil you can," said the captain, laughing. "You are much cleverer than most people, then, for he has only just arrived from the country, and hasn't been in London for several years before."

The servant then shut to and bolted the front door.

He next touched a bell that communicated with some room upstairs.

On the instant Morris heard the heavy bolt drawn of a second door in the passage, and the way upstairs was clear.

Morris laughed at the precautions resorted to by the gamblers, but the captain laughed as he said—

"We are more particular now than we used to be, you know, Morris; the police can't get in upon us before we are prepared for them."

"So I perceive."

"The front door is opened, and unless the visitors ars are well known, or introduced by some one who frequents the place, the second floor is not opened at all. That little bell you heard communicates with the principal card-room upstairs; one ring signifies that all is right, three rings alarm every one; the card, dice, dominoes, and the like are destroyed, so that if the police do come upon us they cannot discover aught on which to convict us."

These particulars were given to Morris by the captain in a whisper, and the officer smiled.

They all went upstairs.

In the front room on the first floor were some half-dozen card-tables lit by gas lights.

Frimley and the captain were quickly recognised and welcomed.

But several black-whiskered, fierce-looking foreigners rose from their seats, and narrowly scanned the features of Morris, and were not fully satisfied as to him until the captain whispered to one of them in French.

"All right, an old 'pigeon' of mine; he's immensely rich, come in for a terrific fortune. Use him gently for a night or two so as to drown his suspicions."

A significant nod was the answer.

After much coaxing Morris consented to sit down and have a game or two with the foreign-looking rascal that the captain had whispered to.

The captain himself was deeply engaged with young Frimley at a side table.

Morris had perfectly understood what Williams had whispered to the Frenchman.

As a matter of course, then, Morris was allowed to win several games, and ere an hour had elapsed he had put twenty or thirty pounds into his pocket.

"This will do very nicely," thought Morris; "they will let me win like this for a night or two in hopes that during the week they may completely fleece me at one sitting; but I'll take care they don't, though. It is a game of diamond cut diamond now, and I am the sharpest of the lot."

The Hon. Charles Frimley, however, was not so lucky.

He lost heavily, and began to get very angry, and drank a deal of wine.

Morris was so close to him that he heard all that was said, and, more than that, he could plainly see that the "Right Hon. Captain" was cheating him.

This was more than he dared to insinuate, however.

It would have been more than his life was worth to have hinted such a thing in the company of such a room full of black-legs, sharpers and desperadoes.

It was past two o'clock in the morning ere the Hon. Charles Frimley rose from the card-table.

He was very much the worse for drink, and staggered about.

Morris had taken a little, and pretended to be intoxicated also, but, as we know, he was not so.

A cab was called, but ere it came the Hon. Charles sank into a chair, and looked the very picture of a desperate youth who has lost his all.

Morris pretended to be sleepy, and sat in a chair likewise.

"How did you and that countryman, Morris, get along together?" asked the "captain" of the French-looking gentleman.

"Oh! very well. I did as you told me."

"How much did you let him win?"

"About £30."

"Rather heavy; but we shall be sure to get it all back in a night or two."

"How do you know that?"

"As I have said before he has been left £30,000, and has come up to town to draw it. He can't do so, however, until a day or two."

"I see; I see."

"We will let him win once or twice more, and, when we know for certain that he has drawn his money, why, then——"

"We'll fleece him of every penny."

"Just the plan I wish you to act upon, but you must draw it mild with him just at first, for I have plucked him once several years since, and he might tumble to our game if we are in too great a hurry."

At that moment the cab was announced.

Morris volunteered to see the Hon. Charles to his residence in Grosvenor Square.

They both got into the vehicle as best they could, and it drove off.

"You'll come to-morrow night, Morris?" said the captain, as they parted.

# THE BOY SOLDIER; OR, GARIBALDI'S YOUNG CAPTAIN.

DON'T KNOCK: I HAVE THE KEY!—(*See next Number.*)

"Oh yes," said Matty, "I have often seen him and Barney together."

"Up in your room?"

"Yes."

"And did they send you out of the room for anything?"

"Yes, for beer, and pipes and gin."

"The cabby can drink a great deal of gin, I hear?"

"So he can, Mr. Gale, more than any half dozen old washerwomen I have seen in my whole life."

"And you didn't catch what they were after?"

"No, sir; but I always thought it very funny that he should have taken such a liking to Barney all at once."

"Did you ever listen outside the door, Matty?"

"Listen, Mr. Gale?" said Matty, grinning.

"Why, yes; all women are fond of listening at times."

"Well, I did listen once, Mr. Gale. They say eavesdroppers never hear any good of themselves."

"Nor did you, I suppose?"

"No, I didn't; for I heard the old cabman say he didn't like the 'cut of my jib,' and advised Barney to get me 'lagged' out of the way."

"Did you hear nothing else?"

"Oh, yes; I heard the cabby talking of the night of old Mr. Ford's murder, and about some things which Barney gave him to pawn or sell."

'What things were they?"

"A set of silver knives, forks, and spoons."

"That belonged to Old Ford?"

"Yes, I always supposed they came from the Red House."

"And did he pawn them or sell them?"

"Yes, he pawned them, or at least the cabman did."

"Fo r how much?"

"For several pounds."

"Where?"

"At a Jew's in Shoreditch."

"The name?"

"Emanuel, I think."

Gale put the name down in his note-book, and appeared much pleased with the information.

"Well, what else?"

"Why they quarrelled over the money. The cabman swore he had lost the ticket, and therefore Barney couldn't find out how much they had been pawned for."

"Very clever of cabby, very," said Gale.

"Oh, he's an artful dodger," said Matty, "but he wasn't quite quick enough for me."

"How's that?"

"Why he used to pump Barney about me, and then on the quiet would turn round and try to pump me about Barney."

"I know the gentleman very well," said Gale; "he has been a long time running about loose, but

PUBLISHER'S NOTE.

PP. 306-313 AND PP. 330-331 ARE MISSING.

he'll fall into my hands ripe enough one of these fine mornings."

"Well, if he does I should feel very happy, for he's been the cause of many a girl getting transported."

"Indeed."

"No doubt about it, Mr. Gale; for when he sees a drunken gentleman in company with some fast woman, he winks to the girl, gets them to ride in his cab, and when the girl leaves it for a moment to get soda and brandy for her companion, Mr. Cabby perhaps drives off, robs the gentleman, puts him down anywhere, and then if there is any bother made about it he blames the girl, gives her discription, swears against her, and all that, and then the poor wretch gets transported."

Matty's face was all a-glow as she spoke these words.

But Gale only bit his lip, as he said—

"What's become of all Barney's pals, Matty?"

"Most of them have turned him up, Mr. Gale," said Matty.

"But do you mean to say he has been working without them for the last few months?"

"Oh, no; he's got quite a school of young 'uns, who met at the 'Cock and Bottle' every night."

"I know that; he's the teacher."

"And gets the most of any one."

"Trust him for that," said Gale, "it is the way with them all. But what I meant to say, Matty, is this; have *all* his cracksmen pals thrown him over?"

"No, there's two who used to work with Barney."

"What's their names?"

"Bandy Bob and Alf Green."

Gale put these names down in his note-book, as well as the address which was—

"No. 29, Ash Alley, Whitechapel."

"Have you seen either of them lately?"

"No; they never came to my place."

"But Barney used to meet them though?"

"Oh, yes; and the cabman also. I saw them all one night in the tap-room of the 'Cock and Bottle.' They were alone; and Barney was chalking out something like a house on the table. When I went in, there was none there but themselves, and Barney made a blow at me with a quart pot for daring to interrupt him. They were making out a plan of some house in the country."

"How do you know it was in the country?"

"Because I heard Barney say one night that he and Bandy Bob were going away bird catching for a few days."

"How long were they away?"

"Four days that time."

"They brought a lot of birds home with them, I suppose?" said Gale, grinning.

"No they didn't though; not one."

"Did they go again?"

"Yes; the next time they were away three days; and the next time only two days; but then the last time they rode home in the cab."

"You are sure of this, Matty?"

"I am."

"How do you know that the cabman was with them the last time?"

"Because his wife came to my place bullying, and swore that he and Barney were up to no good together, and that if she liked to open her mouth she could transport both of them."

"But have you no other proof?"

"Yes; the cabby and Barney got dead drunk the night they came home, and boasted of what a jovial time they had down in Kent."

"Very jovial, I dare say; had they much money?"

"Yes; they both appeared to have plenty of coin."

"Did Bandy or Alf come with them to your place?"

"No; they sent a boy to say they would wait in the tap of the 'Cock and Bottle' until Barney and the cabby went to them. The cabby began to swear, and said if he was Barney he wouldn't give them a penny, for they hadn't done the job as they ought to have done—they hadn't made a clean sweep of the lot he said."

"A clean sweep were his words, eh?"

"Yes."

"But he went to them, did he not?"

"Yes, and a rare old quarrel they had over the money."

"What did you suppose the money came from, Matty?"

"I didn't know for certain, Mr. Gale; but I thought, nay, made sure they had been up to some robbery or other."

"I know they had been," said Gale, laughing. "I know all about it."

"Then why ask me, Mr. Gale?"

"Because I am not quite ready with the case, Matty, that is all."

"You won't bring me into it?"

"No, Matty. You are safe enough; but let me ask, did you ever find out who they sold their plunder to? It wasn't to old Moss, was it?"

"No, I think not."

"Then, to whom?"

"I don't know as how they sold anything, but I only guess so."

"You guess right, then. They sold a very valuable lot of goods, but to whom is a dead mystery as yet."

"I heard Barney say as how old Moss had always swindled him, and he wouldn't go there any more, and the cabby said in a whisper,—'Why not try old Hautwig the smasher?'"

When Gale heard this name, he seemed greatly astonished.

"Old Hautwig," said Gale, several times. "Are you certain of that?"

"Yes, positive."

"I never thought that."

"It is true, though."

"And are you sure old Hautwig *is* a smasher?" said Gale.

"Why, of course he is."

"I never heard that before."

"No, but *I* did."

"And was Barney mixed up with him in the smashing line?"

"Yes, and Bandy Bob, and Alf Green also."

"But they never did anything of that sort in London, I think, Matty, or else the officers of the Mint would have been on their track long ago."

"No, Mr. Gale, I don't think as how they passed off bad money in London much, but——"

"Oh, I see, they 'worked' the country."

"Yes, at fairs, and all such places."

"Very good; go on."

"Old Haulwig is one of the leaders. When there are no fairs in winter, he stays at home, at his rag and bottle warehouse, doing the thing very nicely as a good 'fence,' but in the summer he is always off with his friends to the country fairs."

"A very clever dodge," said Gale, smiling. "They can pass off their base metal better on the yokels than on cockneys."

"So they say, and in the hurry and confusion of the fair, no one stops much to examine his change."

"Is old Haulwig rich, then?"

"He is, or ought to be," said Matty; "for I've heard Barney say he's been up to his capers for the last ten years."

"The devil!"

"I'm certain he is rich," said Matty, "for I heard Alf Green say as how the old man thought of retiring from business."

"From business, eh?" said Gale, smiling. "A pretty business it is, surely; perhaps he'll have to 'retire' somewhere else if he's not very clever," said Gale.

After a pause, Gale asked,

"And Barney used to travel with him, eh?"

"Yes; Hautwig, and some one else had shares in a sparring booth."

"And Barney, of course, was one of the principal boxers?"

"Oh, yes, he thought himself very clever with the gloves."

"And what part did Bandy Bob take?"

"He was in the 'swim' with old Haulwig in the thimble-rigging dodge."

"And of Green?"

"He did anything that was wanted."

"A very pretty rogue, indeed," said Gale, laughing; "but it strikes me very forcibly that I must put a stop to this nice little game of theirs; they little think that at this moment they are 'wanted' at Bow Street."

"But you won't split on me will you, Mr. Gale?" asked Matty.

"No, my girl, I have no such intentions I can assure you. On the contrary, you will receive £100 reward if I am only successful in capturing these vagabonds."

"I didn't tell you all this for money, sir."

"No, I know you did not, my good girl; but these rascals are all more or less concerned in the affair of old Ford, and a large reward is offered for each and every one."

"I should like to see Barney transported," said Matty, "for he has been a great villain towards me."

"And to many others besides you, Matty."

"I will go in search of this old Hautwig," said the officer.

"I don't think you'll find him at home, sir."

"Why not?"

"Because it is summer time now, and there are lots of fairs on."

"So there are, Matty."

"Greenwich Fair used to be a rare place for old Hautwig."

"Perhaps he and his pals are there, then?"

"More than likely."

"Then, keep your own council, Matty, until my return."

"Where are you going, sir? When shall I see you again?"

"Perhaps to-morrow or the next day. I am now going off to Greenwich Fair."

So saying, Gale placed a sovereign in Matty's hands, and left her.

## CHAPTER CVII.

DETECTIVE GALE GOES TO GREENWICH FAIR, AND KEEPS A SHARP LOOK OUT FOR OLD HAUTWIG AND OTHERS.

On passing down Cannon Street, dressed in an excellent disguise, the first person that met Gale was an athletic, surly, hodman-looking fellow, walking up and down with a large placard on his back, on which was displayed in large letters, the words "Greenwich Fair."

"Greenwich Fair, ma'am; Greenwich Fair, sir," growl the placard bearer, as he stared in the face of every one passing by.

"Has the steam-boat started yet?" asked Gale, in the tone and with the manner of a countryman.

"Not yet, sir, not yet; but it's just on the point of starting; you'd better make haste and get your ticket. Down that narrow lane, sir; you'll find the boat at the bottom."

"That ain't the right boat, sir," said an opposition agent; "*this* is the right way."

"No, it ain't," said the first. "You do as I tells you, sir, and you'll be all right."

"Don't go on their boat, sir," repeated the opposition agent, "they are overcrowded, and will sink."

"Don't mind him, sir; he's telling you all lies; *our* boats are the best and safest on the river."

Gale seemed to enjoy the joke.

He was shoved and hustled about first by one and then by another of the opposition agents, and laughed right heartily as they swore all manner of things at one another.

"This way, sir!"

"No, that way, sir!"

"We only charge sixpence!"

"Ours is a gentleman's boat, and we charge ninepence!" said the other.

After a great scramble between two agents, who, at last, from very high words got to downright fighting, Gale went down the narrow lane towards the sixpenny boat, thinking, as it was cheaper, he would have more fun than on the other.

Rare fellows are these clever detectives for fun or frolic, and well they may be.

All the money they spend is paid back to them, and with interest; therefore, when they are out on "business," which also means "pleasure" as well, they are very free-handed, and delight in nothing better than to have a jollification on the quiet, and mix with noisy holiday-making crowds.

The sixpenny boat had its steam up, and was ready to start that moment.

It was crowded with persons.

There was scarcely standing room, so dense was the mass on board.

Some were laughing, smoking, singing, and shouting.

Girls tittered, and seemed very happy in the company of their sweethearts.

Servant girls, apprentices, and errand boys; fathers and mothers, with their children, all were huddled together above and below, so much so that the hands on board could scarcely move about to man and work the vessel.

Some had bottles and glasses, others large baskets filled with eatables.

All were calmly drinking, or doing something to amuse themselves; nor must it be forgotten that the everlasting fiddle and harp were there also, which were performed upon by two red-nosed individuals, with shining hats, who appeared to have lived for the past half century on pennyworth's of fried fish and half-pints of gin.

What these two musicians played no one cared to know.

The only thing remarkable was that at the end of every tune the fiddler would go round among the passengers, and shove his hat under the nose of every one present, and, as one fellow said, "couldn't be choked off," under any consideration.

Nothing in particular occurred on the voyage down the river, except that a young, foppish-looking fellow, who had too much to say, lost his best beaver, and was unmercifully joked, laughed at, and jeered by dozens of rollicking boys and apprentices, who were sucking oranges, smoking penny pickwicks, and the like.

"Vy don't yer take off yer tile, young 'un?" asked one in a bantering tone.

"He can show his false curls, now," said another.

"What a fine 'ead o' 'air he's got."

"Like bristles," another grunted.

"He's quite the dandy, oh! He's quite the dandy, oh!" sung out another.

After a pleasant run down the river, the overburdened vessel, puffing and groaning with its human freight, stopped at the pier, and great was the rush of all on board to get on shore and hurry to the fair.

As Gale, full of fun, approached the scene of the fair, he soon became convinced that "three shies a penny" was one of the chief amusements of all.

Within half-a-mile from the fair, Gale counted no less than forty of these "Old Aunt Sallys'," and every one of them appeared to be up to their eyes in business, and a very profitable business it seemed to be, for Gale never saw but one man at the forty stands who managed to knock down a cocoa-nut or doll.

Gale, as he was on business, as well as pleasure, took care to have his eyes wide open, on the look out for Hautwig, Bandy Bob, or Alf Green.

He therefore sauntered about the forty "three shies a penny," or "old Aunt Sallys'," as they are now called, but he did not see either one of the persons he was in search of.

"Can *I* try at any o' the sticks I likes?" asked a tall countryman, of a proprietor of one of the "Aunt Sallys'."

"In course you can," said a rough, hairy-capped fellow. "Any on 'em you likes, squire. Give us your brown, and here's the three sticks."

"May I throw at the middle one, with the cocoanut on it?" asked the countryman.

"Jest w'ichever you pleases, young man."

"Well, then, I'll have a go. Here's the penny, and give us the sticks. Get out o' the way, there," said the countryman, tucking up his sleeves, and spitting on the palm of his hand, as if he were about to slay a young ox.

The young countryman "took deadly aim," so to speak, at the cocoa-nut, and knocked the stick from under it.

"It's in the hole, upon my soul!" said the rough-looking proprietor.

"Come, let's have none o' that 'ere," said the countryman. "I have knocked it down, and it's mine fairly enough."

"Well, I'm blamed!" said the proprietor, "you *is* green, and no mistake."

"Whoever heard o' such a thing?" said another

The countryman could not for a long time see why he should not have the cocoa-nut, and scratched his head for an idea.

"Try again, sir; better luck next time, sir."

The yokel tried again, and threw the remaining two sticks with such force through the air, that the proprietor of the "Aunt Sally" got rather frightened.

The countryman missed, of course, and was in a great rage thereat, and swore most lustily.

"Try another penn'orth, squire," said hairy-cap; "better luck next time."

"You can't expect to win always, you know, squire," said another; "try again."

The countryman bought three pennyworth of sticks, and began to throw them with great force, and without the slightest judgment, at the pincushions, cocoa-nuts, and the like, to the great amusement of the bystanders.

But with all his endeavours, he did not win a farthing's worth.

"Try agin, sir, try agin; there's nothing like pluck, my young squire."

"He couldn't hit a hay-stack, I think," said hairy-cap, laughing.

"Couldn't I though?" thought the countryman, who had overheard the last remark. "Couldn't I though; I'll let you all see."

Mr. Hairy-cap began to bob up and down, gathering the sticks, and laughing at the "yokel," when the countryman gave one more penny, received three sticks, and at the first shy split a cocoa-nut into a hundred pieces, most of which flew in the face of hairy-cap, and before any one could say a word, he threw a second time, and the stick came into such a violent collision with hairy-cap's ribs, that it made him howl again.

"Give me my cocoa-nut," said the countryman.

"I'll give you a punch in the head," said Hairy-cap, "if you you ain't off."

"Will you, though?" said the countryman. "I don't think you will. You are all a parcel of cheats."

At this, Hairy-cap "put up his hand," and set about thrashing the countryman, aud a regular fight ensued among the bystanders, most of whom took the countryman's part.

But in less than five minutes the countryman gave the bully such a hiding, that he was glad to get out of the row.

"I think I have seen that countryman before," said Gale, to himself. "His face looks familiar to me."

In less than five minutes after Gale had left the spot, the countryman overtook him.

"Ain't your name Bagshaw?" asked Gale.

"Yes," said the other.

He was a detective.

"What made you take notice of that hairy-capped fellow for?"

"Oh, for fun, that's all," said Bagshaw, grinning.

"Fun, eh? I don't think there is much fun in fighting such a ruffian as he appeared to be."

"Perhaps not; but you don't know him as well as I do. Last year, he and two others were very near cheating a gentleman out of £100 at thimble rigging; but because I put a sudden stop to their pretty little game, they got two bullies I did not know, to waylay me, which they did, and almost killed me into the bargain."

"And that's how you take your revenge."

"Yes, and a very good way, too, I think."

"Didn't he know you again?"

"No, not a bit. I am too well disguised. You didn't know me at first, I think."

"I did not. You take the character of a young countryman to perfection."

Bagshaw laughed as he said,

"I came down to-day thinking that the hairy-capped gentleman would be up to his old game of thimble rig; but I am disappointed. I've got it for him if ever I get a chance."

"Has he got any pals?"

"Yes, he has three or four. Barney, a half-bred fighting man, used to work with him, besides a bandy-legged cove they call Bandy Bob, and another whose name is Alf Green."

Gale did not make any remark.

"We must not be seen together," said Bagshaw.

"No, quite right. Are there many of our men down here?"

"About a dozen, in all sorts of disguises; some are dressed like swells, one or two are countrymen like myself; there is one half-washed blacksmith among us, and several others. But what brings *you* down here, Mr. Gale? Especial business, I suppose?"

"Yes, very important business."

"Will you want any assistance?"

"No, I think not; but if I do, what is the 'password' among our men, so that I may know them."

"'Squally,' is the word. If you get into any difficulty say that one word, and half the police upon the ground will be around you."

"Thanks," said Gale. "But what are all of you up to down here? Is there anything in particular on hand?"

"Yes."

"What?"

"Last year there was a lot of base coin put afloat at this fair, and we haven't been able to trace the gentlemen ever since."

"Haven't you had suspicions?"

"Yes; but could never make anything out of them."

"Perhaps I might be able to enlighten you on that point," said Gale.

"Indeed!"

"Yes; but not now. If you see me in the fair about nine o'clock to-night, and I give you the wink, follow me."

"I will."

The two detectives separated.

Whichever way Mr. Gale went his ears were assailed with deafening noises.

Some were shooting at targets for nuts, others were firing with rifles; shows were everywhere.

Organs were playing, the proprietor of the "Fat Boy" and the only "Living Giant" was beating on a gong.

The circus, with its band of music was playing away, "the learned pig," "the calf with three heads," "the ring-tail swing-tail monkey," "the crocodile from the Nile," "the living skeleton, who played upon the banjo and sang songs," "the wild bull from the wilderness, which had taken ten long years to tame," "the miraculous dwarf, who would turn, move, and dance about in a doll's house;" these, and a thousand other things, were shouted in your ears whichever way you went.

The "bearded lady," the "man with four eyes," the "white bear" from the Polar Regions, the "baboon" from the jungles of Africa; each and all these wonderful things and personages were painted on flaming canvas outside.

One showman was shouting against another till both got almost black in the face.

"They are now coming out," shrieked one, with staring eyes, while his partner began to bray through a brass horn, and beat on a big drum.

"Walk up! walk up! just in time, ladies and gentlemen, just in time! we are now just about to commence!" roared a fat man, who had wonderful "performing dogs." "Just in time! just in time! and for the small charge of one penny; one penny only to see the most wonderful feats in all nature."

The circus performers in another part were swinging on slack ropes.

"An "Indian queen," just from Calcutta, was about to dance on the tight rope; but they did not say that she came all the way from St. Giles's.

Signor Browni, the strongest man in the world, and Morris Hercules Sampson Johnsoni, his rival opposite, were balancing chairs, iron bars, cart wheels, and the like, to give a taste, or insight, of the performances inside their respective establishments, which performances altogether were forgotten when the customers got inside.

The travelling theatre, with a dozen or more of painted and extravagantly attired performers strutting about like kings and queens, and the poor, broken-winded clown tossing and rolling about, seemed to be the great centre of attraction.

"Hamlet" and "Richard III," with "Ophelia" and "Queen Anne," danced a polka together.

The "Brigand of the Black Forest" and his mortal enemy, the "Murderer of the Danube," were drinking a pot of beer together behind the money-taker's door.

"Be in time! be in time!"

"Just about to commence!"

"They are now coming out!"

"Only one penny!"

"The small charge of one halfpenny."

These were the shouts and cries on every hand, which, mingled with the discordant sounds of drums, and organs, trumpets, hurdy-gurdys, Punch and Judy, and the din of half-a-dozen brass bands, made the fair into which Mr. Gale entered a perfect Babel of confusion.

Boxing or sparing booths seemed to be extensively patronised; and outside stood men in flannel shirts and hairy caps, or tight trousers and capacious coats, who, with hands to mouth, roared out—

"Yer you are, gents! yer you are! Come and see young 'Stony, the Smasher,' and the 'Terror of the Dials' set to! They are just about to commence! Walk up! walk up!"

Then the proprietor, a bull-headed, thick-necked, sturdy, red-faced fellow, would step forward with a speaking-trumpet, through which, with pudding-looking cheeks, he bawled with all his might—

"This way, genelmen, this way, this way; come and see the noble hart displayed by the best talent in all England. Men who have fought, and can fight again. Walk up and look at the 'Pimlico Annihilator.' We have the finest stud of boxers in all the world; men of all weights and sizes can be accommodated—walk up—walk up."

And having tired himself, the "Annihilator," the "Smasher," the "Terror," "Young Stingo," and "Old Bouncer," would successively show themselves to the public, and shout with stentorian lungs, each moment in danger of bursting some blood-vessel, or having their heads knocked off.

But in all his walk through the fair, Mr. Gale had not as yet discovered the objects of his search.

Bandy Bob and Alf Green were nowhere to be seen.

For many hours Gale sauntered here and there, first into this show, and then into another, without finding Hautwig or his friends; and he almost began to think that, perhaps, Matty might have been mistaken in what she had told him.

The fair towards night became densely crowded.

Thousands from London and other places poured in by trains and boats, until at last it was scarcely possible to move about at all through the dense mass of holiday-makers on every side.

Gas-lights, candles, links, torches, in fact every sort of light was now used to illuminate the different shows and stalls.

People, drunk, were rolling about here and there.

Fights were of frequent occurrence, and the jargon of tongues—shouts, yells, and screams—on all sides were more than deafening, they stunned a person.

Yet the fair was at its height, and as night went on, the confusion, uproar, and unearthly din became greater and greater each moment.

Everywhere Gale went, gambling was going on at a furious rate.

Whether for large or small sums, it was all the same; those standing around seemed to be unusually excited at the losses or winnings of their friends or acquaintances.

Roulette, hazard, wheels of fortune, and other games of chance seemed to be greatly patronized, and whenever a secluded spot could be obtained for the game so as not to be seen by the police, "thimble rigging" was in full sway.

Gale, with a sharp eye, soon detected one of these spots, and walked up towards the players in a cool, unconcerned manner and looked on.

His simple attire and more simple manner threw the gambling gentlemen off their guard.

"Who lifts the thimble that kivers the pea this time?" was the everlasting question of the proprietor of the pea, the three thimbles, and the small common deal table upon which the game was played.

And, as he thus challenged the company to "try their luck," he moved about the pea and the three thimbles with almost marvellous dexterity.

But what surprised Gale most of all was that the owner of the gambling apparatus was none other than the person he was in search of, namely, Bandy Bob himself.

Gale looked about among the crowd, but could nowhere see Alf Green.

"Who'll make a bet? Who'll make a bet?" said Bob, shuffling the pea about. "Who'll make a bet? Anything you likes, gentlemen, from a 'tanner' to a 'quid.'"

"I knows which thimble it's under," says a greenhorn, in a half-whisper, to a friend.

"Are you sure?"

"Certain, could swear to it."

"Then what a fool you are not to bet."

Thus appealed to, the greenhorn stakes half-a-crown.

Bandy Bob lifts the thimble which the greenhorn had chosen, when, strange to say, no pea was there!

The countryman was thunderstruck.

He could have staked his life that the pea had been under that thimble a moment before.

And yet it had vanished!

"Try again, gentleman, try again; it's all the fortune of war. You can't expect to win every time; try again; better luck next time."

In a moment afterwards a stranger pushed his way towards the table, and laid five shillings.

The thimble was raised.

It was there!

"Here's the money, my gallant friend," said Bob, throwing down a five-shilling-piece; "I'm always willing to pay when I loses, but would rather win, of course."

The "gallant friend" tried his hand once or twice more, and to the amazement of all won each time, and more than before.

The yellow, shining, gold-looking pieces, however, which Bandy Bob threw down, were not sovereigns or half sovereigns either, as Gale quickly perceived.

They were only "dummies," yet they looked so much like genuine coin, that few would have detected the difference by candle-light, save Gale.

But the detective was as sharp as a hawk.

He understood all the tricks of the trade as well as the gamblers themselves.

"So that's your little game, eh, is it, Bandy?" he thought. "Well, I won't disturb you yet awhile, but have some fun out of you."

He cast his eyes round, and perceived Alf Green, who had joined the crowd that moment.

Alf was dressed very stylishly, and seemed to be in league with the person who had won several times before.

"I'll try the metal of these gentlemen," thought Gale.

"Won't you have a try?" said Bandy Bob, addressing Gale; "it is all fair here, I assure you."

Gale did not answer, but rattled a handful of silver in his pockets, as if in hesitation whether to play or not.

Alf Green and his friend heard the sound of the money, and it made them very uneasy.

Alf approached Gale, and said,

"Suppose you and I go halves and have a try; we can't lose it; I'm always very lucky at that game."

"I dare say you are," said Gale; "but I always like to play alone."

With that he advanced towards the table and staked a crown.

He lifted the thimble.

The pea was under it.

"Suppose you go half a sovereign next time," said Bob.

"I don't mind," said Gale.

And he staked his money and won.

This surprised Master Bob and all present.

But Bandy was satisfied to lose a trifle in order to draw on the stranger to play for still higher stakes.

"Suppose we go higher," said Bob.

"With all my heart," was the reply.

Gale now staked five sovereigns, and, despite all he could do to the contrary, Bob lost.

He rose from the table as if shot.

"Why, how the devil is this?" he growled. "The pea wasn't under that thimble at all."

"Yes it was, yes it was."

"We saw it."

"All fair, governor, all fair," said the crowd.

"Go on, and win all he's got," said many; "he's won enough from us; now let him lose a little."

"I say it isn't fair," said Bob, striking the table. "The pea wasn't under that thimble at all!"

"Yes it was! yes it was!"

"We saw it!" shouted the crowd.

"Then, which thimble is it under?" said Gale, laughing. "Let some one in the crowd lift the other two thimbles and see."

"Aye, aye, that's fair enough!"

"Nothing could be fairer!"

"I object!" said Bob.

But before he could perceive it the other two thimbles were raised, but the pea was under neither.

Bob knew this well enough, for when he had raised the first thimble he very cleverly extracted the pea from under it without being perceived by any one.

But Gale knew the trick of old, and quite as cleverly had placed another one under it.

It was this that alarmed Bandy Bob.

He knew that he had extracted the pea himself in the first instance, and at the moment that Gale had made his five pound bet there was no pea under either of them, for he himself had it that moment in the palm of his right hand.

But he did not dare to tell the crowd of it, or they would have smashed his table, and, perhaps, have half killed him.

He looked and stared at Gale, but could make nothing more of him, for the detective had won every shilling he had.

At that moment Bob winked at Alf Green, and, at the same moment, slapped his pocket, telling him in plain words that he was short of money.

Alf understood the sign, and hurried away.

In a short time he returned, and, without being perceived, handed a very bulky purse to Bandy.

This was perceived by Gale.

"Now come the dummies," thought the detective. "I wonder where they get it from? I must find out."

"Well, old man," said he, "are you going to play, any more?"

"Look here, my friend," said Alf Green, nudging Gale. "I want to speak to you."

They left the crowd and went some distance apart.

"Was that little game of yours in fun or in earnest?"

"What little game?"

"Why, placing a second pea under the thimble."

"In earnest?"

"Ah! I see; you are too clever by half."

"Am I?"

"Yes. Why do you come around robbing us of our money in that way for?"

"Robbing *you?*"

"Yes, me."

"You are in partnership, then?"

"It doesn't matter whether I am or not," said Alf Green, surlily. "Why do you and your friend come robbing poor, hard-working people, for, then?"

"It ain't robbing."

"Yes it is; and for two pins, I'd call the attention of the police to you."

"You had better not."

"Why, not."

"There are too many of us, and besides, we have 'spotted' for the last half-hour."

"You might 'spot,' as you call it, for a whole week for all I care," said Gale.

"Are you going to play again?"

"I don't know; why?"

"How much will you take to square it, and not play any more?"

"Oh, about a pound or two."

"Well, then, here it is," said Alf, giving him two spurious coins, which looked very much like sovereigns.

"Can't you give me some silver for one of' em?" said Gale.

"Yes, I don't mind," said Alf.

And he took the counterfeit sovereign, and gave Gale several pieces in pewter metal instead.

After a few moments of further conversation they separated.

"Very good," thought Gale, "I have won some good money, and I have also got a good many counterfeits, both from Bandy and Alf."

He walked away chuckling to himself as he said,

"Now, if I could only find out old Hautwig, and pounce upon his base metal, I should do very well."

At that moment, and while standing in the shadow of a booth, Gale perceived Alf Green conversing with a long-faced, cunning-looking old man.

"That must be Hautwig," he thought.

When the two friends had separated, he followed the old man, and found out that he occupied a travelling van, around which a vast crowd of persons were gathered, admiring some flaring canvas pictures, whereon was painted a group of barbarous North American Indians, who were fighting over some handsome girl.

At the door stood a loud-mouthed fellow who was describing the great attractions of the show inside.

"Real wild Indians, gentlemen, every one, the greatest novelty of the age; can never be tamed, and have to be fed twice a day on raw beef, like animals in the Zoological Gardens. Walk up, walk up—be in time. Hear them rattling their chains, ladies and gentlemen; hear them rattling their chains? No humbug about this; they have to be stirred up with a red hot poker before they'll obey. Walk up, be in time, be in time! and for the small sum of one penny."

When he had done old Hautwig took up the strain and described the immense cage and stout iron bars which had been made expressly for these North American Indians.

At the same time, to excite the curiosity of those outside still more and more, one of Hautwig's gang came out upon the steps of the waggon, and flourished a red hot poker, which he said would be swallowed by one of the Indians.

A thrill ran through the crowd, and the red hot poker argument was so very powerful that crowds rushed up the steps.

"Be in time! be in time, ladies and gentlemen, be in time! the last time to-night, positively the last time, and the only occasion for the next forty-eight hours in which the Indian chief will swallow the poker. Hear the chains rattling, gentlemen! hear the chains! real chains, gentlemen! real poker! real Indians! Walk up! be in time! at the low charge of one penny!"

Gale mixed among those who were going up the steps to see the show.

Many of them gave old Hautwig half crowns, florins, shillings, and sixpences to change, and so much hurry were they in to secure good seats in order to see the "red hot poker trick" that they took little notice of what sort of money the old showman returned to his customers.

Gale pretended to be reeling drunk, and when he clambered up the steps he presented a good sovereign to old Hautwig, who gave him 19s. 6d. in bad money, and fivepence in copper.

"Very neatly done," thought Gale, as he staggered into the show. "Old Hautwig little knows who I am, or he would swallow the red hot poker himself."

But, as he expected, the real, live, barbarous North American Indians in their iron cage was all an imposition.

The "Indians" were real live specimens of humanity from the Seven Dials.

But they were painted and trimmed up in a very extraordinary manner, and, in all truth, looked very hideous indeed.

They were chained up in their iron cage, and pitched the chains about very noisily in order to get up a good effect.

When touched by sticks or canes, they screamed and howled most awfully, and jumped at the iron bars (left loose on purpose), and shook them with such energy that many of the simple spectators thought it was all real.

After going through some performance, not worth mentioning, and after listening to five minutes' description of the "wild men," and the enormous price Hautwig had paid for their capture, their ferocious habits, and such like, the curtain was let down upon the "savages," who returned immediately to their pipes and beer.

The door was thrown open, amid loud cries of—

"They are now coming out! they are now coming out! Ask them if they are not satisfied! If any one is not so, he shall have his money back! Be in time! be in time! we will show once more to-night! Be in time! be in time!"

And thus old Hautwig continued his show for two or three hours longer.

But, meanwhile, Gale was laying his plans to capture the whole lot of swindlers.

He sauntered through the fair, never, for a moment losing sight of one of them; and, from all appearances, old Hautwig was doing a flourishing business with his real wild North American Indians, and passing of a great amount of spurious coin.

## CHAPTER CVIII.

IN WHICH THERE IS A SUDDEN COMMOTION AMONG THE WILD AMERICAN INDIANS—HAUTWIG PERFORMS THE RED HOT POKER TRICK.

THE fair had closed, and it was past midnight.

The poor clowns who had been jumping about all the live-long day, and endeavouring to attract the notice and patronage of admiring audiences, had tumbled for the last time.

Mr. Merryman, in the circus, to use his own phrase, was "regularly done up," and another "flip-flap" was not in him.

In truth, save here and there an expiring faggot or flickering lamp, all the fair was wrapt in slumber, or behind the scenes were regaling themselves with beef-steaks and beer, after the arduous labours of the day.

Gale went his rounds through the deserted fair, and after dodging about for some time, he got under old Hautwig's caravan, and secreted himself.

Hautwig, and his real wild North American Indians (now, of course, liberated from their chains, and captivity), were enjoying themselves over an Irish stew, and from the clattering of plates, and the continual roars of laughter, Gale began to think the wild Indians, after all, were jolly, jovial sort of fellows, and were humbugging the credulous public to very great advantage, both to themselves and old Hautwig.

"Pass along some more o' that 'ere stew," said one of the Indians. "I likes it amazin' well."

"Didn't we take in the greenhorns?" said another.

"A rare old thing we made on it to-day, Hautwig," said a third.

"Ah!" said the proprietor of the show, with a deep sigh, "all ain't gold that glitters, my lads; it ain't because you sees the show full o' people every time that we are making a good thing on it. No, not by any means."

"Oh! that's always the tale," said one.

"It don't matter how much you make, you is always losing," said another. "I never see such a chap as you is, old Hautwig; I didn't, so help my tater."

Gale heard all of this, concealed as he was under the cart, and as it now began to rain, he covered himself up in an old tarpauling he found there, and listened still longer.

"I know what old Hautwig is growling about," thought Gale; "he and Bandy Bob go shares in the thimble-rigging job, and he has heard long before this that I won five pounds. It will take all the gilt off their gingerbread for a few days, I think."

But from all he heard, he made sure that the poor devils who were hired at two shillings per day and their grub to "do" the wild Indian business, were not at all aware of the rascality of their employer.

He felt confident that they were totally unaware of the passing or dealing in spurious coin carried on by old Hautwig; and, therefore, he made up his mind to have nothing to do with them, come what might.

He remained in his place of concealment some time, when in the distance Gale perceived Bandy Bob, trudging along through the rain and mud towards old Hautwig's caravan.

He whistled twice or thrice, and Gale heard Hautwig over head, shuffling towards the caravan door, which he opened.

"That you, Bob?"

"Yes."

"Can't come in, yet, my joker; these ere Indians o' mine are having their supper; they'll soon wash up and go off to their lodgings."

"All right."

"It's just as well not to let every one know what we've been up to."

"Just so; but come down, I wants to speak to you; only a minute or two."

This conversation was carried on between the two rascals in an undertone, and in slang words peculiar to themselves, so that the wild Indians inside, if even they had heard it, could not understand the meaning of it.

Hautwig came down the steps, and the rain began to fall heavily.

He and Bandy Bob got underneath the caravan, and sat on the straw, not more than six feet from Gale, who was curled up under the tarpaulin.

"Have you seen Alf Green?" said Bob.

"Yes."

"In course he told you how I was done out of a 'fiver?'"

"He did, more's the pity; bad luck to the man who fleeced us, I say."

"It's knocked off all our earnings for the next two days."

"So it has, Bobby, so it has. If Alf hadn't seen it I wouldn't have believed it."

"I was forced to pay, or the crowd would have broken my head."

"Oh!"

"But I made sure he'd play again. He didn't though."

"An artful cove whoever he was, and no mistake."

"Alf Green followed him, and tried 'to bounce' him out of the money again; but it was no go, he showed fight, so Alf says, and gathered a rare crowd around him, who took his part, else Alf would have knocked him down and eased him of the lot."

Now, as we know, this was all a lie.

Being a bit of a fighting man he had intended to pick a quarrel with the stranger, Gale; but when the detective appeared ready for it, and willing, Alf's craven heart grew faint.

He didn't like the brightness of the stranger's eye, nor the muscular development of his arms and broad chest.

Hence, as we have previously seen, he "squared" it with the unknown detective for a spurious half sovereign.

To keep his credit good with Bandy Bob, however, Alf trumped up the tale told to Hautwig.

Gale, as he lay concealed, and listening, could not but smile as Bob continued,

"Things are getting worser and worser. How's it with you, have you done much to day?"

# THE BOY SOLDIER; OR, GARIBALDI'S YOUNG CAPTAIN.

A STRICKEN HOME.

"Oh! 'mazin' well! Them chaps from the Dials take A 1. I never had such capital wild men in all my life, only, you know, Bob, they eats so much. Lor' bless yer! you have no notion how them ere coves can eat—two pounds o' steak every day, and two pots o' malt arter every performance. I struck dead against the malt twice to-day, but how can a cove get over them? They threatened, if I stopped their beer, they'd leave off growlin', and fightin', and rolling o' their chains; that's were they has me, you know. If it warn't for their dreadful noises and horrible faces they pulls, it wouldn't go at all. The beer though livens 'em up, and they goes it as fierce and true as life; even I think, sometimes, they must be rale genuine savages."

"But how have you got along with the coin?"

"Oh, pretty tidy."

"Have you any more?"

"Yes, plenty. How have you got along with it? Did you palm much on it off on the yokels?"

"Yes, pretty fair; but not so much as I should like. Alf Green ain't as near a good 'un as Barney was."

"Ain't he, though?"

"No, he ain't got the bounce in him which the Pug had."

"Poor devil! What's become on him, I wonder?"

"Lagged, you may depend on it, for summat."

"Come, now, then, you chaps," said old Hautwig, calling to the wild Indians, "don't you lie there all night."

At this moment Alf Green made his appearance.

Bob whistled, and he joined them under the cart.

"Well, how goes it, Alf?" said Hautwig. "Did you get rid of your 'stuff?'"

"Yes, nearly all; I sold a 'quid's' worth to Young Stingo, at the sparring booth, and he shoved off in no time."

"Did he buy any more?"

"Yes; took ten bob's worth."

"That's capital!"

"And promised to take more to-morrow."

"Ah," said Hautwig, "Young Stingo would make a rare good pal. Wouldn't he, bob?"

"I believe you, old 'un. His werry appearance would frighten any one. Just fancy a countryman accusing *him* of doing such a thing; it would be more than his head was worth. He's an awful bruiser."

"He had a turn up with a bloak about it to-day," said Alf.

"Did he, though?"

"Yes, and it was all a ball. 'Me pass bad money?' said Stingo, getting red in the face, 'me give you a bad half-crown !" he said, and afore you could think of it he let the poor yokel have it between the eyes, and knocked him down as flat as a herring.

"Bravo for Stingo," said Hautwig; "ah! he's a rare good customer he is."

"Did you see many 'slops' about?" asked Bob.

"No," said Alf; "I never see the fair with so few on 'em."

"None in private clothes?" asked Hautwig.

"No, or I should have known 'em. I don't believe I see one plain clothes man in the whole fair."

"Well, let's go inside," said Bob: "it's no manner o' good staying outside here in the wet."

"I wants them wild Indians o' mine out on it first," said Hautwig. "I must pack 'em off to their lodgings."

"Oh, let 'em alone for a time," said Alf Green; "you can't expect the lads to go out in such a shower as this."

"But how can we talk o' business afore such as them?"

"Put it off till the rain is over, and they have gone. Come," said Bob, "I shall make a move inside."

"And so shall I."

"I hope you've got summat nice an' hot, old 'un," said Bob; "I'm almost famished."

Without more words the trio left their place of shelter, and went into the caravan.

"This is lucky," said Gale, when they had gone. "I have found out more than I expected. So, young Stingo, the fighting man, is one of the gang, eh? Ah, well, I always thought he couldn't flash and spree about as he did upon honest money. I will have all or none. There is no need of any very great hurry, though."

Gale crept out of his place of concealment, and went out into the rain.

He still kept his eye on old Hautwig's caravan, and, ere long, he met a policeman.

"Where are our men staying?" asked Gale.

"Some of 'em are in yonder public-house, sir," said the officer, when he had fully satisfied himself who and what Gale really was.

"Then you stand here until my return. Keep your eye on that caravan yonder; if any one comes out or goes in, tell me when I return. I shall not be gone more than ten minutes. Stand beside this booth; don't let any one see you watching."

Gale made his way through the mud and rain, and soon reached the public-house.

He called for sixpenny-worth of brandy and hot water, and began to talk about the weather as if he did not know a single soul then present.

In a few minutes he went away, and the men in the parlour left the place one by one.

Gale waited for them outside, and then directed each what to do.

"Where does young Stingo live?" he asked.

"In the public-house we have just left."

"All right," said Gale; "you go on and do as I tell you; I will follow quickly."

Gale then went to the public-house, and left word with the landlord that young Stingo was wanted by Alf Green, at old Hautwig's caravan, and must come directly.

Stingo was very angry at being disturbed out of his drunken slumber, but as he thought that the message concerned a further and cheap supply of base coin, he shuffled along through the wet, and soon reached Hautwig's caravan.

He knocked and entered.

In the meantime, however, Gale had made every disposition for the capture of the whole party.

Several detectives were concealed beneath the caravan, and others were hiding behind a neighbouring booth.

"Don't touch the wild men," said Gale, "for the poor devils have nothing to do with it; but directly this young Stingo enters the caravan, do your duty, and be prepared for the very worst, for I fear there will be a desperate struggle, and some of us may get hurt, seriously hurt."

In a few moments after this, young Stingo approached.

He was accompanied by Hairy Cap, who, as we have seen, was soundly thrashed by the detective, Bradshaw, in the morning.

"How lucky," said Bradshaw.

"Hush!" said Gale. "They are now going up the steps of the caravan. They have entered."

## CHAPTER CIX.

### DETECTIVE GALE AND THE COINERS.

Directly Gale saw that the person he wished to capture had entered old Hautwig's caravan, he gave the appointed signal, and all the constables gradually closed round the waggon, in such a manner that it was almost a matter of impossibility for any one of them to escape.

Gale was now about to mount the steps and knock at the door, when one of the constables hastily approached him, saying—

"Not yet, Mr. Gale, not yet."

"Why not?"

"I see two other parties approaching who are concerned with old Hautwig."

"Do you know them?"

"Yes."

"Who are they?"

"Old Smith, the dog man, and his brother."

"The dog man! who do you mean?"

"Why that old chap that goes about with performing dogs, and all that sort of thing, you know."

"Are you certain he's one of 'em?"

"Quite so."

"And what name does he go by?"

"Old Jemmy."

"All right," said Gale; "we can afford to wait a little while; if we only succeed in securing all the lot, it will be a good night's work."

So speaking, Gale got off the steps, and hid himself under the caravan again.

In a few moments old Jemmy approached, wet through to the skin.

He walked up the steps like a man who was perfectly at home, and he ushered himself in without ceremony.

"Hillo, Jemmy, that you?" said all at once.

"Aye, lads, what's left on me."

"You look down in the mouth, my lad."

"And well I may be, Hautwig."

"Don't the dogs 'take' now, as well as usual?"

"Take!" said Jemmy, in disgust, "take! the devil, no; things are all changing now. You see, the tastes of the rising generation used to be for dogs and monkeys, and all that sort o' thing; but it's no go now; they wants something more sensational now by half."

And as he spoke, old Jemmy, the dog man, helped himself to the contents of a quart pot near by, and almost drained it to the dregs ere he let it go.

It will be seen that before old Jemmy arrived,

Hautwig and his friends had transacted all their secret business without taking the "wild Indians" into their confidence.

For it takes but a minute for coiners and utterers to pass a roll of base metal one to the other.

Therefore, having transacted what they had to do, they were in a merry mood, and hailed old Jemmy's arrival with great applause.

"Ah!" said Jemmy, "things ain't what they used to be; the 'wild' business is what tells now. Give me half-a-dozen wild Indians," said Jemmy, "they are better than all your dogs and monkeys."

Hautwig smiled, as he said—

"Why, I thought you had a long engagement at Cross's penny gaff, over in the Boro'."

"So I did; but it didn't pay very well arter I got the job."

"How was that?"

"Well, I'll tell you all about it if you'll listen," said old Jemmy, filling a pipe.

"You see, when I left you, Hautwig——"

"Which you never had any occasion to do if you hadn't been so thick-headed."

"Never mind talking about that now," said Jemmy, "that time is past and gone."

"Well, go on now about your engagement with Cross."

"Well, I was sitting down arter dinner having a pipe in my lodgings at Lambeth, and was growling a good deal about the hardness of the times, when all at once I hears a rat-tat at the door, and arter a minute or two in walks Cross of the Royal Penny Gaff.

"Jist as usual he walks in as if he were always playing the ghost in Hamlet, and I offers him a chair.

"He sits down as if he were Macbeth, and puts his arms akimbo, and says, in a awful, sepulchra tone—

"'Jemmy Smith,' says he, 'I've called about those dorgs o' yourn.'

"'My good sir,' says I, 'they is werry wonderful creturs, as everybody knows.'

"'Yes, I have heard they are clever,' said Cross.

"'Clever?' says I, 'you may well say that. There ain't two sich animals anywhere's breathing as my dogs Jupiter and Juno.'

"'You have been out of an engagement for a long time, I hear?' said Cross, artful as ever.

"'Out of a engagement, sir?' says I. 'You must be mistaken entirely in the party,' says I. '*My* dogs are *never* out on a engagement!'

"It wouldn't do, you see, to let him know as how I wasn't performing, or his price wouldn't be so much by half.

"Arter a moment or two of solemn silence, Cross picks his teeth and, says he,

"'What terms would you propose for the use of them at my theatre over in the Borough?'

"For how long—a week or a fortnight, or what?" says I, "for I closes a engagement with a certain party this werry evening, and it's the last time I plays for him for some time to come. How long for, Mr. Cross?" says I, "for a fortnight of successive nights?"

"'Jest so,' said Cross, throwing out his legs in such a grand style that you'd a thought 'his theatre,' as he called it, was not less, and nothing inferior to her Majesty's Opera House, at least.

"'For a fortnight of successive nights?' said I, considering.

"'Yes, jest so.'

"'We had ten bob a night at Sadlers Wells,' says I.

"'Ah!' said the great manager; 'but you must remember that while the price of admission to the boxes of Sadler's Wells is half-a-crown, the pit one shilling, and the gallery sixpence, I have got neither boxes nor pit at my establishment as yet, and the price of admission is—ah! you know.'

"'I understand yer,' said I, stopping his stuttering, 'I understand yer. It's "Walk up! walk up! jest about to commence! The last time to-night! For the sole charge of one penny," and all that,' said I, imitating a country fair.

"But this I adds in a quiet way,

"'Why you see, Mr. Cross, I've played at sich first-rate places, that I'm not quite sure it would be quite the correct thing to appear on the boards of such a penny establishment as yourn.'

"There's nothing like cheek, you know Hautwig," said Jem, again helping himself to the porter.

"'Ahem,' said Cross, very loudly, and getting rather red, for what I said took all the starch of Hamlet's ghost out on him, and humbled him a bit.

"But he presently got red, plucked up his courage, and says he,

"'Well, Smith, you astonish me. You do, most certainly; you astonish me really. This is the first time I've ever heard anything said about the respectability of dogs.'

"'Do you mean to say as how we ain't respectable?' said I.

"'Not at all, Smith: I assure you nothing could be further from my intentions as far as regards yourself personally; I only referred to your dogs, you know.'

"'My dogs, sir,' said I, in a loud tragic voice, and looking at Cross full in the face.

"'Yes, Smith, *only* your dogs, you know.'

"'*Only* my dogs?' said I, bursting with indignation. 'I tell you what it is, Mr. Cross, my dogs are very respectable animals, and I wish that all animals with two legs could always behave themselves as Jupiter and Juno does.'

"I felt so awfully wild, I felt inclined to kick Cross out of the room.

"'Do you mean any reflection on *me*, sir?' said the penny-gaff proprietor, rising. 'Do you mean to insinuate, sir, that your dogs are more respectable than *me*?'

"'I means to say this,' said I, 'I shall never stand by and hear my dogs called in question.'

"'You seem to be labouring under a misconception, Smith,' said Cross, 'it was never my intention to underrate the capability of your animals.'

"'Then, you *do* admit they are respectable?' said I.

"'Yes, I have no doubt they are in their way.'

"'Ah,' said I, 'that's talking like a man. And now, Mr. Cross,' said I, with the air of a man who has lots of money, 'now,' says I, 'if you wishes to engage us, my terms to you, considering you have only a penny gaff, are eight bob a-night.'

"'Eight shillings a-night? What! that will come to sixteen shillings for them both.'

"'You are mistaken,' says I; 'that will just make it a guinea.'

"'A what?'

"'A guinea.'

"'How do you make *that* out? You have only two dogs.'

"'Very true,' said I; 'but, then, there's *me*.'

"'Oh, but it's not necessary to have *you*, Smith.'

"'The devil it ain't,' said I, getting red.

"'No,' said he, as cool as ice, 'no; there isn't the slightest occasion to have you, for you don't act, you know.'

"'Don't I, though?' says I.

"'No, not in the least.'

"'What, then, do you call it, Mr. Cross?' said I, boiling over with professional fury.

"'You only say one or two words to the animals from time to time, which I or anybody could say just as well.'

"'Mr. Cross,' says I, bursting with rage, 'sir,' said I, 'if we don't go together we don't go at all. Mark that, sir.'

"'That's quite unreasonable.' says he.

"'No matter,' says I. 'Me and my dogs, sir, or no dogs at all; *that's* my bargain.'

"'But why can you object?'

"'The animals won't perform their most extraordinary and wonderful tricks with anyone else but me.'

"'I don't see why they shouldn't, Smith,' said he.

"'But I tell you they won't, and so that's flat,' said I.

"'Have you any objections to let me try them?' said Cross at last, after a long time spent in thinking over it.

"'Try 'em? Oh! none in the least; I have no objections.'

"'Well, then, Smith, suppose you call in Jupiter, and see whether, on my running across the room and repeating the words you are in the habit of using, the animal does not seize me by the neck of my coat without doing me any injury.'

"'Very well,' says I, 'very well; I have no objections, not the least in the world. Here Jupiter, Jupiter!'

"In a few moments a large Newfoundland dog galloped out of the yard into the room, and stood wagging its tail before Smith.

"'Now,' said Cross, 'I am ready.'

"He ran across the room in a staggering manner, shouting—

"'Ah! ah! the deed is done! Revenge! revenge! revenge!'

"These were the words always used by Smith, but on this occasion the dog did not stir a foot.

"Cross seemed astonished that the animal did not recognise the last word as he usually did, and seize him by the coat collar as he always did to me, his master.

"'Well, sir,' says I, 'perhaps you'll admit now that the animal will *not* perform without me.'

"'I don't know that, Smith,' said he, annoyed; 'it strikes me that if you were to say to the dog, "go, sir," in a harsh tone, when I repeat the last "revenge," Jupiter would at once understand it, and perform the trick.'

"'Very well,' says I, grinning, 'just as you please, Mr. Cross; if you wishes to try it again, why do so, with all my heart.'

"Mr. Cross made a move across the room a second time, shouting, 'Ah, ah! the deed is done! revenge, revenge, revenge!'

"At the proper moment I says in a gruff voice to Jupiter, 'Go, sir.'

"In an instant Jupiter bounded away, and collared Cross, threw him down on the ground, tore all his coat, and then Jupiter and the gaff manager rolled together on the floor, all among the slops and dirt."

"And what did you do?" asked one.

"Why I thought I should have died from laughing, for Jupiter, mind you, didn't bite Cross at all, but he scarcely left a garment on his back but what was torn almost into shreds.

"'Murder, murder!' shouted Cross, as he lay rolling on the floor. 'Murder! the dog is strangling me; for mercy sake, Smith, take him off, and I'll give you a large salary.'

"'A large salary, Mr. Cross,' says I.

"'Yes,' says he, 'only take this beast of a dog from off my stomach.'

"I called away Jupiter, who wagged his tail, and considered the whole proceeding to be nothing else but a dress rehearsal.

"Poor Cross was in a fearful plight.

"He was red and dirty, and bruised and torn, and presented such a pitiable appearance that I had to lend him some clothes to go home in.

"He did not forget Jupiter's cleverness, however, and next morning I went over with my two dogs to the Royal Penny Gaff, and, over some stout, Cross joked about the adventure of the day before.

"'Don't mention it to any one, Smith,' said he; 'don't, for goodness sake, or else I shall never hear the last of it.'

"'But how about the extra pay?' said I.

"'Oh, you shall have it,' said Cross. 'Come to-night and begin your engagement.'

"I began my engagement, and the gaff was filled almost to suffocation every night; yes, several times every night."

"But you didn't give your own name, did you?"

"It wasn't likely. I called myself Sig. Mirini, and the dogs were called Hercules and Prospero."

"Well, and how did the engagement end?"

"Why, at the end of the week, Cross began to grumble and only paid me just one-half what I ought to have received."

"He didn't speak again about the extra pay, I suppose?"

"No, not a word, but I made up my mind to have it by hook or by crook."

"And did you get it?"

"Yes, and more than I expected."

"How?"

"I had been instructing Jupiter in a new trick, and he performed it to perfection."

"What was it?"

"You shall hear. During my engagement I found out that Cross always paid a visit to the money-taker's place every half-hour, and put it into his leather bag.

"This leather bag he invariably put into a breast-pocket inside his waistcoat.

"Having found out this, I began to instruct Jupiter in his new trick, but before I tried it, I says to Cross 'How about my pay; shall I have it all to-night or how?'

"He didn't answer, so I made up my mind that after all he was trying to swindle me.

"It was Saturday night, and my last appearance with the dogs.

"The gaff was crowded to suffocation, and Cross was in great good humour with the large amount of silver that had been taken during the evening.

"It was about eleven o'clock, and the last act was over.

"I says to Cross, who was playing the murderer in the piece, says I—

"'How about that money, Cross? Am I to get it or not?'

"No answer.

"'All right,' says I; so just at that moment, when Jupiter should have seized the murderer by the collar and dragged him down, he seized Cross so suddenly about the chest that it was a long time before he discovered his loss.

"Jupiter had snatched the leather purse from the pocket and brought it to me."

"Which you of course kept?"

"As a matter of course. But when Cross discovered the loss of his money, he jumped up again and began to curse and swear in such a manner that he was hissed and hooted at by all of the audience.

"'Finish the piece! Finish the piece!' they yelled with all their might.

"But Cross rushed about here and there like a wild man, looking for his missing purse, but could nowhere find it.

"The audience, however, were bound to have some kind of fun for their money, and so began to tear up the benches, and jumped upon the stage and had a battle on a small scale between themselves and the company, tearing and breaking whatever came in their way, and causing such a riot that it took half-a-dozen policemen to restore order.

"Cross was marched off to the station, and had ten days' hard labour for creating a disturbance; but Jemmy Smith and his dogs went home and enjoyed ourselves out of the contents of his purse, without thinking it any way wrong either."

Loud laughter greeted old Jemmy on the conclusion of his story, in which the wild Indians joined most heartily.

Indeed, inside the caravan all was comfortable and snug; outside the rain was pouring in torrents, and each one felt very much inclined to remain where he was and not trust himself out in the deluge of rain.

"There's nothing like humbug, Jemmy," said old Hautwig. "Look at me, see what a roaring business I am doing."

"Which way?" said the old dog man, with a knowing wink.

"You knows all about it, I see," said Young Stingo, laughing.

"I do," said Jemmy; "but *I'd* raythor trust to my two dogs than get into the hands of the bobbies."

"Oh, gammon, Jemmy!" said Hautwig, with a scornful laugh. "Do you mean to say that you have never done anything in our peculiar line?"

"No, my lads, nor I shouldn't like to do so either. I can tell you you will be 'copped' sooner or later; that's what I always say."

"And what brings you here now, then?" said several.

"Why, to bring you very unpleasant news."

"Unpleasant news?" said all, in a breath. "Why, what do you mean?"

"Mean?" said Jemmy. "Why, I mean to say this: that if the fair to-day wasn't watched by half a score of policemen in disguise, you can shoot me."

"Half a score?"

"Yes, not one less."

"Then I'm off," said Young Stingo.

At that moment the door opened and Gale entered.

No one knew him; but all felt greatly surprised, and there was something so very peculiar in his looks that they felt sure he could be no friend.

"Who are you?" asked one.

"What do you want here?"

"What's your name!" said first one and then another.

"Well, gentlemen, my name is Gale. I am an officer, and I come to arrest every one of you for being concerned in robbery, and in uttering base coin."

The four wild men no sooner heard that he was an officer, than they clambered through the windows and ran away like lunatics.

Nor were they stopped.

For, as we have seen, Gale had given special orders that not one of them should be molested, for he had good reasons for supposing that neither of them had had any hand in the wicked practices of their employer, Hautwig.

Young Stingo, when he heard the name and occupation of Gale, made a violent blow at that officer, but Gale dodged, and young Stingo fell right into the arms of two constables, who were that moment advancing up the ladder.

As quick as thought old Hautwig made a rush towards a drawer, in which was a very large quantity of spurious coin.

He was in the act of unlocking it, when Gale gave him a violent blow on the knuckles which rendered him almost helpless.

In a few moments the caravan was filled with officers, and the fight became general.

Young Stingo, Bandy Bob, and Alf Green, fought like furies.

Old Jemmy fell flat upon his back, and let them fight it out as best they could, without endeavouring to help either one party or the other.

In less than five minutes, however, all the coiners were arrested and handcuffed.

They were taken away through the rain, and safely lodged in gaol, after having been searched.

Gale and another officer remained behind to search the caravan, and greatly to their astonishment they discovered not only large quantities of base coin, but a perfect apparatus for making it.

It is needless to say that no one was more taken aback than old Hautwig himself.

When he was placed in a cell by himself, and began to realize the awful position in which he was placed, all his former merriment and indifference seemed to change into rank despair.

He could have committed suicide, so keenly, acutely did he feel, and thoroughly understand his position.

But, like a cunning old rogue as he was, he made up his mind to turn informer, and tell all he knew.

Therefore, when Gale had returned with a light cart filled with all manner of things taken out of the caravan, Hautwig sent for him.

Gale went to the cell.

"Well, Hautwig, we have got you at last."

"*Me*, Mr. Gale?" said the old sinner, in a whining tone. "Why, what have *I* done?"

"You!"

"Yes, me."

"Why, everything, Hautwig," said Gale, looking the old rascal straight in the eye. "What have you done, eh? Why, everything, you cunning old rascal. Why, I have ferreted out more than a hundred weight of property concealed in different parts of your caravan."

"Ah, Mr. Gale, it must have been planted there unknown to me."

"Planted, eh? You are a fine old humbug to talk of planting, like as if you haven't been making a fortune for the past ten years from the proceeds of robbery. How about that base coin I found in your drawers?"

"What base coin, Mr. Gale?"

"There, there," said the officer, in disgust, "don't try to play the innocent over me; I know you too well, Hautwig."

"Don't say that, Mr. Gale," whined the old man; "I have never injured you in all my life."

"No; but you have injured, nay, ruined dozens in your time."

"Look you here, Mr. Gale," old Hautwig began. "I intend to make a clean breast of it, and tell you all."

"If you take my advice, Hautwig, you'll say

nothing, for whatever you say may be used against you."

"Yes, I know, Mr. Gale, I know; but it's no use playing the innocent any longer, for I find I have been betrayed."

"Betrayed?"

"Yes, Mr. Gale. You could never have found me out if some villain had not 'rounded' on me."

"Do you suspect any one?"

"Yes—Barney the Pug, or else the cabman."

"Barney did not; and, as to the cabman, I am on the look-out for him, and have been for the last month."

"You do not mean that?" said old Hautwig, with glittering eyes. "After him, eh! What for?"

"For the robbery down in the country, which you, Barney, Bandy Bob, and Alf Green are concerned in."

Old Hautwig turned pale.

He swore until almost black in the face that he knew nothing about it; but Gale detailed so many circumstances regarding it, that the old man could not refute him.

"You might as well make a clean breast of it."

"And do you intend to arrest the cabman?"

"The first moment I see him."

"And prosecute him?"

"Yes, have the old villain transported if I can."

"Ah, Mr. Gale," whined old Hautwig; "I fear our game is up."

"I know it is. I have been a long time after first one and then another of you, but I hope shortly to have every one of you hung or lagged, Hautwig."

"You won't press it very hard against me if I tells you all, will you, Mr. Gale?"

"I can promise nothing."

"But you'll try and poke in a good word for me, now wont you?"

Gale did not answer.

This was always the cry of those who had enjoyed a long career in crime, and were accidentally captured.

And Mr. Gale found out from long experience, despite whatever may be said about "honor among thieves," that nine out of every ten convicted rogues would willingly turn queen's evidence, if by so doing they could lessen their own punishment.

It was with this knowledge and conviction that Gale stood outside the cell door conversing with old Hautwig, whom he called the prince of rogues and humbugs.

He knew very well that the old man was dying to disclose everything that he knew about his companions if only to ease his own mind. Hence, after a time, he begged that Mr. Gale would procure pen, ink, and paper, and take notes of all he said.

This the detective willingly acceded to, and old Hautwig detailed to him such a catalogue of crime, in which he had taken part, or of which he had been from time to time cognizant, that it made Gale fairly unwell.

The officer did not much care to hear anything about Barney; but when old Hautwig began to speak of the old cabman and his doings at night, it fairly startled him, detective as he was.

---

## CHAPTER CX.

### THE DARK DOINGS OF A NIGHT CABMAN.

"You have no notion, Mr. Gale, what a villain that old cabby is."

"I have suspected he wasn't altogether on the square for years," said Gale.

"And many others besides you, Mr. Gale; but he has been too clever all along for all of you officers, and even now I very much doubt you could prove any case against him, he is so deep and cunning."

"I know he is, and have heard that he glories in defying all the police."

"So he does; and I have heard him tell some strange stories. There has been more than one dead body which has ridden inside his cab."

Gale looked up in surprise and horror as he said, "You don't mean that, Hautwig?"

"I do, though. It has been used several times by the body-snatchers and others."

"Horrible! and do you know the names of any of the bodies which they have removed?"

"Only one."

"And who was that?"

"Old Ford, the gentleman who was murdered in the Red House."

"Was that removed from the cemetery?"

"It was."

"By whom?"

"Barney, and another person named Warner."

"You are sure of this?"

"And sure also that the body was conveyed backwards and forwards in the cab."

"Horrible! but tell me, Hautwig, did they sell you any trifles which belonged to the dead man?"

"Yes."

"What were they?"

"Two gold rings, set with diamonds. I bought them with the fingers still in them."

"What!"

Barney and his friend cut off the fingers to save time and trouble.

"I had to saw them off the joints afterwards,' said Hautwig.

"Monsters!" said Gale.

"The body was afterwards sold for twenty pounds to some medical students. When they had done with it various parts were placed in brown paper parcels, and thrown into the sewers or rivers at night time."

"What barbarism!"

"Oh! Barney, to my knowledge, has been a capital hand at body snatching for years."

"The villain!"

"He first finds out what rich people are dead, where they are going to be buried, and such like; in fact, he often attends, or rather follows, the funeral, and then, having laid all his plans, he and cabby do the trick very nicely, for your real gentlefolk are always buried with their rings on."

"Hautwig, you astonish me!"

"It would astonish you much more if you knew as much as I do about him."

"I suppose so; but then, perhaps, he may have told you lies."

"Oh, I have heard it from Barney as well. One night he was called off the cab rank by an elderly gentleman who had a young woman with him.

"'Drive to Hampstead,' said the stranger, winking at cabby.

"Cabby winks back, and drives them to Hampstead.

"When they got there the gentleman orders him to drive five miles farther on.

"He does so; but when he stops, the gentleman has disappered, and the young girl inside is stone dead!

"Cabby finds a purse on the seat and that's all.

"Where or how the gentleman had got out was a mystery which cabby didn't care about solving."

"What did he do with the body? Was the girl's throat cut or anything of that sort?"

"No; it must have been done by poison of some

sort; and so cabby came to the conclusion that he would throw the body into the canal, instead of making a hue and cry about it."

"And did he do so?"

"Yes."

"And what became of the affair? do you know?"

"I have heard that the body was discovered next day, and in three days afterwards identified by a gentleman as that of his only child. The loss of his daughter preyed so much upon the father that he blew out his brains, and strange to say the title and estates went into the hands of some old lawyer."

"Did you hear his name?"

"I did, but forget. All I know now is that cabby received a small parcel shortly afterwards, in which the unknown gentleman *thanked* him for the wise and discreet manner in which he had acted. The parcel contained, among other things, £100 in gold."

"And what did cabby do with it?"

"Drank it, or gambled it away."

For a few moments Gale did not speak, but at last he said,

"Did you hear whether these estates were in England or the continent?"

"I know that the title and estates were both foreign."

"The gentleman's title, then, would be Count Schmidt, would it not?" asked Gale, referring to his note-book. "And the estates are or were situated near Manheim?"

"Now I come to recollect, I think you are right.'

"This old gentleman must have been a lawyer, then?"

"That I know not."

"But I am sure of it," said Gale, "and his true name is Flint. I am after both father and son. When *they* are captured all my work is done."

Whether the brave and restless detective Gale succeeded in his designs and wishes, we shall presently see in another chapter of startling incidents and revelations.

## CHAPTER CXI.

### FRANK FORD'S LETTER TO HIS BROTHER TOM.

WHILE Captain Tom Ford was roaming the high seas in quest of adventure, and capturing or destroying everything which bore the flag of Maximilian, the usurper, and would-be emperor of Mexico, his brother Frank, and his brave band of Boy Soldiers, were much occupied in guarding the upper fords of the river, to prevent the French from crossing, and cutting off the supplies of men and material from the brave little army of liberation, under President Juarez.

Frank, by a private letter, learned that his brother Tom was cruizing about in the Atlantic, and, instead of sending his letters to England, as he had been in the habit of doing before, he wrote to Tom, and directed his epistle to the Island of St. Thomas, in the care of the American consul there, with instructions for it to he left there until called for.

Now Tom was of an active turn of mind and body, and when he had nothing particular to do on sea, he invariably put into some near port in order to ascertain, if possible, the movements of Maximilian's vessels.

When, therefore, he called at the Island of St. Thomas for fresh water and provisions of all kinds, he was delighted to find awaiting him a long letter from the brave leader of the Boy Soldiers, which, in substance, was as follows:—

"DEAR TOM,—Since last I wrote to you from this, our station, on the upper falls of the river which we are guarding, we have had very strange adventures. not with animals this time, but with men—real live Comanche Indians.

"After our battles with lions, bears, wolves, and such like, we were allowed a little peace and leisure from the 'varmints,' as our tall American trapper persists in calling them; but in a few nights we were doomed to a great surprise.

"The tall Yankee who had been out hunting one whole day, returned without killing or bringing anything home with him.

"This very much surprised us all, for, to speak the truth, the trapper is a dead shot, and one of the best hunters I ever heard of.

"Instead of bringing home any game he returned dusty and weary.

"His head was bound up with a handkerchief.

"He was bleeding from several flesh wounds in his head, arms, and thighs.

"His mustang pony was blowing and all covered with foam, and quivered, poor beast, in every limb, and almost tottered from weakness as it hobbled into our camps.

"The trapper had used all his powder and ball.

"He had but one charge, and that was already in his rifle, ready for use.

"I knew that something was up; so, after giving him some fresh meat, I questioned him in private, in order that the whole camp might not be aroused unnecessarily.

"'You look very tired,' I said to him.

"'Yes, I guess I am,' said Long Legs, yawning, and stretching himself on my bed of dried grass. 'I calculate as how any one would be dead beat if they had gone through what I have to-day.'

"'Why, what happened?' I asked.

"'Oh! nothing much,' he grinned; 'I've only had a right smart brush with the red devils.'

"'How did that occur?'

"'Why, when I left our camp early this morning, I took a path by the river, and went up about fifteen miles.

"'When I halted, and began to look about for game, which I knew was plentiful up there, I perceived, not fifty yards from me, a party of redskins crossing the river.

"'In fact, I had almost ridden right into an encampment of redskins without being observed by them.

"'There was no way to escape except the path I had come by, and I thought of retracing my steps, when, lo and behold! the path was occupied by half-a-dozen powerful redskins.

"'Hillo!' thought I, 'they must have discovered me, and perhaps are now surrounding me.'

"'There was nothing for it but a determined fight, I imagined, so made up my mind for the worst.

"'I heard them jabbering away among themselves like a lot of monkeys, and, as I understood something of their lingo, I listened.'

"'What Indians were they?'

"'Comanches—d—d cut-throats every one. I knew them well of old.'

"'And what did they say?'

"'From what I could gather of their patter, it seemed that one of their chiefs had been across the river, and had got into communication with the French, and the Indians had made a bargain with them to destroy us.'

"'Very polite of them, I'm sure—very.'

"'The redskins had new blankets and new rifles,

and appeared to be on the best of terms with themselves.

"'After a bit I watched them all more keenly than before, and in less than half-an-hour I heard great shouting from the other side of the river.

"'I peeped through the thick foliage of a copse, in which I was concealed, and could perceive another party of Indians, and with them several French officers, and some Indian interpreters.

"'In a moment or two, the river was swarming with boats, which shot out from among the rushes on both sides of the river, and the Frenchmen with their Indians crossed over.

"'These last Indians were a war-party of Blackfeet.

"'The Frenchmen brought with them several canoe loads of presents, and odds and ends, and in less than half-an-hour they were all sitting round a great council fire, having a long and noisy 'pow wow' about what was to be done.

"'From what I could learn, the Comanches and Blackfeet, although they had been for many years at war one with another, were so much pleased with the numerous presents which the French had given them, that they agreed to forget their old quarrels, and each send out a war-party to scour the country, and kill every soul of us."

"'That is if they could,' I remarked.

"'Just so,' said the trapper.

"'Well, what then?'

"'After the Frenchmen had gone over the river again, the two war-parties of Indians still sat round their council-fires smoking, but I could see it would have taken very little to arouse them, and cause a sanguinary battle among themselves, for from the looks of the treacherous Blackfeet, and the gestures of the Comanches, it even now appeared that a quarrel was brewing among them about the fair and honest division of the gifts which the Frenchmen had brought over.

"'When they had done smoking one of the Comanche chiefs rose up and said that as his was the oldest and bravest tribe he should have the first choice.

"'He, therefore, seized a rifle on the instant.

"'The Blackfeet, perceiving that there was treachery on foot, jumped to their feet and helped themselves to whatever they liked.

"'The Comanches were taken somewhat unawares, but, in a moment, they all rushed forward to seize something, and a general fight commenced among them.

"'Such shouting, yelling, screaming and cursing you never heard in all your life.

"'They looked like so many devils, dancing about and fighting like furies.

"'I have seen a great deal of Indians,' said the trapper, 'but I never saw anything to equal that.

"'Neither side would give in.

"'They were about equal in numbers, and they fought with the bitterness and obstinacy of so many inhuman monsters.

"'Some were scalped, others had their heads cut off, more than half-a-dozen were riddled with balls, and yet for more than an hour they fought the fight went on without abating the least in fury.'

"'But what did you do?' I asked the Trapper.

"'Why, you see,' the Trapper answered, 'my blood began to boil when I saw so much barbarity, and I made up my mind to mount the mustang and hook it off as best I could, for one white man among so many red devils stands no chance at all. I jumps on the mustang, and was well nigh clear of the fight as I thought, when I was met by another party of Comanches, who were advancing to take part in the fight against the Blackfeet.'

"'Then it was a planned affair?' I said.

"'So it appeared to me, for the Comanches had evidently made up their minds to rob and murder the Blackfeet, and had assistance in ambush, not many miles off; but then their chief had commenced the fight too soon, and were getting the worst of it, for the Blackfeet fought like demons.'

"'Well, what happened to you?'

"'Finding my passage debarred by this second party of Comanches, I made up my mind to retreat.

"'But they discovered me, and let fly a shower of balls at my head.

"'This wasn't very pleasant, you may be sure.

"'Hang it, thought I, they shan't kill me for nothing, so I lets fly at 'em right and left and knocks over two of their greatest braves at one shot.

"'I don't like the Blackfeet any more than the Comanches, you know, Captain Tom,' the trapper said, 'but as the former were less numerous than the latter, I determined to help 'em a little bit, and fight my way out of the scrimmage as best I could.

"'And tough work it was, you can bet,' said the Yankee.'

"'When the Blackfeet saw me gallop in among them, they all turned towards me, vowing vengeance against the pale-face, and I fully made sure they would massacre me.

"'I made signs to them, however, and when they saw me fire among and kill several of the Comanches, they yelled with delight and danced for joy.

"'The Comanches rushed at me right and left.

"'Every weapon was directed at me, and how I escaped from the shower of bullets seems a miracle.

"'My cap was knocked off; my saddle was almost riddled; several shots struck my arms, thighs, and head, and blood poured out from a dozen flesh wounds.

"'The Blackfeet warriors, however, fought well, but they were not sufficiently numerous to beat back their enemies, who were now swarming on every side.

"'Arrows, tomahawks, and war clubs flew thick and fast through the air.

"'A dozen times did a tall, war-like brave gallop up and attempt to strike me down.

"'But he nearly always got more than he gave, and at last I knocked him off his horse with a heavy blow from the butt end of my rifle, and left him sprawling more dead than alive.

"'Perceiving that the Blackfeet could not fight much longer I stopped one of their chiefs, and told him he and his followers had better take to their boats, or else steal the Comanche horses, and thus escape.

"'For, strange to say, the fight had begun so suddenly, and had been continued with such vengeance, that most of the Comanches forgot all about their horses, and fought on foot.

"'My advice was received in good part.

"'Pale-face,' said the Blackfeet brave, 'we have met before. You are, and never have been a friend to the red men of our tribe; but I forget all that for what you have done to-day. Your advice is good; we will fly, but to return swiftly again, yea, as swiftly as an arrow from the bow."

"'He galloped away among his followers, and told them what to do.

"'In a few moments several of the Blackfeet braves fell flat among the grass.

# THE BOY SOLDIER; OR, GARIBALDI'S YOUNG CAPTAIN.

THE SHIPWRECK—(*See next Number*).

"'Several of the Comanches, thinking they were killed, galloped up, and dismounted, in order to scalp them.

"'But on the instant the Blackfeet crawled through the tall grass like snakes, suddenly uprose, killed the Comanches, and mounted their horses.

"'This trick was played several times very successfully, and at last nearly every one of the Blackfeet managed to get a mount at the expense of their adversaries, who were now more bitterly enraged than ever.

"'Those who could not get horses managed to escape to their boats, while their comrades galloped away.

"'But the Comanches were not to be thus thwarted of their vengeance.

"'I was the last one to attempt to escape, and they swore I should not.

"'They surrounded me.

"'My ammunition was nearly all gone.

"'Yet I made every bullet tell.

"'Every time I fired one of the Comanches tumbled in the grass, until at last I became giddy and exhausted.

"'I knew not what I did.

"'Yet in my madness I fought like a devil, and at each stroke I made with my knife or hatchet I clove the skull or broke the ribs of some red devil.

"'Captain Frank,' said the Trapper, 'you have no notion of what a real good Indian fight is.

"'Your soldiers in the field, fighting one regiment against regiment, or one company against company, is all very well.

"'In a battle of that sort it is all fair play compared to the Indians.

"'They dodge about in the grass, tumble off their horses, throw up their hands, and all those sort of tricks to make you believe they are wounded or hurt.

"'But lor' bless you,' said the Trapper, 'it is all deceit nine cases out of ten.

"'When you ride up to scalp 'em, they are no more dead than you or I am; but laugh in their sleeve, and at the first chance will pop you over like a squirrel.

"'I know them of old.

"'Many a good brush have I had with 'em. I wish I had as many dollars as I have knocked over redskins in my time, I should be a rich man long before now.

"'Well, sir,' continued the Trapper, 'I almost began to think my time was come, so exhausted did I feel.

"'I fought my way on all sides like a madman; and while the Comanches exist as a tribe they'll never forget the 'Red Devil,' as they call me, for my arm was dripping with blood, which trickled off my tomahawk and knife.

"'At last I broke through their lines, and with a terrific yell they pursued me.

"'It was now a ride for life!

"'I thought once or twice that my mustang pony would fall under me, so weak was he.

"'Showers of arrows were sent after me, and more than one rifle-ball grazed my limbs; but I stood on my horse's back like a circus-rider, a trick brave lads, word was brought that two Indians had been observed crawling through our camp.

"They could have been captured very easily, but I forbade any one to molest them, but on the other hand not to pretend that we had seen them.

"As night approached, and long before any fires were lighted, I selected a party of men, and placed them up in the trees, with orders not to fire until they heard the signal from me.

"After this we got all the old clothes we could find, stuffed them with grass, and made a great number of dummies.

"These were placed in reclining positions around the fires, as if they were men asleep.

"Others were put against trees, and, when all was prepared, we lighted our fires, and prepared our supper.

"After we had eaten it we piled a large quantity of wood upon each of the fires, and laid down, as if to rest.

"When the fires grew dim, however, every living man and woman crawled away, and climbed into the trees.

"In truth, about ten o'clock, there was not a single human being of our party who were in the camp, but all perched out of sight in the trees.

"All was death-like silence.

"The moon had gone down.

"We expected the approach of the Indians each moment, and were fully prepared.

"We had not to wait long, however.

"The waving of the long grass in the distance told us they were not far off.

"Red Jacket, the trapper, volunteered to be our look-out man, and in consequence he was placed in one of the trees nearest to the path by which the Indians would come.

"The signal he gave us was an excellent imitation of an owl.

"When we heard this 'coo-hoot! coo-hoot!' we knew very well that the Redskins were not far off.

"Nor were we mistaken.

"They divided their forces into two parties.

"The first division, under the chief, remained where they were, just outside our camps.

"The other division went round to cut off our retreat, and to advance in a different direction.

"We did not dare to breathe a word to each other for fear of being heard.

"From our place of concealment in the trees, however, we could plainly see the stealthy movements of our dusky and treacherous enemies.

"Beside the old chief I could perceive my faithful half-breed standing.

"He was the one who was to lead this division into our camp.

"Presently the second division gave a loud shout, and advanced into our camp from the south.

"Immediately this was heard, our half-breed and his party responded to it with a yell, and rushed into the camp on the north side.

"But in running over the uneven ground, our half-breed purposely stumbled, and fell into one of our newly-made 'graves,' right upon Master Fatty and Buttons, who were crouching down in it ready to fire.

"The old Indian and his followers did not stop for a moment, but rushed headlong forward, brandishing their clubs, and knives, and tomahawks.

"At that instant, and when every single one of the Indians could be plainly seen in the dim fire light, I gave the word to fire!

"The crash that followed is beyond all description.

"The aim of each one was deadly, and more than a score of the Indian braves bit the dust at the first volley.

"How could we help killing them?

"From the newly-made 'graves,' or rifle-pits, two of our best shots rose up and took deliberate aim at the Redskins in the camp, while from overhead we poured upon them an incessant shower of shot.

"They were struck with amazement.

"They expected to find us all asleep.

"But once they got into our camp, from every side poured in upon them a deadly shower of bullets and small shot.

"Taken by surprise, they attempted to escape by retreating, but on whichever side they ran, they were met by a sturdy body of Boy Soldiers, who, shoulder to shoulder, now advanced with levelled bayonets.

"The screams, and yells, and noise of the Indians were terrific.

"They were caught in their own snare, and dozens of them were already dyeing the turf with their life blood.

"Unable to restrain my brave lads any more, we all descended from the trees, and the fight now became from hand to hand.

"The Comanches fought like fiends, and many of our Mexican friends were knocked over and scalped.

"But not one of our Boy Soldiers were hurt, for they were in a compact body, and moved hither or thither, obeying my orders as calmly as if only engaged in an ordinary drill.

"It was useless to endeavour to restrain the fury of Red Jacket, the trapper, however, for, directly he saw the Indian chief, he dashed forward, and a fearful hand-to-hand struggle ensued between them.

"'Surrender! surrender!' we shouted, on all sides; but the red devils only yelled out defiance, and fought on to the very last.

"I did not like to see blood unnecessarily shed, so I gave order to Hugh Tracy, the count, and Caspar, to move up their men in conjunction with mine, and thus form a circle.

"This we did, and enclosed not only the Indians, but many of our fellows who were still fighting with them.

"By degrees we made the circle smaller and smaller, until at last we hemmed in both friend and foe, from which there was no escape.

"'Cease firing!' I cried out, loudly.

"The Indians stood calm, determined, and prepared to die.

"They expected nothing else but death at our hands.

"Judge of their surprise, therefore, when I ordered out of the circle every man except the Indians, and procuring an interpreter among the Mexicans (not the half-breed, for it would have been too great an insult), and spoke a few words to them thus:—

"'Indians, Comanche braves! you have been caught in your own snares.

"'You came to destroy us, and are yourselves defeated; but why should you treat us as enemies? We wish to be friends. We are fighting for

Mexican independence, and nothing more. We came not to disturb you in your hunting ground; and, in token of the truth of what I say, I will make a league with you, offensive and defensive, which shall date from this day and for evermore. We will live together henceforth in peace and without envy or distrust.'

"These words, and many acts of kindness, soon convinced the Indians of the truth of my intentions. They had a week to consider my proposal, but in less than six hours they agreed to all my terms and smoked the pipe of peace.

"We are now the best of friends, and our adventures with them my next letter will show.

"In haste,
"Your Brother,
"FRANK FORD."

---

## CHAPTER CXII.

THE MEETING OF JOEL, OLD FLINT AND WARNER —STRANGE CHANGES OF FORTUNE—JOEL IS REDUCED TO BEGGARY AND KICKED OUT OF DOORS BY HIS OWN SERVANTS.

IT will be remembered that in a previous chapter the sudden intrusion of Warner upon old Flint and his son was fully described, and how much astonished the two rogues were at the unexpected and unwelcome visit.

At first Joel thought to strike awe into his visitor by assuming a very savage and determined air.

But Warner was much too old a rascal to be imposed upon by any such tricks, and, as we have before described, he not only forced Joel and his father to remain seated, but drew his revolver, saying,

"Dare to stir, either of you, make the least noise or give an alarm, and I will blow the brains out of both of you."

There was something so determined, and yet, at the same time, so cool, in Warner's manner, that it chilled the blood of both father and son.

Joel, in all his life had never felt so uneasy as he now did under the determined eye of the intruder.

There was a deadly devilish twinkle in the stranger's eyes, truly, which neither father nor son could look upon or withstand.

They cast down their eyes to the floor like guilty things, but spoke not a single word.

This was the moment of Warner's triumph.

He smiled on the two villains, and exhibited his white teeth, which shone like the fangs of some monster.

He next approached the table, and helped himself to a draught of brandy.

Yet all the time he kept an eye on the lawyer and his son, and held his revolver, firmly in the right hand.

For he knew of old how slimy and treacherous the lawyer had proved to him.

He felt certain that if he only turned his back upon either of them for a single moment they would stab or shoot him.

Seating himself in such a manner at the corner of a table that he had a good view of what each of them were doing or likely to do, he pulled out a cigar, lit it, and began to smoke with all the nonchalence in the world.

"So we have met again, eh, Flint?" said Warner. "You managed to escape, then, from the cords with which I bound you?"

"Well, and if I have, what of that?" the lawyer replied, in a surly manner, feeling confident once more that he would be still able to escape from Warner.

"And so you have found out your long-lost son, I find?"

"He has, sir," answered Joel, proudly; "and what of that? Can it concern you in any way, might I ask?"

"Oh, yes, a very great deal, I can assure you," said Warner, laughing. "You are rich, you know."

"Who told you so, sir?"

"Why, the appearance of your luxuriously-furnished apartments, your servants, and such-like, tell me that without asking any questions."

"Well, sir, and if I am rich, it cannot concern you," said Joel. "I know not what business you have here with my father; but as to me, I know you cannot have anything to do. In fact, sir," said Joel, with the airs of a very superior person, "if you must know, I have just returned from abroad, where I have realized a vast fortune."

"Yes, a vast fortune," said the father, rubbing his hands in great glee at his son's ready lie. "Yes, a vast fortune, acquired abroad."

"Oh, indeed," said Warner, with an incredulous smile; "he has been luckier than you or I, then, eh, old Flint?" said he.

"I made my fortune, sir, by extensive speculations in California and other places."

"You were never in Italy, perhaps, were you?" asked Warner, with a slight smile.

"Yes, I was, sir; I have travelled there."

"And never met any one of the name of Tom or Frank Ford, I suppose?"

"No, never; but if I had done so, it would have given me great pleasure in thrashing both of them," said Joel, with a flushed face. "I remember both of them at Bromley Hall, and——"

"You also remember, perhaps, how often you were thrashed by Tom Ford, don't you?" said Warner. "I have heard all about it."

Joel looked at Warner as if astonished.

"Know all about it?" said he. "Know all about what?"

"Why, Tomasso, the detective; the fire in the Custom House building; the wreck, and the——"

"Stop," said Joel, rising hastily. "Stop," he said, red with rage. "Who told you all this nonsense?"

"Nonsense, you call it, eh?" said Warner. "You would not think it nonsense, perhaps, if you knew as I do that the detectives have discovered that you were *not* drowned on the wreck of the 'Dolphin,' and that the two officers who came over from Leghorn with you are even now trying to trace you."

"Impossible! All that you say, or insinuate about my son, is pure invention, Warner," said old Flint, in a sudden burst of anger. "He has made his fortune honourably, and has returned to England to enjoy it, like a true gentleman; and more than that, he doesn't want to be annoyed by——"

"Any such beggars as you are, I suppose," said Warner, laughing. "I understand, and small blame to him, either, for of all the miserable, miserly old scoundrels who ever lived, Flint, you are the greatest."

From the turn conversation was now taking, it was evident to Joel that bitter feelings animated both Warner and his father.

Under the pretext of leaving the room for a few minutes, he rose from his chair.

But Warner, in a determined tone, bade him remain where he was, and Joel sat down again.

"This is no time for jokes," sail Joel. "What do you want with me, Mr. Warner, or whatever your name is?"

"I will tell you in one word."

"And what is that one word?"

"Simply this. Are you prepared to divide the treasure of the chest, or must we use force?"

"Use force?" said Joel, with a quivering lip.

"Aye force, in two ways. First make you disgorge my share of the plunder, and, if you are not civil, afterwards send information to all the police stations of your whereabouts."

"You talk very boldly, sir," said Joel.

"Not half as boldly as I should act if you don't follow my advice. It is better to part with half than to lose all."

"Half?" gasped old Flint, in amazement.

"Half?" said Joel, turning pale.

"Yes. Nothing less than that amount will satisfy me," said Warner; "so if you are wise you will hand over to me a portion immediately."

"I refuse," said Joel.

"And so do I," exclaimed Flint.

"You do, eh?" said Warner, smiling. "Well, I'll give you five minutes to think of it. Where is the treasure chest?"

"It is not here."

"Where is it?"

"In a place of safety, miles away," said Joel.

"You are lying, both of you!" said Warner. "The treasure is in this house—in that back room."

"It is not."

"I will go and see," said Warner, rising.

But Joel reached the door first, and rushed into the back room.

The next instant he turned deadly pale, and reeled into a chair.

"Hullo! what's the matter?" said Warner with a quiet smile. "What ails you?"

"It is gone!" gasped Joel.

"Gone!" almost shrieked his father.

"Gone? What is gone?" asked Warner, with a quiet smile.

"The treasure!" said Joel. "We are ruined!"

"Why, I thought you said just now that the treasure was not in the house?" remarked Warner.

"It was here not half an hour ago!" gasped Joel.

"Then you told me a wilful lie."

"I know I did."

"You had done better by telling the truth, and taking half," said Warner, smiling, and drinking more brandy. "How could it have been abstracted from the room?"

"I know not."

"No one has entered the back room since I have been here. None that I am aware of," said Joel, "except it were the devil himself."

During the conversation the footman entered the room.

"Count," said he, respectfully, addressing Joel, "there is a carman and a cabman waiting outside to be paid."

"Paid? paid for what?" said Joel, astonished.

"For conveying the four gentlemen who called on you about ten minutes ago, count."

"Four gentlemen!" said Joel.

"Four gentlemen! Very mysterious affair this," said Warner.

"Fo-ur gentlemen!" said old Flint. "Why, the servant must be mad. No four gentlemen have been here."

"They called at the house, and were admitted by me, sir."

"By you?"

"Yes, count; they said they were old school-fellows of yours, and did not need my services in announcing them, so went upstairs alone."

Joel did not know what to think or what to say. He and his father looked as pale as ghosts.

"And what can the carman want?" said Joel, in a faint voice. "I have not employed any one of that sort."

"But the four gentlemen did, Count."

"They did? And for what, pray?"

"They brought some heavy piece of furniture downstairs, and——"

The light now began to dawn on the minds of all, and each one seemed surprised as the footman continued to speak.

"What sort of furniture was it?" asked Joel.

"I could not tell, sir; it was wrapped round with carpet so that I couldn't well see it."

"What did you say to them?"

"'Oh, it's all right,' said they; 'we have just purchased this from our friend, the Count.'"

"How long were they in the house?"

"From the time I opened the door until they left with the bulky piece of furniture was not more than ten minutes."

"I am ruined!" gasped Joel. "I have not now scarcely a penny in the word!"

"Very singular; but from the footman's account there seems to have been a clear case of robbery," said Warner, picking his teeth very quietly. "The thieves must have been very clever, indeed. How were they dressed, John?" speaking to the footman.

"Oh, in the latest style of fashion, sir."

"I suppose so. And had they whiskers?"

"Yes, sir, fine bushy whiskers; and great swells, take them altogether."

"And so, after robbing your master, these rascals have the impudence to send in their bill for cab hire and cartage, eh? Well, well, that beats all I ever heard of before. Who ever heard of such impudence? It is adding insult to injury."

And as he spoke he laughed loudly at old Flint, who was trembling with excitement, and as pale as ashes.

"Call the cabman and carman up here," said Joel; "I wish to speak to them."

These two knights of the whip soon came upon the scene, and answered all the questions put to them in a very dry manner.

"Four toffish lookin' gents came in my keb, and told me to wait for 'em. I did so; and soon arter this carman comes up, and he waits outside also. Presently the four gents comes out o' this house wi' something bulky wrapped up in a carpet, or summat o' that sort, and puts it on that chap's cart, and orders him to drive to a certain place, which he did. The four gents gets into my keb again, and I drives 'em off to an oyster-room, where they had a jolly good feed of oysters, and when they had done, they writes a note and gives it to the waiter, who gives it to me, and the note said I was to call here for my money, as they had none. I goes into the oyster-room to try and find 'em, but the master was in a worse stew than I was; for his customers had eaten four dozen natives each, besides ale and stout, and when the waiter returned from giving the note to me, the four coves had hooked it out by the back way without paying a rap."

Warner listened to what the cabman had to say, but "for the life of him," he said, he couldn't help laughing.

The carman gave his testimony in a similar manner.

He had been hired by two gentlemen to carry away a heavy piece of furniture; what it was he didn't know. He took it to a warehouse down by the Thames, and waited there some time. The two gentlemen came at last, took charge of the goods, whatever they were, and gave him a note to Joel for his charges.

"I know nothing of the whole business at all," said Joel.

"Except this, that I have been robbed of every penny I possessed in the world, and now, instead of being what I was but two hours ago, wealthy and independent, I am now as poor as the poorest beggar can be, and without means or income of any kind."

For a moment all present maintained a dead silence.

Old Flint sighed deeply, and could scarce believe it possible that such a great loss and so vast a misfortune could have fallen upon him so suddenly.

But a few moments before Warner's arrival, he had been congratulating himself on what he and Joel would be able to do with the large sum which was in their possession.

And now, as he looked across the room at Warner, who sat smiling, with a look of inhuman triumph, he felt certain in his own mind that he had been privy to the scheme which the four unknown men had carried out.

Joel's countenance was the very picture of blank despair.

He was penniless, and knew not what to do.

The cabman and carman also pressed him very hard for their money, but, save a very small amount in silver, he had nothing wherewith to pay them.

In this emergency, and with a laugh, Warner came to the rescue.

"I don't like to see tired, honest men like you are done out of your money," said he, "and rather than you should suffer, I will pay you myself."

And Warner put his hand into his pocket and pulled out such a large handful of silver and gold that made Joel's avaricious eyes twinkle again with envy.

Old Flint, however, was now certain that Warner knew something of the sudden and mysterious robbery.

He bit his lips with anger, and rolled his old eyes about in a wild manner.

"I always thought that devil Warner would prove more than a match for me," the lawyer thought.

But he did not give his impressions any expression in words.

"If I were you, sir," said the cabman, politely, "I would call in the police, and tell them all about it."

"So would I, sir," said the footman, very respectfully.

"Yes, so would I," said Warner; "let us call in the police by all means."

Old Flint gnashed his teeth at this remark.

Joel's blood curdled in his veins at the word "police," and he sat in an arm chair, pale as a sheet, and biting his finger nails in impotent rage.

When the cabman, carman, and footman left the apartment, old Flint tried to smile, as he observed,

"Well, luck is against us this time; we have played the game, and have lost, my son."

"You have played the game for a long time and very successfully, I think," observed Warner, "for I haven't touched a single farthing of the booty yet."

"Nor I," said old Flint.

"It was no fault of yours that you did not, though," said Warner; "but you were too clever by half, old man. Instead of dealing fairly with me, you have always played the rogue and vagabond, and now you are reduced to your proper station—you are a penniless beggar. I always told you I would have revenge," said Warner, bitterly, "and so I have."

He rose to depart, and as he did so old Flint approached him, to whisper.

"What is it you want?" said Warner, in a surly tone.

"I want to ask a favour of you."

"What is it?—to get a rope to hang yourself with?"

"No, not that exactly," said old Flint, with a faint smile upon his face. "You were always fond of joking, you know, but the real truth is, my dear friend, I haven't a shilling in the world, and——"

"Yes, I dare say, but you don't get anything out of me—no, not one farthing."

And as he spoke these words, there was a world of fierce hatred flashing from his small dark eyes, that caused Flint to wince again.

"No, Flint, if you were drowning and one halfpenny would save your life, that half-penny I would not give to you. We part now and for ever. While I thought you had old Ford's riches in your keeping, I would have followed you like your own shadow all the days of your life; but now that you have lost it and every hope of recovering it, you are harmless; you can go your way and totter into the workhouse."

"Harmless, am I?" said old Flint, with a vindictive look "no I am *not* harmless. Warner, beware! I am an old man, but I can bite like a reptile, and in the dark too."

"Can you? ha, ha," laughed Warner, scornfully. "Perhaps you would like to turn informer?"

"It matters not what I intend to do, but you must remember, I have not yet forgotten all the insults and bodily injury you have inflicted on me, nor will I to my dying day. You will hang yet, mark my words for it."

"Indeed! and for what, pray? Our little job at the Red House, perhaps, you mean?"

"I do."

"Then there will be four of us who will hang together; you, I, Jonathan, and ——"

"Who else?"

"Why, your son, yonder, the grand, penniless imposter, Count Schmidt, ha, ha! Count, eh, what next? Not much account now, I think. Good-day, Flint; take care of yourself, Count."

And with a loud laugh Warner slammed the door of the room and went downstairs.

He met the footman in the hall, to whom he said—

"My man, if you will take my best advice, go and demand your wages and leave the house; the Count upstairs is an impostor, and is not worth a single farthing."

"Indeed, sir!" said "Jeames," in amazement. "You astonish me. Why, I always thought he was possessed of thousands."

"It is not so. He has not enough to pay for a night's lodging, I tell you. Besides, he and the old man, his father, upstairs, are thieves."

"Thieves?"

"Nothing less, I assure you."

"You frighten me, sir. Why, there are dozens of tradesmen in the neighbourhood who have trusted him for large amounts."

"Then, tell them to send in their accounts at once—or, what is better, have the two knaves arrested."

Thus describing Flint and his son, Warner left the house.

"Jeames" was not long in informing the household of all that he knew and suspected.

The servants were up in arms in no time.

The man cook threw his pots and pans about in a phrenzied fury.

He pulled his whiskers, got red in the face, cursed and swore, and flourished a large carving knife in a most desperate manner, threatening all manner of things to everybody.

The females ran upstairs, and packed their boxes in great haste, while "Jeames," the footman, tucked up his sleeves, and prepared himself to punch somebody's head.

In the meantime, however, old Flint and his son had not been idle.

They prepared for instant departure.

"It won't do for us to remain here a single hour longer," said the old man. "If the police get wind of this affair, both of us will be discovered, and then it's all up."

Joel packed his boxes hastily, and crammed into them everything he possibly could.

In less than twenty minutes he had closely packed several trunks with everything of value, and then rang the bell for "Jeames."

The summons was not attended to.

He rang again and again.

But still there was no response.

"This is strange," thought Joel; "but an hour ago these servants would almost fly to obey my wishes; but now they are all as deaf as door posts."

"I wonder if that villain, Warner, has divulged any secret," said old Flint.

"No, it cannot be," said Joel. "I wish I had shot him."

"That would have made too much noise; a knife would have done it more quietly."

"Then why didn't you do it?" growled Joel.

"He was too powerful for one man, or for two either."

Joel sneered at his aged parent, and rang the bell again more violently than ever.

"Jeames," if the truth must be told, had been so much overcome with Warner's strange news that he had visited the wine cellar, and helped himself so liberally to wines and other liquids that he was half drunk.

At last, however, he heard the bell, and in his shirt-sleeves, and a bottle in hand, he struggled upstairs.

"What means this?" demanded Joel, in angry tones. "Where is your coat, sir? and what means that bottle in your hand?"

"It means this," said "Jeames," stuttering and spluttering; "it means this 'ere. I want's my wages and extras, right down on the nail, and, if you don't let me have it, I shall be under the painful necessity of punching your head, for I've found out you're no account at all, and there's an end on it, and no better than a chimney-sweep in disguise. There, them's my sentiments!"

"Rascal!" gasped Joel.

"Knock the drunken villain down," said old Flint, very valorously.

"You'd better come and try it on, old 'un," said the tall footman, holding up his hands in a pugilistic attitude. "I've got plenty of friends to back me; here they come."

At that moment, all the servants in the house came clamouring into the room.

Seeing the footmen in his shirt sleeves, and in fighting attitude, the servants made sure he had been struck by some one; and, therefore, encouraged him on by shouting—

"Give it to 'em, Jeames."

"Hit 'em in the eyes."

"Call the police."

"Jeames" squared up to his late master, and, although not sober, he quickly knocked the count sprawling upon the floor.

Old Flint, hearing the alarming cry of "police," rushed through the angry group of servants, and managed to reach the head of the stairs.

When there, however, he encountered the man cook, who administered such a vigorous kick, that it sent old Flint headlong down stairs.

Neither Joel nor his father dare shout for help, for fear of attracting any attention from officers in the streets; and this was the reason why they bore their punishment so meekly and silently.

But directly Joel got upon his legs again he pulled out a dirk knife, and, with sundry horrible oaths, threatened to kill all who came near him.

One of the maid-servants, however, with a broom-handle struck his arm so violently that the knife fell harmlessly upon the ground and made Joel dance again with pain.

He knew not what to do.

To stay among his infuriated domestics would have been madness, he thought; and yet what must he do?

Leave all his luggage behind?

This was a sad thought to Joel, whose sole wealth in the world now consisted of clothes and the like.

"Go and fetch a constable," said the footman; "he shan't use knives among us English people!"

One of the servants ran downstairs with this intention, when, with a sudden bound, Joel burst from the circle of his tormentors, and cleared the stairs a dozen at a time, his hair all dishevelled, his coat and trousers torn, a bloody nose, and a black-eye.

In this unenviable guise he ran forth into the street, his servants shouting and bawling at his heels like so many wild animals.

"Stop thief! stop thief!" was the cry.

But Joel, with the swiftness of a startled hare, ran down a mews, and, disappearing in a dirty, narrow court, filled with costermongers' barrows and baskets, he was lost to view.

Breathless, tattered, and now reduced to beggary, the lawyer's son was a guilty fugitive on the face of the earth, despised by all and hateful even to himself.

# THE BOY SOLDIER; OR, GARIBALDI'S YOUNG CAPTAIN.

"I KNOCKED AT THE DOOR."

## CHAPTER CXIII.

CAPTAIN TOM FORD ENCOUNTERS A TERRIBLE STORM—CAUGHT IN A CYCLONE—THE GRAPHIC ACCOUNT THEREOF.

THE stirring events narrated in a preceding chapter were scarcely over, and Captain Frank's camp was once more put into regular order, when, tired and worn out with their fighting and watchings, most of the lads lay down to sleep round their camp fires.

During the night a strange horseman rode up, and, without much ceremony, made his way up to Captain Frank's tent, and delivered various letters, one of which was from his brother Tom.

As might be supposed Frank for a moment threw aside all other letters, and eagerly scanned that of his brother, which ran as follows:—

"In my last letter to you I recounted our various encounters and adventures with the enemy on the sea, and, in continuation, have now to say that when I had taken my own vessel and prizes into a neutral South American port I determined to sell both my ship and the prizes in order to purchase a small, swift-sailing English iron clad, which was for sale in the harbour of Havannah.

"Having stored my guns and other valuables on shore, I and a great number of my best men took passage in a British mail steamer for Cuba, but had not left the port of Carthagena long when we encountered one of the most terrific storms man ever heard of, an account of which I now send to you.



"In regular order, then, I may say that H. M.'s royal mail steam-ship 'Antelope' left Carthagena with a gentle breeze, and, as she passed out of harbour, looking so seaworthy, so taut, and so trim, received and returned the hearty cheers of the crews of the British man-of-war 'Bengal' and 'Carnatic,' at anchor there.

"Little did we then suppose that in a very short space of time our noble vessel would be in the most imminent danger, combating, to her utmost strength, with a cyclone of no ordinary violence.

"The time of the year, and the appearance of the weather, did not, in the least, lead the oldest sailor to even dream of such an event.

"At 4 A.M. on Friday we had a light breeze, fine weather, and a long, heavy swell from the north-east, light breeze and cloudy, with a rainy appearance and heavy sea.

"All the port holes were now shut, and plain sail set. Showers of rain, and breeze freshening, but nothing particularly threatening.

"The swell on the sea was supposed to be the result of wind on the ocean some days previous, we being then in the gulf.

"9 A.M.—Barometer rapidly falling, breeze and swell increasing, the anchors were now secured inward, and quarter-boats hoisted close up. Breakfast being well over, we were chiefly on deck, with just that little amount of interest amongst us that is occasioned by seeing the wind increasing, and the top-gallant sails furling, with a second reef taken in the top-sails.

"10 A.M.—The wind came in such hard squalls that the foresail could not be reefed, and the fore-topsail was blown to pieces.

"11 A.M.—Matters looked very serious; ladies and most of the passengers below; mizentopsail blown to ribbons; the hard squalls rapidly increasing to a very heavy gale. The atmosphere all round, to a landsman, even, looked very threatening, with a kind of thick, hazy appearance.

NOON.—We are now in a terrific gale, shipping very large quantities of water down the *stoke*-hole; the sea washed off the battened tarpauling from the skid grating; maintopsail blown out of the bolt ropes; port quarter boat blown away from the davits, and jolly-boat washed from the stern.

"The scene on deck now was striking; the comfortable steamer, with its awnings and comfortable chairs everywhere on its roomy decks, had, as if by the wand of a magician, been changed in a short two hours into a perfect chaos of desolation—ropes stretched here and there across the deck to enable the sailors to hold on by; the awnings gone, after cracking themselves to pieces and firing as it were vollies over their own graves; the chairs and benches smashed to pieces, and the noise of the elements heightened by the sharp reports of cracking sails and splitting masts.

"The barometer falling rapidly; the ship lurching heavily and shipping tons of water over her lee gunwale and quarter; starboard life boat and quarter boats carried away, taking the massive iron stancheons with them; forecastle at times almost buried by the sea and filling the lower forecastle.

"The ship was evidently running into a cyclone; the captain, therefore, determined to round the ship to with her head N.N.E. This dangerous operation he performed very successfully, and also managed to lash and secure the rudder. The sea which curled over her when she dipped her stern carried our captain completely off his legs, providentially inboard, and a Chinaman caught him.

"1.30.—Our jib-boom was carried away, taking the foretopgallant mast with it. The sea was now tremendous, and, if anything, increasing.

"The scenes below in the cabins on the starboard side were not exhilarating to passengers.

"The water which had been pouring down forward on the main deck, found its way aft, and literally filled the cabins.

"With each lurch of the vessel the water in the cabins ran up the sides, washing up the lower berths, upsetting the apparently heavy wash-hand stands with their marble tops, and sending all the trunks and boxes with tremendous force backwards and forwards. It was not possible to stand in these cabins for an instant, without the greatest liability of getting a leg broken from something dashing against it.

"The ladies were collected in the cabin on the port side, and nothing could surpass their patient endurance at this alarming time.

"On our upper deck the work of devastation still going on; the starboard cat-head was now washed away, taking the best bower-anchor off the forecastle; the anchor remained hanging by the shank-painter or chain, and beat against the side of the ship, knocking a hole some eight inches in diameter.

"The weather rendered all attempts to secure the anchor utterly useless.

"2 P.M.—The barometer showing a tendency to rise a little; wind veering round to the S.W. with the same force, and *blowing* inboard the weather life-boat, bringing the forest iron davit with it, and fetching up again the funnel; the gig and quarter-boat turned over by the same squall.

"3 P.M.—The mizenmast-head carried away, the wreck hanging about to leeward against the rigging.

"Maintopmast went short off by the rigging; water increasing fast in the stoke-hole and engine-room; the ship labouring heavily; all the deck gear washed in and smashed; lee bulwarks gone in many places, awning-booms, lower booms, coops, and ladders.

Every exertion was now made to overcome the rapidly increasing water between decks, and in the engine-room and stoke-hole, by baling and pumping, and to keep the seas out by getting tarpaulings stretched over the gratings.

"In this last operation the second officer was carried away to leeward, and his leg badly broken in two places by a hen-coop.

"The passengers' cabins on the starboard side were by this time nearly demolished, as to fittings and their contents; with each lurch of the ship the water rushed in and out in volumes, sweeping everything, and beating up everything into one mass of pulp and *débris.*

"4 P.M.—We had now seven feet of water in our stoke-hole and engine-room, but forward only eighteen inches; the water not increasing, but washing about with such violence that the stoke-hole plates and fire-bars were absolutely washed up, and the *fires put out.*

"It is a very unpleasant fact to learn in a steamer in a hurricane that our greatest power for controlling the vessel is gone.

"What would we now have given to have heard and felt that vibrating screw which, in ordinary occasions, is such a nuisance.

"Still the captain, who never for an instant left the 'con' (*i.e.*, watching the steering), kept us well up against the storm, and, by his skill, effected as easy a position for the vessel as it was possible.

"Not a stitch of canvas could we show, but, by our yards, kept her head well up, all hands hard at work baling and pumping; but the best pump of all on the upper deck, called the 'Dountons,' could not be got to work at all for a long time.

"When dirt, bits of coal, &c., are washing about down below in a gale, as must be often the case, it seems these pumps are very liable to get the 'hose' at the end of the pipe choked up, and as in our case the rose was seven feet under water, it was at present inaccessible—the pipe was accordingly cut above the rose and corked well down to that depth.

"Subsequently the second engineer and the carpenter did, though with that great depth of water, get down and cleared the 'hose;' this difficult and dangerous operation was most valuable to us, and they deserve great credit for it.

"From this time up to 7 o'clock every effort was directed to getting the water under.

"7 P.M.—Ship a complete wreck. Fires had been out for some time, and daylight gone; sea and wind still very high.

"8 P.M.—Gale decreasing, but shipping large quantities of water to leeward: ship labouring very much from the water in her.

"9 P.M.—Weather moderating, but little impression made on the water in the ship: squalls still very heavy, but at long intervals.

"SATURDAY MORNING.—How long and weary and anxious was that Friday night; but the first dawn of Saturday was cheering, for though the sea was still very high the gale was decidedly moderating,

"6 A.M.—The barometer inclined to fall, and the weather looked very squally, with thunder and lightning.

"8 A.M.—All working hard, and the 'Dounton' pump doing its duty—water not decreasing—and some leak supposed to exist, though not a large one.

"10 A.M.—The anchor before mentioned we were now able to secure, and to move about more freely on the deck.

"How shorn of its beauty did our noble ship appear.

"Forward, in addition to the damage already mentioned, the bob stays and lee bowsprit shrouds were broken; iron outriggers bent double, all the rigging very slack; traces and lifts carried away to leeward, and in knots, with the remnant of the sails, rudder chain gone and jammed on the screw, starboard quarter galley swept away.

"7 P.M.—Reduced the water to five feet in the engine-room and stoke-hole.

"A little before this we got the 'donkey engine' at work below, and on deck, about 4.30 p.m., the steam had helped a little working of the 'Dounton' pump. How refreshing to the passengers was the sound of 'steam,' a sure relief to the really very hard work at the pumps.

"11 P.M.—The engines began working very slowly, and we felt our troubles would now soon be lightened if only we could keep the fires lit and steam up.

"12 P.M.—Fine weather; but ship with a strong list to starboard, and rolling heavily.

SUNDAY, May 1st.—Engines working slowly; pumping still going on and baling; the crew very exhausted, and but little impression being made on the water in the ship.

"We could not get up sufficient steam to throw much of their labour of pumping on the engines; and, therefore, considering all the circumstances, the captain, at 5 a.m., resolved to return to port.

"In the wisdom of this all concurred—neither passengers, crew, nor ship were in a fit condition to encounter another severe gale, and the weather looked far from settled.

"The passengers formed a strong able-bodied force, and very fortunate it was for the safety of the ship and for themselves that they were so strong, for, unquestionably, the unaided efforts of the crew and stewards could never have so far reduced the water as to get the fires lit.

"It was a pleasant sight to see passengers of all ranks and ages working vigorously at the pumps and baling.

"We formed ourselves into gangs and worked in succession, each gang doing a fixed number of strokes.

"In the great heat the work was very conducive to intense thirst, and the number of refreshing jugs of 'shandy gaff,' made and brought to us by a young member of our community, will always be gratefully remembered.

"The party of engineers of the Royal Navy, coming from China, were very valuable, from their hearty working and help at the pumps.

"On this morning, the last task falling to the passengers was to form sanitary gangs, and clear the debris out of the cabins.

"This duty performed, the saloon was a little more bearable; but the cabins still remained very offensive from the smell of wet clothes, boards, &c.

"2 P.M.—I fancy few steamers or ships have gone through such severe weather coming so suddenly on them.

"She is a splendid ship, and stood wonderfully the tremendous blows which she constantly received from the sea, making her tremble from head to stern—had we shipped seas to windward we must have foundered.

"Such severe weather is, I believe, seldom known, and, on account of the heat, these mail ships have a great number of large openings along the upper deck and main deck.

"Caught thus suddenly in a cyclone, the seas effect an entrance before it is possible to securely cover in the said openings. *

"The admirable skill, energy, and pluck of the Mexican captain and his officers are worthy of all praise.

"The crew undoubtedly was completely cowed, but the European officers came out more than equal to the emergency.

They were everywhere at the right time, doing the right thing.

"They and they only made gallant, but vain attempts, in the first tremendous gusts of the hurricane, to take in the sails.

"The chief officer, and chief engineer, were very prominent in their devotion to their duty, and it is difficult to say which service presented the most danger—the attempts to keep the engines going, whilst the sea was pouring down into the engine-room, and steam flying almost in every direction, or that on deck where the wind had its full swing, and blocks, ropes, spars, boats, hen-coops, &c., were dashing about in all directions.

"The passengers have marked their sense of the services of the captain, officers, and steward, by presenting the captain with a letter and a sum of £100 to purchase a piece of plate; the chief officer and chief engineers with letters and sums of £50 to each; and the stewards with a sum of £90 divided amongst them. I must not omit to note that the value of a body of strong able-bodied stewards was fully shown; no men could have worked better, more cheerfully, or more willingly. The stewardesses received separate presents, having lost all their effects. Many of the officers of the ship have lost all their baggage, and the passengers on the starboard side have suffered severely. The married parties especially on that side of the ship have lost, on an average, by luggage utterly ruined, not less than £80 each.

"When we arrived at Carthagena once more, I took passage for one of the Texan ports, and by stress of weather we were obliged to run into the little harbor of San Patricio, where we now are.

"I have not time to write a longer letter this time, for the winds have moderated and we shall sail again in less than an hour, perhaps, for Galveston.

"Thinking that a few lines from me would be agreeable, and hoping at the same time that both you and our gallant little band of Boy Soldiers are well and hearty up the country.

"I remain, your Brother,

"TOM FORD.

"N.B.—I send this letter by an American who is on his way to join the republican army in search of a brother of his, a trapper, who has long been in the Comanche and Blackfeet country.

"He is a gallant fellow, and if he finds you in his rambles, make him welcome for my sake. When I reach Havanah, I shall write again, for I am in a great hurry to get a good ship, for the other had

*Some ship, supposed, on account of the number of silk bales floating about, to be a China ship, apparently was lost in the "cyclone." On Monday morning we passed bales, and the body of a lascar lashed to a mast.

been so knocked about by wind, storm, and cannon-shot, that it was scarcely sea-worthy. When I get the iron-clad, however, I shall give the enemy 'pepper,' you may be sure. "T. F."

## CHAPTER CXIV.

### YANKEE SAM—THE SCOUT AND SPY—STIRRING ADVENTURES.

The next letter which Captain Frank opened proved to be an order from Juarez, which commanded him to leave the part he was then guarding and to descend the river as fast as possible, for the French were about to attack him in great force.

Captain Frank did as he was commanded.

His camps were struck that same night.

Before morning he was a long way from where he had had such a sanguinary and midnight meeting with the Comanches.

The Indians, however, as we have seen, swore friendship with the Boy Band; and how they fulfilled their promise will be seen in another chapter of startling interest.

When, therefore, the company of Boy Soldiers had joined the main body of the Republican army, they were constantly on the move to and fro, for the English boys were favourites with Juarez, who had great faith in their bravery, and accordingly employed them always on the most hazardous enterprises.

There were several American volunteers who had joined Frank's company, and they proved excellent soldiers; but if they had one fault more than another, it was their fondness for scouting and acting as spies.

But there was one called "Yankee Sam," a spy, who had rendered great service to the whole Republican army, and to Frank's company of boys on more than one occasion, and saved them from the treachery of the French or their renegade Mexican followers.

This Yankee Sam was, or rather had been, a person of property before the coming of Maximilian and the French; but rather than oppose the cause of the people, he left his Mexican estates, and joined Juarez even as a private soldier.

Yankee Sam, the scout and spy, was the talk of the whole army, and his exploits on his famous grey mare, "Nancy," were numerous and almost beyond belief for daring.

It is not our intention in this place to speak much personally of this famous spy, but an account written by Captain Frank Ford to his friends in England contains many things about Sam which are well worth remembering.

In one of his letters Frank says:—

"We had just pitched tents one evening, after a long march in the cold winds, over hills, through woods, and immense quantities of mud, when, lying down smoking on a bundle of hay by the camp fire, we heard the jingling of spurs and harness, and looking up saw Yankee Sam and his grey wearily ambling by.

"The invitation to take a cup of coffee was eagerly accepted by our old acquaintance, and his mare being properly provided for he was so charmed with the savour of sundry beefsteaks broiling on the coals that he consented to take up his quarters with us for the night.

"With a circle of some twenty officers and men we made a pleasant party round the immense fire of blazing oak logs.

"Some were engaged with cards, others wrote letters home.

"A fiddle was not far distant, with a laughing crowd of dancers going through a cotillon.

"Many were cooking, eating, sleeping, and picket guards were going out on duty.

"'What's the news, Sam?' asked one.

"'How's all the girls in Mexico?' chimed in another.

"'How much is whisky over there, Sam,' questioned a third, and so on.

"'I'm mighty tired, boys,' said the scout, smoking and reclining; 'but we had a first-rate time of it. We fooled the French as usual, and had a jolly old spree in Mexico city; danced with the girls, had lots of tip-top whisky and cigars, and brought back letters for the fellows; went wherever we darned pleased; seized two of General Bazaine's orderlies with despatches—found them in bed a little way back—and brought them over the river safely, papers and all.

"'We had some difficulty in crossing at the old place, so while some of our videttes were fussing about and attracting attention, four of us, in Yankee costume, swam our horses, and soon reaching a friendly house changed clothes, and put out again, for we could heard the French galloping about furiously in all directions. Our boys took to the woods, and never left it until within thirty miles of Mexico city.

"'Talk of the Mexicans taking Maximilian, 'tis all bosh! I've lived there for fifteen years, and should know something about it, and am positive that ninety-nine out of every hundred are true Mexicans if they only had a fair chance to express themselves.

"'Freedom of speech, indeed! or freedom of the press!—it is all nonsense.

"'None dare speak openly, and should the newspapers even hint at French tyranny, a prison is assigned them without judge or jury.

"'As to habeas corpus—that is a thing of the past.

"'While I was in the capital the members of the Legislature and Senate arrived, and every one in the least suspected of true national feeling was waited upon as he landed from the car or at his hotel, and, without the slightest explanation, conducted to dungeons.

"'There are fortifications of immense strength overlooking the city, and every gun in every battery is shotted, and pointed at the city.

"'As the French confess, with a laugh, "all these works were raised, not to protect your city, but to destroy and lay it in one indistinguishable heap of ashes should the slightest indication of a revolt betray itself."

"'And they claim that Mexicans are loyal, and have brotherly love for them.

"'Yes, as much love as the lamb bears the wolf.

"'A lady cannot walk the streets in a dress of her own choice without its being noticed and commented upon by hundreds of red-breeched soldiers or spies, and should she wear any colours indicative of Mexican sentiment, is immediately arrested and insulted.

"'As to taking the "oath of allegiance to Maximilian," so called, thousands have done so from sheer necessity; but argue that it is forced, and that they do not, and will not, consider themselves faithful to those who have proved unfaithful to every compact and every instrument.

"'And they are right. What can the thousands of Mexicans do?

"'Is not the country overrun by all the villains and spies the French can control or hire?

"'Are the masses armed?

"'Can they organize?

"'Can they, without shackles, boldly declare their sentiments or wishes to a civilized world?

"'What would you have them do?

"'Can they escape across the borders or the rivers into the United States?

"'All the railroads and boats are in French hands, and you cannot travel ten miles round your birth-place without a "pass" in your pocket, or be dodged or accompanied by an armed spy.

"'Can we even pray in our churches unrestrained?

"'No; several ministers are now already in jail, not for denouncing Maximilian in public or private, but simply from being suspected of cherishing ideas antagonistic to these of the French.

"'What must the people do?

"'Without a legislature of their own free choice; without civil tribunals of common justice, with no appeal to higher authority than the will of the French; without implements of war, resources, or place of meeting—what would we have them do?

"'Rise like raving, unarmed fools, to be mercilessly butchered by trained bands of hirelings—the offscourings of the earth?

"'Better as it is.

"''Tis now a game of 'diamond cut diamond'—play hypocrite with hypocrites.

"'But the day will come when the true sentiments of Mexicans will be fully known.'

"'Yes, that's all very good, Sam; no one disputes it. We know that the Mexicans are "sound" enough, but take a drink out of the count's canteen—prime old Rye, too—and go on with your trip,' said one, who was yawning, and wanted something exciting to keep him awake.

"'Well, boys,' continued Sam, refilling his pipe, 'one of my scouting trips is much like all of them, and not very interesting; but to go on.'

"'When we approached the city I told the boys we had better separate, and meet as strangers at one of the hotels.

"'We did so, and as the guard was not over vigilant around, or in town, I got along very well, and met several friends—but avoided some acquaintance from foreboding suspicion.

"'Having stabled my mare at an out-of-the-way place, I called on an old friend, and was surprised to find him giving a party to some dozen French officers.

"'He laughed, and introduced me as a friend, and before long we passed the bottle freely, and got along swimmingly. I bore out my character as a Yankee admirably, and spoke splendidly about the Empire, and a hundred other bygone catch-lines, and was put down by the French as a 'regular brick," &c.

"'I did not drink much, but danced with the girls, condoled with them on the trials and privations of the times, and procured a large amount of information, dropped in scraps from the half-intoxicated French, nearly all pertaining to the number and disposition of their troops, and slept at my friend's house that night.

"'According to promise, I called on one of the French next morning, and as he was officer of the day we walked arm-in-arm over the fortifications, everything being explained to me, and by well-put questions I extracted all the information possible, and by comparing statements arrived at pretty accurate facts and figures.

"'From a friend I obtained the "sign" and "countersign," by which regularly initiated Mexicans might detect each other, and by this means spent several days very agreeably in the city.

"'I was surprised, however, to find so many belonging to the secret Mexican organisation, for I could not be in any assembly long ere signs were exchanged, and I have not unfrequently heard staunch members of the Club speaking very loudly in favour of Max in the presence of the French, when at the same moment signs to the contrary were frequently passed between us.

"'They manage this thing well in Mexico city, and have plenty of funds to assist our needy sympathisers who come under their notice.

"'Constant correspondence is maintained with Juarez, and semi-weekly dispatchés sent to them by ways and means which the French authorities can never discover.

"'But of all the Mexicans, the women are the most ardent and open in the expression of feeling.

"'When officers ask them to play or sing, they usually comply by performing the most rebellious kinds of music, in the most modest and artless manner, causing the visitors to sit uneasy in their seats, and look very serio-comic.

"'Not that all such things can be done with impunity, by any means.

"'I know some and have heard of other instances where our female friends have been taken up and put into gaol for speaking or singing seditious sentiments, or causing excitement by wearing party colours upon the stage or in the streets.

The theatres, however, being organs of public taste, were under the protection and guidance of the French, and nightly crowded by soldiers, who sat hour after hour applauding clap-trap pieces, in which French soldiers accomplished miracles of heroism; or when dying, did so wrapped up in the red, white and blue flag, with a flourish of trumpets.

"'It strikes me that the Frenchman proper may be truthfully termed a theatrical and imaginative being, and be wrought upon by "effect."

"'From childhood they are supplied with a multitude of books of equivocal taste and morality.

"'Their historians are partial; their swarms of novelists persons of fervid imaginations reared in all forms of atheism, and decidedly unreal in all things.

"'Their theatres, also, are the public expounders of prejudice and bad taste.

"'Until of late all battle-pieces had for subject the wars with Great Britain, and we know that one Frenchman was always considered equal to a dozen Englishman, and on the stage, like Samson, they slew their thousands with loud applause, and ended with a large expenditure of "blue fire," and a waving of banners.'

"'That is all very good, Sam,' broke in a fat old captain; 'but go on with the narrative, "taps" will sound presently, and I must be off to my guard.'

"When our party had sufficiently enjoyed themselves, and effected the purposes intended, we met and devised plans for the return.

"From the information of a trusty friend, it was deemed advisable to be extremely cautious, as everything on the Rio Grande indicated movements of importance, and the different forts were doubly guarded.

"General Mezia, Maximilian's right-hand man, had been in secret conference with the authorities for several days, and in private circles bragged of what he was going to do.

"*He* was not going into winter quarters until the vile 'rebels' were driven from his front, and they did so at rebel expense, &c.

"As General Mezia acted in conjunction with General Lopez, at Matamoras, across the river a piece, it was not a matter of much doubt whence the blow was likely to come, so we hastened back again as speedily as possible.

"The nearer we approached the river, the more difficult it was to proceed.

"The French had so many men lying along the main roads, that it was almost impossible to travel.

"We picketed our horses in the woods when near Matamoras, and held a council of war.

"I proposed to procure the countersign by stratagem, if possible, and go into Matamoras.

"The rest of the party vehemently dissented from such an adventure, but promised to stay at the house of a friend till my return.

"I had resumed my half-French uniform, and proceeded cautiously along the road, according to the directions of friends, and as it was just sunset saw innumerable camp-fires in every direction.

"From a distance I perceived picket guards round a fire, at the forks of the road, and was compelled to halt.

"Hitching the grey mare in the woods, I proceeded on foot, and crept among the brushwood until within thirty paces of the nearest guard.

"Having lain there for an hour or more, some one approached, and I faintly heard the countersign of 'Puebla,' given, and, being satisfied, cautiously returned, mounted the mare, and galloped along the road, roaring the Marsellaise.

"'Halt!' shouted the picket, as I unceremoniously approached.

"'Who comes there?'

"'A friend with the countersign,' I answered, hiccuping, and pretended to reel in the saddle.

"'Advance, friend, and give the countersign,' replied the sentry, with a laugh, for, thinking me an officer returning from a jollification, he scarcely noticed the countersign.

"Passing along I could not help lingering near my old estates.

"Regiments of Frenchmen were camped upon them; my woods, fences, and barns were all destroyed, and they had converted the dwellings into guard-houses, where dozens were howling in intoxication.

"Possessed of the countersign, I found no difficulty in passing from place to place, and enjoyed myself until midnight with a lot of officers who were bent on a drinking bout.

"One of them had brought important despatches from General Bazaine, and was to return before sunrise.

"'But,' said he, 'if they think I am going to travel thirty miles again to-night, the general is much mistaken. I shall just go out of town, and put up at Paulo's for the night; what say you, Smidt?' said he to another aide, a Belgian.

"'You are not going on with your papers to-night, eh? They'll keep, man, they ain't important, so let's make a night of it, and put in an excuse of lame horses!'

"Both agreed to the plan, and about an hour afterwards proceeded on their way together.

"I knew P——'s plantation very well, and resolved that both their persons and papers should visit *this* side of the river, and immediately started for my party, awaiting me.

"Having watched in which room these worthies were domiciled, we lay in wait, and I hit upon the idea of separating them.

"Accordingly, I rode up to the house and inquired if Captain Smidt was there. I had been told he was, and had been sent by General Mejia to call him immediately.

"Smidt soon made his appearance, cursing and swearing in every dialect of Dutch and English.

"'Some cot dem tyful hat watched him, sure unt he was a gone schicken, else how old Mejia know him not gone?'

"I condoled with Smidt, and ere we had gone many paces, he was seized and secured without a show of resistance.

"When Paulo was about to blow out the candle, I knocked again.

"He was in a terrible temper, and when he shoved the candlestick close in my face to see who it was, almost staggered with astonishment. (See cut in this Number.

"He fully recognised me, but presenting a revolver at his head, and placing a finger on my lip, I passed in, and a companion stood guard over him, while I went upstairs.

"Knocking at the door, Smidt's companion answered, and I entered.

"He was surprised, but glad to see me. I had heard him state his intention to stay at Paulo's all night, when in the tavern, and thought I'd follow suit, intending to go on and join my regiment in the morning.

"After smoking and partaking of some brandy I had with me, we talked for a long time on the subject of arms and accoutrements.

"He had a magnificent pair of revolvers, and it was my ambition to effect his capture without bloodshed. I handed over for inspection my self-cocker, empty, and he pushed across the table his loaded weapons.

"I fingered them coolly for several minutes, and with apparent thoughtlessness, cocked them both.

"Presenting them at his head suddenly, I informed him who I was, and commanded him to dress immediately and follow me.

"'Resistance is useless,' I remarked, 'the house is surrounded.'

"Deadly pale and almost paralyzed, the courier dressed and was conducted to his horse.

"We started off without a whisper, and soon arrived at the spot where Smidt was guarded.

"In my absence the boys had gagged him, to stop his eternal prattle, and when he recognized his companion, handcuffed, I thought his hair would stand on end with astonishment.

"With our prisoners in the centre, we briskly trotted along the bright moonlit road, and ere long caught a distant view of our camp fires.

"The river, we knew, was well guarded at nearly all points; hence, for the sake of caution, we stole through the woods and made up a plan.

"Two of our party were to advance boldly to the river, give the countersign, and say that they had volunteered to cross to reconnoitre the Republican army.

"This news would spread up and down the bank, and the mounted men especially feel anxious to converse with their comrades, and attended little to their posts meanwhile.

"The ruse answered admirably, and, while I saw one particular spot deserted, our party issued from the woods and swam their horses across.

"No resistance was offered by our prisoners.

"We had explained to them the importance of silence and obedience, while revolvers were always pointed to enforce submission.

"We had scarcely crossed, however, when in the distance we saw two squadrons of the enemy dashing along the river bank in great commotion.

"'Twas lucky we had used all expedition, as some one at Paulo's must have informed on us.

"As I stood in a thicket, listening to their angry conversation, I could not help laughing heartily at their annoyance, and they must have heard it, for one said,

"'That's him; I know his voice, major.'

"'That you, Yankee Sam?'

"'Yes, that's me. How are you, major? Fine night, isn't it? I shall give you another call shortly.'

"I could scarcely get out of the way before a perfect shower of shot was dropping all around me."

"Yankee Sam's narrative was listened to with great interest by the Boy Soldiers, for it was well known that the brave fellow had lost nearly all his property in Mexico, on account of the war, although had he not taken up arms he might have retained every acre of all he was posessed."

## CHAPTER CXV.

### THE BATTLE OF MATAMORAS—THE VICTORY OF THE REPUBLICANS.

In another part of this present letter which Captain Frank wrote to his brother, the brave young fellow describes what happened a few days after the narrative given by the tall Yankee round the camp fire in the boys' camp.

He says, speaking of that part of the Republican army to which he was attached in a more particular manner:—

"I thought at first to write but a short account of our doings here; but as important events have taken place within the past forty-eight hours, I cannot allow the mail messenger to go without saying a few words regarding them.

"And although we are in high spirits at having soundly thrashed one of Maximilian's best generals here near Matamoras, our sufferings have been extreme throughout the entire campaign; but, though troubling and inconveniencing us, to some degree, have tended to doubly harden and make our limbs as tough as steel.

"Continually marching through non-inhabited districts, we had to depend upon Fortune for supplies, as our stores were few, and the departments particularly 'slow' in such 'fast' times as *we* have experienced.

"Over mountains, through 'gaps,' across rivers, streams, creeks, &c., our progress was toilsome and weary.

"But few doctors meddled with any one.

"'A good tough march' was the prescription for all, and not more than a hundred could be found upon the sick lists at any time during our frequent and rapid journeyings to and fro, continually harassing the enemy, cutting off supply trains, 'bush-whacking' for whole days with them, scouting and scouring the whole country was our constant occupation.

"Cavalry led a hard life, and must have been made of brass to support the trials incident to their daily duty.

"Among the mountains a party of these partisan horse would watch all the roads, conceal their fires, and hang around the enemy with pertinacious watchfulness, and at the least opportunity dash into them, capturing and destroying as they went, living as best they might, and doing whatever they pleased, generally.

"As scouts these men were invaluable. They were here, and there, and everywhere.

"No track could be kept of them.

"Their dress was of skins or anything that came to hand, and so long as grass was found for their hardy, wiry, Indian horses, the riders cared little for food, dress, leisure or relief from duty.

"The enemy were watched like mice, and no movement could take place from the Upper Rio Grande to the mountain regions, but some of these 'irregulars' were fully aware of it, and informed Juarez thereof.

"The enemy vowed vengeance against these hardy fellows, and sought to train *their* horsemen to the wild, half-Indian kind of life practised by ours.

"But just imagine obese Dutchmen, such as Maximilian had brought over with him, rivalling the swiftness, daring, and endurance of our wiry frontiersmen!

"They were posted on mountains and in the passes,' guarded fords, bridges, and roads, as ours did; but their loss was continual, and the mysterious disappearance of stores, horses, waggons, and men, unaccountable; so that they were withdrawn, and the experiment abandoned as an expensive and fruitless one.

"Entirely masters of the roads, and every route by land or water, our horse and foot had lively times on outpost duty, and stood all fatigues without grumbling, but rather enjoying it, seldom troubling Juarez for supplies of any kind, save ammunition, but frequently driving into camp large numbers of beeves, hogs, fodder, corn, and whatever could be purloined from the enemy.

"Flanks, front or rear, the Imperialists hardly dared to move, except in large bodies. Our guerillas lay in every bush, and many an enemy was found lying dead at his post without a trace of those who did the deed.

"These partisan horsemen were remorseless.

"They expected little mercy if captured, and spared but few found in arms against them.

"Some of our men, falling into the hands of the enemy, were hung on the spot; but this only heightened the animosity on either side, and when French soldiers were found dangling from trees by the roadside, the enemy thought it wise to recognise these Partisan Liberty Rangers as legitimate soldiers.

"After our Rangers had hung a score or more of the red-legged Frenchmen, or Mexican renegades, the enemy began to think it wise to deal with all prisoners who fell in their hands with the common usages of war.

The reason why Juarez called us from the Upper Rio Grande down to Matamoras in such haste was soon apparent to us all.

"The truth was, that General Mejia, with a strong force of French, and Mexican traitors, was marching down to take us by surprise, if they could, and capture the city.

"They had to cross the San Juan river in order to get at us—a stream not very far from the city, and, as the bed of the stream was often perfectly dry, they anticipated very little trouble in getting at us.

"But the San Juan is one of the most unreliable streams in all the world.

"In twenty hours it will rise twenty feet high, from immense floods which flow occasionally from the mountains inland.

"As it happened, the bed of the river was perfectly dry when Mejia was only a few leagues distant, and, to prevent him from crossing it, our generals thought it wise to keep their troops continually moving to and from, in order to prevent it.

"As might be supposed, then, Juarez, gave us very little rest, and marched us about both night and day.

"While we were away from Matamoras, however, dodging the enemy, the San Juan suddenly rose to a great height, and prevented Mejia from advancing further, at least, for some time.

"But while we were away, however, several spies left the city, swam the San Juan, and fully informed Mejia of our doings, whereabouts, and total numbers.

"So well had they managed matters in our absence, that several French engineer officers crossed the San Juan and mapped out all the country round about the city.

"The good people of Matamoras, however, little dreamed of what our real intentions were.

"Our company of Boy Soldiers were ordered back to the city, and encamped not far from the walls, outside in the fields.

"This, our sudden return, took many of the citizens by surprise, nor could they make it out why so few of us should now appear to dispute the advance of the French, who, all very well knew, were not far off.

"We did not satisfy their curiosity, however, by giving any explanations, but kept our mouths closed.

"Judge of the surprise of all, however, when at sunset the next (Saturday) evening, our whole force marched back unexpectedly, and camped on the same ground which they had done a month before.

"I felt very glad to see the return of all our force, for I now was sure that much of the fatiguing, guard, and other duties would be taken off our hands.

"But I was doomed to disappointment once more, and so were all our gallant boys.

"About three a.m. on the next (Sunday) morning while I and the boys were doing camp guard, one of our generals rode into our camp very hastily.

"Not a drum was beaten, not a bugle sounded, yet in ten minutes all the tents disappeared, and the army waggons moved off on the road to Monterey.

"The troops were drawn up ready to move at a moment's notice, and what all this sudden change might mean none of us could tell without it was that we were ordered to retreat once more,

"The doubt, however, was soon cleared up.

"Juarez and his staff of generals were soon heard approaching.

"All our men being formed, one of the generals rode up and said :

"'Mexican patriots, the enemy are approaching; they have, or will, perhaps, soon cross the San Juan.

"'As you know, they greatly outnumber us, but we must fight, yes, and fight hard, for there is not a single road by which we can retreat with safety, and we need not expect reinforcements, for there are none nearer to us than ten leagues. The enemy, I understand, muster fourteen or fifteen thousand men in two bodies, and are well off for artillery.

"'As I said before, there is no hope for us except in fighting in a determined manner, and Mexico expects that in the approaching combat every man will do his duty, and let your cry be for "victory or death.'"

"These few words, hurriedly spoken, gave great courage to our men, and if they had been allowed, they would have made the welkin ring again with their shouts.

"At the word of command we marched after our generals and were on foot many hours.

"We ascertained from scouts and spies that the enemy had crossed the river much higher up than we expected, and were committing all manner of depredations on all those who in any way countenanced the Republican cause.

"Taking up the line of march, we passed northwards through the most picturesque and delightful farming country the eye, perhaps, ever beheld.

"All was decidedly pleasant in aspect, and the people remarkably so.

"The lands were highly cultivated, the cattle fat and of superior stock ; farm-houses, out-houses, and servants' quarters were all regularly, substantially, and neatly built, scrupulously clean, and possessing an air of comfort and contentment superior to anything I had ever seen on the continent.

"Mountains and valleys, hills and dales, fine springs and majestic woods came into view at every turn of the road, while overloaded barns and corn-cribs, neat school-houses and rustic churches by the wayside, cosy villages, and strong, masculine, rosy-cheeked inhabitants, contrasted favourably with the tumble-down appearance, sallow, fever-and-agueish aspect of the immensely wealthy, but careless and fast-living cities by the sea.

"The habits, dress, look, language, and all things reminded me much of Spain ; but nothing more so than the buxom, rosy-faced, and white-aproned mothers and daughters who lined the wayside, and brought out all their stock and store to entertain our merry, dusty, and weary soldiery toiling up the hills of this beautiful region.

"Our reception by the inhabitants was enthusiastic and cheering. It was rumoured that the country was nought else but a den of traitors, but, certainly, their cordial behaviour fully contradicted the whisper.

"As this country was in the north-eastern corner of the state, it was mountainous and rolling. The river ran on two sides, north and east, while in the north-west we could see the mountains which separated us from the road to Monterey.

"The ferry lay under the northern extremity of the heights, the San Juan washed its foot, while on the opposite bank towered perpendicularly the heights of Monterey.

"The distance by the river (unnavigable here) from Matamoras to the Ferry was about forty miles.

"The land route was about thirty-five miles, with two or three very small towns in the valleys. Pontsville being but four miles from the Ferry, and on the south bank, a body of the enemy were reported in possession of this last-mentioned place, and to questions our general grinned good-humouredly, and promised to 'shake them out one of these fine mornings!'

# THE BOY SOLDIER; OR, GARIBALDI'S YOUNG CAPTAIN.

THE ACCIDENT.

"The whole aspect of the country was unbroken rolling land, but to the north stood a cluster of three hills, all alone in the landscape, the tallest and most conspicuous of which was called the Peak. The Imperialists occupied this on our approach, and had a full view of all that transpired on our side of the river, the distance being but twenty-five miles to their forces.

"Their pickets lined the whole river, from the Ferry to Pontsville, and it was impossible for any to approach the San Juan without the fact being instantly telegraphed from post to post to General Mejia, who now was chief in command. Our general, to deceive the enemy, had divided his force into small parties, with an over allowance of tents.

"And as white canvas-covered waggons were continually seen moving about over the hills, and as our various camps were wide spread and plentifully supplied with fuel, it was thought by their journals that Juarez was in chief command of us, and had not less than from 30,000 to 40,000 men.

"Our whole force, however, did not number more than 3,000 infantry, four light field-pieces, and a squadron of cavalry. Our general, however, moved us about continually.

"Now we marched opposite the Peak, our tents still standing in the old camp ground, near Matamoras.

"Next day would find us in some other direction.



"So that at last the enemy were completely deceived as to our number or position, and were even on the *qui vive.*

"Such were our movements that scouts daily informed us of the enemy's counter-movements, who, with whole brigades and divisions, were continually moving from place to place to prevent our supposed attempts at crossing.

"The Imperial commander Mejia was an old school-fellow with Juarez, and smart messages, it is said, were frequently passed between the rival commanders across the river.

"Picket firing was constantly maintained between the guards on opposite banks of the stream, with more animosity, however, than any decided effect.

"The enemy was still on our side of the San Juan at Pontsville, and it was determined first to entice them into the interior and then surround them, if possible.

"Scouts came in daily, correctly informing us of the position, number, and depredations of the enemy, but we were sorry to learn that the inhabitants of the surrounding country patronized them.

"They had on several occasions betrayed our men to the enemy.

"Our general had warned them to desist harbouring the foe, but they replied by concocting a plan to destroy all our cavalry in the neighbourhood.

"An old broad-brim proprietor of an antiquated hotel, invited the captain of cavalry to halt and refresh his men.

"The soldier willingly did so, but while engaged at dinner the whole premises were surrounded by several hostile squadrons.

"Our men mounted and fought their way out as best they could, but lost half their number in killed and missing.

"Exasperated at the perfidy of these fanatics, our general summoned his brigade, and leaving camps standing, to deceive the telegraph at the Peak, sallied forth towards Pontsville long before day.

"When the sun rose we had just halted on a lofty hill, and lay in the woods. The scenery on either hand was enrapturing. East of us lay a wide expanse bathed in gold, while the San Juan and Rio Grande, winding to the sea, were covered with a dense white vapour that sparkled like molten silver.

"Clouds capped the Peak, while to the west rose dark lines of mist-covered hills and mountains, with snow-white villages dotting the undulating landscape, while the distant crowings of early fowl could be faintly heard upon the morning air.

"The column pushed rapidly forward, but ere midday large black clouds gathered on the mountains, and tremendous rain poured into the valley, deluging everything, and swelling the streams.

"At 'secure arms' all manfully trudged forward through mire and flood, but as we approached our destination horsemen could be seen hovering and rapidly disappearing in the distance.

"With our cavalry to the front we moved forward at a quick pace, but could never secure any of the horsemen we saw moving on the hills. Halting within a mile of Pontsville our cavalry unexpectedly came upon a large body of horse, and, without hesitation, charged them.

"A desperate encounter ensued.

"The enemy gave way.

"A running fight took place, friend and foe simultaneously charging through town, in great confusion and fury, the enemy being at last driven into the river in sight of their whole force drawn up on the opposite bank.

"'Finding the place deserted, and malcontents fled, we departed next morning without damaging the village, although both officers and men were sufficiently incensed to have burned the miserable place to the ground.

"Long excursions of this nature were of weekly occurrence, for our general seemed to delight in keeping his men moving.

"But what the causes might have been we never knew, and to the remonstrances of sundry fat old officers, who did not much relish marching and countermarching, retreating and advancing, the general swore roundly, and threatened to kick them out of his office.

"It cannot be denied that our position was a critical one, and required great caution.

"The enemy were now fully aware we did not meditate crossing, and massed their troops at different points to dislodge us, if possible, from our fertile region.

"All our reinforcements were leagues distant, and from the state of the country it was impossible to bring up supplies or receive reinforcements.

"Our general was told to 'hold the place at all hazards,' and such instructions to a 'fighting general,' were likely to be fulfilled to the letter.

"In other points of view the possession of Matamoras was of paramount importance.

"It was populous, wealthy, and the most fruitful in supplies of any county in the State.

"It had been somewhat disaffected, but that had all passed, and now none were more enthusiastic for independence.

"The rail and other roads ran through the town, and should it fall, a large area of fruitful country would come into Imperial hands, with its accumulated crops—a consummation devoutly wished by the Imperialists, as the country they were then inhabiting, beyond the San Juan, was incapable of supplying wants, keenly felt.

"They had, moreover, to *pay* for all things among their 'friends,' whereas by being quartered among the 'Republican rebels,' all things would follow, and save vast inconvenience and expense.

"These considerations made our service very irksome and arduous.

"With a river front of over forty miles to guard against a superior force, and a multitude of spies, required the utmost vigilance and self denial.

"Our videts, who were young and inexperienced, occasioned much annoyance and unnecessary marching.

"Such was our habitual life of excitement that we could not call a single hour our own.

"Night or day reports would come in of some 'imaginary advance,' or 'crossing,' and night or day, fair or foul, we marched to the threatened point, to find our supicions undeceived, until at last, our general, in great wrath and with tremendous oaths, vowed to hang the first cavalry man that brought in false alarms, and the officer commanding likewise, for permitting it.

"After this informal order, we were much relieved, and enjoyed our leisure hours as best we might in town, or country if furnished with a 'pass,' from the provost marshal or officer of the day.

"Once, however, the cavalry were correct in their reports.

"Some of Mejia's men were in the habit of crossing in large boats, and despoiling the country.

"All kinds of things were stolen by them.

"They committed all manner of outrage upon unoffending women and children, whose fathers or brothers were in our army, and not unfrequently burned the house above their heads.

"Our company of foot was sent up, and lay perdu in the woods for more than a week without success.

"At last two large scows were seen approaching containing more than a hundred individuals, some of them being renegades, but most of them French soldiers, and all well armed.

"Two other scows, similarly freighted, were descried crossing higher up.

"Both landing-places were in full view of us, and when most of them had departed on their depredatory excursions, the guards at the boats were surrounded, and surrendered at discretion.

"The prisoners were secured in the woods, and we awaited the return of the marauders.

"After a few hours, one of the parties approached in a body, well laden, but, probably, informed of our being in the neighbourhood, observed military order against a surprise.

"When they had unconsciously advanced within our ambuscade, I stepped forward, and demanded a surrender.

"I was answered with a volley, but before they could reload, every man was weltering in his blood, dead or wounded.

"The second boat's party, hearing the firing, rushed towards the landing-place.

"Our heroes fell back some few paces, and awaited their approach.

"Having to pass the spot where their companions lay, they halted and gazed with horror on the destruction before them.

"At the same moment I called on them to surrender.

"The dead and wounded were placed in a scow, and two men, paroled, conveyed them across.

"We had captured in this little affair 150 fine English rifles, 60 revolvers, 6 swords, and over 100 prisoners, besides having killed or wounded 75 others.

"We procured waggons for all those things the rascals had stolen, together with arms, accoutrements, &c., and marched our prisoners to town—the civilian renegades in front.

"Not a man in our party was scratched in this meeting, and received with modesty the encomiums of our general, who sarcastically remarked, on hearing an account of the affair,

"'Mejia, the scoundrel, will learn to keep his thieves at home in future.'

"This and several other successful affairs very much embittered the feeling between pickets on the river bank, and the firing was incessant.

"Indeed, they brought down whole regiments to oppose our guards, and maintained an incessant fusilade from sunrise till dark.

"Not only this, they brought forward field-pieces and endeavoured to disperse our pickets by destroying every tent or hut that might be in range.

"In fact they asked no questions, but smashed everything within reach, and unhoused several poor farmers and labourers who had not wherein to lay their heads.

"More than this, their firing was mere waste of ammunition, and betrayed but little skill.

"When *our* artillery answered, they invariably retired, and at last mounted some heavy pieces on a rising ground back of the Ferry, and incessantly shelled, in the vain hope of destroying our camp, which they had not manhood enough to attempt to take.

"Their numerous shells, however, from some unknown cause, although rifled and of very best quality, always fell short.

"Being out on picket, we enjoyed ourselves amazingly among the farmers, who willingly furnished all things needful, and as our camps were near the little town of Rainford, many pleasant hours were spent there among the pretty quakeresses and widows—the latter being very numerous and handsome.

"With their little town of one street screened by surrounding hills, the inhabitants seemed perfectly happy and contented, for they possessed a fine mill, two woollen cloth factories, several tanneries; had a large meeting-house, two small chapels, a newspaper, and excellent grazing land all around them.

"In general aspect it looked much like a Spanish village, only that the inhabitants were even prouder in step, wore better goods, and had rosy, well-cut features that plainly indicated the best of 'blood.'

"Many of the males had decamped to Maximilian's army; but the women, Heaven bless them! were as true as steel, and behaved like heroines on all occasions. Sweet little Village of the Hills, long may ye flourish!

"From deserted and intercepted travellers we gleaned particles of information occasionally which left little doubt that recent acts of boldness were but forerunners of mischief, and every day witnessed greater vigilance and caution on the part of officers.

"The more distant detachments were called in, and save a picket guard, under special instructions, our whole force fell back nearer to Matamoras, at which point all flanking forces must necessarily first appear.

"This ruse was resorted to to bewilder the enemy, who were accurately informed of all our movements by spies among the townspeople.

"What this habitual retreating and advancing might mean none could tell.

"It sufficed that our general ordered it, and the men obeyed cheerfully, although frequently marching in drenching rains and impassable mud.

"In order to be positively informed of the enemy's movements and intentions, several bold fellows in our command volunteered to cross the river, dodge the pickets, and push into the interior as far as Mexico city.

"One of the three brave men was no other than our old friend, the Yankee trapper, the same who had befriended the Boy Band in so many ways, and had earned for himself the name of Red Devil among the Indians.

"He mounted a favourite mare of mine, which I had loaned him for the purpose, and started out at midnight.

"He managed to elude the enemy's guards, and passed through them unobserved.

"He reached Pontsville, and engaged himself for an hour or two, and then made his way to the river San Juan.

"He arrived on the banks in safety, and swam his horse across.

"Prowling around the camps of Mejia, he obtained very valuable information, and was about to return to our camps again, when some rascal or other, who was paid for the information, divulged the secret that the Red Devil was not an Imperialist, but a staunch Republican, and formed one of my own company of Boy Soldiers as a volunteer.

"Red Devil was totally unaware of this, and after he had recrossed the San Juan again in safety, he was suddenly chased by a whole squadron of light cavalry.

"His position was a most perilous one; but putting spurs to his mare he galloped madly onward.

"Meanwhile, however, shots were whistling round him.

"One, who took more accurate aim than the rest, hit Red Devil in the shoulder.

"Yet he was not unhorsed.

"The wound was a most painful one, and he lost much blood.

"Yet onward he sped like the wind, the hussar squadron in full chase after him.

"While jumping a ditch, however, some one of the soldiers in pursuit fired again.

"This time Red Devil was hurt in the thigh, and so great was the pain and so great his weakness that he fell from the saddle, and with one leg in a stirrup, was dragged along the ground. (See cut in present Number).

"How long the brave fellow might have been dragged along the ground no one can tell, had it not been that at that moment a party of mounted Republicans, headed by Sam Gale, advanced to the rescue, and thus saved Red Devil from certain death.

"Sam Gale was not aware of the presence of the hussars, for he and his friends were at that moment returning from a scouting expedition.

"But directly they saw how things were, they raised a shout, charged the hussars, and drove them off successfully.

"Yankee Sam, and his friend the 'Red Devil,' felt so much annoyed at their mishaps that they resolved to gather two or three hundred volunteers, who should be well mounted, and thus penetrate into the lines of General Mejia around Pontsville.

'I need not tell you that such a proposal was received by our brave boys with loud cheers, all of whom procured good horses, and were eager for the fray.

"Myself, the Count, Major Caspar, Hugh Tracy, the 'Red Devil,' and Yankee Sam, were chosen the leaders of this party, and, having procured several small pieces of light cannon to serve as 'flying artillery,' we filled our havresacks with food, and our canteens with wine, ready for the expedition.

"We remained in camp several days, waiting for favourable weather, and in the meantime sent out scouts to see 'how the land lay' around us, and on our destined route.

"From scouts, out several days before, it was ascertained the enemy had a strong force of cavalry quartered on the proposed route, and that a fight would be inevitable.

"Rising with the sun, our men dashed along the roads, and, as the enemy's pickets were unable to tell what this immense cloud of dust meant that rose on the distant landscape, our force actually rode through one of their cavalry encampments before the alarm was given.

"The enemy were for the most part absent at the time, and sustained but little loss save the total destruction of their stores, capture of spare horses, and a few prisoners.

"These latter, being mounted, were placed in charge of the rear guard, and the excursion proceeded.

"The delay at this camp had given the enemy warning, and, when we progressed some miles further, several squadrons of dragoons were observed drawn up on a slope ready to receive us.

"A halt was sounded, two squadrons were sent forward, who dashed at the enemy full gallop.

"The Imperialists remained long enough to discharge their revolvers, and not attempting to charge down hill, broke and fled precipitously.

"Their officers were the last to retire, and seemed disgusted with the poltroons they commanded.

"A few accoutrements, pistols, horses, &c., were found here, and in a neighbouring camp, and on we dashed as gaily as ever.

"We had not proceeded many miles when a strong body of the enemy were discovered admirably posted, with skirmishers thrown out in front.

"Our advance, consisting of one squadron, went ahead, drove in the outposts, and rode in full view of the enemy, five squadrons strong, and attempted to draw them out.

"The commander, not observing our whole force screened in woods a mile distant, sallied forth to exterminate our advance.

"The latter, however, returned up the hill, over it, and, when half-way down, were met by another squadron—both advanced again, and met the enemy advancing up on the other side.

"Sam gave the word, and our horsemen, spurring their steeds into a maddening gallop, charged among the enemy, and were sabreing and pistolling right and left before they fully recovered from astonishment.

"The conflict was hand to hand, and conspicuous in our foremost ranks were the Count and Caspar.

"The fight lasted about ten minutes, and ended in the Imperialists' flight, who dispersed in all directions, and would not heed their trumpets sounding the rally.

"As our men advanced down into the level plain they were again attacked by a fresh body of horse.

"But a third company coming to our assistance made the combat more equal, and finally routed them with loss.

"We captured many prisoners, a lot of fine horses, sabres, trumpets, and pistols, together with their well-provisioned camps found a half-mile further on, with all things as their owners left them.

"And among other articles lots of superior saddles and harness were immediately appropriated, and not allowed to be burned with all things else.

"Having refreshed our men, and remounted many, we continued on our travels, and were cheered on every hand by the country people, who, informed of things by the frightened Imperialists, lined the road-side and waved hats and handkerchiefs in high glee.

"'I told 'em you'd come along one of these fine mornings' said a fine old gentleman, standing at his door with two daughters, and shaking with laughter. 'Take care of my son, Yankee Sam, and drive all the skunks into the river!'

"'Hurry on, boys, hurry on! the varmint ain't more nor a mile ahead! We're all Imperialists (!) down here, you know. One of their camps is just over the hill, and has lots of horses. Darn 'em! Go in, boys, give 'em the devil!'

"'Hold on,' said a fine young girl, with a gun in her hand, 'I've got four of the rascals in my house; they thought to hide until you passed, but seeing your boys coming, I made them deliver up their weapons, and stood guard till you arrived.'

"Sure enough the Imperialists were there, but soon accommodated with horses, and being placed in charge of the rear-guard, on went the column again; clouds of dust rising on every hand, and artillery jingling along the roads. Rustics on fences, negroes on door-steps and wood piles, others at the plough or spade; all rushed forward, yelling and clapping hands like madmen.

"'Pile in on 'em, Massa; 'we ain't no Imperialists down dese diggins!—fotch it to 'em, white folks, and make 'em clar out of Mexico. We want none ob em among dese chickens.'

"Such were their acclamations as we passed on in our circuit of the country.

"As the whole rear of Mejia's army was by this time fully alarmed by fugitives flying in all directions, it would have been madness in us to have followed the usual roads in its vicinity, we therefore pushed towards the routes of their depôts and intercepted large waggon trains approaching, laden with stores of every description, and destroyed them.

"The horses and mules were entrusted to the rear-guard, and so proceedings continued.

"Waggon trains were seized on all the roads leading to depôts and head-quarters, and burned; their guards and drivers accommodated with spare horses, and sent to our rear. Approaching villages, all French and Imperial property was burned, and prisoners seized.

"Several army surgeons, captains, quarter-masters, commissaries, &c., were obliged to mount mules and follow, much to their astonishment and chagrin.

"Approaching the river railroad the command was divided to scour all the roads, and appointed to meet at a designated rendezvous.

"Several schooners espied at anchor were seized and burnt, together with valuable cargoes of clothing, stores, &c., but several slipped cables and escaped.

"Some half-dozen waggon yards, with scores of vehicles of all kinds, were fired, and teamsters added to our list of prisoners, when plans were laid for capturing the afternoon train then due.

"As the locomotive was heard approaching, and not sufficient time to tear up any portion of the track, troopers lined the sides of the road, and were ordered to take dead aim at the engineer.

"Such of our men commenced firing when the engine was fully a hundred yards distant, and as the driver suspected foul play of some kind he turned on steam, rushed past the station, and shoved off several logs placed on the rails.

"Many of the passengers, to escape the hailstorm of shot, jumped off the train and were crippled.

"Some few ran to the woods, but were picked up by our men, together with many who ran from the station on our first approach.

"All were taken, but the train escaped, although many on it were killed or wounded; the cars being, for the most part, uncovered, or freight trucks.

"The gallant fellow who drove the engine was also killed by an accurate shot, but his bravery and foresight deserved a better fate.

"Continuing our raid in all directions, our parties destroyed property to the amount of several million dollars, but always secured whatever arms, horses, or prisoners, fell in our way, until, wearied with labour, the gallant troopers made for the appointed rendezvous, which was not far from a small village where several main roads joined.

"The first party that arrived found that the place contained several finely furnished sutlers' stores, and depôts of goods deposited thus far in the rear of the army, to be conveyed up to the front as circumstances demanded.

"They were, in fact, central or wholesale establishments, to furnish regimental sutlers, and elegantly stocked with everything necessity might require; having tasteful bar-rooms attached, in which were sold champagne, and all sorts of expensive wines and liquors.

"When a party of our fatigued and dusty men hitched horses and entered, they were so unprepossessing and unpresentable, that all present rose, including several officers who had trotted to the rear 'to spend the day' convivially.

"'Brandy, gentlemen?' inquired the fat proprietor, urbanely. 'Certainly!'

And, presenting decanters, our men began to imbibe freely.

"'Might I enquire to what cavalry you belong, gentlemen?' asked the proprietor, acutely surveying our dusty figures from head to foot.

"'We?' answered one, laying violent hands on a box of havannas, and emptying the decanter. 'Oh, we are Imperial cavalry, just arrived; a new regiment raised in Tampico, just returned on a scouting party after the rebel leader, Yankee Sam.'

"'Yankee Sam, eh? You don't mean to say that *he* is in our lines, do you? Well, let him come, that's all, and although I'm not in the army, I'll show him a thing or two, just see if I don't.'

"And as his eye glanced over a fine case of revolvers exposed for sale, he seemed as valiant as Ajax.

"The rest of the company were dressed too finely to shake hands with our dusty fellows, and smoked and talked apart in dignified reserve.

"Hearing the approach of a squadron, our troopers went to the door, and the landlord prepared bottles and glasses for his expected visitors.

"'Are these some of your party, gentlemen?'

"'Yes,' was the reply, 'and as 'tis no use of fooling any more—*we* are Yankee Sam's cavalry!'

"Every one present was struck dumb with astonishment, but soon disarmed and made prisoners, being seated on mules and delivered to the rear-guard approaching.

"As there were four or five large establishments of this kind in the neighbourhood, our commander paid attention to all, providing them with shoes, clothes, new weapons, and literally 'ate out' the establishments, until not a box of sardines or can of oysters or preserves remained on the premises.

"Such a feast our men had not enjoyed for many months.

"All took whatever articles were needed, and the rest destroyed.

"Fruits, preserves, sardines, oysters, bread, fine biscuits, crackers, champagne, brandy, whisky, and ale, &c. &c., were all consumed; but none of our men forgot their perilous situation, and remained sober.

"Horses were fed, and about midnight, all prepared for the start home.

"'Twas foolish to attempt to return by the same route, so, as he had entered on the right of Mejia's lines, Yankee Sam determined to make the grand tour, and make his way out by the left.

"The whole army was aroused, and cavalry patrolled all the roads; but none knew the country half so well as Sam, so that he rapidly and quietly pushed forward by unfrequented lanes and paths, and safely arrived on the banks of the San Juan.

"No bridges being near, Sam swam his horse across, and all followed save the artillery.

"An old farmer had witnessed the crossing, and showed the way to a broken bridge a little way up stream.

"This was quickly repaired with logs and underbrush, and just as the first dawn of morning topped the trees, the whole command was safely on the south bank, and cautiously picking their way, for they were still in the enemy's lines, and at the most difficult stage of the journey, being gradually approaching their encampments.

"The main body followed a by-path through the woods, but scouts were sent out ahead, and on the flanks.

"'Who goes there?' and a shot was the almost instant challenge.

"Our scouts rapidly fell back to the main body as directed, and as the Imperial mounted outposts pursued, were in the midst of us, and secured.

"This occurred on several occasions, but, by good fortune and daring, the whole command reached the main road, and, utterly exhausted, halted on the outskirts of our lines, the enemy being within a mile, and in full force.

"Excitement had strung both man and beast since their start.

"But now that all were safely through the adventure, and passed on their way to camp, their appearance was most jaded, care-worn and dusty, having been many hours in the saddle without dismounting or drawing rein.

"The fruits of this excursion were several hundred head of horses and mules, more than a hundred prisoners, a perfect knowledge of Mejia's position, force, and resources, and the destruction of property to the value of several millions.

"The enemy were signally defeated on several occasions in combats with an inferior force.

"We killed and wounded many, remounted all that required it, furnished the command with fine weapons, saddles, harness, and clothes, and lost but one man in the last combat.

"Many of the prisoners took the affair good-humouredly, mounted on mules as they were, but several doctors were apostrophizing Jupiter and all the gods about the cruelty of placing them on saddleless animals with sharp vertebræ, and swore roundly against riding sixty miles without rest or food!

"Grumbling was of no use.

"Ride they *must*, and the chop-fallen, wretched appearance of these sons of Galen was ludicrous in the extreme, and their horsemanship wonderful under the circumstances.

"The appearance of this gallant band was certainly very unprepossessing, for the men were dusty, dirty, and looked more like negroes than whites.

"Their horses could scarcely move, and riders had overweighted them by hanging on saddle-bows, strings of shoes, bundles of blankets, new weapons of various kinds, the horse and entire outfit being not unfrequently Imperial property.

"Several of them were scarred or cut, but manfully sat their saddle, and took no heed of hurts, and marched along through our lines as gaily as possible, saying 'they would not have missed the trip for anything.'

"Such an adventure was worthy of remembrance, and those who participated had right to feel proud; for here was a small band, commanded by a dashing horseman, who had been for more than sixty hours within the enemy's lines, capturing and destroying as they went, and though engaged in several combats, with superior force, had returned with the loss of but one man.

"Mejia felt humbled, as any general would have been, but resorted to his old practice of telling but half the truth; and in his despatches, spoke of it as a trivial affair, and scarcely worthy of mention.

"In retaliation, the French cavalry made frequent incursions into counties within the limits of their *own* lines, though never attempting to cross *ours*, and spoke of each exploit as wonderful affairs.

"Had they crossed *our* line, and committed *half* the havoc acknowledged to have been done within their *own*, their achievements might have been worthy of mention; but they knew too well the character of our men to attempt any such adventure.

"However, from those constantly arriving in camp, it was ascertained beyond a doubt that Mejia was strongly fortifying on the river, so as to serve as a safe base of operations, whence supplies could be easily transported into the interior by their extensive waggon trains, boats, &c. Pontsville was held by a French colonel, Burgos, and a strong force, was strongly fortified, and being on high ground commanded all approaches from the interior, the river being open for the transit of any number of troops.

"Juarez determined to march forward and attack it, but was informed that large bands of outlaws and others were devastating the whole country on his left, and threatened to get in his rear.

"Suddenly diverging from his proper route, Juarez sent an officer up in that direction with a small force of hardened determined men, and so secretly was the expedition conducted that they unexpectedly came upon the renegade Mexicans at a creek called La Palma, and after a confused fight of some hours, drove the enemy from the field, pushed forward to their head-quarters, and captured it, with everything left intact.

"Joining the column under Juarez again, our army of 5,000 effectives and five guns pushed forward again towards Pontsville, and arrived in the vicinity.

"Our 'irregular' horse, Yankee Sam's (for I can call them nothing else) did good service in scouring the country for supplies, and keeping the enemy within the lines of the town, and although frequently inviting combats, the noble Imperialists remained quietly within their chain of breastworks, and refused every offer.

"By the 18th our ammunition waggons and artillery had arrived, infantry were rested, and Juarez broke up encampment at the Fair Grounds, two miles from town, and advanced against the city.

"The Fair Grounds was an admirable position for us had the enemy ventured to attack, for it was surmised that upon hearing of us at Pontsville, Marshal Bazaine would have collected his available force, and coming up in boats, reinforced Colonel Burgos, and chased us out of the country.

"His genius was befogged.

"He did nothing of the kind, but quietly remained where he was, enjoying serenades, balls, parties, &c., in the blissful state of vice-regal pomp and parade, being quite oblivious of everything save waltzes, bands, and perfecting the trappings of his renegade 'incapables.'

"Driving in the enemy's outposts round the outskirts, Juarez was fully aware of the strength of the place, and made dispositions accordingly.

"He knew that there were several boats under the bluff, which keep open communion with the north bank of the river, and that the enemy's supply of water depended entirely upon the river.

"Assaults could be of little use, as all advance upon the place was by an up grade, and that the public buildings and other strong edifices had been converted into forts, strongly fortified, and mounted, sweeping every approach.

"His men knew, however, that there were immense supplies of all kinds in the place, together with cannon, horses, waggons, ambulances, thousands of small arms, important state documents, and much specie, which had been robbed from various places throughout the country.

"As all were in the highest spirits, and held the enemy remarkably 'cheap,' dispositions were immediately made for commencing the siege.

"Many thought that officers were too slow and careful in approaching through the outskirts, and resolved to charge the enemy's line of intrenchments placed higher up in town.

"They made the trial, and suffered considerably, so that it was evident cautious measures were the best.

"One part of our force moved forward, and, without much opposition, occupied a good position north-north-east of the breastworks, and with two batteries maintained an effective and destructive fire upon them from which there was no escape.

"Another command, also, moved up south-south-west, and was also favourably posted.

"Each of these brigades had supports within call should the enemy sally down from the hill, and attempt to dislodge them from hastily-constructed field-works.

"While a heavy body of sharp-shooters were thrown out in front, harassing and cutting off their gunners, and such as dare appear in sight, carrying water from the river, wells, &c., a gradual approach was made upon the foe, who lost every hour from the deadly accuracy of our skirmishers, and made several faint attempts to dislodge them.

"But the enemy would scarcely appear ere rapid volleys were fired into them, completely smashing up all such bold intentions, and they would wildly rush back to houses, breastworks, &c., to get out of the way of further loss.

"While all this was progressing in and around town, Juarez received word that Colonel Saunders, a Mexican renegade, was coming down the north bank of the river to oppose him.

"When this force reached a point twenty-five miles above the city, Saunders crossed 2,000 of them, leaving an officer in charge of the remainder.

"Our men, however, knew these renegades of old, in many a fight, and, taking to the woods, maintained such a murderous fire that they were soon routed, with a loss of more than 200, while we lost but 10.

"We formed a junction with Juarez, and instilled new ardour into the whole army.

"But, although Saunders was badly whipped, it was known that others were approaching, also, on the north bank, thinking to cross over and assist Burgos with over 1,500 cavalry, depending upon the ferry-boats for transportation.

"But these boats, lying snugly under the bluff, Juarez determined to capture at all cost, particularly as a large steamboat, also lying there, was reported to contain considerable quantities of stores, &c.

"Directing an officer to this point, he carefully approached from the west, along the river's edge, within part view of the fortifications, and effected the important capture in gallant style, removing the vessels beyond reach of destruction.

"Mejia saw the manœuvre when too late, but opened a vigorous fire upon the party, and as many men fell, on account of the enemy's possession of a house on top of the bluff, several companies were detailed to attack it.

"Although advancing under a deadly fire from musketry and artillery, our men took it in gallant style, but with loss.

"As this house was within 150 yards of his main works, and could be made to command them, Mejia collected a strong force, sallied forth, and retook it, slaughtering every one without mercy.

"The enemy were not long in possession of the strong dwelling, ere our forces attacked and carried the high grounds north of it, and pounded the house so much that the enemy vacated it as untenable.

"Thus we were gaining ground on all sides, and the enemy's position becoming more and more circumscribed every hour.

"Our artillery, moving upon conquered positions, blazed away right and left, sweeping everything before them.

"Mejia's position, however, was still a strong one, and he could have held out for a long time; but being completely cut off from water, his men were failing in strength every hour.

"Hearing that Bazaine was fast approaching the north ferry landing, Juarez got up steam on his captured boats, and transported a strong force on that side, and managed the enterprise so warily, that Bazaine barely escaped capture, his whole command retreating in the wildest disorder, leaving hundreds of tents, camp equipage, and large stores behind untouched.

"Since the first opening skirmishes on the 13th, we had gradually worked our way through town.

"But 'real' business, as I have said, commenced on the 18th, with great success on every hand.

"And it now being the 20th, over fifty hours of incessant fire had been maintained on both sides, *their* loss being very considerable.

"When Mejia found that his boats were captured, and that, instead of fighting their way to him, had 'skedaddled' in all directions, he gave evident signs of giving up all hope of resisting the gradual approach of Juarez around him, since it was impossible to obtain water for his men on constant duty night and day.

"Still fearful of some other's arrival to raise the siege or reinforce, our men redoubled their efforts in every way, and maintained a heavy fire from all points.

"So that, being perpetually powerless, Mejia hoisted a white flag on his works towards 4 P.M. on the 20th; firing ceased in all directions, and loud, deafening yells from all points of the compass informed us that Mejia had unconditionally surrendered!

Seeing the hopelessness of the defence, Mejia fled from the town himself, leaving Colonel Burgos a prisoner in our hands.

"When the enemy stacked arms, and marched out, we found that we had captured 4,000 effectives, rank and file, 120 commissioned officers, several stands of colours, brass bands, &c., two mortars, five rifled guns, over 4,000 stand of arms, scores of sabres, lots of cavalry and waggon harness, 800 horses, waggons, mules, ambulances, medical outfits numerous.

"Immense supplies of every description; much clothing, shoes, tents, ammunition, camp utensils, &c., &c., together with about 1,000,000 dollars, stolen from various banks, which were instantly returned.

"Burgo's sword was instantly returned to him by Juarez, in a 'neat speech,' and all the prisoners being paroled, were immediately sent on their way rejoicing.

"Such jubilation as was in every camp, you have no conception.

"As I informed you, Yankee Sam's arm was wounded in his escape from pursuit, and he suffered much pain therefrom.

"To keep my promise I partly wrote and partly dictated this scrawl, so that you may form some accurate idea of our doings.

"The mails between us are few and far between, but I look for a letter from you every day.

"Love to all your boys and any old friends, for I suppose you meet old schoolmates every day in various parts.

"I do not know how long Juarez will remain here, but judging from reports, suspect he will be again moving—heaven only knows where—in a few days.

"Frequently during the battle I saw several hundred citizens drive their vehicles near the battle grounds, and convey away the wounded.

"And to see a muddy, ragged, bandaged soldier lolling in a fine silk-trimmed carriage was no uncommon sight.

"In fact, such was the anxiety of citizens to carry off the wounded, that one of their omnibuses, approaching too near the enemy's lines, was captured by an ambuscading party, and carried off in great triumph as a trophy.

"This omnibus was but one of many furnished for this humane purpose, and several were capsized in the mud, and rendered useless for all future service.

"The poor fellows seemed perfectly contented with their treatment, and lay up in bed smoking cigars or drinking 'brandy toddy,' as happy as lords.

"In fact, many of them liked the change, and would not exchange their honourable scars for any amount.

"Cigars, brandy, find food and raiment were different from rags, constant duty, hard fare, and incessant marching.

"I could not help smiling at the striking contrast exhibited between the wounded and the unhurt.

"The former would loll at parlour windows or in comfortable hospitals at Matamoras, reading and smoking.

"And those who could not move always had visitors beside them, chatting to or reading for them.

"Some who came out of camps to visit would look round with almost a jealous eye upon the many comforts provided for invalids.

"Ragged, sunburnt, and ill-fed as they were, many could but jocularly smile, and good-humouredly wish some friendly bullet had thrown *them* into such comfortable quarters.

"When the wounded visited their comrades in camp, their appearance was so much improved, they looked so bright and cheerful, and had so many stories to tell about pleasures and pastimes, that our doctors caught many feigning sickness, so as to be sent to hospitals in town.

"Theatres were the great temptation, and as convalescents were permitted to attend them, with properly signed 'passes,' these places were nightly crowded with military audiences, scores having arms in slings or bandaged heads.

"Such pieces, such music, such yelling and laughter were never heard before, and poor musicians in the orchestra were tired to death, the audience accompanying with vocal efforts, or embellishing them with a running accompaniment of stamps and howling.

"'Blood and thunder' productions were greatly in vogue, and those pieces wherein most of the characters were killed rose decidedly in the ascendant.

"A 'tip-top fight' was what the boys delighted in, and an unlucky hero would never fall without an accompanying yell,

"'Bring on your coffins!'

"Had these men free access to liquor, its effect would have been disastrous; but thanks to the viligance of the provost-marshal, a spoonful could not be obtained for love nor money.

"This liberty granted to convalescents, therefore, was productive of good, and a greater per centum returned to camp, and much sooner than they would have done if strictly confined to the limits of hospitals.

"As it was, those who were unfortunate enough to be confined in military hospitals recovered more slowly, and the men betrayed an evident dislike to return to camp.

"Some of our generals, however, did not approve these theatrical entertainments, and on one occasion, posted a cavalry picket around the doors, and all who belonged to his division were marched unceremoniously to camp!

"For a few nights following, few attended, but as this was considered too severe upon the sick and wounded, the boys received their 'passes' again, and theatres were filled.

"No convalescent, however, was allowed more than a week to run around, but as soon as money vanished, he preferred camp to town, and soon returned.

"The wounded and sick were always treated with marked politeness and kindness, and should any attend church, the place of honour was always assigned them.

"Great affection seemed to be lavished upon privates.

"Officers, for the most part, were treated coldly by the masses, and allowed to shift for themselves as best they might.

"It was considered far more honourable to carry a musket than to loiter round in expensive gold-corded caps and coats.

"Much could be written upon the great kindness shown to our troops by the ladies; but although the women of other places did much for the common cause, their noble-hearted and open-handed sisters of Matamoras far surpassed them all.

"Nothing that human nature could do was left undone.

"And, although much of this kindness and care were thrown away upon rude, uncouth objects, their humanity, patience, and unceasing solicitude are beyond all praise and requital.

# THE BOY SOLDIER; OR, GARIBALDI'S YOUNG CAPTAIN.

THE LEAVE TAKING.

## CHAPTER CXVI.

CAPTAIN FRANK FORD STILL WRITES OF WAR OPERATIONS IN MEXICO—WHAT TOOK PLACE AFTER THE FALL OF PONTSVILLE AND THE CAPTURE OF THE IMPERIAL GARRISON — A GRAND SEA FIGHT—ONE REPUBLICAN IRON-CLAD FIGHTS AGAINST AND DEFEATS MANY SHIPS OF THE IMPERIALISTS.

"DEAR BROTHER,—In continuation of my last letter, I may add that after the fall of Pontsville all went well with our little army.

"But what gave us all great pain was that the Imperialists were in strong force at the mouth of the Rio Grande, and shut out all our communication at sea.

"Knowing full well that the French and Imperialists would soon attempt to ascend the river and capture Matamoras in that way, we therefore immediately began to build a raft to retard their progress, and put bounds to Imperial curiosity.

"Hence many old rafts of huge cypress logs, found moored in the river and tributaries, were floated down.

"Woodmen were busy in the timber at various places, cutting down immense trees, the sound of whose fall, crashing in the forest, was like distant thunder.

"In less than a week a raft was formed in two



parts, which, when made fast, would stand 'butting' from all the 'rams' in the world.

"Nor could the enemy fire it, for the timber was so green, or so perfectly saturated from months and years of exposure in the water, it could defy all the turpentine Mexico might produce in a century to kindle a single stick of it.

"This being speedily and excellently accomplished, the enemy being safely placed at a respectable distance, Captain Parker, an English volunteer, and his officers razed one of the vessels, and began the formation of the ungainly 'Juarez.'

"Carpenters, wood-choppers, sawyers, and blacksmiths voluntarily gave a hand to expedite proceedings.

"An old engine was placed in her, and the work of plating commenced very vigorously.

"But how could we get plates, bolts, screws, machinery, &c., &c., when the scene of construction was far away from all supplies of every nature, in an out-of-the-way river, and close to a very small town, devoid of everything but pretty women?

"By superhuman exertions, however, many things were procured, and having four large guns aboard, and plenty of ammunition, volunteers were not wanting to man her, particularly as it was certain she would have terrible fighting to do ere reaching Bagdad, at the mouth of the Rio, her point of destination.

"When finished and ready for service, I visited her, and from the use of much indifferent material in structure, supposed she would be sent to the bottom in quick time, when opposed to the magnificent rams and iron-clads watching for her at the mouth, or drawn up in parallel lines to receive her when passing the channel of the river.

"She was large, rough, strong, and ungainly—vulnerable in many places, and the top imperfectly covered.

"So that, should a stray shell drop through the roof, her destruction was almost certain, as the magazine was somewhat exposed.

"Many were desirous of commanding, as it was hoped she might eclipse the doings of all others; but after a little reflection Captain Parker gave her in charge of a Mexican.

This officer grumbled much at the deficiencies apparent in the craft, and particularly of the engines, which were old, and of doubtful capacity.

"'Do you refuse to command, sir?' asked the captain. 'If there is anything you object to in her, state it, and I will go myself—either you or I must command!'

"'I do not object, sir,' was the quick reply. 'If you take command, I only ask to be captain of a gun, for I'm bound to go in her, one capacity or other.'

"'Very well, sir,' said the captain, going ashore in his quiet manner, 'make things ship-shape immediately, and wait for orders!'

"Things were soon prepared, and orders received.

"It was deemed advisable to keep the hour of her departure a secret.

"Yet it became known in some way to the enemy at the mouth, who steamed off and on all the time.

"At night the raft was unexpectedly opened by a few volunteers, and the 'Juarez' slowly and noiselessly floated several miles down stream, and was perfectly lost in the dense fogs which fall at evening.

"Next morning, at the first rays of the sun, steam was raised, and by keeping close to the heavily-timbered banks, she cautiously proceeded, and as the fog lifted, espied three of the enemy's finest gunboats in the river, near the mouth.

"Two of them backed down, while the largest opened fire immediately, and very briskly.

"The 'Juarez' was moving slowly from defective engines, but fired deliberately and with telling effect, crippling the enemy at the first broadside, who ran the magnificent craft upon the bank, and struck colours at the moment our boat was passing.

"The captain, finding his engines to be useless, depended solely upon the stream, and could not stop to take the splendid prize.

"For he knew many boats would soon appear to oppose his exit from the mouth.

"So that, although using more steam than could be generated, boldly pushed into the broad stream, rapidly firing at the two gunboats retreating before him.

"It was at this point of the action that we could discern all that transpired from batteries on the bluffs.

"As soon as the 'Juarez' rounded, the whole Imperial fleet hoisted anchor, and were in two lines—one each side of the channel at the sea mouth.

"Frigates, rams, gunboats—all were ready to annihilate that iron-clad mass of timber slowly floating towards them.

"Presently an iron-clad left her position, and boldly steaming up between the lines of dark hulls opened fire at a considerable distance.

"The 'Juarez' was silent.

"And nought was seen but a rush of steam as the monster slowly entered the channel, which seemed to please the single enemy, who steamed up nearer and fired again.

"In an instant the bow gun of the rebel replied, smashed the boiler and machinery of the enemy—men jumped overboard, and the vessel sank immediately.

"This exasperated the fleet, which now opened with a terrific roar from both squadrons until the side of the 'Juarez' looked like a mass of sparks floating between parallel lines of curling smoke.

"Few dared approach, however, and those so timorous received such fearful handling that they immediately put back, and were content to fire at a distance.

"To us, on the bluff, spectators of the scene, the slowness of the 'Juarez' was unaccountable, for she seemed encircled with fire and doomed to destruction ere emerging from the ordeal.

"'What's the matter with her?'

"'Why don't she clap on steam and rush through them?'

"'They'll sink her in three minutes!' &c. were the remarks of all.

"Yet onward she went, slowly picking her way, the enemy believing she was only enticing them in her way by apparent slowness!

"'Twas not the case.

"Her engines were worthless, and audacity alone was carrying her through.

"Still fighting at long range, the Imperial fleet slowly followed, and the nearer she approached the bluff the quicker the 'Juarez' fought, until finding her safely under our guns at Bagdad, the enemy gave up the chase, and amid our cheers on the bluff, and a salvo of guns, the 'Juarez' slowly turned the points and was moored before the city!

"From commotion visible among the enemy's vessels of all classes, the activity of small boats passing to and fro, and succession of signals exchanged between commanders, it was evident that many of them were badly crippled, for several were towed to the banks and run upon the sand.

"One vessel had sunk, several were towed away, while the vigorous working of pumps among them testified that shots had penetrated in different quarters, and that they felt infinite relief in her escape.

"Various fragments of wreck soon floated down from the scene of conflict, which proved that chance shot had visited more than one unlucky transport, while with glasses we could perceive two powerful gunboats, which, like ants, were dragging their crippled companion out of further danger.

"'Twas vexatious to think that all the spoil was escaping us, and all felt particularly annoyed that the gunboat which had struck her colours to the 'Juarez' should thus easily escape, for it was the finest in the fleet.

"It could not be helped, however, and when the truth became known, regarding the utter failure of our engines, and the danger to which she had been exposed every moment during her passage, all felt surprised she had done so well, and inflicted such loss upon the enemy; for had the fleets known the true cause of her slow progress, not a fragment of her would ever have floated down so majestically and triumphantly.

"From preparations visible among the fleets, it was conjectured some important undertaking was afoot among them, and every precaution taken to prevent a surprise, or mar the lustre of the day's doings, so that when we saw many of their transports moving up the river towards evening, and the gunboats cleaning up and clearing decks, it seemed to indicate that powder and ball were intended for us in earnest.

"As night closed in, none expected an engagement of any kind, but alarm-guns warned the garrison to be on the alert; when sooner than expected, several vessels appeared before our batteries, and the engagement opened with great fury.

"While the bluff batteries were contending with most of the fleet, several of the Imperial squadron ran past, and opened with an awful roar upon the 'Juarez,' lying broadside to shore; while several boats from below engaged our guns south of the town, and such was the awful uproar and activity of gunners, both friend and foe, that although quite dark, everything could be plainly seen from the frequent and rapid flashes.

"The noise was astounding.

"The bluff batteries above and south batteries below the town seemed all on fire, while the 'Juarez,' engaged with several heavy gunboats and frigates, was rocking from the immense weight of metal hurled at her every moment.

"But as she was bound fast to shore, and the enemy could not remain stationary in the stream, their vessels slowly drifted past towards the lower batteries.

"For a long time this unearthly noise was maintained on both sides, and it was once supposed that the Imperial boats would grapple with the 'Juarez,' and take her.

"But such was her steady and destructive fire, that they slunk off in the darkness to longer distance, and never seemed inclined to try it again.

"The woods facing Bagdad were literally blown down by chance shots from our side.

"While the river was all afoam with hundreds of water columns rising and falling every minute from the same cause.

"And 'tis more than probable, had not our batteries concentrated their fire upon the enemy engaged with our solitary iron-clad, it would have fallen into their hands.

"But such a shower of shot and shell assailed them from three points, and so numerous were small shot pouring into their ports and decks, it was impossible for a human being to appear without instant loss of life.

"So that after a fierce and obstinate engagement the enemy's boats escaped down the river in a crippled condition, while the upper fleet moved up stream with great expedition amid the long and enthusiastic cheers of our garrison and citizens, who lined the works in great glee, making night hideous with their wild and defiant shrieks and shouts.

"Thus ended the first bombardment of Bagdad, and although nought but glory can attach to all engaged, I am sorry to say not less than four or five were killed and some half-dozen wounded on board the gallant iron-clad, most of them receiving injuries in the night attack of the enemy's gunboats.

"But beyond these casualties I hear of none whatever throughout the garrison, for all are in high spirits, and desirous of meeting the enemy again at any time and in any number.

"After the affair of Pontsville, Juarez re-formed his army, and remained some short time where he was, but subsequently fell back, for it was known that Bazaine's force of 4,000 were hurrying on to join 8,000 strong, who were about to cross the river, and drive us by degrees into the Gulf of Mexico, or some other place.

"He had already crossed the river as we fell back, and was camped at a place rejoicing in some dozen houses, and having Paxtillo for its name.

"Juarez gathered every man he could, and marched out to give battle.

"We camped within five miles of Paxtillo, and could plainly see the long line of camp fires.

"Our cavalry had been closer for many days before our arrival, and were noticed by the enemy, but not molested.

"Early next morning (Sunday), and long before dawn, our line of battle was quietly formed, and as we had no camp fires, our presence was not known.

"Marching in three grand divisions, we approached nearer to the enemy's camps, deployed columns, and commenced the attack.

"When about two miles distant from Paxtillo, the enemy had seen us, and a general alarm was raised—such drum beatings, trumpetings, signal guns, rockets, &c, you could never imagine.

"But although this confusion might appear on one part of their line, Bazaine was informed of our vicinity the night before.

"As we approached nearer, sunlight began to appear.

"Clouds of sharp-shooters fanned out in our front, and little puffs of smoke innumerable dotted the dark green landscape over which our dark lines were rapidly moving.

Presently long curls of smoke from the wooded hillocks to our front were answered by screaming shells and loud reports, and artillery bugles were sounding up and down our line.

"We galloped to the front, and opened a brisk fire, while to the extreme right and left we could faintly hear pattering vollies of musketry.

"The sun now rose in true Mexican brilliancy, and shortly became intensely warm.

"At all events, it so seemed to the artillery, for we pulled off coats and jackets, strapped them on to caissons, and, rolling up our sleeves, began to 'roll into' the Imperialists with great gusto.

"Such a noise you never heard, and I am deaf even now.

"But feeling determined to pay off old Bazaine for our scrape at Puebla, our onset was fierce and dashing, and the continual command was 'forward, boys, forward.'

"Sometimes we moved up a few hundred yards, unlimbered and worked away awhile.

"Then moved forward again and again, until at last we found ourselves blazing away among the tents of a division, having to withstand the fire of not less than twelve pieces.

While all that remained was three out of our four, the fourth gun having been upset by a stray shell, and rendered unserviceable.

"Ammunition was fast giving out, and supplies were far to the rear.

"And, as our infantry were now rushing through the camps, we stopped firing, and retired to a patch of wood to cool the guns.

"'Hold on a while, boys,' our brigadier said in passing, 'the boys are hard at it in front, and we shall find some better guns for you in a few moments.'

"In half-an-hour the musketry fire somewhat subsided to our front.

"Orders came to unhitch teams, and select a set of guns from some twenty that had been captured.

"We did so, and claimed for our use four splendid brass fellows—two six-pound rifles, and two twelve-pound howitzers.

"Having found lots of ammunition, we were ordered in again, and went forward at a gallop, the horses being much superior to our old mules, and powerful in harness—thus you see us re-equipped on the battle-field—and turned the enemy's guns on them.

"It was now nearly eleven o'clock.

"Reports from different parts of the field represented our generals as having driven the enemy pell-mell before them, capturing camp after camp, and immense supplies of all kinds.

"From the continual change of scene, from field to wood, from camp to camp, and incessant fighting, I could not realize the lapse of time, and could not believe it to be more than 7 A.M.

"The heat, however, began to be very oppressive, and, as we gradually became short-handed, officers dismounted, and served the guns with right goodwill.

"Our progress now became much slower than before.

"The enemy had collected in great force towards our front, and had several powerful batteries in full play against our further advance.

"Had we not been reinforced in time, our little battery would have been snuffed out; but Escobedo, under whose care all artillery had been placed, sent ample succour, and the duel between us became hot and determined.

"By continually changing position in the open ground we escaped much loss, but we made the woods in front smoke again.

"I had noticed our infantry cautiously moving up through woods on their flank, and orders came to cease firing.

"The enemy saw the danger, and moved up their infantry.

"With a sudden movement up rose several regiments of ours, gave a shout as usual, and ran across the open the open ground and up the slope without firing, but dozens of them knocked over by artillery every moment.

"On they went, however, colonels and colours in front, until they got near to the infantry, when volley upon volley greeted them in quick and savage style.

"The artillery fight lasted full half-an-hour.

"Reinforcements went up rapidly until at last the guns were silenced.

"A wild yell rent the air, and immediately the order came,

"'Artillery to the front.'

"We moved forward rapidly and passed the scene of the fierce engagement I have described, and found not less than twelve guns deserted, as many more having been drawn off during the fight.

"The loss in infantry seemed large. The enemy had received an awful lesson, but fought to the last.

"Our opponents at this point were Frenchmen, fellows of true grit, and fought like heroes, disputing every inch of ground with great determination and valour.

"We came to a place where the Mexicans had encountered some German regiments; it was like a slaughter-house for the poor gunners, few of ours being visible anywhere.

"The fight was not over, however, by any means, as incessant musketry on our flanks fully proved.

"It seemed, from the line of fire, that our wings were out-flanking the enemy, or that they had been fighting too fast for us in the centre.

"After a little breathing time we commenced the onward movement a third time, deserted camps being to the right, left, and on every side of us.

"The temptation of so much plunder led scores of our young troops to halt on some excuse or other.

"And the result was that hundreds were lost to their respective regiments, and hung behind for purposes of spoil.

"I was sorry to see this, and remonstrated with many.

"But their excuses were so natural or plausible I could do nothing with them.

"The majority had not been from home more than a month, and having beaten the enemy in their immediate front, thought the game was all over for that day.

"Many were footsore.

"Others famished, and not a few perfectly exhausted.

"Driving rapidly through the camps, the scene of slaughter was plain on every hand.

"The enemy had re-formed their line again, and the roar of artillery opened immediately.

"We had scarcely got into position before six pieces opened on us with great fury, and, in fact, all along the line.

"The first shot killed several horses, and smashed up an empty caisson.

"We changed position somewhat, and got within better range of our friends, whose horses and caissons were behind an old farm-house.

"We hammered away at the house and blew the roof off, knocked in the walls, and got a sight at the caissons.

"We did not much care about the guns, for they were firing very rapidly and wildly.

"After a little manœuvring we pointed fairly at the caissons, and were about to fire.

"'Hold on!' shouted our general; 'point at the guns until ordered—there is a little game on foot.'

"The 'game' aforesaid was concocted by the colonel of our supports.

"The infantry were to creep up on all fours, while we maintained a furious fire, and being concealed by the smoke, should wait until all our shot was concentrated on the caissons, and blowing them up, the infantry should make a sudden rush and secure the guns.

"The plan succeeded admirably.

"We suddenly charged on the caissons, and blew most of them up; but before the guns could be removed, the infantry were upon them, and desperately engaged with opposing regiments.

"The guns were ours, and proved very elegant and costly.

"The line was temporarily broken; but fresh troops came pouring in, and ultimately forced to retire.

"Yet in strengthening one part of their line they weakened another.

"And by a vigorous push our infantry and artillery made a wide gap lower down to our left, and rushed through it like a torrent.

"The fighting now became very confused.

"Different sections of the enemy's line wavered and broke, and were crowded into a very small space by large masses in their rear, which seemed undecided which way to go or what to do.

"Of course our generals did not give them much time to consider, but poured in upon them, and drove them in confused masses towards the river.

"The fight was desperately maintained by the Frenchmen, who fought like panthers.

"But it was of no avail; our admirable plan of battle was still maintained by the quickness and coolness of our several chiefs, among whom I would especially mention the count and Caspar.

"The former, of course, was ever with his fond artillery, and seemed as cool as a cucumber among thirty pieces blazing away like furies.

"Caspar, however, had achieved a great success in capturing prisoners.

"But while all were in high spirits at our evident success, and at the prospect of soon driving the enemy into the river, couriers looking pale and sad passed by reporting that Juarez was wounded while personally leading an attack on a powerful battery.

"This news wrought us all up to madness, and without leave or licence all pushed forward and assailed the enemy with irresistible fury, driving them down to the edge of the river in utter confusion and disorder.

"It was now about four o'clock, and reinforcements were reported as rapidly advancing to Bazaine's relief, but were yet several miles from the river's edge.

"From some cause I could never ascertain a halt was sounded, and when the remnants of the enemy's divisions had stacked arms on the river's edge preparatory to surrender, no one stirred to finish the business by a final assault.

"It was evidently 'drown or surrender' with them.

"And they had prepared for the latter, until seeing our inactivity, their gunboats opened furiously, and, save a short cannonade, all subsided into quietness along our lines.

"Night came on, and great confusion reigned among us.

"Thousands were out in quest of plunder.

"Hundreds had escorted prisoners and wounded.

"Scores were intoxicated with wines and liquors found.

"Yet still the gunboats continued their bombardment, and reinforcements arriving in haste, crossed the river, and formed line of battle for the morrow.

"It could not be denied that we had gained a great victory.

"Thousands of prisoners were in our hands, including many officers of all ranks.

"We captured many pieces of cannon, enormous quantities of ammunition, and stores of every sort.

"Many hundreds of tents, camp equipage, hundreds of horses and waggons, much clothing, and eatables of every possible description.

Many standards were ours, and in fact, waggon-loads of everything pertaining to the camps and commissariat of a superabundantly and lavishly supplied enemy.

"But where were our men?

"With the exception of a few thousands of well-disciplined men under Escobedo, and others, our whole army had scattered far and near, as very young and raw troops always will, if not kept firmly in hand.

"And yet our outposts brought word hourly that large masses of the enemy were moving across our whole front, and it could not be doubted that ere the sun again rose, the whole of Bazaine's forces combined would be hurled upon us, weak, wounded, and scattered as we were.

"Although Escobedo had committed a great mistake in not pushing the enemy to conclusions the day before, he exerted himself untiringly for the morrow.

"Stragglers were gathered, positions taken, and the greatest exertions made to secure the invaluable spoil of the battle-field.

"Every spare horse and waggon in the service was employed in the work, and property worth many millions was conveyed to the rear during the night.

"The artillery were sorely taxed.

"Their horses were occasionally used in transporting supplies during the night, and could scarcely get an hour's rest.

"Couriers and orderlies were dashing to and fro all night, inquiring for this general or that, who could not be found.

"Despatch bearers looking for Escobedo and other chiefs.

"Thousands of wounded were moaning and groaning all around us.

"Large fires were consuming everything that could not be transported.

"And so it continued until cocks on neighbouring farms crowed the hour of midnight.

"Wearied beyond all expression, I lay down on bundles of straw, with my feet to the fire, and soon was fast asleep.

"I know not how long I slept, but it seemed that in my dreams, I heard constant picket-firing going, hurried voices, and clanking of chains.

"When I was awakened, the battery was about to move off.

"So shaking myself, I saddled, and was soon on the move.

"It seems that battle was inevitable.

"And although not yet twilight, our men were moving to and fro, and all seemed inspired with new life and confidence.

"Everywhere large fires indicated the destruction of property, which plainly showed that Escobedo did not consider himself strong enough to hold the ground any longer

"Just at dawn picket fighting became angry and rapid.

"In an hour after sunrise we fired our first shot.

"Bazaine had gathered his shattered regiments and brigades as best he could.

"But when our men met them, they gave ground, and every one thought for some time that victory would crown our efforts a second time.

"But after we had wasted our newly-regained strength on the dispirited battalions of the day before, in came fresh troops, and terrible fighting ensued.

"In some places we drove them by unexampled feats of valour.

"But man is nothing more than bone and blood, and sheer exhaustion was hourly telling upon both man and beast.

"Until about noon we retained the ground heroically.

"But it became evident every moment that numbers and strength *must* prevail.

"So that although we had gained everything up to this hour, a retreat was ordered.

"Escobedo had prepared all the roads for this movement.

"There was no hurry or confusion.

"Everything was conducted as if in review. We slowly fell back, leaving little of consequence behind.

"We thus in an orderly manner fell back about two miles, and obtaining a favourable position for our small force, re-formed line of battle, and waited several hours.

"The enemy did not stir.

"They seemed content to hold the field and not pursue, and did not move five hundred yards from their original position of the morning.

"It having become known during the night that the enemy had despatched a strong force to cut off our retreat, Caspar was sent off with a respectable number of men to drive them from Pontsville Ferry, which they occupied. We were ordered to go in another direction for the same purpose with two guns; the count was in charge of Caspar's infantry, but Caspar had sole control of the cavalry.

"At 4 A.M. next morning, we cautiously took up the line of march, and when within a mile of the Ferry abruptly left the main road and approached the heights.

"We could distinctly see the tall bold rock at the Ferry, encircled by mists and clouds.

"And as we journeyed quietly through the forest and ascended the steep wood-covered mountains, the sun rose, revealing the swiftly-flowing river, as I have elsewhere described, with here and there a white dwelling of the town sleeping in the quiet morning air, at the base of the gigantic rocks which overhang the Ferry.

"With excessive labour we pulled the pieces up the face of the hill, and had them in an ambushed position overlooking the town long before the enemy had sounded reveille.

"Their camps about the Ferry were distinctly seen.

"Various trenches, forts, and earth-works were counted and examined with glasses; the whole panorama of the valley lay several hundred feet below us.

"While on every road leading to and from we saw numerous picket fires and videttes.

"There was no sign of Caspar or his command.

"When the mists of morning cleared away, and the distant woods were visible, small faint columns of smoke indicated where his forces lay along the main road.

"At the base of the hill on which we were a streamlet ran towards and emptied into the river, a mile northward at the foot of the town.

"So that on the north and east, two different rivers ran winding through the landscape, while beyond the first-named stream in the valley lay a picturesque village, where the commandant of the post and merchants delighted to dwell in the peculation times of old.

"The chief buildings, however, were now converted into barracks and storehouses, establishments that Caspar had long beheld with a jealous and covetous eye.

"About 7 a.m. I observed several horsemen dash from the distant woods and approach the village in great haste.

"The drums began to beat very wildly.

"Shortly afterwards clouds of dust indicated Caspar's approach.

"At 8 a.m. to a minute he halted on the main road, and fired a shot at the infantry barracks.

"This was a signal to us.

"We hoisted a flag, and two shots answered that all was right.

"The enemy were not long in assembling, and could be seen swarming into their field works and rifle pits.

"Skirmishers were sent out by both parties, and little puffs of smoke and faint reports told that they were hotly engaged.

"The enemy did not seem inclined to leave his fortifications.

"Yet to draw Caspar forward, sent out two regiments as decoys.

"They were saluted with round shot and shell, and quickly turned and fled to the woods south-west of the village.

"They were mistaken in their calculation.

"For as they approached the timber, volleys saluted them, and a squadron of cavalry dashing forward on their flank, cut down many, and dispersed the rest in wild confusion.

"Caspar now advanced several hundred yards nearer.

"The foe brought forward field pieces and fresh regiments to oppose him.

"While this was progressing our artillerists had taken accurate range of the chief storehouse, mills, &c., and then shelled very fast into them.

"This unexpected assault seemed to discomfort the enemy within the town and suburbs.

"And although they endeavoured to save their stores, most of them were fired, and the buildings smashed.

"Had they ascended the opposite heights (not more than half a mile across the river), our position would have proved untenable.

"For they were much higher than those on which we were.

"They did not.

"Our cannonade was maintained with great vigour.

"Every object within reach being smashed up in succession.

"The enemy now began to cross the river on flats at different points.

"Observing it, a few shell were directed towards them with decided effect.

"The flats capsized, and submerged the parties on them.

"Still the enemy advanced, and still Caspar held his ground.

"As the Imperialists advanced in line of battle he put forth a few to meet them; but the latter, at the first fire, broke and fled.

"The Imperialists seeing this, gave a tremendous cheer, and ran forward with the bayonet, but in confusion and with broken lines.

"And as they advanced towards the woods out came a regiment of cavalry, and was among the Imperialists in a few moments, pistoling and slashing awkwardly with sabres.

"The cavalry attack was made in great confusion, and most of the enemy effected their escape by running into a very large fortified house used for barracks in the village.

"Caspar observed this place, and stealing along the road with his 24-pounder on waggon axles, directed a few well-aimed shells at it, broke the walls, blew off the roof, and the refugees sallied out to their nearest lines in great confusion, and with loss.

"This unsatisfactory style of fighting was maintained with fluctuating success until noon, when a courier swam the rivulet, ascended the mountains, and begged us to bring our force into the valley, and assail the enemy on the right, while Caspar pushed the centre.

"Our orders forbade—we dare not go; and although the men crowded round me and begged to be led against the enemy, I was compelled to refuse.

"The cannonade was renewed with great fury by either party, and many shells came screaming over and on to the heights on which we stood, but with no effect.

"Caspar, seeing that the enemy greatly outnumbered, and were endeavouring to surround him, used his field pieces with so much destruction as to hold them in check while he drew off his small force to a better position.

"The rustics Caspar had with him becoming accustomed to the thing, gallantly advanced and repulsed the enemy; while Caspar, conspicuous on a white horse, led on the cavalry, and made several very brilliant charges.

"Having effected his main object, viz., of destroying the mills, storehouses, bridges, &c., Caspar slowly retired, having captured several hundred stands of arms, some prisoners, much ammunition, stores, &c.

"For while he had attracted the enemy's attention by fighting, and driving in their advance, his troopers were scouring the country in all directions, seizing waggons, and vast quantities of commissary stores, &c., unprotected.

"As he retired behind the woods, scouts came in and reported the enemy endeavouring to cut off our retreat.

"But by expedition and coolness we soon descended the mountains, and, reaching the main road, occupied the point crossing a hill, and placed our pieces in position ready for a determined fight.

"For although few, the men were truly desperate, and, to use their own expression, 'spoiling for a fight.'

"The enemy perceived the strong position, and over-estimating our force, retired without firing a shot.

"While bivouacked that night, a courier came dashing towards us, and brought the stirring news that Bazaine, with a heavy force, was marching to cut off Escobedo.

"The latter had hastily retreated, bag and baggage, ten miles; we must immediately follow him as best we could.

"If the enemy had really entered, a courier would inform us of it on the road, and give time to branch off towards Matamoras to get under protection.

"This indeed was startling news.

"The men had travelled much and were excessively weary.

"I decided not to call them up for a few hours, but gave them rest.

"Towards twilight all were quietly awakened and informed of the state of things.

"The men good-humouredly arriving at the conclusion that we had better 'up stakes and dust' out of the neighbourhood in 'a mighty big hurry.'

"Our waggons were sent out of the way by a road leading south-east, with directions to halt at a certain point for further orders.

"We marched through villages like shadows—all were abed, and not a dog barked—and continued at a great pace towards Matamoras.

"Towards evening we halted on a large hill overlooking the town, and received orders to keep to the woods and proceed on to our brigade.

"The rain fell in torrents, and the roads were awful, as all roads in Mexico are at this reason.

"When within a mile of our resting-place a courier brought orders to halt for the night, and proceed to Matamoras at break of day.

"With much swearing and grumbling at Escobedo's idea of strategy, the order was obeyed, and foot-sore, and dirty, and shoeless, we pitched tents on our old camping-ground, one of the companies being detailed to hold the mudwork on the hill, called by the dignified term of 'Fort Escobedo,' though it had no guns, and was not pierced for any.

"This company, together with the other three, detailed men to picket at the river as usual, and were instructed to wait until further orders.

"First from one place, then to another, up and down hills, over mountains, moving away during the night from one place, and returning next day—everlastingly on the move—thus we live out here.

"If this eternal marching through mud, rains, and snow, means 'strategy,' Escobedo possesses more of it than our whole army put together.

"We first moved here, next day moved back, in a few days moved back again, thence from one place to another, until at last I began to imagine we were commanded by some peripatetic philosophical madman, whose *forte* is pedestrianism.

"With little or no baggage, we are a roving, hungry, hardy lot of fellows, and are not patronized at all by parsons or doctors.

"The latter have a perfect sinecure, and I would wager that all the medical stores in our department don't amount to more than a dozen doses of blue mass.

"In fact, we don't want medicines, and have not time to get sick.

"Up one mountain and down another.

"Now watching this 'pass,' next night watching some 'gap,' or 'ford,' or 'bridge.'

"In fine, we seem to do nothing else than 'gap' it, 'ford' it, 'bridge' it.

"But there is no such thing as 'passing' it, for we are but few, and every man must stick to his post or the general will very quickly want to know the reason why.

"He may be a very fine old gentleman, and an honest, good-tempered, industrious man, but I should admire him much more in a state of rest than continually seeing him moving in the front.

"And such a dry old stick, too!

"As to uniform, he has none.

"His wardrobe isn't worth a dollar, and his horse is the only valuable and presentable feature about him.

"And don't he keep his aids moving about!

"Thirty miles' ride at night through the mud is nothing of a job; and if they don't come up to time, I'd as soon face the devil, for he takes no excuses when duty is on hand.

"He is about 45 years old, medium height, strongly built, solemn and thoughtful, speaks but little, and always in a calm, decided tone.

"From what he says there is no appeal.

"He seems to know every hole and corner of this country as if he made it, or at least designed it for his own use.

"He knows all the distances, all the roads, even to cowpaths through the woods, and goat-tracks along the hills.

"He sits his horse very awkwardly, although, generally speaking, all Mexicans are fine horsemen, and has a fashion of holding his head very high, and chin up, as if searching for something skywards.

"Yet although you can never see his eyes for the cap peak drawn down over them, *he* sees everything and nothing escapes him.

"His movements are sudden and unaccountable.

"His staff don't pretend to keep up with him.

"Consequently, he is frequently seen alone, poking about in all sorts of holes and corners, at all times of night and day.

"I have frequently seen him approach in the dead of night, and enter into conversation with sentinels, and ride off through the darkness without saying 'God bless you,' or anything civil to the officers.

"The consequence is, officers are scared, and the men love him.

"He was a student in France, but never remarkable for any brilliancy.

"What service he has seen was in Texas, where he served as lieutenant of artillery.

"At one of the battles there, his captain was about to withdraw the guns, because of the loss suffered by the battery, and also because the range was too great.

"This did not suit our hero.

"He advanced his piece several hundred yards, and 'shortened the distance,' dismounted his opponent's guns, and remained master of the position.

"He left the army, and was professor of mathematics and tactics in the University of Mexico, but was generally looked upon by the students as an old fogey of little talent, and not over-gifted any way.

"It is my opinion, that this man will assuredly make his mark in this war.

"For his untiring industry, and eternal watchfulness, *must* tell upon a numerous enemy unacquainted with the country, and incommoded by large baggage trains.

"Escobedo evidently intends to supply himself at the enemy's expense, and, as he is a true fire-eater, and an invincible believer in our 'manifest destiny,' poor Maximilian will find him a disagreeable opponent to confront in the mountain passes or at the many fords.

"The Mexicans have an idea that he is veritably 'the coming man,' and from the numbers joining him, it looks as if he meant mischief.

"But to form an accurate idea of the doings of this man, it is necessary to state in proper order the various affairs in which he has been engaged since last I heard from you.

"When we reached Matamoras I was glad to hear that a fresh division had formed a junction with us.

"Within a few days we learned that tremendous forces combined under command of Marshal Bazaine, were again slowly advancing, swarming over the country like locusts, eating or destroying everything, carrying off property, capturing negroes, and impressing them into service; driving in our pickets, &c. and had camped about three miles off.

"This was a startling position for us, truly!

"Our main line of communication was in their possession, and we obliged to travel many miles round to keep open intercourse!

"We have but two lines of road, and both were taxed to the utmost.

"But what could we do with but one, while the enemy had several outlets by land and rivers for advance or supplies?

"To add to our misfortunes, Matamoras was a miserable site for encampments, utterly destitute of water, good or bad, and what little could be obtained was scooped up from the sand, or from pools fed by occasional rains.

"You fully know the place and are aware that, although there were then not more than ten thousand camped here, the water was so bad many frequently gave money for a gallon from indifferent wells.

"Except to keep open free traffic with the south, Escobedo would not hold the place five minutes, particularly as out of fifteen thousand men present, the heat, insufficient and bad food, wretched water, and other causes, had reduced our effective strength to about ten thousand.

"Add to these disagreeable things the fact that Marshal Bazaine did not seem inclined to fight us in our breastworks, but occupied ground north of the town, which, you know, was higher than ours, and began intrenching, depending on time and patience to work up till within shelling distance, and then destroy us at leisure.

"Notwithstanding our small force, and the tremendous odds against us, Escobedo put a bold face upon matters; frequently marched out and offered battle, but, to our surprise, he found them unwilling to leave their entrenchments, which grew larger and more numerous every day.

"But if things looked so discouraging in our little army, among troops born on the soil and accustomed to the heats, rains, sudden changes, and abominable water, what must be said of the French general's losses from similar causes in his numerous and well-appointed army of men, who were never before in such a climate in their lives?

"Their loss was truly appalling—it is beyond conception!

"As long as Marshal Bazaine held the road to our front and another on our left flank, he seemed sufficiently contented to advance slowly upon us, and having more or less completed a vast line of elaborate breastworks, began to manœuvre on our right, so as to gain possession of the other road; thus leaving Escobedo in possession of but one line to the south, viz., the south branch road.

"Such intention was early perceived by Escobedo, who moved counter to the design, without weakening Matamoras itself.

"The labour and pertinacity of Bazaine were wonderful.

"Having to build roads as he advanced into the interior, he employed large bodies of men, and when trenches were opened before Matamoras, his army had completed several fine military roads to his immediate front, by which ponderous guns and immense trains of supplies were regularly moving to and from his base of operations.

"For a distance of thirty miles or more, ox, horse and mule teams, were unceasingly moving night and day, much facilitating the speedy construction of his works, miles in extent.

"Sickness, however, greatly weakened his forces, and chills, fevers, chronic disorders, and agues, filled the hospitals, and occasioned large ambulance trains to move to and from the river continually.

"His sanitary system was much superior to ours, and scores of deep wells were bored, and an ample supply of water obtained, while we in Matamoras were almost decimated for the want of a sufficient quantity, and the surrounding country filled by our sick men, too weak to stand, reduced to skeletons from heat, exposure, chills, &c., &c.

"Indications became apparent, however, that since Bazaine would not advance from his works, Escobedo must be compelled to retreat at no distant day, or be massacred at discretion by the enemy's guns, which every day approached nearer and nearer with apparent impunity.

The Imperialists were sorely afraid we would retreat.

"In that case all their mammoth trench and road-building would be vain, and nought left to compensate them for their patience and sufferings.

"Immense roads, as I have said, were dug and levelled through miles of timber.

"Unheard of supplies of shot, shell, and mammoth mortar batteries had been brought to the front with infinite labour, and much sacrifice of life and money, when early one morning all our army quietly decamped towards Monterey, and, ere the mists had risen were beyond sight or hearing.

"A few regiments were thrown out to our front as usual, and maintained picket firing, but were much surprised to receive orders to fall back, and could not believe the army had left.

"For the movement had taken place so quietly, orderly, and unexpectedly, that it required ocular proof to convince them of the fact.

"When the pickets retired from the front the enemy quickly perceived it, and, though much astonished, prepared to pursue.

# THE BOY SOLDIER; OR, GARIBALDI'S YOUNG CAPTAIN.

THE DEATH STRUGGLE!

"Mortified at their failure, the enemy followed our trail vigorously, and, owing to some miscarriage of orders, two waggon trains of miscellaneous, but not valuable baggage, fell into their hands, together with several hundred sick, and a few old arms.

"I do not know, but believe we did not lose a single gun, caisson, or pound of ammunition; for, when we had left, it proved Bazaine had been quietly withdrawing from Matamoras for a space of three weeks, but so strictly had all orders been fulfilled, and so secretly, that three-fourths of the army could not realize and would not believe it.

"It was true, nevertheless, and, had it not been for the accidental capture of the two small baggage trains, through wilful carelessness, this retreat would perhaps stand unrivalled in the history of warfare, as being the most secret, successful, and disastrous blow which a feeble army ever dealt to an all-powerful and confident enemy.

"Escobedo proved most expert, and deserves credit, for you are aware that miles of fine roads and mammoth earth-works had been erected at great cost, to within four hundred yards of us.

"Bazaine had stored his camps with immense supplies, destroying hundreds and hundreds of horses, waggons, mules, carts, &c., in transportation.

"He had prepared for a bombardment of an indefinite period, built magazines, barracks, repaired railroads, built bridges, &c., thus occupying the whole spring in preparation.

"In one moment all these plans were thwarted, and the hot season too far advanced for them to move a mile farther into the interior.

"Thus all the labour, expectation, patience, loss in life, immense expense, and fruitless strategy of Bazaine proved worthless, and his army weakened by sickness, far more than could ever have been from actual battle.

"Save a few hundred sick, and the baggage trains mentioned, we lost scarcely anything worth mentioning, and arrived at Monterey without adventures of any kind, save flying rumours from the rear, where the enemy was following us up, shelling the woods furiously on every hand, but never approaching within gun-shot of our rear-guard.

The distance was twenty-five miles south of Matamoras, and the place selected for our stand an excellent one.

"The enemy did not follow, however; the season was unfavourable, so that finding a supply of good water, and eligible sites for fortifications, we were comfortably placed, and not fearful of consequences.

"You can very well imagine Bazaine's chagrin at Escobedo's retreat, and, as might be expected, the French were railing at us for running away, calling us 'cowards,' &c., for not remaining to be shelled out at discretion.

"Much comment exists in the army regarding this movement, and it took all by surprise.

"Opinions differ materially, and it is said that

Juarez blames Escobedo extravagantly for allowing himself to be driven to any such necessity.

"I doubt this report.

"We had scarcely arrived at Monterey ere it was known that fleets were approaching, to unite in silencing the batteries at Bagdad—the only town on the river which blockaded navigation to the enemy—and as it was thought a land force would co-operate with the gunboats, our brigade was sent to assist in its defence.

"I was appointed to command the post, and did everything in my power to place the Bagdad a good posture for defence.

"Bagdad is situated on the south bank of the river, and did good service as a depôt during the war, being the only safe crossing upon the river.

"Thousands of men, supplies, and materials were continually passing to and fro.

"Much of our provisions, &c., for the armies in the east and west being derived from Texas and other parts.

"So that, could the enemy silence our batteries and seize that town, all the agricultural products of the north and west would pass down to them unmolested to the Gulf.

"It would give them free access to the whole river front, supply them abundantly with all things, and, having us fairly on the flanks, they could operate with impunity upon numberless points, divide our forces, and subjugate us piecemeal.

"The north bank of the river, for several miles above Bagdad, gradually rises higher than the common level.

"So that immediately above Bagdad there are high bluffs, which command the river, north and south, cover the town, and can sweep the peninsula across the stream, formed as it is by windings of the river, and which is much lower land than the east side, and subject to overflows.

"The Rio Grande, above Bagdad, runs north to south, and suddenly bends.

"So that the point of this peninsula came immediately under our guns at the bluffs, and few boats could pass or repass without receiving damage, since the stream at that point was not one half mile across, and the usual channel immediately under our batteries.

"As will be seen at a glance, Bagdad was an all-important point to the enemy, who, aside from military ends, desired free navigation for their commerce.

"It was a vital position to us for the same reasons, independent of the fact that its occupation would throw that country into the hands of the enemy, and cut us off from regular and large receipts of stores.

"As the enemy had swept everything before them on the river, except at Bagdad, it was considered we could make but feeble resistance, as the country around was nought but a district, short of agricultural supplies, and connected with the interior and main army at Monterey by a single road much over worked and unsound.

"When June advanced, and rivers began to rise, the smoke of numerous boats below the city, reconnoitring, was daily observed to be slowly approaching.

"Our foundries and other shops were busy night and day.

"Timber was hewn on every side for breastworks, magazines, and hospitals.

"Within a few days, formidable breastworks, earthworks, and rifle-pits were dug on every hand, and the river bank lined with marksmen to sweep the decks, should an enemy appear.

"The streets running parallel with, and at right angles to, the stream, were cleared of all combustible material, and orders given for women and children to leave immediately.

"Women, for the most part, refused to go, and many dug holes in the ground, made them bomb-proof and comfortable, so that, if forced by the boats, they could seek refuge therein.

"The whole town was burning with patriotism, and the women were more fierce, if possible, than the men.

"Everything was prepared for a bombardment.

"Yet business progressed as of old, to some extent.

"There was nothing of that flurry and excitement visible among the people which thoughts of a cannonade might naturally create.

"Batteries on the bluff were manned night and day, but so concealed it was impossible to discover the position or number of pieces.

"In truth, we had not more than twenty guns and the artillerists perfect novices.

"They were eager for the 'fun,' however, and ably supported by some splendid troops, who would 'rather fight than eat.'

"The women seemed to have changed their feminine natures.

"They wished every building crushed to powder rather than give up.

"And if any of the French soldiery could have seen them, young and old, arming for the worst, and bent on mischief, it would not have given them pleasing ideas of the warm reception prepared for an Imperial landing.

"Everything ingenuity could devise was resorted to by dames to facilitate military preparations.

"Expense, loss, fatigue, and danger were despised.

"All were in rivalry to make sacrifices for the common cause, and even stripped sheets and blankets from beds for the use of the sick.

"More than this.

"It was announced the commandant of the town needed flannel for ammunition, and none could be obtained.

"In less than an hour several hundred flannel petticoats were sent to him, with compliments of the late wearers.

"While on picket duty one morning at the river bank, south of the town, a gunboat was seen coming up round the bend, with a white flag flying, and much speculation ensued as to the cause.

"A boat soon landed at the wharf, and communicated with the commandant, asking for the surrender of Bagdad, in the name of Maximilian.

"The answer was instant—

"'We never surrender!'

"The gunboat departed.

"All now knew what was in store, and began cleaning arms, preparing for the combined attack of both fleets, which none could doubt would attempt to unite and destroy us.

"The following day, from bluffs above town and on high grounds, a few miles from Bagdad, we could plainly see the fleet of gunboats and transports steaming towards us, and at evening saw smoke ascending from ther funnels, while anchoring west of the peninsula before described.

"From the character of the river's winding, this peninsula faces—or, as the sailors would say, 'lies broadside to'—Bagdad, being about one half-mile across.

"So that were it not for woods a vessel would be in sight for twenty miles or more ere rounding the point and passing under the bluffs.

"A day or two after an answer had been returned the Imperial commodore, one of his iron-clads was signalled from below, and, soon after appearing round the southern bend, put on steam, and advanced rapidly and boldly towards us, evidently bent on running the gauntlet of our guns.

"Coming within distance, it was perceived she carried numerous and heavy guns, was shot-proof, and had no one visible on deck.

"When nearing the town, under full head of steam, one of her ports opened, and a head thrust out, shouted to pickets on the bank,

"'Oh, you republican rascals!' and a torrent of such-like compliments.

"He was instantly answered by a volley of small arms, and quickly dropped the port screen.

"When abreast of the city, and steaming boldly to round the point, three or four white puffs were visible on the bluffs, and simultaneous roars accompanied, while round shot plunged about the gunboat, spurting up jets and columns of water around her.

"Still pushing forward, her helm answered readily, and when rounding the point and abreast of the bluffs, a quick succession of bright flashes glanced from her dark sides, and, amid deafening roars, the ground was ploughed up in all directions round our guns, while quick answers from our side made the water spout around her, as if a thousand whales were blowing.

"Thus it continued for some time, without intermission.

"The gunboat was throwing shells, and our batteries vomiting round shot.

"Though not disabled, it was clear she had been repeatedly struck.

"Yet, when rounding the point and getting out of danger, she gallantly presented her larboard to the batteries, and giving a parting broadside, was soon from view behind the trees, safely anchored.

"It was now apparent that we could do but little with the enemy's ships, for our shot glanced from their sides in showers of sparks, and damaged them but slightly.

"So that it was deemed necessary to erect a strong battery south of the town for the better reception of other visitors.

"They were not long in coming.

"Being informed of the inefficiency or insufficiency of our batteries, several others ran past, inflicting no injury, but, in many cases receiving much.

"The fleets having now formed a junction, prepared to bombard the town.

"And, by way of preliminary, to get the range, sent several dozen eleven-inch shell across the peninsula, which, save a horrible screaming noise, did little harm more than throw up tremendous clouds of dust and sand wherever they chanced to fall.

"Their transports now began to assemble rapidly, until a truly formidable fleet was gathered, and all imagined them heavily freighted with troops, destined to co-operate on land.

"Had the peninsula been less thickly timbered, our batteries could have played sad havoc among them, for the distance was not more than a mile in a direct line.

"Yet every shell thrown by us was waste of ammunition, since the vessels were so close in shore that it required more skill than our gunners possessed to clear the woods with nicety, and drop shell among them, drawn up as they were in single line, broadside to the beach.

"But while the enemy in early morning or cool of evening would favour the city with a few hundred shells and even amuse themselves long after starlight with such pastime, a few young naval officers were up a branch of the Rio, and having blockaded the passage to the enemy with immense rafts, cut in and floated down from extensive forests in that vast region of swamps, were actively engaged in building a huge iron-clad, which was destined to sally out and drive off the enemy.

"The enemy were fully aware of our activity up that river, and correctly informed of all our doings with the ships and craft which had taken refuge there.

"To keep fully informed of our mysterious doings up that branch of the Rio, three of the finest boats were detached from the fleet to carefully watch the mouth of the tributary.

"And for this purpose they always kept up steam both night and day for fear of any sudden movement.

"Yet the fleet daily maintained a hot and vigorous cannonade upon Bagdad at all hours, save during the intense heat of mid-day.

"Their troops were landed from transports, but never came within view.

"Yet from scouts and spies we ascertained the enemy had seized hundreds of poor Mexicans in that part, and were actually digging a canal across the peninsula, which it was hoped would divert the waters of the river from its proper bed, and leave Bagdad high and dry as an inland city.

"The idea was a bold one.

"The present undertaking, however, did not promise good results.

"The stream was too strong, and could not be diverted.

"So that although numbers of their men sunk and died under their labour—being several miles long— it was not prosecuted, hundreds having found early graves in that low, marshy, and deathly climate.

"Yet still the bombardment continued daily, and thousands of shell, round shot, and other missiles were hurled at our city.

"But strange to say, except in some half-dozen instances, I know not one house which was more than slightly injured.

"One shell entered the church on the hill, and made a large hole above the great window, but passed out through a window, and buried itself in a sandhill.

"Another struck the school house on the southwest corner, ranged through the building, and made the interior like a basket of chips, subsequently exploding in an engine house hard by, carrying off the roof to parts unknown.

"A small frame building was fired near the ferry landing, and, being old, was allowed to burn to the ground.

"Yet, considering the number of shells thrown, and the streets of wooden houses towards the river, it is extraordinary how any escaped, or how the city was saved from daily conflagrations.

"Three shells entered the hotel, and upset the dinner things—slightly.

"A hundred shot were fired at the court-house, many feet above the level of the river.

"From its position on a hill, with a large banner continually floating there, was a conspicuous mark for the enemy.

"They made some capital shots at it, truly, and one entered the dome, two feet below the flag-staff, ranged downwards to the entrance hall, and—fizzled!

"The wharf-boat at the landing was partly sunk in the first days of the bombardment.

"And I am happy to state that a row of wooden buildings on the levee, owned by a race of sleek Jews, was knocked into a mass of splinters, and no longer recognizable.

"A few evenings since I saw a Mr. Moss standing behind a house, gazing on the ruins of his 'Cheap Store' and 'Emporium,' soliloquizing.

"I might have heard what he said, but a distant explosion informed Mr. Moss the enemy were still inclined for business, and he had better run—which he did in great haste—away.

"Yet what had the enemy effected by this bombardment?

"Comparatively nothing.

"They could not pass our batteries without great loss or damage.

"And although thousands of shells had been hurled at the town, not a house of importance had fallen.

"Business was continued to some extent, and people moved about, dodging the shells as best they could.

"Our batteries were intact.

"Two guns were all they had dismounted, and we were now better prepared than ever.

"We had not lost a man from the bombardment.

"Save a good old lady who was killed while carrying refreshments to the sick, and an old man watching the distant fleet, not a drop of blood was shed, despite all the noise and great exertions of the enemy.

"When shells came thickly, those who had dug caves in the ground retired to them, and suffered nought but inconvenience from the enemy.

"And, strange as it may seem, during the whole cannonade, which lasted a long time, they never fairly got the range of our batteries on the bluff, although continually firing in that direction.

"The bombardment, however, was not without intermission.

"Sometimes we were favoured with an uninterrupted tornado of shot and shell for many hours, and then all would subside again, and people reappear in the streets as if nothing had taken place.

"Occasionally, the spectacle was truly beautiful.

"Standing on a hill two miles from the bluffs, the whole scene was delightful, when witnessed in the cool of evening.

"For the snow-white houses of the quiet town, with flags flying in every direction, stood out in bold relief against the rich dark green of the landscape, or in striking contrast of the light-blue skies, with rising stars.

"While from the west, behind the thickly-wooded peninsula, thick clouds of sulphurous smoke curled from the dark sides of the fleets, as monster shells by scores were screaming through the air in all directions, bursting in town, or ploughing up the ground all around our lofty batteries.

"For many hours after sunset would the strife continue.

"And long after the moon had dipped beyond the dark lines of forest fringing the broad, swift waters of the Rio Grande, bright flashes lit up the heavens to the west, and earth-shaking reports succeeded, as scores of shells and iron bolts were vomited forth from invisible vessels, pyrotechnically coursing through or exploding in the air, bursting over the town into a shower of parti-coloured, meteoric fragments, leaving vapoury circles of sulphurous smoke sensitively trembling in the starlight.

"How long the enemy intended to remain in position before the town was a matter of conjecture, though not of anxious inquiry.

"For as long as ammunition lasted, we cared little for their obstinacy and waste of powder against us, since experience had taught all to laugh at their noise.

"Yet, although despising their efforts to destroy the place, we were careful to husband our resources.

"For although material was inexhaustible with them, it was difficult to procure with us, owing to the lack of waggons and resources.

"Our gunners never fired at random, and seldom failed to hit the object intended.

"This the enemy knew, and although the gunboats had passed up without positive destruction, experience taught Imperial and French commodores it would not be safe or wise to try the experiment a second time.

"For our men had become wonderfully expert, and tried their rapid advance in gunnery to the great annoyance of the enemy on more than one occasion, and with destructive effect.

"It thus seemed, therefore, that the commodores would not allow more vessels to run the blockade from the south, although several were in view desirous of attempting it.

"They were perforce obliged to stand off and cannonade, independently maintaining a cross fire upon the town.

"The intense heat had now passed, and sickly weather came in with fevers among the unacclimated enemy, cooped up in their ships amid smoke, heat, confinement, deathly night vapours of the lands and water.

"And though suffering extremely in every way, they were farther from realizing their hopes than ever.

"It was computed they had at anchor more than twenty boats playing on the city, together with a land force of several thousands, scores of transports, flats, &c.

"And ordnance officers affirmed that they had fired more than 5,000 shells during the bombardment, without counting rockets, round shot, iron bolts, &c.

"For a few days they were inactive, but did not prepare to depart.

"They had abandoned the canal project, after digging more than a mile, and spies informed us their wheelbarrows, tools, &c., were scattered around the peninsula, and every house was an hospital.

"The commodores were nonplussed.

"And as their large fleet lay at anchor on the ripless, copper-coloured river, with a cloudless sky, under the scorching sun, without the echo of a voice, without the motion of a leaf, or flapping of ensigns from a breath of air, the cries of sand-cranes coming to and fro reminded one of some river of death, with hospitals for ships, and spectres for crews."

## CHAPTER CXVII.

### THE STORY OF YOUNG DON CARLOS AND ELVINA.

ONE evening during a cessation of hostilities, the Boy Soldiers were much amused by the stories told by old Mexicans who had flocked to the standard of the people.

But of all who assembled round the watchfires of Young Frank, none were more welcome than old Don Roberto, who seemed to have at his fingers end the whole history of Mexico from the time of Montezuma down.

"You never heard, I suppose, how young Don Carlos (Don Toros' son) won his fame and fortune, did you?"

"No," said all, "but we have read of him in history."

"I dare say you have," said Don Roberto, "but I am nearly one hundred years old now and know more of such things than most people, therefore if you will poke up the fire and pass the wine around I will tell you a story of more than passing interest about young Carlos and the first Spanish settlers in Mexico."

"Hear, hear," said all.

And old Roberto began:—

"The tall black towers of Toros Castle loomed out in grim and bold relief against the moonlit sky.

"Watchfires flickered and flamed on its many-gabled battlements.

"A solitary banner floated lazily in the soft September wind, and all was still.

"The vale, with its green and mossy hills, stood out in the far perspective of ethery blue, where twinkling stars sparkled and shone with ever-changing ray.

"While midway in the blooming, undulating landscape of a thicket and dense forest, the river wound round and round like a silvery thread that marked the bloodstained borders of Mexico and Texas.

"All the earth seemed sleeping in the lap of loveliness and peace.

"The very air was laden with the perfumes of field and forest.

"The mocking-bird, with thrilling song, warbled on bush and tree.

"Save this, and the gently moaning night winds, naught caught the ears of trusty sentinels who, with sword and spear, battle-axe and mace, walked their nightly rounds on the castle walls of Don Toros, the lord and bold defender of far-famed Rio Grande.

"The draw-bridge was up.

"The castle, towering to the midnight skies, was silent as the vaults of death.

"Two steel-clad trusty knights stood watch and ward at the massive gates without, the deep moat rippled sluggishly in the moonlight, reflecting myriads of twinkling stars.

"Yet within, and close to that black and massive gate, there slumbered in picturesque carelessness and confusion a hundred grim and valient men-at-arms, who, in an instant and at a single word, would have been ready to contest the right and with their dearest blood any who dared insult or assail that solemn portal with unwarranted rudeness.

"Silence reigned in all the spacious courtyards of the castle.

"None but the steel-capped sentinel, with flashing sword or spear, walked in the granite-paved, far-echoing, moonlit galleries or cloisters.

"The banquet hall, a common resort of knights and squires, pages and attendants, had lost its busy appearance of feasting and revelry.

"Long oak tables were rolled against the lofty walls, where flapped in fitful gusts of wind a hundred victorious banners, and where flashed in the twilight a hundred shields of far-famed knights and lords, who did homage and gave service to the warrior, Don Toras.

"Around the blazing faggots of the banquet-hall gathered gallant knights in dazzling armour.

"Some told the tale of wars, of wounds and scars received in battle, while attendant squires and pages, highly born, whispered apart in silence, or in secret sighed for the long-sought time when they should have won their 'golden spurs' on the field of victory and honour.

"Weary stag-hounds lay on the rush-covered floor, soundly sleeping at their masters' feet.

"Yet, even in slumber, they dreamily growled as if then engaged in some exciting chase in the well-known forests of Texas.

"Knights and nobles were there, indeed, clothed in steel from head to heel, with swords of ponderous length and weight belted on their thighs, and nodded drowsily in the fire-light, or walked to and fro.

"For none knew at what moment the alarm might be raised from the watch-towers or postern gates that the enemy had burst across the border, bent as usual on some predatory inroad, and prepared to destroy or kill with fire or sword all who dared oppose their ravaging march through the adjacent country.

"Horses in the stables were always saddled, and ready for instant use.

"Knights themselves, and all in Toros Castle, were wont to stand prepared for conflict both night or day.

"Nor was it an uncommon sight to see lords sit at the banquet table cased in mail, to carve the baron of beef with gloves of steel, raise golden goblets and quaff ruby wine through their visor-bars, or, with corselet laced, to lay them down to rest beside the faggot fire, and pillow their heads on cold, hard bucklers.

"Such was the warlike custom rendered necessary at every castle and stronghold through the restless violence of the merciless Borderers, and at no place were such preparations on a grander scale than at Toros Castle, for it was famed as being the most formidable one along the Rio Grande.

"Yet, while all was still in that grim, gigantic pile of battlements and towers—while the old don slumbered peacefully in his gorgeous chamber, forgetful alike of foreign wars, of intrigues at home, or the incessant inroads into his domains by ruthless hordes of marauders, there was a youth who paced his chamber with restless step, and could not slumber.

"It was young Don Carlos.

"A bold and handsome youth was he, of feature fair, and flowing raven hair.

"His step was elastic.

"His form and figure noble.

"There was fire in his eye.

"A dilating nostril and a stately manner which bespoke alike both his descent from kings, and an unbrooked ambition and fiery temper.

"Again and again did he gaze from his lofty casement upon the far-off silvery Rio, splashing and flashing and sparkling like a mass of many-coloured diamonds twinkling in a bed of green.

"But he sighed, and waited hour after hour.

"Yet left he not his post of midnight observation.

"In this chamber also a noble, fair-faced youth lay upon a couch of sable furs.

"The book had dropped from his sleepy hands.

"He was fast bound in slumber, and smiled unconsciously in his sleep.

"This was his faithful companion and friend.

"Young Don Carlos again and again looked forth from the lofty turret far away towards the towering hills of Texas, but saw not that which his keen eyes so eagerly sought.

"'He will not come to-night,' sighed Carlos, and left his apartment thoughtfully and slowly.

"He had resolved to proceed along the long stone corridors, and ascend the loftiest battlements in order to have a still more extended view of the surrounding country.

"When young Spinola, with a loud shout, awoke from his sleep, looking startled and deadly pale.

"With clammy brow and flashing eyes he darted from the chamber, and sought his friend, companion, and lord, and Don Carlos.

"Carlos, however, unknown to him, had ascended the watch-tower stairs, and at that moment stood on the loftiest pinnacle of the castle!

"'What of the night, guard?' asked Don Carlos, with a troubled brow, pacing up and down.

"'All is quiet without, my lord,' said the sentinel, in tones of genuine reverence and respect.

"'You have well scanned the high roads that run through the forest across the Rio?'

"'Yes, in truth, most noble Carlos; such were the orders of the captain of the watch.'

"'And have seen nothing?'

"'Nothing, good my lord.'

"'Strange! 'tis very strange,' mused Carlos, with a heavy heart.

"'Are you sure that while on guard you have neither seen nor heard ought?'

"'No, in truth, my good lord."

"'Nor your comrades of the night-watch either? I expected a trusty yeoman messenger to-night, one who was ever faithful and true; he tarries long, and comes not far from the border.'

"Even while thus he spoke, and peered over the moonlit battlements, he saw that which at first seemed to please and afterwards to startle him.

"''Tis he! it is! it must be Hubert!' he said. 'See yonder, or do my eyes deceive me, guard?' said Carlos.

"In the distance, far, very far away, a small black speck was seen crossing the moonlit landscape, and speeding hastily to the covert of the forest.

"Presently this unknown object was observed to be closely followed by four others!

"Onwards they come! it is an exciting scene; it seems to be a race for life or death.

"The five small black objects become larger and more distinct each moment.

"The first one seems almost overtaken by the others.

"'Poor Hubert! brave, gallant Hubert! it must be he! it must be he! the border ruffians give him chase.'

"'My good lord, did you see their rude weapons flash in the moonlight?'

"'See! there it is again,' said one.

"'He falls!'

"'No; he cuts his way through, and dashes away from them!'

"'He seeks the forest shelter.'

"'They are now lost to view, Don Carlos.'

"'I saw one fall.'

"'Yea two, good, my lord.'

"'They must be robbers assailing some laggard traveller, for he had a white horse under him.'

"Such were the several exclamations of the guard and officers of the night-watch who had witnessed the exciting chase in the moonlit plain below.

"'A white horse, say you?' Carlos asked, in doubt.

"'Yes, my good lord.'

"'Then it was not Hubert,' said Carlos; 'he will come to-morrow with the dawn. What we have now seen must have been an affair with forest cut-throats.'

"As thus he spoke, and turned away from the group of guards, young Spinola walked up to him hastily on the castle walls, looking pale and troubled.

* * * * *

"'Why, my faithful Spinola, what would ye with me?' said Carlos, in a jocose tone, as he shook his young companion by the hand. 'Thou look'st as if some frightful ghost or goblin had disturbed thy wits and slumber.'

"'So there has, Don Carlos,' young Spinola coolly replied.

"'Why, man, what mean ye?' said Carlos, laughing. 'Surely my friend, Spinola, has not turned old dame, that he believes in dreams and witchery? What ails thee? Could'st not sleep without me, then? Come, come, look pleased again; don't be angry with me. I love thee too well to see thy comely face so sorrow-laden. Come, I'll watch no more to-night. Let us to bed; thou shalt pour into my ear the dreadful dream which hath paled thy rosy cheek, and, when Hubert arrives in the morning, we will——'

"'What of the morning, Don Carlos?' Spinola thoughtfully asked.

"'Why, off we are to the hills, and merrily slay the deer.'

"'Methinks good Hubert will never more return.'

"'What say you?' said Don Carlos, the colour mounting to his face. 'Not return! what mean you?'

"'Indeed methinks he will not. I feel certain he will not.'

"'Suppose you, then, that he has turned a dastardly traitor, and revealed all my secrets across the Border? It cannot be. You know not Hubert so well as I. He would serve me with his heart's blood.'

"'He never will more.'

"'What mean ye?' young Carlos asked, striking his foot impatiently on the ground. 'You were not wont to speak in riddles thus. What reason have you to doubt good Hubert?'

"'I do not doubt him; he is, and has ever been, the very pink of honour itself—never a truer or more faithful yeoman hired to serve Don Toros or his son.'

"'Right glad am I thus to hear my bosom friend so speak of him.'

"'But still for all he will never return, Don Carlos.'

"'What prompts you to think so? He is the best forester on the whole Border; none can track or catch him. He it was who taught me how and where to hunt, and now I know all the range from these walls far across the Rio, aye, up to the battlements of Bexar; a stouter heart or braver man ne'er pulled bow or threw a spear. I would trust my soul's fortune in his hands. He it is, as you know,' continued young Carlos, 'who is my messenger to Elvina, our old enemy's fair daughter.'

"'And Elvina has caused his death,' said Spinola, in a half whisper.

"Don Carlos started back at the words which Spinola had so solemnly uttered, and gazed on his friend's pale face like one just starting from a dream.

"At that moment, however, and while they yet stood on the battlements, the thoughtful mood of Carlos was broken by the clanking footsteps of a man in mail who approached him with a slip of parchment in hand.

"'Don Carlos,' said the young knight, bowing gracefully, and saluting, 'at first methought this mission was for my lord, your father; but the messenger who is called Hubert——'

"'Enough,' said young Carlos, taking the small strip of parchment from the knight's mailed hand, and which was covered with and secured by full a dozen waxen ends. 'Thanks, brave sir, your native wit hath taught thee that *all* which comes by messenger is not intended for my father.'

"The knight smiled grimly, and was about to retire.

"'Stay, Sir Knight,' young Carlos said, opening the note, and eagerly reading it by the ruddy glare of the turret watch-fire, which, like a blood-red flag, flapped and waved against the rapidly darkening sky. 'Stay, good sir, stay; methinks this note requires instant answer. Would you——'

"'I am at your bidding, my good lord,' the knight replied. 'The messenger requires an answer, so he told me, and with immediate dispatch would post away again.'

"'Excellent fellow! Brave Hubert, my heart yearns towards him for his fidelity and love,' young Carlos said, with a countenance flushed with joy.

"'Shall I wait for an answer, sir?' the knight asked.

"'One word from me is all sufficient. Tell him not to tarry on the road, and my message is, that I will fly, at the proper moment, to the place that is named.'

"'That you will fly at the proper moment to the place that is named, such is your verbal message, Don Carlos?'

"'It is; and you might add, as the matter is of moment, that I will write and send a messenger forthwith, but that at the moment my impatience is too great.'

"The knight bowed and retired.

"For a few moments neither Carlos nor young Spinola spoke; but walked slowly and silently to their chamber.

"Carlos cast himself upon a downy lounge, and by the lamplight read again and again the precious message which had been brought to him.

"His eyes seemed to dance with joy, and his face was flushed with excitement.

* * * * *

"Long before morning broke, while even yet the stars struggled with approaching twilight, young Don Carlos arose from his sleepless couch.

"He went into the apartment of his dear and faithful young friend, Spinola.

"'He sleeps sweetly,' said Carlos, thoughtfully, and with a smile.

"'No one would dream of his faithfulness to me; yet Spinola believes in dreams, and that is childish.'

"'I do not sleep, Don Carlos,' said the youth, opening his eyes; 'nor do I lay too much stress upon the importance of dreams.'

"After a pause, he added—

"'You call it childish and silly to believe in the warnings which may visit us in sleep, but *I* do not. If glad tidings ever come to me in slumber, I heed them not; but, if I am warned of danger, I always heed the message, whatever it be.'

"Young Spinola's manner was so unusually calm, composed, and strange, that young Carlos felt a sort of sorrow for his companion's fears.

"'But you told me, Spinola, that good Hubert would never return.'

"'I did so.'

"'And this warning you say occurred in a dream?'

"'It did.'

"'Then for once you must confess yourself wrong.'

"'I do not, Don Carlos.'

"'No.'

"'I do not.'

"'But Hubert not only returned, as you know; but has gone forth again on another message for me to the fair Elvina.'

"'Did you see him?'

"'See him?'

"'Yes, see him.'

"'I did not.'

"'Then why still persist in saying that my predictions are still untrue?'

"'Did he not arrive at the castle gates? Did I not receive his message and send another? Did I not?'

"'Did you *see* him, I ask again?' said young Spinola.

"'I did not.'

"'Then I am still right, for Hubert has *not* returned.'

"'It was his ghost, then.'

"'It might have been his ghost, or anything you may please to fancy; but it was *not* Hubert!'

"'Not Hubert.'

"'No.'

"'Then who else?'

"'That I know not.'

"'A friend, think you?'

"'Perhaps so.'

"'Or an enemy?'

"'Possibly an enemy in the guise of a friend.'

"'Impossible. I cannot—I will not believe, it Spinola.'

"'As you please, Don Carlos.'

"After another pause, young Spinola laid his hand gently on the shoulder of Don Carlos, and said—

"'Carlos, did I ever wrong you?'

"'No, never.'

"'Or ever give you other than brotherly advice?'

"'You did not. I prized your friendship more than that of any person living.'

"Spinola smiled, as he said again—

"'Did I ever refuse to accompany you in any expedition?'

"'You never have.'

"'In your hunting excursions, where traps were laid for you by the native Mexican princes, have I always fought by your side?'

"'Yes, ever.'

"'And yet, for all this, Don Carlos, although in a measure we have been reared and grown up together, I find of late that you have distrusted me, spurned my advice, and looked coldly upon me.'

"'Nay, Spinola, you wrong me.'

"'No, Carlos, I do not; you do not love me as you did.'

"Carlos did not reply.

"'I know you do not, and because I have always dissuaded you from continuing this attachment with Elvina.'

"'Mention not her name in words so cold, Spinola,' said Carlos, passionately. 'I love her dearly, devotedly, and almost to distraction.'

"'I know you do—you have always done so. But what of that?'

"'What of that, say you? Why, she loves me in return.'

"'That may or may not be.'

"'Do you doubt it?'

"'I do.'

"'Then, Spinola,' said Carlos, reddening, 'if you doubt the truth of her devotedness to me, you are not my friend.'

"'I thought you would say as much,' said Spinola, with a quiet smile. 'All men have their ambition, and if any one steps in to thwart it, that one is considered an enemy.'

"'What reasons have you for supposing that she does not love me?'

"'Many.'

"'Name them.'

"'Is not your father, Don Toros, a Spanish invader of this soil?'

"'He is, and many others beside.'

"'What made him rear this castle with so much care and expense?'

"'As a safeguard against the natives and their Indian allies.'

"'True.'

"'But what of that?' said Carlos, in doubt.

"'Why, this: if these native princes and their Indian allies were so peaceably inclined, if they bowed willingly to the yoke which the Spaniards had thrust upon them, why build strong castles, and why retain scores of armed knights and military adventurers around us?'

"'For fear of treachey.'

"'That is the very word, Don Carlos—treachery! Beware of it; for not all the strong places in the world could defeat the cunning of these native princes and their Indian friends if they once made up their minds to destroy us.'

"'You are raving, Spinola! The descendants of Montezuma have been thoroughly subdued long ago.'

"'They have not, Carlos. Their constant dream is for the liberation of the land from the Spanish invaders.'

"'And what are dreams worth?' said Carlos, laughing.

"Spinola did not heed the laugh, but asked—

"'Has Don Toras, your father, ever visited this prince Catalka, whose daughter, Elvina, so much enraptures you?'

"'He has not.'

"'The last time they met was in the battle field?'

"'It was.'

"'Catalka and his forces were routed by your father, Don Toras?'

"'They were; and my father was raised in rank in consequence.'

"'But Don Toras knows nought of this your love for Elvina?'

"'He does not.'

"'Nor would he approve of it?'

"'Perhaps he would not; and, for this reason, I have always observed the greatest caution and secresy about it.'

"'More than once,' said Spinola, 'I have been tempted to act the true friend in this matter, but you would have looked upon me as an enemy had I done so.'

"'What then did you meditate?'

"'To tell your father the whole secret.'

"'But you did not?' said Carlos, rising in anger.

"'I did not; but I say, again and again, that I fear Catalka, Elvina's father, knows of the whole affair.'

"'And what if he does?'

"'He will, if he has not already, take advantage of it to ensnare you, and perhaps slaughter every Spaniard in this part of his former dominions.'

"'Dreaming again,' said Carlos, with a hearty laugh.

"'No, I am not dreaming, Carlos. You do me wrong—a grievous wrong! And to prove my friendship I will do aught you wish; go wherever you bid me, or even lay down my life if you will prove the truth of my attachment.'

"'I do not need fresh proof of your love, Spinola,' said Carlos, "but I came here to speak to you on particular business.'

"'Name it.'

"'It is hazardous.'

"'That matters not.'

"'It also requires the greatest secresy.'

"'It is of love, then?'

"'It is. I have resolved to visit Elvina once more, and bear her away from her cruel father.'

"'And bring her hither?'

"'No.'

"'Where else would you convey her, then?'

"'Anywhere, but not here; it would entail certain death on both, for Don Toros, my father, hates the name of Catalka, and all who belongs to him.'

"'That fact is well known,' said Spinola. 'No two enemies ever hated each other with such intensity as they do; and why, therefore, prosecute this wild passion?—it can never end in good.'

"'She is so beautiful,' Carlos exclaimed, in a rapture.

"'But you dare not return to your father's halls with her.'

"'I know it. I have made every preparation to fly to Spain.'

"Madcap that you are, Carlos! This wild adventure will bring ruin on us all.'

"'I care not,' said Carlos. 'None but the brave deserve the fair. I have sworn that Elvina shall be mine, so there's an end of it.'

* * * * *

"Half-an-hour had not elapsed after this communication, when two gallant young horsemen were seen to emerge from the gate of Don Toro's castle.

"They were none other than Don Carlos and his faithful friend, Spinola.

"They were splendidly mounted, and their horses neighed and pranced along the lonely road in splendid style.

"'How far is it to Catalka's castle?' asked Spinola.

"'Several leagues.'

"'It will be broad daylight ere we reach it.'

"'No, not if we ride fast.'

"So saying, they spurred onwards in the beautiful twilight, and their glistening spears and shields were soon lost in the depths of a dense forest through which they had to pass.

"They did not observe anything particular as they journeyed along, so intent was Don Carlos in dilating upon the charms of his ladylove.

"But at the very moment they had left the gates of Don Toro's castle, several mysterious lights could have been seen flittering about on adjacent hills.

"The winds sighed mournfully.

"The trees shook in the breeze with a melancholy murmur.

"The calm around made both Carlos and Spinola thoughtful as they entered the forest.

"They cantered along, however, and soon left the forest far behind.

"In a short time they arrived at the mouth of a mountain gorge through which it was necessary to pass.

"This gorge was the common boundary between the domains of Catalka, the native Mexican prince, and Don Toros.

# THE BOY SOLDIER; OR, GARIBALDI'S YOUNG CAPTAIN.

THE ACCIDENT.

"It was called Wolf Gorge by the natives.

"Skeletons of animals were plentiful on every hand.

"The place was dark, gloomy, treacherous, and deadly in appearance.

"It was truly named Wolf Gorge, for it was dangerous alike to man and beast, so numerous were ferocious animals in and around it.

"In this cheerless place, however, Elvina had often met her lover, and Don Carlos knew all its windings well.

"Spinola turned pale as he entered the gorge, but revealed not his fears.

"The screams and yells of all sorts of wild animals now greeted their ears on all sides, making the lofty and craggy rocks echo again and again with the dismal noises.

"Onward they went, however, and were about in the centre of the gorge, when Carlos stopped his horse.

"'For the first time in my life I fear treachery,' said he, half aloud.

"'Have you seen anything, then?'

"'No, nothing unusual. I have often been here before, but never felt such gloomy foreboding as I do now.'

"'Then let us return, Carlos. I beg of you to return; not for my sake, but for your own.'

"'No,' said Carlos, 'I have come thus far, and will not think of such a thing; it would be unmanly, and unworthy of a Castilian to do so.'

"The place they now were in was not more than twenty feet wide.

"On either side rose perpendicular rocks covered with bushes and stunted trees.

"The place was as dark as pitch, and save a faint streak of starlit sky overhead, nothing cheerful was to be seen.

"For some time they journeyed onwards.

"At last in the distance Don Carlos perceived, or thought he perceived, an object dressed in white which waved its hand towards him.

"His heart beat high with expectation.

"'It is, it is Elvina,' he said. 'She is on horseback, and is beckoning me onward.'

"With these words he clapped spurs to his good steed, and hurried onward.

"He and Spinola had not proceeded far, however, when dreadful shouts assailed their ears on all sides.

"They were entrapped—they were ensnared!

"Both the youths drew their swords, prepared to fight hard for their lives.

"But at that instant some villains, with a loud laugh of mockery, threw their lassoes with unerring aim, and both Don Carlos and Spinola were dragged to the earth insensible and almost strangled.

"They had fallen alive into the hands of Prince Catalka and his Indian allies!

"But this was not all.

"A deeper plot was laid for old Don Toros.

"Catalka was much more cunning than ever old Don Toros had ever imagined.

"This plot which Catalka was now developing, had long been in the mind of the crafty native.

"It is true that he and his people had been defeated in battle more than once by the Spanish invaders of that part of the country, under the guidance of old Toros.

"Part of his lands, in truth most of them, had been seized by Toros; and the native prince, though pretending submission and obedience to the newly-arrived ruler, had vowed in his heart not to rest either night or day until he had taken signal revenge.

"And the method of his proceeding was simple enough.

"He had discovered, through the agency of an Indian spy, that young Don Carlos was enamoured of his only daughter, Elvina, and that they had often met secretly in the lonely mountain gorge.

"When sufficient time had been allowed to pass, Catalka imagined that the passion of young Carlos was inflamed, and thus he had entrapped him and young Spinola, yet not before all his plans were fully prepared for immediate execution.

"The watch-fires, which Don Carlos had not observed at the moment of departing from his father's castle, were for no other purpose than to signal to Catalka's friends to act the part they were each intended to play, and to inform them that the present moment was the one agreed upon.

"The method and plan of Catalka was this.

"Directly the two youths had left the castle—which he felt certain Don Carlos himself would do, upon receipt of the fictitious despatch from Elvina, Hubert, the trusty messenger, having been stopped and killed, according to Spinola's dream—a large party of Indians were ordered to appear suddenly before the castle of Don Toros, and invite an attack.

"This the Indians did.

"As soon as old Toros was informed of this he laughed good-humouredly.

"He did not think it possible that mere Indians would dare to oppose his knights, and other armed men.

"Nor was he incorrect.

"For when Don Toros ordered out a party of armed men, the Indians fled towards the defiles of neighbouring mountains, closely pursued by the old Don's adherents.

"When this was accomplished, however, a courier arrived at the castle-gates, post haste, and almost out of breath, informed Don Toros that the party of knights and soldiers who had but recently gone forth, were almost surrounded by Catalka's whole force.

"But this information was not wholly true.

"The Indians enticed the Don's retainers and friends into a mountainous defile, and a fierce fight ensued.

"Had the Indians stood their ground there they would have been exterminated by the knights.

"Be this as it may, old Toros, in a great rage, rose from his couch, and, gathering all his men together, he sallied forth from the castle, bent upon slaughtering not only the Indians but the whole of Catalka's forces.

"He took a different route from that pursued by the first detachment, and left the castle almost without a guard.

"It was at this moment that Prince Catalka himself, at the head of a select and brave body of natives, suddenly appeared before the gates of the castle, smashed in the gates and gained possession, to the dismay and horror of its inmates.

"Thus, at one and the same time, so craftily had he arranged all his plans, Catalka not only secured young Carlos, but enticed the whole force out of old Toros's stronghold, and then captured it.

"Leaving a strong guard behind, Catalka in less than an hour sallied forth from the conquered stronghold, and marched straight towards the mountain pass in which his Indian allies were hotly engaging those sent after them.

"Thus taken in front and rear, Don Toros's followers could not successfully contend with their numerous opponents.

"In less than half an hour Catalka gained the victory.

"Many of the Spaniards, both of high and low rank, were killed or captured, and the natives took up the line of march to the spot where the false guide had taken Don Toros and the last of his men.

"Old Toros and his followers had unwisely followed the guide up a narrow ravine, which ended (at the distance of several miles) very abruptly in a solid wall of rock, through which there was no passage at all.

"Of this old Toros was not aware, nor would he have followed the Indian guide at all unless the latter had expressly and most solemnly assured the old Don that Catalka and his whole force were there concealed.

After wending their way up this treacherous ravine for more than a mile, the guide slipped from his horse, disappeared among the brushwood, and escaped.

"Old Toros was now convinced that he had been deceived.

He, nevertheless, cheered on his men, and made every preparation in case he was attacked.

Still proceeding farther and farther up the ravine, in order to reach more quickly the territories of Prince Catalka, which, he knew, were just beyond the mountain range, his vanguard galloped back with the startling information that there was no outlet of any kind.

"With dreadful maledictions on the heads of Catalka, and all who had aided him, Don Toros prepared to retreat.

"But at that moment fearful sounds reached his ears.

"It was like that of distant thunder.

"What could it mean?

"No one could tell.

"Not a man dared whisper his suspicions.

"Again and again the sounds recurred, and they reverberated along the broad, dry, and timber-edged ravine, with sudden and loud explosions.

"The nearer they approached the mouth of the ravine the more frequent and ominous were the sounds which fell upon the ears of the benighted Spaniards.

"The mystery was soon explained.

"Catalka and his men, now joined by all their forces, having in their midst young Carlos and Spinola, had allowed old Toros to pursue his way as far up the ravine as he pleased, knowing full well that there was no outlet.

"In the meantime, however, all of his available forces were busily engaged in chopping down the heavy trees which grew on each side of the ravine.

"In this manner they prevented the retreat of Don Toros.

"Dozens of immense trees fell with a loud crash across the ravine bed.

"This was the cause of those loud sounds which the Spaniards had heard.

"When, therefore, they approached the place of exit, old Toros found himself helpless and unable to proceed.

"Nor could his men get at Catalka's forces on account of the obstructions.

"In addition to this the native prince had posted scores of his Indian allies on projecting rocks, whence, at a given signal, they hurled down showers of stones and arrows upon the heads of the devoted Spaniards.

"For one or two hours this sort of fight was carried on, until at last Catalka thought it time for himself to personally engage in the conflict.

"He feared death, it is true; and he knew beyond a doubt that if old Toros could get near him, the desperate and despairing Spanish chief would hew his way through scores of men to get at him.

"Cunning-like, he ordered some of his men to mount an adjacent rock, and there, in the morning light just dawning, to exhibit the captive son before his own father's eyes.

"This was done.

"The sight was unexpected by any of the Spaniards, and least of all by Don Toros.

"The old chief gazed on his son as if he was an apparition.

"It struck more terrors to his soul than all the weapons of Catalka's army.

"'Surrender!' shouted Catalka, in a voice of thunder.

"And as he spoke, an arm was upraised to slay the youth before his father's eyes.

"The old Spaniard's heart sank within him.

"Carlos was his only child, and he loved him to distraction.

"Paternal love, and soldierly pride were waging in his battle-scarred breast.

"He would save his son, but yet would rather die than sully his honour, particularly at such a moment as that, when death was staring him in the face.

"Catalka was triumphant.

"He and his followers made the ravine ring again with their shouts.

"But suddenly Catalka's cheek turns pale.

"He is about to sacrifice Carlos before the father's eyes, when at an unexpected moment, his daughter Elvina, who, unknown to her father, had followed the expedition, crept through the dense brushwood, and frantically running towards Don Toros, threw herself at his feet.

"'I am Catalka's only daughter,' she said, aloud, and in a wild proud manner, 'and have been the innocent cause of all this bloody strife. Don Toros, I love your son and he loves me! If my father is intent upon murder, here is my bare neck; raise your sword and despatch me also!'

"For a moment an awful pause ensued in the ranks of all.

"Both fathers were subdued.

"What strife could not attain love achieved.

"The combat ended.

"The lovers were united.

"Catalka and Don Toros shook hands, and never since that time has there existed strife of any important character between the Spaniards or their descendants and the natives of this part of the Rio Grande."

Thus ended the strange story of old Roberto, concerning one of the fiercest feuds which ever existed in Mexico.

---

## CHAPTER CXVIII.

CAPTAIN FORD'S LAST LETTER FROM MEXICO—BLOODY BATTLES AND DEEDS OF DARING—THE LAST FIGHT—THE OVERTHROW AND CAPTURE OF MAXIMILIAN — THE FALL OF QUERETERO—GREAT REJOICINGS AMONG THE LIBERATED PEOPLE.

"DEAR BROTHER, — In my last last letter I described to you all that had happened to myself and the gallant band of Boy Soldiers, which I have the honor and pleasure to command.

"I now proceed to relate the last and most desperate battles in which we have been lately engaged, which sanguinary conflicts, I am happy to say, have at last resulted in the capture of the Emperor Maximilian himself, and the overthrow of the throne which he wished to raise up in a foreign land against the wishes of the Mexican people.

"My last letter informed you that, after the action, we were on our way near to Potosi to recruit and organize.

"We had not remained in this wilderness of a place many days when information was brought that Maximilian had suddenly stopped, and was somewhat bewildered by the unexpected discomfiture of his generals.

"Instead, therefore, of following up the advance they halted, and formed a junction at Potosi, having a total of some twelve or fifteen thousand men, well armed, disciplined, and counting among them a heavy force of German and Belgian regulars of arms

"Escobedo, however, was daily receiving re-inforcements, and in a few days could count upwards of nine thousand in his command.

"But thousands had no arms whatever, and had to depend upon chance or fortune for them.

"It seemed to be determined by our generals to advance upon the enemy.

"But there soon arose much bickering among the officers regarding precedence in command. Escobedo and Lopez did not muster more than 4,000 men; but because the former had been appointed brigadier-general by the authorities, and Lopez had not yet been recognized at all by them, he claimed that precedence of command belonged to *him*, although Lopez's troops mustered 10,000, had been successful, their general had distinguished himself in former wars, as in this; whereas, it was said, Escobedo had not yet shown any signs of genius or capacity.

"Lopez waived every distinction, and was willing to take *any* command, or do *anything* which might tend to overthrow the power of the enemy, and rid the country of its oppressors.

"Many generals, however, were averse to advancing on the enemy at all, but desired to fall back, so as to draw the enemy away from their base of operations.

"But Escobedo argued that the enemy were comparatively weak to what they *would* be in a short time, our men were anxious to advance, and that the country ahead of them would prove rich in supplies, and successful battles do much towards arming the hundreds rallying to their standards; while by giving up the country we had conquered, the 'moral' effect upon the country at large would prove distressing.

"Finding Lopez averse to advancing, Escobedo asked him to loan a few thousand stand of arms for his men, and "he would fight alone."

"This Lopez refused; but receiving peremptory orders to advance upon Maximilian, he acquiesced with a bad grace, and the march for Potosi commenced.

"Such a march, and such an army, you could never conceive.

"We were equipped in every way that chance or circumstances permitted.

"There were all kinds of weapons, and every sort of attire; so that had a stranger beheld us, toiling along over hill and dale, through dust, &c., day by day, he would scarcely have thought there was any 'discipline' or 'fight' in us.

"There was not much of the former, it is true, but any quantity of the latter.

"All were terribly pugnacious; but, except ourselves, there were few regiments that had reliable arms, most of the men carrying with them the old flint lock muskets and rifles brought from home, and devoid of bayonet.

"They all had hunting knives, which would have answered very well in a hand-to-hand encounter.

"But from the character of the enemy it was thought they would present few opportunities for using them.

"Provision was also very scarce.

"Our commissary and quarter-master's departments, but recently organized, were very indifferent, and it was very seldom the men drew full rations of anything.

"They made up for all deficiencies, however, by laying violent hands on everything that came within reach, appropriating large quantities of corn, and eating it.

"They also extensively patronized the various corn-cribs on their several routes; and, shelling the corn, pounded it between rocks until reduced to powder, and then made bread.

"Hogs were plentiful, as also beef cattle; and farmers, being friendly to our cause, willingly sold all things for Republican paper.

So that this much relieved the commissariat, and eased the line of march.

"Lopez, with his column, led the way; Caravajal followed; at last, came the hero and patriot, Escobedo, with his ragged, half-fed, and ill-armed band of Mexicans.

"After many days of toilsome travel we approached a point thirty miles south of Potosi, where it was reported Maximilian's forces were encamped on hills beside the road.

"We halted.

"Next morning, we cautiously advanced again, but found that the enemy had decamped, and gone in the direction of Potosi.

"Their strength we could not ascertain with precision, but learned they had at least 10,000 men, well-armed, excellently drilled, and counting thousands of mercenaries among them.

"They also had a strong force of cavalry, and some twenty pieces of artillery, Mejia's battery being considered one of the best in their army.

"Our effective force amounted to about 5,000 ill-armed, badly-drilled men, and some 6,000 horsemen, who were, for politeness sake, called cavalry.

"But they had not a particle of discipline among them, being armed as best they could, with every imaginable weapon, and their horses resembling skeletons, more than anything else.

"They had been drilled to serve on foot, but no drilling in the world could effect systematic action among them.

"Finding that the enemy had fallen back the day previous before our advance-guard, we hurried forward in pursuit, and marched over twenty miles as best we could, the roads and hills being dusty and heavy, and the men completely broken down with fatigue, and from want of proper or sufficient supplies.

"We camped at a creek about ten miles south of Potosi.

"And the whole country was scoured for every and any sort of provision that could be collected.

"Everything that fields produced was instantly appropriated, and many of us were thankful for the abundance of green corn, and such like, which neighbouring farms produced.

"Lopez had halted his advance on the right of the road, assisted by Caravajal; while Escobedo was on the left of it; and thoughtless of danger—in fact, never dreaming of Maximilian being in the vicinity at all—threw out no pickets; or, if any were in advance, they were few indeed. During the evening, little was thought of but fun and frolic, as indeed all our evenings were.

"Most of the men were dancing and kicking up their heels until a late hour as lively as if the enemy were a thousand miles away.

"Early in the morning, before the sun had risen, the sharp report of fire-arms on our right and rear awoke every one.

"The word passed from mouth to mouth,

"'They are here!'

"'Fall in! fall in, we are surprised!'

"'Quick! quick! we are surrounded!'

"'Fall in! fall in!'

"Lopez was surprised, as none will venture to deny.

"And before his line was formed, loud drumming in Escobedo's command convinced him that we were all in a precarious condition.

"One of the enemy's generals was attacking our right and rear with great vigour.

"And his shot and shell were bouncing into our camps, knocking everything about in great confusion.

"Such a scene of excitement and hurry no mortal man could ever conceive as reigned in our midst on that eventful morning.

"Soon as the men recovered from excitement, thrown on their accoutrements, and formed line, things began to mend.

"But the enemy by this time had advanced some distance, and was playing the mischief with us in our quarter.

"Maximilian, however, hearing that his general was fairly engaged on our right, pushed the centre and left with great energy.

"The Mejias' battery was admirably posted on an eminence, and ploughed up the ground in our front with mischievous earnestness.

"Sustaining the onset as best he could, Escobedo rode up and down the line with hair streaming in the wind, cheering, forming, encouraging his ragged musketeers, and posting them as well as might be done, to prevent further encroachments of the enemy.

"And by their incessant discharges and accurate

aim, they stopped advance, and equalized the fight in the centre and left, while Lopez was stemming the storm on the right and rear.

"Finding that some of their guns were playing havoc with our men, Lopez determined to make a bold dash and drive them.

"Collecting a few men, he rushed to the right and rear, but found one of our batteries already engaged in that quarter, and by accuracy of fire had disabled them.

"Taking advantage of their confusion, Lopez dashed forward with his companies, and before the enemy could recover from astonishment, five guns fell into our hands.

"Other forces instantly following up the movement, our horse dashed in upon them with terrific shouts and yells, discharging their shot—guns, rifles, and revolvers, at short distance; captured the sixth, their last gun, and begun cutting and slashing about them with wild vengeance and fury.

"The enemy in this quarter was totally routed!

"His infantry, opposed to ours, were not better than Dutchmen usually are.

"Their flight was expedited by artillery, which hammered away at them, dropping shell into little groups of them, and clearing our whole front in that direction.

"But if things were thus successfully progressing on our right, Maximilian was pushing Escobedo with great vigour in the centre and left.

"Our artillery manfully stood to their guns against the accurate and deadly fire of the Belgian 'regulars.'

"But the loss was considerable.

"The enemy occupied a hill, and all advances upon them were opposed by tremendous discharges from their whole force, occupying that elevated position.

"But as reinforcements arrived from our right, together with artillery, Maximilian perceived that we were determined to win the field, and that nothing short of desperate courage could turn the tide setting against him.

"Rallying his forces in a gallant manner, he rode to their front, and waving a handkerchief, cheered them on, making himself a conspicuous mark for our marksmen.

"He had been wounded in the leg early in the day, but rode to the rear, had it dressed, and laughingly observed that 'all was going on well, and he'd turn up trumps before night,' &c.

"He rode forward to the front again; but by this time, our whole force was pushing a-head vigorously, and gradually advancing up hill.

"The idea seemed to be that Escobedo was endeavouring to capture Mejias' batteries.

"But they were gradually withdrawn, and changed position.

"Masses of infantry gallantly rushed forward to dispute our advance.

"Their vollies were deafening.

"The whole hill seemed to be vomiting forth fire.

"Clouds of smoke hung over all, and our advance was extremely difficult.

"The men were in fine spirits, and rushed boldly to the attack, cheering, shouting, yelling, and keeping up an accurate fire of musketry.

"Cannon to the rear sent shell and round shot whizzing over head, and making great slaughter among the enemy.

"Maximilian (whom I recognised on the field) was dashing about in great haste, from point to point, cheering and leading his men.

"But as we reached the top of the hill, I never saw him afterwards, but thought he must have fallen, for every one was aiming at him, as he rode about so fearlessly.

"As soon as we reached the brow of the hill, the enemy were found strongly posted, and seemed determined to make a stout resistance.

"We cheered, and made a rush for the guns.

"But masses of their infantry came forward and protected the retreat.

"It was not until our whole force was collected and hurled at this point, that they finally gave way, and left the field in great confusion.

"Having secured the field, the wildest excitement ensued.

"Our cavalry were sent forward to follow them up; but little was effected.

"We captured many prisoners, arms, ammunition, stores, &c.

"After pursuing several miles, we returned to camp, and made ourselves comfortable on the good things which had fallen to our lot.

"Binos, a bosom friend of Maximilian, was found among some two thousand killed, wounded, and prisoners, and was decently coffined and sent on for interment.

"When the body of this officer was found upon the field, it was discovered that two small buckshot had penetrated, one above, and the other below, the left nipple, having caused almost instant death.

"When conveyed to the rear in a dying state, he exclaimed to his servant—

"'I'm afraid all is over for Maximilan!'

"He was not more than forty-five years of age, small in stature, wiry, active, dark hair and complexion, small black eyes, fond of military pomp, but an excellent, though restless, and ambitious officer.

"His great activity in aiding the suppression of Republican feeling in Mexico city endeared him to the Imperialists.

"He seized the arsenal, erected defences round the city, disarmed all Republican sympathizers, and rapidly rose from captain to major-general in two months.

"His cruelty to all suspected Republican sentiments, and conscienceless behaviour in the administration of affairs, will long be remembered by all who had the misfortune to live under his brief and arbitrary rule.

"He was brave, and had his troops imitated his reckless daring, things might have been very unfavourable to us.

"His body was deserted by every one, and was interred by us in a metallic coffin, but subsequently given to his friends, who removed it to Belgium, where it now reposes beneath a costly monument.

"We captured six cannon, many waggons, stores, and five or six hundred stand of arms.

"Our loss was estimated at 250 killed, and 1,000 wounded and missing.

"Of these Escobedo claims to have lost 150 killed, and 500 wounded.

"Of the battle-field I can say little.

"Our generals had but a shadow of true discipline in their commands.

"But the men fought well, and that was all that saved us.

"Had it not been for their impetuosity and valour we might all have been in Jericho or some other foreign country, as both General Binot and Maximilian crept upon us during night, and took up commanding positions, from which the latter was driven with much difficulty, and not until after an obstinate and bloody fight.

"We ought to thank our stars that things turned out so favourably to us, as the most sanguine could never have anticipated such a complete overthrow.

"It had great effect among thousands of 'wavering' minds, and many rushed to our camps from all quarters, so much so, indeed, that Escobedo knew not what to do with them.

"He had already thousands around him without arms, but as other forces in the south-east were daily augmenting, it was thought that arms in plenty would be forthcoming for all, though none had any idea whence.

"We were not like other armies.

"Our arsenals did not contain a single musket save several hundred muskets captured at this present battle ground, which is called Silver Hills.

"Escobedo's men had nothing but what they had originally brought from home with them, having no regular cartridges, and nothing in which to keep those they made in camp.

"Many had to put ammunition in their hats or pockets, to protect it from the weather, a proceeding extremely wasteful and unsafe, but which could not be avoided.

"This late battle, however, had brought us many useful things, and among others, a few tents, which gave our encampments some little appearance of military habitations.

"But they were so few, that nine-tenths of us slept under the bare canopy of heaven, in all weathers, which, though very romantic in ideal illustrations of wars, is a very uncomfortable state of affairs in 'real' life.

"But, worse than all, there seemed to be a jealousy growing up between commanders, and division in their councils.

"Mexicans were daily flocking to Escobedo, and his name seemed a talisman among them, while Lopez was scarcely mentioned except among his own immediate friends.

"Nor was his capacity as commander looked upon so confidently as that of Escobedo, whose desire seemed to be to 'push a-head,' and not give the enemy breathing time, but follow up every success, and strike terror into them by rapidity of movement, and invincible energy.

"Lopez did not seem to me to be the whole-souled patriot that Escobedo did.

"For his quibbling about precedence of command, and his flat refusal to advance without it was conferred upon him, leaked out among the men, and his own troops saw selfish ambition at the bottom of all, with no record of educated talent to sustain it.

"Escobedo, however, has acquired historic fame by his deeds in Mexico, and has learned the art of war from experience.

"His recent acts and clear-sightedness gives evidence that nothing was lost from age, but that increase of years had only added greater coolness and circumspection to all his acts.

"When our troops had fully rested themselves, therefore, and various departments reduced to a better system of daily routine, Escobedo desired the whole army should move towards Queretero, seize the enemy's stores, supply the unarmed with weapons, and, if need be, procure them upon the battle field, ere the foe could recover from late defeats, and mature plans.

"For information was constantly reaching us that Maximilian now was actively engaged in forming a large army near Queretero, and, having funds and supplies, was determined to put his forces into the field in a style of imposing grandeur and portentous strength.

"Lopez did not approve advancing to meet the enemy, but wished to fall back on the frontier, and allow the enemy to weary themselves in hunting for him.

"Here was a difference of opinion, and no unanimity of sentiment or action.

"Escobedo now was amazed and annoyed.

"He collected all the men and arms he could, indeed, nearly all we had, and left and pushed forward alone towards Queretero, being hailed everywhere as the chief and father of all.

"You never saw such patriotism as was displayed on every hand.

"And although, at least, we were a poor undrilled body of adventurers living upon the public, and trusting to heaven for supplies, our regiments and brigades were animated with a burning enthusiasm for action, and an unbounded confidence in our leader, which were enough to carry us through any enterprize.

"Everywhere we went, however, signs were numerous of the wanton waste and wicked recklessness of Dutch dastards and fanatics in the pay of Maximilian.

"Truly the barbarities of our foes are beyond al description.

"All law, save military law, is suspended.

"Banks robbed of specie, wealthy men 'compelled' to contribute largely for the wholesale destruction of friends, relatives, and rights.

"Prisons full in every city where their rule is paramount.

"All law is laughed at, dwellings seized, property confiscated, sold, and carried away.

"Farms destroyed, cattle driven off, barns, houses, &c., burned before their owner's eyes.

"While mothers, wives, sisters, or daughters are insulted and disgraced, and oftentimes murdered.

"All this is true.

"And I do not exaggerate, for things are bad enough.

"They could *not* be worse, with all the colouring in the world.

"Our whole march has presented harrowing sights.

"Widows, wives, children, and the aged, standing houseless by the wayside, their homes in flames and ruins, 'because the Republicans are coming, and it is a military necessity.'

"Are these *men* who do all this?

"You know their character too well to suppose it.

"It is those valiant Belgian and Dutch heroes of Maximilian, runaways from battle-fields, who show their paltry spite to helpless little ones, whose fathers and brothers are fighting for freedom.

"These are the worthies—the offscourings of Germany and Holland—who, in uniform, dog the heels of Maximilian; who are thus brave and ferocious to women and children, and dare not stand before half their own number of men on the battle-field!

"Not that the name of Mexicans should be placed on such a record.

"Yet there are ambitious leaders among them, who riot in rack and ruin, and care not who perish, so they may rule.

"Think you that kings and others dare show themselves as military leaders of those they gather from all quarters, and pay to cut our throats?

"Not they!

"Such men stay at home, talk much, realize immense fortunes by peculation and politics, but do not practise what they preach or some might excuse them.

"The Republicans put bullets in their rifles, and they know it too well to approach within a less distance than thousands of miles.

"Here, in this unhappy country, a German empire is dreamed of among the enemy, and already their generals are assuming all the trumpery and airs of foreign courts, without any of their talents or worth to sustain him.

"Maximilian already travels in state, has a German body-guard, and tricked out in what appears to be the cast-off finery of a third-class theatrical wardrobe, with paste diamonds and glass bugles thrown in to add to the ferocity and ugliness of his precious corps of Dutch butchers and sausage makers.

"When he travels on the river an entire steamboat is sufficient to accommodate his majesty.

"Guards pace before his door night and day.

"Servants in gay livery hand around wine on silver waiters.

"Grooms and orderlies are shadows, and poor imitations of the same class of servants in German cities, while the ruling language of the court is *very* low Dutch.

"When will all this farce end? Not while money lasts.

"And, even if Maximilian had not unlimited powers conferred by those at Paris, his audacity is sufficient to keep up the spirits of his obese, greasy-looking and tipsy revellers to a considerable length of time.

"Such is an outline of things as learned from two of our friends just arrived from the city of Mexico, who add that 'riff raff' from all Europe are enlisting under Maximilian, and daily parading through the streets to the music of German bands.

"But to return to the pursuit of Maximilian, and of other battles in which we were engaged, not forgetting the last and greatest of all which terminated our stay in Mexico and Maximilian's empire, namely the battle of Queretero.

"About midnight, and after we had had a good rest, all of Escobedo's preparations being completed, we began to move on, and felt certain that Maximilian would dispute every mile of ground on our way to his great and last stronghold at Queretero.

"The old count's command in advance hugged the river, and his troops halted in a wooded slope near the stream, and within five hundred yards of the position the enemy had retreated to.

"The movement was silently effected, and in the dim light I could plainly see the work before us.

"A farm house was situated about half a mile from the river, on high ground, which sloped towards the bank.

"A creek ran in front of the dwellings, and at right angles to the river.

"No bridges were discovered on which to cross and get in the rear, where rose majestic woods filled with troops.

"The 'rise' was crowned with strong breastworks, commanding all approaches, and rifle pits on the flanks covering the creek!

"Caspar and his command occupied higher grounds to the left of this position, screened by woods, while the entire front was open fields.

"The count commanding, had been to consult with superior officers, and returning, found the enemy had discovered his covert, and were vigorously shelling it.

"His men jumped to their arms, and advanced in the twilight.

"The mound to the left in front, the banks of the creek on the flank, and elevated rifle pits to the rear, were soon crowned with rapid flashes of artillery and musketry.

"The disparity of numbers and position would have appalled any troops but those selected to storm the place.

"Skirmishers advanced to the front, and, occupying bushes on the edge of the creek, maintained a brisk and deadly fire, and cleared the opposite bank in little time, while the main body advanced with loud shouts to attack.

"Volunteers constructed temporary bridges on which to cross, but the passage was obstinately disputed, and resulted in loss.

"Once across, the infantry fight became animated.

"While three companies of artillery poured showers of shell into their works, and silenced several guns.

"Caspar, on the left, was slow in his advance; but the old count, riding over, soon had them in rapid motion.

"And as our right had pushed some distance a-head, they assailed the right with terrific yells, and finding a passage across the creek, were soon on a line with our right.

"The enemy's infantry, though numerous, seemed disinclined to venture on open ground.

"While our wings held theirs in check, an assault in front was determined upon; but Caspar, estimating our force insufficient, sent for reinforcements unknown to the count, so that when I came on the scene with my gallant boys, the chief command devolved on me.

"Waiving it, however, our artillery opened at shorter range with terrific noise.

"But, suddenly ceasing, up rose the centre, rushed across the creek, up the 'rise,' over the dry ditch, and were swarming over the parapet, shooting and bayoneting the troops defending it!

"The sight was grand.

"Men standing on the parapet were fighting in every conceivable attitude.

"And as the sun brilliantly rose over the tree tops, illumining the scene, the semicircular line of fight, with its streams of fire, bursting of caissons, shouts, yells, and charging on the right and left—the centre occupied by the strong redoubt, crowds of combatants rushing in and out, with a sea of heads swaying to and fro round our banner floating on the wall,—all was soul-stirring, sublime, and horrible.

"The fight on and around the hill, supports advancing from the woods, the volley and rush of ours to prevent it—the occasional discharge of cannon in the works—men clambering up and tumbling from parapets, the yells, shrieks, and shouts of friend and foe in that central position, clouded with vapour, all spoke of a terrible attack and a desperate resistance.

"One wild shout!

"Out poured the enemy.

"And as they rushed across the open ground to the woods, then came our men through the opening in pursuit—reeling, bleeding, shouting, powder-blackened, and fainting,—madly firing random shots, and sinking from fatigue.

Quickly the line was formed in rear of the works—all joined in the final charge—cannon belched forth grape and cannister into the woods, tearing down limbs and trees, when one ringing shout passed along the line.

"Double quick" was the order given.

"Our men fired at fifty yards, yelled, charged into the timber, and scattered them like chaff before the wind.

"All was over!

"They hastily retreated through the wood, and our cavalry could not follow.

"Cannon, small arms, prisoners, and stores were the trophies of victory; but wearied with several hours' severe fighting and loss I took up the advance, while the others rested round the well-fought redoubt.

"Our troops began to move in strong columns, shouting and yelling vigorously as they passed, and saw guns, prisoners and stores strewn on every side, with fatigued, dusty and ragged brigades, resting in the shade.

"Haste was evidently an object with General Escobedo. He knew that Maximilian had endeavoured to force his men into an energetic resistance thus far, so as to gain time to protect his main army in the neighbourhood of Queretero, near the river.

"Cavalry scouts were therefore rapidly pushed ahead, and infantry followed, batteries being at hand to withstand any sudden exhibition of force, and open the fight, should they feel desirous of trying the fortunes of war in any of the very large open farms intervening between us.

"The advance, therefore, was prosecuted with vigour, and it was scarcely 9 a.m. ere the several divisions were rapidly approaching the enemy. In order the three columns proceeded through the country towards Queretero, but were frequently halted and formed in line to invite a combat with the enemy in fair open ground.

"They would not accept our frequent challenges, however, but slowly retired through the woods, feeling confident in the strength of their position at the city.

"Arriving at a plantation or ranche, one and a-half miles west of the city, General Escobedo took up temporary quarters there, while the columns halted in the open to await the arrival of others. Unacquainted as I was with the various roads, escapes were frequent from horse pickets stationed on the roads, through dense woods, so that having run the gauntlet of pistol shots more than once for intruding upon disputed territory, and not inclined to be hurt through mere motives of curiosity, I returned to our lines, scattered through the woods, and hitched my horse among scores of others round the house, where Escobedo and a crowd of officers were gathered in council upon the doorsteps and grassy sward. I had never seen so many of our generals before, and amused myself by smoking a cigar.

"Escobedo's temporary quarters were not far from the river, and I could distinctly see our batteries and troops on the south bank, and in a direct line across.

"'Twas now about 1 p.m., and as we had full possession of both banks of the river thus far, several couriers rode over, and heavy batteries immediately opened upon the woods on the north bank, about a mile to our immediate front, so as to clear the way for our further advance.

"Our skirmishers were far in advance, popping away in the timber, and occasional discharges of field-pieces told us that we were gradually working towards Queretero.

"The enemy had abandoned a fine field-work at the ranche, and several other important structures still closer to the river, which had frequently contended with our cannon.

This house was badly shattered by our shot and shell, and seemed to be very shaky.

In the upper rooms we saw large stains of blood near where a shell had entered, and prisoners said that Maximilian had used the place sometimes in his journeys along the lines, and that on one occasion, while all were abed, a shell came whizzing across, and cleared its way completely through the walls, killing one aide-de-camp and severely wounding another.

"Be this as it may, *some one* was killed at this spot during our frequent artillery duels, for outhouses bore every evidence of being used for hospitals, while numerous mounds of earth spoke of sepulture.

"The whole yard and orchard were now occupied by officers, aids, couriers, and prisoners.

"Escobedo sat in the south portico, buried in reflection, neatly dressed, his fine, calm, open countenance and grey hair being purely military in caste, and, as he leaned his head in thought, presented an excellent opportunity for an artist to sketch.

Juarez sat in an old garden chair, at the foot of the steps, under shady trees, busily engaged in disposing of sandwiches, and his canteen of water, with feet thrown against a tree; he presented a true type of the hardy campaigner.

His gay uniform had changed to brown, with many a button missing, his riding-boots were dusty and worn, but his pistols and sabre had a bright polish by his side, while his charger stood near, anxiously looking at him.

With uniform buttoned up, though a very warm day, Juarez refreshed himself, and conversed freely with all.

"Maximilian's position was admirably chosen, and well fortified.

"To defend it he had brought over many troops from the south bank of the river by bridges not more than a mile away, protected from all attack by a strongly fortified camp and hill in the south-eastern corner of the place, its foot being washed by the creek before mentioned, which empties here into the main stream.

"When the divisions, therefore, debouched from the woods near Queretero, the Imperialists were plainly visible in battle array on the high grounds, while the glitter of bayonets in the blazing sun of a June afternoon was dazzling.

"A few shells were sent, as compliments, at the head of our column, but missed; but they never fired a shot from the belt of timber crowning the ascent from the centre, west, and north-western boundaries of their position.

"They wished to deceive and lead us to suppose the passage to the north-western quarter would be undisputed, and that all they desired was a fair, open fight, when we reached the plateau.

# THE BOY SOLDIER; OR, GARIBALDI'S YOUNG CAPTAIN.

"It was now afternoon, and having opened the fight to the left, the Count and Caspar moved through the woods to the west, and having got sufficiently under the hill to prevent loss from shell thrown from the north-eastern quarter, each commander gathered his troops well together, gave the word, and under a storm of lead from the hill, ran eastward, parallel with a brook, gave the word 'by the left flank—double quick!' and in less than three minutes Caspar on the right, the count in the centre, and myself on the left, were rushing along the open towards the brook, descended the 'dip,' jumped into the brook, tumbling and clambering over logs and brushwood, and contending with a heavy force of the enemy defending a long breastwork, and rifle-pits on higher ground, to the rear.

"The character of this approach was the best that could be devised, for had these troops marched in the fields, instead of creeping through the woods and hollows, to the west of this 'rise,' few of them would have survived the hailstorm which awaited them.

"By cautiously approaching at right angles with the brook, until near it, giving the word 'file right, double quick' until each had got into position in line, and then 'by the left flank—double quick!' it brought the troops directly under the rising ground, protected from the fire of the north-eastern quarter.

"And by rapidly moving they got so near the brook, that cannon on the rise to the rear could not be depressed sufficiently to hit without killing their own men, who were now hand to hand with ours at the brook, and obstinately defending their line of breastworks.

"In such a position, and on such broken ground, officers saw it would be impossible to ride, and, as many horses had been shot in the morning, we left our steeds in the woods, where they had been quietly drawn up.

"And when orders came to advance we dismounted, buttoned up coats, pressed down hats, drew swords, and dashed forward on foot, and in front, giving commands in loud tones, which the troops heard audibly amid the roar of the enemy's musketry.

"Though many fell in the rush while filing right from the woods across the open, down the dip to the brook, none faltered.

"Ranks closed up as soon as broken.

"Each brigade seemed emulous of the others in keeping a straight and unbroken front as if executing 'double quick' movements in a divisional drill.

"There was much confusion at the brook.

"For it had been deepened and every impediment thrown in the way against our passage.

"But having safely conducted our commands fairly under the hill and safe from numerous field-pieces whose shell harmlessly screamed and whizzed overhead, officers soon restored a perfect front.

"Once across the brook our men scaled the wooden and earthern line of wall that overlooked it, and were soon desperately engaged with masses of infantry who retired up the hill and kept up a deafening roar of musketry upon our further advance.

"The situation was critical.

"But while our skirmishers 'fanned out' in front, and from behind every tree fired into whole regiments before them, lines were reformed, and cheers told of our advancing again.

"Concealed in bushes their swarm of skirmishers disputed the ground inch by inch, while an unbroken line behind them on higher ground fired over the heads of their sharpshooters upon us.

"In fact, there were thousands of combatants opposed to us; first, a dense body of skirmishers.

"Next, a few yards to the rear, and on higher ground, an unbroken line of battle.

"Thirdly, still further behind, and on the edge of the unwooded plateau, a line of cannon, which, depressed as much as possible, fairly shaved our heads, blew off our caps, and broke bayonet points!

"'Warm work, this!' one remarked, as he ran in our rear towards the right, with a regiment to meet a flanking force entering the woods from the north-eastern plateau. 'Warm work, colonel, but push them hard, sir, for everything depends on *us*.'

"This admonition was not necessary to stir up our men.

"They knew that fewer would fall from rushing to 'close quarters' than by advancing slowly, and firing from 'long taw.'

"Accordingly, the word rang out from wing to to wing: 'forward, march!'

"With indescribable yells, the advance began.

"The woods were soon completely filled with smoke, so much so that the position of the enemy could only be ascertained by a sudden flash of light across our front.

"Standing erect our men would reply with a deliberate volley, at fifty yards; rush forward, crouch and load, while the return volley swept over our heads, cart-loads of leaves and branches falling, well-nigh burying us.

"Our men instantly aimed up hill, but sufficiently low, at the line of legs just visible under the smoke.

"And such was their precision, that as we steadily advanced, we had to stride over bodies which lay just as they had fallen, in regular line, but seldom with faces turned towards us.

"The destructiveness of our fire far surpassed anything I have ever witnessed; but owing to the Indian style of fighting instinctively adopted by our men—viz. of standing erect, taking deliberate aim, and firing; instantly bending low, or crawling several yards to the front; rapidly loading, waiting for a "return;" and judging distance by the line of legs visible under the dense vapour, which did not fall within two feet of the ground—our casualties were unaccountably few, and those mostly shot in the hand or arm, owing to the overshooting of the enemy.

"But while things were thus progressing with this portion of the field, with the enemy gradually falling back through the woods to the plateau, Escobedo was vigorously pushing the centre of the line, and some of his forces coming into action on the left, by a road approaching the field in the north-west.

"Being driven from the wood and up the hill on to the plateau by our right and centre, they fell back, and threw forward a heavy force of artillery which swept the open field and tore down the edge of the captured woods in which our forces were resting and reforming.

"Fatigued and torn as we were, the most difficult and desperate fighting was yet before us.

"For in the north-east their heavy masses of infantry stood in admirable order, half a mile away.

"And the array of shining bayonets, waving banners, and a perfect circle of artillery flame rapidly shelling north and south-west, plainly indicated that before we could advance through their still standing camps many thousands would inevitably fall.

The count attempted to move forward in the centre, but his division, thoroughly exhausted by hard marching and constant fighting, was unequal to the task, and was drawn in favour of my own boys.

"The troops succoured Casper on the left, and had been actively engaged since the combat opened, but the regiment of Frontier men was held in reserve, and as this was the 'great fight' in which they had participated, a desperate part was assigned them to act.

"While dispositions were being made for the final struggle, the sun sank upon the scene, and perhaps mistaking the causes for our inactivity, Maximilian moved up heavy masses of infantry to drive us from the woods.

"This was too much of a joke.

"For our infantry, now fully rested and reformed, calmly remained in the edge of the forest, and awaited their approach.

"Their advance was beautiful, and as they came on in unbroken line, with colours waving, and men cheering, a thrill of admiration was felt by all.

"When within a hundred yards our men lay close to the ground.

"They received the volley, and rose to their feet at a 'ready.'

"Imperial commanders jumped to the front, and led on their men to the 'charge.'

"They advanced a few yards in unbroken lines.

"A few paces nearer their line began to waver, and swayed from wing to wing like a curving wave.

"But ere they recovered from apparent indecision—while colours rushed to the front, and commanders pranced about and shouted—our whole line delivered an accurate and deadly volley, which seemed without end, and simultaneously yelling, dashed out from the edge of the woods, rushed headlong through their own smoke, and were upon the disorganized masses of the enemy bayoneting, pistolling, and knifing, in the wildest manner, driving them in the utmost confusion through their camps, seizing many guns, and approaching within a few yards of cannon hastily thrown forward to cover the fugitive masses.

"Much was gained by this charge, but as not a single piece of our artillery had yet been brought into action.

"The lands were flat and open.

"Their guns opened upon us with redoubled fury.

"The left of their lines was still held by powerful earthworks, and our right exposed to a flank movement.

"This latter they attempted to achieve, but the old count, in withdrawing from the centre, had marched by our rear, and lay in wait, under cover of the conquered strip of woods, so that when their forces appeared on our right, up rose the brave old count to meet them.

"They were apparently astonished.

"But while engaged in reforming their lines, and bringing forward fresh forces to make a desperate effort to restore the lost equilibrium of things, their right was assailed with great fury by our left.

"Another force, assured of our victory, was rapidly marching through country to their right and rear.

"The absence of artillery sorely perplexed us, and particularly on the left, where their cannon were sweeping all approach with canister and grape.

"Several regiments had been thrown forward to capture these pieces on their right, but, having proceeded to some distance, they were exhausted and baffled by the enemy changing position and gradually retiring.

"Occasionally rising to their feet, our thinned and bleeding regiments staggered forward a short distance further, but suffering severely, they again fell on their faces, and picked off scores of cannoniers, completely unmanning several guns.

"As to the advance of their infantry, they cared not a jot.

"It was exactly what they desired.

"Their cavalry charged; but, without forming square, our men closed up their broken files, and received them with such unerring aim that they never essayed to gallop down upon us again.

"Their infantry next appeared; but without waiting for them, our men rushed forward and fired, while they rushed back again in unmanageable confusion.

"Again and again their guns fired; it was evident they were gradually preparing to retreat, but while several regiments were annoying their guns and killing scores of gunners, a wild shout arose to the rear.

"On came the Frontier-men at a run, officers in front charging among their redoubts and guns—smashed up their right—and while desperately engaged against great odds, the whole line closed up, and a hand to hand conflict ensued at all points!

"Clouds of dust, woods smoking on every hand, long lines of musketry fire, the deafening roar of artillery, and piercing yells, arose on every hand.

"The dark, dense mass of the enemy slowly retired through their camps, across the creek and though the woods in the north-east part of the field; bursting of caissons, and explosion of ammunition waggons, lighting up the scene on every hand.

"But while myself and others were hurling our commands at the stubborn enemy, and rapidly capturing guns, munitions, and prisoners at every turn, the distant roar of cannon, miles away to our front, breaks upon the ear, and news is soon brought that Escobedo in person is breaking their line of retreat towards their fortified camps on the north bank of the river, and has already captured several thousand prisoners, including cannon, waggons, and officers of all ranks.

"And thus the battle of Queretero was over, and the victory ours!

"Couriers and generals and regiments moving to and fro told that the enemy were to be hard pushed, and nothing left undone to completely annihilate those which had been opposed to us.

"So that, though the roar of musketry to our front, and southward across the creek, told that we were driving them closely towards their fortified hills and camps near the city, it was certain these movements and preparations were in anticipation of hostilities on the morrow, should Maximilian essay a second attempt to maintain possession of the city, under cover of his numerous fortifications still untouched, several of which in the distance could be seen, not more than a mile away, with camp fires burning and rockets quickly ascending in the star-lit sky.

"The field was rich in booty.

"I myself counted several magnificent brass guns pointed south-west and north-west, with caissons, and horses, and dozens of cannoniers, just as they were left by vanquished owners. Camps, clothing, thousands of prisoners, and immense quantities of small arms, banners, drums, etc., etc., were gathered in a few hours, while most of the troops lay where they had halted, and fast asleep; many using a dead man for a pillow!

"The destruction was certainly awful, and, if many guns fell into our hands, heaps of men round them told that they had been heroically defended.

"Many horses were shot, but the enemy finding themselves unable to carry off the guns had deliberately cut the throats of uninjured animals to prevent them falling into our hands.

"Without giving the enemy breathing time, a council of war was held, and a vigorous pursuit was resolved upon.

"This determination on the part of Escobedo and our other generals was a wise one.

"Spies from the city of Queretero came out in dozens, and informed us of the state of affairs in that city.

"It was ascertained from these men that the Emperor Maximilian had staked almost his very existence on the result of the battle just fought.

"He was reported to have said that if the combat should take an unfavourable turn, that there and then would be a termination to his hopes of empire.

"He is said to have raved and sworn like a madman because of the departure of the French troops for Europe.

"But Maximilian was deceived by the impostors who surrounded him.

"They told him that the Mexican people loved him, and desired the establishment of an empire among them, and that they would not desert him.

"All this was false.

"The people as a nation absolutely abhorred the very idea of an empire founded by an Austrian prince, and resolved to die in defence, not of him, but of their own national rights.

"That this was the true sentiment of the people cannot now be doubted.

"A succession of bloody encounters in all quarters proved to Maximilian that the masses were heart and soul with Juarez and the Republicans, despite the petty intrigues of Lopez and a few others who wished to sow the seed of desertion in the ranks of the peoples' army.

"The people of Queretero were burning with impatience for the advance of Escobedo and our gallant men.

"Without taking much time to consider, therefore, our army marched boldly towards the city of Queretero.

"And after a hot siege and many sanguinary encounters, we assaulted, and would have taken the place at the point of the bayonet, but Maximilian and his staff, giving up all hope of assistance or success of any kind, surrended himself to Escobedo amid the enthusiastic rejoicings of all Mexico.

"Thus, my dear brother, I have recounted to you all that has happened to myself and my gallant band of Boy Soldiers in Mexico, and it remains for me to add but a few words more regarding several individuals whom you know, and to say in very brief tones what has become of them.

"In the first place, the old count, who had been with us so long, and distinguished himself so very much in this war, has been offered a command of importance, under General Escobedo, in the regular Republican army.

"He did not at first think of accepting it, but the smiles of a famous Mexican beauty won him over.

"He at last resolved to settle in the country, and I believe has done so.

"May a loag life and joy be his share through life, for none of us can forget the white-haired gentleman, or his kindness and gallantry on al occasions.

"Caspar was also invited to stay in the country, but he refused, and the reason was this :—

"A few weeks ago he received a very important communication from a legal gentleman in England, who discovered, after much labour, that Caspar had been cheated out of a large fortune by knavish relations.

"Caspar did not leave us for seveual weeks, for he could not believe in his good fortune.

"In the meantime, however, a second letter came, telling him that those who had so long deprived him of his just rights had been seized, cast into prison for forgery, and that they had made a full confession, to the effect that Caspar was the only son of Sir Robert Caspar Phillips, in Wales, and that, when a child, he was stole away, and never afterwards heard of, until discovered through the exertions of Mr. Ferret, attorney, of London.

"Caspar, as might be expected, departed for Europe at once, bent upon marrying his old sweetheart, and no doubt will arrive in London long ere this reaches you.

"The two American trappers who have so long and faithfully accompanied us in our varied fortunes have left the army, and are now in the city of Mexico—dancing, and singing, and spending their money like princes.

"Fatty, after many troubles, dangers, and lots of frolic, has at last succumbed to the winning ways of a rich young Mexican widow, and married her.

"He intends to visit England, he says, and resolves to astonish every one of his relatives in his costly gold-laced Mexican garments.

"The young widow seems very fond of Master Tony, and not many years hence we may expect he will be the happy father of a large family of bouncing boys.

"He struts about with gold spurs and riding-whip, sombrero trimmed with gold tassels, and styles himself—Don Antonio Waddleduck.

"Young Buttons was loth to part with Tony, but does not like Mexico, he says, but prefers to get a sweetheart in merry old England, and hence returns home with me.

"If I am at all succesful with uncle's affairs when I return, I shall reward the faithfulness of Buttons most handsomely, for he shall never want for anything while I live. I have grown to like the merry little imp so much that I could not now part with him.

"Hugh Tracy, than whom a nobler, braver English youth never breathed, is at present unsettled, and has not made up his mind what to do.

"Escobedo points him out to all as the finest specimen of a gallant soldier in the whole army.

"Juarez has, three or four times, had interviews with him, and endeavoured to prevail upon Hugh to stay in Mexico; but has not won him over as yet.

"All sorts of honours would be showered down upon Hugh Tracy if he were to stay; but from what Hugh says, I think he will go with us to Europe to see his friends once more, and then, perhaps, he may return to Mexico, and settle down for life.

"As to myself, I will not say much.

"Suffice it for you to know that when Juarez and Escobedo heard of my determination to depart for Europe, they got into a terrible rage, and swore that they would not part with me on any consideration.

"One of the grandest and most responsible positions in the Republic has been repeatedly offered for my acceptance; but I have declined them all, for I could never think of leaving old England for ever. You know how ardently I have loved Nelly Lancaster for years. How, then, can the smiles of any fair one, however noble or wealthy, make me prove false to her?

"No, Tom, a true soldier is also true to his plighted word. I love Nelly Lancaster, and I care not who knows it; and, be she now sick or poor, she is the same to me, and have her for a wife I will, if it costs me my life.

"While finishing this letter, I cannot but reflect and feel some regret at the number of our gallant boys who have fallen in this war.

"The Boy Soldiers were ever foremost on all occasions, and, as a consequence, many, very many, have fallen on the field of glory.

"Few, very few, of those gallant lads who followed me from Bromley Hall School, have lived to see the end of this bloody war; but those that are alive, though bearing many honourable scars, and entitled to rich rewards for their heroism, have determined to return home with me, and, in the bosom of their families, tell the tale of distant wars around the merry crackling fires in their own homesteads.

"At this moment, and before I close, I have received a commission sent you by Juarez, who wishes you to take a command in the Republican navy. Whether you will do this or not remains with yourself to decide.

"One word more, and I close this, my last letter.

"We are coming to England by the next mail steamer.

"Each and all of us that remain of the Boy Soldiers have been handsomely rewarded with honours, decorations, gold, and continual feasting, and all we can say as our parting word is—

"'Success to the Republic of Mexico, and its brave people!'

"Yours, &c.,

"FRANK FORD."

## CHAPTER THE LAST.

### IN WHICH INNOCENCE IS TRIUMPHANT, AND VILLANY MEETS A JUST REWARD!

BUT while the stirring events narrated in the preceding chapter were transpiring far beyond the sea, let us glance at the sudden change in affairs at home.

Gale, the detective, now that he had old Jonathan, Barney, and others in custody, worked night and day to capture every one who in any way had anything to do with the murder of old Ford at the Red House.

Slowly but surely he got upon the trail of the two miserable fugitives, Lawyer Flint and his rascally son Joel, alias Count Schmidt.

With the instinct of a bloodhound, he followed them from place to place, and, when least expected, he pounced down upon them, and lodged them in one of the strongest prison cells in Bow Street.

The old cabman was next looked after, and in less than a week was discovered one night waiting for a part of the Bromley gang of housebreakers, who, at that moment, were engaged in robbing a bank situated in a dark, lonely and unfrequented street in the city.

Gale recognised the old cabman at a glance.

He did not raise any alarm at the moment, but procured the assistance of several other officers, who waited until the burglars had finished their work.

Their plunder was quickly placed in the cab, and when the driver was just in the act of whipping his horse to start off, Gale and his officers pounced down upon the vehicle, surrounded it, and, after a severe fight, in which knives and pistols were freely used against the officers, the villains were all secured, and conveyed to Bow Street handcuffed.

Gale was wounded in this encounter, but not dangerously.

But, judge of his joy when he discovered among these desperate characters no less a person than—

Warner!

Gale forgot all about his wound, and felt so much rejoiced that he had at last captured every one concerned in the murder at the Red House, that he stopped out all night on the spree.

The case was now completed.

Yet one important part remained to be discovered.

Where was the treasure chest?

This thought gave Gale much trouble for an hour or two.

For it is always a rule of honour with expert detectives to secure not only whatever prisoners they are in search of, but the treasure also.

Believing that Warner and his friends of the Bromley gang might know more about the immense wealth which had been so mysteriously stolen from young Flint's lodgings than any one else, he visited the cells and had a confidential chat with one of the Bromley men who seemed more chicken-hearted than the rest.

As this fellow did not much relish the idea of penal servitude for life, he told Gale all that he knew about the expert robbery, which, in a few moments, had reduced "Count Schmidt" from opulence to extreme poverty.

When the hiding-place of this treasure was thus discovered, Gale lost no time in securing it.

This, then, was the end of the brave detective's labours in ferreting out all concerned in the barbarous robbery and murder of old Ford at the Red House.

When informed of the whole matter, Captain Tom Ford danced about the room for joy.

He felt very impatient for the arrival of Frank in England, and the trial might have been put off for some time but for an accident.

Warner was so enraged against old Flint, Jonathan, and Joel, that he sent for Gale, and made a full confession of the whole affair unknown to Flint.

The lawyer, in turn, to save, as he thought, his old neck from the gallows, made a confession also to the prison chaplain, wrote it out and signed it with his own hand.

But he did not mention a single word of what part he had taken in the murder long ago of the bride and bridegroom at Bromley Hall.

But this was supplied by old Jonathan himself.

Ever since the old villain had been in prison, he seemed haunted both night and day by frightful spectres.

His oaths and blasphemy were appalling to hear.

His hair turned gradually to a snowy whiteness, his teeth chattered, his eyes rolled, and he danced about like a maniac.

In his fury he accused old Flint of every crime he could imagine, and when, in a temporary state of calmness, he told the tale of horror concerning his own and old Flint's horrible deeds at Bromley Hall, he made the officers around him shudder again.

Not only this, but he acknowledged the murder of old Flint's clerk in Green Court, and of his systematic cruelty and brutality to sundry children who had died under his hands at Bromley Hall.

When these horrible revelations had been made, old Jonathan was seized with sudden cramping pains during the dead of night, in his cold cell.

Thinking that the old villain was only raving, as usual, no notice was taken of him.

But next morning revealed a most horrible spectacle.

He was lying on the floor of his cell, curled up like a ball.

His eyes were protruding, and he had torn the flesh from his arms with his teeth, in some intolerable agony.

He was dead!

A more horrible sight could not be imagined than this.

But of the rest, they lived to stand their trial for wilful murder.

Barney, Warner, old Flint and his son, were severally placed in the dock, and their own confessions were more than sufficient to condemn them.

Flint and Joel were condemned to be hung.

As they left the court, Joel stopped for a moment and seemed to shiver in every limb.

His gaze encountered that of the handsome youth, Captain Frank Ford, and several of the Boy Soldiers, who had returned to England but a few days before.

Joel stared, and a volley of insane curses poured from his lips, but he was hurried to his cell and heavily ironed.

Warner and Barney were also condemned to die for murdering the policeman in old Flint's office, but even to the last Warner preserved his coolness, and even smiled in triumph as he stood on the gallows, side by side with old Flint.

The fatal bolt was drawn; four human beings were launched into eternity; Calcraft got his money and grinned!

But what shall we say of the brave man, Gale?

He was promoted and made a superintendent in the detective force, and after many years of useful and indefatigable services, he retired from active life, rewarded, as he should be, with a handsome pension. But the most pleasant moments of his life, Gale was wont to say, were passed in the company of Captain Frank Ford and his beautiful young wife, Nelly Lancaster, who, with Captain Tom and Caspar (now also married to his faithful sweetheart) were in the habit of giving frequent balls and parties at their residence in Belgravia.

And old Lancaster, who once had detested the mere mention of young Frank Ford, was now often heard to say to his friends,

"The best day's work I ever did was to give my consent to the marriage of my daughter to young Frank Ford, for he is one of the most handsome, gallant, and opulent gentlemen in the kingdom, and Nelly loves him ardently."

To which the company rising would often rejoin,

"Fill your glasses to the brim, and let us drink long life and happiness to all the Boy Soldiers; and of times since to Frank Ford, the Boy Soldier, Garibaldi's young captain."

THE END.

www.ingramcontent.com/pod-product-compliance
Lightning Source LLC
Chambersburg PA
CBHW080819020726
47501CB00009B/2345
* 9 7 8 1 5 3 5 8 1 2 0 4 7 *